The lure of magic . . .

Mikhyel reached a curious fingertip to the nearest leythium pillar. He had no sense of texture, nothing of liquid or solid, only of warmth and a rhythmic throb . . . like a heartbeat. He pressed deeper. His entire hand disappeared.

But that warmth slid away from him, down his arm and off his fingertip, leaving no sense of residual substance, only a memory.

For the first time, that *presence* took firm mental form. Directly before him, seemingly solid leythium expanded upward, twisting, contorting into a vaguely, human-like form.

Fangs, scales—or perhaps the crystalline webbing that fluttered so freely all around them—faceted eyes . . . utterly inhuman, utterly beautiful.

The creature extended a graceful hand, palm upward. A sense of attraction. Interest. . . . Hunger. *This* was the source of the curiosity latent in the very air Mikhyel breathed.

{Come . . .}

"No . . ." Mikhyel whispered, having no breath for more, and he took a blind step backward. The ground gave beneath his bare foot, but he quickly steadied himself, determinedly human in the face of this inhuman entity. This creature wanted him, not the other way around. *He* would dictate the terms of this encounter, not this creature of the ley. And with that decision, his fear vanished along with the shrinking uncertainty.

Humor filled the air, his mind, his body. Rich, internal, full-bodied laughter.

{Where have you been?} The creature's mind asked.

"Right overhead."

JANE FANCHER

Dance of the Rings
RING OF LIGHTNING
RING OF INTRIGUE
RING OF DESTINY*

*Forthcoming from DAW Books

RING OF INTRIGUE

Jane S. Fancher

Dance of the Rings: Book Two

DAW BOOKS, INC.
DONALD A. WOLLHEIM, FOUNDER
375 Hudson Street, New York, NY 10014

ELIZABETH R. WOLLHEIM
SHEILA E. GILBERT
PUBLISHERS

To my siblings.
Those I was born with and
those I've acquired along the way . . .

SECTION
ONE

Chapter One

Dusk was closing rapidly as the small entourage approached the outer wall of Rhomatum. A strangely deep dusk—the leyroad lights, once bright beacons leading to the city, glimmered feebly in the distance. Even Tower Hill, an architectural mountain rising above foothills of concentric rooftops, seemed subdued, fewer lights and dimmer shining from those oldest, most elegant buildings of the city of Rhomatum.

Only the highest point in the City gleamed with undiminished silver leylight: the Rhomatum Ringchamber, uppermost room within Rhomatum Tower itself. Home of the Rhomatum Rings.

The source for all those other, failing, lights.

Lightning clouds roared in from the north. An hour before, just as the entourage had crossed the Oreno leyline, the storm that had rumbled in the distance all afternoon had suddenly broken pattern, gaining organization and direction, forming a line of blinding ferocity, a constant barrage of ground strikes that chased the open carriage and its handful of outriders down the valley.

It was a race now to see whether they could reach Trisini Gate before the solid mass of atmospheric fury overtook them.

Deymorin had kept the team to their steady, running trot as long as he dared. Bracing his feet against the forward rail of the driver's box, he gave the anxious horses the signal they eagerly awaited, tired as they were.

Fool, he called himself, and worse, as he guided galloping horses grimly over and around the ruts and potholes of the cattle trail; fool, for choosing this side track over the smooth-graveled Trisini Leyroad.

In choosing the anonymity of off-ley roads, he'd made their trip from Armayel overlong and dangerously slow. He should have known that despite the clear morning skies, the storms that had made the last month an unpredictable, living hell for the valley would arrive before nightfall.

At least the storm would keep Anheliaa, or whoever was in control of Rhomatum Tower these days far too busy protecting the city to notice their arrival. So he trusted the seasoned team's instincts, and hoped he didn't shed a carriage wheel or a brother in this final mad dash.

Kiyrstin, he'd never lose, so long as he had a coattail for her to grasp.

To the front and sides, the outsiders kept pace, calling out warning of ruts and mud holes. Nikki, a quiet and sane presence—in every sense—brought up the rear and cast Deymorin silent reassurances regarding his passenger's safety.

Huddled in the back seat with Kiyrstin, Mikhyel was a black sink of nonemotion. Awake, holding his thoughts his own, that was all a brother could ask, a brother whose mind could afford no distractions.

The trail branched, one road toward the stockyards, the other toward the leyroad and the gate. The horses surged uphill, and the ground beneath the wheels rattled and bounced, then settled onto the smooth surface of a leyroad. A mental sigh of relief reached him: Nikki's thought, Mikhyel's, or both; or perhaps just his own.

But it was a short-lived relief. At the gate, chaos reigned, delivery vehicles jammed the opening, the silk balloons that normally rose above them, taking the strain off the axles, lay limp over the cargo or deflated even as they watched; further evidence, if they needed it, that the node's power umbrella was rapidly failing.

Or perhaps, Deymorin thought, as he raised his eyes to see stormclouds gathering above the city, that energy was being redirected.

"The Tower, Deymorin! Has the storm reached the Tower?" Mikhyel's voice pierced the near-deafening rumble. He spoke aloud, as was not altogether necessary, except from a brother who sought to hide his horror of the lightning.

Deymorin looked beyond the immediate area to the sky above the Tower.

"It's all right," he shouted back over his shoulder. "The sky's clear beyond the old wall."

Words or mental image penetrated the thunder and darkness, and Mikhyel's relief filtered back: a conscious leak in the blackness.

A relief all well and good for the safety of the rings and those individuals within the perimeter of the old wall, but the immediate danger to themselves and all those milling about them remained. The old wall, that marker of an earlier limit of the city's power umbrella, was a mile and more yet ahead.

But they didn't need to reach the umbrella. Not far from Trisini Gate lay their salvation, if only they could get to it.

As the lightning bore down on them, Deymorin added his voice to the general cacophony, ordering his men to help clear the vehicles and get the horses and their handlers inside the wall, and never mind the cargo.

"Can't, sir!" one shouted back. "Gatekeeper's demanding to see papers!"

Deymorin cursed, then yelled at Nikki to change places with him. Handing the team off to his youngest brother, he made a flying mount into the saddle and forced the big horse through the mill to confront the gatekeeper personally.

"Papers!" the man shouted at him, and held out a hand, wide-eyed and automated as a mechanical doll.

"Don't be a fool!" Deymorin shouted back, and pointed at the approaching wall of lightning. "These people are going to fry, and you'll fry with them! Get them and the stock through the gate and into the underground. *Now!*"

The man stared at him blankly, obviously terrified into idiocy. Ignoring him, Deymorin began shouting orders at anyone within earshot. He found a man—one of the idiot's assistants—familiar with the nearest entrance into Old Rhomatum, and set him at the forwardmost team, with orders to get the men and animals under cover.

"After hours, sir!" The man shouted. "Locked!"

"Then break the damned doors down!" Deymorin answered.

"Yes, sir!"

In a few moments, the frightened horses, free of harness, were forming a steady stream toward the underground city and stables, the oldest legacy of Darius' followers, and newly restored for the delight and amusement of tourists.

Tourists be damned, it got *them* out of the storm.

Deymorin spotted Nikki with his unharnessed team in hand, waved him into line, then searched the madness for Kiyrstin and Mikhyel. Targeting on Kiyrstn's red hair, a spot of color in the lightning glare, he pushed his way through to them.

"We're all right, JD," Kiyrstin shouted, and Mikhyel's determined calm seeped past the gut-jolting thunder. "We'll get underground, wait for you there!"

Meaning *I'll get your shattering brother to safety, and don't you dare waste time worrying about us.*

Deymorin grabbed a fistful of her hair long enough to press his lips hard to hers.

As the rain began to fall, he let her go, then shouted, *"Love you!"*, and ran to help free another panicked team from wind-whipped balloon silk.

§   §   §

"I remind you, our identification is all in that carriage outside. Do *you* care to go retrieve it?"

Mikhyel dunMheric's velvety voice carried a hint of contempt that could cut through the most imperturbable individual's confidence.

The keeper of Trisini Gate was not what one would call imperturbable.

"I—it doesn't matter. The law says—"

"I know full well what the law says. I wrote it. Shall I quote it for you?"

Somewhere beneath the city of Rhomatum, Kiyrstine romGaretti, estranged wife of Ringmaster Garetti romMaurii of Mauritum, leaned against a stack of hay bales and watched the Trisini gatekeeper squirm.

"Better yet," Mikhyel continued, and he held out his hand. "I'll read it to you."

The gatekeeper stared at him.

"Naturally you have the paperwork you are by law required to hand out to every individual entering the city without proper identification, do you not?" Mikhyel asked, and Kiyrstin bit her lip to keep from smiling, then winced as her teeth encountered the bruise left there by Deymorin's parting kiss.

His adrenaline rush, or her own—hard to recall, in retrospect, which was responsible. They were still learning each other's limits.

As her exploring tongue found the misaligned tooth responsible for her bruised lip and marked it for future reference, the brown-eyed visage that lurked constantly at the back of her mind crept forward. Kiyrstin made no effort to push the image back. Mikhyel didn't need her at the moment. Mikhyel's keen mind was back on track, now they were out of the storm, and she had total confidence in his ability to win so minor a skirmish.

And as it had a tendency to do these days when relieved of other distractions, Kiyrstin's mind, like a pubescent schoolgirl's, turned to Deymorin Rhomandi dunMheric.

Deymorin presented an intriguing dichotomy. She'd known the man only two months—*less* than two months in Rhomatum's odd calendar—and yet it seemed, at times, as if she'd known him all her life. At others, it seemed that three lifetimes wouldn't be long enough.

Raised to be the head of the Rhomandi Family, premier Family in the Rhomatum Web, Deymorin exuded a confidence and power to command she'd witnessed in only a handful of individuals in a lifetime among the rich and powerful of Rhomatum's rival nation, Mauritum.

There could be no doubt, at times such as this, where men seeking an anchor in time of crisis reacted with instinctive trust to his deep-voiced confidence, that he was comfortable with that fate.

And yet he was a virtual stranger to his own people. Years ago, for a complexity of reasons that no one outside the family could ever understand in their entirety, Deymorin had abdicated his inherited responsibilities to Mikhyel and retired to the Rhomandi country estates. Consequently, while Deymorin was still in every legal sense the Rhomandi of Rhomatum, Mikhyel's face was far better known to the Rhomatumin populace.

Or should have been. Kiyrstin couldn't blame the confused gatekeeper for questioning Mikhyel's identity claims. She'd seen some of the popular renditions of Mikhyel dunMheric, and cartoonists and serious portraitists alike had clung to Mikhyel's elegant, feature-defining beard and mustache as his distinguishing characteristic, a look, Deymorin had told her, that had spawned a new fashion throughout the City.

And now Mikhyel dunMheric was as smooth-faced as a child, the hope that his facial hair would return fading with each passing day. Four long Rhomatumin weeks had passed since the battle at Boreton turnout, four weeks since Mikhyel had fallen from the sky, burned almost beyond recognition and nearly dead.

He had survived, had healed miraculously unscarred—on the outside—but his body hair was gone. Everything, he'd revealed once in answer to her unabashed query, except his eyebrows and lashes, and the silky black mane confined now in a braid at his back.

Black-haired and gray-eyed, with his black clothing and beard, and that indefinable attitude, he must have once made an imposing figure, despite his average height. These days he looked more like a harassed cleric. Handsome enough, if a woman's taste ran toward light-boned and slender, and with a look about his eyes that could, when he was distracted, become sad and a bit haunted.

But his eyes were keen enough now, gleaming with engaged intellect, and neither the loss of a beard nor this strange venue could undermine the effect of a voice seasoned in the courts of Rhomatum.

The gatekeeper's worries had passed beyond the Rhomandi brothers to the chaos of men and animals and legalities of forced entry into city property. Leaving Mikhyel to persuade the harassed civil servant that the way to handle the situation was *not* to incarcerate each and every one of the individuals trapped in this underground museum, Kiyrstin edged toward the aisle down which she thought she'd heard Deymorin's voice.

There were stalls, and she saw Nikki's blond head bobbing on the far side of a broad horse-back, but no Deymorin. The sound must have been an echo from somewhere else in this strange underground maze.

She leaned crossed arms on a stony outcrop, and scanned this newest revelation of Rhomatum. The decor was unique, to say the least. Stable, those around her had called it. Except that in addition to stalls and hay, there were restaurants and gift shops lining the entrance corridor and a sign beside the hay bales that read: *Tours start here.*

The light came from oil lamps rather than the ley crystal bulbs she would expect to light the shadows within a node's power umbrella. Oil lamps were a curious affectation within a Node City's limits, but a welcome one, considering this city's currently-constricted power.

She'd hate to be caught in the absolute black that must exist here when those lamps were extinguished. A honeycomb of stone, organic shapes that bore no resemblance to any rooms she'd ever known, sounds that echoed endlessly . . . a person could be lost very quickly in this maze with no hope of logicking herself free.

"Well, we've a respite, at least," Mikhyel's velvet voice said at her shoulder. The gatekeeper had left. "When the storm has passed, he'll send a messenger to the Tower. They'll have someone come down to identify us."

"What about the box in the carriage? The papers Anheliaa sent? Deymorin's seal—"

Mikhyel's black brows knit.

"I . . . very much fear it won't be there."

"You think someone will steal it?"

"No. I—" He seemed uncharacteristically reluctant to meet her eyes. "Rings, I can't believe I'm such a fool. I had it. And then, the lightning, the jostling . . . I lost it somewhere, Kiyrstin." He waved a hand toward the stony ceiling. "Somewhere up there."

That hand was shaking. He was. Cold. Shock. Reaction to the lightning and the storm. Perhaps just the chill of the rain that had caught them at the last. And possibly a relapse of the debilitating weakness that had plagued him off and on since the incident at the Boreton turnout.

"Anything in the box that could be dangerous in the wrong hands?" she asked.

"Not really. None of those papers Anheliaa sent are much good if you can't match our signatures."

"And the seal?"

"Old. Outdated by about a hundred years. It might turn the right person a handsome profit on the black market, but nothing else." He rubbed a hand across his eyes, and swept stray hair back from his face. "We deliberately avoided including anything compromising. Only such items as might, along with the papers, support our claims to someone like—"

He tipped his head in the general direction of the gatekeeper.

"Then I suggest you sit down and relax. Looking a bit pale around the gills, laddybuck."

Mikhyel smiled wryly. "That's news?"

"I wish it were. Sit, Khyel. Before you fall."

She led him to a spot among the hay bales and pushed him down, wrapping his cloak around him, fussing about him, until he laughed and grabbed her wrist and pulled her down beside him.

It was hard to remember, sometimes, that Mikhyel only appeared fragile, with that bruised look about his eyes and with features that were so different from his older brother's. There was a steel core to Mikhyel dunMheric; a core tempered in a childhood as Mheric Rhomandi's second son, and honed to a fine edge by Anheliaa, Mheric's father's sister, and Ringmaster of Rhomatum.

And Mikhyel had met Deymorin head to head in the political arena and won. At least, the result of that long-ago debate had been the event that drove Deymorin out of Rhomatum.

He'd make a fierce and dangerous enemy in defense of his ideals—if he didn't burn himself out first. She sincerely hoped, for Deymorin's sake as well as Mikhyel's own, that events would not push those ideals beyond his physical limits.

Mikhyel's eyes closed, and, with a shiver, he pulled his cloak more tightly about his shoulders, tucking his chin into the folds. After a moment, his eyes lifted and stared unfocused down a corridor of walls.

Odd eyes. Unique, in her experience. Gray with pale green around the edges.

"So, what's he up to?" Kiyrstin asked.

A blink, and he as back to her. "Horses," he said flatly, and his mouth tightened into a slight smile. "What else? But he's going to be cold. Actually, he already is and doesn't know it."

Which meant, Deymorin had gotten wet and chilled, and Mikhyel was inheriting that discomfort, absorbing it like a sponge.

"You do him no favor, you know," she said, and Mikhyel laughed, a short, bitter sound.

"Believe me, if I could not, I would not. Do me a favor, and take him his damned cloak, would you?" He shivered again and pulled his own cloak up around his ears. "Before *I* freeze to death."

🌀 🌀 🌀

"Hot poultices on the hock tonight, a bit of salve on the cut to keep it moist, and it should heal without a scar."

Deymorin Rhomandi dunMheric, erstwhile Princeps of Rhomatum, stood up and slapped the big roan's rump. "He nicked the coronet, but not, I think, deep enough to affect the hoof growth." He let his hand drift along the curve of solid muscle as he moved behind the draft horse, and gave the cropped tail a gentle tug on the way to his next patient.

Not that he could add significantly more than reinforcement of decisions already made. For the most part, the drivers were competent horsemen. Heavy-handed whips didn't last long with any reputable hauling company; horses were too expensive to keep along the leys for that investment to be risked through carelessness or abuse.

Still, any man appreciated endorsement, especially from a higher authority, a position these men had seemed determined to set upon him from the moment he'd challenged the gatekeeper and won.

He wouldn't object, if it eased their minds; still, he gave them his first name only, as was his habit with strangers, having learned that the Rhomandi title tended to build a wall between himself and others. And thanks to his parents' choice of name for their firstborn, "Deymorin" was a fairly common name among Rhomatumin men of his age.

Besides, he had no time or energy to waste in explanations. Princeps he'd been: the Rhomandi, patriarch of the Rhomandi Family. For thirteen years—until his youngest brother's marriage to Lidye dunTarim of Shantum Node.

Now, according to their great-aunt Anheliaa, eldest living Rhomandi, Ringmaster of Rhomatum, and one evil-smelling breath short of her long-overdue death and immersion, seventeen-year-old *Nikki,* youngest of the Rhomandi brothers, was Princeps, because *she* had chosen *Nikki's* wife as *her* replacement in Rhomatum Tower.

Some situations in life truly defied explanation. Far simpler to let these men draw their own assumptions regarding their companions in adventure.

They'd been lucky. Despite the panic, none of the horses had been badly injured. Bumps and scrapes mostly: The worst they'd had to deal with was a fear-induced colic in an overbred, overgrained saddle horse, who'd come in at the last

minute. Even that crisis had been solved by more than half
when they shoved the horse's wild-eyed owner out the door.

Some people just never learned that *self*-control was the
main battle to win when dealing with horses or any other
instinct-driven creature—including children.

It occurred to him, as so many things reminded him now
of the past, that an uncontrolled, angry horse had killed his
father—shortly after his father had nearly killed Mikhyel.

Strange, to gain such an intimate perspective about a
parent, so long after that parent's death. Hard not to want
to make up for Mheric's cruelty to Mikhyel. Harder to remember that Mikhyel was no longer the bruised and broken child they had pulled from a closet the day Mheric
died, and that the man Mikhyel had become might well
resent such a gesture.

Limestone arched overhead in capricious curves. Ancient, massive . . . and as beautiful and natural as the water
and ley that had created them.

Some people found these old stables and the entire underground city to be oppressive, even frightening; Deymorin loved them. The land beneath Rhomatum was a vast
honeycomb of huge caverns, and tiny eddy-formed niches.
It was a vast maze of tunnels, man-made and natural, filled
with wonders. There were mineral stalactites and stalag-
mites, as one found in any mountain cave, veils and lumps
and impossible structures formed over centuries of dripping water.

However, in ground formed and transformed by the
nearby leythium node, the cave-lurker had the added bonus
of the rare, sudden burst of rainbow color when he chanced
upon a ley-crystal bud, unmined and grown enormous over
years of disuse.

Unused—now. But once these caverns had provided the
founders of Rhomatum the same sort of haven they provided a handful of men and horses tonight. Their ancestors
had forgotten that first Rhomatum once they moved to
their surface, leylit homes. They'd forgotten the underground altogether, except to turn the largest caverns into a
prison to house the individuals the law-abiding citizens of
the Rhomatum Web could do without.

They'd forgotten the underground until a handful of
youths found the caverns and reminded a history-starved
populace about them. That reminder had sparked a burst

of mass nostalgia that had opened the old city to public tours and renewal programs.

Fortunately, this stable, which was the staging area for one of the major tour routes, was kept stocked and prepared as if in constant use. It wasn't, of course, in use, and they'd had to move a plaster horse or two to make way for the real thing, but hay was hay, and straw for ambiance made welcome bedding for tired, frightened horses.

And there was water, and cots and blankets, and even food, in those restaurants, for the horses' equally exhausted handlers.

They could worry about reimbursing the owners later.

For himself, as the last occupied stall passed his scrutiny, as the last grateful horseman gripped his hand, sleep seemed far away. He should be exhausted; instead, he was exhilarated, his blood was boiling through his veins, and showed no signs of abating. He ducked into a darkened niche to catch his breath, and quiet his heartbeat, seeking serenity in the unyielding stone.

And jumped nearly out of his skin as arms closed around his waist.

"Show 'ee m' ankles fer a copper, zur." Warm breath brushed his ear, carrying that low whisper.

Deymorin chuckled and twisted in the circle of arms. "Not interested in ankles, Shepherdess," he whispered in return, and slumped backward, dragging Kiyrstin with him. As his arms closed around her, he realized how . . . light . . . his head felt, how completely free of his brothers' thoughts his mind was. He buried his face in her neck, and her scent added to his light-headedness.

"Shepherdess," he called her, in memory of their first mountain meadow encounter, and Shepherdess she remained, as he was JD, or Rags, or any number of other disrespectful intimacies. Terms that reminded them constantly of their unique relationship, that kept them grounded in each other and not the political posturing that drove so many other aspects of their lives.

"Sweet, *sweet* Maurii," she whispered, throwing her head back, exposing her neck to his kiss.

He buried both hands in her cropped, windblown hair, and fastened his lips on hers, met a demanding passion and vigor that matched his own. Unfortunately, this was neither the time nor the place, and with a final, penetrating caress, he reluctantly disengaged.

"I thought you were tending Mikhyel," he murmured, busying his fingers straightening her hair.

She pulled a strand from her mouth. "Khyel's fine." She leaned back long enough to free herself of a heavy cloak, and work it around his shoulders. "*You* are cold."

"I'm cold," he repeated flatly, thinking nothing could be farther from the truth. Wet, yes, but cold?

"So he informs me."

A moment's reflection brought realization. "Damn," he said, and settled the cloak more securely. "I don't feel him at all."

"Obviously, the effect is not mutual." She insinuated her hands past his coat and began toying with his shirt buttons. "He sent me to remedy the problem, after he explained to that poor bemused gatekeeper why we have no papers. — Oops." A button went flying, clattered to earth somewhere in the shadows. "Silly law, Rags. Who're you afraid of?"

"One of Mikhyel's ideas, back when he was still an idiot." His cold (according to Mikhyel) hands found their way to her linen-covered breasts. Kiyrstin's gasp confirmed Mikhyel's assessment.

It was a man's shirt she wore, one of Mikhyel's, as were her supple, black leather breeches. Both an admirable fit, though her decidedly feminine rump posed a greater and more interesting challenge to their seams than Mikhyel's half-starved hips.

"I cannot imagine—" Another clatter. "—Oops, again, Rags. I can't imagine why you left him to run the City all on his own."

Her own chill fingers gained entrance to his chest. He twitched, but Kiyrstin sighed and flattened her hands, then breathed on them, hot, moist air that was nearly as maddening as the cold.

"He was good at it, Shepherdess. Good at getting things done. I only—" His breath caught as her mouth followed her hands, and he finished, quickly and past a suddenly tightened throat. "—antagonized everyone."

"Nonsense," she said, tipping back to catch his eyes. "I saw you out there, JD. Just Deymio, hell. Who do you think you're fooling? You're the Rhomandi every time you inhale, Princeps of Rhomatum when you exhale. No *man*

judges by the name you give. Any *man* would follow you
to the ends of the world, if you asked."

His breath grew short, facing that challenge, the look in
her eyes. "And you, Shepherdess? Would you follow me?"

Her mouth twitched, breaking the spell. "I won't *follow*
you anywhere, Rags, unless it's to enjoy the view."

He choked on laughter and crushed her to him. He could
understand that. He'd follow her for the same reasons. Her
swinging, long-strided walk made his blood move faster just
thinking about it.

Seeking a way past the full shirt, fitted pants and wide
cummerbund that showed off her figure so very admirably,
he began to realize, on limited time and with even greater
limits on movement and privacy, that there were vexatious
restrictions to the clothing arrangement.

He cursed softly and pulled her hands away from his
waistband. "Never mind."

Kiyrstin laughed, low in her throat, and pressing full
against him, pushed him into the deepest shadows. "Your
brother's freezing, remember?" she murmured, and pulled
his voluminous cloak to her back with orders for him to
hold it there. "What say we warm the poor laddy up?"

Her hands steadied his face where her lips could reach
it, then moved downward. Kneading fingers caressed temples, ears, neck and lower, easing tension he didn't realize
he was carrying. Warm palms smoothed his chest and
slipped around his waist, under his shirt. He twitched when
her strong fingers pressed his lower back, finding aches ten
years in the making.

"Ah," she murmured, "thought that was bothering you.
We'll fix it later, laddybuck. For now . . ." A warm breeze,
her breath, crossed skin that shouldn't be bare. Her
fingers—

"Kiyrstin, I—"

"Just say thank you, Rags, then shut up."

And being a tolerably reasonable man, he did as he
was told.

§   §   §

The one unqualifiable truth of this moment in time was
that Mikhyel dunMheric was useless where it came to

horses. It was a shortcoming he truly regretted, for the first time in his life, considering Deymorin's current occupation.

Mikhyel shut his eyes and leaned back into the surprising comfort of stacked hay bales, crossed his legs and flipped his cloak over his lap, presenting, to all the world, the image of an exhausted man.

Damn Kiyrstin anyway, he thought wryly. His brother's lady was an amazing woman, one whose advice—and quiet mind—he'd turned to quite frequently these past weeks. They'd spent many hours in the gardens of Armayel, just talking . . . about his brothers, his father, Garetti and Mauritum, similarities and differences—

And Kiyrstin knew damn good and well what she was doing to him at the moment. Kiyrstin thought him too . . . detached. Kiyrstin, in great good humor, sought at every viable opportunity to shake him out of his indifference to what she considered basic human needs.

Beneath the twin cloaks of wool and nonchalance, he fought Deymorin's reflected passion, striving with every iota of energy remaining to leave Deymorin and his lady with their privacy.

He chilled his mind and his body with thoughts of Anheliaa and the implications of the storm raging directly overhead.

The power umbrella remained, diminished but intact, to the edge of the old wall. Or so Deymorin's final images of the City had implied. The gatekeeper had said the Khoratum expansion, that section of Rhomatum between the old wall and the new, had not regained power since the collapse of the web a month ago.

The collapse of the web. It was a horrifying thought, to a man whose life had been structured around the firm belief that nothing could disrupt the power of the Rhomatum Web. But there was no denying the fact it had happened. Likely, though he couldn't be absolutely certain until he spoke to Anheliaa, as a result of the battle at Boreton.

Horrifying, indeed, but not so horrifying as what might have happened had the Mauritumin intruders succeeded in their plan to get their lightning-generating machine into the Tower of Rhomatum.

Lightning and the ley did not mix. Sparks off clothing could disrupt the smooth flow of energy from the Rhomatum Rings. The Mauritumin machine had been capable of using the power of lightning to create light in wires the way the ley created light in leythium crystals. To put it in the Tower . . . to activate it . . .

Mikhyel shuddered. It might have destroyed the Rhomatum Rings. Without Rhomatum, the entire web would collapse. Without the web, storms would rage down the valley, and hundreds of thousands of people would die.

But that machine had never made it to Rhomatum. Anheliaa had attacked the Mauritumins as they camped at a nowhere spot in the road, a spot known locally as the Boreton Turnout. Using the Rhomatum Rings, the power of the ley, and (by some means they still didn't understand) that link between himself and his brothers, Anheliaa had generated a localized maelstrom that had destroyed the machine along with the men who had brought it into the valley.

She'd nearly destroyed her nephews in the bargain. Somehow, he doubted Anheliaa would have minded the loss. But they *had* escaped and made their way to Armayel, the largest of the Rhomandi holdings and the one nearest Rhomatum itself. From there, they'd sent careful probes, men loyal to Deymorin for years, into the City.

At first, those men had come back with tales of riots and chaos and fear. Later, they'd brought back street flyers proclaiming the end of life as Rhomatumins knew it, and finally with newspapers that gave lists of the dead and damage reports.

As order returned, they'd risked a letter to Anheliaa.

Anheliaa had answered. Immediately. Anheliaa had expressed relief at their survival of the (so-called) Boreton Firestorm, and delight at their well-being. And Anheliaa had issued an urgent and heartfelt request for their immediate return.

They'd taken *that* request at face value: Anheliaa had no heart. At least, not one that mattered.

So, this morning—weeks later—when *they* were ready and without formal announcement to Anheliaa, they'd set out for Rhomatum. They'd taken a circuitous route in, staying as much as possible beyond reach of Anheliaa's awareness, which meant off the leylines. And they'd chosen to enter at Trisini Gate where she'd logically expect them to use Oreno.

All to limit Anheliaa's preparation time.

Considering the chaos greeting them now, it would seem

they were overly cautious. Difficult to believe that Anheliaa was wasting overmuch energy on her prodigal nephews' whereabouts, when storms such as the one raging overhead were bearing down on Rhomatum.

Anheliaa's letters had said the power had faltered the day of the Boreton Firestorm; she hadn't said the web had gone completely down.

Anheliaa had expressed concern at the diminished power available, had said that the communication links with the other nodes were erratic at best, that she couldn't tell, from the Tower, exactly what damage had taken place.

But the clear demarcation at the old wall that marked the pre-Khoratum expansion limit did suggest to Mikhyel a different possibility, one which Anheliaa, trapped in the Tower as her physical disabilities kept her, might not have noticed.

It was possible they'd simply lost Khoratum.

The Khoratum leyline *was* the largest line in the vicinity of Boreton, and Anheliaa had always said Khoratum was the strongest satellite node, the hardest to cap, and the most difficult to hold after it had been capped. If *that* line had gone, or even if it was severely damaged, it could account for the web's erratic behavior.

Hard to judge which would be more devastating to the security and cohesion of the Rhomatum Web Syndicate of Nodes: a general collapse, or the failure of only that newest highly controversial link.

Thirty-three years ago, when Anheliaa first seriously contemplated capping Khoratum, she had made certain promises to the other seventeen satellite nodes in the Syndicate whose cooperation, and power, she'd needed for the venture. Considering the promises contained in those contracts, the repercussions of a drop in available energy, and the rights of the satellites to demand compensation, three prodigal nephews might well be the least of Anheliaa's current concerns.

She might, in fact, welcome them home with open arms— as alternate targets for the Syndicate's fury. Particularly Mikhyel dunMheric, who was her primary voice to that august body.

He shifted uncomfortably, Deymorin' growing sexual excitement penetrating his consciousness despite his speculative exercises. He was happy for his brother, he truly was.

Deymorin was a robust fellow, libidinous to the point of obsession, to his way of thinking. To have found a woman whose appetite matched his own had only improved his overall disposition.

But a brother who preferred a calm and celibate life would far rather endure the pain of Nikki's healing shoulder, or Deymorin's aching leg, or the cold, or . . . *anything*.

Somewhere, Nikki was radiating concern for a horse that was "foundering," a term he'd heard his brothers use and never truly understood. Mikhyel opened himself willingly to Nikki, and a satisfying complex of images and emotions and thoughts flooded his mind.

And still his body, with an appalling lack of consideration for his peace of mind, responded along with Deymorin's.

The cursed link was worse here, far more intense than it had been at Armayel, where he'd been aware of Deymorin's . . . activities . . . but only as a half-dream, easily ignored.

He curled over, pressing his fists to his temples.

"Mikhyel dunMheric?"

The voice was harsh. Unfamiliar. And agreeably outside his head. He looked up. Dropped his hands.

The voice belonged to a man who, by his demeanor and the rather forceful-looking individuals at his back, was official. It was a guard. Several guards, only a handful of whom wore the Rhomatum constabulary's midnight blue. The others were markedly *not* in uniform.

He drew a breath and stood up, drawing his cloak about him as he did so, painfully, distractingly aware of Deymorin.

"Yes?"

"Do you have your papers, Mikhyel dunMheric?"

And suddenly, despite his brother, past the plain clothing, he recognized the man asking the questions, and his blood froze.

"I explained to the gate—"

"Do you have your papers, Mikhyel dunMheric?" the man persisted.

The man's name was Sironi.

"I—No, I—"

He was gorTarim. Nikki's new wife's *father's* man.

"Then I'm afraid I must place you under arrest."

Chapter Two

Deymio!

Deymorin jumped.

"Sorry, Rags," Kiyrstin said. "Too hard?"

"I— No. Fine."

"Fine? That's it? Just—fine?"

"No! Magnificent. Perfect. But—"

{Gods, Deymio, I need—} *Mikhyel's* voice. In his head. He blinked. "Did you hear—"

{Deymorin!} The thoughts were as clear as words, and fraught with embarrassment. {If you hear me . . . Papers . . .}

He cursed again, not at all softly. "It's Khyel. Something about the damned papers."

He gasped as, with a whispered, *"Khyel can take care of himself,"* Kiyrstin returned to her previous pursuit.

But he'd never "heard" Mikhyel from so great a distance, and he feared more than identity papers had put that edge of panic into Mikhyel's thoughts. A residual impression of green-and-gold-uniformed men sent a wave of ice through him that overwhelmed all other emotions.

She cursed softly, and her eyes glittered up at him. "Trouble?"

He nodded.

"Damn. Sorry." She stood up. "You get your clothes. I'll look for the buttons."

"Under arrest?" Deymorin repeated, doing his best to assume at least the appearance of outraged innocence. "On what charge? By whose order?"

Heads appeared in stable doorways; Deymorin frowned at them, and a few disappeared. Many did not, as vulgar curiosity unerringly sensed a feeding frenzy.

"Deymorin, please," Mikhyel said, and an urge for caution filled that underneath sense. "Perhaps we should just go with them. Straighten this out in private."

The leader of this mixed guard smiled faintly. Two men in Rhomatum constabulary blue, three men in practical Outsider clothing, all openly armed, and this businesslike leader, who, by his moves, carried his own hidden arsenal beneath his middle-class clothing.

Deymorin found something profoundly disturbing about city constables taking orders from such an anonymous source.

But there was no sign of the green-and-gold uniforms he'd thought he'd seen in Mikhyel's mind, colors that he associated with Lidye Fericci dunTarim—now Lidye romNikeanor.

"What's this all about?" Nikki, flanked by two men, appeared from a side tunnel down which their horses had been stabled. His voice held the shrill edge of adolescent nerves. "Do you know who I am?"

Deymorin heard Mikhyel's soft groan, and Deymorin thought, or perhaps it was Mikhyel's thought: *Not now, brother.*

"I know who this man says you are, boy." The leader's eyes ran rudely over Nikki's rumpled figure, over clothing that had been a dandy's pride this morning, before wild rides through storms and horses that needed grooming had taken their ruthless toll.

"Nikaenor Rhomandi dunMheric," the leader said, referring ostentatiously to the gatekeeper's note. "The third I've arrested this week."

"Third?" Nikki repeated and blinked, the arrogance fading. "What are you talking about?"

"Surely you don't believe you're the only one to hear the rumors that the Lady Lidye's husband survived the valley holocaust? I will say, you're the most *complete* group of imposters we've arrested so far. I don't suppose you have your papers. No? The Rhomandi seal ring, perhaps?" The man's brows rose expectantly, his gaze moving again from one to the other of them.

In vain, as it happened. The family ring to which he referred had surely melted, along with the Mauritumin hand illegally bearing it, in a blast of ley-induced lightning. That "holocaust" to which this fellow so blithely referred. The Boreton Turnout had been a horror, but the devastation had been exceedingly localized. And this official was calling it a holocaust? One did have to wonder at the sources of the rumors and the panic, when officials were using such language in the presence of ordinary citizens.

But Deymorin held his peace. There were procedures for them to go through, papers to fill out . . . hell, they'd send to the Tower for someone to come identify them and have their release authorized by the time they finished those forms.

The leader referred again to the gatekeeper's notes. "It says here that you are the Rhomandi, Deymorin, dun-Mheric, Princeps of Rhomatum. That this woman is Kiyrstine romGaretti, first wife of Garetti of Mauritum, and that these are your brothers, Mikhyel and Nikaenor, both of House Rhomandi, both dunMheric. Is that correct?"

"That's correct," Deymorin answered shortly.

"You *are* the Rhomandi?" the man repeated, and Deymorin paused.

The Rhomandi. As if he were still the family patriarch. Mikhyel had *not* made that claim. Wouldn't, meticulous bastard that he was—*that* much hadn't changed. The gatekeeper, or this man himself, had inferred it, meaning Nikki's ascendance to the title was not yet public knowledge.

They'd all agreed, at Armayel, that in all practical senses, Deymorin was still the Rhomandi, but they'd never imagined the issue coming up under quite these circumstances, and considering Nikki's belligerent *do you know who I am* . . . Deymorin was no longer certain how to answer.

Yet even as he hesitated, that sense they shared carried Mikhyel's support, as well as Nikki's to acknowledge his title, and so Deymorin nodded once, briefly and without losing eye contact with the leader.

The man's eyes narrowed, and he seemed momentarily taken aback. But only for a moment.

"In that case," he stated firmly, "I must insist that you follow me."

§   §   §

They didn't give her time to collect her cloak—by the time Kiyrstin thought of that dereliction, it was far too late to remedy the situation.

The guards led them to an iron-barred passageway, the only such gateway she'd seen in this stony maze. While the leader unlocked the gate, the guards collected torches from the floor, old-fashioned light sources that flared at the touch of the punk left simmering in a pot beside the doorway.

The grim-faced leader ordered them to sort themselves, two and two, and then led the way into the wide tunnel. They followed, Nikki and Deymorin to the front, herself and Mikhyel behind. It was a conscious sort, at least on her part, and, from the look he cast her, an arrangement Mikhyel welcomed.

Mikhyel claimed he found her presence restful. Of course, considering her competition for the honor, she didn't set overmuch store on Mikhyel's choice of adjectives. There were times, Mikhyel had revealed to her at Armayel, when his brothers' thoughts could nearly overwhelm his own thinking.

She could well imagine that this was one of those times.

Mikhyel stumbled; she caught his elbow and steadied him.

"Thanks," he murmured.

"My pleasure," she murmured back; and when the guards failed to object, she ventured, "Is it Deymorin?"

He nodded.

"His leg?"

"In part."

"How bad is it?"

"Worse than at Armayel."

"His leg? Or just how much you're picking up on him?"

"Both." Gray eyes shifted toward her in a low, sidelong stare fraught with innuendo. And Kiyrstin thought of what she'd been doing with Deymorin, and who Mikhyel had been talking to at that same moment.

"Oh, dear," she said. "I'm sorry, Mikhyel. Truly."

"Could have been worse."

"By another minute?"

A momentary pause, then his shoulders began to shake. "You might say that."

Another stumble. This time she was ready.

"Damn you, Deymorin!"

She barely caught his muttered whisper.

"What's going on?"

"He's *worried* about me. *Again.* Rings, I get tired of it. He's afraid I'll collapse, or something, and sometimes . . . sometimes my knees just give. It's as if his thoughts—" A curse coincided with another catch in his stride. "Bad enough to be hauled off to Sparingate. I'd prefer to make the trip with some remnants of dignity."

"You don't sound particularly concerned."

"I'm not exactly overjoyed, but there's little we can do until they tell us why we've been arrested. It could just be formality. I can think of several good reasons for processing anyone claiming to be a Rhomandi very carefully into the City, particularly if there are unknown individuals trying to impersonate us. On the other hand, you should know that these men—" He glanced at his side, where a man in a blue uniform walked, eyes straight forward, pointedly granting them privacy. "Most of them, at least, are Ferricci."

"Lidye's father's men?"

"The web was down. The City's resources might well have been overtaxed, the constabulary willing to accept help from any quarter. Lidye's father was here for the wedding. Her husband disappeared the day after. I'm not surprised he's remained, considering what's at stake."

"Considering his daughter might just rule in Rhomatum? Under the right circumstances, of course. Such as the Rhomandi brothers in prison? And Anheliaa dead?"

Another long look, and a stride steadied before the rhythm could be disrupted.

"If Deymorin doesn't get you free of Garetti and marry you soon," Mikhyel said, "I'll do it myself."

"To keep you on your feet?"

His mouth twitched, and for a moment, she was almost sorry her heart had already been swallowed by his older brother.

"I thought you were promised to that young Giephaetum woman—Nethaalye," she reminded him.

"Well, there is that." His face took on a mournful look, then brightened. "Would you consider being a second?"

"Khyel," she said reprovingly. "I've been first wife to Garetti of Mauritum for fifteen years. Much as I love you, I'd have to decline."

"Better to be the Rhomandi's mistress, than the Rhomandi's brother's second, eh?"

"Sad, what the standards of the world are coming to, isn't it?"

He laughed outright this time, which drew a startled look from the guards.

"Rings," he muttered, and his head turned away from her. When he turned back, his face was grim.

"The man in charge?" His lips barely moved, but she caught the question and nodded. "Sironi gorTarim."

*Gor*Tarim. A surname that indicated a man sworn for life to Tarim Ferricci. More than a hired guard. Much more. GorTarim meant that Sironi, if faced with conflict between Rhomatumin law and Tarim's direct orders, would follow Tarim's orders without question.

Tarim's orders. Lidye's father's. Not Lidye's.

And Sironi gorTarim had deliberately avoided stating the reason for their arrest, for all his allusions to imposters. Sironi would have stood at Tarim's back at all public events here in Rhomatum. Sironi should recognize Nikki, even if he didn't recognize the other two.

"It has to be an arrest *because* of who you are," she murmured back.

He raised a brow. "One would think. On the other hand, considering my rather . . . befuddled answers, he might well believe he was dealing with a half-wit, if not an outright imposter. With all due respect, my charming almost-sister, this most recent demonstration of filial rapport only verifies my conviction that when the time comes for me to face the Council—or any other official body, singular or plural—my two brothers are going to be as far away as possible. Preferably alone. Preferably asleep."

"Ah, but sleep brings dreams," she pointed out.

"True. Math, perhaps? A good set of calculus problems would keep them occupied."

"Or *put* them to sleep."

"Drugged!" He lifted a finger for emphasis. "*That* would be . . . nice."

His voice trailed off. He was staring straight ahead, a rather puzzled expression in eyes that were quite, quite unfocused.

She held her hand just off his elbow—just in case—and waited for him to return to her.

He was staring at the back of the guards, wondering to whom those men might belong, knowing it was important. He should know. . . .

He *did* know, and the guard was ahead of Deymorin, not himself. Mikhyel sent a sharp-edged thought upstream against the ignorance:

{GorTarim, Deymorin. Sironi gor*Tarim*. Captain.}

And knew he'd been heard when Deymorin's head jerked. And on the thread back to him came acknowledgment. Apology.

Anger. Against Tarim.

But anger wasn't in order. Yet. Mikhyel counseled Deymorin silently against assuming Tarim was responsible. There were other possibilities, and falsely accusing Tarim might well turn Sironi actively against them.

Deymorin's broad shoulders relaxed.

So much depended upon who was actually in control of the Tower. If Anheliaa was in charge, their processing should be fairly straightforward. If he could just get to the Tower and talk, face-to-face with his aunt, their differences could be put rapidly into perspective. It wasn't as if they'd returned to Rhomatum to throw her out, he would argue. With only Lidye romNikaenor to replace her in the Tower, they'd be fools to try to overthrow Anheliaa.

Anheliaa would understand that level of paranoid reasoning.

But Anheliaa's death was, of course, the eventuality Lidye's father awaited. And Lidye's father's man was marching them toward Sparingate. Lidye's father might well want their return to the City kept from Anheliaa. Possibly even from Lidye.

Lidye was, from his observations of her, a weak and easily swayed individual. A father might well want strong-minded Rhomandis kept away from her—at least until he had firmly established his own power base within Rhomatum.

Laughter burst from Nikki and Deymorin, sauntering arm in arm ahead of him. The mental thread that was a constant in his life these days carried images of other tunnels, other underground rooms, and shared adventures.

And a determinedly cheerful outlook from Deymorin. Deymorin didn't want Nikki worrying, he wanted them all to project confidence to their guards, not concern.

Mikhyel was doubly glad, then, that Kiyrstin had chosen to walk beside him. Pairing Deymorin with Nikki not only prevented Nikki from intercepting Mikhyel's dark thoughts, it gave his brothers this opportunity, however contrived, to share fond memories.

There'd been too much of himself and Deymorin and black history in recent days.

Deymorin and his adolescent friends had combed these tunnels for years. Nikki, born with the soul of a historian and infected early with Deymorin's capacity for getting into trouble, had been losing himself in them ever since Deymorin first brought him here nearly ten years ago. But Mikhyel had never been part of those youthful explorations. Not Deymorin's earliest ones, not the later ventures with Nikki.

Possibly he'd been invited, he couldn't say for certain that he had not, but his life had been quite ruthlessly disciplined in those days, by his own choice as much as anyone's ordering.

He stumbled yet again, would have gone to his knees but for Kiyrstin's hand on his elbow. Not Deymorin's doing this time, just an irregularity underfoot and his own graceless self. Kiyrstin's hands steadied him, and Kiyrstin's voice reassured his brothers—quickly enough, convincingly enough—that Deymorin never thought to worry.

"I should let you make my case to him all the time," Mikhyel murmured to her, when Deymorin's attention had returned to Nikki.

"I wasn't certain. You looked very distracted for a moment."

"I was. I'm fine now."

She tipped her head as if to see him better. "Truth?"

"Truth," he answered firmly.

She gave a quick nod, declaring the topic closed, and slipped her hand in his, lacing their fingers together. Friendship. Support. And respect for his privacy.

Unorthodox in her appearance, uncompromising in her opinions, this Mauritumin lady of Deymorin's was nonetheless a very comfortable sort of person, and Mikhyel welcomed her as an almost-sister. Welcomed, as well, her custody of his hand that gave him an anchor to his immediate surroundings.

"What is all this?" she asked, squinting past him at a blocked side tunnel bearing an official nonentry sign. Beyond the blockade, barely visible in the flickering torchlight, were signs of in-progress renovations.

"The first Rhomatum."

"Underground? Grandfather Darius *was* a bit of an eccentric, wasn't he?"

A hint of laughter touched her voice: deliberately, he was certain. Kiyrstin, like Deymorin, had decided to let Sironi worry about why his prisoners were *not* worried.

"Actually," he answered, striving to match her tone, "I'm quite certain it was a good idea at the time. If Darius is to be believed, the little squall that chased us in was a spring shower compared to the storms that ravaged this valley when the exiles first arrived. These caverns are natural. They were here, ready to be occupied in those days. And safe."

"How far do they go?"

"We don't know yet. It's only recently been rediscovered. Historians are still piecing together what we've located with the old records. We do know these tunnels extend for miles into the Khoramali Range and toward Tower Hill, though the vast majority of the living areas appear to be in this area. They connect natural caverns of all sizes that the first citizens adapted for use as everything from stables to whorehouses to hospitals."

"How long?" The laughter was gone. Her voice held a hushed awe Mikhyel did not believe contrived. "How long did they have to live down here?"

"Years. For some families, generations. Until Rhomatum was capped, these warrens were all that kept them alive. Even then, Darius had to control Shatum and Giephaetum before major construction could begin above ground. And that would have been . . . oh, the better part of thirty years."

"Thirty *years*?"

"Eighteen years to recuperate from capping Rhomatum. Twelve after Shatum. Life was not easy on Darius, Kiyrstin."

"But . . . but there were *thousands* involved in the exodus."

"Thousands?" Mikhyel asked, honestly amused this time. There'd been five or six hundred—including the children—who originally followed Darius out of Mauritum.

"And thousands more followed," Kiyrstin continued, and that much was true. "Refugees from all *over* Maurislan.

Where did they *put* all those people? How did they make room? How did they *feed* them."

"With shovels, I should imagine," he answered lightly, finding the mood contagious. "And sheep. *Lots* of sheep."

She cast him a suspicious sideways look.

"Sometimes, Mikhyel dunMheric, you do remind me of your brother."

"My apologies, dear lady."

"Accepted. And my sympathy, dear lord, for your affliction."

"I do thank you."

Their joint laughter roused more interest from his brothers, who demanded enlightenment, to which Kiyrstin replied, "Mind your own business."

Deymorin shrugged, but his gaze slid down to their clasped hands, pointedly lingering there. Without quite knowing how, Mikhyel found his arm draped around Kiyrstin's shoulders, and hers around his waist, for all the world like moon-touched lovers.

Which had to be Kiyrstin's doing, because it certainly wasn't his.

"Deymio, I—"

Deymorin just shook his head and turned away. "My sympathy, little brother."

His almost-echo of Kiyrstin's words prompted another fit of laughter, which Deymorin picked up, and then Nikki, in a self-feeding loop that bordered on hysteria.

A prod from a frustrated guardsman wrenched Mikhyel almost painfully free of the loop. Once free, he slammed a wall down between himself and Deymorin, and walked for a time in grim silence.

"Seriously, Khyel," Kiyrstin's voice disrupted his darkening thoughts. "Where *did* they put all the people?"

"The prisons," he answered abruptly.

"Friendly."

Which might have referred to the ancient distribution, and might refer to his attitude. Repentant, he elaborated. "They weren't prisons then."

"Old Darius must have been trying to discourage them into going back to Mauritum." Deymorin joined their conversation without looking back. "Caverns. Huge ones. A whole series of them. They're the only part of the Old City that have remained in permanent use since the Founding.

When the City grew above, so did the crime—especially
since Mauritum insisted on sending us all the chaff. A few
well-placed cave-ins, and you've as secure a prison as any
warden could ask for. Thanks to Darius, we get the scut
from all over the web. 'Specially in the Crypt." He glanced
back with a wicked grin. "Better hope we don't get sent
there, Barrister."

"Rings, brother, don't even *joke* about it."

"Crypt," Kiyrstin repeated. "Dare I ask?"

"The more grievous the crime," Deymorin answered,
"the deeper they send you. The Crypt's the worst. And
guess who sentenced each and every one of those charming
individuals? Lovely place, Khyel. Primitive. Cold. Damp.
No privacy."

"Speaking from personal experience, Rags?" Kiyrstin
asked lightly.

"Of course."

"Aha, the plot thickens," she said. "What was he in
for, Khyel?"

"I—"

"Murder, Khyel," Deymorin prompted. "Tell her it was
for *successful* murder."

"I—" Mikhyel felt the hysteria building again and fought
it down.

"Oh, never mind. For a politician, fry, you're an amazingly second-rate liar. I was a professional inmate, Shepherdess. Never made it any lower than the Pit, fortunately.
Most of the nonsense I was convicted of I even committed,
though not necessarily at the same time they took me in
for it. Not a bad system, actually. Get drunk, get a bit
rowdy, wake up in the Pit, and spend the next few days
repairing what you almost remember breaking. Learned a
lot about carpentry and plumbing that way, I assure you.
Civilized my cronies in a hurry."

"You took a bit more convincing, I take it," Kiyrstin
commented.

"Naturally," Deymorin said, and turned back to Nikki.

"Sweet Maurii," Kiyrstin shook her head. "The things
we don't know."

"We?" Mikhyel asked.

"Mauritum."

"That the Princeps-to-be of Rhomatum was a delinquent
juvenile? Because that's all it was, I assure you. We treat

our adult criminals rather less kindly. Why should you know? We did our best to hide the fact, particularly from hostile spies."

She chuckled. "Rest easy, O keeper of Rhomatum's self-respect. No, just that the image Mauritum maintains of early Rhomatum is, shall we say, far different."

She tucked her arm in his, and led him off into a discussion of those differences, and he ceased his attempts to direct the conversation otherwise. The relationship between Kiyrstin and Deymorin baffled him. He admired it. He even envied Deymorin a woman who could joke with him under such circumstances.

But he didn't understand it.

Sometimes he wondered if he ever would.

Their path rose slowly but steadily from the stables toward the prison, a pathway dry and sweet-smelling. Modern engineers, marveling at the drainage and ventilation of the Old City, had searched in vain for the plans, refusing to believe happenstance and luck had created it.

The earliest settlements had been tents set up in the caverns to the northeast of the node, their location chosen more for the natural benefits *above* ground than proximity to the node itself. From here, the tunnels had once stretched clear to the heart of what had become Tower Hill and far into the Khoramali foothills, and the gardens and sheep pastures that had, indeed, kept generations alive.

Over the years, as surface life became increasingly remote, those underground tents had become houses, and ultimately apartments and even businesses, built farther and farther away from the community caves, as refugees continued to pour out of the Mauritum Web.

Tunnels had grown between all the areas into a huge maze of which only the segment that lay beneath the Khoratum expansion had been extensively explored.

Officially. He'd never asked how far Nikki had gotten on his solo expeditions.

They passed through one guarded doorway, and past a door that appeared to be a lift platform.

Another guarded doorway, and then two lamps flickering ahead indicated the path they followed branched. One angled up, the other down.

One, Mikhyel knew from those maps, would lead to the

prison offices, and those wards for minor offenses—
Deymorin's Pit, the Womb, which was the female equivalent of the Pit, and other, smaller holding areas.

The other, the downward path, led to the Crypt.

As they approached the branch, the guards closed in at
last, demanding silence.

And herded them toward the downward slope.

Chapter Three

His name was Thyerri. He'd had another name once, as he'd had another life . . . once.

"Boy? Boy! I want your skinny Khoratumin ass over here, and I want it *now*!"

Once, a handful of weeks and a lifetime ago, he'd been a dancer, in every sense of the word. Now . . .

Thyerri balanced the final mug atop three of its companions, swept the double-stacked tray off the counter and over his head, then slid his way past crowded tables and hands determined to impede his progress. One particularly eager set of fingers nearly succeeded in toppling his tray, but he sidestepped smoothly and in two toe-tipped strides made the corner booth, where he distributed mugs and plates with the economy of movement one mastered in the first day on the job, else one didn't have a second—not in Bharlon's Tavern.

"Well, what have we here?" A fifth uniformed man had joined a booth already overcrowded with large bodies, padded clothing, and steel weapons. "*Boy*, you said, dunMarn? How can you tell with these slick-chinned hillers?"

The man called dunMarn laughed. "The prettiest are always men, captain, as you'll discover soon enough. After the first handful of mistakes."

"Everything else looks too damned *young* to fuck," another man grumbled.

"Oh, I don't know . . ." the newest addition to the booth drawled, and his bored gaze traveled the room, like a consumer studying the merchandise. His uniform had a leather band emblazoned with an insignia of some sort. Captain, so the other had called him, and new to Khoratum, from their talk.

Not that it mattered to Thyerri. New faces, new accents: one ceased after a time to try and place them—assuming one had ever cared in the first place. To Thyerri, they were all foreigners, invaders of Khoratum. Lowlanders. Valleyfolk. *Rijhili.*

And Thyerri hated them, all of them, with the singular bitterness of the dispossessed. In that former life, he'd been nearly oblivious to them. They'd been nothing but names and political concepts, invaders of the mountain, destroyers of the village. Curiosities at best, with their complex political intrigues.

Most of all, they had been the source of the dance rings.

In this life, that invasion, the associated destruction was all too personal. In this life, a life without the Dance, the faces changed, the accents changed, but the bold hands remained the same.

"Ah, sirs," Thyerri said, forcing his voice to the pleasant tone one had to use with customers, "you insult my lady friends." He swayed out of range of the captain, who seemed determined to challenge his companion's judgment regarding Thyerri's anatomy, and pointed with his chin to a voluptuous woman weaving among the tables. "Khani, there, is worth a dozen of my humble self, don't you agree?"

Not to mention she'd be more than willing to take the lot on between one order and the next, for the right price. Khani was Khorandi, born and reared, and she was accustomed to rijhili looks and touches . . . and fond of rijhili coin. As if sensing their eyes on her, Khani tossed her mane of artificially curled hair back over a bare shoulder and winked at Thyerri, before turning back to her customer.

"Your tastes are too flamboyant, boy," the captain drawled. "A man of breeding might choose, instead, a secretive air, and charms somewhat less openly offered."

This time the captain had judged accurately: Sakhithe, whose lithe movements his avaricious gaze followed, was indeed a woman—as much as any ex-dancer was man or woman.

Like Thyerri, Sakhithe wore the loose trousers and tunic of the hill-folk. But while Thyerri's elbows gained a few more threads toward freedom each night, and his tunic sported blotches of inexplicable tenacity, Sakhithe's garments had delicate embroidery at hem and throat, and seemed utterly impervious to stain.

Spare-fleshed, light-boned and black-haired, Sakhithe

was like enough to be Thyerri's sister. Alike enough to make him wonder if the man, whose jaded gaze had shifted back to Thyerri, was deliberately goading him.

The captain missed his mark in one sense: the physical similarity was only that. Thyerri was not, at least to his knowledge, directly related to Sakhithe. But Thyerri owed his presence here in Bharlori's to Sakhithe's timely intervention in his life, and he wasn't about to encourage this coarse lowlander's interest in her.

"Exquisite, sir, I agree," he replied, and assumed a forlorn expression. "However, as her five large brothers would take extreme exception to my suit, I keep my distance."

"And advise others to do likewise, eh, boy?" But the captain's eyes drifted back to Sakhithe, a predatory gaze that sent a warning shiver down Thyerri's spine.

Sakhithe's shorn hair and formless clothing, her very movements, should have cued the man she wasn't for hire. But this rijhili captain might not recognize the trademarks of an ex-radical dancer of Khoratum. And even if he did recognize the signs, this foreigner might not realize how disinterested a radical learned to be, here in the newest satellite node of Rhomatum.

And not likely to care if he did realize.

With some bitterness, Thyerri noted that dunMarn, who had been so quick to correct the captain's first incorrect assumption regarding hillers did not as eagerly correct this new error.

Another hail, this time from the room's far side.

"Your order, sir?" Thyerri asked, and when the captain seemed not to hear him, "*Sir*, your order? I've other ta—"

A slit-eyed warning sent him an involuntary step backward. "Ale, scut, if it's drinkable. And one of those, whatever it is." Pointing to a plate of *merifin* tubers and chicken. "The rest looks like hog slop."

"*Boy!*"

Armed with empty mugs and another round ordered, Thyerri hurried over to the impatient table, added their order to his memory, and acknowledged a third party's arrival before escaping to the kitchen, where Cook was waging war with her temporary help.

He gave Cook the numbers, dodged a flying soup bone, and ducked back out to draw the ales himself. Zelin, the elderly bartender, was occupied at the counter's far end, scrubbing mugs as fast as his hands would fly.

Business was, according to Bharlori, out of hand—though one didn't hear the harried owner complain overmuch. Uphill, in Greater Khoratum, most of the kitchens were down, their modern, ley-powered heating elements sitting dark and dead ever since the collapse of the Rhomatum Web.

Khoratum Tower being new and sometimes less than reliable, those buildings had hearths for emergency heating and therefore they had the *means* to cook their own meals. It was even possible the highly paid rijhili chefs retained in those valley-style dwellings might even recall what to *do* with an open fire.

But you couldn't tell that from Bharlori's vantage in Lesser Khoratum. Bharlori's wood fires needed no web to boil water and bake bread. Neither did Lhuiini's Bar, Bharlori's competition here on the outermost fringes of Khoratum. Consequently, for four weeks, ever since the collapse, those occupants of the modern uphill mansions had descended upon the tavern. From dawn to dusk and late into the night, a steady stream of customers—rich owners, maids, and stableboys—had inundated Bharlori's for everything from a multicourse feast to a bowl of soup.

A stream for which Thyerri, ex-apprentice radical dancer of Khoratum, was exceedingly thankful.

"Oh, Thyerri! Bless the Mother, may I take these? You're wonderful."

A whirlwind of skirts, Khani, he thought, swept past, taking his mugs with her.

He opened his mouth to protest, but she was gone. He sighed, and jumped up on the counter to lean across after clean mugs. A hand grabbed his shirt tail and pulled him back.

"Guess who's out there?" Mishthi whispered in his ear, and before he could answer: "Rhyys! I'm *sure* of it this time. Please, Thyerri, is it?"

Mishthi served Rhyys at least twice a week. . . .

Except it never was. Rhyys dunTarec, Ringmaster of Khoratum, would die of starvation before openly acknowledging a use for Lesser Khoratum.

Thyerri, feigning the excitement Mishthi craved, strained up on the points of his toes to see the customer (who bore little if any resemblance to the Khoratum Ringmaster) and dropped down again. "Sorry, Mishthi. I don't think so."

"Oh, well." She sighed, picked up her tray and hurried back to her customers.

Rhyys *dunTarec*.

Thyerri opened the tap on another mug.

The surname, dunTarec, was fabricated, as was the family name Thyerri couldn't at the moment recall. Valley names, valley associations. To hear Rhyys talk, to see his clothing, one would think him as foreign to Khoratum as a foreigner who seriously considered soliciting a Khoratum radical dancer.

Never mind Rhyys had been born in one of the thatch-roofed huts visible from Bharlori's front porch.

Leaving the tap open, Thyerri exchanged mugs without spilling a drop.

Bharlori's Tavern lay in the outermost edges of the Khoratum umbrella, where even at its best, the power fluctuated. The wood-and-stone buildings here were old, the last vestiges of the flourishing village of Khorandi, displaced fifteen years ago when Anheliaa of Rhomatum announced the plan to add Khoratum at last to her Syndicate of Node Cities.

Even before the capping, rijhili from all over the Rhomatum Web had swarmed up the mountain to consume the small village of Khorandi. Not to live there, not to savor the beauty of the surrounding mountains, but to build Khorandi into something foreign and ugly.

Tiny Khorandi had had no say in the matter. The more fortunate, such as Bharlori, had kept their business by virtue of their unfavorable location to the Khoratum Node. Those farther uphill, those residences and businesses solidly within the new power umbrella, had had no defense at all against the rijhili developers.

Those who actually invested in the new node lived elsewhere, sending lesser family members to handle their interests here. Petty people. Sniping people. People resentful of their exile into the barbarous climate of the Khoramali Mountains. People who cozied up to Rhyys in hopes of escaping the cold winds, giving Rhyys a false legitimacy, a respect he hadn't earned, save for being Anheliaa's choice to master the Khoratum Rings.

Thyerri dived across the counter after more mugs, as those he'd filled again disappeared.

Thyerri didn't care—particularly—about Khorandi. The village had welcomed the rijhili invaders, seeing in them false hopes of personal prosperity. Thyerri did care about the trees that had died with the capping of Khoratum, and he cared about the rapacious squandering of the ley that was the essence of the earth itself for purposes so foolish as cooking Rhyys dunTarec's stew.

But without the invaders, without the capping, without the rings spinning in the Tower uphill, the dance rings would never have come to the Khoramali. Thyerri had never known whether to bless or to curse Rakshi for that gift.

Rakshi, the hillers' god of chance—the spirit that goaded the true radical dancer to the edge of sanity . . . from the moment Thyerri had seen the dance rings spinning and held his breath as the first dancer flew among them, he'd known the spirit of Rakshi had touched his heart. He'd dreamed of those spinning silver rings flashing in the sunlight, felt the brush of the ring-swept air against his cheek, the tug of his hair as a ring flew past.

Rakshi's call, and only that, he knew now, had brought him out of his beloved mountains and into the foreigner's new city. And because of that call, he was alone now, condemned to a life that was not even a shadow of his former existence.

Fifteen years ago. Thyerri had been seven . . . or perhaps six, when the first invaders came to the mountain village. It was possible he'd been born in Khorandi; he didn't remember. It was possible he'd had a human mother. He didn't remember that either.

He'd had a grandmother in the earliest memories of that former life. And after that . . . after that, Thyerri had lived in the hills. That was all he remembered; that was all he allowed himself to remember.

"Boy!"

A glancing blow to the side of his head brought Thyerri to a sense of ale slopping over his hand and growing a puddle on the floor. Horrified, he shut the tap.

"Out of your supper, hill-boy." Bharlori filled the last mug and shoved him toward the cramped and smoky room. "We've customers crowding the door, dreamer. Ale. Food. Silver and out the door. You know the rules."

Music caressed his ears as he hoisted the tray overhead

and pushed through the swinging half-door. Pipes and lute, those were a given, evenings at Bharlori's, but Kharmier and Trahdio had brought friends tonight. A drummer, whose beat a dancer's feet matched without benefit of thought, a guitarist and flautist. It was a mix these valley-born invaders likely found odd, but a mix this "hill-boy" relished with every breath he drew.

Hill-boy. The hill-folk had a different name for themselves; as they had another, less flattering term, for the invaders; and a worse one still for such as Bharlori and Rhyys, who were hill-folk before they styled themselves and their lives after the valley-men.

But Thyerri had learned words couldn't hurt, had learned that not all invaders were rijhili, and that Bharlori was not Rhyys. Bharlori had given him this job and a safe, warm place to sleep, and good food and honest pay for honest work.

Which, when all was said and done, was a better bargain than any Rhyys had ever offered.

Chapter Four

Sparingate Crypt; the maximum security ward reserved for the most dangerous of criminals. Deymorin halted at the first security gate, outraged; Mikhyel cast him a rueful glance and moved through the doorway.

"You can't be serious!" Deymorin protested both the order and Mikhyel's acceptance.

"We have our orders," said the leader. Sironi, Mikhyel's thoughts had named him. And gorTarim, honor-bonded captain of Tarim's personal bodyguard.

"And we have our gods-be-damned rights! We've not even been charged! What about a trial? What about notification of our kin? This cursed farce has gone sour. I want a messenger sent to the Tower. Immediately!"

"At this hour?" the Shatumin captain responded. "I'm afraid that's not possible. We have our orders."

As if at a signal, his two guards again heaved him toward the door. Deymorin slammed palms to the iron-reinforced frame and heaved back.

"Where's Oshram? I demand to see Warden Oshram."

Their answer was a third synchronous shove, but he had his leverage now, and their efforts were in vain.

"Whose orders, Captain Sironi?" Mikhyel asked, past Deymorin's set feet and braced elbows.

There was a pause, and Deymorin chanced a glance over his shoulder. Sironi's face had a startled look, then his eyes narrowed, trying, Deymorin thought, to see past him to Mikhyel. The next moment, a blow to the back of his weak leg buckled Deymorin's knee, and he stumbled through the door, into Mikhyel, who flattened himself against the tunnel wall and extended a steadying hand.

"All right, man," Deymorin gasped, using Mikhyel's hold to pull himself upright and resting his weight lightly on the traitorous leg. "All right," he repeated, as Nikki passed through, and guards followed. "But *not* the woman! Not here!"

Sironi smiled. "Of course not. We'll take very *special* care of her."

Forgetting his leg, Deymorin took a step toward the captain, who fell back, his smile fading.

But Deymorin reached past him, hooked Kiyrstin by the waist and pulled her close for a declaration of proprietorship that left them both gasping for breath.

"See that you do," Deymorin said to Sironi as he released her. "It's possible, of course, that you are right, that we *are* imposters. Then again, we might not be."

Something in his face must have convinced the captain, who blanched and inhaled sharply before assuring him, "She'll be taken to the women's cavern, obviously. Given private quarters, away from the whores—"

"Thanks just the same," Kiyrstin said, eyeing the captain with open suspicion, "I'll take my chances with the local ladies."

"M'lady, I *assure* you," the captain began, but Deymorin laughed, which simply made the captain squirm more.

Deymorin kissed Kiyrstin again, casually, confidently, and said, "Try not to antagonize him, m'love."

"What do you mean, antagonize?"

"Don't bite him." He turned on his heel, and swaggered down the narrow tunnel in his brothers' wake, forcing himself not to look back at her, exuding a confidence he by no means felt.

ᔓ   ᔓ   ᔓ

More than ever, as Deymorin limped out of sight, Kiyrstin envied the brothers their silent communication. She wished she could have five minutes alone with him, to help the pain in his leg, to reassure him, to tell him not to worry about her—or his brothers.

And with that thought, she was afraid, truly afraid, for the first time since they'd left Armayel that morning, more frightened than she'd been since she met Deymorin. Deymorin would kill himself trying to protect his brothers in such a place, Mikhyel from resentful offenders, Nikki from his own youthful stupidity.

But there was nothing she could do for him except keep

herself prepared to recognize opportunity should it arise. And to take care of herself, that most of all, so that next time, he'd have that much more confidence in her, that much less he felt he had to worry about.

And *she* had to trust *Deymorin* to realize that his life in exchange for his brothers' temporary comfort was no bargain.

Trust. It all came down to trusting one another.

Take care of yourself, JD. . . .

A hand gripped her arm: Sironi. Kiyrstin let her gaze move directly from his hand to his face.

"Tell me, Captain Sironi," she asked, "have you any intention of using that hand again?"

His eyes widened, ever so slightly, and he released her arm. Abruptly. Then he jerked his head, motioning her down the tunnel, away from the Crypt, away from Deymorin.

§ § §

As Deymorin's limp eased, Mikhyel tried not to begin. It was Deymorin's pain, he kept repeating to himself, *his* limping would do nothing to ease the sensation. Besides, if Deymorin's leg truly was injured, Deymorin needed to know now, not after it was too late.

They'd discovered that unpleasant fact at Armayel, when the shoulder wound Nikki had acquired before the battle at Boreton festered. Unknown to them all, Mikhyel had grown weak fighting *Nikki's* pain, but until Nikki collapsed they'd none of them imagined how dangerously infected the wound had become.

It was an unpleasant and unkind gift he'd acquired, unkind to himself, and to his brothers. Nikki might have died had the wound gone untreated much longer. Mikhyel didn't know which was worse, the pain and festering, or the anger and accusations, once Nikki was strong enough to argue: Deymorin accusing Nikki of selfishly willing the pain to Mikhyel's keeping, Nikki yelling that Mikhyel shouldn't take it if he didn't want it, and Mikhyel wishing they'd both shut up and go away and let him die in peace.

And in all the arguing, no one had pointed the finger at the true culprit: this insidious rapport that took no effort to create, and everything to stop, that kept Nikki from knowing how sick he was until almost too late, and kept Mikhyel's own mind so preoccupied, that his logic skewed wildly.

This time, it was Deymorin's body that invaded his, and the throb in his leg increased with each step. Beginning to wonder if perhaps the guard's heavy boot *had* done serous damage, he tried to catch a glimpse of Deymorin's leg past the heavy cloak—

And threw his weight onto what should have been a perfectly sound leg, but wasn't. He stumbled. Deymorin's hands caught and steadied him. The pain shot through in full force, and his leg collapsed.

"Nikki?" He gasped, and reached for his younger brother. And Nikki was there, holding him on his feet, and Deymorin was cursing him for a fool, and the pain in his leg flowed out through the arm Deymorin retained, so rapidly he could almost see the flow, so rapidly, the relief left him light-headed.

{Damn you, Mikhyel dunMheric, *say* something next time!}

Deymorin's thoughts flared and then the pain was gone, for the most part, and his head was clearer and the guards were urging them on.

Of the five men still with them, two wore City blue. From their obvious discomfort they, at least, resented the actions they were being forced to take against the Rhomandi brothers.

Factions. Someone, Sironi, Tarim, Lidye, possibly even Anheliaa herself, was trying very hard to create factions within Rhomatum. These men in City blue were being told to follow orders or . . . what? Power was shifting hands . . . but to where?

Sironi shouldn't be here, shouldn't be taking them to the Crypt, certainly shouldn't be bypassing all established legal procedures. *Rhomatumin* law.

It had been a gamble, calling Sironi by name. Mikhyel had hoped it might prove their claim—and in that, he might have achieved his goal.

But Sironi knew, now, that he'd been recognized. And that, Mikhyel thought, as the heavy door to the Crypt swung open, might not have been the smartest revelation of Mikhyel dunMheric's career.

*   *   *

The smell alone on the dank air rising out of the black depths beyond the oak and iron door was enough to destroy any remaining delusions regarding the nature of their home for the night.

A crypt indeed.

Mikhyel paused in the doorway, overwhelmed, wondering what had become of the marvel of engineering that kept the tunnels so fresh.

He knew what lay below him, as he'd known the lay of the tunnels they'd walked. He'd seen maps of the tunnels, floor plans of the wards. Had read treatises on the humane care and feeding of the prisoners. He knew what he sent men into when he signed the sentencing papers.

But lines on a paper had little in common with reality. The vast cavern swallowed the light from the tunnel. Or perhaps, he thought, in cold analysis, that distant flickering light in the tunnel was set precisely *so* the new inmate received the most chilling introduction to his new abode.

A gauntleted hand between his shoulder blades sent him stumbling into that darkness. He fought for balance, felt a foot slip over an edge and threw his weight backward, into arms that caught and held him.

Deymorin: the thought/sense/awareness that was indefinably his brother came through even the adrenaline-induced panic that gripped him. He could see the edge then, a darkness against a deeper black. They'd come in at the head of a staircase. Stone-cut and foot-worn, open at least on one side, those stairs extended far past the reach of the doorway's dim light.

Gas lamps, jets protruding from the walls, made eerily flickering pools of light among the irregular contours of the cavern. Men gathered in those pools, passing the hours as men did in places such as this.

Lighting was carefully controlled within the cavern, according to those treatises. The intensity levels shifted at regular intervals to simulate the passage of time above ground. They were in evening now, late evening. Soon, even these pools, for the most part, would disappear.

Tables, littered (as was the floor around them) with remnants of meals, supported card games and dice. To his left, barely visible past curving limestone, the light-pool glinted with running water.

The latrine, his mental map recalled. The one spot in

the cavern that would remain in full-light the entire night. Complete facilities with circulating bathing pool, and other provisions for personal hygiene and comfort.

These men chose to live in the filth his senses insisted lay below him; they were not forced into it.

Where that limited light failed to reach, darkness more complete than any he'd ever known swirled and eddied. Those private niches radiated sounds one didn't care to investigate further.

Criminals, the Council maintained and Mikhyel had always agreed, should be discouraged from ever going to prison again. On the other hand, a man cast here who considered himself innocent of wrongdoing might well feel sorely used.

It seemed that lately his life had been filled with new perspectives.

Without warning his sense of *Deymorin* vanished, that gauntleted hand struck a second time—

And he was falling.

(Lightning flashed.

(That which had been, was, or would be Mikhyel, 2nd son of Mheric, 16th Princeps of Rhomatum, hung suspended in the rarified air inside the spinning leythium-coated rings of Rhomatum. Their hum surrounded him, engulfed him, penetrated to his very core, until, body and soul, he was one with the ley.

(Body. Soul. Only his mind was exempt: observing, calculating.

(Aware.

(A second flash, blinding bright, and he hovered in the cloudless sky above a city that pulsed with the energy of the node buried deep in the earth below Tower Hill, power that rose and coalesced at the bidding of the Rhomatum Rings—and the madwoman who commanded them: Anheliaa, descendant of Darius.

(Anheliaa: powerful, mad—who had had the shaping of himself as she had shaped the web to her bidding.

(That power radiated outward, unseen to ordinary mortal eyes, but not to his ley-sensitized vision, a throbbing opalescence that rippled to the limits of the Rhomatum power umbrella and beyond, confined, now, to eighteen treeless leylines with their pristine, fine-graveled highways: supernatural spider-threads linking Rhomatum Node to her eighteen satellite nodes.

(Eighteen buds to Rhomatum's mature bloom.

(A return swell: enhanced radiance from those satellite nodes coalescing within Rhomatum. The satellites lending power to the hub.

(A third blast that he realized now was not lightning at all, but iridescent flames that pressed Rhomatum's perimeter, flames not from without, but from within, flames that billowed out of Rhomatum Tower, coalesced into a single raging finger, and reached Outside—

(Toward a point *between* leylines, toward areas that appeared night-black to ley-awareness, areas that the mind insisted the ley could not reach.

(Toward Boreton.

(But body and soul denied that reason. The flames reached and strained, striving for a point within the darkness where there lurked an absence of light darker than the darkest night.

(For Boreton. For the Mauritumin machine that lurked in the shadows.

(Anti-ley machine.

(Harnessed lightning.

(The iridescent pulse arced from Rhomatum a fourth time, and a fifth, in rapid succession, until the pulse became a steady stream flowing irresistibly toward that anti-ley source, destruction its objective.

(A stream whose origin was not Rhomatum, but the satellites, which continued to send wave upon opalescent wave down the leylines toward their parent node, who sent that fire blazing outward.

(Toward Boreton.

(All to destroy that tiny point of nonlight.

(And in the center of that target: his brothers. Another part of his being, not body, not mind, not soul, knew that without question, as his mind reasoned that the Tower-generated force bent upon destruction would take them with it.

(Unless he intervened, that unidentified portion cried, and his mind answered, *How?* then self-reasoned: The alternative? To live while those two died.

(Unacceptable.

(He dove into the pulsing stream—

(—and the valley disappeared in a flash of utter darkness.)

Screams filled the air. His. And Deymorin's curses.

"Damn you, get the light out of his eyes!"

Boreton. Boreton. Boreton . . .

And Deymorin's arms lifted him, held him against the residual tremors that always took hold of him following this newest nightmare. And {Quiet, Khyel . . .} filled his mind.

Invaded his mind.

Because of Boreton.

"Damn you, Anheliaa! Damn Garetti! Damn you all to—"

{Khyel, shut up.}

Firm. Commanding.

Deymorin.

Whom he'd saved.

Deymorin.

Who hadn't let him die.

When he should have.

Damn you, Deymorin dunMheric.

He closed his mouth and the screams ended.

Slowly, his head cleared to madness surrounding him. To men with lamps. Men with torches. Far more men than the handful that had brought him here. Perhaps, he thought in a surge of groundless optimism, men from the Tower, to take them out of here. To take them home, to the Tower . . . and Anheliaa.

Before the men incarcerated in Sparingate Crypt recognized him. Somehow, even Anheliaa was preferable to that fate.

There were lights again, shining into his eyes, and someone rolled his head this way and that, until, with a curse, he pushed himself up and out of Deymorin's arms, away from Deymorin's oppressive concern that was the real weight holding him down. He was feeling well enough—except for a myriad of aches and bruises (his own for a change)—and not hesitant about saying as much.

"You'll do, little brother." Deymorin laughed, with relief instead of humor, and the inner pressure eased, only to flare again into a black anger that was directed up the stairs at the lighted doorway. "No thanks to that murderous scut. I want that man's name and identification number logged

with our arrest entry, Oshram," Deymorin said to the
shadow standing next to him. "Along with a willful attempt
to cause life-threatening injury. If Khyel has suffered any
significant damage, that guard's going to be held personally accountable."

"It'll be done, Deymio-lad," the shadow answered in a
low voice, "but I doubt it will make—" The voice broke
off. Mikhyel could wish that statement completed.

Oshram. The Warden of Sparingate. Who was (Why was
he not surprised?) on a familiar name basis with his disreputable older brother. A Rhomatumin warden who was
afraid to speak his mind in front of these Shatumin guards.

"Oshram?" Mikhyel reached a hand to Nikki, who
grabbed it and hauled him to his feet, then steadied him
when his balance wavered. "Dare I hope that you can by
any chance get us out of here?"

Oshram stepped closer, a puzzled look on his face. And
his gaze shifted from himself to Nikki and up to Deymorin,
before coming back to him, still puzzled. The man didn't
recognize him, for all the Warden of Sparingate had been
present in the High Court innumerable times.

Or he did recognize him and was prudently saying nothing the inmates slowly edging closer might hear. Which caution did not bode well for their immediate removal from
this ward.

"Can you at least tell us why we're here?" Deymorin
asked, and Mikhyel felt his brother's impatience rising, sent
cautionary thought back.

Oshram's eyes flickered toward the shadowy inmates, the
surrounding guards at the top of the stairs and keeping
those inmates back. "Well, *Deymio,* since Sironi didn't see
fit to tell 'ee, I can't see m' own way t' doin' it."

"Why should a visiting dignitary's guard's dereliction of
duty keep *you* from following proper *Rhomatum* procedure?" Mikhyel asked pointedly.

Another flicker of eyes—toward the guards, Mikhyel
would swear it was wariness of the guards, not the inmates.
"I—If 'ee don' mind, Deymio m' lad, I'd like ye t' come
wi' me t' th' office. Get me the partic'lars on the situation."

A silent question permeated the link: Deymorin wondering if he should go with Oshram, or send Mikhyel. He
thought that Mikhyel would be safer with Oshram, but that
Oshram might speak more freely to him than to Mikhyel.

Mikhyel's immediate {Go!} intersected Nikki's agreement and support, and the whole formed a dizzying, multifaceted decision process that culminated in Deymorin's departure with Oshram.

But as he followed Oshram out the door, Deymorin's concern nearly deafened Mikhyel. Concern for Mikhyel, alone among these men he'd sentenced, for Nikki, so very young, and in many ways naive. And Deymorin's demand for them to stick together, and a concern that they'd already been too free in their use of names and associations.

Too free, indeed. He, who was their greatest liability in this place of convicts, had been babbling like a half-wit when he came to. He could excuse his actions on the grounds that his brains had been addled by the fall, but excuses wouldn't make him any healthier, if the inmates had heard and decided today's revenge was worth tomorrow's price.

As Mikhyel's sense of *Deymorin* dissipated, a gnawing pressure below his gut grew all-consuming, and for a moment he seriously considered (tired as he was) relieving himself where he stood. From the smell, he wouldn't be the first.

And then he realized that pressure wasn't his, any more than the embarrassment surrounding it was his.

"Excuse me," he said to Nikki, and thought deliberately of that mental map he had of this place, and of the latrine he'd noted from above.

"Thanks," Nikki muttered, and darted into the shadows. Gods knew what Nikki had been watching as *he* came down the stairs. Too late, Mikhyel recalled Deymorin's admonition to stick together, which was only common sense, but decided he'd rather risk Deymorin's wrath than Nikki's.

Besides, at the moment, he seriously had to sit down.

The step met his tailbone rather more abruptly than he could wish, but the minor discomfort seemed to clear his brothers from his mind. At least for a moment. He buried his head in crossed arms, limp and sore, needing all his remaining strength simply to stay awake.

That was all he asked, now. Because as long as he was awake, his thoughts were his own. Once he fell asleep, the Nightmare lurked, waiting to suck them all in.

Fell asleep . . . or passed out.

Or panicked. He was a damned pistol on a leyroad, wait-

ing to explode at random. That nightmare had affected all
three of them more than once this past month. And it radiated from his mind with a force that penetrated even
Nikki's resistant mind.

The dream was all he personally remembered of the firestorm. Deymorin had filled in details, such as he understood them, but enormous gaps still plagued him.

He'd been in the Tower . . . Anheliaa had had him
brought to the Tower. He'd forgotten that. Brolucci gorAn-
heliaa, captain of Anheliaa's Tower Guard, had pulled him
from his bed and taken him to the ringchamber. There,
using the imaging sphere in the center of the Rhomatum
Rings and his then-embryonic link with his brothers, Anheliaa had seen Deymorin at Boreton. And Nikki. In the
wagon. Injured. Scared.

And Anheliaa had seen the Mauritumin machine, recognized its danger, and determined to destroy it—at any cost.
Her desire—or his own—had sent him through, had caused
him to transfer instantly from Rhomatum Tower to the
Boreton Turnout. Somehow, that transfer had completed a
bridge to Rhomatum and Anheliaa's Tower-generated fire
had destroyed the machine and all those around it.

Only he and his brothers and Kiyrstin had escaped.

Deymorin's mind pictures held images of the aftermath
of that firestorm. And of himself, sprawled naked on the
ground. And thoughts of *parnicci* salve that had healed
those unnaturally acquired burns, save for a handful of
scars on his back. . . .

Salve that healed his skin but stripped it of all the hair
that proclaimed a man no longer a child. Stripped him most
noticeably of the beard he'd worn all his adult life. The
beard whose absence now caused even his brothers to forget sometimes who he was.

He cursed that loss as he cursed the link that plagued
him night and day, that stole his autonomy from him as the
too-smooth face stole his painfully acquired individuality.

Deymorin had used that link, forged in the fires of Boreton, to enter his mind and draw him out of an equitable
(damn it all) escape from a life filled with compromises and
mistakes, a life finally justified in that single action that had
saved his brothers.

He'd told Deymorin once, when Nikki balanced on
death's door and Mikhyel himself was nearly mindless with

pain, that he wished this cursed link with his brothers had never happened. While Deymorin had tried to understand, had said all the right words, his injured feelings had permeated and overwhelmed Mikhyel's objections, and Mikhyel had never again broached the subject.

Deymorin was convinced they were all better for the link. Deymorin talked of memories shared, pointed out their new understanding that would have been impossible without this damnable connection. And if that was the case, if that forgotten (on his part) sharing accounted for his revitalized relationship with Deymorin, he supposed he was grateful, overall.

On the other hand, he could guess what memories Deymorin had tapped, and there were times he wished they were back to where they'd been a year ago, sniping suspiciously at each other, but private individuals, responsible only to their own conscience. Their thoughts—particularly their memories—their own.

His own.

"Well, well, well, what have we here?"

It was a deep voice, with a cultured veneer to the accent. Eastern . . . Fharatumin, or Khoratumin, or perhaps neither. City of origin hardly mattered here.

"Pretty hair." That was a different voice. Closer. Common in every sense. "Washed it this mornin', 'less I misses m' bet."

"Sureties find no takers, Adris. And I doubt that's all he washed." The first voice, and overhead. Given that much warning, Mikhyel managed not to flinch when a hand brushed lightly over his head, then lifted the braid lying heavy between his shoulder blades. A tug, not so light. "Give us a looksee, Suds."

Curious how in all his concerns about what he might encounter here, he'd overlooked the most obvious.

Mikhyel lifted his head slowly, then recoiled from a lamp thrust toward his face. The owner of the first voice whistled softly through his teeth, and the hand left his hair to grip his chin, holding him still for that lamplit inspection.

For his part, his eyes still over-sensitive to light, Mikhyel could see nothing, not even shadows, beyond that blinding glare. The callused fingers released his chin at last, and rubbed his cheek curiously.

"Smooth as a baby's butt. Funny, you don't look that young."

"Hill-boy, Ganfrion, that's what he is. Smooth chin. Black hair. Gray eyes—"

"Gray? I thought they were green. Open wide, Suds."

Mikhyel frowned, and jerked away. The callused fingers slapped him lightly, and gripped his chin again. "I said *open*."

He set his jaw and blinked into the light, his eyes beginning to water.

Panic was his enemy, he understood the ways of Sparingate well enough to know that. And while they might push, this early in the game, to push too hard, too fast was to waste a valuable commodity—amusement—in a place where amusements were at a premium and time was in oversupply.

The first voice, Ganfrion, grunted. "Telling tales on your keeper, were you, Suds? Thought they kept the whore-spies upstairs—away from corrupting influences. Who's the giant Osh'm ran off with. Your owner?"

Whore-spies and keepers. Better, Mikhyel thought, than the truth.

"Hill-boy, I tell you. Look here." Someone jerked at his forearm, tore the lace away and gripped the wrist. "Break it with one hand, I could. Whaddya think, prison-scut? Any takers?"

Real fear gripped him then. He fought it down, knowing his panic would consume his brothers as well.

But this new hazard threatened his calm in a way Ganfrion's innuendo did not. Forced sex, that was to be expected here, amusement and dominance established in one economical act. Even an honest beating or two, for the same purpose. In that sense, nothing these men could do could be worse than what he'd survived at Mheric's hands.

He'd learned there was a spot inside, as quiet and safe as the closet at Armayel. Safer, not even Mheric could find him there. And when he came out, it was over.

But the thought of broken bones, here, where setting might be days away, if at all, of infection and lingering death . . . He shuddered—then cursed his own cowardice as the man holding his wrist laughed and tightened his grip.

Nikki, golden-haired, handsome . . . young, so very

young . . . was only a handful of steps away. If he panicked, Nikki would hear. Nikki would come. . . .

He forced himself calm, found the safe spot within, and felt his arm relax. Such as he could past Ganfrion's immobilizing hold on his chin, he shifted his gaze to meet the other inmate's lizard-eyes, the fetid grin waiting for him to beg.

The grin faltered, the face went lax, and the clamp on his wrist eased.

"Let go, Brydn," the first voice, Ganfrion, ordered, in a quiet tone, a tone that *expected* obedience.

The face hardened. The vise-grip clenched again.

"Huh? Got bets, Gan—"

The hand dropped his chin.

"I said let—go—"

Mikhyel's hand fell and struck the stone stair before he had the wit to stop it, and Ganfrion, with a handful of cloak that caught the coat beneath as well, hauled him to his feet, held him there when his balance wavered.

The inmate was as tall as Deymorin. Mikhyel stared, unfocused, uncaring, at the ragged-edged collar. Not bad material, he thought absently. Faded stains, as if attempts had been made toward personal maintenance.

As a hand—Ganfrion's, he supposed—smoothed his hair back from his face, he found himself drifting, as he'd learned to do years ago . . .

"So, Suds, you and your friends sleepy?"

. . . found himself wondering where Nikki was . . .

"First night's easy, Suds."

. . . wondering how long Deymorin would be . . .

"If you cooperate."

. . . knowing it would be too long . . .

"Second night— Well, depends on how good you are, now, doesn't it?"

. . . and not giving a hell-sent damn.

Chapter Five

Late in the evening, as the final supper crowd cleared and the dedicated drinkers began accumulating to discuss the day's events, the rijhili captain—dunKarlon, Thyerri heard someone call him—returned, obviously on the prowl, as obviously having set upon Sakhithe as his chosen prey.

Thyerri tried to catch her eye, but she was laughing with a customer and he had an order to get back to the kitchen. He paused at the bar to order a glass of mountain *cari'li,* on the house, which meant from his wages, but it was a gesture that, with luck, would distract the hunter from the hunt.

He dashed to the kitchen to leave the order, and dashed back—

Too late. Sakhithe's wrist was already imprisoned in the man's hand and tucked up behind her back, forcing her hip-first against his side.

Frustrated, but unable to halt the inevitable, Thyerri gathered the tray bearing a handful of ales and half his evening wages, and began a circuitous route through the tables.

Over in the musicians' corner, Kharmier, Trahdio, and their friends had left the standard melodies behind and began improvising. The unknown drummer picked up her beat, taking control from Kharmier's pipes with single-handed, heartbeat-regular taps. Then, with her other hand, she teased a counterpoint of a mountain lark's triple-beat coo from the flautist. Slowly insinuating into the new pattern, Trahdio wove his pipes in and around, like wind dancing among the leaves. And beneath them all, the guitar swelled into a relentless rumble, a mountain river in a flash flood.

Thyerri found his feet moving with the insidious rhythms,

instinctive actions that soon drew the rest of his body into motion.

The nearby customers grew silent, then joined their hands to the symphony. At first, their clapping hands followed the drummer, then led her, challenging the musicians to make the music more complex, *too* complex for a simple hiller waiter.

But a hiller waiter who had danced the rings could anticipate anything mere mortal hands could devise, and now it was Thyerri's turn to lead with nothing but the subtle movements of his hips, the tilt of his head or the flick of a fingertip.

He glided among the tables, tray balanced on one hand, oblivious to everything around him except as wrinkles in his dancing space, cognizant only of the *thrum* vibrating along his spine, the lyrical trill in his head.

Then the tray was gone, his movement unimpeded, and he dipped and swirled among the flute's cascading tones, the sounds more tangible to him than the rough-wood floor beneath his feet.

Dancer. He was, first, foremost and always, a dancer. Man or woman, human or beast, alive or dead, clothing, hair, name—such distinctions became irrelevant adjacent that single truth. He'd forgotten that, in his mind, in some foolish human preference for survival, but his heart remembered, and heart ruled his body now.

"Thyerri . . ." Words, soft and gentle as the flute's breath.

"Thyerri? . . ." Sakhithe, his mind whispered, and the word became a lyrical counterpoint to the flute.

He reached out to embrace that counterpoint.

A touch: Sakhithe's hand on his.

A moment's perception: dunKarlon's eyes on him.

A grasp of his fingers: Sakhithe was free and spinning across the floor, in a dancer's controlled tumble.

Thyerri laughed, swirled in a sweeping spiral that carried him up and around, and down to settle, gently as a falling leaf, in a half-crouch facing Sakhithe, arms outstretched, beckoning.

Sakhithe rose slowly to her feet.

Join me . . . Thyerri invited her silently. A dancer needed no words. He spun about, stretched toward the ceiling . . . and when his arms descended, she was in them.

Thyerri was drunk with the music and his personal resurrection. With Sakhithe, instinct discovered a whole new mode of expression. He'd danced the rings, he'd danced the mountain, he'd danced the wind and the rain, even the ley itself. As a radical in training, he'd danced choreographed partnerships.

But he'd never danced another radical.

Sakhithe added a new random factor. Sakhithe found different complexities within the music, moving sometimes as one with him, sometimes on a different, seemingly dissociate course, only to return to his arms without a single discordant step.

Time had no meaning. Space had none. There was the Music. There was Sakhithe. And there was Thyerri. Together, they wove a pattern that was in their time and their space absolute Truth.

Only when Sakhithe stumbled and collapsed against him did the world's Truth infringe on theirs. Exhaustion: Thyerri's and Sakhithe's. Holding Sakhithe close, Thyerri spun the drumbeats to a spiraling, continuous roll that rose to a climactic peak, then imploded as he and Sakhithe collapsed in a tangle on the floor.

Silence. Then pandemonium. Applause, cheers, stomping feet—but nothing that could drown out the laboring of his own heart.

It had been the exquisite madness of a frenzy dance, the like of which Rijhili couldn't imagine, let alone experience. The like of which Thyerri himself hadn't, except in lonely, hillside moments where his music was the birds and the wind and a waterfall's rumble.

Sakhithe hugged him, right there on the floor, and gasped blessings in his ear. Crying. Sakhithe, six years his senior, whose dance must have been as dead within her as his had been within his own heart.

Something small and hard struck his shoulder, another his knee. Still more *pinged* off the floorboards behind him.

Hail? His mind wondered dimly, spinning back to those hillside dementias, and he buried his face in Sakhithe's shoulder, protecting both their heads with his arms.

But he was inside . . .

Not hail. Coins. A hail of coins clattering all around them. Hands reached and touched, raised them to their feet. Someone drew Sakhithe from his arms. Or him from hers. She was lost in a sea of bodies. Another wave pulled him about, exclaiming in wonder and pressing on him the strange printed notes that substituted for coins in other nodes.

Other nodes.

Foreigners.

Valley-folk.

Rijhilii.

Thyerri let himself be passed from one table to the next, wondering vaguely what had become of his tray and the glass of cari'li, for which he would still have to pay.

An exhausted haze settled over his vision and his thoughts. He was out of condition, embarrassed. His dance had not *been* for them. Not for their cheers, certainly not for their money.

Even aiding Sakhithe had been nothing but happenstance. She'd been there, an addition, not an encumbrance, to the dance.

His dance.

But they didn't know. Strangers. Rijhilii. They didn't understand that to reward a frenzy with money was tantamount to insult. So he accepted the notes they tucked into his sash, or thrust into the overlapped front of his tunic, thanked them blindly, and escaped at last to the kitchen.

Sakhithe was there before him, perched on a stool beside Bharlori. On the table before them was a scattering of coins and notes, piles that grew as the other employees darted into the kitchen between orders.

Sakhithe hopped down when she saw him, her face glowing with excitement. She hugged him, hard, and whispered, "Thank you!"

Their embrace crackled; she stepped back, taking his hands and holding them wide.

"Look at you!" She laughed. "Thyerri the money tree!"

She pulled him over to the table and emptied his tunic, exclaiming over the inscribed values on the notes. And there was gold among the copper and silver on the table.

Dazed, Thyerri wondered if he ought not return the money: a true frenzy was said to disrupt the sanity of the viewers, and he had to believe that this generosity would be regretted in the morning.

For all he knew, it was illegal to accept the offerings.

But such moral and legal decisions were not his concern. This treasure, as did all the customer gratuities, belonged to Bharlori, and as ownership went, so followed conscience.

He said something he hoped appropriate, and returned to his customers, only to discover they no longer wanted ale or food, but *him*. Some wanted to flood him with praises. Some wanted to know who he was and was he available for intimate parties.

A few simply wanted to buy him for the night.

Panicked, he tried not to insult anyone, and with a plea to Khani to take his tables, escaped a second time, slipping out a side door and into the back alley, where a feeble oil lamp granted safe anonymity.

There, beside the midden box, the cool, mountain air rushed between the buildings and cleansed him of the smoke and heat of Bharlori's.

Panic faded, Thyerri's heart slowed, and as his gut recalled the music of his heart, his body swayed in small, stationary dance.

"So this is where you bolted," a voice said out of the darkness, and dunKarlon stepped into the dim light beneath the lamp. Two others appeared at his flanks, almost, but not quite, barring Thyerri from the door.

But Thyerri was no fool. Even were he a fighter, which he was not, he'd have no chance against three men, each of whom was half-again his size. Even had he a chance, he'd be a fool to challenge one of Bharlori's paying customers: better bruises than back on the streets.

Thyerri forced indifference into his voice. "I warned you, sir, three large brothers. I had to interfere. I didn't want them angry at me."

"I thought there were five."

"How clever you are." Despite his efforts, Thyerri's contempt for dunKarlon and all his ilk crept into his voice. In fear, then, of his own unruly tongue, he moved a step toward the almost-opening. "If you please—"

His attempt came a heartbeat too soon, a shade to eagerly. DunKarlon's arm intercepted him, and shoved him up against the wall.

The midden-box pressed against his leg.

"You needn't worry about the hiller-bitch's brothers. I'm not interested. Not in her."

"Very wis—" Thyerri's voice caught as dunKarlon's gloved hand gripped his chin, and two gloved fingers pressed into his neck. And Thyerri wondered if Rakshi had given him back his dance just so he could die.

But he didn't want to die. Not any more.

"Sir," he whispered, "I—"

DunKarlon hissed. "You owe me, whore."

"I—I don't underst—"

"No *man* moves like that." DunKarlon released his throat, holding him captive with his hips. One gloved hand gripped his hair and jerked his head back, the other invaded the tunic, pulling the plackets apart, exposing him to that dim light.

Thyerri, confused, frightened—and angry—didn't move. The gloved hand groped lower, past the tunic, past the drawstring waist—

And stopped.

Gripped hard enough to bring tears, but Thyerri clenched his jaw and smothered a protest.

"Damn!" dunKarlon hissed with all the fury of a man who had just made a fool of himself.

Thyerri laughed, half-hysterically, thinking the incident closed.

He never saw the blow that sent him reeling. Reflexes responded late, but turned the stumbling fall into a tumble that brought him back to his feet in a blind, instinctive dash for the shadows down the alley.

But legs as uncertain as his reflexes faltered, and the men were on him. He struck wildly—futilely. There were too many of them.

And he was no fighter.

"Thyerri?"

Feminine voice, shrill above the clamor.

"Thyerri!"

A scream that would wake a corpse.

And his attackers were gone. Nothing but booted feet scuffling and thudding all around him. Dazed, aching, Thyerri curled around his bruised and aching ribs, trying to protect his head from those heavy boots.

"Thyerri, *help*!"

Sakhithe. Without thought, Thyerri threw himself toward the voice. His arms encountered booted legs and clamped tight.

Sakhithe screamed. The boot kicked, trying to shake him off. He clung with both arms and bit—hard—clamping his teeth into the flesh behind the man's knee. Clinging like a wolf to a boar.

A roaring curse overhead: dunKarlon.

The captain kicked again. Thyerri dug his feet into the mud and lunged all his weight against that knee. A *snap* next to his ear. Another roar, this time of pain, and Dun-Karlon fell, with Sakhithe, into a pile of arms and legs.

And all the while, Thyerri clung, hands and teeth, to that leg, while the other rijhili kicked him and cursed, while breathing grew difficult, and blood filled his mouth.

And the world grew quiet.

A sharp, slicing pain along his cheek brought Thyerri back to his senses.

"And don't come back. —*Ever.*"

That was Bharlori.

Pounding feet: the rijhili running away, and Thyerri wanted, insanely, to chase them, for all he couldn't find his feet. And he fought that anger, fearing such blind stupidity more than he feared the blood bubbling in his mouth.

"Thyerri!" Sakhithe's hands fluttered over him.

Then Bharlori's voice ordered her aside and the tavern owner's powerful arms surrounded him, lifted him against a barrel chest. And Bharlori's voice boomed above his head, "Out of the way—all of you!"

Bharlori swayed, a sickening twist that put Thyerri's head low. The blood bubbled and he began to choke.

"Get the damn door! *Now!*"

Thyerri grasped blindly for Bharlori's shoulders, trying to bring his head up.

"You! Fresh straw for his pallet. Extra pillows and blankets—"

"But—"

"Your *own,* dammit!"

Thyerri tried to object, tried to get Bharlori to put him down. Terrified at that moment that the customers were all leaving and Bharlori would blame him and he'd lose his job because he couldn't work, not with the blood bubbling down his face.

"Khani," Bharlori said, "fetch Brishini. *Now.*"

Brishini. The local physician.

"No," Thyerri whispered, then with more strength than he thought he had left, "No! I'm fine. Please, sir, let me down!"

But Bharlori wouldn't let him go. Bharlori hauled him

into that back room he shared with the girls and Besho, and set him gently on his pallet. And put pillows at his back to keep his head up.

"Rest easy, son," Bharlori said, which Bharlori never called anyone, and there was a strange tone in his voice. "We'll take care of you. And never you worry about the cost."

"I will, Thyerri," said Sakhithe, suddenly there beside him. And seemingly unhurt, though it was difficult to tell with one eye swelling shut. "I can take care of him, Master Bharlo. He's from the hills. He won't be wanting a valley doctor."

Which argument (along with a promise to call the physician in an instant, should Thyerri's condition worsen) got him at least a reprieve, and his own pallet, and his privacy, save for Sakhithe who was part of his privacy these days.

"Sakhithe," he whispered, as she knelt beside him, holding a mug of spirit-laced, herbal tea, "is Bharlo going to fire me?"

"Fire you?" She rocked backward, as if to see him better. "Why would he do that?"

"I . . . They were customers. . . . I know b—better. I tried not to fight, Sakhithe. I truly did, but—"

"Fight?" she repeated, and he could tell she was trying hard not to laugh. "Thyerri, dear, *that* was not a fight." She smoothed his hair back from his face; hair that was stiff from the hated dye, wet and evil-smelling from the mud beside the midden. He winced as her touch brushed a rising mouse on the point of his cheek. "No, sweet, after tonight, it will take much more than that little squabble to convince Bharlo to turn us out."

He didn't really understand, but Sakhithe wouldn't lie to him, not about something so important, so he didn't ask her to explain.

"You really should learn to protect yourself, Thy," Sakhithe continued, as she smoothed an aromatic paste over the cut on his cheek. "You're too small to stand up to the like of that rijhili. Talk to Zelin. Last year, he won all the festival wrestling matches, and he's not very big. Bigger than you, but . . ."

"I'm not a fighter, Sakhi," he mumbled around his mug, putting an end to her murmured advice.

He finished the tea, and lay back, willing the herbs to

ease his aches, anxious to find sleep among his chaotic thoughts.

Sakhithe sighed, and rested a hand on his chest, and said she understood, and told him to sleep, now.

But he could tell from her voice, the issue was not yet closed.

Chapter Six

The guards called it the Womb. Kiyrstin would wager the ladies interned there had a different name for it.

By any name, Kiyrstin decided, settling onto her assigned cot, it was undoubtedly more welcoming than the Crypt toward which Deymorin and his brothers had descended.

The Womb's central cavern had fairly well swallowed the light of the handful of lamps lining its walls, but had given hints of tables and a variety of amusements: board games, a painting easel, stitching frames—decidedly *not* hardened criminals in this ward.

Sironi had led her through that cavern and down a tunnel, past a latrine and bathing facility, and into a honeycomb of small cubby holes containing cots. And then, Sironi had just . . . left.

She was, Kiyrstin decided, at an unpleasant disadvantage where it came to information: *not* her preferred position. One reason she'd put up with being romGaretti as long as she had was that being the wife of the High Priest of Maurii put her in a position to know more than any woman and most men in Mauritum about the forces ruling their lives.

She threw herself back into the pillow and swung her booted feet up onto the cot, wishing she had the cloak she'd left lying beside a stack of hay, not to mention the bag of personal essentials she'd somehow hauled out of the carriage. That bastard Sironi hadn't given them a moment to think, hadn't let them gather *anything* before he hustled them off through the tunnels.

Afraid they'd say something to someone.

A kohl-rimmed eye peeked around a curve of stone.

"Hello," Kiyrstin said.

The eye flitted away. A moment of whispers and sounds of a scuffle, then the eye and its attached young woman came stumbling in. Shoved, Kiyrstin would guess.

She was a rather flagrantly pretty young woman, who clutched an armload of blankets to her ample bosom. From the paint-job on her face, she'd obviously arrived with substantially more personal effects than Sironi had allowed Kiyrstin.

Kiyrstin swung her feet back to the floor and propped her elbows on her knees.

"Can I help you?"

The girl stared, eyes wide. And again glanced toward the door.

"Are those for me?" Kiyrstin tried again, and the young woman inched over to the cot and flung them at the point farthest from Kiyrstin, then backed quickly away.

Kiyrstin tried very hard not to laugh. Miss black-eyes only substantiated her impression of the main cavern, and the quality of her cell mates.

"What's your name?"

"B–Beauvina, sir. *Ma'am.* M'Lady!" Breathy voice. Panicked.

"Sir." Kiyrstin glanced down at her leather-clad legs and high boots. "Oh, dear." She smiled, trying to set the girl's fears at ease. "It's all right, child," she said gently, feeling old as Maurii.

The young woman chewed her lip.

"So, Beauvina," Kiyrstin tried again, "what didn't *you* do?"

A blink.

Kiyrstin sighed. "Why are you in here, child?"

Her mouth made a little *oh.* "I didn't do nothing wrong."

"Of course not."

"Well, I don't *think* it was wrong, anyway. But one of m' fellas— I'm a legal lady, m'lord. Uh, ma'am—m'lady."

"Call me Kiyrsti, child."

Beauvina's shoulders heaved in a sigh. "Yes, 'm. Mistress Kiyrsti. And I'm Vina, if you like."

"I very much like, Vina." Kiyrstin pulled her knees up and crossed her arms comfortably over them. "And what did your fella do, Vina?"

"Give me a . . . well, a real pretty bauble. I shoulda knowed. But I thought it wasn't *real,* don't you know?"

"Ah. Stole your present from somebody else, did he?"

"I can't say that, Mistress Kiyrsti. Mebbe he bought it from summun who stole it. Can't say, now, can I? Warn't there. And there was lotsa lootin' goin' on, just after th' lights went off, now warn't there?"

"You've the makings of a lawyer, Vina. —So, if someone gave you the bauble, why are *you* in here?"

" 'Cuz it were stole from one o' my other fellas."

"Ah. And *he* saw you wearing it and assumed *you* had taken it."

She nodded vigorously.

"An' he were *important,* up on th' hill, y'know."

"Ah. And have you many important fellas, Vina?"

Another vigorous nod. "None of 'em as nice as Nikki, though."

"Nikki?" Her attention pricked at the familiar name.

Beauvina's eyes went dreamy. "Nikaenor Rhomandi dunMheric."

The syllables of Nikki's name floated off her tongue without a hint of the common accent that colored her other speech. She must have practiced saying it every day for a month.

"One of *the* Rhomandis?" Kiyrstin asked.

Her nod this time was more a tilting sway of her head, and Kiyrstin sensed that *her* mind was about to be distracted.

"Excuse me a moment," she said, and rising from the cot, edged past Beauvina to the opening. Just beyond a curve of stone, a bevy of older women lay in waiting.

"Sent the rookie in to do the work, did you?" Kiyrstin asked.

Glances were exchanged, then one woman thrust her shoulders back and swaggered forward. "Yeah. So?"

"I've no complaints." Kiyrstin let her gaze wander the lot of them. "But I don't speak to hidden audiences. You want to know anything about me, you leave. Now. Beauvina and I will have a pleasant little chat this evening, and I'll talk to the rest of you in the morning. *If* I like what Beauvina tells me about you all. —I *do* hope you've been nice to her."

There were grumbles and loud complaints, but the woman who looked to be their leader ordered them away, and with a final under-the-brows glare at Kiyrstin, she left as well.

Definitely the minor delinquents ward: Sironi must have taken Deymorin's warning to heart. Or Sironi knew exactly who he was dealing with and was taking no chances with Garetti's wife, no matter how estranged her relationship with Garetti.

Kiyrstin slipped back into the room. Beauvina hadn't moved.

Kiyrstin took a blanket from the cot, tossed it toward the wall and settled with it cushioning her behind and the smooth stone supporting her back. She waved a hand toward the cot. "Please, Beauvina, sit."

Beauvina glanced toward the door.

"If you want to leave, I won't stop you, but I'd like someone to talk to."

Wide eyes turned to her.

"Of the local options, I definitely prefer my present company."

With a hesitant smile, the girl sat gingerly on the cot, hands folded in her lap.

"You were telling me about Nikki." Kiyrstin reminded her. "What was he like?"

"Beautiful. The most *bee-u*-tiful creature I ever did see."

"Oh, my," she said appropriately.

"*And* he writes poetry."

"Oh. My." The girl was making it very difficult to keep the enthusiasm up. "How was he in bed?"

She blinked. "He stood on it well."

"Stood." The concept astounded even her.

"He was a *wonderful* kisser."

"Oh, that's promising. Did you do a great deal of kissing?"

She nodded, head tilted, eyes misting.

"How many times did you see him?" Kiyrstin prompted.

"Only once. But that once was . . . special."

"How delightful for you."

"It was his birthday."

"I see."

"I was—" A heavy sigh, and Beauvina hugged herself gently. "I was his birthday present."

"How lovely. His friends bought you for him?"

A slow shake of the head. "He had no friends." Another sigh. "I was his present to himself." And a sniff. "I think that's very sad."

Oddly enough, Kiyrstin found herself in agreement. She'd heard about the night of Nikki's seventeenth birthday, but never from Nikki. Only from Deymorin, who had laughed, and Mikhyel, who had been appalled. For once, she wondered how Nikki felt about it.

"Mostly, he talked."

That figured.

"What about?"

A suspicious look, and tight-pressed lips.

"Come, Vina," Kiyrstin encouraged her. "If we're to be friends, you *can't* keep such a wonderful time to yourself."

"I dunno if I should say . . ."

"Oh. Did he reveal great secrets to you, then?"

She shook her head. "No, nothing like that. He talked about his brothers."

"Not himself?"

"No. Not really. Except that he wished they would get along, and that Mikhyel would let him do more. And that he loved them very much. He made me cry."

That figured as well.

"He didn't seem at all the way I thought he'd be."

"And how did you think he'd be?"

"Well, you know, talk was, he was more useless than his older brother."

"Mikhyel?"

"Oh, no. Everybody *knows* Mikhyel dunMheric is so smart *nobody* can understand him. No, his brother Deymorin. The farmer, you know."

"Farmer."

She nodded. "And an *Outsider*." Another wise nod.

"I see."

"But Madam Tirise, my em-*ploy*-er, she says all that talk is stupid. That mostly it's the Councillors who want something out of Mikhyel and he won't give it to them. Then they blame *Deymorin,* don't you see? And Madame Tirise, she'd know. *She's* known Deymorin Rhomandi for*ever.*"

Yet a third nonstartling revelation.

"*I* don't think Deymorin is at all the way they say either. Not from what Nikki said about him."

"And you believe Nikki."

"Absolutely."

"Well, Vina, you're right to believe Nikki about Deymorin."

Her eyes narrowed. "How would you know?"

"Because I know Deymorin, too."

"Know him?" A pucker appeared between her eyes, then disappeared. "Like *I* know Nikki?"

"Well . . ."

"And did he stand on the bed, too?"

"Frequently," Kiyrstin responded with a wink.

"Oh, how *wonderful*!" Beauvina held her hands to her mouth, and seemed to be thinking. Then she began to bounce excitedly. She waved to Kiyrstin, and patted the cot beside her.

After calming her down, Kiyrstin settled next to her. Gingerly. At least until the rope suspension and straw mattress proved able to support both of them.

Beavina sent a suspicious glance toward the door, then dug carefully into her bodice. She pulled out a crumpled, many-times folded envelope and began resurrecting the contents.

A letter. From Nikki, undoubtedly. Kiyrstin wasn't certain she was up to reading the contents.

Beauvina slid the tightly penned pages out, and smoothed them open on her lap, then paused, biting her lower lip.

"I'm not sure . . ." She flickered a look up at Kiyrstin. "What if you're not telling me the truth?"

"Are there secrets in that letter, then?"

She pressed her lips together.

"Well, Vina. If I wasn't to be trusted, and I wanted to read it, I'd just take it from you right now, wouldn't I?"

Her eyes widened and she clutched the sheets to her bosom. Kiyrstin swallowed hard, and clenched her teeth on the brewing laughter.

"But I won't, Vina. I'm your friend, whether you believe me or not. I won't try to read that letter, I won't tell anyone about it or about what you've told me, until you want me to. But—"

She paused; Beauvina slowly leaned forward, her soft mouth opening ever so slightly. Waiting.

"You see, Vina, I *do* know Deymorin. And Nikki, and even Mikhyel. And I believe you about your fellas. And as soon as Deymorin gets me out of here, I'll talk to him about your fellas and the bauble, and maybe we can get you out of here. Would you like that?"

Beauvina just looked at her for a moment, then:

"You're trying to trick me."

Kiyrstin gave a shout of laughter. "You're absolutely right, child. But I won't try again. I promise. You can keep your letter. Nikki wrote it to you, and he meant all those pretty words for your eyes, not mine. But if I get out before you, I'll still see if I can't get you out as well."

Beavina smoothed the papers. "They're not all pretty words for me."

"No?"

Her eyes flickered up and she held out the letter. "I think, maybe he'd like me to share them with you."

§   §   §

Nikki was nowhere in sight when, on a sheepish apology, Oshram shot the heavy iron bolt behind Deymorin. Neither was Mikhyel. More ominously, that sense Deymorin had come to expect inside his skull remained utterly silent.

He tried not to panic. The guards outside the door had reported the Crypt secure. Quiet. Nikki *couldn't* be subdued quietly—he'd taught the boy better than that. And had the animals incarcerated here attacked Mikhyel, Nikki would have been in the middle of it.

Besides, whatever had happened, or was happening, he had to find his brothers before he could do anything about it, and thanks to that link, *his* panic might well set his brothers to something stupid. Therefore, torn between *concerned* and *irritated,* Deymorin opted for *cautious* as he made his way down the steps.

The prison was even darker than before, at least half the wall lamps had been cut completely, and the remainder were turned way back. A handful of lamps such as the one Oshram had pressed into his hand at the last moment formed islands of light in a black sea.

In one such island, a game of chance separated one man from his money or perhaps tomorrow's meat ration; in another, three friends (or at least temporary business associates) passed a bottle from hand to hand taking reverent sips; and in a far recess, a male prostitute was busy negotiating a warm haven for the night with several of the local residents.

Deymorin looked away, disturbed that so innocuous an offender should be housed here—until he reminded himself he and his brothers were also here. Reminded himself as well to assume nothing about his fellow inmates, including that man, whose crime might well be the most heinous of the lot.

But nowhere did he see his brothers, and still that inner sense failed him. The sense had faded the farther he'd gotten from the Crypt. By the time he'd reached Oshram's office, there'd been nothing.

Except for one brief, disturbing contact.

Panic. From Mikhyel. He was learning, slowly, to sort out the sensations, though the nature of the link seemed to shift constantly according to the give and take of their own personalities.

There was Mikhyel relaxed, which was a faint sense of position, an occasional hint of emotion; there was Mikhyel in his "touch me at your own risk" mode. And there was Mikhyel when he *wanted*—either consciously or unconsciously—to be heard, which was damned near inescapable. Everything else he got from Mikhyel was a variation on one of those modes. Sometimes with the clarity of speech, other times, just impressions.

Nikki radiated constantly: thoughts, images, emotions. Any or all of them, scatter shot and difficult to track, until Nikki began thinking hard, and then he became a deluge of information, his need to be understood sending everything uncontrollably outward. When they were all tracking the same thought, as when Deymorin had been trying to decide whether or not to go with Oshram, Nikki's impressions came through quite clearly.

But right now, that spot that should hold his brothers, in one form or another, was simply empty.

Deymorin walked the nature-carved labyrinth slowly, seeking some sign, visual or otherwise, of either brother.

He groped within that dark, seeking his brothers with that inner sense, wishing he had more control of it.

If only he'd been able to convince Mikhyel to investigate their link more thoroughly during their time at Armayel. Mikhyel had resisted, afraid, Deymorin suspected, that some slip on his part would expose the last of his secrets. Reserved, priggish and intensely proud, Mikhyel had found it difficult enough to share those secrets with his older brother—though that sharing had saved Mikhyel's life. To share them with Nikki as well . . . Deymorin supposed that might well destroy Mikhyel.

Which meant he probed blindly, his mind marginally more reliable than the small lamp at illuminating darkened corners. Except to make certain his brothers weren't involved, he avoided the various activities he encountered, many of them rough and unpleasant, their participants all too ready to include passersby.

It was clear the rules here were different than the roughhouse jollying of the wards he'd frequented in his misspent youth. He sincerely hoped he and his brothers would not be incarcerated long enough to learn those rules.

Keep low, he told himself and tried to shout it to his brothers' minds. {Keep low. Keep quiet.}

Survive.

🔉 🔉 🔉

{*In the closet, Nikki.*} Mikhyel sang over and over in his head. {*Get in the closet and stay there until I come for you.*}

The shadows closed around him, comforting and safe, not scary like the city brats said. City brats were scared stupid of their own shadows. Deymorin said so, and then tossed him high in the air and called him a fearless, freshwater fry.

But he didn't need Deymorin to tell him his closet was safe, Nikki thought, and pressed himself into the welcoming darkness. He and Mikhyel had been hiding in its depths since—

Except he wasn't at Darhaven. And he was seventeen years old. And he was in—

{*Find the closet, Nikki. Stay there until I come for you.*}

*Mikhyel said if he was very, very quiet, he could hear
the Tamshirin in the woodwork, and someday, if he was
very, very patient, they might even come out and play
with him.*

Tamshirin? He *had* seen a Tamshi. Mother was Tamshi. Why—

{*Find the closet, Nikki. Find the safe place and stay there
until I come for you.*}

*His feet were tingling, and he wanted to leave the closet
to wake them up, but Mikhyel's voice shouted in his head:
{You stay there, Nikki. Don't you come out. Don't you move
or you'll scare the Tamshirin away!}*

*He froze then, there in the featureless dark, and wiggled
his toes in his fuzzy house boots, and made faces at the
shadows, because that made the Tamshirin laugh, Mikhyel
said so.*

Mikhyel said. Deymorin said. Dammit! Nikki shook his
head, trying to rid himself of the images, the memories. His
head struck stone. Hard stone. Bringing tears to his eyes.

He was in Sparingate. In the Crypt, and—

{*Wait for me, Nikki . . .*}

He didn't want to wait. He was cold. He was hungry. It
was dark. And the stone pressed around him like a
giant's fist.

{*Don't you dare move, Nikki . . .*}

Move? He couldn't move!

{*Don't be scared, Nikki. Hold still, Nikki. I'll come for
you . . .*}

And he always had. Sometimes it took a while, but Mikhyel had always come for him. And then they'd sit in the
silent dark and listen for Tamshirin until Mikhyel stopped
shivering, and then Mikhyel would tell him stories, in a
quiet, whispery voice that Nikki was sure made the Tamshirin come and listen, there in the shadows between the
shelves of toys and fancy-clothes mannequins.

{*That's right, Nikki. Be good. Relax. I love you . . .*}

*But Mikhyel was taking a boring long time, and he was
angry, and the Tamshirin weren't laughing or making any
noise at all, and he wished very, very hard that Mikhyel
would come and tell him a story, or that Deymorin would
come and toss him in the—*

"Nikki?" Deymorin's voice, and a blinding light that
made his eyes burn. And he screamed, remembering Mikhyel,

and the lightning and the eyes that were nothing but seared flesh.

"Nikki, get out of there!" And Deymorin's hand grasped his shoulder and hauled him free of the darkness. "Dammit, boy, *where's Khyel*?"

Chapter Seven

Nikki yelped, and eyes that were all distended pupils flinched from the lamp.

"Sorry," Deymorin said, and pulled the lamp back. Then he leaned into the narrow opening and called Mikhyel's name, for all he knew Mikhyel wasn't there.

Nikki had found a bolt hole, a barely man-sized pit. He couldn't imagine how the fry had squeezed into it. He'd have gone right past, had Nikki's silent petition not enveloped him as he passed.

But Mikhyel wasn't there. Of Mikhyel, there was only that cold, impenetrable wall, and Deymorin's heart began to race in sudden fear.

"Where is he, Nikaenor?"

Nikki blinked. His eyes were still huge. He seemed not to hear or see Deymorin at all. Deymorin set the lamp down, and shook Nikki by the shoulders.

"Dammit, boy, wake up!"

{Find the closet, Nikki . . .}

Deymorin jerked his hands away, and the voice, *Mikhyel's* voice, vanished from his head.

Find the closet. Wait for me. He knew then what depths of childhood Nikki roamed, sent there at Mikhyel's behest. Mikhyel at his most powerful. His will undeniable. Driving Nikki back to their childhood when Nikki hid, safe in the closet, while Mikhyel intercepted their father's ferocity.

Keep Nikki safe: Mikhyel's prime motivation since the day their mother died.

"Dammit!" Deymorin slapped Nikki's face hard enough to sting. {Nikki, *wake—up!*}

Nikki cried out, and slumped, nearly taking Deymorin down with him. Deymorin braced himself and hauled him back upright.

Nikki's face was corpse-white.

"Where is he, Nikki?" Deymorin demanded, feeling no sympathy.

"Where is . . . Mikhyel?" Nikki blinked eyes that were slowly returning to normal. "Isn't he back . . . ?" Confusion spread across Nikki's face. He looked around, taking in the tight quarters, the lamplit opening of his bolt hole. "Where . . . Why are we . . ." He raised a hand to his head. "Rings, my *head* . . ."

Deymorin shook him again.

"I don't give a *damn* about your head. *Where's Khyel?*"

Nikki gripped Deymorin's arms, and closed his eyes, and Deymorin felt his effort to draw himself together. To remember. . . .

The discomfort of a full bladder, amused directions from Mikhyel, and the latrine.

Dammit, why hadn't they stayed together?

An image then, of Mikhyel slumped on the stair, of men standing around him; and that same fear-hazed impression he'd received in Oshram's office, followed by a coldly indifferent wall.

And then: *Go to the closet, Nikki . . .*

Nikki's hand fell, and Deymorin released Nikki's shoulder, painfully aware of the endless shadowed corners, any one of which could contain his brother.

{*Khyel!*}

Nikki cried out, then added his silent call to Deymorin's. {*Khyel, where are you?*}

Reassurance flowed past the wall, and was as quickly masked. Mikhyel: alive, then, and aware of his return and his thoughts.

A hint of images seeped past the wall along with the specific message, and Deymorin knew beyond doubt, then, which pool held his brother. He grabbed Nikki's sleeve in one hand, the lamp in the other, and headed down the narrow aisle toward the entrance stairs. But:

{Damn you, Deymorin! Keep Nikki away!}

Clear and fiercely proud. Unashamed—but determined to spare Nikki the brutally clear images that burst past the barrier along with that command.

Deymorin surged forward.

{Damn you, Rhomandi. It's under control!}

And Khyel didn't *need* his older brother's help, that was very clear, except to keep his younger brother ignorant.

Well, damn what Khyel wanted. He ran on, Nikki, ignorant, but trusting, at his heels.

Ice flowed through his brain, chilling the anger. Freezing *him* to the core. He couldn't move. For a moment, he couldn't breathe.

Nikki slammed into his back. As suddenly as it had appeared, the chill was gone.

Deymorin staggered to the stairs, dragging Nikki after him, his mind a seething mass of images from Mikhyel, his own anger and frustration, and fears for Mikhyel.

Keep Nikki ignorant. As if Nikki *wouldn't* know. It didn't take any mind picture to guess what Mikhyel was facing at this moment.

"What was that all about?" Nikki asked. "Where's Mikhyel? I left him right here."

"It's . . . all right," he said, the only explanation he could think of. He didn't add why the hell had Nikki left him alone.

"What do you mean, 'all right'?" Nikki repeated, indignantly shaking his arm free and smoothing his sleeve. He'd taken his time in the latrine: face and hands spotless, hair combed into submission, and beneath his cloak, his fancy coat showed little evidence of the day's adventures. "What's all right? Where's Mikhyel?"

Taken his time and left Mikhyel to those damned wolves. Anger flared again. Anger against the wolves, anger toward Nikki, who should have known the trouble Mikhyel could find here.

Anger against Mikhyel for keeping *him* here now. Ignorant. Impotent to help. He clenched his fists and beat his own knee. Waiting.

"Dammit, Deymio, what's going on? One minute, I'm going back to find Khyel—I *thought* he'd had the sense to follow me. I couldn't damnwell piss in the corner, now could I? The next, I'm in the dark, in a filthy hole, and I can't move! Khyel's voice is yelling in my head, making me stay 'in the closet,' but it *wasn't* the damned closet! It's *Sparingate!*"

So, Nikki *didn't* know. Had caught none of those images, hadn't realized the significance of what he *had* seen.

Deymorin clenched his jaw on a sarcastic retort. Such ignorance made a man wonder how he'd come to raise so naive a child.

And on a second thought wonder if he had the right to condemn Nikki so quickly. He thought of his own frozen muscles. And: *Go to the closet, Nikki. Stay there until I come for you.*

Just like the old days at Darhaven. With Mheric. And at the moment, what Mikhyel was enduring wasn't a beating.

Bile rose. He fought it down. In the hours after Boreton, he'd shared Mikhyel's mind. He'd thought he knew everything about his father. He'd thought all Mikhyel's dark secrets had been revealed.

Now, he wasn't so certain.

He tried to smother the thoughts and speculations. Mikhyel had never told Nikki about their father, had demanded a promise from Deymorin never to reveal to Nikki what he'd discovered during the sharing of their minds. However much Deymorin might disagree with that decision, they were Mikhyel's experiences to share or not, as he chose.

But what Mikhyel was facing now . . . at this moment . . .

"Deymio," Nikki asked, "shouldn't we find Khyel? What if he's —"

"Khyel is fine, Nikki," Mikhyel himself answered out of the shadows, and in the shadows he stayed, propping himself casually against a cornerstone just beyond the ring of light.

His cloak, an expensive, gold-embroidered garment, draped negligently from one arm, and his hair was hanging loose behind his shoulders. Deymorin couldn't remember the last time he'd seen Mikhyel fully dressed with his hair loose.

The effect was . . . chilling.

He'd thought he knew everything of significance there was to be known about Mikhyel dunMheric. Now, seeing him standing there, knowing what he'd just done, Deymorin wasn't certain he knew his brother at all.

"Where have you been?" Nikki demanded.

Mikhyel's easy laugh sent another shiver down Deymorin's spine.

"Negotiating with the locals," Mikhyel said, and tugged a strand of loose hair, as if suggesting the price of his negotiations had been the silver and enamel pin that had held his braid in place. "This area—" He kicked a chunk of loose mortar toward the shadows beneath the stairs.

"—has been declared ours for the night. Beyond that, I'm counting on Kiyrstin's Just Deymio to . . . hold . . ."

Mikhyel's head lifted, looking beyond Deymorin. That inner sense radiated a private warning: Mikhyel's attitude issued a clear challenge.

Deymorin twisted to look over his shoulder, and surged to his feet to face the man stepping into their circle of light.

Few men could look Deymorin Rhomandi straight in the eye. Fewer still would dare. Deymorin was a large man, tall and powerful. He was also clever, well-trained in the arts of self-defense and offense. And he had been born to be the Rhomandi.

Those were the facts of his personal existence, facts he'd never seriously questioned. He'd grown up in utter confidence that there were few men he couldn't at least hold his own against, one on one, in a battle of wits or of strength.

With this man . . . {Ganfrion} Mikhyel's mind supplied the name, and if a mind could spit, Mikhyel's spat . . . he'd be inclined to caution.

It was a rare sensation.

He wasn't at all certain he liked it. Not here. Not with *this* man.

"How much?" the man—Ganfrion—asked, in a surprisingly civil voice, and Mikhyel answered:

"I told you—"

"I'm not talking to you, Suds." Indifferent. Patronizing. Delivered without so much as a blink in Mikhyel's direction.

Even Nikki flinched from the anger that flared throughout the link. Anger, Deymorin noted, surprised, that originated with Mikhyel, not himself. But Mikhyel controlled that blaze immediately, and Deymorin received a clear demand to play along with the man's notions.

Which evidently meant (he assumed when Mikhyel's brow tightened in response to the thought) that wringing the man's thick neck was not an option.

"How much?" Ganfrion repeated, speaking directly to Deymorin, this time fingering the money pouch openly displayed at his belt. The pouch was heavy, bulging; one assumed with coins.

And no one, the open display declared, dared take it from him.

"How—much." Impatience tinged the rough voice.

"Not for sale," Deymorin answered flatly.

"Come, man, I've only five months left in this sty. You'll have him back. I've a fancy for cleanliness, and Suds, here, smells as good as any woman. Certainly better than anything that's come down those steps since I arrived."

"My answer stands."

"Too bad." Ganfrion clucked and shook his head, looking toward Mikhyel's shadows for the first time. "Don't say I didn't try to give you a civilized option, Suds." He began to turn away, caught Deymorin's eye, and paused. Hostility flared one way and the other. Then Ganfrion's scarred lip lifted in a sneer. "The hill boy has settled your tab for tonight. Beyond that, well, you might find yourself defending your territory." His sidelong gaze drifted indifferently across Nikki, then settled on Mikhyel, still standing in his shadows. "*All* your territory."

"I think I can manage," Deymorin replied, relaxing now the stage had been set and the players identified.

"One man against seven. Brave words."

"Three," Nikki said, and Deymorin glared at him, willing him to keep his mouth shut.

"Three," Nikki insisted, ignoring him. "Where's *your* seven?"

The man scanned Nikki briefly. "A fop, a whore, and . . ." Returning to Deymorin: ". . . just what are you, friend, other than very large?"

"What am I?" Deymorin bared his teeth. "Definitely not your friend. Now, if you don't mind, my unfriend, Suds, the fop, and I have had a long day. A *very* long day. So . . . go play with your pack, will you? —Thanks ever so." And when the man hesitated, Deymorin repeated, "Go, go, go!" And shooed him away with several flips of his hand.

Ganfrion pulled back, narrow-eyed—startled, perhaps. Deymorin noted the shift of weight, the mouth that opened slightly, preparing a retort that was left unrealized. Accustomed, more than like, to different results from his intimidation tactics. But the inmate shrugged, and sauntered off into the shadows.

"Fop?" Nikki sputtered when Ganfrion was gone.

"What's he babbling about? *Who's* a whore? Khyel, who was he?"

"Deymio?" Mikhyel's voice quivered around the edges; Deymorin felt sick, knew it for spillover and answered: "Go! Trust me."

His final words echoed to empty space. Mikhyel had disappeared into the darkness toward the latrine, leaving his gratitude floating in the air Deymorin breathed, and his cloak in a glittering heap on the littered floor.

It was some few moments before Deymorin could trust his own stomach enough to say: "Don't ask questions, Nikki. At least, not just now. Khyel negotiated us out of a very unpleasant—"

Spasms ripped through Deymorin's gut. Instinct said protect himself, shut Mikhyel out. But instinct be damned. Twenty-seven years of being Khyel's older brother said his churning gut was no accident: Mikhyel *had* kept the reality of the last hour from him, as he he'd kept a hell of a lot else private, even during those moments of uncompromising truth a month ago.

Whatever prompted Mikhyel to let this much through, whether anger, or spite, or just a desperate need for understanding, trust was close behind. Trust that Deymorin would understand. Trust that Deymorin would help. Trust that Deymorin wouldn't reject him regardless of his reasons.

Either that, or Mikhyel sought to drive him away in total disgust. Perhaps Ganfrion wasn't the only one receiving a challenge tonight from Mikhyel dunMheric.

And with sensations as real as if he stood in the latrine beside Mikhyel, he had his arms around Mikhyel, holding him steady against the involuntary spasms, controlling his own rising bile, sending that control through his touch to Mikhyel.

{Doesn't matter, Barrister,} he thought as clearly and emphatically as he knew how. {Doesn't matter. I'm here, brother. Always.}

A return swell of relief and gratitude failed to mask Mikhyel's residual resentment. Old resentment: a sense of disbelief. Distrust based on a lifetime of Deymorin not being there. Of being left to face Mheric . . . Anheliaa . . .

And an almost overwhelming fear that his assurances

were just words. That tomorrow, he'd be gone. Again. And
it would be Mikhyel alone . . . again.

"I'm sorry, fry," Deymorin whispered out loud, for all
there was no blame he could assume. Not this time. He
couldn't have stood between Mikhyel and Ganfrion, and
been with Oshram as well—

Another spasm; a sense of bitterness, of frustration and
self-anger. And he felt Mikhyel sink to his knees, felt the
damp stone against his brow.

Deymorin clenched his fists. There was nothing he could
do, short of following Mikhyel to the latrine. And for that,
Mikhyel would never forgive him.

"Deymio?" Nikki asked softly, and gripped his elbow,
then pulled away as if stung. "Rings, Deymio, what's
going on?"

"Felt that, did you?" Deymorin swallowed hard. "I don't
think Mikhyel meant you to. He's still unwell, Nikki. Those
men, well, you heard the one. His name is Ganfrion.
They've made some assumptions about Mikhyel and myself—perhaps you as well. You be careful who you turn
your back on, hear me? Mikhyel has . . . promoted those
assumptions because it's far simpler than the truth."

"Not to mention safer," Mikhyel finished firmly, returning to their small pool of light, radiating self-assurance.
{They mustn't learn who we are, Nikki.}

But Nikki just shook his head, and his half-understanding,
his frustration, permeated that underneath sense. Nikki
didn't hear as clearly as Deymorin did, not even when
Mikhyel wanted him to, although he'd heard well enough
when Mikhyel had demanded he hear.

And Nikki still hadn't figured out what had happened,
that was crystal clear from the half-thoughts and images he
spewed like a flood-driven fountain.

Hell, Deymorin thought, *he* hadn't put all the pieces into
their proper places. He only knew he'd never felt so useless
in all his life.

Mikhyel drew closer and continued, aloud, but very
softly, and Deymorin felt it in his head as well: a dual
expression that Nikki did apparently follow. At least his
confused frustration eased from his corner of the mind-
triangle.

"But why did he call you a hill-boy? What did you tell
him?"

"Nothing, Nikki. They— He decided that on his own. I saw no reason to correct him. Whatever misconceptions these men make can't be as dangerous to us as their associating us with the High Court that sent them here. They're not really very happy with Mikhyel dunMheric, and there's no way of telling what they'd do to his brothers to get at him. They've little enough to lose at this point, and the simple fact that we're here means *someone* wouldn't be all that upset if we never left."

"But what did they—"

"Nothing you need to know about, Nikki. Just, for all our sakes, stay close to Deymio. You're young. You're—" {Innocent/ignorant} filled the underneath, but Mikhyel didn't say the words, and because Mikhyel didn't say, Nikki didn't hear. "That's like blood in the water to these men."

Deymorin opened his mouth to object that ignorance was not an asset here, but Mikhyel had turned away, mentally as well as physically.

"Well, fop and unfriend, I'm for bed, such as it is," Mikhyel said, in natural tones, and picked up his cloak in two-fingered repugnance. "The sooner to sleep, the sooner morning and light."

He disappeared under the steps into their negotiated territory, leaving behind a shadowy need for conference—at least in Deymorin's mind. Deymorin caught Nikki's eye and jerked his head to follow.

Closer examination revealed the area, as promised, unoccupied, for reasons that rapidly came clear. Cold air rushed in from several narrow openings in the stone, pumped in, one end in the air circulation system.

Cursing loudly to satisfy the hardened humor of the inmates who had hustled them, they found a spot near the corner where they could huddle together in fair comfort. Nikki dropped down next to Deymorin.

Mikhyel kept apart. Standing.

"So, Deymio," Mikhyel began, in that bilevel voice, "what did your friend Oshram have to say about our arrest?"

"Tower orders."

"Official?"

Deymorin nodded.

"You saw the documents?"

"I'm not that ignorant, Barrister. She signed them."

"Forgery?"

"That scrawl of hers? Possible. Not likely. Who would dare?"

"Lidye?"

Nikki twitched.

"To gain what?" Deymorin asked.

"Time?"

"If Anheliaa's dead, who's to argue?"

"If Anheliaa's *not* dead?"

Deymorin opened his mouth. Closed it again.

"Those letters held words, Deymorin. Things I'd *swear* only Anheliaa would know."

"Clues?"

"Only to their authenticity."

"Would she have passed those keys on to Lidye?"

"I wouldn't think so. It was . . . *our* code."

"You didn't say anything about that before."

Mikhyel shrugged.

"What *other* secrets are you keeping, Mikhyel?"

"What other secrets are *you* keeping, Deymorin?"

Deymorin frowned. There would always be secrets. But in the end, only one thing mattered.

"Trust me?" he asked.

"Absolutely. Trust me?"

Deymorin waited for some pressure—reassurance or pressure to comply—to manifest underneath, but Mikhyel had placed the cold wall between them. Trust him. Or don't trust him.

"Absolutely," Deymorin echoed him.

"I *believed*, Deymorin, that those clues indicated she was alive. I still do. But Ferricci's men are worrisome."

"They're in charge."

"Obviously. Their orders?"

"Signed by Anheliaa," Deymorin said. "Not unreasonable. When the city panicked, the Constabulary would need all the help it could get."

"Did you ask Oshram about the power umbrella?"

"The whole city went dark for three days. He said that when the lights came back, the Khoratum expansion remained dark, and that afterward, the dark started creeping inward from the old wall."

"As if the web were deteriorating."

Deymorin shrugged.

"The Khoratum expansion again . . ." Mikhyel murmured, and he leaned back against the wall, arms crossed, one hand cupping his chin.

"What are you thinking?"

"Boreton is on the Khoratum line . . . If the web is deteriorating . . . But you said the sky was clear over the old wall."

"As far as I could see. I wouldn't trust my analytic precision. There *were* just a few distractions at the time."

"Granted. But what if the Khoratum line was actually damaged. I mean, physically, there near Boreton. Could that account for what we're seeing?"

"You're asking me?"

"Sorry." Mikhyel gave a wry chuckle. "And our arrest? It wasn't the identity papers. Not considering everything else."

"I still don't know. Oshram's been cut out. But he said that Ferricci men have been bringing in one poor sod after another vaguely matching our descriptions, on a variety of charges, generally unfounded, and always dropped within a day. That was one reason he took so long to get down here."

"We guessed wrong," Mikhyel stated the obvious, still in an undertone, but louder, that inner sense gone suddenly blank. "They've expected us to try to sneak into the City."

"They? Who? Who the hell do you think is in charge here?"

"Anheliaa. Lidye. Tarim. What difference does it make who wants us out of the way? We know Anheliaa hired at least one man to kill you; perhaps there were others. We thought that danger minimal, that there was enough at stake she'd at least listen first. But what if we were wrong? That man who pushed me down the stairs . . . What if that wasn't an accident?"

"And she dropped us in here to disappear? We'll just have to disappoint her, now won't we?"

"Her? Anheliaa? or Lidye?"

"I'd as soon disappoint them both."

Mikhyel's mouth twitched. "I've no inclination to argue with that. We've got to get a message out. I've got people, JD. People I trust."

"I know, Barrister. Oshram's grandson is going to try. I

decided Raulind would be best to contact. And the boy's just asking him to come here."

Mikhyel agreed with a nod and a slight smile. An image crept through, a sense of absolute trust in the man who had been companion and servant to Mikhyel since Mheric's death. The depth of that faith came as something of a surprise to Deymorin, but confirmed his choice.

"Any of my people will recognize Raul," Mikhyel said. "He'll get someone here to help."

"I'm counting on it," Deymorin answered. "Nikki?"

"Who?" Nikki gave a grossly exaggerated start. "Oh . . . me. Sorry. I'd forgotten I was here. Yes?"

"Stop it, Nikki."

"Sorry. Thought I was injecting a little humor," Nikki spoke out loud, apparently making no attempt at their private conversation. "Lightening the mood, you know."

"And horses have wings. We can tell differently, boy."

"So you claim."

"What do you mean?"

"I *mean*—o eldest brother who hears my every thought—I hardly hear you at all—cither of you. Even now, half the time you are a buzz. How do I know you can 'tell differently'? How do I know you're both not just willfully misunderstanding what I say just to give yourselves the excuse of not considering my opinions? What about *my* resources? Why Raulind? Why not Jerri? Because Jerri is *my* man? Because Jerri is just a *boy*, like me? A selfish fool, like *me*? You never used to think such disgusting things of me, but you've got each other now, haven't you? You don't need me anymore, so you can insult me, and you can insult my friends, and accuse my wife and her father, and ignore me because I don't matter, do I?" Nikki was on his feet, the words flowing from him, rising to a shout, unchecked by any real thought. "*Nikki's* just a problem. *Nikki's* just a boy who doesn't understand . . . *anything*. Go to the closet, Nikki. Get out of the way, Nikki. Let big brother take care of everything, Nikki."

Deymorin thrust himself to his feet, buried his fist in Nikki's fancy coat and shoved his brother up against the stone. He filled his own mind with the need for caution and the inmates closing in, and *Deymorin's* fist laying Nikki out cold if he didn't damn well shut up, then thrust that image toward Nikki.

Let him claim he didn't hear that one.

Mikhyel cried out. Nikki's face went white. And Deymorin experienced a moment of contrition. But they couldn't afford the delicacy of genteel behavior here. Better that Nikki learned it from him now than from Ganfrion a week from now.

"Let him go now, Deymio." Mikhyel was beside them, his hand on Deymorin's arm. "You've made your point." {So has Nikki.}

Deymorin's anger faded, his arm relaxed, almost without his willing it, and Nikki slipped free. This time, when Nikki sat down, he sat alone. Mikhyel leaned against the stone, rubbing his temples.

Headache. And Nikki was still pale. And not half an hour ago, Mikhyel had stopped him in his tracks—with a thought.

Damn, they were fools. Deymorin sighed, and slid back into his former spot. In conceding to Mikhyel's privacy, just how much potential—for good and ill—had they overlooked?

In the first few days following Boreton, he and Nikki had played games with the link, trying to determine its limits. They'd decided it was more curiosity than value.

They weren't playing games any longer. And in retrospect, Deymorin realized that any test that did not include Mikhyel was no test at all.

"Nikki," Mikhyel said softly, "did you recognize the man who arrested us?"

Nikki just looked confused.

"Sironi, Nikki. Sironi gorTarim."

Awareness dawned in Nikki's face and in the underneath sense, and a moment of embarrassment that he hadn't noticed. Then Nikki's jaw set stubbornly. "So. Lidye's father's man. That means it's my fault we're here, I suppose. I married the wrong woman, too. Let's see, what else can we blame on Nikki?"

"Is that what you truly believe, Nikaenor?" Deymorin asked. "That we blame everything on you? That we consider you and your perceptions unimportant?"

"Yes!" Sulky tone. Hurt. While underneath Nikki radiated absolute conviction to the contrary, colored with a blatant desire to hear Deymorin admit as much.

And suddenly, Deymorin was tired of Nikki's childish

notions, tired of giving little brother Nikki the benefit of every doubt. Tired of treading daintily past Nikki's vulnerable ego.

"Fine," he replied bluntly. "You're wrong, of course, but you know that. You know you're actually quite important. You're Lidye's husband. A Rhomandi. Whether *the* Rhomandi or not, makes no difference to Lidye. Or to Anheliaa. Your existence grants Lidye validity."

"They don't need me anymore. Lidye's carrying my child! *That's* the only Rhomandi they need!"

"And if it dies? What if it doesn't even exist? Wake up, Nikki. How could they know? Anheliaa's *hoping* Lidye's pregnant, but she still needs you—just in case she's mistaken. Mikhyel knew that. I did. We granted you the dignity of *assuming* that *you* realized it as well. Apparently we were mistaken."

Nikki opened his mouth to protest; Deymorin ignored him.

"If it makes you feel special to believe you're the victim of some gross conspiracy on our part to cut you out, there's little I can say, is there? Moreover, there's nothing I care say."

Shock. Frustration. Confusion. But nothing of hurt. Nothing of shame or self-evaluation. That would come later—if Nikki were indeed the man Deymorin believed him to be.

Nikki glowered at him, at Mikhyel, then back at him.

Deymorin ignored him. Mikhyel's barrister face was solidly in place.

Without warning, Nikki flung himself to his feet and stalked off into the dark. Mikhyel started to follow, but Deymorin raised a hand to stop him. Old resentments flared, differences of opinion regarding how to handle Nikki.

{Curse you, Deymorin, you *know* what's out there!}

{Sometimes, Barrister, you've got to take the risk. If he needs us, he can damnwell call.}

{And *you* could have kept those names to yourself!}

{The damage was done. Nikki had already—}

{Nikki's a *boy*!}

{Nikki can't afford to be a boy. Not any longer.}

Nonetheless, relief flooded him as Nikki returned, barely visible behind an armful of straw, bits trailing behind, more bits falling toward their small lamp.

96 Jane S. Fancher

"Dammit, fry." Deymorin rescued the lamp. "Be careful!"

Another silent objection from Mikhyel, which he ignored. His head hurt. He wasn't interested in any more discussions on child-rearing.

Nikki flung the armload down and stalked off again. Several more such trips had a sizable pile from which Nikki built himself a nest. Then he wrapped himself in his cloak and threw himself down, leaving the majority of the straw still in a pile.

For them.

And underneath, *real* concern that his gift would be rejected.

Deymorin met Mikhyel's glance, and Mikhyel's barrister face slipped away, leaving a sense of relieved amusement. Deymorin went to Nikki's excess pile to throw an armload toward Mikhyel, who began arranging it against the wall. A second armful landed where he'd been sitting. A third . . . Deymorin snuck a glance at Nikki, found one half-lidded blue eye watching him, felt the hope surge underneath . . .

And tossed the third armful on top of Nikki—nest, cloak and all.

Nikki sputtered upright, visually indignant; Deymorin smiled, and said softly, "Thanks, fry."

Nikki burrowed back into his nest, and out of the tangle of hair, straw, and young man came a simple, muttered, "Welcome."

Deymorin plucked a straw free of the blond curls, and returned to arrange his own nest, not to sleep, but as protection against the chill and to cushion the hard stone. He settled, upright, fully intending to spend the night awake.

"That's not necessary," Mikhyel said.

"Didn't say it was. I'm just not exactly sleepy."

He didn't add that he wasn't running the risk of Ganfrion coming anywhere near his brother, or that a part of him hoped the damned rapist would try. Mikhyel frowned, and turned toward the stone, a black shadow among shadows.

"Khyel, I'm . . ."

"Sorry? I know that, Deymio." Weariness permeated Mikhyel's voice and the underneath as well. "I . . . know that."

Deymorin slumped into his own mound of straw. He

couldn't imagine what Mikhyel must be feeling behind that wall of nonemotion. He feared what ancient nightmares lurked within Mikhyel, ready to plague them all tonight. He wanted Mikhyel to know, deep within, that it wouldn't happen again. He wanted the nightmares, Ganfrion . . . all of it—he wanted that gone—purged from Mikhyel's soul forever.

And all the wanting in the world wouldn't make it go away.

He wanted to hate Mheric. But the Mheric of his memories was too different for Mikhyel's memories to take solid root in his own mind. He couldn't make the man who had been his father, who had taught him to ride, and wrestled with him, and laughed with him—he couldn't make that man capable of the acts the evidence increasingly suggested.

Besides, Mheric was gone.

So in the absence of Mheric, he hated Ganfrion and all his ilk. Hated those who took pleasure in another's humiliation and pain. He thought of what Ganfrion had forced his reserved and frail brother to do, and he thought of what he'd do to Ganfrion, should the opportunity arise. . . .

And found in those plans some relief from past guilt.

Mikhyel's shadow rippled. Pale fingers and a fall of torn lace appeared, slipped toward the cloak, caught the hem . . . and froze.

Images seeped into Deymorin's mind. Glitter of gold braid, black wool padding his knees . . . Mikhyel's knees. Matte weave turning sleek and shiny as fresh-oiled leather. Water, or some other liquid, oozing through the wool, wicking through black, kidskin breeches.

The wall slammed down between them. The cloak slipped free, the white hand vanished, and Mikhyel burrowed into the bare straw.

Only a blind man would need an interpreter.

Deymorin unfastened his cloak; Mikhyel jerked. A frowning eye appeared over a narrow shoulder.

{Keep your damned clothes—*and your pity*—to yourself, Rhomandi.} The words hissed in his mind.

"Don't be a fool," Deymorin said, deliberately aloud. Steadfastly ordinary. "I don't need it. Yours is soaked." He tried not to think of how it came to be that way: a foolish gesture, doomed to failure. The eye disappeared.

{Go to hell.}

"For the love of Darius, *I* don't need it. You do. You've been ill, remember?"

The shadow shifted, gained eyes and a pale face.

"We need you, Barrister."

The eyes disappeared, this time behind lowered lids. Deymorin sensed compromise and raised an arm.

"Share it?"

Mikhyel pushed himself upright, braced his elbow on his knee, cupped his chin in his hand, and frowned across at Deymorin. Then he buried his face in both hands, and his shoulders began to heave: laughter, Deymorin realized in some bemusement.

He raised his arm again, hopefully, and with a final shake of his head that set his hair to rippling in the faint light, Mikhyel relented. As his arm closed around Mikhyel's shoulders, Deymorin felt bone beneath the layers of clothing, and beneath the layers of self-control . . .

Rings, he thought, *no wonder Mikhyel kept himself separate.*

Exhaustion. Cold. Consumed with fear that he'd fail everyone, his brothers, his city, just when they needed him the most.

But nothing about this most recent humiliation. There was no self-pity beneath Deymorin's arm, and no regrets. Nothing of Mheric or Ganfrion or anything that Deymorin had expected. The Barrister had done what the Barrister had to do. For his brothers. For the City.

As the Barrister always had.

Deymorin had coined the phrase Hell's Barrister for the cold-eyed advocate who had faced him before the Syndicate and won. Khyel had been seventeen. Younger, by several months, than Nikki was now.

And the Barrister had been Mikhyel's armor ever since. Deymorin realized that now. He knew that, as much as he hated that facade, *Mikhyel* needed it. Desperately.

And he conjured the image now, using it to counter the self-doubt, picturing the Barrister outmaneuvering his elders in the Council, controlling the debates through his eloquence, his scholarship, and the unnerving figure he cut on the rostrum.

"Rings, Deymorin," Mikhyel whispered aloud, keeping

his inner-self sacrosanct. "How would you know? You were never there."

"Wasn't I?" And he thought of those times he'd come to Rhomatum, unannounced, and stood in the Council Chamber, listening from the crowd as the acting Rhomandi bent the City to his will.

"Damn you, Rhomandi," came the uneven whisper. "You could have told me."

Deymorin shrugged.

Mikhyel sighed heavily, and sagged against him, and Deymorin could almost feel him wrapping himself in Deymorin's fraternal reassurance as surely as he wrapped his body in Deymorin's cloak.

Across the pool of light, beyond the final flickerings of their tiny lamp, Nikki lay alone, radiating rejection, then self-pity, then guilt for feeling sorry for himself, then feeling sorry for Mikhyel, because he was sick, and then jealousy because Deymorin could make Mikhyel feel better and Nikki could only make him worse, and jealousy for Mikhyel, lying there sharing Deymorin's cloak with Deymorin's arm around him, and for that warm feeling they exuded.

Not in words; Deymorin rarely received anything so coherent from Nikki. But Mikhyel was trying to sleep, his head sinking deeper into the cloak, and Deymorin tried to think of himself as a cloak against Nikki's thoughts, as the cloth shielded Mikhyel from Nikki's curious eyes.

Thoughts that soon turned to Ganfrion, curiosity that centered around the inmate's comments. Images of Mikhyel and Deymorin, and a sense of wondering if it could be true; wondering about the years before he'd arrived, trying to imagine the two of them together. . . .

A new image then, of two men beneath one cloak, of Deymorin's arm around Mikhyel. And Deymorin's hand brushing Mikhyel's hair. And Deymorin's head bending over Mikhyel's—like a lover's.

And from under his arm, out of the haze of exhaustion and near sleep, came need. Desire. Hope. Emotions that mingled uncomfortably with those images from Nikki.

And vanished, as Mikhyel came awake.

Mikhyel pushed away, escaping Deymorin's touch, and Deymorins' cloak. Gathering his soiled and damp garment off the stone floor, Mikhyel moved away from the circle of light, isolating his feelings from the cocktail Nikki was serving them all.

Nikki watched him go, despair and self-loathing adding themselves to the mix.

"Damn you, Nikki," Deymorin said slowly, deliberately, and realized with a marked lack of surprise how little Nikki's stricken look moved him, realizing, at that moment, how amazingly simple it would be to hate his youngest brother.

Chapter Eight

Mikhyel clenched his fists and squeezed his eyes closed, trying to force Nikki's formless anguish from his mind. He wished Deymorin would take his recriminations back, would leave Nikki his comfortable illusions, the easy security of love without reservations, without conditions, if not for Nikki's sake, then to quiet all their minds.

But that, he knew, wasn't possible. Not for Deymorin. For Deymorin, love—true adult love—was never unconditional, it was a by-product of respect and admiration of a person toward whom he was predisposed to feel affection.

Never mind he'd raised Nikki to expect otherwise. Never mind they both had.

Anger, betrayal, curiosity: all those and more flowed from Nikki. Strongest of all was fear. Nikki had realized at last what Mikhyel had done, and he was scared, his conjured images far more horrific than actual fact had been. Nikki didn't understand that the deal was made, that he was safe for the night.

At first Mikhyel passively accepted that flow of brotherly anguish. Then he actively sought it, drawing it out like poison from a wound. The effort left his pounding head filled with uncertainty and strange images of himself and Deymorin and Ganfrion, but he could mark those images as Nikki's and ignore them.

And he could send back to Nikki a soothing salve of reassurance, of safety. His reward, as his younger brother finally settled into exhausted, quiet sleep, was his own peace. Peace and—

Deymorin. Within arm's reach, an instant and instinct short of making that contact that would grant him undeniable access to Mikhyel's thoughts.

Deymorin was trying to stay quiet, trying to control those instincts to eradicate the pain and the humiliation that he believed Mikhyel *must* be experiencing, but despite those valiant efforts, Deymorin's concerns filled the air like a thick, cloying smoke.

Deymorin's concerns. Deymorin's guilt. Mikhyel wished he could explain to Nikki that once Deymorin ceased reliving the past, life—all their lives—would return to something akin to normal.

Deymorin wondered whether he should leave Mikhyel to his private thoughts or push him to purge those thoughts with expression. And Deymorin was worried that, if he chose incorrectly, poor, violated Mikhyel might fall over the edge into some pit of self-hatred that would destroy him forever.

And on a more basic level, Deymorin couldn't understand Mikhyel's reactions now. Deymorin wanted him to break down, or to turn Deymorin loose on Ganfrion. Mikhyel's cold acceptance of the incident . . . frightened Deymorin. An assessment Mikhyel doubted *Deymorin* would make of the emotions he radiated.

More importantly to Mikhyel, those memories of Mheric that Deymorin believed Mikhyel needed to purge were as far off the mark of past truths as Nikki's imaginings were regarding Ganfrion's pack.

Speculation. Deymorin *hadn't* gotten as much of Mikhyel's past as he'd thought.

For which ignorance Mikhyel was exceedingly thankful.

"Nikki's an ass," came out of that turmoil at last.

"He just hasn't figured out how to keep quiet yet. He tries hard—too hard, I sometimes think. Maybe *that's* why he can't hear us." He shrugged, for all it was too dark for Deymorin to see. "Who knows?"

"And you don't care to find out."

"Not at the moment."

"Doesn't excuse what else he was throwing around."

"What was he supposed to think, when you coddle me more than you do Kiyrstin, whom you supposedly love so deeply?"

"Kiyrstin doesn't need coddling."

"Neither do I."

"Looked in a mirror lately?"

" 'Fry'? Why don't you complete the question . . . big brother?"

"I wasn't thinking that."

"No? You could have fooled me. Poor little fry. The closet was a damned long time ago, JD."

"The closet. What makes you think I care spit about the closet?"

"I don't think, I *know*! For the past month, every time we're in the same *room* that damned outdated image floats between us."

Even as he spoke, the black hole that was the door of the closet at Darhaven flashed in Deymorin's mind. An instant later, it was gone, a conscious shut-down from Deymorin. But he was too late.

"You think *I'm* responsible for it being there?" Deymorin asked.

"Who else?"

"And I suppose *I'm* the one who sent Nikki to the closet tonight," Deymorin said, from behind that blank spot his mind had become. And this time, though Mikhyel consciously sought a deeper explanation, the fickle link had closed Deymorin's thoughts to him.

"What do you mean?" he asked finally.

"You don't know?"

"If I did, I wouldn't ask!"

"I found him in a bolt hole, Khy." Deymorin's voice was low, with that internal augmentation they'd discovered. "*Your* voice was in his head, *demanding* he stay there. *In the closet.*"

"Then that's . . . *That's* why he was so angry. 'Go to the closet, Nikki, get out of the way, Nikki, let big brother take care of everything, Nikki.' " Mikhyel rubbed a hand across his eyes. "Rings, who can blame him? I was forcing him right back into childhood."

"And you, Khy? What forced you back?" It was a tentative probe, silent as well as verbal, seeking the truth about Mheric. Mikhyel evaded, "What *doesn't* any more? The dark. The fear . . ." An image of Ganfrion, sharp and clear. Those imaginings about Mheric superimposed. Questions. Confusions.

Mikhyel choked on something between laughter and a curse. "Nothing so dramatic, I assure you. One of them threatened to break my wrist, that's all. I panicked. Your brother's an abject coward, JD, you'd better learn to live with it."

"Coward?" Deymorin repeated slowly, and in his mind

was a kaleidoscope of truth and supposition about Mikhyel's life, ancient history and recent. "You're possibly the bravest man I've ever met."

"You're coddling again," Mikhyel said.

"Hell if I am," Deymorin retorted. "I know coddling."

"So do I. You coddle me."

"Maybe I do. Maybe I don't. Maybe I just want an *excuse* to coddle someone."

"Then try coddling *Nikki*. He'd love it."

"Nikki doesn't need coddling."

"Neither do I!" The words exploded out of him. Irritation at this newest twist in Deymorin's misconceptions, reaction to the increasing pressure to supply Deymorin with information he damn well didn't want Deymorin to have.

"So, what you're saying is, I should have left you to keep us awake with your shivering, rattling bones."

"It would have spared us the rest of what Nikki's 'throwing around.'"

"I've got news for both of you. Even if *Kiyrstin* needed coddling, sex would be the farthest thing from my mind. You . . . I don't know how to break this to you, Barrister, but you're just not quite my style."

It was an honest enough attempt at humor, but Mikhyel's attempt at laughter choked on his bitterness.

On the other hand, it was a natural enough speculation, considering what else Nikki had learned about him tonight.

"What do you mean?" Deymorin asked, and Mikhyel realized he'd spoken aloud . . . or thought too clearly. "There's nothing *natural* about it!"

He shrugged.

"Had to learn somewhere, didn't I?"

"Learn?" Deymorin repeated. "Learn what? You've left me behind in the swamp."

"Rings—*sex,* JD. Men with men. You're his source for all such information." Mikhyel drew a steadying breath. "Nikki has some quite amazing notions regarding what did or did not happen between myself and Ganfrion tonight. If I were Nikki, with Nikki's overly romantic, rather confused notions about sex and love, I'd probably prefer to think that my brother had had some . . . pleasant experience before facing a pack of Sparingate wolves."

"Experience," Deymorin repeated flatly. "Sex." A pause for a response that Mikhyel didn't make. "With me."

"Far more palatable than the available options, isn't it?"

"We were *children*."

"We aren't now."

"We haven't spoken to each other in years without fighting."

"We have in the last month."

"But—there was never anything of that nature between us. Not even the thought . . . Or at least . . . Rings, Khyel, was there? Did you . . . ?"

Surprise came through to Mikhyel, along with an image of himself, asexual, almost androgynous. And on its heels, another image, as he'd appeared this evening, hair down, challenging—shockingly (to Deymorin) sultry. But he sensed nothing of loathing. Nothing of revulsion. Curiosity . . . that, perhaps.

"Did I want to be with you?" Mikhyel asked. "Sexually? I don't think so, but I don't really know. I'm not certain I know what it means to want . . . Certainly I've never desired you the way you desire Kiyrstin."

"Kiyrstin?"

Mikhyel acknowledged silently. "In the past month, your feelings for her have provided me with a . . . a benchmark for feelings I don't believe I've ever understood. When I spoke of Nikki's notions about sex and love, it was in philosophical abstracts. What Nikki expects out of life, what you feel with Kiyrstin . . . frankly, Deymorin, makes no sense whatsoever to me."

"And Ganfrion? Did that make sense, Mikhyel?"

Sharp. Direct. That question had been brewing for an hour and more. Unnecessary concern on Deymorin's part; it had been humiliating to capitulate to the wolves of Sparingate, but nothing more.

"Only in economic terms, Deymorin. And in that sense . . . in that sense there were times . . ." His voice grew hoarse with humiliation. "There were times that . . . Darius forgive me, I'd have filled your bed in an instant, if that would have kept you in Rhomatum."

"For the love of Darius, *why*?"

"I don't—" He realized too late the memories he tapped, tried to stop the mental images, but he was too tired, and too slow. Memories of being a child with Deymorin, of swimming in the mountain lakes, and of playing in the snow. Of a warm body to huddle close to at night.

He'd been nine when Nikki was born. Deymorin had been twelve. Nothing had been the same since. But in the years since, even after Mheric's death, that desire to have Deymorin near, the resentment every time he left Rhomatum, had never faded.

"In Rhomatum," Deymorin repeated out of those thoughts. "But not for yourself? Your own desire?"

"Desire, no. Friendship . . . that very possibly. Alliance. Advice—definitely. But not desire. I've no appetite for it, man or woman. Never have had."

"No appetite . . ." And Deymorin's thoughts were on the woman Deymorin himself had placed in Mikhyel's bed on Mikhyel's seventeenth birthday. "Man . . . or woman." And of the sight he'd seen when Anheliaa threw open Mikhyel's bedroom door. "Don't lie to me, Khyel." And of a three-way sharing on Nikki's wedding night. "Not now."

"I'm human, Deymorin. Cut me, and I bleed."

A long pause.

"It's a strange metaphor you choose."

"Is it? Perhaps. And perhaps it's just one more bodily function I'd rather live without."

A longer pause, during which Mikhyel fought the instinct to invade Deymorin's mind to find out exactly what his brother was thinking and feeling. Fought until the blood pounded in his head, and the bile rose in his throat.

How could he expect Deymorin to understand? Deymorin, for whom women and sex and children were the essence of being alive.

Then, suddenly, Deymorin sighed exaggeratedly. "Thank the ley. Kiyrstin would not, I fear, be inclined to share."

Out of the pain, out of the embarrassment, the fear of consequence, came laughter, full and heartfelt, his own or Deymorin's, it didn't matter. Mikhyel released his internal control; and as Deymorin's arm fell around his shoulders, heavy, strong, and natural, he found Deymorin's thoughts, and his own, quiet at last.

§   §   §

"And this one?" A long fingernail bearing a hoarded vestige of chipped enamel pointed to a word in the last tightly penned paragraph.

"Beguiling," Kiyrstin read the word aloud.

"Beguiling," Beauvina echoed. "Is that good?"

"Very."

The girl smiled, then repeated the word. Once aloud, twice more to herself, while looking at the word, then read the entire sentence silently, though her polished lips moved.

It was quite a letter Nikki had sent the young woman. A letter written shortly after Nikki's seventeenth birthday, the day after Nikki had promised to wed Lidye dunTarim.

And quite a young woman he'd sent it to. The letter had arrived in an envelope marked *private,* and Beauvina had respected that request. In the months since she'd received it, she had taught herself to read just so she could make sense of that so-intimate letter. And no one else knew she had it. Except her employer, of whom Beauvina seemed to think very highly.

And since that employer, knowing Beauvina couldn't read, had delivered that envelope marked *private* still safely sealed with Nikki's Rhomandi stamp, and afterward never pried into that envelope's contents, Kiyrstin was inclined to agree with Beauvina's assessment.

Not that Nikki had revealed anything particularly indiscreet. He'd written to thank Beauvina for making his birthday special, and to explain why he wouldn't be back to see her as he'd promised, because he was honorbound now to wed Another, and he intended to love his wife as a husband should, and that didn't include falling in love with Beauvina, so he'd best never see her again.

And then Nikki had simply poured his heart out in terms only a seventeen-year-old whose life had been turned inside out on the most important day of his life could use.

And through a letter intended for someone in whose good opinion Nikki had no stake, Kiyrstin began to see, for the first time, the young man Deymorin and Mikhyel had loved, the young man who had existed before that link among the brothers had exposed so ruthlessly the chaotic inner processes of his young mind to his very worldly brothers.

A young man who had cared so deeply for his older brothers and longed so greatly for their reconciliation, that sometimes, he'd work for weeks just to contrive a single evening together without an argument, fearing every time that something would happen to drive one or the other of them out of his life forever.

To Nikki's mind, on his seventeenth birthday, the very day he'd come of legal age, that long-dreaded eventuality had come to pass. The morning after his party, he'd awakened to discover Deymorin gone, and for the next half year, Nikki had been allowed to believe that exile had been of Deymorin's own choosing.

That misrepresentation had been Mikhyel's doing, as much as Anheliaa's. And out of well-meant necessity. But that fact hadn't made the truth any easier to accept, when that truth had come out.

In the letter, Nikki had confessed his belief that Mikhyel and Deymorin had far more in common than they had differences. And now that fate had proven Nikki correct, Nikki found himself left out, or at least forced to share his brothers in a way he'd never imagined.

This letter left no doubt that prior to his wedding night, Nikki had held out hope that he and his future wife would be everything to one another: romantically, politically, and spiritually.

Hope. And naivete. The letter swam with both. But Kiyrstin could hardly blame Nikki for that.

Kiyrstin had managed, from the day she'd been married at sixteen, to keep sex and friendship and hatred in what she'd always believed were their proper perspective. She'd married with no thought of romance or love, only family and responsibility and power. At thirty-two, she'd believed herself immune to the insidious influences of that mental enigma called love.

Deymorin had annihilated that self-delusion and warped the perspective, and thanks to his insidious charm, she found herself allied with Garetti's enemies-by-tradition, dodging lightning bolts on a regular basis, and currently in danger of spending the rest of her life in Sparingate Prison.

Better that than sitting in Garetti's Mauritum villa having babies and making doilies.

Better for her. Better for Deymorin. But for Nikki . . . Nikki the poet, Nikki the romantic had had to face that perfect love of theirs daily. Probably been forced to share, to some unknown extent, Deymorin's feelings when Deymorin was with her, possibly as intimately at times as Mikhyel. She wouldn't know; Nikki didn't talk to her the way Mikhyel did.

In fact, Nikki hadn't talked to any of them much over the past month. It had to hurt, to be seventeen, and to experience that perfect love he'd sought vicariously, knowing what awaited him in his own marriage bed.

And now he'd arrived in Rhomatum to have that same wife, or her father, have him thrown into Sparingate Crypt. Not exactly the marriage he'd imagined, back when he'd written that letter.

Beauvina read the letter through again, then dabbed at her eyes with her already damp handkerchief. There'd been a fair number of tears. Beauvina's was a romantic heart, and Nikki's story one to inspire such waterworks. Sometime since, she'd excused herself and come back soft-eyed, washed free of makeup . . . the image of common sense and common understanding.

"I think, he's really a very nice young man," Beauvina said quietly.

"I think, Vina, that you're right."

"I wish I could help him . . . somehow."

"I think you already have, Vina."

"I'm . . . glad."

Kiyrstin smiled, and Beauvina smiled back, then leaned back against the wall, the letter pressed to her bosom. Her eyes grew dreamy, then drooped closed, and she slid slowly down onto her side on the cot. Kiyrstin chuckled, and spread a blanket over her.

Perhaps the most revealing aspect of the letter was the fact that the only person Nikki had had to confide his concerns to was a nearly illiterate prostitute he'd met only once.

Knowingly or not, Deymorin and Mikhyel had worked hard over the years to see that what Nikki wanted to be true, was, and Nikki had learned to act on the assumption that the world was the way he wanted it to be. He'd never really had to reach beyond his brothers because, overall, his world had made sense. Because his world was his brothers. When that structure collapsed, he was left without any alternate support, and he struggled now to keep that new world stable.

Interesting, she had to admit. She'd judged him based on

other seventeen-year-olds she'd known. And, for the most part, her reservations still held: he *was* spoiled, and self-centered, and thoughtless.

He also wanted to be more than that. Someday, he might well become more.

If he lived long enough to grow up.

Chapter Nine

{Nikki . . . Nikki . . . Nikki? Nikki, keep—}

"Wake up, dunMheric! You're leaving."

{Calm, Nikki. It's all right, Nikki. Don't fight . . .}

Fight? Why should he—

Fingers bit into Nikki's shoulder and hauled him upright. Light flared in his face and he flinched, throwing an arm out to ward off his assailants. A club struck his wrist, driving it back toward his face.

His mind reeled with the images flooding it from a source other than his own light-blind eyes. Men in uniforms, some in Tower black, most in Fericci green and gold. None in City blue.

"Deymio?" he called to Deymorin with voices internal and external, and for a moment, he thought he had an answer, then the sound of flesh meeting flesh, a grunt, and a thud. "Deymorin!"

Hands jerked him to his feet and held him there as his balance wavered. When he could stand on his own, he strained to see past the guards to Deymorin's pile of straw. It was empty. And he remembered Deymorin had left him, had said he hated him and then followed Mikhyel and not come back.

Fear surged.

"Deymorin!" he cried and: "Mikhyel!" And he reached for both of them, *wanting* to hear them.

{Nikki, it's all right. . . .}

{Deymio!} But—

{Mikhyel,} filtered back, calm and remote. And he could see now, into Mikhyel's dark corner, and Mikhyel himself, who was also flanked by men dressed in green and gold.

Deymorin was sprawled on the stone floor, facedown. Limp.

Panic threatened, but {Unconscious,} invaded his head

along with Mikhyel's engulfing calm. Panic died, overpowered by Mikhyel's cool detachment, even as logic challenged how Mikhyel could possibly know.

"What's going on?" Nikki asked aloud.

"These men have come for you, Nikki," Mikhyel said, as if commenting on the weather. And underneath, clear and pointed: {To take you to the Tower.}

The *Tower*. And Deymorin had been trying to stop them.

"Deymio!" Nikki broke free of his guards, and dropped down beside Deymorin.

Conscious of all eyes following his efforts, he rolled Deymorin over and lifted Deymorin's head and shoulders into his lap, an undertaking far simpler in theory than in practice, Deymorin being a large man and Nikki being seventeen and not yet to his adult strength.

Still, he managed despite their veiled derision, and when he had Deymorin braced on his arm and lap, he patted Deymorin's face lightly, calling his name, trying with all his might to *feel* his brother, to reach into his mind and draw him out of unconsciousness and the brink of death, the way Deymorin had once done for Mikhyel.

And wonder of wonders, there *was* a flicker in the darkness, and Deymorin's head grew lighter on his arm. Deymorin cursed softly, and Nikki *heard* Mikhyel whispering to Deymorin, filling him in and heard Deymorin answering—confused, disgusted—half in his head, half outside.

{Deymorin!} Nikki screamed in his head, desperate that Deymorin hear. {They want to take me to the Tower. What should I do if she wants me for the Rhomandi, and to—}

{Dammit!} Deymorin's arm swung wildly about, sideswiping Nikki's jaw. Nikki dropped his hold, and Deymorin slid back to the floor.

Deymorin cursed again, and other curses answered him from the shadows beyond the guards' flickering torches. Curses less soft and more articulate: inmates complaining at the light and the noise, yelling at the guards to get out and let condemned men sleep.

And the guards cursed back at the shadows, then cursed at Nikki and hauled him to his feet, impatient with his delays.

And Mikhyel's thoughts invaded his {Calm, Nikki. Keep calm.}

Voices in his head, voices in the shadow, voices and hands pulling at him, one way and another, one moment, a torch in his face, the next, black shadows.

{Get out!} he shouted inside. And aloud: "Wait!"

He shook himself free, staggering back to where he could *see*, dammit. And screamed into the shadows: *"Shut up, damn you all!"*

And amazingly, for a brief moment, there was respite. He brushed his sleeves free of straw, shook the dust from his hair, taking a moment to pull the comb from his pocket and force it through the curls, and when *he* was composed, he asked, "What about my brothers?"

One of the guards said, "Our orders cited only you, if you are indeed Nikaenor Rhomandi dunMheric."

"Maybe I am, maybe I'm not."

Mikhyel's protest rattled in his head. He ignored it. Stubbornly not interested in Mikhyel's opinion. He *wasn't* arbitrarily leaving with these men.

"Whose orders?" he demanded.

"The lady Lidye Fericci romNikaenor, Ringmaster of Rhomatum."

Lidye—ringmaster? Suddenly, he was shaking. Surely he'd heard that wrong. The Tower was Anheliaa. That was the order of the universe, never mind he knew one day it wouldn't be true. But when he left, Lidye and Anheliaa were working together, but Lidye as ringmaster meant Anheliaa was dead.

And Sironi gorTarim had brought them here, where Mikhyel had been pushed down the stairs and left to Those Men, and Deymorin lay senseless on the floor.

This time, there was no outside control for him his pain. He'd thrust Mikhyel out, and couldn't get him back, no matter how much he wanted him to be there.

Lidye had married him, thinking she could control him. Anheliaa had made him Princeps in Deymorin's place, thinking *she* could control him. But he'd left. He'd defied them both. And now *he* was being singled out, taken to the Tower. Under guard. Lidye's *father's* men.

Lidye's father, who owned controlling interest in the Shatum Rings. Tarim Fericci, who wanted a figurehead in Rhomatum. Tarim was out to rule the web, and he'd do it by controlling Nikaenor dunMheric. With the determination of the truly terrified, Nikki reached underneath for his broth-

ers, stretching mental hands toward both. And it was as if
hands clasped his, cool and sure.

{Go with them.} He could feel the relief in Mikhyel's
thought as it burst into his head. {Get yourself out
first. Free us later, if you can, but you're no good
inside here.}

But what if he couldn't free them? What if he tried to
argue for that, and Lidye got mad and sent him through
the rings to some unknown mountain lake as Anheliaa had
done to Deymorin? He'd *seen* Mikhyel on the other side
of that transition, and for him there'd be no Mother, no
Kiyrstin, no magic potion, only pain and death and—

{Get control of yourself, boy!}

Like a slap to the face, that chastisement rocked him out
of his panic-driven fears. And another voice in his head:

{Stop whining. If the bitch wanted you dead, there are
easier ways. Don't play hero, just get out, keep safe, and
keep alive.}

{Deymorin!} he shouted inside, and felt it echo clear to
his toes. But Deymorin's groan followed, and Deymorin's
thought went all black and fuzzy.

{Deymorin?}

{All right.} Mikhyel again. {Go, Nikki. Don't cause trouble. Get outside. Get safe.}

Outside. Where *they* didn't have to worry about him. He
could figure that much without Mikhyel's saying anything.
Stop whining, Deymorin had said. Well, he wasn't whining
now. And if Mikhyel thought his input useless beyond
keeping his own skin in one piece, well, Nikaenor Rhomandi dunMheric, *Princeps of Rhomatum*, would prove
them both wrong. He'd prove he had the right to his title,
same as either of them. He'd go with these guards who
belonged to his wife's father, and he'd free Mikhyel and
Deymorin, *and* he'd have Lidye under control and supper
waiting before they reached the Tower.

He lifted his head and preceded the guards up the stairs
and out of Sparingate Crypt.

§   §   §

The door closed behind Nikki and the torches, casting
the prison back into darkness. But no door could close
Nikki off completely from Mikhyel.

Mikhyel wished his younger brother safe, continued sending advice though he could tell Nikki was ignoring him again by the feeling he got of beating his head against a noisy wall. Finally, he gave up the effort that gained him nothing and left him with a pounding, sickening headache. He sank down to his knees, pressing his fingers against his temples, striving to maintain consciousness against the pain, that was his own, and the lure toward insensibility that was Deymorin.

Deymorin's mind was a velvety black that wasn't consciousness, or sleep, and wasn't death. Mikhyel could feel Deymorin breathing. Mikhyel knew Deymorin's heart was beating, because if he let it, his own heart strove to echo Deymorin's.

But the velvet gave Deymorin position and substance within the lightless room, and allowed Mikhyel to work his way over to his brother's prone body.

"Deymorin?" he whispered, and sought his brother's face with his fingertips. He brushed dirt and straw from Deymorin's lax mouth, and, closing his eyes to eliminate the illusion of sight, searched by touch alone, finding a sticky-damp spot among the hair: blood.

He tried to straighten Deymorin's body, to get his head up, and to protect the rising lump from further mishap.

"And then there were two."

A whisper in the dark at his back.

"Well, Suds," the whisper continued, "your bodyguard is dwindling fast. Doesn't look too good, does it?" A hand touched his hair, fingertips that caught the strands and pulled them back from his face. "It'll be morning soon. The clock's spinning down. Why don't you just tell your boyfriend here to bow out gracefully?"

"I might," Mikhyel answered. "Unfortunately, he rarely listens to my advice."

"Oh, I doubt that. Have you told him, yet, what you did?"

"He knows."

"Does he, now?" An inexplicably savage tone laced the whisper. "And I'm still alive? Doesn't speak well for your champion, does it . . . Suds."

"He's not my champion. Therein lies the error of your logic."

"Saves that for blondie, does he?" The hatred increased. "Grown too old for him, have you?"

Mikhyel said nothing. He told himself that Ganfrion was simply probing after information, hoping to goad him into revealing something useful.

"Or is it just that . . . hill-boys . . . are expendable?"

But in the process, the inmate revealed a curious animosity . . . toward Deymorin. It was an unexpected twist. He had anticipated his own discovery. The effect of Deymorin's own personality on these men might prove a far greater complication.

The voice shifted to his other side. Drew closer. "And does he know the whole of it, Suds? Did you tell him how it was your idea? *Your* deal? Might change his opinion of his property. Might not be so eager to keep so willingly popular a commodity."

"I doubt it."

"Doubt. Which?"

"Take your choice."

"Ah. Perhaps I can convince him."

And the presence rustled at his side. Mikhyel leaned forward, intercepting Ganfrion's touch.

"Keep your hands off him."

"How sweet." Once again, the tone shifted. Became mocking. "And how do you intend to stop me, my skinny little friend?"

"We had an agreement."

"Ah, yes. Crypt honor, and all that. Until tomorrow, then." The hand he'd stopped slid along his shoulder, and lifted his hair to an audible sniff. "Mmmmmm, yes. Tomorrow. After that, I fear you'll smell like all the rest and I might well lose interest." The hand tightened and pulled, just enough to remind Mikhyel it could be worse, and when he spoke again, his voice had shed that assumed disinterest. "I can protect you, Suds. Men like you burn out fast without a protector."

"Like me?" he repeated advisedly.

"Too skinny. Too clean. Too frail. The wolves love the weak ones, while they last."

"Wolves? Like you."

"Maybe. Then again, maybe not. But wouldn't you rather a lone wolf than a pack?"

"Maybe. Then again, maybe not. Looks can be deceptive, wolf."

"You think you can handle that pack? You think you can handle me?"

"I think we had a deal, and I'd like to get some sleep."

The presence leaned close; a chuckle stirred the shorter hairs around his ear. "Sweet dreams, Suds.'"

Interlude

Comes a time when every mother must release her young to the world. Fledgling birds must fly, salmon must swim to the sea, fawns must run the high meadows, butterflies must burst from their cocoons, tadpoles become frogs, aphids and bees—

Well . . . Mother wasn't a bug.

Ever.

Comes a time when every mother's energy wanes, when she must retreat to her own private haven to renew her essence, to restore the vitality she expends nurturing her young, helping them mature to that state of adult independence.

And sometimes, she gets just a little too much interference from her own progenitor. Just when she'd gotten her buds maturing nicely—despite that monstrosity overhead, just when she was beginning to seriously connive her own independence, that *creature* down in the valley had to go and argue with a misplaced lightning bolt.

Now, thanks to her progenitor's bad taste, Mother was *wounded,* her tap root to the original Source damaged, and her greedy siblings were stealing all Mother's vitality.

So it was that Mother came to be in her caves deep within the heart of Mount Khoratum, drifting lazily among the ragged-edge veils of crystalline-leythium lace, her toe-webs immersed in the nurturing ooze of liquid ley. Relaxing. Renewing.

And bored.

So it was that when one of her surface-dwelling children thought of her with gratitude and longing—and that indefinably human *need*—Mother welcomed the diversion. She located the point of activity, a shimmering mote within the fainter glow of the universal pattern, and answered with an impulse of Motherly interest. She fed the need with reassurance of Mother's cognizance and a promise of Motherly aid . . . when she got around to it.

Ridiculous, she thought and yawned widely, drawing the motes of vaporized leythium into her lungs. One *tiny* little brush with the surface world, and she was exhausted.

Mother hadn't felt this lethargic in aeons. For the last few earthly heartbeats, she'd walked the surface world quite freely, mixing with all the various species, running as a deer one season, a wolf the next.

And with her humans, of course.

Her humans amused her most of all. They fed her with their love, their faith . . . and their chickens. Thanks to her darling children, Mother had grown in strength and power until she had been ready to claim her own independence, to free herself, to *burst* from her own cocoon.

To leave her obnoxious, over-bearing progenitor to the valley muck and slime he loved so well.

The soothingly-warm/briskly-chill leythium shimmered liquid rainbows in response to Mother's delicate shudder. Sucks-pond-water had grown Old without ever enjoying Youth.

Mother rolled the concepts about her tongue—concepts she'd learned from her darling humans—enjoying the flavor.

There he sat, an ancient source beneath an eroded mountain, progenitor to eighteen other sources (of which, Mother reluctantly admitted to herself, she was one), a lump in the valley floor, absorbing, *relishing* the essence of the humans sitting on his head.

Any humans.

Another shimmering shiver; Mother would melt first. She chose *her* humans with utmost care.

Never mind the human-built stone and wood now sitting over Mother's head like an ugly, too-heavy crown. Never mind the leythium rings spinning within the tallest of those buildings, directing (or so the unwelcome, unChosen humans liked to believe) Mother's essence. That city, the abomination the unwanted humans called Khoratum, wouldn't be there forever; Mother would see to that.

Eventually.

Somehow.

Mother had been small when her humans first arrived

within her sphere of awareness. Young, compared to Sucks-pond-water. Young even compared to her siblings.

And perhaps because she was (at the time) small, perhaps because her surface manifestation was (at the time) confined to a bubbling spring atop a tiny barren hillock, the humans had climbed the mountain to reach her, ignoring the great leythium source in the valley.

The humans' lively thoughts had filled her sphere with energies—colors, tastes, and smells—she'd never imagined, when it was just the birds and the wolves overhead. And fear.

Fear unlike the fear of prey whose cycle had ended. The humans' clever imaginations created Unnatural, Unreasoning fears that disrupted the energies within the ley and disturbed Mother's existence, that sent uncontrollable ripples through the leythium lace and turned her chambers to unpleasant yellows and violent flashes of red.

And so it was that when the humans cried for fear of the storms that raged in the skies over their heads, Mother came to study the patterns in the leythium above *her* head, noting how those shifting veils reflected the fury of the surface storm as well as the humans' cries.

She'd played with those patterns in the ley, using her essence to create waves to counteract the human-generated ripples and to send the storm's fury to her periphery. Her humans' fears had eased, and the surface storm pattern modified as well, which had been a curious thing. She'd tried, then, to shift those leythium patterns deliberately, to shunt the fury off toward her siblings, who were too dull and stupid to object.

The subsequent gratitude and love of her humans had proven intoxicating.

That unexpected exhilaration, combined with her already roused curiosity, encouraged her to try other, more subtle tweaks of the storms using her essence. Such efforts were at first enormously tiring, but over time she'd grown in strength and skill until now she could swim the clouds and dance the lightning as deftly as she swam and danced the ley.

Other human requests had proven more difficult. They'd begged her to heal their sick, which was a much more curious thing than sending storms away, because living creatures contained internal rhythms: conception, gestation, birth, growth, life, death, sickness, health . . . all things that occurred according to their own schedule, and it seemed quite silly to desire it to be otherwise. And in lives so fleeting, Mother had had to wonder what difference a handful of season-cycles could truly make.

Still she'd answered those calls . . . when she heard. When she wasn't exhausted from dancing with the lightning, that being, in those early times, far more exciting than anything her humans could offer. She'd learned to brush their wounds with the sweet nourishment of the ley, adding its essence to their own natural healing powers.

Miracles, her humans had called her efforts—eventually—as they eventually called her Mother, and Goddess.

They had very different words for her earliest attempts; there were some things even *Mother* needed to learn. But she'd cleaned up after herself. . . .

Mother paused in her reflections long enough to lick her lips.

For some reason her fastidiousness had disturbed her humans more than her mistakes. For a time, they feared her greatly and called her "evil" and "demon" and endeavored to cast "spells" to keep her away.

But still they called for help, and when she eventually inferred the advantageous procedure for healing, they began to call upon *her* to keep *herself* away.

Ah, her silly children. Her silly, fickle humans.

A glimmer in the web. Another child was thinking of its Mother. A very young child. Mother touched that receptive mind and nurtured it with the scent of Mother, the taste of joy, the warmth of optimism, before her interest waned and she returned in all senses to the world cave.

How she longed to walk the surface world, to watch her children perform their incomprehensible but amusing antics, to taste the wind, the rain . . . the chickens. To experience the *real* sweetness, the *real* crunch of *real* aphids on *real* drenal leaves rather than making do with the recreated sensations on her tongue.

Which she might also have created, for all she didn't quite remember making her tongue for the first time.

But then, Mother's sense of time had been severely disrupted—recently, she believed, though who could say, considering?

Mother thought, perhaps, there were thoughts she should

be thinking, concerns she should be concerning herself with, but Mother was tired. Thinking, concerning, remembering, those required more energy than dancing with the lightning.

So Mother floated. Mother drifted. Mother waited for the ley to surge through her once again. Waited for total restoration. Mother could feel the moment coming.

Soon. Very soon.

Unlike the old days.

Mother had been a bit slow back . . . then. She'd redirect a storm, then sink her toes into the ley to rejuvenate until she heard a call, and then she'd surface to heal some poor child with a chicken to spare.

She'd learned later that her moment's rest might have been, in human terms, days, weeks, years, or even human generations. But with practice, and as the leythium web grew, expanding its liquid and crystalline structure in all directions, sending tendrils out to gather the world's essence and channel it to her caverns deep in her mountain's belly, she'd visited the surface world with increasing frequency.

She grew quite fond of her humans. For all they were a bit silly, for all their goals were irrational and shortsighted, they were decidedly more amusing than her own slow-thinking offspring percolating within the surrounding leythium caverns, and infinitely more attentive than her progenitor.

She'd even brought some of her humans into her world cave, to teach them to dance the ley. The clumsy ones fell between the strands, and into the pools to become one with the ley. Some took fright when they witnessed the fate of the clumsy and ran, only to find *their* steps mired in liquified leythium, their feet dissolving beneath them.

But one had reveled in the dance, flying with joy among the strands, even laughing at her when she dared to challenge him with a sudden dissolution of the strand between his fingers.

Rakshi. Her first Dancer-child.

Rakshi returned to the surface to beget others who, like Rakshi himself, could dance the ley. And as the human generations turned, a precious few learned to draw on the ley, a precious few who could, like Mother, sink themselves into the leythium pool and draw its essence to them, rather than be consumed by it.

Those, her special children, she cherished beyond measure.

When she remembered them.

SECTION TWO

Chapter One

Mornings in Bharlori's back room were invariably noisy. With little to do until mid-morning, it was a time of sharing the gossip gleaned from customers the previous night. Gossip similar to that in Rhyys' court, only rather more accurately recounted, here in Lower Khoratum, where the only ears to overhear were hiller peasants, whose influence was nil, and so whose opinions didn't matter.

But last night, Bharlori's had created its own fine topic. And that topic felt terrible.

The young women gathered around Thyerri, arguing about the proper care for him. Some were for propping him upright in a nest of pillows, others insisted that he should be lying flat on the hard floor.

They decided on the pillows, then took turns bathing his brow, and feeding him sips of tea and bits of bread. All the while they exclaimed over his bravery, saying how Sakhithe had explained everything, and those awful men would never have attacked him if he hadn't stepped in and rescued her, and how if it had been Biertha (whom no one liked), she'd have only gotten what she deserved, but Sakhithe never sought attention, so she didn't, and he was a fine fellow to have championed her.

Their chatter made Thyerri's head spin all over again, or perhaps it was the spirits they slipped into the tea. Thyerri's attention wandered; the fresh balm on his cuts stung, the fumes made his eyes tear, and he soon decided all he really wanted was to go back to sleep.

He drew his blankets high under his chin, closed his eyes, and tried to see himself hale and well, his cheek smooth, scarless. The balm grew warm, and the sting went away.

But the other aches were worse this morning, even past the drugged tea, and Thyerri grew frightened because he didn't know what that mind-hazing pain meant, and not knowing, couldn't think the pain better.

He'd never been in a fight, never been seriously injured or ill—or if he had, Mother had taken care of it. He had nothing against which to judge the sensations flooding his body. Nothing except the self-knowledge gained as a dancer-in-training. So he sought, in the quiet of his own mind, to assess his wounds.

As he considered the possibilities, the might-have-beens, had this kick been a finger's-breadth lower, or that cut a shade deeper, he began to shake. He remembered hands doubled into fists, booted toes, belts that carried knives . . . swords . . .

And he thought of the anger, the hatred . . . the desire to hurt . . . to . . .

He could be dead.

The blankets slipped from his nerveless fingers; a palsy consumed him, dislodging the carefully placed pillows at his back, and he curled on his side, shaking with fear and cold and horror.

After the Collapse of the web and with his chance at the Dance gone forever, he'd flirted with the notion of death— frequently. But this was different. This death would have been meaningless, the result of a stranger's momentary, senseless anger that sent him over that brink prematurely.

And he knew then—as light feminine voices exclaimed in concern, and gentle hands soothed him, and warm bodies joined him under his blankets, pressing close, shifting him to take the weight off the sore spots, holding him against the shivers that made his joints hurt more than ever, that he truly was not ready to die.

He unwound his arms, clenched as they were to his middle, and curled them around the inviting warmth before him, the humanity that was still so strange to him. He wasn't certain who it was he embraced, only that his need was not rejected.

Strange sensations, and familiar rippled through him. Warmth. Security. He'd known that. Sympathy. Perhaps even understanding . . . that was new. Different.

He'd always known he was different. He was a dancer like no other dancer before him. But then, so were all true Rakshi dancers unique.

He'd wagered everything on that belief, and lost—everything.

Thyerri had been raised not by human hand, but by the wind and the rain, the meadow grass and the mountains. There were early memories, images from before grass and the meadows and the wind, but they faded with time, as life became the dance . . . and Mother.

That which the hillers worshiped in secret, the leymother herself, had kept him alive when he would have died. And Mother had taught him to dance, had, such as she was able, loved him.

Or so he'd always believed.

Following the Collapse, he'd run through the hills calling for her, begging her to answer. But the hills had remained silent. Cold. He'd have transferred to her caverns deep in the mountain's heart, would have risked life itself in the doing, without the ley-touched oil to protect his fragile human skin, but the mountain was closed to him.

Mother had expressed concern in those final days that he had lost touch with his humanity, and losing his humanity he had lost, or so he had extrapolated from her musings, his value to her.

He'd defied Mother once, in hopes of finding that humanity, had risked her love and her goodwill to become, at last, what he believed she desired.

And she'd rejected him.

He'd known beyond doubt, then, that he was lost. The dance was gone. Mother was. There were others for Mother. Other children. There always had been. There would be many still. Others who wouldn't disappoint her.

Aimless, faint with hunger, seduced even then by the dance rings, he'd returned to Khoratum. And there, in the chaos following the collapse, Sakhithe had found him and brought him to Bharlori and bullied the owner into accepting the most inept of raw recruits.

He'd found humanity, found bravery and cowardice, selfishness and selflessness, love and hate . . . but he still didn't know where he fit within that web. For him, life was the Dance. Anything short of the Dance was merely survival.

A hand cradled his head, worked in among the hair still filthy with last night's mud, and pressed his cheek against a full, soft breast. He sighed and nestled there, safe, warm, entwined in a mood that was the antithesis of the anger and hatred that had permeated the alley behind Bharlori's last night.

It was a new sensation, but one to which his bruised and chilled body conformed easily. Naturally. Gratefully. Until the hand on his back began wandering lower.

Thyerri shifted, trying to avoid Mishthi's searching touch, seeking Sakhithe, who knew better. Sore, bruised, muzzy-headed with their potions, he still wanted none of what Mishthi so insistently suggested.

"Sakhi," he whispered, and his voice caught. He didn't know how to tell Mishthi to leave him alone, and her hands were deep into his clothing now.

"Mishthi, behave!" Sakhithe's voice whispered from somewhere above his head. 'You *know* he's a dancer."

"No, he isn't. *Wasn't.*" But Mishthi's hands retreated, to brush along his chest. "He was a novice. But he's not any more. He *failed.* And now, he's ready to become a man, aren't you, pretty, brave, *wonderful* Thyerri?"

"Have pity," he mumbled and grasped Mishthi's wrist. "I feel as if I've been tossed off a cliff, struck by lightning, and poisoned for good measure. There's nothing *left,* Mishthi!"

Instantly remorseful, she cooed and petted, apologized and promised, and he relaxed again into his warm, human-scented cocoon.

But it was just a matter of time before Mishthi, or Khani, or one of the others tried again. Only his own disinterest had kept them at bay this long. He would speak with Sakhithe. Perhaps she could convince them their hopes were in vain. He was twenty-two years old and those feelings Mishthi sought to rouse had never affected him.

For which dearth he was eternally thankful. More than one dancer's career had ended when the body decided, not when the heart had.

He had been an apprentice dancer, yes; and he'd probably never have another chance at the rings, that was also true. But he was still a dancer, last night had reminded him of that simple truth, and as long as he was a dancer, hope remained, however unrealistically, that he still might one day dance the rings.

And for a dancer, those sensations Mishthi sought, the emotions and distractions that came with them, were a death sentence. That was the common knowledge, and not a belief this would-be dancer cared to challenge.

Chapter Two

Waking came with a flare of light and a noisy announcement of breakfast's imminent arrival.

Deymorin, complaining of a headache, stumbled off to the latrine, to return with a wet head and a stream of curses.

"If you will flaunt authority—" Mikhyel began.

"—I should thank my ancestors for giving me a hard head?" Deymorin finished sarcastically.

Mikhyel answered with a lift of one shoulder. The movement disrupted his unsecured braid, and the loose strands slid forward into his face. He silently cursed the man who had claimed his pin, and this time just flung the hair behind his shoulders.

It slid back into his face.

"I swear, I'm going to join the Brothers of Barsitum and shave it off. That would at least give Raul something to do with my razors."

"Count your blessings, brother." Deymorin scratched his stubbled chin. "Would that my leyapult, as Nikki calls it, had done me a similar favor."

"There *are* tweezers in the latrine."

"There's also a cold-water bath. I can still hold you under, and I doubt your new talents include gills. As for shaving your head, *only* if you explain to Kiyrstin that I couldn't stop you. *She* thinks your hair is utterly *splendid.* But frankly, I don't give a rat's ass. Let's go eat."

The prisoners had formed a living wall at an obviously long-established demarcation line, waiting with surprising decorum while double-guarded kitchen aides set piles of loaf-bowls on the tables, then scurried back up the stairs.

When the aides were gone, guards manned a cast-iron cauldron at one table and a spigoted barrel at the other, and at a signal from the captain of the guard, the inmates surged forward.

Mikhyel would have held back, waiting until the others had theirs, but Deymorin hauled him straight into the crush, to establish, so Deymorin conveyed along with the throbbing in his skull, that they were one of the crowd, no better, no worse, and ready to protect their rights.

Deymorin passed two bread-bowls filled with a thick gruel to Mikhyel and grabbed two mugs before chasing Mikhyel back through the milling bodies to their spot beneath the stairs.

The gruel was agreeably palatable, and the bread, fresh-baked, with a hard, water-brushed crust, gave a man's jaws a satisfying fight for supremacy. Mikhyel managed about a third of the gruel, exchanged bowls with Deymorin, and nibbled slowly at the crust of Deymorin's empty bread-bowl. The simple fare proved far more sympathetic to his half-starved gut than the typical five-course spread they'd have faced in Rhomatum Tower this morning.

"Here," Deymorin said, and handed him one of the mugs.

"What is it?"

"Ale. Morning, noon, and night," Deymorin answered, taking a healthy swig.

Mikhyel set the mug down, untasted, uncertain he could face even the smell this early in the morning. After lunch, perhaps. On a hot day. Very hot.

But the bread was dry, and eventually he conceded. He lifted the mug to sniff gingerly, but his overtaxed nose could detect no discernible odor. He eyed his brother's bland expression suspiciously, doubly so when he realized Deymorin's normally emotion-rich essence had gone blank.

A cautious sip found, rather than the threatened ale, a pleasant, dilute fruit juice. Sending Deymorin the glare his brother obviously expected, he drained the mug and went after his own refill.

Whether by chance or design, Ganfrion intercepted him at the barrel. He met the man's look with outward calm, and stepped aside to allow the inmate first access to the barrel, tacit acknowledgment of Ganfrion's superior position within the prison power structure.

A faint smirk tweaked Ganfrion's scar-twisted mouth. He tipped his head in amusement, and pulled the tap. When his mug was only two-thirds full, the stream of liquid dribbled to a halt.

"Oh, dear." Exaggerated gentility dripped from the words. "It appears I've taken the last of it. —Here, Suds." Ganfrion held the mug out. "Have mine. After all, we have you new lads to thank for the fancy fare this morning, don't we?"

Mikhyel turned away. Ganfrion's hand on his elbow stopped him, brought him about to face the barrel again.

"I'll share mine with you."

Suddenly, the tactic was too obvious, the depletion too convenient. Mikhyel reached past the inmate, who refused to move away from the tap, and pulled the lever. Fruit juice sprayed across the man's already stained pantleg.

"Oh, dear," Mikhyel said, mimicking Ganfrion, words and tone. "It appears to have had an air pocket. —Excuse me."

This time, the inmate did move aside. Mikhyel filled his mug and returned to Deymorin's niche, reaching it with his mug still full despite his shaking hands.

Deymorin said nothing, but from the look in his eyes, and the murderous anger underneath, Mikhyel could only hope Raulind—or Nikki—could secure their freedom today. *Soon.* He'd seen the reports on men who had tried to make a lone stand in the Crypt; Deymorin would only get himself seriously hurt—if not killed.

And Deymorin would be alone in such a stand. Mikhyel, when all was said and done, was useless in the sort of encounter Deymorin would provoke.

Morning and a third mug of juice led to natural consequences. Having convinced Deymorin he had been going to the latrine on his own for several years now, and with Deymorin's {Just don't fall in.} echoing in his head, he wended his way in the gas-given daylight to that area of the vast chamber to which his instincts had led him unerringly in last night's dark.

The flames were brighter this morning, and more numerous: the prison's attempt to simulate passage of time. Rhomatum believed in punishing her wrongdoers, but not in outright cruelty. She'd learned constant dim lighting was not, in the long run, economical, as it turned already marginally socialized men into unreasoning animals.

And these daylight levels did make the massive chamber

infinitely less intimidating. What had been a confused montage of suddenly-there stone walls last night became a honeycomb of narrow corridors and antechambers.

Most of those chambers contained straw-filled pallets and crumpled, stained blankets. Substantially more pallets than there were inmates to fill them. If he and Deymorin were forced to spend another night here, it was quite possible that they might do so in slightly more comfort than last night.

Or (images of Ganfrion and his pack intruded) they might not.

There were two men seated side by side in the latrine comparing philosophies of purgatives when he arrived. One voice, at least, belonged to last night's pack.

Mikhyel ducked into the nearest stone pocket to await their departure.

Their conversation drifted from purgatives, to politics, to prostitutes. Based on a mixture of fact, rumor, and innuendo from all over the web, they created a curious kaleidoscopic view of the world above. As Mikhyel waited in increasing discomfort, he decided that if a man truly wanted to test the pulse of the City, he should find just such a spot juxtaposed to the public latrines and set up constant surveillance.

"So, think they'll trip us fer th' fun'ral?"

The second man's response was little more than a mumble, but it roused coarse laughter.

"Hah. Web's fried. Frizzled. Old Annie-girl's dead or near enough as makes no never mind. Sooner th' better, I sez. Ol' bitch runs th' web like it's 'er own friggin' dinkinrod. She goes, th' web goes—" A noise followed Mikhyel did not believe originated in the man's throat. "Ask me if I gives a fuck."

More mumbling.

"Shit, no. I jes hopes she takes that fuckin' asshole of a nevvie with 'er."

A pause for mumbles, then: "Naw. Those ain't the Rhomandi, more's the pity. Jes one more batcha fakes. I 'member that black-haired second. Mean-lookin' bastard. Proud." A pause, then laughter. "This 'un, he had practice."

A pause. Laughter. Mikhyel stared into the shadows and waited, coldly indifferent.

"Yup. Frustrated as 'ell. All prepared fer a bit more personal attention, ol' Gan was. Has a taste fer th' hiller-brats. Too bad blackie *ain't* dunMheric. Mebbe get us pard'ns, each 'n ever' one uv us, bein' so restrained an' all in our urges. '—Say again? Yeah, well leastwise long 'nough t' go t' th' old ringbat's immersin'. 'Ell of a party at'll be. Ever' damn shiny-pocket, tax-eatin' thief in th' web'll be there."

More mumbling.

"*Private* immersin'? That's—that's uncivilized! Cheats th' lightfingers, it does! Big funeral like that 'un *should* be— all the rich-uns, all that weepin' an' wailin'—hells, we'd be set up fer good n' all. Then we get th' 'ell outta here afore they locks us back— Ah-h-h. That's it fer me."

Mumbling and the splash of water, and the area was free. Finally.

The prison's plumbing was simple. Rainwater, collected in cisterns somewhere above ground, exited here in controlled, narrow streams from spouts along the wall. Cupped stone basins received and pooled it for washing, then funneled it to a urinal channel along the wall, flushing liquid waste down past the seats (where the previous users had been so leisurely enthroned) and ultimately, he would suppose, to the ley itself, where such human by-products, in the manner of the ley, disappeared, to nourish the growth of another generation of leythium crystals.

Off to one side, a slate-edged sunken pool provided cool, but clean, bathing water, and piped spigots, filled from somewhere outside the cavern, gave foaming liquid.

Suds. He frowned, irritated that the memory of last night had any power still to disturb his thoughts. No reason a man couldn't stay clean here. Provided, of course, he was allowed to bathe in peace.

He was wondering, as he refastened his clothing, what the odds of that happening might be, when a blow between his shoulders sent him up against the stone wall. He rebounded, scrambling for balance on the shallow conduit's slick stone.

A hand imprisoned his wrist and twisted his arm back and up between his shoulders. A large body pressed him hard against the stone.

"You *are* left-handed, aren't you, Suds?"

He hadn't the breath to answer, even had he been so inclined. Anger flared. And fear, as Deymorin sensed his anger and surged to his feet, out there beneath the stairs. Ignoring his captor, Mikhyel wished Deymorin to be calm, to stay where he was, and he knew relief when Deymorin settled.

"You don't have to answer," the voice—Ganfrion—was saying. "I know. I remember those white fingers—signing my death sentence."

So, the secret was no longer. He said nothing, still thinking primarily of Deymorin and calm. But *that* was patently false. He remembered *every* man he'd ever sentenced to death, and this Ganfrion was not one of them. Ganfrion was trying to goad him into—

Another twist threatened every joint in his arm. He clamped his jaw on a cry of protest.

"I could take you here and now, dun*Mheric*." Spittle dribbled a cold, slimy trail down his neck. "I could take you and leave you for the rest. They're over there, dunMheric. Waiting. You could be dead before that big brother of yours even missed you."

"I'm not—"

Ganfrion's lower body slammed his into the irregular stone of the wall, obliterating his protest. Ganfrion's other hand buried itself in his hair, took a twist and pulled, arching his head back, forcing eye contact. The too-close face swam in time with the throb in his head and body. He stared through the image, thinking of Deymorin and calm.

"I know who you are, Lord Supreme High Justice Mikhyel Rhomandi dunMheric." The hissed whisper was for his ear alone. "That smooth chin threw me off at first, but I remember that look of yours, lawyer-man, and your Tower-born airs, and I'm here to tell you, it did my heart good to see you on your knees in front of me, you arrogant son-of-a-whore."

Another driving thrust of hip and arm sent shafts of pain through his body and drove the air from his lungs. Mikhyel pressed his face against the cold stone, closing his eyes against gray-and-gold swirls that seemed to surge toward him and fall away at one and the same time.

{Stay where you are, Deymorin. Stay calm. Mikhyel is fine.} The thought became a litany in his mind.

The pressure eased enough for him to draw breath.

"Do you remember me, dunMheric? Or do you throw

so many lives away they all blur together? Do you remember? Do you know why I'm here?"

That was almost too easy. Only a handful of offenses could legitimately land a man in this particular grotto.

"Murder, I should imagine." His gasping after breath robbed the comment of the indifference he sought, and Ganfrion chuckled, a throaty, mocking sound.

"Not rape? You wound my pride, lawyer-man."

"On the con—" His answer collapsed in a grunt, as someone entered the latrine and Ganfrion leaned his full weight on him.

His arm and shoulders were on fire, his feet were going numb. He fought for balance against slippery stone and Ganfrion's deliberately shifting weight, while the unknown inmate urinated quickly, and as quickly departed, politely ignoring their presence.

When they were alone, the pressure eased, and Mikhyel continued on a gasping intake of breath, "—trary. I was implying your pleasure didn't require force."

"Funny man. Clever man," said the whisper in his ear.

With a parting thrust, the massive weight let up. The hold on his wrist relaxed and guided the numb limb to a controlled drop. But he wasn't fool enough to believe himself free.

"Assassin, as happens," Ganfrion continued. "Politically felicitous elimination. The system taking a good dump. Hardly the same thing as common murder."

"If you insist."

"And do you know who hired me?" The hand worked its way up his arm, rubbing gently. Solicitously. Mocking his weakness. "Do you know who promised, *on her honor,* I'd not be prosecuted if I were caught?"

"Should I care?"

"Oh, yes, Lord Justice, I think you should."

The answer was suddenly obvious. Mikhyel glanced back. "Anheliaa."

"Clever, clever, lad, Suds." Fingers infiltrated his hair to caress his scalp, paused and took a ruthless twist. "And do you know who I was hired to kill?"

"Me?" It was an embarrassingly small, choked sound he made, but the fingers smoothed his hair aside, hooking it over his shoulder, then slid down and around his waist. "Now, Suds, you know better than that. Try again."

"Deymorin." Again, obvious. And it meant Ganfrion had been here a minimum of seven months. Likely longer.

"Very good, Suds."

He tried to remember back. Tried to remember the man's name, his face. Certainly, he'd never have forgotten the charge. If Ganfrion were telling the truth—

Warm breath on his cheek, a brush of rough-trimmed beard. "Still so smooth. What do you do, Lord Justice, wear a fake to hide the fact you haven't the *balls* to grow your own?"

Mikhyel stared straight ahead, ignoring that touch, ignoring the taunt, both intended to shake him from the fact that the man's story didn't fit. Assassin: possible. Hired by Anheliaa: also possible. But an attempt on Deymorin . . .

"You're lying," he stated firmly. "I sentence no one arbitrarily, I would remember—"

He swallowed the rest as Ganfrion's hand slipped the first button on his breeches.

"Auntie got the charges changed, Suds. She kept her promise at least that far. And since an attempt on the Princeps of Rhomatum *would* have been a death sentence, I suppose I should thank her for that."

That still didn't explain why— "You didn't recognize him."

"Didn't I?"

The hand slipped the last button and invaded his clothing; Mikhyel fought to keep Deymorin out of his head and seated on the stairs.

"But I had to wonder, Suds, when you three showed up. Did she intend me to finish the job? Do you suppose after they took your bodies from here, I'd be free? —Or dead?"

He said nothing.

"I heard baby brother and big brother arguing last night. Appears you lads have a problem."

"Nothing we can't work out."

"No? I suppose not. You and big brother Deymio can work out everything, can't you? Brother Nikki. Who runs the city. Who fucks brother Khyel . . ."

Mikhyel's heart beat loudly in his ears. Ganfrion's hand rested quietly on his flank, a tactic as unexpected as it was, considering the alternatives, welcome. But Mikhyel didn't trust that restraint, and he wondered when the pretense— both physical and verbal—would drop.

"Why am I still alive . . . Barrister? What kind of *brother* is he? Is he a true brother at all? Or just Mheric's son? Does *he* enjoy seeing you humiliated, too?"

Mikhyel closed his eyes and calmed his breathing, concentrating on Deymorin and stairs, not the fantasies of a man who couldn't begin to know the truth of his outlandish accusations.

"Perhaps the whore would like to see the unfriend humiliated—"

"Touch him, and you'll regret it."

"Really? Such loyalty. And toward someone who sat on the stairs while you . . . well, we won't talk about that any more, will we? And what will you do, little hill-boy whore? You'll get no sympathy from anyone here. The lads will laugh while they're fucking you to death."

"You seem to take your own death very lightly. Because when this is all straightened out, if I'm dead, if Deymorin is, Nikki is capable of having the lot of you executed. And there are those in the Council who will support that."

"Ah, yes. Death. That's a powerful card, lawyer-man." Its passivity at an end, the hand began to inch its way randomly along his skin. "And Nikki-boy *is* gone, now. Green and gold took him, along with the Tower black. A man interested in living would have to wonder what that means. Tarim in control? Would Tarim want his daughter's husband's competition taken out? Or would he fear the Lord Justice more? What do you think, Suds? Which would you choose?"

"Deymorin's never wanted Rhomatum," Mikhyel answered, without hesitation. "He'd pose no competition to Nikki's position."

The hand paused.

"So you would eliminate the Lord Justice? If you were I?"

"If my goal was to curry favor with Tarim. Yes."

"Curious. On the other hand . . . perhaps I don't have to choose. Perhaps if both of you—"

Temper flared, without warning.

"Damn you!" he hissed into the stone, then realized the temper for Deymorin's, and shut them both down.

"You presume too soon, Suds. Tarim's is not the only game. Anheliaa's isn't. What if I leave you—and your brother—alone? What if I keep the others off you? You might be out of here before nightfall. Or perhaps tomorrow. Perhaps a week, but you will be free, won't you? If you're alive. Your kind, you slick and powerful scum, never stay, regardless of your crimes, regardless of the Family's current little power games."

Temper flared again. Deymorin's, perhaps, or his own at this indictment against the system in which he took great personal pride.

"If I take care of you, one day, you'll be here, the next, you'll be back in your courtroom sending men to this hellhole. —And pardoning them."

Mikhyel set his jaw against the retort that rose to his lips. Deymorin, he told himself firmly. It was Deymorin's anger, not his.

"If I were you, dunMheric, I'd remember this day. Remember this very moment. Remember what I know about you. Remember I could have made your life a living hell—and didn't. Remember I kept these animals away from you, and that I didn't press your brother for the fight that would kill him with no questions asked. You owe me, dunMheric, and you'll either pay that debt, or the world—and your brother—will know how you survived last night. Do you understand me?"

He should say something—he was supposed to be so clever—but his mind was blank.

"Do you?"

"I'm not—" His breath exploded as once again Ganfrion leaned full against him.

Yet another inmate had entered the latrine, this time with some rude comment about needing more time than a woman, and Ganfrion's hand was again moving, never minding the other inmate's presence.

Or, perhaps, because of it. The touch was almost clinical in its examination of his unnaturally smooth flesh.

A grunt, of surprise—or perhaps, of confirmation. Either was possible. But when those callused fingers surrounded him, Mikhyel felt that inner wall that kept him separate from Deymorin fracture.

"Do you hear, little man?" The words were a breath in his ear.

He fought the wall furiously back into solidarity and whispered: "I hear you, Ganfrion."

The hand squeezed. "And you owe me, word of a Rhomandi."

"Damn y—"

"Your word, *Rhomandi*."

"I—owe you."

"Good." With a final, almost tender, caress, Ganfrion released him and walked away, nodding casually at the man who'd settled indifferently on the stone seat.

Forcing his shaking knees to support him, Mikhyel pushed himself free of the stained wall, stumbled to one of the inlets, and held his wrists under the chilly stream, waiting for his head to clear, disgusted at himself for letting Ganfrion's tactics affect him.

It was a reasonable enough negotiation, if somewhat unorthodox in its delivery. Not a stupid man, Ganfrion. Revenge and a way out, all in one controlled act.

But it was over. The deal made. *If* Deymorin would control himself.

Always, if Deymorin would control himself.

When his breath had steadied to his satisfaction, he checked and reinforced that inner wall for which he had no rational explanation or description, secured his clothing, and left the latrine.

§ § §

"I thought I told you not to fall in," Deymorin said, trying to hide his relief at Mikhyel's reappearance.

Mikhyel stopped short, a startled look on his face.

Forcing a grin, Deymorin pointed at his brother's damp boots, endeavoring not to notice the other stains on Mikhyel's clothing. "Miss the drain, did you?"

Mikhyel glanced down, blinked, then laughed and sank into Nikki's pile of straw, his booted feet thrust out in front of him. "Apparently. Looks as if you'd better come along next time. Teach the baby to aim."

"That should be the cheapest entertainment I've had in years." He regretted the words the moment he said them. Trying too hard, just like Nikki. Trying not to invade his brother's pride, and failing miserably. "Khyel, I'm sorry."

Eyes that had gone unfocused, flickered up to him. "Why? Oh, that." A faint shake of the head. "You worry too much, JD. Say what you like. I know what you mean."

Perhaps that was true. But there was a lifetime of words said that shouldn't have been, and nothing could erase those years, just as nothing could wipe from Deymorin's mind the knowledge of who had disappeared toward the latrine right after Mikhyel left.

And nothing could wipe from his mind the knowledge that only Mikhyel's wishes and Mikhyel's blood-chilling thoughts had kept him from joining the pissing party. He'd been sickened by the forced inaction, and resented Mikhyel's passive acceptance of the situation that hampered anything *he* might do to stop it.

Mikhyel's shadow-smile faded. He rubbed his arms as if chilled, but made no move to join Deymorin. His hair was loose again; he pulled the strands forward and separated it into sections. "What do you suppose is happening to him?"

"Nikki?" Deymorin asked, and Mikhyel's head dipped. "Do you really want to speculate?"

"I suppose not. It's just . . . I stopped feeling him when he entered the Tower, and—"

"The *Tower?* Rings, Khyel, just how much *do* you get from us?"

"I—" Shaking hands fouled the braid. Mikhyel cursed softly and finger-combed it free to begin again. What had begun as necessity was rapidly devolving to a nervous tic. "I think this is the first time I've *completely* lost touch of him since his wedding night. Before that—"

"Before?" Deymorin repeated. "You mean, his birthday? When Anheliaa threw me out? That's the first time I noticed anything. I didn't understand at the time, of course, but in retrospect, that's what I think of as the real beginning."

Mikhyel frowned. "There was that, yes. But I'm beginning to think this ability has been with us a very long time. What you said last night, about Nikki and the closet, has had me wondering whether or not it's always been there. Maybe we just never *needed* it enough."

"Or, at least, not since Mheric died. Is that what you're saying?"

Mikhyel nodded, his eyes fixed on some spot just beyond his boots. "When we were children and Mheric would come after me, no matter where Nikki was, he'd end up in the closet, right where I wanted him to be. I remember *yelling* at him to go there, but it was all in my head. Mheric would have killed me if I'd screamed. I'd wish Nikki there in the closet, safe. And he always was. My consciousness of him is clearer now, more constant, but I don't think it's entirely new. Any of it."

"Your consciousness of *him*," Deymorin repeated. "And of me?"

There was a long pause, containing Mikhyel's silent examination of his hands and the repair of a ragged nail. "Who knows? We've been at odds for so long, have gone to such great lengths to misunderstand each other, to think the worst. For all I know, half the problem I had was believing one thing about you based on apparent facts and *knowing* underneath, that I was wrong."

"Says the man who deals daily with politicians."

Gray eyes flickered up at him. "You were my brother, not a Syndic."

"Point, Khyel."

"When we were young—perhaps, though I can't remember. The need wasn't there. Except—"

"Except the time I reset the rings?" Deymorin followed that train of thought, and Mikhyel nodded.

"Terror has been known to work miracles," Deymorin said with a grin.

"True. But the Talent had to be there in order for you to tap it. We snuck into the Tower together. *I* touched them and disrupted their orbits, but I could never have reset them." His eyes dropped. "The rings themselves know, I've tried often enough since. As for the rest of what we have experienced, I can barely recall what my mind was like two months ago. Besides, how can we know what 'normal' is? I'd assumed, because the change was so obvious following Nikki's wedding night, that *that* was the true beginning. But after last night . . . I just don't know any more."

Mikhyel occupied himself again with his fine, slippery hair. Thinking he needed something to keep the end tied, Deymorin pulled Mikhyel's stained cloak into his lap and began plucking at the threads holding the decorative gold braid in place.

Mikhyel's hands slowed, his head tipped, his brows puckered. In someone else, Deymorin would interpret the look as confusion.

"And now?" Deymorin asked. "How much do you get from me these days?"

"I . . ." Mikhyel's gaze flickered and fell away. "Right now? Not much. Other times . . . a great deal, Deymio. Words, when we all seem to want it, but mostly, just . . . things. Things I'd rather not know, things I've no *right* to know. I try not to hear, but . . . sometimes I can't stop it. Sometimes, I . . ."

Mikhyel's voice faded, and his expression grew puzzled, watching Deymorin's hands.

Mikhyel got "things" from Deymorin that he'd rather not know, but evidently not so mundane a thought as why Deymorin was pulling the braid free, one stitch at a time.

Only emotionally charged things bridged spontaneously between them, things a man would most want to keep private. Perhaps the type of impressions he got from Mikhyel on occasion—or the flood he got from Nikki. A wave of resentment flowed through him, a sense of violation.

The look Mikhyel cast across the room to him was pained, uncertain, mirroring the fact that Mikhyel was, to some unknown extent, following his thoughts, his reasoning.

"I didn't know—I didn't know it was *so* different for you." It was all he could think of to say. "So much worse."

"Worse?" Mikhyel shrugged. "Is it worse to know, or be known? I can't honestly answer that."

Thoughts of Nikki, then, and Nikki's constant resentment at being misunderstood—or understood too well—came to Deymorin, along with recollections of how Nikki's resentments had colored and disrupted all their lives. He examined his thoughts and decided he wasn't ashamed of those thoughts or of how he felt, and wasn't afraid for Mikhyel to know.

And with that insight, he banished his own resentment toward Mikhyel and Mikhyel's involuntary perception. Resentment that would never, he sincerely hoped, return, although he was realistic enough to know it would, from time to time.

On the other hand, reserved, self-possessed Mikhyel might well feel a need to conceal his truths, and particularly his feelings.

"I don't get nearly as much from you," he said, feeling obliged to voice that reassurance.

Mikhyel shrugged and slumped back against the wall staring broodingly at his loosely laced fingers.

Deymorin picked another stitch free. "You said you lost Nikki when he went into the Tower?"

Mikhyel nodded, still brooding.

"Distance?"

Hesitation, then a slow shake of the head.

"Something in the door, do you think? Something about the building itself? The fact it's right above the node, maybe?"

Another unspoken negative. The strip of piping came free.

"Well? *Why,* then? Have you any idea?"

A flickering glance. Embarrassment, clear and quickly smothered. Mikhyel had an idea what was keeping him from Nikki's mind, but Mikhyel wasn't saying, because Mikhyel thought it would make him sound stupid.

And since that barrier was, for now, a point about which they could do nothing, *prove* nothing, one way or another, Deymorin was content to let the matter drop. He tossed Mikhyel the strip of gold piping from the cloak, thinking deliberately of Mikhyel's hair.

Mikhyel, without comment, caught the strip and secured his braid.

Just as he'd planned when he began picking that braid free. But Mikhyel's mind hadn't ascertained that simple goal, until he'd deliberately cast the thought along with the braid. And Mikhyel's certainty of Deymorin's thoughts had seemed to waver the entire time he'd been working on that purely functional task.

"You might make it easier on yourself, you know," Deymorin said.

"No, but I'm certain you'll tell me."

"You mean, you're not picking it up?"

"Deymorin, I *try* to leave your head alone, strange as that lack of curiosity might seem. Mostly, I get images. Feelings—emotions as well as touch. Opinions come through as vague pros or cons—I *assume* on the topic under discussion. Since I've a fair number of associations from the past ten minutes, it's far easier to ask than to try to figure it out."

"Interesting. Well, as I was saying—"

"Told you."

"As I was saying, you'd make things much easier on yourself if you'd try confiding once in a while."

"Confiding."

"The important parts of topics on which you don't want us to know everything, and want us speculating even less. You'd keep our curiosity quieter."

"I'm . . . out of the habit."

"Managed tolerably well last night."

Mikhyel's frown was dubious at best.

"You could start with what really happened just now, between you and the ugly unfriend."

Mikhyel's frown deepened, his eyes stared off into dirt-filled corners. Deymorin waited patiently.

It wasn't as if he had any pressing appointments.

"He knows, Deymio."

"Knows?"

"Who we are. He heard us talking last night."

"Careless of us."

"Not necessarily. He'd have recognized me eventually anyway. Or someone would. Occupational hazard. Rule number one: Don't get arrested in your own district."

"I'll commission you a plaque for your wall."

"I appreciate that."

"And?"

"And he's in here for attempted murder."

"Attempted?"

"Of you."

"Oh. I'm glad he only attempted."

"Quite. Anheliaa hired him."

"Another unsurprise."

"And he's keeping the locals off us."

"Out of the goodness of his heart, no doubt. Redemption, perhaps?"

"Favors. Currently unspecified, as I'm still rather limited in value. And he—threatened blackmail."

"About last night?"

Mikhyel shrugged. Last night, but there was something else: guilt, perhaps, but unspecified. A man didn't need the underneath sense to know that. Concern, about what Deymorin *didn't* know, and the unfriend did. Deymorin pulled the cloak to his lap again, and began picking idly at loose threads.

"I have only one question, Khyel," he said, and Mikhyel

looked at him, straightly but with a hint of fear underneath. Uncertainty. Another thread came free. "How did you talk them into it?"

A start. A tightening about the eyes. "You heard?" Mikhyel tapped his temple with one long finger, but Deymorin shrugged.

"No need. No man puts himself willingly between the jaws of a stranger, man or woman, without some sort of guarantee, brother. Must have been the fastest talk of your career."

Mikhyel's mouth opened ever-so-slightly. His breath caught in a little hiccup of a laugh. "You're amazing, Deymorin."

He grinned. "One of these days, I'll remind you you said that."

Laughter happened, reluctantly, at first, and gaining intensity as the tension slipped from their minds, and those internal pressures relaxed at last.

Mikhyel stopped first, and abruptly. And he sat there, staring into emptiness. A freak ray of light made the green rim around his gray eyes gleam.

{Nikki's awake.}

Chapter Three

It was his own room that greeted Nikki when he opened his eyes, and honest sunlight shining through the same windows he'd awakened to most days of his life.

Clothing lay strewn about, same as always after an evening on the outer rings with Jerrik. While he didn't *remember* such an evening (which wasn't unusual), his head didn't hurt (which was).

His guitar rested in its bedside stand, as it always had, the little gray horses on the embroidered strap Anheliaa's servant, Mirym, had given him for his seventeenth birthday shimmered and danced in the sunlight as if they were alive.

The sheer bed curtains floated on a breeze; the windows were open. The bath gurgled beyond the open door. His sheets smelled of fresh rose petals, for all *he* did not.

Another, not particularly unusual, state of existence.

And he wondered, just for a moment, if it had all been a dream: the prison, Mother, the battle, even his wedding.

Perhaps *today* was his seventeenth birthday, and he'd go to breakfast, and Deymorin would have arrived from Darhaven as he'd promised, and they'd spend the day market-grazing, and Deymorin would laugh at his taste in—

But, no, there was the strap Mirym had made for him for his birthday, and the stiffness in his shoulder from a Mauritumin bullet.

"Nikki?" His name was a whispered hiss rising like steam from the sunken bathing room. "Dammit, Nik, aren't you awake *yet*?"

"C'mon in, Jerri," he answered on a jaw-cracking yawn, and sat up, stretching joints that snapped and popped. "Rings, what time is it?"

"Past midday and halfway to dinner," Jerrik dunDaleri's voice answered, still in a whisper. "And keep your voice down!"

"Huh? Jerri, get *out* here."

Jerrik appeared in the bath doorway, and eyed the suite's entrance suspiciously. Bare feet, loose shirt belted over loose hiller trousers—he looked as if he were planning to stay in all day. But his clothes were stained at knees and elbows, and there was a smudge on his cheek.

"What'd you do?" Nikki asked. "Come through the passage?"

"Four weeks since I've seen or heard from you. This morning there're five guards at your door, and I've orders to be ready to dress you at a moment's notice. Damn right I came in the back, and I'll leave the same way, once I've an answer or two out of you, you lazy bastard."

"Guards?" Nikki repeated, a bit dazed.

"Nik, what's wrong with you? I've been stuck in that gods-be-damned room for four gods-be-damned weeks because you wouldn't take me gods-be-damned with you to find your gods-be-damned brother. 'Watch Khyel,' you said. But two days after you left, the hells above Rhomatum rained lightning, the web went down, and Khyel took off to Giephaetum. Now you're back. Alone. Acting the half-wit—"

"The web?" The Rhomatum Web didn't *go* down. *Couldn't* now Khoratum was capped, wasn't that what Anheliaa had always claimed?

"Dark as Outside here for three days. Rioters damn-near—"

"You said, Mikhyel left?" he asked, the most confusing fact in the confusing flow of information. "For Giephaetum?"

"With Nethaalye dunErrif and her father. Not that I saw him before he left. *I* was locked in my room."

"But . . ."

But four weeks ago, Mikhyel had appeared in the sky over his head just before the Rhomatum Web had destroyed the Mauritumin lightning machine in a battle the sounds of which still echoed in Nikki's dreams.

Of course, he hadn't actually *seen* Mikhyel fall, he'd been tied in the back of a wagon under a cloth, but he'd *felt* him—in the old, normal way, not the new—land on top of him. Before the world exploded around him.

"I tell you, Nik, it's been crazy-making. That new wife of yours littered the place with her father's guardsmen. I can't imagine where he was keeping them all. They told me to stay put, and I didn't argue: stay low and keep quiet sounded sensible to me, considering what was going on elsewhere. Besides, I had those maps to copy, and since I can get out of here any time I want—"

"Maps?" he repeated, *trying* to follow Jerrik's account. "Out?"

But a cold feeling was creeping into his gut. He remembered thinking, just last night, that the Mikhyel in the Crypt with Deymorin simply *wasn't* the same as the Mikhyel he'd known all his life, but a changeling. He'd dismissed it as impossible, but if *his* Mikhyel was actually in Giephaetum, then the Crypt . . . Deymorin . . .

He raised a hand to a head strangely scattered.

"Wake *up*, Nik." Jerrik came into the room at last, a look of disgust on his face, hooked a stocking from under a chair with his bare toe, and flipped it up into his hand, then began dealing similarly with other clothing strewn about the room.

Trying to think past the cottony haze that passed for his mind this morning, Nikki remembered leaving his brothers in Sparingate, remembered coming into the Tower just before dawn, under guard, remembered being escorted to his room where they left him alone at last. He remembered a glass of wine, welcome to his chilled toes, and shedding his clothes and falling into bed with his shirt still . . . half . . .

Wine. He stared at the drained and dropped goblet lying beside his bed, and suspicion flared.

Drugged. Someone had drugged the gods-be-damned *wine!*

He stared at Jerrik, wondering if *he* could have done it—a thought as horrifying in its way as the idea that that *person* in the Crypt with Deymorin might not *be* Mikhyel. Jerrik had been his best friend forever. He'd been counting on Jerrik to help him get Deymorin and Mikhyel out. If *Jerrik* was Anheliaa's now, too . . . or Lidye's . . . it was Lidye in charge, now. Or Lidye's father.

He pulled off his half-buttoned shirt and tossed it at Jerrik, who added it to the pile.

"Well?" Jerrik asked, expectantly.

"Is the bath hot?" he asked, and Jerrik eyed him as if he'd gone mad. Of course it was hot. He was in the Tower now, not at Armayel. The baths in the Tower were always hot, always circulating. As long as the web was up, and rings, when *hadn't* it been?

Four weeks ago, a part of him answered.

He headed for the bathing room.

"Nikki—"

"I want a bath. I can't think when I smell like a trapper's outhouse."

He grabbed Jerrik's stained sleeve as he passed. Jerrik followed, still protesting, and Jerrik slapped Nikki's hand away when, in wordless suggestion, he jerked Jerrik's shirt free of its belt.

Nikki shrugged and made a flying dive into the pool.

When he surfaced, Jerrik gave an impatient hiss, pulled the door closed and locked it. Leaving his clothes neatly on the wall hooks, he slid into the swirling water.

"Nikki, I—"

Nikki dove for Jerrik's heels and pulled him under, ending the protest.

Jerrik kicked free and shoved upward. Nikki followed and ducked him again, desperately seeking his old friend, whose help he needed now, more than ever. But desperation faded in a reunion full of wild attempts at mutual drowning. Too large for simple soaking, too small for a proper swim, the pool was sufficiently deep and wide to momentarily drown all questions.

It was all too easy for Nikki to forget, while dodging a faceful of water here, slipping a body tackle there, that his brothers weren't likewise buoyantly occupied, but sitting in a place he'd only heard of yesterday morning, a place whose scent he sought, even now, to eliminate from his nostrils.

Easy, except after the first excited tackle, his healing shoulder began to ache. Easy, except that in the back of one's mind, one remembered the guards and made the reunion abnormally silent.

On that second, disturbing realization, Nikki took a watery blast full in the face. He caught Jerrik's wrist on the rebound, forcing a silent truce.

Panting, they eyed each other across water rippling silver in the leylight, a light he hadn't experienced for weeks. A light that was foreign-feeling, in a way it never had been on other returns from the Outside.

But he was clear-headed now as he hadn't been before,

and plagued with the thought that *someone* had wanted to guarantee he slept very late and woke with addled wits. He *needed* to be certain, above all else, that Jerrik's hand hadn't put that drugged wine beside his bed.

Jerrik was his dearest friend. He'd left Darhaven and moved to Rhomatum four years ago *just* so he could be with Nikki all the time. They'd shared the same tutors, ogled the same women, dreamed the same dreams. . . .

Jerrik's brow tightened, his wrist turned in Nikki's hold to return the grasp. After a moment's silence, Jerrik tugged insistently, pulling Nikki back to the side of the pool, pressing him to sit on the underwater ledge where the pressurized inflow pummeled his lower back.

Jerrik perched behind him on the tiled rim, and began applying foaming oil, scraper, and sponge to his shoulders in a ritual as old as their friendship.

Nikki sighed and let his head drop forward, pretending for a moment more that it was a year ago, and he and Jerrik were getting ready to go down to the market and compare opinions of bright-eyed and willing young ladies, whose willingness he'd never experienced, never so much as tasted.

"I see your lady wife's little love marks are all healed," Jerrik commented. "Planning on renewing them tonight?"

But it wasn't a year ago. He was married, now, tied forever to a flaxen-haired witch who ripped his shoulders with her enameled talons when they embraced.

"Rings," he muttered, "I'd rather be a eunuch."

Jerrik's laugh held real compassion, and he was silent after. The sponge slid up and over Nikki's back, then paused as Jerrik's other hand swiped Nikki's hair aside. The pause grew overlong; the sponge slid free, over Nikki's shoulder, and into the bath, splashing soapy water into his eyes.

"What in the eighteen hells above Rhomatum have you been doing to yourself?"

The half-healed hole in his shoulder. His respite from reality was over.

"My brother used me for target practice," he said sarcastically and twitched away from the pool edge to scoop up the sponge bobbing toward the narrow outlet.

"Target practice," Jerrik repeated in a colorless voice. "Wouldn't put it outside the realm of possibility."

Nikki snapped the sponge in his friend's general direction, a retaliation that missed wildly and sent the sponge skidding behind a warming rack.

"Possible," Jerrik repeated, retrieving the miscast missile. "But somehow, I doubt it."

"What do you think? That I shot myself?"

"Also possible. C'mon, Nik, tell."

"Tell what?"

"Everything! How you got that hole in your shoulder, where Deymorin is—you did find him, didn't you? Why'd you come in in the middle of the night? Why the hell didn't you wake me up? Why are there guards at your door? Dammit, Nik, I knew there'd be trouble the moment you decided to leave me behind. You never did learn which end of a pistol spits the bullet."

"What? Am I a child that I need you to attend me?"

"*Tell* me!"

And he decided, all in a moment, that if he couldn't trust Jerri, he might as well give up all hope of helping his brothers. Mikhyel had negotiated a single night. The price of the second might be far too high: Deymorin would get himself killed protecting Mikhyel from further "negotiations."

"All right." Nikki threw himself back down, sending water over the edge, and pointed toward his shoulders with a crooked thumb. "All right. Rings, where do I start?"

"Did you find Deymio?"

"Yes, but—" That was hardly the beginning.

"Where is he?"

He glared around at Jerrik. "Do you want to know what happened?"

"Of course—"

"Then *shut up!* Deymorin didn't *leave.* Neither did Mikhyel—at least, I don't *think* Mikhyel did. They were thrown out. By Anheliaa . . ."

Here in the Tower, in the silver light of the ley, the horror of that moment when he'd first seen Mikhyel lying seared and broken on the ground faded somehow and the full impact of Anheliaa's accomplishments penetrated. He twisted to catch Jerrik's wrist and stared up at him.

"It's amazing, Jerri. We were halfway between here and Darhaven, on the Boreton Turnout, and he just . . . *appeared* out of the sky on a bolt of lightning! Seconds before, he'd been in the Tower, then, *boom,* there he was, naked as the day he was born! And Deymio went all the way to Persitum Pass!"

Jerrik's eyes widened, suitably astounded.

"It's the ley, Jerri," Nikki said, his enthusiasm growing in proportion to Jerrik's widening eyes. "It can do *wonderful* things. Things we never *dreamed*!"

"Then it's true," Jerrik whispered, but his voice held nothing of awe, only horror.

"What's true?"

"She can make people disappear, just like they say. Nikki, are they alive? Where are they? You said Mikhyel fell from the sky. Is he hurt?"

"Of course they're all right," Nikki snapped, embarrassed. "You think I'd be here if they weren't?"

"Nikki, I don't *know* why you're here!"

"Mikhyel *was* hurt. Badly. But the Tamshi *healed* him, don't you see?"

"Tamshi?" Jerrik drew his legs slowly from the water, and even more slowly, stood up, pulling free of Nikki's light grasp.

"Oh, get back here, I haven't gone mad." Nikki went for Jerrik's ankle instead, gripped it in his excitement at the secrets he was finally able to share with an appreciative audience. "They're *real,* Jerry, just like we always believed. She appeared first as a filthy, disgusting rag-hag, and she touched Khyel and his pain disappeared, and then Dancer—"

"What dancer?"

"Not *what* dancer. *Dancer,* that's Mother's helper. They *healed* Khyel, Jerri, with an oil that gleamed with every color in the rainbow, even there in the shade of the trees. He was burned—all over. He *was* dying, but they saved him."

And now he was in prison, with maybe worse things than death happening to him. Nikki's enthusiasm faded; he released Jerrik's ankle and sank back down.

"Nikki, who shot you?" Jerrik asked, and he answered absently, his mind still with his brothers:

"The Mauritumin spies."

"Mauritum. And Tamshirin." Jerrik eased toward the wall rack, took down a thick robe, and slipped it over his shoulders. "Nikki, you wait here. I'm going for help—"

Snapping back to the Tower, Nikki leaped free of the

water, made it to Jerrik before he reached the door. He spun his friend around, held him by the shoulders, and forced him to look him in the eyes.

"I told you, I'm not crazy! I'm *not* making up tales. Not *this* time. Anheliaa's been trying to get rid of Deymorin. She's even hired assassins. Mauritumin assassins. Mauritum knows we've no replacement for her in the Tower, so they're making a move on Rhomatum. Deymorin didn't just leave. Last fall, when he refused to accept her bride-choice, Anheliaa got mad at him and sent him away. *He* landed in a lake in Persitum Pass about a month ago. *He* landed on Kiyrstin's head, not mine. Mikhyel landed on me."

"Kiyrstin?"

"Garetti's wife."

"Garetti," Jerrik repeated flatly. "Deymorin landed in Persitum on High Priest romMaurii's wife."

"She tried to kill him—Garetti, not Deymio—then ran away with Vandoshin romMaurii. He's the Mauritumin spy that shot me. Now Deymorin's in stupid-love with her, and if she weren't married to Garetti, she'd be my sister, which I *really* don't want her to be, but I'd rather her than lose Deymorin again."

"Nikki, you're making less and less sense."

"It doesn't matter. The important thing is, when I went looking for Deymorin, the rings had shown us he was at Darhaven, so I went there—"

"You *saw* him. At Darhaven. In the Rhomatum rings."

Nikki nodded. "I told you, the ley does things we've never imagined! By the time I got there, Deymorin was on his way here. I ran afoul of romMaurii, and Deymorin talked with Khyel, who told him where I'd gone, so Deymorin went back Outside to find me. But by that time, romMaurii was making his move on the Tower. He had this machine, you see, that tames lightning, and he was going to bring it into Rhomatum and destroy the rings, don't you see?"

"I damnwell do not. Tame lighting, Nikki? And you claim to be sane? Forgive me, old friend, if I don't take your word for it. I've heard your stories before, and this time, it's not funny."

Jerrik flipped the lock and jerked at the door.

Nikki, terrified that his own past stories had destroyed

any credibility he might have had, just when he needed it most, grabbed Jerri's arm and pulled him back, to hold him against the wall.

"But you must believe me, Jerri, because Deymorin and Mikhyel are in the Crypt and *we've* got to get them out."

Chapter Four

The pebble landed in the ring just outside the center of the meticulously constructed straw maze.

"Ha! Got you again, little brother!" Deymorin laughed and shook his head. "Out of practice, fry."

"Call me that one more time," Mikhyel said under his breath, "and the next shot goes down your throat."

Mikhyel edged slowly around the maze, discovering the wild strategies of brazen youth as alien to him now as the flex and release of muscle and bone required to toss the pebble cradled in his palm.

"Which one, *child*?" Deymorin asked, in a voice that grinned and goaded, but Mikhyel ignored him. He found his angle, crouched, and flipped the pebble flat-side down, then snapped it toward the maze. It struck Deymorin's pebble into the fourth ring on the far side, and deflected itself into the center.

He stood up, brushing his hands free of dust, and glanced across the maze at his brother.

"You were saying?"

Deymorin's mouth opened, shut, and he frowned at the maze, moved to Mikhyel's vantage, and grunted. "Luck."

Mikhyel tipped his head. "If you insist. Another?"

Deymorin grunted and began resetting the straws. The game was Dancer in the Maze, a game that had kept the two of them occupied for hours, some twenty years ago. Deymorin had suggested it as a means to pass the time and to take their minds off whatever was happening in the Tower.

He'd heard nothing more from Nikki after that initial hazed awareness, but that slight touch had been sufficient to assure him Nikki was well and in his own room, and at his ease. A simple reality that did much to ease his own mind, at least for the time being, despite the fact that the strange veil had immediately closed between them, shutting Nikki off again.

True to Ganfrion's word, the inmates had left them alone—other than the occasional heckling comment when they began constructing the maze. Even those had stopped, now, and from the occasional argument over rules that echoed through the Crypt, others had been inspired to try their own hands at the ancient child's game.

"Here." Deymorin grabbed his hand and dropped his eighteen stones into his palm. "You go *first* this—"

The door thudded open. Footsteps clattered down the stairs.

"DunMheric!" The name echoed through the mazelike vastness. Murmurs and rude laughter and ruder remarks answered from the dark crannies.

Deymorin's mouth twitched, and he murmured, "Wonder which dunMheric they want?"

Mikhyel just looked at him, then stepped free of their drafty spot beneath the stairs. Regardless who they called, if it was only one dunMheric they wanted, the other would be left down here with no possibly anonymity left.

Deymorin's hand landed firmly on Mikhyel's shoulder.

{I want to hear you, fry.}

He understood then, and didn't flinch away. But he thought of Ganfrion, and the need to keep a cool head, and begged Deymorin not to get himself killed before they could get him out.

{Don't worry about me,} was Deymorin's thought.

{Who's the one laid out cold the last time they were here?}

Amusement. Confidence. Enough of both he longed to grab his brother and shake sense into him.

{I shall endeavor to behave.}

{See that you do, Rhomandi.}

The guards had seen them, and moved to surround them. They were all in Tower black and this time, Mikhyel recognized them all. Anheliaa's men.

Fear flooded him, though he kept his face impassive. Anheliaa *was* alive. Anheliaa wanted him. Wanted to warp his mind and force him to her bidding. Perhaps even to make him order Deymorin's death.

A wave of near hysteria washed through him as he recognized his own thoughts echoing Nikki's panic, when they'd come after him. He fought the fear down, forced rational thinking to the surface.

{Just yell, brat,} Deymorin's thought came through on a surge of confidence. {We stopped her before. We'll do it again.}

"DunMheric?" asked the guard in the lead.

"Yes," he and Deymorin said, as one.

The leader, Hodan, looked momentarily taken aback, then: "Deymorin Rhomandi dunMheric, former Princeps of Rhomatum?"

The panic in the link this time was Deymorin's. Deymorin had been certain they'd come for Mikhyel. Deymorin had been prepared to stay here alone; he wasn't ready to leave Mikhyel in a similar state.

{Hypocrite,} Mikhyel sent down Deymorin's touch, and Deymorin sent back an image of himself, in a circle of men, on his knees before Ganfrion.

{I can't leave you here, Khy!}

He sent back the same image, from ground level, and laced it with details of the encounter in the latrine—and his own indifference.

The guard took Deymorin by the elbow and pulled him around, jerking his hand from Mikhyel's shoulder.

"Secure him." Came the order.

"Dammit, *no*!" Deymorin said and resisted the guards' attempts to force his hands behind his back. "I'll not go through the streets bound like a common criminal!"

{Temper, brother.} Mikhyel touched his arm to be certain he heard. {Don't be a fool.}

{And if Ganfrion decides to favor Anheliaa?}

{He won't.}

{I never took you for a fool, Mikhyel.}

{Just behave yourself and get me out of here as soon as you can.}

"Deymorin!"

Kiyrstin's voice, from above them.

"Kiyrsti?" Deymorin answered and threw his head back, searching for the door. "Kiyrstin, are you all right?"

"Fine, JD. Just quit giving these fellows trouble and get your rear up here, will you?"

{Smart lady.}

{Damn right. But, Khyel, if they're taking her as well—}

Mikhyel gave Deymorin a shove toward the foot of the

stairway, getting him out of any possible physical reach. That might cut his thoughts off from Deymorin, but Deymorin, despite his valiant efforts to the contrary, continued to radiate concern along with those damnable images.

Deymorin should never have seen that. He had and would continue to put far too great an import upon it. Worry too much, waste too much energy.

Yet as he watched Deymorin mount those stairs, watched him greet Kiyrstin much as he'd parted from her, for all his arms were secured behind his back, Mikhyel felt his calm waver.

They knew, now, who he was. Every man he'd consigned to this pit. And accidental death happened so easily here.

Deymorin looked down at him one last time and he forced himself to nod confidently.

The door closed.

And a presence behind him whispered, "And then there was one."

§   §   §

"Dee-nah-ah ees served," Jerrik intoned and bowed low. As he straightened, he made a face at the closed door and the pompous servant who was likely well on his way down the hall by now.

"Well, let's see what he brought." Nikki sighed and pushed himself out of his chair and pulled the top off the tailor's box the servant had thrust into Jerri's hands.

Diaphanous fabric filled the box. Blues and greens . . . dressmaker's flowers and ivy twined among the folds. Nikki met Jerri's eyes, and pulled the creation gingerly from the box.

A card fell as he shook the folds free. He dropped the strange garment back in the box and picked the card up.

Something special for tonight, my husband.

He stared at the script. Lidye's writing, or so he thought.

"What do you think?" Jerrik asked. He'd tossed the box aside and was holding the mostly transparent marvel up against his body. "Wonder what you wear under it?"

Their eyes met again., It required no brotherly link for him to guess Jerrik's lewd thoughts. As one, they burst out laughing. It was a welcome release for the tension that had built inside them both.

"So," Jerrik asked when he'd caught his breath. "You going to change?"

"I . . . think not."

"So, what do we do with it?"

Another look. Another burst of laughter, and Nikki grabbed the atrocity from Jerrik, ran to the pool and flung it into the water. They stood side by side while the garment bobbed, swirled and dipped with the movement of the water, they watched as it reached the outlet and disappeared, soon to become one with the ley.

Like all sewage.

A moment of silence, then Jerrik said quietly, "Time to go, Nik."

He nodded, and followed Jerrik out into the bedroom. He eased his arms into the dinner jacket Jerrik held for him, then extended his arms while Jerrik eased the tailored seams into place. He shook out the lace at his wrists, then stood passively while Jerrik tugged and pressed the folds of his cravat into place.

As it had turned out, they'd had all afternoon, he and Jerrik, to talk. The long hours had let him explain—in sane detail—to Jerrik all that had happened since he'd left in search of Deymorin, and he thought, perhaps, Jerrik actually believed him now, if only for Deymorin's and Mikhyel's sakes.

In the end, however, for all their wishes to the contrary, they'd come up with nothing, no plan that had the least hope of getting Deymorin and Mikhyel free. But then, Deymorin's plan would do no better. Mikhyel's Raulind had been confined to his rooms, same as Jerrik.

Finally, Jerrik pronounced him ready.

"Jerri, I—"

"Nikki, I—"

They laughed, and Nikki motioned for Jerrik to go first. Eyes fastened on his bare toes, Jerrik said, "I'm sorry, Nik. I should never have, well . . ."

"Doubted me?" Nikki finished for him, and Jerrik shifted uncomfortably. "It's my own damn fault, Jerri. I've been fabricating lies all my life, trying to make ordinary things . . . not. Ordinary, I mean. I'm just glad—"

"Yeah, Nik. So'm I." Jerrik held out his hand, and Nikki clasped it tightly. "Good luck, old man."

Nikki nodded, and headed for the door.

"Nikki?"

He turned. And intercepted a slightly scared, slightly worried look that vanished into Jerrik's old, confident grin. "Don't stay out too late."

Dinner was to be an intimate affair in the family dining hall, at a small table, one only large enough for a party of . . . oh . . . twenty. Silver, gold, and crystal glittered in the flickering light of real candles; nuts, fresh fruits, and vegetables from Outside hothouses had been cut and arranged to mimic exotic flowers; wine bubbled down a carved-ice waterfall . . .

All for two people.

Bouquets of roses graced every nook, and as if their scent wasn't enough, a fine mist of perfume puffed periodically from aerators cast to look like the Tamshirin of children's books. In fact, the entire room was draped and dressed to look like those paintings.

Fanciful renderings that fell far short of the real thing.

"I'll wait in the Blue Salon," Nikki informed the servants, and turned on his heel, ordering wine—corked—to be sent to him there.

The Blue Salon was decorated in burgundies and pinks, with hints of pale yellow, a phenomenon no one had ever successfully explained to him. Color notwithstanding, it was comfortable, it was convenient to the dining room, and by its very hypocrisy eminently appropriate.

The wine bottle arrived with a second for when that ran out. Nikki drank and waited, and paced and waited, and sat and stared into the cold hearth—waiting.

There'd been no summons, not from Anheliaa, not from Lidye. Just that announcement and delivery of the costume. Having seen the folly awaiting him in the dining hall, he wondered whether he'd been intended as guest or the main course.

Lidye's father's men had said Lidye was in charge here, but they hadn't actually said Anheliaa was dead. Even Jerrik had been unable to enlighten him. Jerrik had been held a virtual prisoner for the past month. He'd been questioned several times by Brolucci, captain of Anheliaa's Tower guard, and Sironi, Lidye's father's sworn man, both of whom appeared primarily interested in the Outsider army Deymorin was supposedly amassing.

All indications were, Lidye—and Anheliaa, if she was still alive—had no concept of the true scope of the problems facing Rhomatum. If he could, somehow, turn this dinner to his advantage, *use* this opportunity to explain exactly what had happened, to convince whoever came through that door that they were allies, not enemies, to explain to them all those things Mikhyel had said they needed—

"Nikaenor?"

It was a stranger's voice, from far way in space and time, almost as if it didn't belong to his memories at all, but some other Nikaenor's.

"Nikki?"

Closer, and with the brush of fabric over carpet. A pale lavender flounce puffed into his side vision, preceding a feathery touch to his arm. "Please, look at me, Nikki."

Vaguely familiar, now, the voice was soft, but firm, imploring without whining. Not the little girl's voice that had at first fascinated him, then driven him mad with boredom. Neither was it the harshly angry voice that had ordered him out of the bedroom following their wedding night . . . breeding.

It was a woman's voice. Low. Cultured. A bit shaken around the edges. Fear? Of rejection? *His?* Why should she care? Why should it matter?

He let his gaze drift from the fire that wasn't there and around to the woman's face that gazed up at him. Again, he was struck by the feeling that this was not the same woman he'd known. She had too much . . . substance, somehow.

"Lidye," he said, statement of fact, not an address, and her brow puckered.

As if, one was tempted to laugh, he'd hurt her feelings.

"Have I estranged you so thoroughly, then?" Her eyes dropped. "I can't say as I blame you, my gentle husband."

Which total assumption of guilt dangerously undermined his carefully realized determination and indignation.

"Please, Nikki, delay judgment, if you can."

So, she pleaded, as Mikhyel would put it, *Not guilty.* He did laugh, then, bitterly, his anger salvaged. And he asked, without preamble, "Why were we arrested?"

A sharp intake of breath, a flash of pale eyes that disappeared quickly beneath darkened lashes and delicately tinted lids.

"Precaution, Nikki," she answered. "After your brother, Deymorin, was here, threatening to bring that Mauritumin machine into the tower and destroy the rings, Anheliaa was filled with concern. I knew Deymorin had arrived with that Mauritumin woman. I knew that Mikhyel had taken his side in the matter and angered Anheliaa. I needed to know if you were party to the Mauritumin threat, as Deymorin was."

She paused: an opening, he supposed, for him to defend his brothers. But she knew better—or should. Deymorin had told him Lidye had been in the room when Deymorin had confronted Anheliaa. She knew that *Deymorin* had never mentioned the machine, that the root of that fear was Anheliaa's paranoia, not Deymorin's threat.

"I asked them to arrest everyone answering your description," she continued at last. "I had to, Nikki. I had to know when you entered the City. There's been such chaos. And I must say, Nikki, I was very concerned, when Captain Sironi said Deymorin claimed to be the Rhomandi. That was the only reason *you* were arrested. Sironi believed he recognized you, but he didn't know Deymorin. And when the man with you *claimed* to be the Rhomandi, he was confused."

"Confused."

"Deymorin should have *known* that *you* were now the Rhomandi. When Sironi told me, his description of Deymorin certainly matched my own experience, and I was afraid that Deymorin had bullied you. Had forced you to abdicate the title."

"That was foolish of you."

"Was it? I don't know your brother, Nikaenor. I only know you, and your sweet and amicable nature, and I wanted you free of his influence. Free to call me a fool to my face, or to ask for freedom from his domination, if *that* was your wish. I'm sorry if I've done badly."

"Sweet and amicable. Such an opinion you have of me, madam."

"But you are, Nikki. As well as intelligent and reasonable. It speaks well of your brother that you maintain such loyalty to him, but I have yet to see that side of him that inspires that loyalty in you. I trust I shall have the chance."

"Is that why you had us put in the Crypt? So you could . . . *observe* that side of Deymorin?"

"Crypt? What crypt? I thought you were in Sparingate?" For the first time, there was a hint of prevarication to her voice. Nikki raised his chin, and her false face wilted. "Nikki, I *didn't* know. I still don't *know*. But when Sironi described your situation . . . I had you brought from there as soon as I could, Nikki. As soon as I knew."

He said nothing. He waited for her to mention the obvious (to him) omission within that statement.

"Brolucci has been in charge. It was he that suggested the arrests be made upon entry—to give us time. He ordered your disposition, and told me only when your arrests had been confirmed. Another error in judgment, I grant you, but I've had such pressure . . ." Her mouth quivered, then firmed. "No, I won't make excuses. But I had you brought here, as soon as I knew, Nikki, please believe that."

So, she wasn't going to repair the omission. "My *brothers* are still there." He pointed out.

"No longer, Nikki. Deymorin and the Mauritumin woman will be joining us for dinner." Nikki didn't bother to point out the table had been set for two. "I had you brought first because I wanted a chance to speak alone with you. But then I was in the Tower all day—the storm, as I'm sure you know—and so I finally just sent for them. They're in your brother's room now, but—"

"And Mikhyel? Will he be joining us as well?"

"Mikhyel?" She tilted her head at him, puzzled. Or so it appeared; he no longer trusted her expressions.

"Has he returned from *Giephaetum,* my lady wife?"

"Oh." She turned her back—hiding that false face. "Um, no. Not yet."

So, even with him, she sought to maintain the lie that had been spread throughout the house. But why? They'd sent letters to the Tower from Armayel. *Mikhyel* had written those letters; *Anheliaa* had answered. Anheliaa had asked them to return to Rhomatum. And Lidye had known they were coming.

"When will he return—from Giephaetum?"

"Nikki, I—I don't know how . . ." She faced him again, and her delicate features were twisted with uncertainty. "I'm sorry, Nikki. I lied, as you, in your subtle way, accuse.

But I don't know how . . . You see, Nikki, I very much fear your brother Mikhyel is dead."

"Dead?" His head went blank. Then filled with images of the Crypt and that scar-faced inmate and all the things that he'd feared had happened since he left. He groped blindly for his chair.

"Nikki, I'm so sorry . . ."

Her hand touched his shoulder. He flinched away.

"You said." His voice failed him. He fought it angrily back, thinking his brother would be alive, but for this woman. "You said Brolucci ordered us into the Crypt. Brolucci is the captain of *Anheliaa's* guard. The men who arrested us wore your father's colors, madam. The men standing at my bedroom door are not Tower men."

"I had to use those whom I could trust, Nikki. Surely you see that?"

"*You* could trust. *You've* been in the Tower. *You've* had Deymorin and Kiyrstin released. And what of Anheliaa, my lady wife? Where is Anheliaa?"

"That's the problem, Nikki. That's *been* the problem." She sank gracefully into a chair. "Anheliaa has been . . . unavailable . . . since . . . that day."

"Unavailable," he repeated while his mind tripped over the verified facts, to the conclusion: "Dead?"

"No, thank the rings. At least, not yet. But that's why I had to concede some decisions to Brolucci. Anheliaa is comatose, since the day of the Collapse. She's been confined to the Tower. I believe only her instincts have the rings spinning at all."

Another fast mental sort. "What about the letters we received at Armayel? What about our *arrest* papers? Who signed them?"

She bit her lip and stared down at her hands for a moment. Then, without a word, she went to a desk near the window, pulled a sheaf of papers from a drawer, and handed them to him wordlessly.

He stared at the top sheet. Anheliaa's name, her almost-signature repeated over and over.

"Your doing?"

She nodded.

"So we add forgery to your other parlor accomplishments."

She lifted her chin, offered no apology. And perhaps, in all fairness, she'd had no real choice.

Among the pages, one of Mikhyel's letters, written from Armayel. The page blurred, and damp spot appeared in the middle of the letter, followed by a second. Nikki swiped a hand across his eyes and asked, feeling a darker hatred than anything he'd ever felt in his life:

"What happened?"

"To Mikhyel?"

"*Who* killed him? Was it that Ganfrion? Whoever it was, I want him!"

"What do you mean, who killed him?" Lidye stared at him. "The rings—"

"I left him last night in the Crypt, madam, with Deymorin and a number of very unpleasant housemates. I know *Deymorin* didn't kill him. I want to know who did!"

"In the . . ." She held her hand to her forehead, her face losing what little color it had. "No. I don't believe you. He's dead. He couldn't have come in with you."

"Why couldn't he?"

"Sironi said—"

"I don't give a damn *what* Sironi said! He *talked* to Mikhyel first!"

"No . . . Nikki, I . . . Sironi said it was you and Deymorin. That you'd brought another man in with you who *claimed* to be Mikhyel, but it wasn't. He *said* it wasn't!"

"Then Sironi's a damned liar!" He drew a deep breath, seeking calm. "If you didn't know Mikhyel was in the Crypt, then why did you tell me he was dead?"

"I—I saw him disappear, Nikki." She sank to the floor near his chair, one hand resting on the armrest. "And then the rings . . . the lightning . . ." She buried her face in her hands. "It . . . it was . . . horrendous. Nothing caught in that—whatever it was—could have survived, don't you see? When the letters came, I was certain Deymorin must have written them. To make me, I mean, Anheliaa, believe Mikhyel was alive. I mean . . . I was doing that regarding Anheliaa, wasn't I? If *I* was doing it for good reasons, surely . . ." Her voice broke on a sob. "Oh, Nikki, I'm *so* mortified."

Despite his better sense, he rested his hand on her pale hair. And through that touch, almost like sometimes happened with his brothers, he knew the truth of her horror, the depth of the embarrassment she now suffered.

And he began to wonder if perhaps he had been too hasty. Whatever animosity had existed between them, the past month had obviously wrought significant changes in them both.

Her head came up and, still without meeting his eyes, she tipped her cheek into his palm. "When the storms began, I fell to the floor, *hid,* I'm ashamed to say. It seemed hours before it was quiet again. I lifted my head to darkness. Utter, terrible darkness. I thought for a moment I was blind. But I was in a bed, my bed, in my room, not the ringchamber, and Brolucci arrived, with *candles,* and took me to the Tower. I saw . . . I saw . ."

She shuddered and buried her head again, and he pulled his hand back. "I discovered later that I had been unconscious for three days. Anheliaa was laid out in the Tower, her physician adamant about leaving her there. Somehow, I'll never know how, I got the rings up and reset. It was as if I were in a trance. Perhaps I was. Perhaps Anheliaa, even in her unconscious state, knew the rings must be set and took me over to accomplish it. It—" Her voice caught. "It wouldn't be the first time she did that. Once the rings were back in motion, she seemed better. She still hasn't wakened, but the rings seem to have given her strength."

He felt an insidious attraction toward this woman. Her story made sense. And he didn't want to hate her. She was his wife. Rhomatum's future depended on her. Mikhyel had said—

Mikhyel! He shook his head, wondering where his sense had gone.

"Then Mikhyel *isn't* dead!" he exclaimed. "You thought he'd been killed by the rings. But he wasn't. He was *in* the Crypt. He's *still* in the Crypt. I want him out, madam. *Now!*"

"But . . ." She turned tear-stained eyes to him. Her mouth was trembling. She reached her hand for his, and again, that light-headed attraction fuzzed his thinking. "Mikhyel knows . . . so much. He's so . . ."

"Now," he repeated.

"I—I will, Nikki. I'll get him out, I promise you. Just as

soon as I'm sure it's safe. Please, Nikki, understand. So much depends on my judgment. I *must* be cautious."

He fought her allure. He couldn't afford to trust her. Couldn't give in to this charming woman, so different from the wife he'd willingly abandoned to what he'd believed at the time to be her fate-by-choice.

And yet, he couldn't quite bring himself to pull his hand from hers either.

"The power of the rings is uncertain," she said, winding their fingers together, pressing his hand to her cheek. "Simple light is sometimes difficult. I'm ashamed to admit, I have grown ridiculously fearful. I want candles or oil lamps about me at all times. I fear the dark, Nikki. I fear the dark terribly."

"What's wrong? Why doesn't the energy return? *Is* it the Khoratum line?"

"Khoratum? What makes you think it's the Khoratum line?"

"Something Mikhyel said. And the power umbrella is back to the old wall."

"Mikhyel? Well, *I* don't know. As long as Anheliaa is alive and in that chamber, I can't truly take the rings over and seek the cause of the problem. I only hope that—when the time comes, I *can* trace the problem down."

"Why shouldn't you?"

"I—I no longer trust the rings." Her hand tightened to the point of pain, as her fingernails dug into his flesh. "That's a terrible thing for a ringmaster to admit, Nikki, and that's what I very much fear I am soon to be. Anheliaa is so weak. She doesn't wake. I *need* your help, as my husband, and as Princeps of Rhomatum. I need your support. And your brothers'. Mikhyel's—bless the rings he's still alive—perhaps his most of all. The civic leaders, tradesmen, councillors, syndics, they're *all* demanding answers. Compensation. I don't know what all. I don't *know* the laws of Rhomatum, Nikki, only the laws of the ley. And we don't *have* the power. I don't know what happened, but it's not there, and all their wanting it won't make it be there."

Her words made just enough sense to trouble a thoughtful man, a man who desired most of all to be fair, to understand all sides.

"Why not ask your father?"

"Father? Why would I ask his advice?"

"Those are *his* men. Sironi most certainly is."

"I don't know who to ask, Nikki," she whispered, "I don't know who will take advantage of my ignorance. Father—perhaps I distrust him most of all—but he warned me against Mikhyel. He said I should be glad Mikhyel is dead. And in that much, he's right. I *can't* have Mikhyel against me. Not now."

"And I say, madam, your father is wrong. Legally, morally, and practically. You *do* need Mikhyel. And Mikhyel is not against you, not as long as you are not against Rhomatum. Mikhyel is *not* Rhomatum's enemy."

She bit her lip and frowned. "On your word you'll help me with him, I'll send for him immediately."

"Help you? How?"

"Talk to him. Explain to him. Support . . . me?"

Her eyes flickered up to meet his. Worried, but calm. This sudden change in the woman who was legally his wife puzzled him. If not for the words, he'd have a difficult time believing it was the same woman.

"Why did you act as you did?" he asked, out of that thought.

"Which?" she responded without the least hesitation. "The fool, or the termagant?"

"Uh, b-both," he stammered, startled that she'd made the connection, more so by her candid response.

"The fool . . . that was Anheliaa's idea. She insisted you were obsessed with Kharishia, and that that performance would entrance you."

"Obsessed with who?"

"Kharishia. Darius' last wife. The—" Her carefully shaded lip rose in a slight, most unladylike sneer. "—flutter-headed imbiber of ocarshi and other perception-affecting substances."

"Kharishia?" The soft syllables floated across his palate like a fine wine. "Was that her name?"

"How beautifully you say it, Nikki," she whispered, and her perfume flooded his head.

He blinked. "How do you know?" he asked. "Her name isn't recorded anywhere."

"I know many things about her, Nikaenor my dear," she said softly. "Most of all, that fluttering was not at all her

style. It was Anheliaa's notion of her, or perhaps what Anheliaa thought *you* expected."

"How do you know?"

"Anheliaa told me."

"Not that," he said impatiently. "How do you know
about . . . about Kharishia?"

"You mean, you didn't realize her sister was my remote ancestor?"

"Three hundred years remote."

"But Family nonetheless, Nikki, and I've a great interest
in the history of my family." Another shift, this time to a
shy, almost hopeful smile. "We could discuss her—and that
history—at length, my dear, once this crisis is over. If
you'd like . . ."

"I'd—" Like very much, he nearly said. But a wise man
didn't commit, not when his dearest interests were being
used to sway him. *That* was what Mikhyel always told him.
"And the other?"

"You mean our disastrous wedding night? I'm so very
sorry about that, dear, sweet Nikki. Did I hurt you terribly?" She wrung her hands, as if washing them under a
stream of water. Her eyes dropped, and as if startled, she
clasped her hands together to stop them. "I . . . hate to
admit it, because it shows such weakness on my part, but
it was Anheliaa. She was determined to have that child,
and I had no defense against her." She rose and turned
her back to him. "You know how she is. You've firsthand
knowledge of her incentives."

That much was true. He, Deymorin, Mikhyel—they'd all
faced Anheliaa's notions of persuasion.

"She was acting through me, Nikki. I could not stand
against her. And she hates men. She hates their physical
power, and their obsessive sexuality. She—" Even without
seeing her face, he could hear her humiliation. "She never
in her life . . . *knew* a man."

"What man in his right mind would have her?"

Her back stiffened, and her head tilted, looking at him,
though her face remained shadowed. "Quite." She turned
then, and it was compassion he saw. "I don't think any of
us can truly imagine what she lives through every day of
her life. The pain. The *impotence,* in the natural sense of
the word. She's had power of a sort no one, man or woman,
has ever known, but the *world,* the natural world, has been

closed to her since she was a child. Perhaps she wanted to experience . . . well, I presume. She did want the child of Darius' and Kharishia's line, and was determined nothing should prevent its conception."

"And was it worth it? *Are* you with child? *My* child?"

She nodded. "Without question, Nikki. If her vision holds true, I will bear the ringmaster of the ages."

"So she wanted a child." Nikki stared past her to the cold fireplace, remembering those final days with Anheliaa. "And she wanted to punish me. I had defied her. She wasn't about to have me enjoy my end of the bargain. Is that what you're saying?"

"Poor Nikki. Yes, I very much fear so." Her eyes flickered and fell. "It wasn't exactly pleasurable for me either." And raised again, soft, blue, imploring. "Might we try again? I won't say begin. There will never be a first time together, but . . . might we not still find . . . something? Friendship, at the very least?"

He stared at her, wondering if it was the wine making his head soft, or if he was, in fact, seeing the real Lidye for the first time. He'd much rather be married to this calm, elegant woman, who understood what they'd both lost that night, than any of the other options she'd presented him over the past months.

But still . . .

"Why was I drugged?"

"Last night?"

He nodded.

"To sleep, Nikki. I told you, I needed time. But I wanted you safe, as well."

Reasonable. He didn't like it, but reasonable.

"How is it you're able to leave the Tower at all?"

"Anheliaa, even in the state she is, seems able to steady the rings. In fact, there is little to do but wait in case her control falters."

"Where is Nethaalye? Can she help?"

"Gone, Nikki. Her father took her home after Mikhyel disappeared and the web collapsed. He feared war among the nodes. Feared being caught away from home and in— I'm dismayed to say he felt this, however unfounded— enemy hands."

"Mirym? Where is she?"

"With Anheliaa, of course. There are the monitors

who've always aided Anheliaa. Please, don't judge me
harshly. I must rest sometime. Don't ask more of me. I've
had so little . . ."

Her voice was shaking too much to say more.

"I didn't mean that, Lidye. Yes, in the name of Darius,
send for Mikhyel. Rings, what have I been thinking? Get
him out of there now. I'll talk to him—convince him. And
Deymorin—"

{Is right here, fry.}

He jumped, and whirled to face the door, where a footman was announcing Deymorin dunMheric and Kiyrstine
romGaretti. He met Lidye's eyes, thought he saw an imploring flicker . . .

And went at his wife's side to greet his brother.

Chapter Five

"What do you mean, he wasn't there?" Deymorin demanded. "Where else *would* he be?"

"We conducted a thorough search, Lord dunMheric, and—"

"The *name's* Rhomandi, *Captain* Sironi *gor*Tarim. Just Rhomandi. And *we're* going back there and find him."

"I told you, sir, we conducted—"

"Obviously not thorough enough!" Deymorin thrust himself to his feet, and headed for the door. "*Wait* for me in the foyer."

Sironi glanced past him toward Nikki's wife, then moved to block the door.

Deymorin stopped. Whirled. "Well, madam?"

Lidye had risen as well. Trays of appetizers, as pristine as they'd been when the servants delivered them three hours ago, sat in the center of the salon. She reached now for a cube of cheese. "By all means, m'lord, if you feel your efforts will be more successful—go. Captain, please wait downstairs." She bit delicately. Chewed slowly. And when Sironi had gone: "However, while one hates to suggest the possibility, if a thorough search was made—"

"Then I suggest you do not make the suggestion, madam. I suggest you pray intently to whatever gods you believe in that your high-handed assumptions have not resulted in the death of a Rhomandi. —Kiyrstin?"

She had risen and was already moving to his side. "Do you want me to come with you?"

He shook his head. "Just to his room. I want to get him a cloak, some clean clothes."

"Deymorin?" Nikki called across the room. "Should I—"

{Stay here!} Deymorin shouted the thought, *wanting* Nikki to hear, and Nikki's face blanched. Deymorin tried again, more gently. {Keep an eye on Lidye.}

Nikki nodded. Deymorin reached for the door, found himself intercepted a second time by Lidye's father's guards. Openly in uniform, here in the Tower.

Deymorin glared across the room at Lidye. "I go where I please in my own house, Lidye romNikaenor."

"For your own safety, Deymorin dunMheric. And that of the web. They will not hinder your movement, I assure you."

Before he could answer, Nikki said, quietly, but firmly, "If they do, Lidye, there will be no hope for reconciliation. You will lose *all* Rhomandi support."

Lidye's expression hardened, and she swirled to face Nikki, but the fry, to do him credit, didn't flinch.

"Deymorin," Nikki continued, his eyes still locked on her. "I'll send a message to Jerri. He's a good back-man."

"That's hardly necessary," Lidye said impatiently.

"Perhaps not necessary. But reassuring."

"You insult me!"

"On the contrary, I give you the opportunity to demonstrate your good faith."

A momentary pause, then, with a faint smile, Lidye said, "Ah, Nikaenor, the rings chose more wisely, even, than we supposed. Of course. Call your man."

Nikki said, "Go on, Deymorin. Jerri will meet you at the front door."

Deymorin sent Nikki his silent approval as he caught Kiyrstin's hand and left the salon. Jerri or no Jerri, he had to move quickly. Three hours since Lidye had sent Sironi to fetch Mikhyel from Sparingate. Nearing eight since he'd left his brother alone in a prison filled with men well aware, now, that Mikhyel dunMheric was in their midst.

With Kiyrstin on his heels, he headed for Mikhyel's room. "Stay outside!" He snarled at the guards, when they reached the door to Mikhyel's room, and the uniforms didn't argue, but took up smart positions to either side of the door. Silent. Efficient. If they weren't dogging *his* heels, he'd be impressed.

The door swung open before his hand touched the latch.

"Raulind!" The sight of Mikhyel's personal servant brought vast relief. "Thank the gods you're here." He stepped inside, drew Kiyrstin in beside him, and closed the door.

Raulind's thin face was twisted with worry. "M'lord Mikhyel?"

"Did Oshram's boy get through?" Deymorin asked softly, and Raulind nodded.

"I sent a message to Judge Kharmiini," Raulind said. "But the routing is necessarily circuitous, and by the time I received an answer, word had come that you were in the Tower. I waited, assuming Master Khyel had taken Mistress Lidye immediately into conference. But then, Jerri said . . . m'lord Dcc, where is he?"

"Still there."

Raulind's thin face turned pale. "I feared as much. But Jerri said they were going after him."

"Sironi claims they couldn't find him."

"You're going back yourself to search?"

He nodded. "I need a cloak. Clothing—something that goes well with dirt."

"Thank you, m'lord Dee, but there's no need to jest. My wits are back in order." Raulind turned to Kiyrstin. "And is this your brave Mauritumin woman?"

Kiyrstin chuckled. "That's the nicest introduction I've ever had. Mikhyel's told me all about you, Raulind. He holds you in great esteem."

"Thank you, m'lady. He spoke with great admiration of you, before he . . . left." Raulind dipped his head and moved toward the far closet.

Deymorin took Kiyrstin's hands in his. "Kiyrstin, I've *got* to try to find him, but—"

"Might not come back, is that what you're saying, Rags?"

"All depends on *why* he's missing. Tarim placed Sironi under Brolucci's orders, according to Lidye. Brolucci is Anheliaa's, has been for years. There's just no way of knowing how deep the infection runs."

"Will you confront him before you go?"

"What good could it do now, other than bruise my knuckles?"

"Excuse me, m'lord Dee?"

"Yes, Raul?"

"House-word is, his ring is spinning off-orbit."

"Meaning, he's losing influence fast?"

"Yes, m'lord Dee."

"Meaning, I should save my knuckles?"

"Yes, m'lord Dee. Was he in breeches, sir?"

Deymorin blinked. Realized Raulind's revised "he" was Mikhyel, and nodded.

"Ah." Was Raulind's cryptic response, and he turned back to the closet.

"So," Kiyrstin said, in a matter-of-fact tone, "how long do I give you?"

Forever, was the quip that rose to Deymorin's tongue, but never escaped. He was all too aware, at the moment, of just how much he'd begun to take their future together for granted.

"Take that look off your face, Rhomandi," she said softly. "We don't walk a safe path. We haven't since we met."

"Is it so easy for you?"

"Easy? To watch you go out that door, not knowing if you'll come back? Not at all. And it never will be. But neither will I waste time and energy worrying about something over which I have no control." She took his face between her hands. "I love you, JD. I *have* loved you. I look forward to loving you for the rest of my life—or yours. Short or long, that time has been well spent."

She kissed him lingeringly, then let him go with a brisk pat on the cheek. " 'Sides, Deymio-luvie, I don't intend t' stick around if the locals go bad. I'll ditch these fancies, swipe another pair o' Khyel's breeches from under ol' Raulind's nose, and hit the road. Meet you in the woods. Find us a lake or two—wot ye say, luvie?"

He laughed because she expected it.

"Good plan. Except I'd cultivate Raulind's good will. According to Khyel, he's more dangerous than he looks."

"Ah."

"Stay here with him," Deymorin said seriously. "Tell him—hell, tell him everything you think he should know. Trust his judgment, is the best I can advise.—Raulind?"

The valet looked up from the small bag he was packing.

"Staying here is best, m'lady. There are routes from the Tower of which Mistress Lidye's men are quite ignorant. I have sent messages to Master Khyel's allies on the Hill. Should necessity dictate, we will find at least temporary refuge with them."

"I knew I could count on you, Raul," Deymorin replied.

Raulind held out the valise and a cloak. "I'd prefer my efforts be wasted, m'lord Dee. Tell him his bath is waiting."

"I'll do that. —Kiyrsti?"

She stopped him with her lips.

It was dark in the Crypt, long past the final lamp turn-down, and Deymorin ordered the lights left down. No sense, he pointed out to Sironi, in alerting those who might have hidden Mikhyel the first time.

{Khyel?} Deymorin sent out into that blackness. {For the love of Darius, brother, answer me!}

He was there, Deymorin could sense that much, and alive. Relieved, Deymorin paused at the foot of the stairs, closed his eyes and listened to that inner voice. He was vaguely aware that inmates had risen, and were closing in through the dark, but Sironi was there, and Jerrik, with others of Tarim's guard.

In that darkness behind his eyelids: peace, warmth, the quiet of near sleep he'd learned to associate with Mikhyel at his most accessible. Too awake for dreams, too far into sleep for that wall he erected about his conscious self.

And Mikhyel's mind was quiet as it had been only on the best nights at Armayel.

There were vague sensations Deymorin's cognizant mind readily identified: a stout arm for a pillow, a second lying heavy along his side, and the warmth along his back was a large body.

Deymorin controlled the anger that flared, and traced those sensations, clear as a signal fire in the night, to their source. For all instinct demanded he hurry, cold prudence made him commit false probes into one dark warren after another. Sironi had claimed a thorough search had failed to locate Mikhyel; Deymorin's walking straight to wherever Mikhyel lay with that human pillow would raise far too many undesirable questions.

Besides, this way (he shot a deliberate wake-up call to that gradually stirring mind) Mikhyel would have time to prepare.

{Deymorin? *Back here?*} Returned to him, along with a surge of concern.

For him. The dolt. Deymorin caught that mental thread and sent back:

{Come to take you home, fry.}

Relief, then, and a sense of movement, vivid impressions that translated, moments later, to a shadowy figure at the edges of their flickering circle of light.

Two shadowy figures.

Deymorin froze, fists clenched. Mikhyel moved toward them, Ganfrion, an arrogantly-tilted head taller, at his back.

For a moment, Deymorin saw nothing except that dark, scarred face, the challenge issued in Ganfrion's every move. But for all Deymorin longed to plant a fist right in the middle of that arrogance, he couldn't. Ganfrion was a prisoner, without recourse; Deymorin had arrived here with substantial backing.

Which wouldn't stop him from beginning immediate legal inquiries into the past of one Ganfrion of Sparingate Crypt.

Mikhyel stumbled, and thoughts of equity faltered as Ganfrion's blunt-fingered hands steadied his brother's strides. Bare-footed strides. Mikhyel was filthy, his face bruised, and a swelling around one eye threatened to turn purple by morning. And his clothing—

"Where's your coat?" he asked, by way of opening.

Mikhyel stopped.

"It's good to see you, too, Rhomandi," Mikhyel said in a voice as flat as that underneath sense. "And I'm fine, thank you for asking. How's the weather?"

The smallest man in the circle of light, his face as smooth as a twelve-year-old's, no coat, bare feet, his shirt in tatters . . . and he still managed to look down his nose at all of them.

Deymorin stifled a shout of relieved laughter. The Barrister was alive, healthy in all the truly important ways. Ganfrion might have had him in these past hours. Every man down here might have, but they hadn't defeated him. Not by any means.

He could get Mikhyel safely to the Tower, and see to these scum later.

{You'll do nothing, Deymorin.}

{We'll see—}

{*Nothing!*}

{Are you all right, Khy?}

Silence.

"Fancy tailor," Deymorin said, aloud, and stared pointedly at the standard prison-issue gray that hung from Mikhyel's waist, let his eyes drift to the bare feet below. "Changing the Barrister's image?"

Mikhyel's mouth twitched, along with an eyebrow. "Considering the size of the exchange, I don't envy the new owner's feet."

"Subtle as always, eh, Barrister?"

"Deymorin . . . " Mikhyel shook his head, then swept his hair back from his forehead. "Just . . . get me out of here?"

Underneath, Mikhyel was exhausted, and relieved, but little else, other than a sense that if Deymorin was here—with Jerrik—and joking, then all that comprised his world couldn't be collapsing.

"Sure, fry," he said quietly. He shook out the cloak he carried and flung it around Mikhyel's shoulders, setting Ganfrion back a step with a warning scowl.

"Thank you," Mikhyel said, drawing the cloak securely into place.

"Got a whole rig for you up in Oshram's office."

"I don't—" Through his touch on Mikhyel's shoulders, Deymorin received a flashing desire just to be home, in his own bath, followed by a sense of Raulind's spider-fingered touch on his sore back.

{That good, is he?} Deymorin asked silently.

{Rings . . .} At least, he thought that was the essence of Mikhyel's mental sigh.

{Be careful. I'll steal him from you.}

{You can't afford him, brother.}

"So, do you want to just go home?" Deymorin asked, his head beginning to throb with that silent effort.

Temptation. That came through clearly, but he knew his meticulous brother, knew Mikhyel would want to make a dignified entry into the Tower, and so wasn't the least surprised when Mikhyel finally shook his head.

At the top of the staircase, Mikhyel paused and looked down, a slow, guarded scan of the blackness below. That scan paused when it reached Ganfrion, still in reach of the torches. Other shadows, barely visible, were closing in around the big prisoner.

Perhaps he wouldn't have to worry about legal retaliation after all.

Mikhyel's brow tightened, and Deymorin was ashamed of the thought.

But Mikhyel only said, as he turned and stepped out of the Crypt, "I hope to hell Raul remembered a hair clip."

ᔓ   ᔓ   ᔓ

If Raulind ever failed him, Mikhyel would know for certain the universe was coming to an end. A hair clip, indeed, toiletries—including a razor—even a pair of comfortable house boots: everything required to restore himself to basic respectability.

"Obviously—" he waved the razor toward Deymorin, then dropped it back in the bag, "—you haven't told him everything."

"Nothing, Khyel. I'll leave that to you to explain."

"Oh, thank you. I can't even explain it to myself. Sometimes, I touch my chin and could swear the damned thing was back."

"Like a man who's lost a leg," Deymorin said.

Mikhyel frowned at the shirt he lifted free of the valise, reminded unwillingly of the brother who had almost lost a leg once, thanks to his younger brother's stupidity. "The man who lost his leg should resent such a comparison."

"Oh, stuff it, Barrister. *I* wasn't thinking of that night. I only meant I've heard that such men still feel their missing limb, years after they lost it. Their mind expects it to be there, the doctors say. Your mind expects the beard to be there."

"I think that your argument lacks—" Mikhyel vision faded. The shirt slipped from fingers gone suddenly numb. He sat down hard on a nearby chair.

"Khyel?" Deymorin was at his side. "Are you all right?"

Hell, no, he wanted to shout, but there was no reason, nothing to be gained by a show of temper and frustration.

He was tired, that was all, and waked out of a sleep as quiet and sound as he'd had in weeks. As had happened with Nikki, his sense of Deymorin had disappeared once Deymorin passed into Rhomandi House. For all the uncertainty of his situation, despite the fact that his immediate fate had rested in the hands of a single inmate, who had paid handsomely for the honor, he'd been more relaxed at that moment when Deymorin's call had waked him than he'd been since Boreton.

Perhaps longer.

Now, he was back to guarding every thought in *case* Deymorin picked it up, to wasting valuable energy trying (by means of dubious efficacy) to *keep* Deymorin from picking up those thoughts and impressions, and wondering which nonessential bit of seepage was going to set off his brother's reactive nature next.

Be open, Deymorin had advised him. *Tell me, so I won't speculate.* Tell Deymorin what had happened after he left, and Deymorin would blow everything out of proportion and overreact. He knew his brother. In that, Deymorin hadn't changed. In that, Deymorin never *would* change.

Deymorin had picked up the shirt. He slipped it over Mikhyel's shoulders and buttoned it when Mikhyel's hands failed to achieve that basic coordination. Mikhyel managed his own trousers, but let Deymorin braid, twist, and fasten his hair.

As if he were a child, Mikhyel thought sourly, and slid his arms into the black coat Deymorin held for him. But for all the effort it took, for all the frustration of needing Deymorin's help, once his transformation was complete, he left the warden's office in far greater spirits than he'd entered it, able to face the Shatumin guards without embarrassment.

Except, he thought, as he preceded Deymorin into the waiting carriage, and while Sironi and Jerrik settled in beside Deymorin and himself, he hadn't *been* embarrassed.

Relieved, yes. But embarrassed . . . Sironi had left him in the Crypt to suffer indignities, perhaps death. Perhaps that choice had been Sironi's own decision, perhaps based on the orders of Tarim or Tarim's daughter; perhaps, as Deymorin suggested there in Oshram's office, he'd been working on Brolucci's orders.

Whatever prompted leaving Mikhyel dunMheric in the Crypt, there was something to be said for the image of Mikhyel dunMheric standing before them all, unbroken, while confirming, by his physical appearance, the filth and degradation to which they believed they'd consigned him.

In fact, he'd rather looked forward to that little piece of melodramatic grandstanding. The image of his triumphant entry into the Tower had sustained him more than once in the past few hours. Instead, Deymorin had provided everything necessary to *hide* his reality from the world

Deymorin, who could look at him now and not see those

inmate-gray trousers, the bare feet. Who could avoid, now, seeing Ganfrion's shadow looming behind him.

Deymorin's embarrassment was at issue, not Mikhyel's. Deymorin's guilt for not having gotten Mikhyel out with him. Deymorin, who had yet to learn that sometimes, a man simply had to work within the system life provided, not according to some personal, esoteric structure of "right" and "wrong."

Deymorin had done nothing for him because there had been nothing Deymorin *could* do. Deymorin had had no choice. There could be no guilt where there was no option. Perhaps someday Deymorin would learn that sometimes there was no fair answer.

And perhaps some day . . . horses would have wings.

The streets were quiet. Dark. Only the occasional indoor lamp and the light from distant Tower Hill relieved the black of night. A man who had always found comfort in the dark, might welcome those shadows, but a man whose duty it was to keep those streets lighted could not. He could only wonder at the fear that lack of light must be generating, in the leyside dwellings. Could only wonder what it had been like the night of the Boreton Firestorm, the first night of utter darkness in living memory for most of those in the city of Rhomatam.

Within the old wall, there would have been gas lamps, the backup for the leythium streetlamps in the years before the capping of Khoratum. Here, in the Khoratum expansion, such provision had never been necessary. Since Khoratum had been capped, the power had never wavered.

Until now.

Fortunately for the City's coffers, the anticipated population shift toward the new Khoratum ring had never occurred. Speculators had jumped in early, buying the land at exorbitant prices, only to find themselves either stuck with large chunks of unusable land, or faced with the expense and difficulty of long-term development and a slow recuperation of their investment, or selling at a substantial loss.

By the time most of those overeager speculators had finally faced market reality, the initial city-wide interest had faded. Over the past years, buildings had gone up, but slowly. Population had shifted from the inner city. But slowly.

Which meant fewer Rhomatumins than might have been to compensate now for losses due to the collapse. Or at least, fewer to compensate for the *extended* lack of power. If the reports they'd received were accurate—and certainly Lidye's account to Nikki of three days with the rings down would support such accounts—the continued problems of the outer ring were only the beginning of the City's fiscal problems.

They arrived at the inner gate, and were passed through without comment.

Ordinarily, livestock would not be allowed into Rhomatum; obviously, these were not ordinary times. The carriage itself must have been confiscated from one of the internode transport services. He made a mental note to find out which one and make certain they were properly compensated.

It was quiet within the coach. It was even quiet within his head. Deymorin, sitting opposite him, had conveyed everything of substance that he had learned from Nikki during those moments of privacy in Oshram's office. He put the space between them now deliberately, though whether Mikhyel knew that from Deymorin's mind or personal assessment of his brother's character became increasingly indecipherable.

A realization he wasn't certain he appreciated.

But for now, Deymorin's mind was at ease. He had relaxed in the cushioned seat, rocking easily with the motion of the carriage, his eyes at half-mast and staring out the window. He had about him a sense that his concerns, his immediate, personal concerns, were over, at least for the time being. A sense that anything else could wait until tomorrow.

Or such was the interpretation Mikhyel's own mind put on the peace that ebbed and flowed within the carriage.

Within the old wall, the familiar silver of leylight ended the darkness. But it was dim. And the lights on the crossleys were barely brighter than a full moon. There was something about the appearance of the light that suggested it was deliberate, that the bulbs had been purposely misaligned—perhaps to limit the drain on the power umbrella while still reassuring the citizenry that all was under control within the Tower.

Perhaps to disguise the fact that everything was *not* under control within the Tower.

By that light, he began to take painful note of the damage the City had taken. Boarded windows, fire-gutted buildings . . . that appeared to be the worst. Fire was not a common problem within Rhomatum. Heat came from the ley. There *was* no need for open flames. Ever. But the ley had deserted the city. The citizens must have tried to compensate. . . .

Oh, his poor, foolish Rhomatumin, who hadn't, in all their lives, had the need to keep a fire stoked.

He felt a quiver, deep in his gut, and his throat tightened.

"Stop the coach," he said, and when Sironi began to argue: "I said, *stop the damned coach!*"

{Khye . . .} Deymorin started awake.

Mikhyel slammed the handle on the door, and had it half open before the vehicle rocked to a halt.

Deymorin followed him out. Sironi did. He whirled on them both.

"Follow me," he said to Sironi, "and you'd better be gone from Rhomatum in the morning."

He turned on his heel and headed toward one of those gutted buildings. Sironi began to follow. Mikhyel's hand clenched: echo of Deymorin's hand on Sironi's arm. And Deymorin's voice came, half-heard through the link, advising Sironi just how foolish it would be to challenge what was obviously a rapidly shifting power structure.

Within his mind, Deymorin's deafening shout reassured him Sironi had seen reason, and then Deymorin pulled his mind back. Mikhyel acknowledged the message, and at the same time reached a mental hand to stop Deymorin's retreat, extending to him that hold that would reassure him as to Mikhyel's well-being.

How long he walked that street, he couldn't say. What thoughts passed through his mind, what notes his subconscious took, were equally opaque to him. He only knew that, of all the changes in his life, this devastation of Rhomatum was the most unthinkable.

Eventually, he came aware of Deymorin's hand, warm on his shoulder, of concrete, cold beneath his buttocks, and a pile of charred wood and ashes that had once been home to a dozen families.

"Come back, Khyel. We can't rebuild it tonight."

He let Deymorin pull him to his feet and draw him back to the carriage. This time, he sat beside Deymorin, and under cover of the touch that seemed to make their silent communication so much easier, he began quizzing Deymorin regarding Outside resources, everything from places to put those displaced by fire and damage, to lumber and nails.

For rebuilding.

If not tonight, then tomorrow.

Chapter Six

"And then, we were brought here," Kiyrstin said, bringing the tale of the past months to a close. "Deymorin has been, well, frantic."

"He is concerned, no doubt, about leaving Master Khyel alone with the inmates," Raulind commented in his quiet voice, and Kiyrstin nodded.

"Evidently Mikhyel had already had at least one round with them. Deymorin has avoided specifics, for his own sake, I believe, as well as deference to Mikhyel's privacy."

"But you can supply the unsaid words." Statement, not a question. Raulind had judged her—and accurately—from the handful of details she'd given regarding her own past. Kiyrstin nodded.

"And I can't say as I contest Deymorin's concern. The longer he's there alone, the more chance there is that something irreparable will happen to him."

"Master Khyel can take care of himself, m'lady Kiyrstin," Raulind said. "He is quite amazingly strong."

"Certainly his mind is. If they can be talked to reason, he will."

"And his body. Don't be misled by what you see, m'lady. He has as least twice now, by what you said, cheated death."

"Twice?" Taking Deymorin at his word, Kiyrstin had told Raulind everything, from her own past, to her meeting with Deymorin, to the Boreton Firestorm and the brothers' strange new abilities.

Raulind rose to his feet and paced the room slowly, contemplatively. Finally, he turned to her. His thin face was drawn, the skin around his eyes puckered.

"By what you've said, my master has spoken quite freely with you these past weeks."

Kiyrstin nodded, for all it wasn't a question.

"I can believe that. You have that about you that draws a man toward trust, m'lady."

"Thank you, Raulind. I think I know when to keep a secret, if that's what you mean."

"I'm not certain I meant it as a compliment, m'lady."

An easy smile came to her. "Honest man."

"Yes, m'lady."

"You're saying that I've a talent that might be abused."

"And my master is in much need, at times, of understanding."

"Of being understood, you mean."

"That as well. But he needs, at times, to talk in order to understand the world as others see it. He hasn't a good . . . template upon which to build his internal sanctuary."

"And you have provided that template over the years."

"As best I could."

"And you fear my influence."

"Fear. No, not at all. My master is his own man. He reveals his secrets knowing the dangers, and having balanced those dangers against the benefits. But in choosing my personal path, in choosing those whom I will trust, I must understand his reasoning and balance that against my own judgment."

Kiyrstin shook her head. "I begin to see where Mikhyel comes from."

"I take that as a compliment, m'lady."

"It was intended as such. How *did* you come to be with him?"

"He hasn't told you?"

"He said you were one of the Brothers who tended him at Barsitum, after his father died. He said he never understood why you left the Order to accompany him to Rhomatum. He said he didn't know how he would survive without you."

"He would, I have no doubt. I am nonetheless pleased to know my importance to him." A pause, then: "When I first met Master Khyel, he was hanging to life by sheer will alone."

"From the injuries his father inflicted?"

"Injuries. I suppose that's what one must call them." Raulind nodded. "Has Master Khyel told you about Mheric?"

Mheric: as Mikhyel never referred to Mheric as his father, neither did Raulind. She wondered who had learned the trick from whom.

"Honestly, Raulind? Only the barest bones of the situation. I know Mheric was not much of a father. I knew he took his frustration with life out on his son. I suspect a fair amount more, but I can't say that Mikhyel revealed it to me. At least, not intentionally."

A slight smile broke the solemnity of his thin face. "I understand. And I know now why he trusted you. On his thirteenth birthday, he refused to go riding with his father and the crowd of men his father had gathered to witness his second son's . . . emerging manhood. There was one man in particular, whose horse Mikhyel was ordered to share."

"Share?"

"Mikhyel was to ride ahead of him. In the same saddle. It wasn't the first time."

"Sweet Maurii," Kiyrstin whispered.

"I see you understand my young master's dilemma. He refused. Mheric tried to force him, and lost control more thoroughly than usual. He left my mangled master in a closet while he went out and rode with his friends. Mheric did not come back from that ride. By the time they found my young master, he was very nearly dead. He should not have survived the drive to Barsitum. But he did survive, and in the course of the next few months the pools worked the greatest miracle I'd ever seen."

"The pool, and his own will to live," Kiyrstin said, and Raulind nodded.

"The two work together. What you tell me about this newest ability only confirms that which I suspected from the first time I held his head above the leythium. There are those for whom the Barsitumin pools will perform their magic, and those for whom they will not. when Mikhyel floated in them, they . . . came alive. I don't know how else to describe it."

"Don't try," Kiyrstin said. "I'll take your word for it."

Raulind nodded. "He told me things in those months, sometimes out of delirium, sometimes just because he needed to talk to someone. After he recovered, I could not stay in Barsitum. In his desperate innocence, he had granted me keys to his soul that no human being should hold for another. But having those keys, I could not, in

good conscience, leave him to face that to which I knew
he would return."

"But Mheric was dead."

"Mheric was. *Anheliaa* was still very much alive." Raulind paused, seeming to listen. A smile stretched his face.
"They're here."

§   §   §

The door of Rhomandi House, a massive structure of
beveled glass surrounding the web within circles of the
Rhomandi crest, swung open. Even to Mikhyel's light-sensi-
tive eyes, the foyer seemed dim: conservation within the
Tower itself. He hadn't realized that was possible.

Deymorin went in first, and Deymorin's presence vanished. His mind reveled in that giddy freedom for a moment—before his own foot crossed the threshold, and
Deymorin's thoughts, and Nikki's, sent him reeling back
out.

"Khyel?"

He gathered himself together, and made a second attempt on the doorway, prepared, this time, for the
onslaught.

"Whew," Deymorin said, and within Mikhyel's mind, a
ragged stone wall appeared. Deymorin's attempt, he finally
realized, to set a barrier between them.

"Thanks," he murmured.

"Mikhyel! Thank the rings you're all right!" Nikki came
bounding down the stairs. He grasped the hand Mikhyel
extended and pulled him into a quick embrace, radiating
relief, guilt, dismay, horror, and a myriad of other emotions, all of it roiling in the images of what Nikki thought
had been happening to him in the prison.

"Rings," Mikhyel muttered, and pushed Nikki away. The
mental assault continued. He struck out, blindly, and with
a mental shout: {It's all right. Nothing happened. *Calm
down*.}

When his vision cleared, Nikki was standing well out of
arm's reach, one hand raised to his mouth, exuding pain
now and anger. Betrayal.

Mikhyel felt that throb in his own lip, and knew he'd
struck Nikki in his attempts to stop that stream of impres-

sions. And damn it, he had succeeded in that goal, and his little brother could just *keep* his sore lip!

But for all his rational mind tried to stop that flow of sensation from Nikki to himself, it couldn't prevail against habits of a lifetime. In the end, Mikhyel accepted that minor pain, and simultaneously sent reassurance to Nikki, along with explanations.

Nikki's hand dropped, the anger eased, and Mikhyel's lip hurt.

His awareness of his brothers increased with each passing moment. Proximity to the node, he supposed. The commonest folk knew that the closer you came to a node the greater the effects of the ley.

The very air within the Tower seemed different from what he remembered. Alive, somehow. The reflective gleam of leylight off metal or polished wood sparked with hints of color, and Mikhyel wondered whether that effect was visible to everyone and he'd simply never noticed, or just another manifestation of whatever metamorphosis had occurred within himself and his brothers.

Or perhaps it was just his own exhaustion acting on eyes too accustomed to the dark.

"Where's Lidye?" he asked Nikki.

"In the Tower," Nikki answered. "She asked if we would wait for her in the salon. She hopes to make amends, Khyel."

"She couldn't wait until morning?" Deymorin asked.

"In the morning, I'll have a clear head, Deymorin," Mikhyel answered for Nikki. "Much better to make explanations to the sleep-deprived."

"It's not like that, Mikhyel," Nikki protested. "*She's* not."

"I'll take your word for it."

Nevertheless, he accompanied his brothers to the Blue Salon, where he found himself ensconced in a wing chair, with a glass of red wine close at hand, while Deymorin left to get Kiyrstin, and Nikki went to the Tower to get Lidye.

He wet his lips with the wine, set it down again, finding the taste not at all to his liking tonight. As the opulence surrounding him was not. Opulence he'd grown up with. Opulence that was, somehow, excessive. Opulence that could disappear in an instant as easily as that cross-ley apartment.

And if it did, Mikhyel dunMheric and all his dependents could simply move somewhere else. Where had those individuals found refuge? Or had they all died in the inferno that gutted their home?

He closed his eyes, vaguely aware of his brothers' direction, as he was vaguely conscious of their minds. Deymorin had gone to Mikhyel's private suite, where Kiyrstin had been waiting with Raulind. Likely trading secrets. Not that it mattered. Within the next weeks, his whole life would probably appear in *The Gazette*. Once secrets began to emerge, nothing would stop them. Wasn't that what Anheliaa had always stressed to him?

Still, he'd do his best to beat the odds. His life, his past, was his own. Not Deymorin's, not Raulind's, certainly not the average Rhomatumin citizen's.

As his brothers faded, a different pressure built in his mind. A darkness deeper than the Crypt after turndown oozed behind his eyelids. Exhaustion, he thought, coercing sleep on him, and he forced his eyes open, then wondered if it was exhaustion that made the room's shadows seep with that same black malignancy.

He rose to his feet and began to pace, striving to stay awake. There were no papers in the room. No magazines. Plates of food. Wine. But nothing to occupy his mind, nothing to catch him up on the events of the past weeks.

And still the shadows moved inward.

Logic said it was impossible, that the light from the lamps, however subdued, hadn't changed since he entered the room. Logic demanded he challenge that perception for the mental aberration it had to be.

He reached toward the shadow—

§   §   §

Deymorin stepped through the door, cried out, and collapsed as if hamstrung.

"Deymio!" Kiyrstin called out, and was at his side only a stride behind Raulind.

Deymorin stared through them. "Khyel," he whispered, then shouted, "Khyel!" And he was on his feet, racing down the hallway.

Kiyrstin exchanged a startled glance with Raulind, then

lifted her skirts and chased after him, Raulind at her heels.
Down the hall, down the wide spiral staircase—

"Dammit, Khyel, snap out of it!" Deymorin's voice
reached them first. Kiyrstin rounded the curve, and saw him
struggling with Mikhyel before the door to the Tower lift.

"She lied!" Mikhyel's face was dark with anger. "Anheliaa's not only awake, she's in the Tower and *damned*
active."

Kiyrstin stopped, still several steps above the brothers.
Raulind stopped beside her, a worried, pained expression
on his face.

"Rings, Khyel, how do you know?" Deymorin was asking, and his hands were on Mikhyel's shoulders, struggling
to prevent his much smaller brother from calling the lift.

"Are you, blind?" Mikhyel shouted, and held out his
hand. "*Look* at it! There. And there. And there!" He
pointed to seemingly random spots about the room, then
shook that hand in front of Deymorin. "Don't you *feel*
her?"

"Oh, my poor Khy," Raulind whispered, and the agony
in his voice, Kiyrstin knew after the past two hours, was
not contrived.

"Khyel, I see noth—" Deymorin said, and broke off as
Mikhyel caught his hand. His eyes widened, tracing the
path Mikhyel had indicated.

"Rings. All right, Khyel, all *right*." He shook Mikhyel
lightly, and Mikhyel relaxed visibly as silent messages
passed between the two of them.

A quick intake of breath beside her indicated Raulind
had registered that silent shift of attitude, and recognized
in it the truth of what she'd told him regarding the brothers' new ability.

Kiyrstin took the final steps, judging it time to disrupt
their silent tête-à-tête.

"Everything all right?" she asked.

Deymorin blinked at her, then dropped his hands from
Mikhyel's shoulders. Mikhyel looked past her to Raulind,
and the tension drained from his face.

"Welcome home, Master Khyel," Raulind said easily.

And Mikhyel answered in a similar tone, "Thank you,
Raul. It's good to be home."

"Been under some strain, sir?"

"A bit."

"Better after a good night's sleep."

"Undoubtedly. But I must see my aunt first."

"As you will, sir. I'll go make the bath ready."

"Thank you, Raul. I'll be there shortly."

"And will you be wanting a rubdown, sir?"

"About a week without stopping, Raul."

"I understand, sir. Afraid my hands won't last that long. Shall I call in reinforcements?"

Mikhyel laughed. "No, Raul. I'll be lucky if I don't fall asleep and drown. Your hands will have ample time to recuperate."

"Very good, sir. I'll be upstairs."

"I—" Mikhyel's face sobered, and his eyes again drifted toward his hand, then flickered back to Raulind. "I won't be long," he finished firmly.

Raulind nodded and left.

"You're going up to see Anheliaa?" Kiyrstin asked, and Deymorin nodded. "Would I learn anything if I ask why?"

Deymorin shook his head.

"Then I won't bother."

"Good."

"But I will go with you."

"Shepherdess, I don't think—"

With a hiss of venting steam, the lift arrived with Nikki and Lidye aboard.

"Mikhyel!" Lidye exclaimed, and she stepped free before the grill had fully opened, hand extended.

His face stone blank, Mikhyel reached to meet it.

Lidye fell back, eyes wide and startled—and focused on Mikhyel's hand.

"Lidye, what's wrong?" Nikki asked, still half-inside the lift.

Deymorin brushed past Lidye, and pushed Nikki back inside. "We're all going to go see Aunt Anheliaa, Nikki."

"What? Deymorin, why? I just came from there. She's nine-tenths dead."

"Then she can't do anything, can she?" Deymorin said, and followed Nikki into the lift.

Mikhyel followed; Lidye shied back from him, keeping even her dress from contact with him.

Mikhyel stepped into the lift—

And cried out. He swayed. Deymorin grabbed for him,

Nikki did, and Mikhyel's arms shot out, flailing wildly even as his feet staggered without rational direction.

The next instant he collapsed into a twisted heap on the floor, his eyes wide open and staring, his limbs twitching.

၅   ၅   ၅

That which had been Mikhyel dunMheric stared out through that which had been his eyes and saw shapes, blurred images without meaning. His ears collected equally meaningless noises.

He felt nothing.

His arms were no longer his own. His legs were not. Not even his heart beat for itself, and for its own reasons, but because Deymorin's beat. And because Nikki's heart had not stopped.

Deymorin. Nikki. Names. As Mikhyel was a Name. *His* name.

Mikhyel held on to that one truth, as the images tilted and swayed. His arms twitched, his legs did. He was walking, carrying a body that babbled meaningless words and writhed uncontrollably.

No, not him. Someone Else was carrying the body.

Deymorin, was the name supplied, for one or the other.

And still he carried the awkward bundle upward.

Stairs. Endless stairs. And the bundle twitched, thrashed about, and sent him to his knees. He thudded down two steps, and held the bundle close, protecting its head.

And he said something to it, though he didn't know what, and he sent his mind into the whirling maelstrom of the bundle's mind, and he stilled those turbulent waters. He embraced them with godlike scope, contained them.

Contained. Protected those waters from brothers and black malignancy alike.

And slowly, as the malignancy retreated, feeling returned to his limbs.

His name was Mikhyel. He lay draped across Deymorin's lap on the staircase halfway between the first and second floors of Rhomandi House.

"Very good," Deymorin said, and he realized he'd spoken aloud. "And two plus two equals?"

"Ask me in the morning." He groaned and pulled himself upright and onto the stair beside Deymorin. "What happened?"

"I'd assumed you could tell me."

Kiyrstin was on the step beneath them. Otherwise, the staircase was empty. "Where's Nikki?" he asked, then realized he *should* have known.

"He's gone with Lidye up to the Tower."

He didn't feel Deymorin, except in the old, normal way. He touched Deymorin's hand, and wondered, if somehow, some crisis point had been reached and—

"Sorry, brother," Deymorin said, and his voice was strained. "It's not gone. I . . ."

He understood, then, what the images meant. He looked at his hand, free, now, of the black stain, though the shadows still crept in the corners. Deymorin's doing, that freedom of his mind from Anheliaa—and everything else. And Deymorin was turning green beneath his tan from the effort.

"Let it go, Deymorin."

"Khyel, you don't understand. You'll—"

"Be fine. I'm ready for her now."

Deymorin held out his hand. After a moment, Mikhyel took it. Only then, when he had that solid contact, did Deymorin begin to ease his hold on Mikhyel's mind.

It felt as if Deymorin took down a wall, stone by stone. A wall around Mikhyel. Not stacked stones, but solid granite between himself and the rest of that underneath world.

At one point, Mikhyel felt Anheliaa surge, that *presence* that sought to consume him, and the wall was back. Another drop, another surge, and Deymorin's anger swelled, violent red that flared between Mikhyel and Anheliaa, and the blackness curled in on itself with a near-palpable scream.

This time, when the wall came down, it was only Deymorin's mind waiting to touch him.

Chapter Seven

Thyerri closed the door and shot the bolt behind the last customer. With a heavy sigh, he collapsed into the nearest chair and buried his head in his arms, ready to fall asleep right then and there.

"Thy?" Sakhithe's voice roused him. "You all right?"

He nodded, the barest movement of his head, since anything more made the room spin. "Tired."

She moved behind him and began to rub his shoulders and neck. "Shouldn't have come out."

"Couldn't sleep. You needed the help."

"Can't deny that. Thank you."

"My—" He yawned widely, and let his head fall again. "—pleasure."

"Is that what you call it?" She chuckled, and continued rubbing. Thyerri's neck relaxed, and his head began to sway with the motion of her hands.

"So, this is our young warrior, eh?" Zelin's voice jarred him awake.

The barkeeper fell into a neighboring chair and swept a towel across his face. The towel left a damp sheen in its wake. Zelin wiped his hands next, then tossed the towel into the middle of the round table.

"Sakhi said she talked to you about what happened," Zelin said.

Thyerri shrugged, embarrassed.

"She said you might want it not to happen again."

The bar towel remained in the center of the table. Thyerri laid a claim and buried his head in a pillow formed of its cool damp folds. He was ready to sleep, not at all concerned about tomorrow.

"Thyerri, behave!" Sakhithe grabbed a fistful of his hair and hauled his head up.

"Sakhi, I'm not a fighter!" Thyerri groaned in protest, and tried unsuccessfully to pull free.

"No sane man is, boy," Zelin said, and his voice was cold. He stood up. "Never mind, Sakhi. Let him go."

She released his hair and Thyerri's head fell, nearly to the table, he was that tired. But she didn't seem to notice. She just left him there, and walked with Zelin toward the back door.

"Sakhi?" he called to her, but she didn't stop. He stumbled to his feet and followed her. "Please, Sakhi, wait."

She spun about, but Zelin kept walking. "Why? What do you want me to say? It's all right, Thyerri? It won't happen again, Thyerri? Well, it *will* happen. Again and again and again."

"Not . . . not if I don't ever dance again."

It was as if he twisted a knife in his own gut. It was defeat. But his dance had caused the fight. Had roused passions and anger. If he didn't dance, it wouldn't happen.

And he would die.

"Do you think it was just the dance? Wake *up*, Thyerri. You're not in the Tower any longer. There's no way to stop it. Not out here."

She was frightening him. He was tired and sore and he couldn't think straight.

"Sakhi, what did I do?" His voice shamed him, quivering like a child's. He tried to steady it. "Why are you so angry?"

Her shoulders sagged. "I'm not angry, Thy. I'm frightened. For you. I had no idea you were so . . . so helpless."

"I'm *not*." The very idea was revolting. "I'm not a fighter, but—"

"Helpless," she repeated firmly. "Vulnerable. I didn't know, Thyerri. I'd never seen you dance before. And . . . your dance is dangerous, Thyerri."

"I know. I made them crazy. That's why—"

"Not to others, Thyerri, to yourself. You're too open. Everything that is Thyerri is laid out for them to know—and to destroy. And they will, Thyerri. They'll try to destroy it, because they can't have it. And what they'll do . . . it's worse than death, Thyerri."

"They? Sakhi, you're confusing me."

She bit her lip, looked away, her face growing red.

"What? Sakhi, *tell* me!"

Taking his hand, she led him back to the table. "Thyerri, I realize now, you aren't like the rest of us."

"But I am, Sakhi." He slumped back in his chair. Drawing his braid forward, he jerked the tie loose and finger-combed the strands free. Long hair was a dancer's pride, its whipping tail as much a part of the radical dance as the dancer's well-trained body. "I know, I never cut it, but I don't *really* figure I'll ever get another chance at the rings. It's just . . ."

"A dream? That's the difference, Thy. I don't even dream of dancing the rings any more—except for the night-mares. I never *want* to dance that way again. None of us do. At least, not those who survive. This—" She ran a hand through her own cropped hair. "—is not castration, Thyerri, but freedom. For me, Rakshi's touch would be a curse, not a blessing." She reached out and freed his hand from his hair to hold it. "What happened last night, Thyerri, that was a bonus. For me, it is truly enough. But it's not the rings. It's not the maze. It's not . . . it's not reaching out to Rakshi and having him hold you in his hand."

He just stared at her, resisting the ache inside.

"Thyerri, it's still there for you. You could no more stop dancing—whether on the rings or down the street—than you can stop breathing. That does something to certain people, people like that dunKarlon man—"

"That? That what, Sakhi?"

"The way you move. The exaltation of life. The challenge you send to some people, just by *being*. It seems like some people just have to possess that. Or destroy it. I don't know how to explain it. But I've seen it happen. And *that's* why you must let Zelin help you. I don't want to lose you."

He chewed his lip, wondering how all this revelation had come about, when all he'd really wanted was to fall asleep. "I—I didn't say no, Sakhi."

"Does that mean. . . ?"

He shrugged. "I said I wasn't a fighter. I didn't say I wasn't willing to learn."

Her face lit, she squeezed his hand, and ran out the door in search of Zelin.

He didn't remember her return.

Interlude

A glimmer in the web. A child, frightened. Mother fed it, felt herself drawn along the delicate strand of perception, and realized a moment's disorientation as she recognized a special child. A part longed to extend arms to hold it, to make it not frightened. But she'd done that before, a part of her reminded, and lost the child altogether.

Another glimmer, reaching to her without awareness. Mother traced that glimmer to its source: the valley, near the progenitor. Very near.

Strange, that she should hear it, with her drastically curtailed awareness.

She opened her awareness further, expending more energy than was necessarily wise, in her weakened state. But curiosity had always outweighed wisdom, at least, since she'd discovered curiosity, and a mystery existed only to be solved.

As Mother brushed the glimmer with a mental feather, she recognized the glimmer for the new node, that strange conglomerate that had first appeared in the pattern a human generation ago, and then flared into its majority . . . sometime.

Recently.

A node that tasted, vaguely, of the past.

Not too long ago—some three hundred or so seasonal cycles, a part of her supplied—a human from beyond the land's edge had invaded Sucks-pond-water's sphere of awareness and had taken control of Sucks-pond-water's source. Mother had never imagined such a thing was possible, though she'd subsequently learned of other sources similarly human-confined, blasphemous as the notion was.

Initially, she'd been amused: the old miser chained, his growth contained, halted. And in the following years, as Mother's siblings' sources were similarly confined, Mother grew more than amused, Mother grew ecstatic, deliriously, orgasmically fulfilled as more earthly essence than she'd imagined could exist in all the world flooded to her source: essence to strengthen her web, for her to grow, for her offspring to grow and bud sources of their own.

Her consciousness had likewise expanded.

Following connections through source after source, Mother had learned the shape of the world web. She'd sensed others like herself, distant kin, but with a paltry sense of self, and even less curiosity for their world. It was a trail that inevitably brought her back to her own world-cave.

And from her humans, she learned what had occurred to Sucks-pond-water, and she'd learned to fear. She'd rapidly deduced it was only a matter of time before the valley humans came to *her* mountain to contain *her* source. Capping her node, they called it.

Ugly sounds for an ugly deed.

Just as ugly was the destruction of *her* humans. The invaders brought new ways, ways that made outcasts of her chosen ones, her darling dancers, and drove many of them away, across the mountains and into the inadequate care of her torpid kin.

Mother had put all her energy then into strengthening her node, determined to match Sucks-pond-water's potential. Only then could she break free of her progenitor. Only then could she keep the humans from capping her node.

The ley shimmered, disgust and dismay rippling in uncertain hues about her.

She'd failed. Her final buds had been mere suggestions, runners tracing through the mountain's stone, barely beginning to crystallize on their far ends when the creature that controlled the progenitor in the valley had come to Mother's mountain. Together with its ringmaster horde, those humans who controlled Mother's vacuous siblings, the creature had forced Mother to capitulate, had forced the energies flowing through her into directions of its choosing.

Temporarily.

Had reduced Mother's world awareness to the narrow confines of the immediate web, blinding her to the universe.

Temporarily.

Put a human fool in charge of her.

Temporarily.

For Mother had learned to plan. Mother had set a pattern in motion twenty human years ago that would see fruition.

Someday.

Mother had time. Humans thought in terms of seasonal cycles, Mother in terms of worldly cycles, and twenty years was nothing, less than nothing.

Except where it concerned those humans Mother had taken to her bosom. Those children Mother had nourished for their own sakes and her own purposes. For them, for their lives and the love she bore them, Mother might find herself moved to act, even past exhaustion's lethargy.

Exhaustion. That was the most boring aspect of her current situation.

For one accustomed to walking the surface, for one accustomed to basking in the adulation of her humans, it was a lonely time. All of Mother's children had deserted her, following their paths to wherever fate and the ley had chosen, forgetting their Mother, uncaring that she grew thin, that her glow faded.

She had given all she had to protect her humans, to set them on the path of enlightened understanding of the cosmos, and now she must rest, rejuvenate in the radiant pools beneath her mountain peak.

Without one single chicken to ease the gurgle in her belly.

SECTION THREE

Chapter One

It had been three days since he'd been pulled from the Crypt and brought in secrecy to Rhomandi House. Three days, and he'd already been subpoenaed, resubpoenaed, and served with a contempt fine for failure to appear before the Rhomatum Council Conduct Committee.

Another, similar procedure was in progress for the syndicate.

Mikhyel set the contempt papers back on the tray, and reached for the glass of chilled fruit juice.

"Why wasn't I told?"

Another stroke of the brush through his hair, and Raulind answered:

"You were sleeping."

Difficult to argue with facts. Toast. And butter. Then: "Where are my brothers?"

He'd long since grown accustomed to the fact that Raulind always seemed to know such things.

"Master Nikaenor has gone to the stables, sir. Master Deymorin has taken the lady Kiyrstin to the market. It appears she requires, ah, *things* to prepare for her part in today's inquiry."

"*Her* part?"

"It appears that she has been summoned to appear as well."

The image of Kiyrstine romGaretti standing before the council in *his* breeches and *his* shirt, with her red hair flying wildly about her head flashed through his mind, and suddenly breakfast lost all appeal. Mikhyel pushed the tray aside and sat upright in the grooming chair, pulling his hair free of Raulind's fingers.

"Sir!" Raulind admonished.

"I'm sorry." He set a contrite hand to his valet's shoulder as he passed, a concession to an old friend's feelings that

nearly gave Raulind a far more onerous task than re-
working his braid.

When his stomach had ceased turning itself inside out,
Raulind was beside him with a cool cloth and supporting
hands. And when he was back on the grooming couch, with
that cool cloth on his forehead, and a heated bathsheet
draped over the rest of him, Raulind disappeared. Off to
his own quarters, Mikhyel supposed, to brew the stomach-
settling concoction the secret of which only Raulind knew.

He had explained everything to Raulind, in those rare
few hours that he'd surfaced from the depths of exhausted
sleep. Nikki's wedding, Anheliaa, and the Boreton
Firestorm . . . he'd explained everything he could remember. Raulind had accepted his story with typical serenity,
up to and including his implausible mental link with his
brothers, not because Raulind was a gullible fool, but because Raulind had never, in all their years together, questioned Mikhyel's veracity.

But then, Mikhyel would never consider lying to Raulind.

Raulind's matter-of-fact attitude, coupled with his steam-
ing potion of stimulating herbs, helped Mikhyel settle his
nerves and his stomach enough, at least, to sample the
breakfast Raulind had personally supervised, and to hold
it down while Raulind worked his hair loose, combed, and
rebraided it.

And all the while, the summons lurked on the table beside him. The Council would want answers. They'd want to
know where he'd been and what had happened to the web,
and how soon it would be fully functional.

And he had no answers for them. Neither did Lidye.
According to Deymorin, Lidye had not been able to probe
the web, because Anheliaa was still in control.

Or so she'd told Deymorin three days ago.

"Has there been any change?" he asked.

Raulind, who had been able to follow his thoughts for
years, even without brotherly links answered, "Your aunt
has not yet roused from her coma. Your brother Deymorin
was lamenting the fact this morning. He said he wished she
would make up her mind and either wake up and tell them
what was wrong with the web, or die."

He was almost tempted to ask how Raulind had come
to have that particular piece of information, but he held

his tongue. The servants' information web was too valuable to tamper with.

But Deymorin was right. Even comatose, Anheliaa would have located the force that was destroying her web. If she were, indeed, comatose.

Despite Deymorin's efforts to protect his sleep, nightmares of that malignancy seeping from the shadows to engulf his hand had haunted his subconscious mind. Ever since that moment three days ago, when Deymorin's anger had flared against the encroaching shadow and shriveled it into nothingness, Mikhyel had questioned his own perceptions.

Deymorin had gone on to the Tower that night, after leaving him in Raulind's hands. Deymorin had seen Anheliaa's comatose body, and had shared that image with Mikhyel by that means Mikhyel couldn't disbelieve.

And yet . . .

"I'm going to visit the Tower," Mikhyel announced, when the pin that held his hair had been secured.

"Do you think that wise, sir?" Raulind asked, as he was inclined to do when Mikhyel contemplated something stupid.

"At the moment, Raul, my brothers are nothing more than mist in my mind. I think, if it is ever to be safe, now is the time to see her for myself."

"And seeing Anheliaa for yourself is, of course, of paramount importance."

He met Raul's eyes in the mirror.

"Yes, Raul, it is."

"Very good, sir. I'll lay out your clothes."

There were guards outside his door. Guards dressed in Fericci green and gold.

Raulind had explained, and Deymorin had confirmed that the guards were precautionary only. That they were Lidye's means of monitoring their activities until she was assured of their common goals.

Which sounded to him like amazing good sense from someone he'd thought lacking in the most basic instincts. He wondered if it were her idea . . . or Tarim's.

But then, for all they were Tarim's men, Tarim himself was housed elsewhere on the Hill. As Sironi was. And Lidye *was* the woman who, rather than openly declare Anheliaa incapacitated and herself in charge, had had the uncommon sense to pretend to *be* Anheliaa, as a stop-gap, solidarity measure.

For all Nikki had sought to excuse his wife's subterfuge to him, Mikhyel could appreciate the motives for the deception, particularly considering the fact she'd readily admitted her counterfeit to Nikki at the first challenge.

Understanding did not, however, mean he considered the present situation acceptable. He would not be a prisoner within his home—or *any*where within *his* City, for that matter.

At the Tower lift, Lidye's green and golds stepped aside and Anheliaa's guard, in somber black and with far more ominous expression, replaced them at his back.

Over the years, he'd occasionally wondered if Anheliaa had purposefully chosen guards who were a head taller than he. He'd further wondered, if it *was* a conscious choice, if she'd thought to intimidate him, or to teach him not to care.

One never knew. Not with Anheliaa.

Inside the lift, Anheliaa's presence surrounded him like the folds of a too-heavy cloak. While it wasn't the black malignancy of three days ago, her ambition and purpose filled the air like the heavy perfume she favored.

Likely Raulind was correct, and he was a fool to come here. But sometimes a man had to be a fool, if he was going to live with himself. He was awake now, and clear-headed, and as he would not live surrounded by Lidye's guards, neither would he live in terror of what dwelt overhead.

The lift reached the top floor, the ringchamber itself, and the guard beside the controls brought it to a smooth halt. The grillwork slid back, and he stepped out into the chamber.

Anheliaa lay still as death on a linen-draped bier. Light from the Tower's beveled-glass windows cast bands of unnatural color across the unnatural color of her withered, painted features. Flickering shadows from the rotating rings that dominated the room added an equally unnatural sense of movement to her massive form.

She was grotesque.

Mikhyel wondered why, in all the years of forced association he'd never realized that simple fact. Perhaps, in fairness to his own perceptions, he was only now—as an adult and seeing her for the first time with her autocratic personality laid low—able to acknowledge that which he'd always known.

He stood beside her, knowing better than to touch, feeling no inclination to do so. That it was the rings keeping her alive was beyond doubt. Anheliaa neither ate nor drank, yet her physical status had remained unchanged ever since Lidye had reset the rings.

Twice before, following the capping of Khoratum and again only a few weeks ago, Anheliaa had used the rings to regenerate a nearly destroyed body. Mikhyel hadn't seen her those other times, but Anheliaa's own physician, Diorak, insisted the same process was in operation this time. And yet, her comatose state had never lasted so long, the draw on the ley had never been so great, and even Diorak was beginning to lose hope of her recovery.

Hope. He supposed the possibility existed that someone other than Diorak hoped she would survive. Likely Brolucci, captain of Anheliaa's guard, hoped she would. If he did not, he was a fool.

Deymorin had met with Brolucci to challenge their incarceration. The captain insisted he had been operating under a standing order from Anheliaa, and as long as Anheliaa lived, Brolucci was immune to investigation and prosecution. Once Anheliaa died, unless Lidye took him as her captain, his immunity ended.

And Lidye assured them all she had no interest in keeping Brolucci in any sense.

If Mikhyel were the captain, he'd be sincerely hopeful of Anheliaa's recovery.

Himself—Mikhyel dunMheric would believe Anheliaa's damnable existence was over when he set her adrift in the Rhomandi hypogeum, and not a moment sooner.

Perhaps not even then.

A hand touched his arm for attention. Its partner held a mug of fresh tea before him. He accepted the tea and for the first time met the gaze of Anheliaa's wraithlike personal servant. Mirym pressed his hand—silently, as she did everything without words—then returned to her needlework stand on the far side of Anheliaa's bed.

Mikhyel cradled the tea in both hands, hardly knowing

where to look. His eyes caught Mirym's and she smiled easily, as if it were just one more morning visit to Anheliaa's ringchamber.

They'd seen one another often enough since Mirym came to live and work in Rhomandi House almost three years ago. He'd come to the ringchamber every morning, and every morning, she'd be at Anheliaa's side. Silent. Attentive. But their relationship now was far different than it had been the last time Mikhyel had paid his regular morning visit.

While Mikhyel's memories of the days surrounding the firestorm were hazy, the handful of hours surrounding Nikki's wedding were ruthlessly clear, and those memories involved this young woman in ways necessarily awkward to them both now.

When the rings had chosen Lidye dunTarim of Shatum Node as the appropriate spouse for Nikki, Anheliaa claimed they'd chosen, not their new master, but a stopgap, that Lidye was primarily an incubator for the next true master. Anheliaa had refused to leave the web in the hands of a second-rank spinner, and with typical Rhomandi arrogance, she had refused to believe that anyone outside the Rhomandi line could be anything *but* second rank.

But Nikki had set the price of his marriage high: the rings' help in locating Deymorin, and leave to depart from Rhomatum the day following his marriage to find and rescue his brother. A quest from which, Anheliaa would have been forced to acknowledge the possibility, Nikki might never have returned—a circumstance that would have put her Darian child's inception at some risk.

That night, when Nikki's passion for his new bride proved less than adequate, Anheliaa had stepped in with her mind-bending rings to resolve the biological deficit. Her efforts had proven rather more effective than even she had supposed. Through Nikki's erstwhile tentative connection with his brothers, Anheliaa had driven them all into a breeding madness. Nikki and Lidye, by agreement, Deymorin and Kiyrstin, who had been nearly to that point already, himself and . . . Mirym, whose only crime had been attending *his* sickbed at the wrong moment.

Mirym's reproachless presence recalled that night with brutal clarity. Nikki's cry of protest ringing in his mind, the sense of easing into Nikki's skin as he would into a too-

hot bath. There'd been a startled moment as he realized
the sheer unadulterated power of his younger brother's
body, the vigor, and the intoxicating rush of energy the like
of which he'd never before experienced.

And the utterly foreign sensation of a body primed and
ready for sex.

Sensations that had surged anew as Nikki looked out
through *his* eyes and saw sweet, gentle Mirym . . . framed
by Mikhyel's black-edged sheets.

And then—

Mikhyel frowned, disgusted, and gulped tea that burned
his mouth with satisfying real pain. He did not envy his
brother his new wife. What *he* had seen in Lidye's face that
night had been all too reminiscent of Anheliaa at her worst.

And when Anheliaa was finally gone from his life, he
wanted her *gone* . . . forever.

To his knowledge, Mirym had revealed nothing to anyone about that night. Certainly she hadn't made the allegations against him the situation would justify. She seemed
to be inclined to forget his behavior that night.

But for all the ease she radiated in his presence now, he
couldn't forget. Whatever outside force had prompted his
actions, those actions had been beyond all bounds of propriety and human decency, and he couldn't shake the feeling that he *should* have been capable of stopping himself.

Worst of all, he couldn't throw off the sense that he'd
been a performer for the grotesque lump lying silent as
death before him. He'd seen the images Anheliaa had been
able to pull up on the central viewing sphere of the Rhomatum Rings; he didn't appreciate being included in her reper-
toire of dupes.

And he had to wonder what was going on within her
mind now, as her body lay immobile. Did she even need
the viewing sphere? Or could she send her mind out along
the lines? Could she see the weaknesses? Could she look
into his bedroom, or Deymorin's or some poor Councillor
who had dared deny her proper homage?

He clenched his hands on the mug and sipped again,
schooling the bitterness and the anger.

Difficult to say what he'd hoped to find, here in the
Tower. Perhaps a replaying of the night of his arrival, ending, perhaps, with Anheliaa's melodramatic death, and an
end to the suspense. Or perhaps he'd hoped she would

rouse while he stood here beside her, to return his world, at least in that sense, to what it had been all his life.

Pure logic advised it would be best if she rallied long enough and well enough to make a smooth generational transition within the Tower. But such a transition would never take place. Anheliaa would never admit she was dying, for all she'd bemoaned her lack of an heir daily for the past twenty years. Anheliaa would never make those final adjustments, never reveal those final secrets to the person who could then replace her.

Even so, a part of him wished, desperately, that she would rouse enough at least to explain what was happening in the web. Was it the Khoratum line alone? Was the node itself failing? Was it Khoratum at all? The web was suffering, depleted and unreliable, and the Council wanted ans—

{Don't . . . worry . . .}

A vague awareness: a light touch on his arm.

{. . . all . . . right . . .}

{She's *dying!*} He answered reflexively, then jolted back to the present. A present where his brothers were far away, the faintest shadow in his mind. Here in the Tower, there were only the guards . . . and Anheliaa's supposedly mute servant.

Mirym was at his side again, her hand on his arm. He stepped away from her, confused, uncertain whether that voice in his head had been real or imagined. Mirym pursued him, reached again, this time for his bare hand, lacing their fingers, palm to palm.

{You . . . hear . . . don't you?}

He hesitated, sensing unknown hazard in any admission to a skill he'd never imagined a month ago, and with which this young woman seemed uncomfortably familiar.

{Some.}

Amusement came through, and a hint of condescension.

{Thought so. I'll think more slowly. —Better?}

He didn't answer, aware of the guards staring at them; guards who might report to Lidye the strange behavior of Mikhyel dunMheric with Anheliaa's servant. Wondering on a different score if Nikki still coveted tender feelings for Mirym, and whether Lidye might not use the guards' reports to rouse Nikki against him.

And confounding it all, the memory of this young woman

lying warm and pleasant in his arms, in the aftermath of Nikki's wedding.

More silent amusement, that contrasted sharply with an outward appearance that now involved trembling lips, and incipient tears. It was a contradiction which endorsed his own limited experience with women in general, but which jarred, somehow, with his experience of this woman in particular.

{Can't you see I'm in terrible need of comfort, you silly man?}

Without conscious thought, he wrapped his arm around her shoulders and murmured encouraging words to her.

{Better.} A touch of surprise, and an image of himself: a proud, distant man, seated in this chamber, facing Anheliaa's atrocities with cool detachment.

Not the sort a woman would naturally turn to, he supposed.

{How little you know of women, Mikhyel dunMheric. Remember, I knew her as well. Of course, she's dying. But the rings will not go down with her. Lidye, the monitors below, I—}

Her thought-words garbled. Conveniently so, he thought, behind what he hoped was an equally effective mental shield.

{You?} He pressed the issue. {Can *you* control the rings, Mirym?}

{I make no such claims, but I'm not indifferent to what occurs within this chamber. I know that at the moment Anheliaa is drawing heavily on the ley, attempting a resurrection. It's a battle she's losing. Soon, she'll be gone and the web will be free to rejuvenate itself rather than Anheliaa dunMoren.}

Then perhaps they should take Anheliaa out of here. If Mirym was correct—

{Safest to leave her for now. In her desperation, she might destroy the rings, possibly even the source itself. Let her linger as she can. She *will* go. Time is on our side.}

He found her response to thoughts he had believed secure disturbing, and he wondered how much else she was picking up.

Silent laughter told him nothing.

Time is on our side. . . . But how long did they really

have? The Syndicate was angry, restless. Dissolution
threatened.

{Time,} her thought responded. {We are obsessed with it,
aren't we? A day, a year, a decade . . . those are moments
in the life of the ley. It could take time, a long time, for
the web to rejuvenate. We must be patient.}

Source? Rejuvenate?

The Syndicate's mood was suddenly far from his mind as
out of this formerly silent woman's mind came a seemingly
vast knowledge, confidently expressed in terms he'd never
heard, not from Anheliaa, not from the experts who studied
the ley and its patterns and behavior.

{How do you know?} he sent the question deliberately,
along with his own view of her: small, pale-haired servant
to Anheliaa, always with her needlework, ever silent. In all,
the very model of a relation to one of the house servants
come to Rhomandi House to better her situation, perhaps
to find a husband among the other well-paid servants.

{*Husband?*} Indignation and an image so overwhelmingly
powerful, so beautiful, so enthralling, that for a moment,
the ringchamber vanished altogether from his senses. Leythium crystal: draped in shimmering, shifting curtains, hanging in immense, incandescent chandeliers; pools of liquid
leythium, more viscous than water, oozing, bubbling, growing and shifting into towering organic shapes.

And color. In places, soft, subtle shades of white, in others, a brilliance so pure, there was no human term, no
earthly paradigm to describe it. The image faded, leaving
him with eyes tearing for want of blinking.

Beyond that tear-distortion, Mirym was staring at him.
{What need *I* of a husband?}

And with such an imagination, perhaps—

{*Imagination?* How *dare* you, Mikhyel dunMheric? I
know because I've *seen* them!} She jerked away.

But how could he believe her? How could she know
things no one else . . .

Unless Anheliaa knew. Unless Anheliaa, with some hidden agenda had gone *wherever* that care was, and taken
Mirym with her.

There were dangerous gaps in his knowledge of this
young woman, who had so quietly infiltrated his home. Anheliaa had brought her in as she had all the other Tower
servants before her. He'd believed her enforced silence was

part of Anheliaa's satisfaction with her. Now, he had to wonder what other uses Anheliaa had had for her.

Nikki and Mirym. The haze dissipated from certain areas of his memory, and he recalled watching them once and marveling at Nikki's ability to interpret the mute girl's hand gestures. That memory in turn led him to wonder if Nikki's entrancement with Mirym was, in part, her ability to communicate this way.

And on the heels of those memories came details of another night in the Tower. A night he'd awakened, filled with nightmares, to be given a draught—a potent sleeping potion—from this girl's hands. When next he'd awakened, it had been for the sole purpose of being dragged, still groggy from that drug, to Anheliaa's ringchamber for questioning.

And from there—his mind veered away from the lightning and the flame.

{I did what I had to do,} came her silent answer, with the force to carry it between them without benefit of touch. {For my own safety, and that of *my* family. *My* node. *My* source.}

He held out his left hand, and when she returned hers to it, covered it with his right and asked, {Who are you?}

{Mirym.}

{Where are you from? What node?}

{Does it matter?}

{*Ye—*}

Suddenly, a hand clutched his wrist. A hand that was *not* Mirym's. Enameled nails, filed to talons, cut deep. A lifetime of training kept him from flinching, kept his eyes directed at Mirym even as he felt the blood seep along the palm of his hand.

{*Say you love me, boy!*}

It was a familiar hiss that echoed in his mind, though Anheliaa had never before spoken to him thus. He closed his eyes on a world that tended to swim.

{*Say it!*} The thorny grip tightened, and his view of the chamber shifted, taking in himself, Mirym, and Anheliaa . . . as if the image came from the rings.

{I . . . love you, Aunt Liaa.}

{*And I'll miss you, Aunt Liaa.*}

{The web!} he battled his thoughts into coherency, recall-

ing the upcoming meeting, the desperate need to know:
{Anheliaa, what's wrong with it? Show—}

{*Say it!*}

The thought drove into his mind with the strength to
stagger him. He forced his eyes open, insisted they see the
room as he did, not as Anheliaa did. His jaw ached around
clenched teeth. He wanted to damn her to the eighteen,
lightning-blasted hells above Rhomatum, wanted to put his
hands around her neck and squeeze what life remained into
whatever void of hereafter she endorsed, and take his
chances with the future.

Laughter in his mind, shrill and mocking. But desperate
as well. Pleading. It was an old demand, one she'd first
pressed upon him almost fourteen years ago, when he'd
been brought to her following Mheric's death. Anheliaa
needed to be remembered, not in records and in history
books, but in living minds. Anheliaa wanted to be certain
that even when she was gone, she'd control him.

Mirym's eyes gleamed across at him, deep with understanding, but without pity. *I did what I had to do . . .*

And he knew then he dared not give way to that dark
fury seething within him. That, as he had in the past, for
the sake of Rhomatum and the life and responsibilities that
were his by accident of birth, he must bend.

{I'll . . . miss you, Aunt Liaa.}

Triumph flared, then dissolved into indifference.

{Anheliaa! The web . . .}

The talons released his wrist, and Anheliaa's hand
dropped the short distance to her side, as motionless as
before. Humiliated, cheated, fighting to hide his revulsion,
he stepped away, avoiding the guards' looks, avoiding
Mirym's.

But as the lift carried him downward, a lingering image,
a scent of roses in the morning sun permeated his being.
Roses with a gentle hint of raspberries. And a touch, clean
and honest, surrounded his congealing wrist and took away
the sting.

Chapter Two

"Inhale," Zelin ordered. And Thyerri drew a deep breath.

"I said inhale, not sniff!"

A sharp blow between his shoulders made Thyerri gasp.

"Better. Now hold it."

Fingers probed his ribs, gut, and back, seeking reaction, seeking weakness, but the aches were gone.

Mostly.

Thyerri flinched as those strong fingers dug deeper.

But he didn't exhale.

And Zelin laughed.

"You'll do, lad," the old man said and told him he could breathe now, if he wanted, and Thyerri did want.

Badly.

While he gasped after breath, Zelin asked about legs, arms, head, and any other residual aches, but there was nothing Thyerri would even consider mentioning.

Zelin gave a brief nod, then jerked his head toward Bharlori's back door, where the afternoon sun's slanting rays warmed the wooden steps.

When they'd settled, Zelin turned to him and asked, "Well, boy, what is it you want?"

"Want? I . . . don't know. I *don't* want to get pounded into the ground again."

"Do you simply want to escape?"

He shrugged, uncertain. Put that way, it sounded cowardly.

"To stop your attackers?"

He nodded emphatically.

"To punish your attackers?"

He chewed his lip. He didn't really want to hurt anyone.

"Kill?"

"*No!*"

Even the thought revolted him.

Zelin stared at him, eyes narrowed, then jerked his head in a quick nod and pushed himself to his feet.

"Stand up," he commanded. "And face me."

Standing opposite him, Zelin was, Thyerri realized, shorter than he expected: of a size with Thyerri, but broad. The sort of body that challenged the perceptive line between dangerous and merely immovable.

Neither was he as old as Thyerri once assumed. Silver-gray hair and lined face notwithstanding, he moved with the grace and lightness of foot of a man in his prime.

Zelin lunged toward him; Thyerri dodged, startled.

A sudden whirl, and a foot flew outward from Zelin's body like a bucket on a rope.

Thyerri leaped backward.

Another pause. Then he commanded, "Face me, boy, and shadow my moves."

It was like a dance exercise. Don't think. Follow. Let the body sense the shifts of weight, the follow-through that must occur. A sweep of the arm, fall back. Lunge forward, ease left. Rock heel to ball to toe—and thrust. Toes catch the weight, ankle absorbs the momentum. And thrust again.

Side, side, forward, fall back. Turn and thrust, turn and hop . . . and turn and turn and turn and drop.

Thyerri, crouched on the ground panting, laughed.

Zelin, three turns back, frowned.

Possibly, he shouldn't have added his embellishments.

Zelin pointed at the ground in front of him. Feeling the heat rise in his face, Thyerri shuffled silently back and stood facing the older man.

"This time," Zelin said, "countermove."

The patterns changed, and changed again, growing faster, more complex. Shadow again, and counter. Shadow. Counter.

And Zelin's frown never eased. Finally Zelin barked, "Enough!" and dropped to the step, red-faced and sweating.

Thyerri stood, panting, hands braced on his knees. The moment his breathing eased, he began stretching, light moves, to keep his muscles from stiffening.

And all the while, Zelin simply watched him. Until—

"Give me your hand, boy," Zelin commanded.

Thyerri hesitated, then shrugged and obeyed. Zelin turned his hand over, examining the calluses, the tiny, white

scars that were his only visible legacy, constant reminders
of the dance rings' honed edges.

"You were a dancer."

Thyerri shrugged.

Zelin set their hands palm to palm. Like the rest of him,
Zelin's hand was short and broad. Thyerri's was slender,
with long, supple fingers.

Zelin stood, and gripped Thyerri's chin, holding his face
for a closer examination.

"Raise your arms to the side," he said, in a tone not to
be questioned, and he extended his strange examination to
Thyerri's torso, running his hands down ribs, waist and hips.
Abruptly he said, "That will be all for today."

"But—"

"I must think on what I've seen!" Zelin said sharply.
"Not all students can be trained alike, ex-dancer of Khoratum. You move differently. Strangely. I must think how to
direct that strange motion. Now leave me to think!"

Different. Strange.

Thunder rumbled to the west, and Thyerri glanced
toward distant, darkening skies, wondering what he was
going to tell Sakhithe when she asked how the lesson went.

Another rumble, a flash of distant lightning, a pause, and
another rumble.

Because she *would* ask, as surely as they would have rain
before nightfall.

§   §   §

Lightning flashed to the north and west. There'd be another storm before the day was out. But Lidye insisted
the storms were diminishing in both ferocity and number,
evidence, Mikhyel dunMheric sincerely hoped, that the web
was growing more stable, if not stronger.

Outside the window of the Rhomandi floater-coach, the
buildings of Tower Hill passed in antique splendor. Marble
statuary, stately columns, rose gardens, and fountains . . .
it was a splendor for which Mikhyel dunMheric had an
insatiable appetite.

Over the years, Anheliaa had reminded him daily that
his family owed the City nothing, that Rhomatum would
not exist without Darius and his descendants, and as long

as the rings kept spinning, the Rhomandi had fulfilled their side of the eternal bargain.

She had reminded him, but she'd never convinced him. A Rhomandi had led the exodus out of Mauritum three hundred years ago. Those believers and their descendants had looked to a Rhomandi ever since for leadership.

Mikhyel had learned, long before his life with Anheliaa, the *true* value of Darius' modern descendants, and had decided that neither his father's cavalier ways nor his aunt's ruthless attitudes would be his own. His duty, his life, *did* belong to the City and the web.

And he was content with that arrangement.

He had no wife, no children, and had never felt the lack. He'd been engaged as a child to Nethaalye dunErrif of Giephaetum Node. While he'd had no objection to the match, neither had he felt compelled to pursue it, as any normal man might. And now, Nethalye had retreated to Giephaetum with her father, and would, he fully expected, declare their engagement off.

And his only reaction to that realization was a vague regret for the loss of her friendship. At times he wondered if he was unnatural in some way, and then he wondered, if he were normal, like Deymorin or Nikki, who would fill out the City's paperwork?

Another flash of lightning. The floater-coach simultaneously lurched and swayed. Coincidence, not cause and effect. He knew from previous experience that the track was flawed at that point, a less-than-perfect connection he'd reported to City maintenance almost two months ago.

Normally, such routine maintenance would have been repaired within a week. Of course, when that section worked free and sent a floater careening out of control about the Hill, someone might no longer consider it a minor problem.

Priorities. Within the next handful of days, all Rhomatum's priorities would have to be reexamined, as would those of all the Node Cities. Mikhyel wondered how many of those now in power would survive the upcoming changes, changes that must come if *any* of them were to survive.

His single greatest obstacle to everything he needed to accomplish was, as it had always been, Anheliaa. Anheliaa and whatever private deals she might have made over the years to secure private as well as Syndicate support for her obsessions.

The most recent of those contracts and the one of most personal note, was Nikki's marriage contract. Mikhyel had wondered, as he'd structured that contract according to Anheliaa's specifications, why his aunt had bothered choosing women from other nodes for her nephews' spouses. After declaring the marriage would solidify faltering Syndicate relations, she'd turned about and insisted on including the precise clauses guaranteed to demean the gesture.

By that contract, *Lidye* could never negate the contract, and any offspring were exclusively Rhomandi. Lidye's family—and Shatum—relinquished any claim to the children, and to their inheritance.

Which agreement had made Mikhyel wonder, with the future of the Syndicate on the line, what Anheliaa might have promised Shatum in private in order to secure those clauses, and to wonder what might be the unwritten subtext in a marriage contract made, not with Lidye, not with Lidye's father, but with the entire Shatumin Guild Alliance.

In the days leading up to Nikki's wedding, Mikhyel had looked for evidence of such agreements, but even as he searched drawers and archives alike for notes or secret contracts, he'd known the effort wasted. He'd known Anheliaa to sign such agreements, if signing was the price of her desire, but Anheliaa would never keep a copy.

If Anheliaa decided not to honor her side of a bargain, she would require the other party to come to her to collect the debt. Few had ever had the courage to face her again, let alone challenge her. But once she was gone, once a weaker master ruled in Rhomatum Tower, those past agreements might rise to haunt them all.

Mikhyel had become all too familiar with Anheliaa's tactics over the years. Since Mheric had died, Mikhyel had spent every morning and two full days out of every week at Anheliaa's side, first as her companion, and then, when he'd grown past childhood, as her lawyer and adviser.

In adult retrospect, he recognized his presence in the Tower as one more ploy in the game of a master manipulator. By impressing on him from childhood the fruitlessness of opposing her, she'd endeavored to create the perfect tool, her voice in all matters outside Rhomandi House. As an adult, Mikhyel could resent that control of his mind and body, but as a Rhomandi, he could understand the urgency Anheliaa had felt to create such a tool.

Because Anheliaa was trapped inside the Tower, partially by choice, but physically as well. Some ringmasters controlled the rings without personal repercussion; Anheliaa was not one of those lucky individuals. She'd entered the Tower for the first time as a child, and by the time she had taken control of the Tower at seventeen, the rings had already begun to take a massive toll on her health.

By the time she'd capped Khoratum, her arthritis-riddled body had had to be carried all the way to the mountain node, and the capping itself had completed the crippling of her body.

Confined to mobility chairs and Rhomandi House, Anheliaa had desperately needed someone to present and push through her Tower-enhancing policies. And since, in Anheliaa's philosophy, the sole purpose of the Rhomandi Family *was* the enhancement of the Rhomatum Rings, she'd undoubtedly felt fully justified in all her actions.

As he had matured, Mikhyel had supplied that voice. His presence, and his logic had given her plans a legitimacy they otherwise lacked. And if any Councillor or Syndic or influential citizen had argued with him, balked, she'd have that opposition brought to her ringchamber for reasoning.

Rather as she'd had criminals brought to her.

And criminal and Councillor alike had been given similar options.

Her only witness to all these confrontations had been Mikhyel. He'd been there, he eventually realized, to act as judge and jury. *His* had been the authority to deem her acts justified. He'd never revealed what he'd seen, not to Deymorin, or anyone else, but he had argued with Anheliaa over the ethics of her "necessary experimentation".

Somehow, she'd invariably swayed his thinking.

He could see that dynamic now, with a perspective of time and distance and following whole days where his life was not dictated by Anheliaa dunMoren. And after a month of mental intervention on the part of his brothers' desires, he wondered whether his acquiescence to Anheliaa's demands might also have been part of her "experimentation," wondered whether any opinion he'd ever taken from the Tower had been his alone.

And yet even in the coldest of blood, he *could* understand her. He could comprehend the necessity governing everything Anheliaa had done throughout her long tenure as Rhomatum Ringmaster, including Nikki's marriage to a woman several years his senior.

The Rhomatum Web, completed at such great personal sacrifice on her part, was Anheliaa's legacy, the only child she'd ever have. Every project she had supported, every experiment she had made had been to enhance that legacy. Blackmail, physical threats, bribery—even Nikki's wedding night abomination—such tactics had simply been expedient means for protecting and nurturing that leythium-coated child.

Her child. As Rhomatum was his.

"Nearly there, sir." The pedaler's announcement came through the speaking tube.

Mikhyel acknowledged, then leaned forward to catch his first glimpse of the Pharmonelli Building, eager for the comfort of its stark, familiar walls, for the smell of ink that sometimes filtered up from the presses in the basement levels and mixed with the rose bouquets, the stronger scent of the stimulating *pacciimi* brew that kept busy clerks awake into the early hours of the morning. . . .

Ink, roses, *pacciimi* . . . perhaps it was just the scent of power that set Pharmonelli apart: those who had it, those who wanted it, and those who believed it resided beneath every rosebush. Pharmonelli housed the elite of both Syndicate and Council. Deals and decisions were made here.

The anchor caught and the coach touched down smoothly into a docking berth.

He was home.

Chapter Three

"Oh, come, Rags. Big fellow like you can do better than that."

Deymorin cursed under his breath, set his feet, and pulled. Hard. The strings snapped and Deymorin stumbled backward to come up against a dressing table.

Kiyrstin turned, disgust on her face.

"Oops," he said as he held up the two ends. "Sorry. I guess we should have accepted Lidye's offer of her lady's maid. Shall I send a message?"

"Only for another set of corset strings. You insisted you could manage, and you're going to manage." She slid into a chair before the mirrored dressing table and began studying the array of cosmetics they'd found in the market that morning. "Unless, of course, you want me to send a message to Madame Tirise."

"We got the girl out of Sparingate and settled her debts. Do I have to invite her to dinner as well?"

She shrugged and picked up the largest jar. "Seems to me she'd liven things up around here."

"I think we can leave Mistress Beauvina right where she is," Deymorin said firmly.

"If you say so, luvvie," Kiyrstin sighed heavily and began applying blue-green slime to her face.

Which meant he should probably start checking in the corners for Beauvina.

Deymorin pulled the bell cord to summon a footman, then leaned on the back of her chair and propped his chin on her head to stare at her increasingly blue-green image. "Charming."

He reached over her shoulder and stuck a cautious finger in the jar, raised the slime to his nose, and sniffed. Green eyes glared at his reflection.

A light chime announced a servant's arrival. Deymorin stuck the finger in his mouth and licked off the slime.

"Yum," he whispered and bit her ear—then dodged for the door.

The wide-eyed junior footman listened solemnly to Deymorin's request, straining all the while to catch a glimpse within the room. Deymorin made him repeat the message twice before he shooed the youngster on his way.

He supposed he should have insisted Kiyrstin use the room Lidye had had prepared for her instead of allowing her to take up residence in his suite, but Kiyrstin had been adamant. She hadn't risked Rhomatum only to be shut up and forgotten.

Besides (she'd argued) hadn't he promised her they were going to set the two greatest cities in the world to gossiping? How could they possibly manage that if they were sleeping in separate rooms?

So here she was and, truth to tell, here Deymorin wanted her to be, even if it meant he had to tie her damned corset strings and watch her perform arcane rituals man was not meant to witness.

He leaned again on the back of her chair, watching those rituals with a morbid fascination.

"What's it do?" he asked, when she'd sat, blue-faced and silent, for several minutes.

"Fades the freckles, so the man claimed."

"No!" He grabbed a cloth and began scrubbing at the slime.

She slapped his hand away and snatched the cloth.

"Take it off!" he cried indignantly, "I've an intimate acquaintance with each and every one of those specks!"

She laughed and dabbed at the slime. "Don't worry, it won't work. This stuff never does." She slid a finger over the exposed flesh. "It just prepares the skin."

Prepares it for what, he wondered, and frowned at the growing spot, pretending to count the freckles as they appeared. When an entire cheek had been reexposed, he leaned over and tested the skin's preparation with his lips.

"Mmmm . . ." She hummed, twisting to meet his kiss—

Leaving a slime trail across his face. He protested and grabbed a towel to rub it off, then splashed lemon-water into a glass and retreated to the bathing room to expectorate in private.

When he returned, she was back at her ritual.

At this rate, to use the entire array of pots and sticks and brushes would consume the balance of the afternoon and well into evening. But he trusted Kiyrstin to know what she was doing. She knew the schedule. Besides, the private Rhomandi House floater-coach was outside, waiting to take them to this Conduct Committee meeting.

"How did the widows take the news?" she asked, and he paused halfway across the room.

"How did you know?"

"Magic, Rags."

He forced a smile, and clasped the hand she stretched toward him.

"I'd have gone with you, if you'd asked, Deymio."

"I know you would have, but it was my duty."

"Actually, it was Nikki's. They were his men. They died while under his command."

"They were lost on my behalf, Shepherdess. I offered."

"*He* should have insisted. He should at least have been with you."

"Perhaps. But I can't blame Nikki. He's been distracted."

"By his wife."

"Even more reason to forgive. She's not at all what he feared, and she's entranced him with her talk of Darius' wife and Tamshirin. You know how he feels about the Tamshi. He'd love to be out in the mountains right now searching for that Tamshi creature that saved Mikhyel."

"We can't always have what we want."

"I know that. So does Nikki. But it's hard to see it that way when one's lifelong fantasies are involved."

"Your brother *lives* in a fantasy world. Someday, Big Brother Deymorin, reality is going to rise up and bite him on the ass."

"It already has."

"Not hard enough!"

He frowned. "He *did* go with me. At least to see Ben's widow."

"How noble of him. Ben died saving his hide."

"And Nikki expressed his sorrow and gratitude very eloquently."

"I should hope so. He's a poet, or so he claims."

"Kiyrstin!"

"And how much of that eloquence did he *really* mean?"

"Every word."

She turned back to the mirror, refusing to meet his eyes. "Lie to me, Deymorin. Just don't lie to yourself."

"I'm not. He *was* sorry. *Is*. He liked Ben a great deal."

Kiyrstin met and held his eyes in the mirror, and it was Deymorin who turned away. He couldn't expect Kiyrstin to understand Nikki to the depth he did, not even if he explained all that had happened in those hours in prison. He'd pressed Nikki's self-confidence too much then. He couldn't press on this issue. At least for now. For everyone's sake.

Arms slipped around his waist, and her head rested between his shoulder blades. "I'm sure he did, Deymorin. And I like Nikki, for all he's convinced otherwise. But you're protecting him from the consequences of his decisions, and that's not good. More than that, it's not fair to Nikki. He *did* nothing wrong. His decisions weren't foolhardy or wrong. But bad things happened. He needs to face that. Accept it as one of the unhappy consequences of leading men into unknown circumstances."

He turned in the circle of her arms, and brushed her cheek with his thumb. She'd finished removing the blue-green slime and the skin *was* marvelously smooth and supple.

"You're protecting him, Deymorin, from growing into the man he can be."

"Is that you talking?" he asked. "Or Mikhyel?"

"Does it matter where the truth comes from?"

He chuckled, and pushed her back into her chair. "Keep going, woman. We're running out of time."

She patted his hand as it rested on her shoulder, and turned to the next pot.

More slime, this time one that matched her lightly tanned, befreckled, skin. It was as if she were preparing for a stage performance.

He supposed, in a sense, she was.

"Why is it," he asked, "that *you're* the one facing those old fools and *I'm* the one whose knees are shaking?"

"Obviously, it's your proximity to my distracting self that has your knees in jeopardy. I find this quite familiar. We had our own old fools in Mauritum, you know. Only ours were all men." She picked up a tiny sponge and smoothed an irregular patch of color. "Besides, your brother has the hard job."

"I wish I'd had a chance to talk with him before he left for his office. Last night, he could barely sit upright."

"Raul says he's fine, just catching up on a lifetime of too little sleep. Raul is quite pleased. Besides, Mikhyel's no fool. He wouldn't have gone this morning if he wasn't prepared."

He picked bits of hair off her shoulders, and brushed his fingers across the bare skin. "You like him, don't you, Shepherdess?"

"Raulind?" Her reflected eyes glittered at him. "Of course."

"Kiyrstin . . ."

"Why do you ask? Worried? Shouldn't be. I already turned down his offer to be second to Nethaalye."

"What?"

She chuckled. "Seriously? How can I not? Don't you?"

He didn't answer. She twisted in her chair to face him.

"Deymorin?"

"I don't know how I feel. Except worried. He's . . . not the man he used to be."

"Are any of you? Sweet Maurii, JD, after what you've been through—"

"You don't understand. In all due respect, you *can't* understand."

"Because I don't hear his thoughts the way you do?"

"Because you're a *woman.*"

"I see."

Fraught with innuendo, those two words. But she didn't know . . . *couldn't.*

"Tell me, JD, has this anything to do with the Crypt?"

He shrugged, avoiding her eyes.

"Come, man, *talk* to me. Ever since you brought Mikhyel out, something's been festering. What happened down there?"

"I don't know."

"Then why—"

"I don't know!"

"You were there, weren't you?"

"No, dammit!" He caught himself shouting and repeated, in a quieter voice, "No. Dammit." He moved a chair to her side and sat down. "The first time . . . I could under-

stand that. Not easily, but it made practical sense. He was
preserving the deception. And from the inmates' continued
interest, he evidently played his part quite satisfactorily."

"Does that bother you? I could replace Beauvina in a
heartbeat, Deymorin."

"Beauvina? Kiyrstin, my love, you could replace Tirise."

It was a moment before he realized the expected laughter
hadn't come.

"And that *doesn't* bother you?" she asked finally.

"Not particularly."

"So it's all right for your mistress to be a whore, but not
your brother."

"I didn't say that."

"No?"

"No!" He rubbed a hand across his eyes, trying to sort
his thoughts. "It's not what he did. It's that . . . he was
able. Where did he learn? How?"

"Same way I did?" Indignation crept into her voice.

"No, Shepherdess." He reached for her hand, and lifted
it to his lips. "I'm sorry for what Garetti did to you. I look
forward to the day when I can express to him exactly my
feelings on that topic, but . . . it's not the same. Somehow.
You're . . . still alive."

"And Khyel's not."

"He *should* have been outraged. Bitter. Angry. Violated.
Horrified. *Anything* but indifferent."

"Sometimes indifference is easier."

"Not for a man!"

She drew her hand away and frowned.

"I'm sorry, Kiyrstin. I didn't mean—"

"Didn't you?"

"No. Dammit, listen to me. You've never hidden your
past, not from me, not from yourself. Whatever happened,
you came out of it healthy. Normal. Able to hate Garetti
for what he did, and able to enjoy life—and love. Khyel . . .
For a man to endure . . . that from another man and come
away content—"

"You said nothing about *content*."

"I said, the first time I could understand. Even the next
morning, when one of the inmates cornered him in the
latrine and roughed him up a bit. That's . . . that's prison
politics. It might make me inclined to kill Ganfrion, but I

can understand, painful as it is, why Mikyhel felt compelled not to start anything. It was later . . ."

"When you went back after him."

He nodded. "I felt him the minute I entered the Crypt. He was . . . *with* Ganfrion."

"And this Ganfrion is still alive?"

He grunted. "*Whatever* had happened was over, more's the pity. I *wish* I'd had the excuse. But Mikyhel was on the edge of sleep, and that *slime* was wrapped around him." A cold chill passed through him at the memory. "I felt his arm under my head, the other wrapped around me and his body pressed up hard against my back . . . And I was relaxed. Content. For the first time in *years.*"

"*You* felt."

He blinked the memory aside. "I mean, Khyel, of course. I called to him, inside. Woke him up and got him out in the open where we could find him."

"And where Sironi wouldn't see what you felt."

He shrugged. "When Mikyhel appeared, he was a mass of dirt and cuts and bruises. For all I could tell, considering the circumstances, his exhaustion and his determined withdrawal from my thoughts, he had been . . . *serviced* by every would-be stud horse in that hell-hole. How could he be *indifferent,* let alone content?"

"Perhaps . . ." She picked up a brush and eased escaped powder into a pile on the table. "Perhaps he was just relieved that whatever happened was over, and he was still alive."

"Then why in the eighteen hells above Rhomatum wasn't he glad to see me?"

"What makes you think he wasn't?"

"I don't think. I *know.* He . . ." Deymorin clenched his fists. "He *resented* my being there."

"That can't be right, Deymorin. You're misreading—"

"Hell if I am. I *know* when I'm not wanted."

"Have you asked him?"

"Damned if I will. I saved his ass when he wanted to die a month ago, and I'll save it again, if I have to, whether *he* wants to live or not."

"Maybe it didn't need saving this time. Maybe he'd settled the situation himself, and was glad for a respite."

"Respite. From me."

"You can be a bit . . . overwhelming at times, JD."

Deymorin turned that over in his mind, and recalled: "*He* says I coddle him."

"Possibly. You unquestionably hover."

"Can you blame me? Most of what's wrong with him is because I *wasn't* there!"

"Is that what this is all about? Guilt? For your absence years ago?"

"No!"

"Why did you want to see him this morning?"

"To make sure he was all right, obviously."

"Not to discuss the meeting. Maybe possible strategies and tactics?"

"Of course not. Mikhyel knows . . ." He clamped his jaw on the rest. "Rings. Point made, Shepherdess. Watching the wrong hand, aren't I?"

"Possibly. Can you handle another question?"

"What now?"

"You said, *most* of what's wrong with him. What do you think is wrong with Mikhyel?"

The sheer number of responses that swelled in answer surprised him, but one thought seemed to summarize the rest. "He should expect more out of life. Personally."

"Perhaps. Certainly he deserves more. I know that. You do."

"But does he?" Deymorin finished for her. "That's the question, isn't it?" He stared at her subtly transforming image as she brushed colored powders on her cheeks. And he thought of how much she'd added to his life and how lost he'd be without her, now he'd found her, and said, out of those thoughts, "I wonder whether perhaps we should send for Nethaalye. If we can just get her down here, let them be together, perhaps she'll still be interested."

"Why?"

"She's Mikhyel's fiancée. Beyond that, they're friends. It's got to bother him that she left under such circumstances."

"Get him a woman and everything will be all right?"

"I didn't say that."

"Does it occur to you that *sex* might not be the answer?"

"It couldn't hurt!"

"Unless he's not interested. Then, you just create more pressure on him to perform to your expectations."

"Of course he's interested."

"That's why they're still engaged rather than married."

"She's his friend. She's bright and clever. She shares his interest in politics."

"If she's such a paragon, why did you turn her down?"

"I *didn't*. I objected to being engaged before I was ten."

"I see. And Mikhyel didn't."

"Mikhyel never objected . . . to . . ."

"Anything?"

"Rings."

"He's twenty-seven, Deymorin. Why hasn't he married her yet? Why hasn't he three or four children of his own running about?"

He said nothing.

"Perhaps, he's just not interested in a quiet, gentle woman, Deymorin."

"He's not like that! He's just confused!"

"Like what? What *are* you talking about? Afraid he prefers men? What's wrong with that?"

"Nothing! I just wish it were that simple. I do know that when he's thought of Nethaalye in the past month, the underneath has been calm. Secure. Surely that's good. Calm, normal . . . someone kind and gentle. Someone who cares about him. What more could a man want?"

"That's what scares you, isn't it? That maybe he's not interested in someone who cares about him?"

"Scared? No. Concerned for Mikhyel, yes. Concerned for the mental stability of the man who holds more keys to the City secrets than anyone I know . . . damned right."

Her mouth opened as if to answer, then snapped shut. She frowned into one of the pots. Then: "You have, my dear Rag'n'Bones, a point."

Upon which history-making concession, the bell chimed, and Deymorin had to leave her to retrieve the corset strings. This time, when he returned, the mirror reflected a one-eyed raccoon.

"Good god," he said, and took a step back.

The tip of her tongue made a rude appearance then disappeared, before she attacked her other eye, matching its decor to the other. She ended the procedure with a polish on her lips.

"Well," she asked, when she'd finished, and she pursed her lips at him. It was, he had to admit, an unusual and very attractive effect. Not the painted mask Anheliaa

RING OF INTRIGUE

sported, not the unabashedly alluring look of the ladies of
Peplondi Street, or the faint touches of color Lidye favored.
But the color, the definition, added a subtle power to her
already strong features.

"This is how the ladies look in Mauritum these days,
is it?"

"Men, too, Rags."

"Oh?" He leaned forward to gaze fondly down her cleavage. "Really?"

She tapped his nose to back him away, and stood up to
face him. "Really." And she kissed him soundly, then
leaned back in his arms and smoothed a finger across his
lips. "There." And tilted slightly so he could see into the
mirror. "What do you think?"

The sight that greeted him was worse than the one-
eyed raccoon.

"I think I'm not going to Mauritum any time soon," he
answered, and used the rag to scrub his lips free of the
pink polish, relieved when it came off almost as readily,
though not as pleasantly, as it had gone on. "Strings, Rags,"
she said and pointed to her back. He began working the
broken strings free, taking his time. The dress waiting on
the form was of Kiyrstin's own ordering.

The design was, so she said, in Rhomatumin fashion, but
with suggestions of Mauritum. Just enough, so she'd said,
to remind them of who they were talking to.

"Do you realize," he said, picking at a knot, "that I've
never seen you in a proper dress?"

"Depends on your definition of proper, doesn't it?"

"I suppose—" He frowned at the knot. "Hold still."

He took a good hold and jerked; she hissed and punched
him in the arm.

"Got it," he said smugly, and held up the broken piece.

"There were other ways!"

"Such as?"

Her face went blank. She leaned forward and picked up
a manicure knife.

He held up a warding hand. "I concede. Next time I'll
ask."

"Clever lad." She tapped his nose with the carved handle, then pointed to her back again. "I suppose, if I truly
wanted to make an impression on the Committee, I should

wear that . . . creation you so generously loaned me the last time."

"It certainly made an impression on Anheliaa—chicken feathers and all."

"Lidye, too. She looks at me like some sort of perverted form of life every time I enter a room."

"And you? What do you think of Lidye?"

"I think it's high time you asked."

He poked her between the laces. She squealed, and stepped backward—placing her shoe's narrow heel squarely on his unshod toes.

She threw him a look over her shoulder. "Oops."

"Well?"

"I think that my first impression of Lidye was possibly as warped as hers of me. I don't *trust* the differences, but a smart person could impersonate the Lidye I first met. That first Lidye could not impersonate the new one. A smart person won't stand in the way of logic. Right now, logic is on your side. Fair enough?"

"Fair enough." He began again on her laces. One-handed. With the other, he traced the curve of her back, the clearly defined muscles so unlike any other woman of his acquaintance. "On the other hand," he said, as he hooked the final section of ragged corset string and pulled it slowly free, "what kind of guarantee does this paint job come with?"

She turned into the circle of his arms.

"I've never thought to ask."

Chapter Four

Words could not describe the chaos within his once-orderly office.

Mikhyel set his jaw against pointless expletives—pointless because there was no one within hearing distance—then closed and relocked the door on the mounds of unopened mail, rifled papers, and ransacked files.

He should have expected something of the sort from the moment he entered the eerily quiet outer office, where six clerks and two secretaries normally sat at their desks, busily, and generally quite chattily, handling the mountain of paperwork his amorphously defined position regularly generated.

The mountain now occupying his theoretically private, theoretically locked office.

Counting his anticipated moments of solitude in familiar surroundings as quite irretrievable, Mikhyel headed downstairs to the personnel office to see what had become of his staff.

He didn't recognize the manager, nor she, him, at least by sight, but that wasn't surprising. Most of his staff had been with him for years, those who had not had been recommended to him by those who had. Several people might well have occupied this particular office since he'd last crossed its threshold.

"They've all been reassigned, Representative dun-Mheric," the manager said, as she sent an aide off to pull the file packets. When the aide returned, the manager spread the pages out across the counter. "As you see."

His entire staff—except Petworin and Kheroli, his oldest, most trusted assistants—had been reassigned to other senior officials within the building. Face neutral, he asked, "Whose order released them from my service?"

Her brow tightened, her expression became suspicious in addition to defensive. "Yours, sir, I assure you."

"I assure you, it was not."

She returned to her desk and brought back a single page, ordering the termination of all his assistants, stamped with the Rhomandi seal, signed with (he had to admit) an authentic-appearing signature (his own).

An upward glance discovered the woman's attention not on his face, not on the files, but on his hands as they turned the pages. More specifically on his wrists where the lace had fallen back, revealing the discreet bandages Raulind had placed on them following his session in Anheliaa's ring chamber.

He flipped the letter to the top of the stack, shook the lace cuffs back over the bandages, and abruptly left the office.

Damn the old woman, anyway. It had been years since she'd dared mark him with those lacquered talons. She'd shaken him, as had no doubt been her semiconscious intent, forced issues and roused emotions belonging to the past in order to disrupt his present.

He headed for Councillor dunTaraway's office, the nearest office housing one of his former staff. The bored-looking individual who answered the bell summons stared at him with a blank expression of nonrecognition, and insisted Paulis dunPaulis, the erstwhile junior clerk he'd traced here, was busy and not to be interrupted.

But Paulis himself emerged, dusty and disheveled, from the depths of a storage closet, shouting, "M'lord Mikhy—"

The rest of his name was lost in open-mouthed confusion. A step closer, a narrow-eyed squint, and a flurry after a handkerchief and dust-covered glasses preceded a more cautious, "It *is* you, sir, isn't it?"

"I certainly hope so," Mikhyel answered.

"They told me you were—" Paulis glanced around the room, crossed to an overstacked desk, and freed hat and coat from the wall-mounted peg beside it. "I'm taking a break," he announced to the room at large, and in an undertone, as he paused beside Mikhyel with his back to the room, "Best we not talk here, sir."

Mikhyel nodded to those throughout the room—who were staring not at him, but at the no-longer bored-looking individual who had opened the door—then preceded Paulis out the door.

"You *are* back, sir? For good?" was Paulis' hopeful query as he closed the door.

"I certainly hope so," Mikhyel repeated.

"They said you were gone, that your younger brother was to be Princeps, and that you'd gone off to Giephaetum with your intended. I—we all—were afraid you were dead. But I see that you aren't, and praise Darius' good name for that, but what now, sir? You aren't dead. You're here, not in Giephaetum. Do you want me back? Is that why you're here? Please, sir, say you do."

Mikhyel held up a hand to slow the eager onslaught, nodded his head in the direction of the staircase, and began walking in that direction.

"I can't promise you anything," he began, once they were safely in his office. "Not yet. I've a meeting with the Conduct Committee in—" he glanced at the clock spinning in the center of the office, realizing in some shock "—less than two hours. I was hoping there'd be something useful— memos from Councillors, requests—in my office, but as you can see . . ."

The stacks on the desk drew both their eyes.

"If you're willing to help me out, I'll make certain your salary's paid, out of my own pocket if need be, and you'll have my sincere gratitude, but I honestly don't know, at this time, how long that position will last, or what the ramifications of your leaving dunTaraway's offices so abruptly will be."

Paulis didn't answer immediately, a fact Mikhyel accepted with mixed emotions. It was the barest of explanations, coming from a man returned from the dead, certainly nothing to inspire confidence and loyalty. But further explanation would, of necessity, have to wait, if he ever gave it.

"I have," Paulis said, at last and slowly, "only one question, sir. May I—"

"Ask."

"Have they cause?"

"None," Mikhyel answered.

"Then I'll stay with you, sir," was the immediate answer, "if you'll have me."

"Thank you," Mikhyel said, relieved and unexpectedly moved by the young man's loyalty. "I promise you, when and if I'm free to explain the events of the past month, you will be among the first to know."

"I'd like to know, but it'll not weigh on my mind. You've never lied to us—and I promise you, sir, we'd know—and if you say your conduct's been legal and ethical, well, I say, those who will be questioning it have a lot more to account for than ever you have, and I'd be willing to stand in court and remind them, if it would help."

Simply said. Quite pragmatically stated. And the thought sent chills down a prudent man's spine.

"Thank you . . . no. If we can just sort this mess, that will be more than sufficient help."

They hauled an extra table into his office and began a rough sort of the mountain. As they worked, Mikhyel asked, keeping his voice casual, "Why did you think I was dead?"

"When they showed up to give us the papers—"

"They? Who told you to leave?"

"Not certain, sir. But Personnel said they had the right."

"Were they liveried?"

"Gold and green, sir. No badge."

Lidye's men. Mikhyel grunted. "Go on."

"They told me—us—you were gone for a week or so, but that you were replacing us all, and we *couldn't* stay in the office—not even without pay, which we all wanted to do. We none of us believed you'd do it like that."

"It?"

"Give us the sack. You'd face us personally. Tell us why. I thought . . . I was *sure* you were dead, and they just weren't saying. I thought the old witch—" Paulis' lips tightened, smothering what sounded distinctly like a curse, and he ducked after escaping papers.

"Indiscreet, to say the least," Mikhyel filled in smoothly.

"Yes, sir," was the mumbled reply that rose from under the table.

"Not, I would think, a remark you would make if my unexpected appearance hadn't startled you deeply."

"No—I mean, yes. Sir. —I think. Sir."

Mikhyel controlled an inclination to chuckle.

"Relax, Paulis. Time's running out. It's impossible to judge what might be useful for me to know. My word, I'll not hold anything you say against you in any way."

That only got a grunt.

"I'm honored, actually, to think that I've roused such loyalty in my staff. Or perhaps, it was only to escape the dusty closet that you came so eagerly to my side."

Which got a shy, bespectacled glance. "Actually, sir, it was that desk. Everything they had to think what to do with, landed on my desk. I'd have gone underground to tend the growth chambers rather than face that desk one more day."

"Oh," Mikhyel said, borrowing Nikki's most mournful tone.

Paulis' eyes went wide. "Sir! I was jok—"

Mikhyel laughed, and after a startled moment, the young clerk joined him. It was a new and different feeling, and Mikhyel was tempted to allow the relaxed formality to extend beyond the proposed hour. They were much of an age, and there'd been few enough individuals in his life he could call friend.

Tempted, but not foolish enough to act upon that temptation. A man who had control over another man's livelihood, owed it to the employee and himself to retain a mutually respectful distance, especially when other livelihoods might one day depend upon his ability to trust or discharge that same man.

He'd learned that particularly difficult lesson when he'd first opened the Tower to his own offices here. At thirteen, there'd been many individuals, at all levels of employment, ready to take advantage of him and his childish innocence. Fortunately for Mikhyel dunMheric *and* his City, Mikhyel dunMheric's childish trust had first been given to Raulind of Barsitum.

And Raulind's caution ruled him still.

"You could start," Mikhyel prodded gently, "by telling me what happened the day the web went down."

A rather blank look came into those bespectacled eyes. "You weren't in that morning." The words came slowly, as if Paulis was trying to piece broken memories together. "You'd left early the day before—taken ill, they said, during the Appropriations Committee meeting."

Mikhyel nodded, acknowledgment of the statement without commitment. Deymorin had arrived during that meeting. And Nikki had been shot . . . in far-off Darhaven. It had been the first time they realized just how invasive their new gift could be. Staggering from Nikki's shock and pain, he might well have appeared ill.

"The next day, I . . . we all . . . came in early—in case you needed help, you know."

Thinking he'd be in early, to make up for time lost the previous day. Hoping, he supposed, to make a good impression on him.

"Unnecessary diligence, I trust you realize," Mikhyel said.

"Perhaps, sir, but what with your older brother being gone, and you having to go Outside all the time, and still do the work here, well, we were getting worried for you, sir, and that's the truth of it."

"That was . . . thoughtful of you all," he said, which was all he could think of to say, embarrassed without quite knowing why.

"Yes, sir. Well, when you didn't show that morning, and we didn't hear, we were that certain you'd truly collapsed this time, and we were worried—"

"About your positions here. I wish I could assure you otherwise, but—"

"*Sir!*" the clerk protested.

"I understand, Paulis," Mikhyel assured him.

"Sir, we were worried about you."

Mikhyel blinked twice and slowly, and finally, when *no* words came to him, handed Paulis a stack of papers.

"The Khendolhari project," he said, and Paulis nodded, adding the stack to one on the table behind him.

"About the Collapse?" Mikhyel prompted, guiding the clerk away from his personal well-being.

"Sometime soon after lunch, someone . . ." Paulis paused, squinting into the unfocused middle-ground, then shook his head. "I can't honestly recall who, sir, came to the door and yelled at us to come see. He said the sky was disappearing above the Tower. We went to look, and sure enough, it was glowing all purple and green with flashes of blue. Bright flashes. Like stars. We thought—"

Paulis paused, removed his spectacles, and rubbed his eyes, hard.

"We thought, Darius save us from our ignorance, we thought, sir, that the lady Anheliaa, was doing some kind of fancy show for the wedding visitors. We just watched and watched, and laughed, and applauded. And then it began to turn. Faster and faster and . . ."

He shuddered, and replaced his spectacles. "And then, it just reached down—this whirling pool of purple and blue and green reached down and touched the Tower, then arced across the sky and disappeared. The people all around—and I, sir, I'm ashamed to admit, was no exception—cheered and laughed and wondered what she'd do next—"

"I'd have done so myself, Paulis," Mikhyel said, to dispel any time-wasting self-incriminations, and Paulis nodded.

"Thank you, sir. But then, the lights went out, and the cheering stopped. Silent as death, it was. The air had stopped circulating . . . I never realized until that moment how noisy the fans are. And then . . . then the lightning began. . . ."

Mikhyel could only imagine how that must have felt to life-long Rhomatumin. The skies above Rhomatum had never, in living memory, contained lightning. The Towers existed to keep the lightning from the node.

"It was—it was so strange, sir. There were no clouds, just the sky pulsing deeper and deeper blue, then purple, then black, and all the while, the lightning had flared and flared, aiming at the Tower. Or—" Paulis paused, folder hanging forgotten from one hand. "Or maybe, thinking on it, sir, the lightning started at the Tower and went up to the cloud. I couldn't say, sir."

Mikhyel hid a smile. At times, his staff were better at lawyerly precision than he was.

Everyone had panicked except, Paulis declared, himself and his fellow staffers. Mikhyel could be proud of all his assistants, the clerk insisted. They'd comported themselves with dignity, retreating to their offices, and locking the doors against the growing insanity of individuals torn between the possible safety of the building, and a need to be with their families.

His staff, bachelors all, had simply hunkered down in the windowless room, and talked to one another in the darkness, discussing the projects they were involved with, the girls they were seeing . . . anything to avoid thinking about what might be happening on the far side of the door.

Eventually, the thunder had died—how long that was, Paulis seemed completely uncertain. An hour, a day, or two days, the clerk insisted, would all be the same. It had seemed forever until the thunder stopped. Kheroli, the senior secretary, had used his key to Mikhyel's office, and they'd opened the door to the first light they'd seen since the storm began.

The pen Paulis was using to mark the file he'd just collated, clattered to the floor. Mikhyel turned from the drawer he was straightening, and found the clerk staring blankly at the tall windows.

"Paulis?" he called softly, and the clerk jerked. Blinked. And exclaimed aloud as he began blotting at the ink-spattered desk. "Paulis," Mikhyel repeated, "What's wrong? What happened here in the office?"

"Not here, sir," the clerk said, and lifted his chin toward the window. "Out there. The citizens, from downhill to the wall—they stormed Tower Hill. They came running from all over, screaming, pounding on the doors, demanding . . . I don't know. Answers? Reassurance?" He gave a shuddering shrug. "They . . . people were mad, that was all, and nothing anyone said seemed to make any difference. Some of those downhill opened their doors . . . before they knew . . ."

Paulis' voice trailed off again, and his face grew pained.

"What then?" Mikhyel asked, keeping his voice coldly neutral.

"We only heard what happened. People died, sir. That's all. It was ugly and barbaric, from what the reports said. Not just the scandal sheets, legitimate news as well. It was awful, sir. Just . . ."

"I'll check the reports, Paulis. What about you? Is your family safe? Your parents? Your sisters?"

"Yes, sir, thank you. They were at home, and they stayed there. The streets finally quieted. For a while, it seemed like everywhere you looked there were armed guards of one kind or another. Colors I've never seen before—came in with the guests for your brother's wedding, so they say. But I think we were lucky they were here. When I went home the first time . . . rings, sir, there were flowers and broken glass and broken statues all over. Next day, we came back determined to have your office spif-spaf for you—only to discover 'our talents were no longer needed.' —Ah, here, sir, I think this might be useful. . . ."

He handed Mikhyel a memo out of Councillor dun-

Yardo's office demanding an immediate priority be given to the city hospitals—which just happened to lie right beyond his district, which meant his constituents would also have priority power. A second memo, from dunBarkhli of Potter's Square detailing the loss in inventory and sales due to the power outage.

By the time the first sort was completed, they had a stack of similar memos and sealed document folders.

Mikhyel gathered the stack into a document case, and picked his coat up from the back of his chair. "That should give you enough to work on until I get back. That's provided, of course, they release me before next week. In the meantime—" He stretched out his hand and Paulis met it, wrist to wrist. "Thank you—for everything."

"Nothing the others wouldn't have done, sir, in my place. May I contact them? Let them know you're back?"

He released the clerk's hand and slipped the case strap over his shoulder. "Let's wait, shall we? At least . . ." He left the rest unsaid, and Paulis nodded.

"Good luck, sir."

Mikhyel pulled the keys to the office from his belt. "Just . . . lock up before you leave, will you?"

With something just short of reverence, Paulis received the ring Mikhyel tossed toward him. It was tacit promotion to a level of trust men ten years Paulis' senior rarely achieved, and never a second-level clerk from a minor Family of the outer ring.

And Paulis' voice, when he answered, trembled at the corners. "You can count on me, sir."

"Naturally," Mikhyel answered as he left.

§ § §

"Are you quite certain, Nikaenor?" Lidye asked.

Nikki pulled the driving gloves through his hands, impatient at the delay Lidye's unexpected appearance was creating. Beyond the beveled glass of the Rhomandi House main entrance, the family floater-coach balloon bobbed, waiting. For him.

"The driver says that Mikhyel sent him back here for his brother's use. And Bharker saw Deymorin leave with Kiyrstin, so *he* won't need it. I planned to go for a drive today, if the horses were sound, but that was before the subpoena came in this morning. Well, the horses are sound, but I wanted to wish Mikhyel luck first, so I came back, but he's gone over early, and he *never* likes me to bother him at the office, so now, if I'm going to drive and get back before he's done, I've got to take the floater, because it takes too long to walk."

"Don't you want to be at the hearing to support Mikhyel?"

Nikki shrugged, avoiding her eyes. "The horses need to get out. They've been cooped in since we arrived."

"Will another day make that much difference?"

"It's a private meeting."

"You could wait outside the chamber for him."

"He doesn't like me there, all right?" Nerves and the necessary lie made him unreasonable. He knew that and tried to temper his voice. "He never has. He says I—make him nervous." More lies.

Of course, she didn't know about the Complication. She didn't understand that he'd been banished from proceedings such as this for reasons as reasonable as they were unpalatable:

Nikki, it's not that we don't want you there.

Ha.

They're old men, Nikki. They didn't like having to accept Mikhyel. They'll simply make you angry. Justifiably, but now isn't the time.

So, when would it be time? When his hair was gray? Or (he shuddered) gone?

Mikhyel must have a clear head, Nikki.

Deymorin didn't want him there because he thought too loudly, felt too passionately. In short, Deymorin didn't trust him. And maybe Deymorin was right. It was a very important hearing for Mikhyel, so even though it hurt, even though it meant he just wouldn't know what was happening, he was leaving. Voluntarily. Going Outside where even Mikhyel's head couldn't follow him.

He hoped.

"I've got to go," he said, and without thinking, asked, "Would you like to come along?"

It was reflex. The sort of question he'd been taught it was polite to ask. It was, he realized too late, grossly out of place to ask her on this day and under these conditions.

"I—I'm sorry. No, of course you can't. The Tower . . . Anheliaa . . ."

"No." Lidye interrupted him, and she had a head-tilted, considering look on her face. "No, Nikki, it's all right. In fact—" Her pale blonde head gave a decided dip. "I'd love to. Let me get my hat."

She glided away, leaving Nikki more confused than ever. Lidye *hated* the Outside, she'd made that abundantly clear on their last outing. He hoped she wasn't reverting to her previous manipulative techniques. He liked this new Lidye much better. But did this mean her arm-clutching fear that had ruined his last drive with her had been assumed as well?

He certainly hoped that was the case. He wanted to enjoy this afternoon. Wanted the sun and wind and smells of Outside to wash away the resentment brewing in his heart.

He stepped out onto the floater dock to wait, slapping his gloves against his thigh nervously. He'd hoped to be on his way by now, had planned to go to Armayel today, when the subpoena came in. Now, it was too late for that, not if he were to get back by the time the meeting was over.

The walk back from the stables had taken far longer than he had anticipated. It seemed as if he'd had to stop every few steps to speak with people, friends he hadn't seen for weeks, people he'd never met who just seemed to recognize him.

He'd never been so conscious of being a Rhomandi. In the past, most folk had seemed content to ignore that fact, if they'd noticed. Now, the anonymity was gone. Everyone wanted answers from him. Some had gotten openly hostile when he had proclaimed ignorance, and he'd been very glad to have Lidye's father's green-and-gold guards around him.

And thanks to those delays, he'd missed Mikhyel after all. So now, he was anxious to get back to the stable as fast as possible, because otherwise, Mikhyel would hear him and get confused, and they'd all be mad at him. . . .

He wished Lidye would hurry.

§   §   §

Deymorin was late; fortunately, so was the Committee. Mikhyel stared out the large window draped in the elaborate style of the mid-second century, hoping to catch a glimpse of the Rhomandi floater-coach's black-and-silver balloon entering the port below. If the cursed link could be trusted, Deymorin had yet to leave Rhomandi House,

And considering that link, he supposed it was just as well Deymorin wasn't here yet. Even before they began thinking at one another, Deymorin had had the unerring capacity to rouse the worst possible uncertainties in him.

Still, he'd feel far more confidence in the outcome of the imminent hearing were he certain what would come through the door when the Committee called on Kiyrstine romGaretti to testify. It wasn't that he didn't retain a great personal respect for the unusual lady who, save for an awkwardly still-extant husband, would be his brother's wife. Kiyrstin was, by his own experience of her, intelligent, sensible, and extremely politically astute.

But her men's clothing, her short-cropped hair and frequently brusque manner would not, he feared, intrigue the conservative group assembling just beyond the towering, double doors that were of greater antiquity than the drapes.

He'd sensed, vaguely, Nikiki's coming and going, his despair that he'd missed Mikhyel. He'd tried to send Nikki reassurance, but Nikki had been concentrating so hard on not interfering in Mikhyel's thoughts, Mikhyel doubted he'd heard. Nikki's presence was no more than a shadow of remembered sensation, now, hinting primarily of Outside and invigorating winds.

Turning from the window, defying his nerves, Mikhyel forced himself to sit rather than pace. He crossed his legs and arranged the lace over the bandages, restraining a second inclination, this one to delve yet one more time into the contents of the document case propped against the chair leg.

For the most part, those documents were no more than he'd expected: memos similar to dunYardo's or that of dunBarkhli. Though couched in a variety of florid terms, threats, and pathetic hardship accounts, they all boiled down to two things: fear and money.

Rhomatumin Councillors, in the names of their constituents, wanted their energy back. They wanted compensation for the loss of production, wanted money for restoration after the riots—for personal as well as civic buildings.

And they wanted to make certain the Rhomandi remembered that they, the Rhomandi, not Rhomatum, were responsible for the damages to the web beyond Rhomatum herself. *Anheliaa* had sworn such a catastrophe was impossible, and backed the claim (the Councillors were one and all quick to remind him in those memos) with the Rhomandi fortune, not Rhomatumin taxes.

And there were concerns expressed about Lidye. To have a Shatumin woman in charge, to have a notable number of Shatumin men-at-arms highly visible throughout the City, had people frightened.

He could appreciate their reservations. He'd had his own this morning. Since then, he'd discovered Lidye rom-Nikaenor (or her representatives) had tampered with his mail and his files and dismissed his staff. While he could conceive of viable reasons for her actions, he did not automatically accept her motivations as benign.

Under the circumstances, she'd have been foolish not to take steps to discover his personal affiliations on the Hill, also, to be cautious about leaving unsupervised individuals in close proximity to the records his office contained.

What she chose to do with the information thus gained was another question. He sincerely hoped she'd had the sense not to act on concerns expressed under duress.

And much depended upon what other documents, other than termination notices, she'd forged with his signature.

There were many questions he wanted to ask Nikki's wife—following this meeting.

Of the eighteen senior Councillors preparing their inquisition behind those doors, two, possibly three would be most inclined to trust him. Men and women with whom he'd planned Rhomatum's future. In private. Individuals who knew and trusted him, who had feared (according to carefully phrased but anxious notes in his packet) for that future when he'd disappeared under such cataclysmic circumstances.

It was, perhaps, their dissension among those eighteen seniors that delayed the start of the inquiry, and left him sitting here.

Eighteen senior Councillors. One for each wedge-shaped section of the City, chosen to their seniority by the other representatives of the section. Men and women twice his age and more, who had listened to him and taken his advice ever since he'd come of legal age.

They'd listened not by choice, but for want of options. He'd been the voice of the Rhomandi, their only link with the Rhomatum Tower. The majority were oblivious to how much he'd intervened, but there were those who knew the narrow ledge he'd walked for years and feared the woman in Rhomatum Tower without himself there to temper her whimsy. Some had come up directly against Anheliaa's bitterness and manipulation, and those were his allies.

But they were not his friends.

And in that sense, he had no doubt that their trust had limits. The rumors of war out of Mauritum had them frightened. And fear made men both brave and stupid. He could, if he so chose, turn that fear to his advantage. Anheliaa was a master of the art of manipulation and Anheliaa had overseen his education. He could convince them their lifestyle and livelihoods were subject now to his whim. Could threaten them with total annihilation of the web.

But he had no desire to intimidate the Council or Syndicate. The facts were on his side, so was logic, and the Councillors were not fools. Neither were the Syndics, those representatives of the satellite nodes who would be after him the moment they'd reorganized their scattered members.

If these leaders persisted, if they insisted on bringing House Rhomandi down . . . Mikhyel stared at his clenched hands, forced them to relax. If the Council thought they were better off without the Rhomandi, let them have it. Let them have it all—the Tower, the Rhomandi fortune . . . the endless headaches.

He'd come to realize these past months that the web provided luxuries, not the necessities of life. He believed in the Syndicate, but he was not about to fight bull-headed stupidity forever. He was tired. Tired of the games. Tired of the constant tightrope. Either they saw sense . . . or they did not.

The Rhomandi brothers had nearly died for the Tower and the City and the web. Even before that, their lives had been subjugated to the Tower and the web since they were conceived. Deymorin's Outside holdings were beyond the Council's reach. The three of them and their servants,

Kiyrstin . . . even Lidye, should Nikki so decide, could survive without Rhomatum.

Whether Rhomatum could survive without the Rhomandi had never been seriously tested.

The elaborately-uniformed doormen swung open the elaborately-carved doors.

As he stood up, Deymorin's thoughts brushed his. He sent an irritated reminder in that direction, fueling it with all his remaining tension. Afterward, he felt purged, Deymorin's and Kiyrstin's roles no longer as important as they once had seemed.

He slung the document case over his shoulder with something approaching Deymorin's flair, and strode toward that gaping double-wide maw.

Chapter Five

The original summons had been to one of the small meeting rooms, but a notice left on the door had directed Mikhyel instead to this, the largest, most ostentatious auditorium in Brinmori Hall, with prime seating for three hundred, and a gallery for twice that number.

All for a meeting with eighteen people.

Intimidation. Anheliaa wasn't the only one skilled with the tactics.

However, in choosing this gallery, those would-be intimidators overplayed their hand. In general, Mikhyel dun-Mheric, representative of House Rhomandi, felt more at ease in the anonymity of this great hall than he ever did in a more intimate setting.

He stepped confidently through the doors and into the great hall, where prismal skylights sent sunlight in shafts to spotlight the podium at the acoustic focal point of the great, semicircular room.

Only as his eyes adjusted to the lighting, did he realize the change of venue was not the only tactical shift on the part of his would-be intimidators. The hall was packed, standing room only, with Councillors, Syndics, and anyone else who could justify their presence.

Defying all rules of protocol, Mikhyel went directly to that central podium and mounted it.

"Ladies and gentlemen of the Rhomatum Web." His voice rang in the eerily, unnaturally silent hall. "The history books describe the Rhomatum Syndicate of Nodes as an economic coalition, a union of legally autonomous city-states joined by a common and irrevocably interdependent energy source.

"That autonomy, my fellow citizens of the web, is our individual strength—and our collective weakness.

"Those same history books show that for the first two

decades of the fourth century After the Founding, the Rhomatum Syndicate dealt with little more than trade disputes and keeping the leyroads clear of criminal activity that might interfere with the movement of goods. One by one, in the name of efficiency and profit, we have eliminated the programs that once guarded our borders against foreign invasion.

"I ask you now to consider what the history books will say fifty years from now regarding the decisions we make today.

"The web, that fragile thread that binds individual cities into a single entity, is faltering. We need look no further than the nearest leylight to assure ourselves of that simple fact. We know the fact; we do not know the precise cause—yet.

"While we can rest assured that our ringmasters will isolate and repair the problem, eventually, even if the web were to be restored to full capacity by the time we finish dinner tonight, the situation that led to our current state would still exist.

"Anheliaa is dying. That can be no surprise to anyone here. Her death will leave an unprecedented void in Rhomatum Tower. We must guard against that void. The mere possibility of a vacancy in Rhomatum has already generated one militant probe out of Mauritum. That immediate threat is gone, but Mauritum remains a very real, long-term complication.

"There can be no question that High Priest Garetti of Mauritum has designs on Rhomatum. He made his interest clear when he sent his junior priest, Vandoshin romMaurii, into Rhomatum along with that probe. Had they managed to coerce their way into the Tower, as was their plan, Vandoshin romMaurii might well have seized control of the rings, securing Rhomatum for his superior.

"Thanks to Anheliaa, and the storm that temporarily took down the web, romMaurii won't be controlling anything. Her actions also resulted, unfortunately, in the chaos and loss of energy we're all of us all too familiar with. However, while concern for our current situation cannot be overlooked, I ask you to consider the possible alternatives. Annihilation of the rings, or Mauritumin rule.

"Thanks to the historical stability of the Rhomatum Syndicate, this first move to test our defenses was hesitant at best. The firestorm destroyed the entire party; there will be no firsthand accounts making their way back to High Priest Garetti. Mauritumin understanding of the event will necessarily be limited to the wildly speculative rumors which have been circulating our own cities for the past month.

"I know the truth of those days, my fellow citizens. I am willing to share that truth with you today. But the Mauritumin probe is only one incident. That which the incident implies is my concern.

"Rhomatum and her Syndicate have gotten careless, there's no other word for it. There is no other excuse for the defenseless state into which we have fallen.

"Other interests, less traditional, but equally anxious to take advantage of Rhomatum's impending vulnerability, might well be organizing similar campaigns. History tells us that in the early years following the capping of Rhomatum, our rich lands attracted a variety of outsiders, both those who had been trying for generations to settle here, only to be driven out by the storms, and those living under the skies to which Darius shunted the valley storms.

"Until the ring of nodes was nearly complete, the Syndicate maintained border watches, and subsidized trained troops that could be ready to leave their farms or kilns or workshops and protect the storm-free corridors against invasion.

"When all the satellites except Khoratum were capped, the effectively continuous storm belt proved a more compelling deterrent than any human sentinel, and those border raids trickled to a virtual halt.

"And then, Anheliaa came to power. Anheliaa, my friends, has had an agenda her entire life. That fact is or should be no news to all of us. Anheliaa wanted Khoratum capped, and over the years she pushed programs that shifted the web's energies and tax monies toward that singular purpose. She needed growth chambers beneath all the nodes, and she needed strong redundancies within all the Towers: she was prepared, my fellow Syndics, to sacrifice every ringmaster within the web to control Khoratum.

"However, Anheliaa *did* cap Khoratum, without the loss of a single life, and we all know the result of that capping has been a decade of absolutely reliable ley-energy.

"A fact that we, as a collective unit, have rather blithely

overlooked, was that Khoratum's capping also brought a significant reduction in the storm belt, both in width and intensity.

"I hope we have not delayed action for too long.

"Because as Anheliaa approaches her final hours, and with the control of Rhomatum Tower in doubt, our relaxed borders will appear increasingly attractive to outsiders. If the Syndicate is to survive in anything approaching its present form, we must reinstate the old patterns, revive the border watches and work as a unified nation, not independent entities.

"I personally accept no small part of the blame for this oversight. The Rhomandi have traditionally represented the interests of the web as a whole, not the interests of an individual node-city—not even Rhomatum. But I have become personally and painfully aware that for a generation, the Rhomandi have provided no true guidance, no vision toward a secure future.

"The Rhomandi are paying now for that dereliction.

"The Rhomandi are also coming to you armed with potential solutions—if you're interested.

"Everyone in this room knows that Anheliaa made individual agreements with every satellite Tower to ensure their cooperation in the capping. Some of those agreements are on record, others are not, though we all know they exist, for all we pretend they are secret.

"If the Syndicate intends to enforce those agreements, my brothers and I will not fight. Once Anheliaa is dead and unable to contest the decision, the Rhomandi fortune will be at your disposal, and the Rhomandi themselves will leave Rhomatum forever. Because such a decision, considering the scope of this unpredictable and unavoidable disaster, would ruin House Rhomandi financially before it satisfied all claims likely to come forward. But if such is the choice of the Syndicate, then the time of the Rhomandi is past, and my brothers and I have agreed that we will not be the source of yet one more division within the Syndicate.

"Obviously, House Rhomandi would wish otherwise. If the web is to continue, we need cooperation, not division. Rebuilding and regrouping, not blind vengeance. I hope, before I leave today, we will have come to an understanding that is best not for any individual, not for any individual node, but for the entire Rhomatum Web."

He paused for breath. . . .

"Whatever questions you have, I shall answer. Willingly."

He could feel their eyes on him. Feel the opposing energies of hope and fear, confidence and distrust.

"Whatever advice I can offer, I shall give. Willingly."

That sensation was nothing new to him.

"If you would like to consider the House Rhomandi solutions, just ask."

It was the energy of life itself.

He let a slight smile curl his lip.

"Ladies and gentlemen of the Rhomatum Web," he ended, in the voice one frustrated critic had said could convince a hungry snake that an egg was a rose, "Mikhyel dunMheric is at your service."

§   §   §

"I told you we should have walked," Deymorin said, as he handed Kiyrstin from the floater-cab to the Brinmori Hall dock.

"Better late than windblown, JD." Kiyrstin swept past him, her skirts held precisely free of the dock. "Politicians understand contempt. Besides, if that brother of yours hadn't run off with the Rhomandi coach, we'd have been here in plenty of time, now wouldn't we?"

Deymorin flipped a coin up to the independent cabby, who single-handed it, tipped his hat, and eased the floater free of the dock, pedaling off in search of another fare.

"You know it was a mistake." Ignoring the throb in his head, he took the stairs two at a time to catch up with her. "Jerrik said Nikki thought we'd gone over already."

"Well, he was wrong, wasn't he?"

"And we were cutting it damned close."

Her mouth twitched. "True." She smoothed the front panels of the form-fitting bodice. "Even?"

"I'll let you know when my head quits vibrating. Rings, the lad can pack a mental punch."

"You three had best sort that out soon and lay down some ground rules, before one of you kills the other."

He grunted. Her point was well taken, but hardly necessary. Mikhyel's kindly reminder to get his ass to the meeting had sent him to his knees on the Rhomandi House threshold. One hesitated to consider what might have happened had he been on horseback, or standing on a Tower balcony.

His hip throbbed in memory of just such a fall that had nearly killed him once and long ago, and on the wake of the thought, a desperate plea from Mikhyel, elsewhere in this building, begging him to shut his head up.

{Sorry,} he sent back, and put forth the effort to block his thoughts, concentrating on the simple, practical aspects of placing one foot in front of the other. The technique wasn't completely effective, but Mikhyel claimed it helped.

And at least he'd gotten, in that brief contact, and the residual awareness of his brother, a sense, almost a flavor, of satisfaction.

"How's the meeting going?" Kiyrstin asked.

"Fi—" He blinked at her, wondering how she'd guessed, but they were at the lift, and he dared not inquire in front of the silver-haired operator. They rode upward in silence, and when they were again alone and headed down the third-floor corridor. "How?"

"Did I know you were talking with Mikhyel? I'm sure I don't know. Perhaps something about the silence, and that vacant, witless look you get, I suppose."

"That obvious?"

"To a stranger, Rags."

"You might have said something before now."

"Waiting for the right moment."

"After the humor wore off?"

She glanced up at him, a seductive challenge.

"Dammit, Kiyrsti, it's not funny. It's one thing for me. *Mikhyel* can't afford to appear a fool."

"*Mikhyel* doesn't."

"Oh. Here it . . ." He stifled the curse that rose, sent a worried query to Mikhyel, received in return a vision of a crowded hall, a demand to hurry, and the first hint of real concern. {On our way, fry.}

He grabbed Kiyrstin's hand and pulled her toward the staircase. When she protested, he said, "He's done it, Kiyrsti, he's *done* it. The lot of them—Syndicate *and* Council—every damned one of them, all there, and he's got them. You, m'love, are his icing." He laughed aloud as he pulled her up the stairs. "He's terrified what's going to come through the door. What *have* you done to the poor lad, Shepherdess? You should *see* the mental image he has of you."

Chapter Six

"They were captivated from the moment she entered the room. She was . . . superb." Mikhyel raised his wine in a toast to Kiyrstine romGaretti, who was seated next to Deymorin at the head of the formal dining table—

Next to where Nikki should, by rights, have been sitting. But Nikki had insisted otherwise, and so sat in his old position, on the table's west side, next to Lidye, his *legal* wife, whose formal dinner arrangements had forced Nikki to make that gesture.

Lidye had meant well—for everyone.

He suspected that she'd sensed his disappointment at being left out of such an important meeting before she ever agreed to accompany him on the drive and that her decision to risk the Tower and go with him had hinged more on *his* need than her desire.

And because he'd suspected that, and trying to be considerate to everyone's needs, he'd cut the drive short and then counted the stitches in the floater-cab on the ride home, thinking *nothing* about politics or his brothers, trying to keep his head quiet, the way Deymorin said he could.

He and Lidye had been sitting in the ringchamber when Mikhyel's exuberant victory announcement had rung in his head. He'd tried to keep that knowledge from Lidye until he could escape from Lidye long enough to have Jerri write a note that he could show Lidye and claim it was from his brothers.

It had all been very complicated. And all because *his* wife couldn't be trusted with their "secret."

On receiving the note, Lidye had immediately set in motion this fine celebration, in part, he was certain, to remind his brothers of the New Order in the household. She meant to imply they should not have left him out. But she just didn't know. She didn't realize it didn't matter *at all* to him that Deymorin was still acting like the Rhomandi.

He only hoped when the time came (after Anheliaa was too dead to contest the reversion) and Mikhyel filed the papers to reinstate Deymorin as Princeps, Lidye wouldn't try to fight the action out of some mistaken sense of loyalty. To him. Which was a pleasant thought, however wrongheaded in this case.

Besides, when Mikhyel had arrived filled with gratitude and praise for Nikki's adult attitude and his thoughtful decision to vacate the city, Nikki had almost forgotten that he had ousted himself from that very important moment. Because he hadn't been there to foul the mental water, Mikhyel had enthralled them all—Syndics, Councillors . . . and Deymorin.

Deymorin had said Mikhyel's eloquence would have dazzled Darius himself.

And thanks to Mikhyel's golden tongue, the Syndics were looking to Mikhyel for leadership through the political maze ahead, as they were looking to the commanding Daymorin to organize the border watch they'd agreed was vital for the web's future safety. As they were looking to Lidye and Anheliaa to stabilize the web.

And to Nikaenor they looked for—nothing. Nikaenor was to stay out of the way. *Everyone's* way.

Nikki sighed and picked up his fork.

"DunHaulkh had already sent a team of examiners to the Boreton Turnout," Mikhyel was explaining. "The *facts* of the destruction were never in question. The factions and forces behind it were. All the equipment that hadn't been burned beyond recognition bore the Darhaven crest."

That was because romMaurii had *stolen* the wagons from Darhaven . . . at the same time romMaurii had taken him prisoner. Nikki wondered if Mikhyel had told them about that. If Mikhyel had told them how his younger brother—the current Princeps of Rhomatum—had been stupid and gotten himself shot and tied up like a pig for slaughter and had had to be *saved* by his older brothers.

". . . and combined with my simultaneous disappearance, they were justifiably suspicious of the Rhomandi. They wanted proof, or at least substantiating evidence of Mauritum's involvement, and Kiyrstin—" Mikhyel kissed his fingers in her direction. *Deymorin's* gesture, not Mikhyel's.

"Kiyrstin provided all they could wish for, and dared them to disbelieve her."

"You'd have loved it, Nikki," Deymorin said, chuckling. "They cited every possible rumor, trying shake her story. Syndic Marighi of Persitum asked about the wanton destruction of one of Rhomatum's largest markets."

Kiyrstin swirled her wine delicately. "I didn't once expose a certain ex-princeps' stupidity in leaving a poor ignorant city-girl in charge of a team of wild horses. But I fear I maligned the characters of a flock of innocent chickens."

"Be that as it may," Deymorin said pompously, and lengthening his face into a caricature of some unknown (to Nikki) Syndic. "Is it the practice of well-born women of Mauritum to have, how should I put this, *relations* with the enemy?"

"Well, you see, gentlemen," Kiyrstin responded in kind, "I could hardly have known him for the enemy. The poor fellow had been dumped in a cold mountain shepherd's pond, as . . ." She blushed delicately and dipped her head behind a modestly raised hand. ". . . exposed as the day he was born."

"And yet," Deymorin continued, "you were attracted, in the physical sense, to this stranger. Does this not question your morals?"

Kiyrstin's eyes widened innocently. "Not if you've met my husband. Garetti had a wife for political favor and blackmail purposes. I've become something of a connoisseur over the years. I *told* you, he appeared before me quite as nature created him." Her eyes blinked twice, expressing amazement without the slightest hint of modesty. "Quite, *quite* impressive on the most reserved of women, and I am not, I fear, what one might term reserved. I would say, rather, that it is a judgment upon the quality of Rhomatumin leaders that, having encountered one of them, I find myself, despite my expectations, satisfied."

Deymorin gave a shout of laughter. "I tell you, Nikki, she had them by their collective hypocrisy. She neither condemned Garetti for despicable actions they've every one of them at least considered in the past, nor begged their forgiveness for taking advantage of fate's benevolence."

"I'm sure it was wonderful," Nikki said, feeling compelled to say something, for all he thought Deymorin didn't really understand the Syndics, saying such cruel things about them. Of course they'd be shocked at Kiyrstin's cavalier attitude.

But Nikki fought to keep his thoughts and emotions to himself, the way Deymorin insisted he could, keeping his mind on silly things, like his wineglass or the shape of his fork. So far he thought he'd done quite well. At least, Mikhyel's cheerful triumph seemed overall undisturbed, except for the occasional puzzled look Mikhyel cast him.

"The old hypocrites want to see Zandy's machine," Deymorin said.

"Not here!" Lidye exclaimed, and Deymorin lifted a hand.

"Of course not, madam. I'm not a fool. They're choosing a delegation to go to Armayel."

Nikki concentrated on his fork's bent tine. He didn't want to think about Alizant of Mauritum, the boy who had come into the Rhomatum Valley with Kiyrstin. Zandy was Deymorin's other recent obsession—besides Mikhyel and Kiyrstin and armies. A misunderstood, poorly used illiterate with a machine that controlled lightning.

"They want to know more about it," Deymorin was saying. "Want to know if it can safely coexist with the ley and if there's any true market value, and they're willing to go Outside to find out. Greed does wonders to offset prejudice."

"I doubt anything will make a Mauritumin peasant boy more palatable to them."

Nikki knew the moment he spoke he'd have been better off keeping silent. He stared at that bent tine, imagining it twisting, contorting into fantastical shapes. And he sensed, underneath, that Mikhyel and Deymorin were arguing about him.

For which disagreement he was sorry. And he was sorry to ruin the mood of the party. but if Zandy had been here, Zandy would have gone to that meeting with Mikhyel and Deymorin and Kiyrstin. Would have spoken to Council in all his illiterate glory. Zandy wouldn't have had to go driving Outside to keep his thoughts from confusing Mikhyel. Wouldn't have all the councillors wondering where Nikki was. Wouldn't have had to wonder and worry for hours and hours and hours—

"Nikki?" Mikhyel's voice interrupted his inner turmoil,

and Nikki, schooling his face and mind into pleasant indifference, answered politely. "Yes?"

"I need your help, Nikki."

Nikki shrugged, refusing to show the relief that charged through him like a horse at a gallop. But Mikhyel must have sensed it, too, because the ghostly smile Mikhyel reserved just for him twitched the corners of Mikhyel's mouth.

"It's a major undertaking, Nikki, but one I think my history-loving brother will enjoy. It will mean a great deal of work. No short cuts. You'll have the help you need to gather information, I'll see you get access to whomever you deem material, but I want *your* take on the information. *Your* evaluations, no one else's."

That didn't sound quite so exciting. "Evaluations? Of what?"

"The nodes. Each and every one of them. I need current statistics, population, geographic variables—you know the sort of thing. I need details of their economy, past and present, politics, same. General history, primary factions past and present. Customs, that in particular. Everything a man might need to avoid insulting the locals."

Nikki shrugged. "I know all that now."

"Write it down for me? Cross-check all your references? Especially of names and associates. Not that I don't trust your memory, but it's very important that I make no mistakes."

"Certainly." He tried to force enthusiasm into his voice. "I'll do anything I can." It sounded like a lot of busy work, but it wasn't as if he had much else to do. "What's it for?"

"As part of their agreement, the Syndics have demanded that a Rhomandi make the rounds of the nodes to explain in person the situation in detail to their various rulers. They claim a discontent among the nodes that no Rhomandi has deigned personally to acknowledge their existence in two generations. It seemed reasonable, and I didn't argue, although I don't like leaving Rhomatum at the moment."

Nikki sat forward eagerly. "I could go, Khyel. I'd be *happy* to go!"

Mikhyel's face went blank. Deymorin and Kiyrstin looked at each other then down at their plates. But Lidye's hand clasped his, on the table, openly supportive.

"Of course he could," she said confidently. "In fact, *should*. He is the Rhomandi after all."

Mikhyel pushed aside his wineglass and leaned forward, elbows on the table, fingers loosely interwoven, chin resting on his thumbs, and rubbed his too-smooth upper lip with a thoughtful forefinger.

"Likely he should. And everyone seated at this table knows he could. But the Syndics requested I go. Not Deymorin, for all they still tend to think of him as the Rhomandi, regardless of Anheliaa's meddling." He met Nikki's eyes squarely. "What do you think, Nikki? Why would they request my going rather than you or Deymorin?"

He knew what Mikhyel was doing. It was a game they'd played since he was a child, and Mikhyel not much beyond childhood in years, but very old in knowledge.

It was a game no one else at this table understood. Mikhyel had rarely demanded things of him. Mikhyel would present the situation and ask: What would you do?

But it was different tonight. Tonight, everyone was staring at him, wondering what was going on. And Deymorin was frowning, not an angry frown, but curious, and Deymorin would be listening to his answer.

Carefully.

And Deymorin already thought him a selfish child.

He scowled down at his own wineglass. Mikhyel was right, of course. Mikhyel was always right. The Syndics asked for Mikhyel because the situation demanded a glib tongue.

More fairly, the job required trust. No one had ever questioned where Mikhyel's loyalties lay.

Deymorin had openly allied with the Outside farmers and miners and such, and he . . .

He was only seventeen. In Rhomatum, that made him a man. In other nodes, under other laws, even Mikhyel was barely considered an adult. In those nodes, *he* would be accorded the same respect as a five-year-old.

Besides, Mikhyel had been the recognized representative of House Rhomandi for ten years.

It wasn't Mikhyel trying to replace him, not Mikhyel trying to push Nikki back into boyhood. It was Mikhyel saying: this is the situation, Nikki, and the only adult answer is . . .

He drained his glass and met Mikhyel's expectant look.

A thread reached him then. A hint of Mikhyel's true feelings behind that look.

Mikhyel would love it if he could send Nikki. Mikhyel didn't want to leave the City again. Mikhyel had been, and still was, afraid of the Outside. The land that lay beyond the reach of the ley-energy held specters for Mikhyel that Nikki didn't pretend to understand.

But Mikhyel loved the Node Cities and the web, in a way Nikki began to suspect neither he nor Deymorin could match. Mikhyel's duty to the web was about to take him Outside again, the way duty to the Rhomandi estates had forced Mikhyel Outside when Deymorin disappeared last fall.

And like the last time, Mikhyel would be true to that duty, not because of his oath to the Council and the Syndicate, not because he was second in line to Deymorin, but because Mikhyel believed in what he was doing.

And damned if *this* brother would make that job any more difficult.

He chewed his lower lip, then asked, "Couldn't Deymorin go for you?"

Which seemed to confuse Deymorin, but not Mikhyel, who sent gratitude on that tenuous thread of awareness.

"Deymorin's going to be busy," Mikhyel explained. "The Syndicate and the Council both have voted the necessary emergency funds to begin restoration of the border watch. Between that and training camps, Deymorin will have his hands full."

Nikki nodded. He'd forgotten about that.

Mikhyel had worried for years about the deals Anheliaa had made with the other nodes. Maybe Mikhyel, away from Rhomatum and the shadow of Anheliaa, could find the answers to those questions. Someone needed to have the entire picture of the political affiliations within the web, and who better to attain that picture than Mikhyel?

"I also hope to get a chance to talk directly with the satellite ringmasters, while I'm there," Mikhyel continued.

"Why?" Lidye asked sharply, and Mikhyel cast her an enigmatic look.

"To see if they can help isolate and repair the precise points of damage within the web," was Mikhyel's cautious reply.

"That's not necessary! When Anheliaa dies—"

"We can't wait that long, Lidye. Since Anheliaa keeps you from accessing the web, we must find other solutions. Besides, I'm seeking consensus. I have developed a . . . curiosity . . . about the web, and how those who use it perceive it."

"Your *curiosity* comes rather late in life, Mikhyel dunMheric."

Nikki eased his hand free of Lidye's, disliking her patronizing tone.

"Events have triggered it, madam. And need. I want every Tower in the web on the alert for when Anheliaa finally dies. It seems only sensible."

Lidye made a sound of patent disbelief, and picked up her wineglass.

"Also," Mikhyel continued, ignoring her, "something must be done about the web. If we can consolidate efforts—both in the boardrooms and the Towers—and put the health of the web first, perhaps we can accelerate the healing."

And so, Nikki thought, Mikhyel had added yet one more concern to his already too-long list. So many different considerations, so many needs to balance. How had Mikhyel learned to see all the variables at once? When had he learned? Did he truly know? Or was he as uncertain as Nikki felt now?

{Sometimes, brother. But over the years, you learn that you can't always win. No matter how much you care, no matter how hard you try, sometimes the most minor oversight brings you down. That's why you can't just dive in headfirst. Not because you can't do it, but because, if it goes wrong, *you* may drown. I don't want you to drown, Nikki.}

Nikki met Mikhyel's eyes and was oddly content. He grinned without any effort at all, and asked, "So, when do you leave?"

§   §   §

"Behind you, boy!"

Thyerri twisted, caught movement in the corner of his eye, and leaped into a high, twisting arc. He felt the *shoosh* of air beneath him, like the passage of a ring, and landed feet first, punched the ground with his toes, jumped straight up this time, beyond the reach of a second swing, touched ground, and rolled beneath the pike's backlash.

Zelin cursed and whirled, swinging his pike across and down, but Thyerri wasn't there. Laughing, having at last the measure of the game they played, he spun away, a tumbling, twirling escape that ended atop the midden wall.

The morning sunlight slanted between Bharlori's and Gep, the shoemaker's, and all the haphazardly arranged surrounding buildings, making a shadowed patchwork of the alleyway.

Zelin let his pike thud to the ground handle first, then leaned on it, panting.

"And just what, in the name of the Mother, was that?"

Thyerri set hands on hips and laughed again. "In the name of the Mother, *that* was an escape. Up and over the rooftops, and I'm free."

"And if you don't? If your first attempt fails, your opponent knows you for a coward and knows your tricks?"

"I'll just have to make certain I don't fail, won't I?" Thyerri jumped down into the cramped spot among the sunbeams.

Zelin just frowned at him as if he'd uncovered a strange new species of bug. And in his long silence, Thyerri began to worry that he'd seriously offended the older man. Sakhithe had said that Zelin was not only the local wrestling champion, but a warrior from beyond the Khoramall. Such a man, the warrior, *would* scoff at a coward's way out, at escape as a priority, and Thyerri—

Zelin's pike lunged toward him, without warning.

Thyerri responded with exactly the same movements, but this time it was Zelin's low-hunched back he sailed above, with the boost of an added punch of his hands to Zelin's bowed shoulders. The first toe-tap sent him deeper into the shadows rather than straight up, and a side-roll brought him up on the far side of a fallen beam.

He came up, breathing a bit harder, but glowing in his victory, only to find Zelin facedown in the dirt. Thyerri vaulted the beam and rushed to Zelin's side.

"Z'lin?" he called softly. *"Z'lin!"* He rolled the bartender over, terrified that the blow to his back had done serious damage.

The body beneath him erupted into movement. Before

he could blink, Thyerri was on his back with a dark mass between himself and the blue sky, and a knife at his throat.

"Still think you know it all, boy?"

Thyerri swallowed hard, wondering where the knife had come from, when he'd never seen Zelin with anything more dangerous than the blunt practice pike, wondering why Zelin looked suddenly so much darker and fiercer than he ever had before.

He felt the knife prick his skin, and grew frightened without knowing exactly why. His voice froze in his throat, his face felt cold and hard as if he were made of ice, his eyes wide open, frozen like the rest of him.

"Hold!" Zelin shouted and raised a warding hand between them. The forgotten knife clattered to the ground beside Thyerri's ear, Zelin lurched away and staggered backward. Thyerri scrambled to his feet and came up hard against the shoemaker's rough-sided hut.

"Z'lin?" he whispered, and then, as his breath returned, "Zelin, what's wrong?"

The hand eased downward and a suspicious peek seemed to reassure his instructor. "Boy, with those moves and those Tamshi eyes of yours, there's nothing more I can teach you."

"Please, Z'lin, *please*, don't stop now." Not under such strange circumstances. "I'm just beginning to—to react rather than think. Isn't that what you've been asking me to do?"

"Instincts, boy, are everything, and yours are—peculiar."

"Oh." So he was . . . peculiar. Nothing new in that, except for the fact that now it seemed to matter to him. Time was Thyerri had treasured his differences. Now those differences stood between himself and the only life left to him.

He sighed heavily and headed for the horse trough and water pump. "Thank you, sir, for trying."

A sigh, heavier even than his own had been, filled the air behind him. "Boy—wait."

He kept walking.

"I said *wait*." Sand and gravel struck his feet and bounced off his pant leg. "Wait, damn your eyes."

Thyerri stopped, since he was beside the trough anyway, and ducked his hands into the water, bringing it up to sluice his sweating face. Cold and clear, it washed some of the sting of the old master's words away along with the dirt.

More than likely, it *was* time to quit. Bharlori would be unlocking the back soon, and he had duties to perform before the tavern opened.

He grabbed his braid to keep it from falling in, drew a breath and ducked his head into the trough.

"Thyerri." Zelin's deep voice rumbled through the water and the old man's hand gripped his shoulder drawing him up. "Thyerri, lad, listen to me. I can teach you a handful of tricks, but what you just did . . . that's far beyond me."

"What I did? What did I *do?* I jumped and rolled. I've done it a dozen times already today!"

Zelin's brow puckered, and he scratched absently at his ribs. "I'm done anyway, if I'm to have anything left for work." He caught Thyerri's elbow. "Come, sit with me in the sun, lest an old man take a chill."

Without protest, Thyerri followed Zelin to a neighbor's steps, shaking the water from his hands and head, and waited while Zelin grunted and stretched, sitting only after the older man had settled where he pleased.

"You're a good lad, Thyerri," Zelin said, which seemed to Thyerri utterly immaterial, especially considering Zelin's expression and the fact that Zelin leaned away from the most casual brush with Thyerri's sleeve.

"Give me your hand, boy," Zelin commanded as he had that first day. This time, Thyerri obeyed without hesitation. Also as he had that day, Zelin turned his hand over, and set them palm to palm, as if to force comparison between Thyerri's narrow bones and his own bulk.

"You were a radical dancer," Zelin said, and Thyerri looked away. "Apprentice, then. But you should have been."

"So would all the apprentices claim, were they the sole judge of the competition."

"Sakhithe says otherwise."

"Sakhi never saw me compete."

"Competition does not determine a true dancer, Thyerri. You know that."

He shrugged. The conversation was painful and pointless. Zelin frowned.

"Tell me, Thyerri, how many of your competitors were of the old blood?"

"Most are hill-folk—"

"Hill-folk, perhaps, but not dancer-blood."

"How could they be? The ringdance came with Darius and his followers."

"Ah, Thyerri." Zelin shook his head. "So ignorant, like all your fellow Khoratumin. The Dance is very old. Much older than Darius."

"Rakshi's dance. The frenzy. Dozens of others, but not the rings."

"Even that. But unless you want to waste time arguing—"

Thyerri shook his head.

"I thought not. Sakhithe told you that I come from beyond the web's border."

Thyerri nodded.

"And that my folk and yours were once the same."

Thyerri shrugged. Some said everyone in the world had come from one child of the gods, a single human that split down the middle to become the first man and woman. By those criterion, they were *all* related.

It seemed a rather distant connection.

"Three hundred years ago, my folk left the Khoramali rather than allow Darius' folk to destroy their ways." Again he took Thyerri's hand and compared them, palm to palm. "That's not just the difference between two men, Thyerri. In my village, we had those like you. They were held apart, not in contempt, but in respect. We were two different peoples living in one village. The dancers bred true for hundreds of years before Darius invaded."

Thyerri bit his lip, finding in Zelin's words a strange twist on an old, old story. He'd been raised in the hills more by the wind and the rain and the leymother than by any human hand; his understanding of his own people had been gleaned from observation and the historian in Rhyys' court, whose scholarship tended more toward fantasy than fact. Thyerri's one true belief had been in Mother and her first dancer-child, Rakshi, whose spirit flitted capriciously from one radical dancer to the next.

Nothing else had mattered. Then. When his world was Mother and the Dance.

"I look at those in the hills now and see that Darius' folk invaded more than the land. There are few of my distant cousins left. Fewer still of the dancers." Zelin enfolded

Thyerri's hand in both of his. "Our legends would have it that the dancers were hunted, like beasts of the forest, when Darius' folk first came."

"By the invaders?" Thyerri asked, finding his voice at last.

But Zelin shook his head. "I don't know. From what I've seen and heard, I'd be more inclined to suspect those hill-folk who welcomed Darius and his new order. Our legends would have my ancestors leaving to escape their neighbors, not Darius. When I came here to die, I never expected to find one such as you, Thyerri."

"Odd." Thyerri jerked to his feet, crossed in two strides to the building opposite, and leaned his shoulder against the corner post. He didn't want to hear any more. Didn't want this information that he might belong somewhere, but that the somewhere was far, *far* from here, and that, whatever he was, the hill-folk he'd always considered his own would kill him for that difference. Unless they'd forgotten the past.

"Thyerri . . ." He jumped. He hadn't heard the old man's movement, wasn't prepared for the rough-skinned hand that cupped his chin and pulled his face around. He tried to avoid the older man's scrutiny, but in the end pride made him meet that gaze.

"Hmph. Normal enough now." He patted Thyerri's cheek and dropped his hand. "Not odd, boy. Special, perhaps, if you knew . . . But you don't. And I don't. Those who *did* know, are, to my knowledge, dead, despite their eyes. Or because of them. Who knows? Perhaps, in this case, ignorance is best."

"Dead?" Thyerri whispered, and his heart twisted for those kin he'd never known. "What happened? What do you mean, you came here to die? Know what? What about my eyes?"

Zelin refused for a moment to look at him. Then slowly, as if the words were being torn from him, he said, "I was born, Thyerri, in a valley on the very edge of the storm-belt. I grew up there, fell in love, had a wife and five beautiful, loving children, three sons, two daughters. When An-heliaa capped Khoratum and the storms eased, the raids began."

"Why?" Thyerri asked, but Zelin shrugged.

"Who can say? People we'd traded with for generations

suddenly decided our homes and fields were more attractive than our goods. Perhaps others were pushing them from their far side. Who knows? We tried to protect ourselves. We united under a rich neighbor, who had a huge estate and many horses to protect, and we drove those invaders back into the lowlands. But the enemy outnumbered us. My comrades died, one by one, and finally, those few remaining returned home, only to find our crops burned, and our families and neighbors dead or taken into slavery."

"Did you go after them?" Thyerri asked.

"To where? How? And once I found them, what good could I do for them?" Zelin shook his head. "There was nothing left, except the dream."

"Dream?"

"Marini and I always wanted to come home to die."

"Home?" Thyerri repeated, confused.

"We always felt out of place, Thyerri. Pashahli Valley lies just across the Khoramali, but it was . . . different. Fertile enough, but hot in the summer. Dry. The wind always blew hard and straight across the wide flat plains to the east."

A faraway look came into Zelin's lined face. "Three hundred years, and the villagers still talked of the mountains of home." His eyes flicked to meet Thyerri's. "I wanted to see those mountains before I died."

Thyerri thought of his mountains, of the feel of the meadow grass between his toes, and sun-warmed rock, all those sensations that once had welcomed him as no one and nothing had since, and blinked tears from his eyes. He could well understand so long-abiding a love, had known personally the heart-sick deprivation.

"Thyerri!" It was Bharlori, calling him to work. Thyerri waved to the owner and turned anxiously back to Zelin.

"But the other, those skills you do know, you will still teach me that, won't you, Z'lin? Please?" When that answer didn't come immediately, he said, "Thank you," on a sigh, and headed toward Bharlori's.

"Thyerri, wait."

He swung around, hope springing.

"There's truly nothing more I can teach you."

He opened his mouth to protest.

"But if you want to meet me here each morning—just to work out . . ."

Thyerri grinned, and skip-danced all the way into Bharlori's.

Chapter Seven

It was a time of Family as Nikki had always dreamed Family could be. Dinner together every evening, followed by discussions about important, world-changing events, or sometimes just quiet reminiscences. Stories that told him more about his brothers than he'd ever known. Not big things. Little things. The important things.

They each had assumed a proper family role. Deymorin, as the Rhomandi (It was official now, or would be the day Anheliaa died.), and beside Deymorin, Kiyrstin, who was (Nikki had to admit) a proper, well-informed partner for the Rhomandi of Rhomatum. And her opinions, when they weren't aimed at destroying a younger brother's credibility, challenged Deymorin to think, to see other sides of an issue, and that, in general, was a good thing.

Mikhyel had returned to his familiar role of cool aesthete for whom such normal, human drives as hunger and sleep . . . and love . . . seemed somehow too commonplace, which was a great relief to Nikki, who had depended forever on Mikhyel for his sensible, distanced insights.

And for himself, Nikki had Lidye.

Lidye, who had asked for *his* understanding, not his brothers', who had defended his rights as Princeps, who shared his love of history, and laughed easily, and played the piano with a skill and pathos he'd never imagined her capable of feeling.

Lidye, who (true to her promise) never touched him, never approached his bed, but who, from their wedding night, nurtured *his* child in her womb.

Nikki had worried, briefly, when Mikhyel spent one entire afternoon closeted with Lidye, the day after his triumphant hearing. But when they'd exited that meeting, exhausted but still speaking, and Mikhyel declared himself satisfied with her responses, Nikki's concerns had vanished.

And if, on occasion, it appeared that the acting Rhomatum Ringmaster neglected her Tower duties to practice the piano or to accompany Nikki on his trips to the library, Lidye insisted that her active presence in the Tower only aggravated Anheliaa into disrupting the rings' stable, if not particularly productive, revolutions. And since Mirym took care of all Anheliaa's physical needs, Lidye insisted her presence in the Tower was unnecessary, and so she might as well be helping him.

Mirym. Anheliaa's servant. The young woman he'd once thought he might love and now remembered only as a pleasant diversion. He felt guilty for that inconstancy sometimes, when he went to the Tower and was faced with her quiet loyalty to Anheliaa's withering hulk, or intercepted Mirym's understanding nod or her reassuring smile. Every time he saw her now, she was washing Anheliaa's wasting body, or stitching her silken pictures, or weaving intricate patterns of lace.

Silently waiting for Anheliaa to die.

As were they all.

It was a *time* of waiting, a time of preparation.

And such preparations. The sense of purpose he'd sought for so long permeated Nikki's every waking moment, as he tracked down the details so vital to Mikhyel's upcoming trip.

Much of the information Mikhyel required truly was in his head, needing only references to verify the particulars. In that, Lidye proved amazingly helpful. She threw herself into his work, accompanying him to the library, staying there and taking notes in a fine, exquisite hand while he went off with Mikhyel to meetings throughout the City.

And oh, those meetings. Mikhyel had never had any intention of ousting him from the important position into which Anheliaa had cast him, he knew that now beyond any doubt.

Using Nikki's information-gathering task as an opening, Mikhyel introduced him to Syndics, Councillors, City engineers . . . important people of every description. Influential people, intimate meetings, one on one, with Mikhyel retiring deftly to the background, using that secret link between them to guide his words, to suggest questions, to give him silent reinforcement and approbation when he acted on his own initiative.

Mikhyel *used* those meetings to show the Syndics that they were dealing with a Rhomandi in every sense of the word when they dealt with Nikaenor Rhomandi dunMheric, that Nikki, like his brothers, *could* be Princeps of Rhomatum and worthy of the title, should that need arise.

And he, in his turn, introduced the most elite of them to Lidye, at meetings in Rhomandi House designed to supplement his report for Mikhyel. He had the pleasure of watching their reservations and suspicions wither under his endorsement and Lidye's own diplomacy. Certainly they were mistrustful of her at first, but no one could doubt her commitment to her new position.

She was, she would insist, present only as Nikki's secretary, taking notes on their conversation, but her subtle presence, her obvious knowledge of their respective nodes, soon won them over.

True to her claims, Lidye knew her history—better (though he quickly learned to mask the fact) than he. And while she said little at those meetings, it was obvious that no name, no historical event referenced, passed unnoticed.

In their private moments, she would lapse into entertaining anecdotes—stories *he'd* never heard—about his own ancestors, though they fit well enough into his understanding of those individuals and the times in which they lived, stories she related with the ease and intimacy of a natural storyteller.

She was eager to accompany him everywhere, whether to the library, the market, even (in sharp contrast to her previous demeanor) on the Outside drives he took to clear his head and exercise his horses, and he found himself increasingly reconciled to a life with her at his side.

He rarely saw Deymorin, except at dinner and afterward. Deymorin was gathering troops and equipment, calling in all those Outsiders he'd trained at facilities financed with his own funds. Men (and even some women) the City Council had once feared, thinking Deymorin was mounting an offensive against the City, and now welcomed as Rhomatum's hope against the Enemy.

Deymorin called those Councillors fickle and self-serving, but better that, he also said, than other options. At least those self-serving City-men were willing to provide the funds for provisioning the incipient troops.

Troops to man the old guard stations on Persitum Pass, troops for the coastal watchtowers—relegated in recent times to peaceful rescue and warning along shipping lanes—preparing them again for their original martial use.

Manning the western coastline against Mauritum.

And those he gathered from the Rhomatumin jurisdiction were only the beginning. Messengers came and went daily, contacts with coastal landholders as well as nodes, large and small, messages from individuals Deymorin would be visiting while Mikhyel made the rounds of the primary satellite nodes.

Providing Mikhyel survived long enough to make the trip.

Mikhyel seemed to grow thinner with each passing day, the lines about his eyes deeper. If Mikhyel slept, Nikki didn't know when. He had meetings all day, and at night, after dinner, he reviewed pending and extant laws with Deymorin and himself, seeking consensus among them, forming, Nikki slowly realized, a basis for future reference, creating meticulous guidelines in a black-bound notebook that grew markedly thicker with each passing day.

Guidelines for himself.

Because Mikhyel was leaving—soon—and Deymorin was leaving shortly after Mikhyel, and it was possible, Nikki realized one night as he stared into the darkness of his room, that Deymorin and Mikhyel might not return. It was the possibility of war they discussed, not romantic battles of the past. The world was in flux and history taught that when stability was threatened, wars frequently followed.

Deymorin might be killed on a battlefield that didn't yet exist. Mikhyel was headed into a world filled with angry and bitter people who might choose to blame Mikhyel personally, or others who would seek power by taking Mikhyel dunMheric down.

Mikhyel had to be aware that while the Syndics might have been swept up into Mikhyel's words and Mikhyel's vision for the future, the nodes themselves might not be. And Nikki thought of that dark and scarred man in Sparingate, and the man who attacked him on his seventeenth birthday right on the supposedly safe streets of Rhomatum, and he realized that the guards Mikhyel interviewed were going along for more than carrying clothing trunks.

But even as that ominous shadow crossed his mind, Mikhyel's thought, a reassuring wisp, fluttered through him, carrying with it a sense of Mikhyel, sitting in his own room, of silver leylight illuminating the notebook that he worked on late into the night, that being the only time left to him to record the day's revelations.

And with that comfortable image, Nikki slept.

§ § §

"Thyerri," Bharlori intercepted him on the way to the kitchen. "Can we talk, lad?"

"O'course, sir. But I've a table—"

"It'll wait, son." Which dereliction Bharlori *never* allowed, but Bharlori took his elbow and urged him toward the back room that served as his office. Thyerri resisted only long enough to pass the order for table seven on to Sakhithe before he forgot.

Bharlori waved toward a chair and Thyerri perched on the edge, hoping this wouldn't take long, hoping, desperately, that he wasn't about to get the sack.

It had been over a week since the dunKarlon incident, and Bharlori had never mentioned the fight—at least to Thyerri—and Thyerri had been working hard, hoping the owner would forget the whole thing. DunKarlon hadn't been back, and, except for customers asking him when he would dance again, everything had seemed to be settled.

"I haven't wanted to say anything," Bharlori began, and Thyerri swallowed hard. The embarrassed tone, Bharlori's patent efforts not to look at him, did not bode well for his future here.

And Bharlori had said to let *his* table wait.

"I—it's all right, sir," Thyerri said to the hands folded in his lap. "I—I understand. I'll leave tonight, after—"

"Leave?" Bharlori swung about. "What makes you think I want you to leave?"

"Isn't that what this is all about, sir? My fighting with one of the customers?"

"Why would you think that?"

"He hasn't been back. His friends haven't. I've lost you business—"

Relieved laughter interrupted him. "Damn right that son-of-a-goat hasn't been back! I told dunGythrii that if that *rijhili* bastard of his ever darkened my door again, his entire staff and household would be refused service."

"Th–then why . . ." Thyerri scratched his head. "What did you want to tell me?"

"I just wanted to ask you if you'd be willing to dance again."

Thyerri stared, dumbfounded.

And having begun, the words seemed to come to Bharlori in a gush. "The customers have been asking. They've told their friends, and they keep coming, hoping, even though I've promised nothing. I wanted to wait until you were quite recovered, you know. Sakhithe said she would, but doesn't think they'd like her alone, which I think is nonsense, but she—"

"I'm not . . ."

"Whatever they give you, after the dance, I'll split, half-to."

"Sir, that's not necessary. I'm your employee. You . . . you gave me a job . . . a place to live, when I didn't *know* anything. I'll do what you ask of me, but the frenzy, well, I'll try, but I don't *think* I can just, well, *do* it. A frenzy *happens* of its own accord."

Bharlori's face glowed.

"I understand that. I didn't mean the frenzy. I just meant for you to dance. And only when you feel like it, Thyerri. Every night. Once a week. Whatever you want. *When*ever you want."

"I—" Thyerri took a moment, while the world settled around him. All he'd hoped for was to be forgiven for disrupting his work that once. To be *asked* to dance, under any circumstances . . . "What can I say, sir? It will be my pleasure."

"And, Thyerri," Bharlori said, and the owner looked quite fierce. "You don't have to worry about that dun-Karlon, or anyone like him, ever again."

Thyerri looked down at his feet, curled his bare toes back under his chair and shrugged.

"Thyerri, I promise you. Not while I live!"

Which sounded very like a challenge to fate . . . to Rak-shi. A chill rippled down Thyerri's back, and all at once Thyerri was frightened. Very, very frightened.

Chapter Eight

On the eighth day of the second week following their return to Rhomatum, and with Mikhyel's departure less than three weeks away, Nikki was in his suite, sorting notes into stacks when, without so much as a pull on the bell-chain to announce her arrival, Lidye burst into his room.

"I *told* you I could find it!" she crowed triumphantly, waving a book through the air. "I just had a feeling where it would be."

Nikki stood courteously, uncomfortably aware of his half-buttoned shirt hanging loose outside his breeches.

"What is it?" He reached for the book. "What did you find?"

"Ah–ah–ah!" She whipped it out of reach and behind her back. "What will you give me for it?"

"I—" He hesitated, more than a little taken aback, her coquettish actions unlike both her early childish posturing and her more recent steady composure. Until he suddenly realized . . . adult teasing, like Deymorin and Kiyrstin.

His breath quickened, an unexpected warmth grew within him. He fought both feelings down. Their relationship had been established, or so he believed, at partnership and nothing more. "What do you want?"

She relaxed, brought the book out of hiding and held it to her bosom between gracefully crossed hands.

"Just a smile, Nikaenor. A smile that's all for me, and—maybe—a little, just a little, approval?"

There was a winsome quality to her tone. A hint of sadness. And Nikki wondered if perhaps she wasn't lonely. She'd been in Rhomatum for the better part of a year now, and for all practical intents, confined to the Tower that entire time. She'd been forced to play a distasteful (he'd come to realize) part for him, and sought acceptance, now, for the woman she truly was.

He could understand that need, and with understanding, the smile she requested came effortlessly. He moved from behind the desk, held out his hand to receive the book, transferred it to the other hand, and reached again, this time for her fingers, drawing her over to a settee near the largest window, a divan deep with cushions, worn and comfortable.

His favorite reading spot.

She fingered a threadbare cushion, and he waited for the inevitable suggestion that it be recovered, but she only met his eyes, smiled a secret little knowing smile, and curled her petite slippered feet up beneath her, the way he would, sitting in that same spot with a favorite book in his lap.

Those excited little fingers flitted along his spine again, and he settled into the other end of the couch, facing her, and tucked up in similar casual comfort.

Only then did he transfer his attention to the book or, more properly speaking, journal. An old journal dedicated to the establishment of the first fourteen satellite nodes. A journal that might have been written with Mikhyel's mission in mind, outlining, as it did, the events surrounding the capping and the backgrounds and philosophies of the founding fathers of the various cities.

His mouth was oddly dry. He closed it, swallowed, and opened it again. "Where did you find this?" he asked in what voice he could muster.

Lidye smiled gently. "Do you think it will be useful?"

"You know the answer to that. Where? Who. . . ?"

"Don't you recognize the hand?"

And then, of course, he did recognize it, from other journals.

"Darius," he said, and she nodded.

"It was in Anheliaa's suite. I *knew* I'd seen it somewhere. There would be a companion work, a continuation—"

"Not likely," Nikki interrupted. "Darius died before . . ." He let the thought trail off as he realized: "He couldn't have written this. At least, not all of it. He died after the capping of Orenum, and that was only the sixth satellite capped."

And around the time of Orenum, the handwriting did shift, but it remained very similar, almost as if there had been a conscious attempt to copy Darius' style.

"His son, Darius II." She shifted to peer at the script upside down. "Amazingly similar, don't you think?"

"That's one way to describe it." He skimmed a few more lines, his familiarity with Darius' antiquated spellings and speech patterns making it easy to absorb. "You say there's more?"

"There certainly ought to be."

"In her suite?"

She nodded. "Bookshelves *full* of ancient journals, Nikaenor. By all the Ringmasters of Rhomatum."

"I'd no idea," he murmured, his mind filling with images of that forbidden landscape that was Anheliaa's apartment. More sacrosanct than the Tower, he'd never entered it. Perhaps these journals were the reason why no one else was allowed in.

But Lidye had seen them. Lidye had been chosen by Anheliaa to inherit those treasures. And Anheliaa had chosen Lidye *for* him, so perhaps . . .

"Do you suppose . . ." He looked up and met her eyes. "I'd like to see them."

"Why not? It will be my suite soon enough. How could it be wrong to access it now, when so much depends upon the knowledge lying within it?"

"How, indeed," Nikki answered, and he bounced to his feet, holding his hands out to draw her up. "Let's go, shall we?"

It was a historical treasure trove, a tiny library without, at first glance, a commercially printed book on its shelves. Some were the originals of books he recognized as published works, some were writings referenced in other works, but generally considered lost.

Of most current interest were the shelves of journals, the handwritten history of his family and their alliances by marriage; but there were other books, books with elegant bindings, leather covers with hand-stamped titling that spoke of uncommon origin. Antique in style, but too elegant for the earliest Rhomatumin binderies.

Nikki drew one from the shelf, traced that impressed lettering with his fingertips, and opened the cover. Unlike the others, it was not handwritten, but the print was uneven, the stamp irregular, and of a style he'd seen only in histories of technology.

Old. *Very* old books. Illegal books. Pre-exodus, Mauritumin books. Some, from the titles, must have been taken from the Tower of Maurii itself.

Nikki's knees turned to water. He staggered, and caught himself against the shelves. A presence at his back steadied him, a slender, graceful hand reached around his shoulder and turned another page.

"I loved this one," Lidye whispered next to his ear, and she turned another page, and another, and he found he was no longer staring blindly, but scanning the words, following the text, absorbed in visuals, hand-tinted plates, images of caves and flowing iridescent water and nonhuman, magical creatures.

Maurislan Tamshi tales.

Rhomatum had had similar stories, handed down by word of mouth, intermingled with hill-folk legends, but these were the originals. These were the stories Darius himself must have heard as a child, pictures he must have looked at.

"Evi—" His voice caught; he cleared his throat and tried again. "Evidently the laws didn't apply to Darius."

"Of course not," Lidye said, her tone echoing some of the reverence he was feeling. "Someone had to retain historical perspective. I imagine he saved all he could before ordering his people to destroy their Mauritumin memories."

He leaned away from her, seeking her eyes. "How many of these have you read?"

Her chin tucked shyly in an appealing half-shrug. "I've had a great deal of time since I came here."

"Rings," he whispered. The book was shaking; so were his hands. He closed the book and sought a nearby chair, then sat there, clutching the book, and gazing blindly about the room. Anheliaa's room. Anheliaa's suite. The suite every Rhomatumin Ringmaster since Darius had lived in. "What other treasures must be kept here?"

Lidye sank down beside him, spreading her skirts sidewise in a graceful, single-handed sweep.

"We could," she began, then bit her lip diffidently.

"We could . . . what?"

"We could investigate the rooms together."

"We could do that."

Her long lashes blinked a single tear free.

"Is it not too late, then? Might we not find . . . something in common still? Nikaenor Rhomandi dunMheric is a man—a *husband*—to be proud of. I want to be proud of us, sweet, sweet, Nikki."

"I—" Somehow, the Lidye he'd first known seemed very far away. The past days flooded his thoughts as her perfume flooded his nostrils. Not the heavy scent he'd associated with her before, but a light, floral scent, like a hillside in spring. Like the Outside.

She'd evinced terror when he'd taken her driving two months ago; he wondered if this perfume perjured that impression, and if yes, what else she had hidden from Anheliaa and so from himself.

The rings, had, after all, matched them.

The book forgotten, he reached to touch her faintly flushed cheek. The color deepened under his stroking thumb. She gave easily to the suggestive pressure of his fingers, swaying toward him.

Their lips brushed, a feathery-light touch that he pressed deeper, drawing her tight as that heat, strange and new and wonderful, flared within him.

§ § §

"Heels down, eyes up!" Deymorin shouted from ring-center. "Man, woman, noble or common, your ass follows your—"

Thump!

"—nose." He cursed softly and walked toward the arena's far end, grabbing the free-flying reins of the free-flying—and rather startled—horse, tugging the gelding to a halt and pulling him to heel. "Are you all right, Shepherdess?"

Green eyes glared at him from under the shock of red hair, the glue she used to plaster the locks in place these days no proof against the wind and dust of horse. Kiyrstin ignored the hand he stretched down to her, pulled her knees up and sat there, brushing her sleeves and shaking her hair free of arena sand.

Their sessions in the newly reinstated training arenas on the outskirts of Rhomatum had become a daily ritual. In part, to improve Kiyrstin's horsemanship, in part, just to find time to be together.

The lessons had been his idea; he wasn't altogether certain Kiyrstin approved of his choice.

The horse attached to the reins bumped his back, an impatient nose demanding attention, worried he'd done something wrong. He reassured the beast with an absentminded scratch.

"All right?" Kiyrstin answered at long last. "I'm fine. Wonderful." She rolled to her knees and, with a fair command of street language, hauled herself to her feet. This time, her glare included the horse. "Evil beast."

"Eyes—"

"Up," she completed for him. "Right. Deymorin, I'm never going to learn. Why don't you admit it, and we can go take a nice warm—"

"Nonsense. You're doing splendidly. Up you go." And denying her time to protest, he tossed her back into the saddle.

"Rags—"

"Just a little line work, Kiyrsti. To loosen you and the horse back up. All right?" Somehow, her assent lacked conviction, but knowing he was right, he snapped the long lines into the bit and started the gelding moving, just a slow walk, at first.

"Have those investors settled on a date for the trip to Armayel yet?" she asked.

"Try dropping the reins, Kiyrsti."

"What?"

"Trust me," he answered, with a laugh, and: "Not yet. Sometime before I leave. Want to go along? See the fry?"

"Why Alizant *endures* that nickname—"

He set the horse to a trot.

"Damn you, Rags—"

"Can—*ter*!" he called out. "Arms out to the sides— *straight*, Kiyrsti. Tighten the arms, not the rest. That's my girl." Her back was loosening up. Her shapely rump settling deep and solid into the seat at last. He shook his mind free of that distracting image and called: "Now, shed the stirrups."

"Go to your seventeen hells."

"Eighteen. You're in Rhomatum. Drop 'em, missus."

This time, her curses covered several languages, but she slid her feet free. When silence greeted his command to close her eyes, he was certain he'd be sleeping in the barn. And then, a soft *"Oh, my . . ."* reached his ears, and he grinned at no one in particular, thinking perhaps his bed was available again.

Her body relaxed and settled the way the gods had intended when they first advised man to top a horse, and Deymorin felt his grin widen. All Nikki's beloved poets couldn't begin to find the words to express the way that felt the first time. Just watching, a man could feel that action beneath him, the sensual, almost sexual thrill of being part of so much power and grace.

"So, Shepherdess," he began after a handful of rounds, "what do you think—"

She swayed, wildly.

"Kiyrstin!" he shouted, and: *"Whoa!"* to the horse, as he dropped the lines and ran toward it. The creature stopped obediently, then shied away from him, startled. Kiyrstin slid inward bonelessly, but he was there to intercept her limp weight before she hit the ground. And still, they nearly went down, his bad leg choosing (with its normal exquisite sense of timing) to protest the effort.

Grooms appeared to intercept the horse, and cradling Kiyrstin in his arms, Deymorin limped out of the arena as rapidly as his leg would bear. He carried her down the wide corridor between stalls to the tack room and a bench covered with carefully sorted strips of leather: a stableboy's afternoon project. With a silent apology, he swept the bench clear with his booted foot and laid Kiyrstin flat, disposing her limbs in what comfort the narrow bench allowed.

She was pale, but her breathing was strong and regular. Deymorin could see no obvious reason for the sudden collapse, no visible injury, but the memory of her first fall plagued his thoughts. For all it had appeared from his vantage to be a simple bounce off into the sand, even the simplest blow, at the wrong angle, had been known to cause irreparable damage to the strongest man.

"Kiyrstin?" A quick-thinking lad provided him a bucket of water and one of the sponges they used for sluicing down the horses after a good workout. He squeezed the sponge and set it to her brow, wiping a drip from her mouth with his thumb.

"Come, girl, talk to me."

"And say what?" she muttered, and damp sprayed on a gust of escaping breath. "Told you so?" She struggled to sit up, swept dripping hair back from her face, then paused, sniffed her fingers, and jerked her head back. "Sweet Maurii."

"Maurii smells like horse, does he?" Deymorin teased, relieved.

"She," Kiyrstin answered, and wrinkled her nose. "And Maurii doesn't have anything to *do* with horses. Maurii is a very well-behaved goddess."

"I thought Maurii was a god."

"Only to men." She brushed his anxious hands aside and stood up. "Don't fuss so, Rhomandi. I told you—I *want* my bath."

"So, this was all a ploy, was it?" he murmured, cupping her face in both hands, examining her eyes for any abnormality.

Her mouth twitched. "Maybe."

He stilled the twitch with his own mouth, her lips opened beneath him and those urges that had flared in the arena returned, in full force.

"Rings, Shepherdess," he whispered, and pressed her back to the wall, striving to control his ridiculously adolescent obsessions.

Kiyrstin laughed against his chest, punched his ribs and rocked a hip forward, an abrupt move from which he instinctively flinched. She ducked away, laughing. He chased her, making an equally noisy show of losing her, but knowing exactly where she was headed.

It was a spot in the loft, private amongst the bales of hay and straw, but far from secret, and the lads in the stable knew well the amusement value could never offset the consequences of spying on whoever happened to be using it.

Kiyrstin was waiting there for him, stretched out in loose straw, hands laced behind her neck, legs crossed comfortably at the ankles. He stood above her, leaning against stacked bales. She eyed him up and down, and *tsked* disapprovingly. "Have you *always* been like this?"

He opened his mouth, closed it again, not knowing how to answer. "I—No, as a matter of fact."

She grinned. "Good!"

And reached for him as he dropped to his knees beside her.

§   §   §

Anheliaa's heavy chest rose and fell in rhythm with the Cardinal ring, outermost of the nineteen concentric rings of Rhomatum. Anheliaa was still alive, if what she experienced could possibly be termed living. Although perhaps having the world pending, waiting for her fate before making a move was, indeed, the ultimate experience—for Anheliaa.

Mikhyel set the stack of letters he'd brought to the Tower with him onto the small writing desk beside Anheliaa's bed, and sank into the chair next to her.

He'd taken to answering his mail here in the ring-chamber. Anheliaa's mind had gone completely opaque to him, after that first visit, and he'd discovered that, as long as his brothers were quiet, so to speak, he could escape their thoughts here as well.

And somehow, the sheer macabre nature of the place attracted him. He waited for her to die, as they all did, and yet, he had to admit that he daily hoped to enter the Tower to discover her small, deep-set eyes open and ready to challenge his independent actions.

To return here was to face the dichotomy that was his life, a dichotomy without resolution until this key element was gone forever.

A flash of green and turquoise at his elbow: a *toshi* lizard, one of several flitting about the ringchamber. He reached for the pot of *ushin* paste, dipped a finger and held steady while the tiny creature eased down his sleeve and began licking the sweet jelly from his fingertip. Male or female, it was impossible to tell without much closer inspection than this little creature was likely to grant him.

Perhaps it was both—some toshi were like that.

Three others soon joined their cousin, and two more, smaller, eyed him from a safe distance. The toshi lizards thrived within the Rhomatum ringchamber. They were accustomed to him, as they weren't to Nikki or Deymorin, and accepted him as a feature of their limited world.

He couldn't recall the first time he'd been brought to the Tower to attend Anheliaa. Even before Mheric's death,

Mikhyel (raised to be more biddable than Deymorin) had been trained to massage the aches from Anheliaa's shoulders, bathe her brow, and brush her hair.

He supposed a normal person with normal sensibilities would shudder at the memories conjured as he sat beside her, waiting, without shame, for her to die. Memories of a child's hands buried in the fleshy folds of Anheliaa's neck and shoulders. Memories of numb fingers seeking the key pressure points they'd learned to recognize on a well-muscled servant. A servant whose slender young body those childish fingers had still barely spanned.

Mikhyel rubbed his fingers, kneaded joints suddenly aching. He recalled wondering once, as he grew older, whether his abnormally long fingers were the result of stretching his child's hands around his great-aunt's body.

Not that it mattered now. Once she was gone, he'd never have to come to *her* Tower. Never again would he be roused from his bed in the middle of the night to ease her mind and her body. Never again would he be forced to listen to the bitter complaints when his best efforts failed to relieve her pain, never again suffer her dry lips against his skin when she was pleased.

A hand touched his, as it rested on the arm of his chair. He jumped, discovered, to his disgust, that he was shaking, inside as well as out. He turned his hand to lace fingers with Mirym, and thanked her silently as they were inclined to communicate, with Brolucci standing watch.

As the days passed, he'd found Mirym a warm, comforting presence. Whatever complex motives and associations might have ruled her actions before the Boreton incident, her actions since had been unwaveringly supportive of the web in general and of himself in particular.

Which was, overall, a good thing, as he'd also grown increasingly aware of her modestly rated Talent. Five days before, a message had arrived from Barsitum begging for more leyflow. A mining accident had flooded the healing node with over a hundred injured. Mirym had cradled Anheliaa's head in her lap, and the rings' steady pattern had shifted, and Barsitum had gotten its increased leyflow.

Lidye had refused to try, had declared any attempt on her part to shift Anheliaa's chosen course would simply cause her unnecessary pain and might erupt in storms such as the one that had chased them into the city.

Difficult to blame Lidye, assuming Anheliaa could affect her the way she claimed, but Mirym had suffered no such fears. Mirym had faced Anheliaa's wrath and won, not through battles of wills, but via some more subtle manipulation he had yet to comprehend.

As he'd grown suspicious these past days of Anheliaa's ability to sway his thinking in the past, so had he examined his comfortable acceptance of this young woman. In part, his visits here had been to watch her, to challenge that calm demeanor, to await some slip. But there'd been nothing, only an increased curiosity on his part, a desire to understand her better.

He wondered if he ever would.

{Don't hold your breath, raven-hair.} Mirym's characteristic humor colored the thought.

Mikhyel laughed, acknowledgment of his discovery, and raised her hand to his lips. On a sudden impulse, he drew her closer still, cupped his hand behind her neck, leaned forward . . .

Came a flux in that sense that held his brothers: infinitely subtle and soft, but undeniable. He paused, his lips so close to Mirym's he could feel her breath. He closed his eyes, and in the star-shot darkness there, he saw Lidye's blonde beauty shimmering before him, and just beyond, Kiyrstin's laughing eyes.

"Rings," he breathed aloud, knowing, then, the source of his uncharacteristic impulse. Mirym's silent laughter seeped up his hand. He held her close, hiding her face in his neck while he gained control.

Damn Nikki and damn his unpredictable, youthful urges.

Chapter Nine

"If you ask me, this is all part of the Mauritumin invasion fantas—" The speaker broke off abruptly and glared at Thyerri, who paused in the open doorway of the smallish room, balancing the large platter with both hands.

"Rings, Tobinsi," a second man said. "It's just Bharlori's boy." The second man, a regular patron whose name was Morshani dunSharn, waved imperiously to Thyerri. "Well? Bring it in, bring it in!"

Thyerri rushed across the room and set down the platter in the perfect center of the long, low table. Acutely aware of the five men's impatience to continue their interrupted conversation, he gathered the empty plates, then darted past the guards and back downstairs to the kitchen, a parting command to return with more wine ringing in his ears.

Bharlori's had expanded. The second-floor rooms, cheap by-the-night lets in the early days of Khoratum, had been transformed into private dining halls, each of a different character and price range. Many of the well-to-do from Greater Khoratum, like dunSharn, had become nightly regulars: the new Khoratumin bringing their other-node guests down to Lesser Khoratum for private conferences and deal-making.

Many, like dunSharn, spoke freely regardless of who was present in the room. Others, like Tobinsi, were patently suspicious. Thyerri had enjoyed, during his days as an apprentice dancer in Rhyys' court, a lively interest in the political maneuverings of the nodes, and at times like this, he found leaving such a gathering very difficult.

The talk was increasingly of dissatisfaction with Rhomatum and Rhomatumin policies. Giephaetum and Orenum had claimed for years that the Syndicate gave special consideration to those nodes on the lucrative Kirish'lan trade routes, ignoring the needs of the hard-working, but less populous, timber and mining nodes of the north. Those rumors of separate dealings with the nodes of the Southern Crescent, always a topic of speculation, had taken on ever more ominous tones since the marriage of Nikaenor Rhomandi to a Shatumin woman *of* that Southern Crescent.

"Do you mean to imply that Persitum intends to drop from the web, Marighi dePers?"

That same angry voice penetrated the walls as Thyerri approached the room laden with wine. Thyerri paused, just out of sight of the guards, wondering if he should wait to enter, curious himself to hear the answer to that question.

"That decision is up to Ringmaster Faris romPersii." That voice would belong to Marighi dePers, who was, Thyerri knew from his title, an official representative of Persitum Node.

"*Rom*Persii?" The first man laughed. "Have they reinstated the Order already in Persitum?"

"We never stopped believing, Tobinsi. The fact that Darius ruled priests out of the Towers in the Rhomatum Web could not end the belief. Three hundred years they've kept it quiet, but the training—and the faith—continued within the ranks of the ringmasters."

One of the guards glanced toward Thyerri's shadow, then, and Thyerri walked boldly forward, as if he'd just arrived, and knocked on the doorframe this time to announce his arrival.

"Come!" dunSharn's voice called, and the local man smiled at Thyerri and waved him in.

"And if Anheliaa fights?" dunSharn asked, as Thyerri moved silently about the room, filling depleted glasses. "If she tries to force Persitum to stay in the web?"

"According to the Rhomandi," another stranger answered, "they do not expect Anheliaa to awaken."

The Rhomandi? Anheliaa dying? There was a time that news would have brought great joy to . . . the person Thyerri had been.

"And if she does?" the first man, Tobinsi, asked. "Or if the Shatumin bitch proves capable?"

"Then Persitum is prepared to collapse the entire node and reset all the rings but Rhomatum's." That was the Persitumin representative, Marighi. He was a long, thin man with graying blond hair, and an air of perpetual perplexity.

He seemed very tired. "They must do something. Anheliaa is draining all of Maurislan!"

"She's draining every node in the web. They say Mauritum will suffer more than Rhomatum, if Persitum withdraws."

"Who can know? It's never happened. No satellite has ever willfully cut itself off from a mother node. Certainly it can't be worse than what's happening."

The words were flying around his head, statements without origin. Thyerri made another slow round of the glasses, delaying his departure.

"Would that *we* had the option," dunSharn growled. "Would that we had *any* true option."

"Perhaps we have," Marighi said.

"You mean the Mauritumin?" dunSharn asked.

Marighi nodded, but Tobinsi glared at Thyerri, and hissed. "Idiots!" And to Thyerri: "Get out. *Now.*"

🌀 🌀 🌀

"Persitum has recalled its representatives."

Mikhyel broke the news in the sitting room after dinner, considering it only polite to allow time for good food to settle.

"They're going to cut us off," Deymorin said.

"Obviously," Mikhyel responded, and sipped his wine.

"Garetti must be ecstatic," Kiyrstin said. "He's been trying to get Persitum to cut off Rhomatum for years."

"Well, one can't blame him now," Mikhyel said. "Anheliaa has been draining the entire web ever since Boreton. It's unconscionable, what she's doing."

Word had come from the other nodes, from the ringmasters with whom Mikhyel hoped to meet, that Anheliaa was indeed drawing hard on their resources. They were, to a Tower, fighting that leeching, and to a Tower, refused to relax that battle until they had far more confidence in the outcome of such a gesture.

"I'd stop her, if I could," said Lidye, from the settee where she'd settled with Nikki. "It's just . . . she's so powerful, and I fear . . ." Her voice trembled, and Nikki took her hand, speaking soothing nonsense.

The fact that Lidye and Nikki had reconciled their differences was impossible to ignore. Beyond the fact that Nikki had taken to sleeping in his wife's bed and disturbing all their sleep with his youthful rutting, Nikki being Nikki and in love with the notion of being in love, he radiated desire and obsessive concern throughout the day as well.

Watching the tender little performance, Mikhyel hoped her actions were less calculated than they appeared to Nikki's rather more cynical brother. Having seen Mirym brave Anheliaa's wrath quite successfully, he had his own opinions on why Lidye chose to put off assuming control of the rings.

Still, considering the obscenity lying moribund in the Tower, he supposed he should sympathize with Lidye's reticence to challenge Anheliaa. There was no knowing how channeling the ley-energy would affect Lidye until she began work, was how Anheliaa had explained the dangers at the pre-engagement interviews; and those physical parameters could change over time or overnight or not at all.

Nor did they know how the Tower work might affect the unborn child Lidye carried. No Rhomatumin master had ever tried. Anheliaa had counted on the child being born before Lidye would be required to control the rings.

Truth to tell, Mikhyel suspected that Anheliaa had planned to live long enough to train the child, and to hand the rings directly down to a Rhomandi after all.

On the other hand, considering that Lidye had married Nikki knowing that Tower work was inherently dangerous, now was hardly the time for second thoughts, excuses . . . or misplaced loyalties.

"Lidye," he said, and she looked up expectantly. "Persitum's pending defection has raised new doubts, and revived old factions within the Syndicate." He sent a mental warning to Nikki to hold quiet, sensed instant resistance, and beat it fiercely down. "The old distrust is welling up between the Northern and Southern Crescents. Your presence here tonight is fueling that suspicion. I will ask this only once, and I trust you realize the ramifications to yourself should I discover at some future date that you lied to me today."

Her brow tightened, but otherwise, her calm face didn't change.

"Are you Rhomandi or are you Fericci?"

It was a direct challenge of her loyalties. Nikki jerked, full of protest, and Mikhyel sent another message, wanting no extraneous commotion. He could almost feel Nikki writhing beneath his hand, but the motion was all invisible, a mental grip, forcing his brother to stay quiet.

Lidye rose to her feet and walked slowly about the room, taking time to consider the question, wisely avoiding the immediate, self-protective response that would simply have confirmed his suspicions. She stopped, looking at Nikki, then said slowly, carefully, "There is no way to answer that question to your absolute satisfaction, Mikhyel dunMheric, as you know full well." That steady blue gaze met his without flinching. "However—and you can believe this or not, as you will—I'm not the same person I was when I arrived here last fall. You cannot connect with the rings and not become committed in a way beyond politics. My life belongs to the web, now, not to any one node. Not to any one Family. My parents assumed otherwise. My parents prepared me with certain objectives should I attain the position I shall soon hold, but my parents are destined to disappointment. I listened to your advice, and your brothers' on choosing my own guard. I also listened to my father's. But ultimately, I followed the advice of the rings. I have sent my father and his men back to Shatum. He was not pleased with that decision, but I was. I found him . . . uncomfortable to have near me. I am *of* this node now, Mikhyel. Irrevocably. I . . . can't explain otherwise. I can only act as seems best for the web in general and this node in particular."

Mikhyel nodded, and released his hold on Nikki, who glowered in angry silence.

{I'm sorry, Nikki.}

{You had no right!}

{I had *every* right. Until you learn to control—}

"Nikki?" Lidye's voice interrupted them. "Nikki, are you all right?"

"Fine," Nikki said abruptly, and his sudden silence rang in Mikhyel's head like a blow. "I apologize for my brother's lack of respect."

"Your desire to protect my feelings does you credit," she said soothingly, "but his concerns were well taken. Surely you must see that as well? This is not the time for misplaced confidence." She looked up to meet Mikhyel's eyes. "I only hope I have allayed some of his fears."

"What I think," Mikhyel said, without inflection, "is that

you had best hold with that stance, if you want to remain Ringmaster of the Rhomatum Web. What we have accomplished so far is acceptance of the situation and the basic goals we set forth for dealing with that situation. However, the Syndicate considers the danger to the web to far outweigh the immediate danger from Mauritum, and seeks reassurances I can't give them. They believe that the only real defense against Mauritum is a solid web with an unshakably loyal and capable ringmaster. I tend to agree with them."

"I can't *do* anything, as long as Anheliaa lives."

"No? And if the satellite ringmasters refuse to cooperate unless you prove dominance? What then? Do we wait while Anheliaa destroys the web?"

"We don't *know* that's happening."

"Don't we?"

"I can't *do* anything. The child—"

"You would be the Ringmaster of Rhomatum, Lidye romNikaenor. Will you master the rings, or won't you?"

Again, he was forced to divide his attention, to hold Nikki quiet while he sought the truth behind Nikki's wife's posturing.

"The risk is too great!" Lidye cried, and her eyes flashed with growing anger.

"Then what do you suggest, you who would be Rhomatum Node's master?"

She drew a deep breath, visibly controlling herself, then answered coldly, "I've already answered that."

"Wait."

She nodded.

"Unacceptable."

"Damn you, Mikhyel dunMheric! Then find another!"

"Mirym?"

Astonishment filled the pale Shatumin features. "Surely you're joking."

So she didn't know about Mirym . . . Unless, of course, the look was contrived.

"What about Nethaalye? As I understood the situation, she had at least some capacity to hold the rings, though she wasn't as skilled as yourself. Is that accurate?"

Lidye shrugged, a single-shoulder, petulant gesture. "She might have."

"In any case, I suggest we ask her to return as soon as

possible. Your Southern association is and has been a real point of contention in any case. *She's* not pregnant. I *know* she has courage, and I *know* her politics favor the web as a whole."

"And if she hasn't the ability? If Anheliaa strikes at her the way Anheliaa strikes at me?"

"We won't know until she tries, will we?"

"You are as cruel as your aunt, Mikhyel dunMheric," Lidye hissed.

"Tell her what you will. Frighten her off from trying if you would like. I won't interfere. My desire is not to replace you, Lidye. My desire is to save the web. I would think you would welcome relief in the Tower, and being from the North, her presence here might reassure the Northern Crescent that we're not favoring one side over another."

"If she'll come back." Lidye cast him a clearly challenging sideways glance from half-lidded eyes.

"Why wouldn't she?"

"She didn't leave on a whim, Mikhyel dunMheric. She left because she was convinced you had deserted her. Rejected her as Anheliaa had rejected her."

"I can't blame her for that. But if I explain . . ."

Lidhye shrugged. "It might be enough."

"But you don't believe so."

"I *told* you. She was quite upset. I tried to talk sense with her, but when her father discovered you'd made that servant girl pregnant—"

"I . . . what? *What* servant girl?"

"Anheliaa's wench. Mirym. She had dizzy spells, fainted in the Tower. Anheliaa's physician said it was too soon to make the determination, but *she* seemed quite certain. Refused to rest, as the physician recommended, saying her response was quite natural."

Nikki was staring at him, his underneath presence, for once, icy quiet. Painfully cold, and Mikhyel released all hold on him.

Deymorin was radiating amusement and gentle mockery. "Should have been more careful, fry."

"You're a fine one to talk, Rags," Kiyrstin said.

"But I didn't . . ." Mikhyel's protest faded into uncertainty. There'd been only that once, and Nethaalye had been gone within days. . . .

"Damn you, Mikhyel," Nikki hissed, "don't lie. I *saw* you with her."

"What do you mean, Shepherdess?" Deymorin was asking Kiyrstin, causing an echo in Mikhyel's head as well as his ears.

"Once, Nikki. There was just that one time—"

"I mean," Kiyrstin hissed in an undertone Mikhyel heard only through Deymorin's ears. "I'm sprouting, you're spinning a new strand on the family web, your gun was loaded—"

"Liar!"

"Nikki, I'm not denying it happened, though I don't know what you were doing in my room that night, but it was just the one time—your wedding night, and she *couldn't* have known that soon—"

"Once is all it takes, fry. —Kiyrstin, do you mean—"

"*Yes,* for Maurii's own sweet sake. I'm in foal . . . breeding . . . *pregnant.*"

Deymorin caught Kiyrstin up in his arms and swung her about the room. His mind, intoxicated with Kiyrstin's revelation, reflected within Mikhyel's. Deymorin was oblivious to all else in the room. Oblivious to talk of other women and other children, his vision and thoughts all on Kiyrstin.

And Mikhyel grew ill with the swirling images overlaying Nikki's angry face, and with the mixture of Deymorin's joy and Nikki's outrage—outrage that surged now past that barrier of mental ice, though why Nikki would care about Mirym, with Lidye warm and close and willing, remained a mystery to Mikhyel.

Kiyrstin's scolding voice, rich and blessedly solid, broke through the internal cacophony. "Let me down, you overgrown . . . Don't you know you're supposed to be *careful* of us when we're in this condition? I expect to be coddled, treated like the most delicate web in the—"

The lights went out.

Someone screamed; perhaps it was Mikhyel himself, for the agony that coursed through him. Agony. Fear. Depletion. Anger. Horror. Resistance.

Death.

Silence then. So complete, Mikhyel wondered if he was the only one still in the room.

Or the only one still alive.

*   *   *

{Khyel?}

Deymorin. And a moment later, Nikki was there as well. A sob.

"Kiyrsti?" Deymorin's whisper, and a rustle of cloth. A sense of warmth and relief.

Carpet rasped his hands when he tried to move them. A sense of gravity, of up and down. Of pressure along his body. The floor.

"Lidye?" Nikki's voice. Broken. There was no answer. *"Lidye!"*

The lights flickered.

And slowly steadied.

Deymorin rose from the floor, drawing Kiyrstin up with him.

Mikhyel pushed himself off the floor, grasped a chair and pulled himself to his feet.

Nikki was likewise swaying upright. Deymorin and Kiyrstin. Lidye . . .

Lidye was standing, to all evidence, unaffected. She was staring at the door, a slight smile on her face.

The door opened: Mirym, out of the Tower for the first time since their return. And it was toward him she looked, a fact Mikhyel realized only after sorting out the three-way image of her. He closed his eyes and angrily shut out his brothers' minds, an effort that left his head pounding, but leaving only one image to contend with.

And when he opened his eyes and met hers, he heard her as he heard his brothers, without the benefit of touch.

Or perhaps, he simply knew.

"Darius save us all," he whispered. "Anheliaa's dead."

Interlude

"Ah-h-h . . ." Mother's sigh fluttered the leythium veils, and shimmered through the air. She inhaled, deep and gasping, the first unadulterated breath of ley that she'd had in two human generations.

Anheliaa was dead.

Mother had only enough time for that realization before the renewing leythium surged toward her in an intoxicating rush of total sensory glut. The tidal crest ebbed, and for an instant Mother sensed the tiniest of her threads vibrating with life again before the tap root that linked her to the progenitor surged a second time, and Mother rode that crest up and out of the pool and danced the ley as she'd never danced before.

SECTION
FOUR

Chapter One

For Mikhyel, second son of Mheric, direct descendant of Darius I, gods and religion were just words—words for culturally ingrained habits designed to ease the sleep of the masses. Death happened, the inevitable consequence of life; if any thing or any one governed either or both sides of that equation, he'd never perceived that it mattered one way or the other to the living.

He'd resolved, when he was nine years old and holding his mother's hand as it turned to ice, that dying and immersion were experiences to be avoided as long as possible. Beyond that, he endeavored not to consider. He knew only that he never wanted to feel another hand do what his mother's had done in those final moments, never wanted to accompany another empty husk into the depths below the City.

His mother had been immersed in the common hypogeum. She'd not been Rhomandi, in the literal sense, and therefore, Anheliaa had claimed and Mheric had not argued, she'd not been worthy of Rhomandi immersion.

Anheliaa's life had been filled with just such petty pronouncements.

Mikhyel thought perhaps that he'd begun to hate Anheliaa that day. His mother had become, in those final years of her life, the focus of his entire life, and when on her dying bed she'd consigned the newborn Nikaenor into Mikhyel's care, the bond between them had been forged for all time.

Anheliaa, by her arbitrary rejection of his mother from the Family hypogeum, had destroyed any chance she might have had of securing Mikhyel's loyalty. From that point, he had endured Anheliaa's decrees, but he'd never accepted them. Or her.

He'd followed his mother's funeral bier down a long tunnel draped with the remnants of some previous procession. Decorations of a joyous party, a cheerful celebration of the life that had been lived. A party that had culminated in a procession into the uppermost cavern, where the ley formed a shallow, faintly glowing lake, waiting to receive the remains of the deceased.

Rather like it daily received the City's sewage.

The same common pool into which Anheliaa insisted his mother would be set adrift.

But there was to be no party for the wife of Mheric, Princeps of Rhomatum. In that, she *was* Rhomandi, Mheric had insisted and Anheliaa had willingly agreed. There would be no redistribution of her wealth, no sharing of her personal treasures and trinkets, no loving reexamination of the life that had been lived. She was to be carried in somber propriety in the final hours of the day and released without ceremony to the ley.

Mikhyel had cried that night, in the privacy of his bedroom. Cried for the mother lost and the honor she'd been denied. And he'd learned the meaning of hate.

Somehow, carrying Anheliaa's bulk down the ancient, hand-operated lift, the thought of setting *her* adrift, didn't affect him in the least.

As with his mother, for Anheliaa dunMoren, the most celebrated of Rhomatum's celebrated ringmasters since Darius himself, there would be no party. There wasn't even a circle of friends and family to attend her immersion. Only their tiny party of four: his brothers, himself, and Nikki's servant, Jerrik, to steady the fourth corner of the bier.

That was the way of the Rhomandi Family. Since Darius I, they had buried their own in private, in a cavern far deeper than the common immersion lake, in a pool that lay directly below the rings themselves, a place as much Rhomandi property as Rhomandi House was.

A place too holy, according to Anheliaa, for Mheric's Outsider wife.

Anheliaa had died with the passage of Persitum from the web. They'd pieced that together, when they had gone to the Tower and discovered Persitum's ring lying dormant on the floor. That Anheliaa's simultaneous demise had not crashed Rhomatum itself was Mirym's doing. So he'd guessed and Mirym had silently verified.

If Lidye realized the source of that stability, she gave no

indication. Lidye claimed the blackout was the result of Anheliaa's battle to keep Persitum from escaping her hold, and attributed the return of the other rings to stable orbits to the inherent stability of Rhomatum Node.

That claim, whether made out of ignorance or willful misdirection, did make him wonder about Lidye's future as Ringmaster of Rhomatum.

However, Lidye was in the Tower now, despite her voiced concerns for her unborn child. Lidye hadn't left the ringchamber in three days. Three days during which she'd neither slept nor eaten.

Three days since Anheliaa's death; three days before Anheliaa's immersion, the minimum wait allowed by laws so old even Darius hadn't dared to challenge them.

Three days, and from the calm skies and steady power, the rings had, indeed, accepted Lidye in Anheliaa's stead.

Perhaps, Mikhyel thought, a happier note on this slow descent into the depths of the Rhomatum Node, it had been Rhomatum's acceptance of Lidye that had put that strange look on Lidye's face the night of Anheliaa's death. Perhaps the node itself had protected its new master from the death scream of its former master.

Perhaps—but Mikhyel had lived too long in Rhomatum Tower to count on any such benign explanation.

Queries had come in already, regarding the improvements in weather and available power, and news reports in general were optimistic for the first time in weeks. Queries had arrived as well from the masters of the satellite rings. They sensed a difference in the web, but no living master could know what their rings felt like without Anheliaa in Rhomatum.

Anheliaa's death made his upcoming task both easier . . . and more urgent.

For the moment, only a handful of people knew the truth, those like Diorak, Anheliaa's personal physician, who had officially pronounced her dead and prepared her body for immersion.

And those like Brolucci, captain of Anheliaa's personal guard. Brolucci had disappeared following an hour in the Tower with Lidye. He'd taken the rest of Anheliaa's guard with him. Lidye had assured Mikhyel via written message, that Brolucci wouldn't—couldn't—talk. And true to her promise, Lidye had replaced Anheliaa's guard with men of both Shatum and Rhomatum, *and* made all of those appointments subject to his, Deymorin's, and Nikki's approval.

Her father's opinion had not been solicited.

Politics, perhaps, but smart politics. And he was inclined to believe Lidye about Brolucci. Even so, he was glad Deymorin had set his own men to following Brolucci, men whose early reports indicated a mind in serious disarray. Kinder, Mikhyel would think, to place the man in permanent custody, but the ringmaster held absolute power over the Tower Guard, a circumstance Brolucci had accepted with open eyes when he accepted Anheliaa's appointment.

It appeared, in retrospect, that Anheliaa had chosen her successor well. He wondered—in retrospect—whether Anheliaa had known *how* well.

Soon, of course, they'd have to issue a public announcement, but until that time they had decided to keep Anheliaa's passing quiet, to show the world that the Rhomatum Web would continue without her—had, in fact, continued for some time before the general public realized she was gone. That was important. He wanted no more riots. No more panic. Anheliaa was gone. Restoration could begin in earnest.

Under Rhomandi control.

The lights inside the lift went out, leaving them in a dark deeper than his own darkest dreams. Mikhyel stifled instinctive panic, even as Deymorin's thought reassured him: the extinction only indicated they neared their goal, a point at which the leyflow required to excite the tiny crystal within the bulbs eddied rather than flowed, making alignment impossible.

It was Mikhyel's first time inside the ancient shaft that pierced the heart of Mount Rhomatum. A lift whose final destination was the Rhomandi hypogeum. Fourteen years ago, while Nikki and Deymorin had participated in Mheric's immersion, Mikhyel had been in Barsitum Hospital fighting for his own life. Nikki had returned here often; Deymorin had, chasing Nikki down. But Mikhyel had refused to enter the private shaft, seeing no reason to go early to his own grave.

The lift jolted to a halt.

A rasp of metal on metal: Deymorin had opened the grating. Mikhyel adjusted the protective pad on his shoulder—a thicker pad than the others' to make up the difference in height—and eased himself under the pall. At Deymorin's murmured signal, they lifted the bier free of the corner supports and moved out into the tunnel.

Mikhyel had some idea what to expect, from Nikki's poetic descriptions of his adventures as well as the many and varied images he'd received from both his brothers for the past three days.

But nothing could truly prepare a man for stepping off a solid platform into utter blackness.

Fortunately, Deymorin moved confidently ahead, and all Mikhyel needed to do was keep pace with his left-front corner.

The bier was lighter than he'd expected. Stylistically simple, following another Rhomandi tradition, it added as little weight as possible to Anheliaa's own bulk. But even she was lighter, her body, once the vitality of the ley ceased to flow through it, evidencing the effects of weeks without normal sustenance.

Effects for which his shoulder was grateful.

His head felt odd. Light. Devoid of his brothers. It was as if a haze had settled about his thoughts when they stepped from the lift into the tunnel, insulating him and his thoughts from his brothers, and theirs from him.

Light touched the edges of his vision, and soft streamers gradually took form and color: a lacework of light covering the tunnel walls. A web. Leythium, growing naturally here, and pulsing with the ebb and flow of ley-energy.

Like blood through living veins.

By that light, he could see Deymorin's profiled face on the far side of the bier. There was a throbbing, a fluctuation of color—as if he could see the blood pulsing just beneath the surface of Deymorin's tanned skin. Throbbing in time with the pulse of the ley.

Mikhyel shuddered and turned his face toward a brighter glow just ahead, beyond a bend in the tunnel, a gentle curve that easily accommodated the bier's length, and then opened out into the hypogeum.

He paused, an involuntary reaction. The bier stopped as well, Deymorin granting him a moment to take in the spectacle—or perhaps, Deymorin himself had been similarly mesmerized.

The cavern's perimeter seemed to fluctuate with that

same pulsating radiance. It was similar to, yet utterly unlike Nikki's poetic depiction. More like Mirym's mental picture, yet not that either. And he wondered, as Deymorin set them into motion, whether Mirym's leythium lace was any more accurate an image than Nikki's improbably perfect round pool.

A luminous pool indeed dominated the cavern floor and illuminated their footing, but unlike Nikki's poetic version, its shore was amorphous, a mass of tendrils that extended into shadowed perimeters. Those tendrils retreated from their feet as they approached.

Deymorin guided them to the right, toward a natural stone bridge spanning the widest tendril. Strange, Mikhyel thought, that he hadn't noticed that bridge before. That bridge, or any of the dozen or more spanning other tendrils. He was just beginning to account himself unobservant, when another scan of the cavern counted fewer bridges, and a third found none.

Except the one toward which they headed. It was as if something had given them a choice, and once that choice had been made eliminated the other options.

Something—or someone. As a sense of Anhheliaa had permeated Rhomandi House upon his return, so now some other presence resonated here. He wanted to ask Deymorin if he felt that presence, wondered if Nikki did, but that mental veil continued to hide their thoughts from him. And he was somehow disinclined to voice the question aloud.

Besides, there was about that presence a sense of vast age, a feeling that had been here since the founding of Rhomatum, probably longer. And Rhomandi had been immersed here without recorded incident since Darius the first. Best, Mikhyel decided, just to finish their business and escape as quickly as possible.

So he kept his gaze on that bridge, willing it to be real as Deymorin set foot on the seemingly solid arch, and sighed with relief when Deymorin indeed rose above that strangely shifting shore. Mikhyel kept pace, watching that stone beneath his feet, the leythium eddying on either side, a substance that was—in this semi-liquid state—near-instant death, absorbing human flesh as easily as it absorbed human waste.

Or so he'd always been told; he'd never had any inclination to test the theory.

As his feet touched the far side of the bridge, the bridge vanished, leaving himself and Deymorin on one side of the tendril, Nikki and Jerrik on the other. Lifting the pall from his shoulder, Mikhyel turned to face Deymorin, who had likewise freed himself.

At Deymorin's signal, they knelt and released the bier to the ley. Mikhyel kept his fingers well away from the pool, but when Deymorin's came dangerously close, the liquid retreated, sank away from his hand as the shoreline had retreated from their feet.

As if the ley wasn't interested in *living* flesh.

Which made a man wonder, as some unseen and inexplicable current caught the bier and carried it out to the center of the pool, where and how his ancestors had learned not to touch it.

Mikhyel supposed, had anyone asked, that he'd expected they would leave Anheliaa's body here, floating, until one day, they'd come back and it would have disappeared, consumed into the ley. That's what happened to those immersed in the upper pool, as he'd learned during his daily visits following his mother's immersion.

He hadn't tried to speak with her: he wasn't like the pilgrims he'd walked among, who came to ask advice of their dead ancestors. He'd just thought someone should be with her as long as there was anything left to be with. That someone should remember her, someone should care. Deymorin and Mheric had left the City the day after the immersion ceremony. Mikhyel had stayed in Rhomatum with baby Nikki and the wet nurse.

And Anheliaa.

Not a day had passed that he hadn't wished that bier had held Mheric instead. Or Anheliaa. Preferably both.

But this wasn't the upper lake. The ley was different here. Thicker, more viscous. And it *was* Anheliaa's body floating, not his mother's. He doubted he'd return to this immersion site other than to assure himself that Anheliaa was, indisputably, gone from his life.

Dark thoughts, filled with bitter memories of Anheliaa and her Tower, memories that were his alone, memories that, had he any say in the matter, would remain his own forever, and he was grateful for the haze that kept his mind apart from his brothers.

From their silence, at this time when tradition dictated

family and friends remember aloud the accomplishments of
the deceased, his brothers shared his dilemma. Let those
who had known her less well extol her life and achievements.

Slowly at first, then with increased purpose, Anheliaa's
bier began to rotate, first one way, then the other. The
leythium, like some living creature, oozed tendrils up and
over the bier, tendrils that began to form the lacy, weblike structure typical of solid leythium—a process that
in the growth chambers took months to form a palm-
sized crystal.

The iridescence flared. The bier soared upward on a
pillar of liquid leythium, lifting Anheliaa's web-covered
body well above their heads, stretching toward the
cavernous—

—ceiling. Mikhyel staggered slightly as his knees turned
liquid. It was Mirym's mind-picture and more. Drapes of
leythium lace bridged every stony contour and dripped
downward in graceful chandeliers, rippling with iridescent
light.

The chamber resounded with oppressive silence; or else,
he thought, distantly horrified, he was deaf. But then, came
a faint ringing, a chiming hum, *inside* him where he heard
his brothers.

The crystal was singing.

A prudent man would run in terror. Instead, Mikhyel
stretched his arms toward that brilliance, that sound, willing
it to shine and reverberate through him.

And the scent—it was a million roses in bloom, the tart
freshness of raspberries, and the bittersweet of fire-blossom
tea. Scents that permeated his body, entering through his
very pores.

He was smelling with his fingertips.

How long it lasted, he'd never know. It was an instant
and a lifetime of glorious exaltation of the sheer essence
of being. And as the leylight coalesced and sank in on itself,
there came a welcoming, an invitation to dive into that
vibrant sensory stream, to follow the bier to the very heart
of the node.

{This is life . . .} that stream whispered, and he took
a step toward the pool. Another. Blindly. Aching for the
fulfillment offered.

"Khyel, *stop!*"

He couldn't move, though his feet strained against the

ceiling—the *floor,* mind insisted—of the cavern. Deymorin, his inner sense assured him: it was Deymorin's hands that stopped him, and Deymorin's hand on his cheek, hard and sharp, a blow that brought him to his senses a step short of the pool's lethal edge.

The greater awareness faded, and before his eyes (Or was it his fingertips that registered the sight?) the pillar collapsed, sucking Anheliaa's bier into a hole of swirling iridescence. The surface of the pool closed over her without splash or reverberating ripple.

Deymorin's eyes were wide with fear. For him, the inner sense confirmed, as the insulating haze vanished. He pressed his hand over Deymorin's, sending reassurance of his sanity, surprised, when he thought on it, at the instinct that guided his communication preferentially into that exotic form.

He dropped to his knees beside the pool, to what his mind said was solid stone. But even that hard surface seemed to accept him, shifting beneath his weight, conforming to his shape, cupping his bony knees in total comfort.

He reached a hand to the pool. Deymorin's protest filled his mind, or his ears, or both. It was irrelevant, both protest and registering agent.

He palmed the semi-liquid.

Or it rose to fill his hand.

He wasn't certain of the actual sequence.

He didn't care.

The sensory cognizance returned. Gentler. Less consuming. And the ley floated there, a liquid rainbow in the palm of his hand, at once briskly chill and soothingly warm. He grew conscious of the sting in his cheek where Deymorin had struck him, and following some instinct—or perhaps some outside suggestion—he raised his leythium-filled palm to that spot.

Deymorin yelled, but the leythium had already oozed up and over his cheek as purposefully as it had entered his hand. Its essence traced his chin; he thought of the beard that once had been so much a part of him, a personal trademark—lost.

A sense—not his feeling, not Deymorin's or Nikki's—of regret. Regret for the pain, for the embarrassment, and a sense that it had been unnecessary. A sense of self-interested healing.

And more, a sense of awakening curiosity—about him.

He lurched to his feet and staggered back from the pool, clutching at the arm Deymorin stretched to support him, thinking belatedly of the leythium that should, even now, be eating his flesh away, and instead had evaporated without a trace.

"Deymorin, do you feel it?" It was his voice, barely audible even to himself, asking that question. He was shaking, a palsy that threatened every joint.

"What?" Deymorin answered, his voice strong, forceful. "I don't feel *anything.*"

Except frustration at him for being a fool. And relief for him that his foolishness had not killed him. Yet. And anger and fear that he—that *Deymorin*—had been held motionless, unable to stop his brother's suicidal actions.

"Get me out of here!" Mikhyel hissed.

"Gladly."

Far across the leythium pool, Nikki was staring at them both, head cocked to one side, his eyes wide, brows drawn. And as they watched, Nikki knelt beside the pool, as he had done; reached, as he had done—

"Nikki, *stop!*" he shouted, and the words echoed back at him, chiming in the chandeliers. And Nikki heard him. Nikki stared right at him, then deliberately thrust his hand into the pool.

"Nikki!" Deymorin shouted, and he dropped Mikhyel's arm to sprint around the pool, whatever force that had kept him from reaching Mikhyel acting now in his favor, creating shortcuts across the tendrils.

But even from his vantage, Mikhyel could tell Nikki was in no danger. The leythium parted, avoiding Nikki's hand, forming a crater in the smooth surface that tracked the rapid sweep of Nikki's fingers as he sought to scoop the leythium into his palm.

Mikhyel's head exploded with Nikki's internal scream of outrage and denial, and Nikki jumped to his feet and ran, away from the pool, away from the hypogeum and his brothers, away from his—as he perceived it—ultimate rejection.

က   က   က

Nikki began running the moment he could squeeze past the lift door. He didn't know where he was, and he didn't care. He just wanted away.

As he stumbled out into the rose-and-orange light of sunset, his brothers' pleas rang in his head, telling him to come back, trying to force him back to where they could gloat, where he'd have to look at Mikhyel over and over again.

Mikhyel, whom the sweet Mother of the Ley had saved from certain death at Boreton; Mikhyel, whose mind now glowed with the power to hold a man helpless. Mikhyel, coldly practical, eminently logical. Mikhyel, whom the ley had welcomed as surely as it had rejected him.

Roads, garden paths, and open courtyards, they were all the same. Nikki just ran until he could run no longer, then staggered to a halt beside a fountain, eyes blinded with sweat, heart pounding, his hands scratched from the roses he'd blundered past. He thrust his hands into the cool, honest water, liquid that ran from his cupped palm the way nature intended. He splashed water into his face, then buried his head in the water.

Instinct alone prevented his drowning.

Instinct, and his brothers whose thoughts followed him and chastised him now for a fool.

He pushed himself up and away from the fountain's stone edge, swept his dripping hair back, only to realize he'd become the center of extremely unwanted attention, as visitors to this small public garden gathered about to see what crazed person had just plowed through the hedgeroses.

"It's Nikaenor dunMheric," someone whispered, and someone else giggled.

Nikki glared from one vulgar face to the next, encountering grins, downcast eyes and open laughter, and wished them all to the eighteen hells above Rhomatum.

{For the love of Darius, boy, *get home!*}

And he knew, then, where he was and how to get to the one place he could both escape his brothers and find a truly sympathetic ear.

Mirym was coming down the staircase as he took the steps two at a time. He crossed to the outside curve, ignoring her, this girl he'd once thought his special friend, who was now pregnant by his brother's seed.

But her hand caught his sleeve as he passed, and as if through that touch he sensed her concern. For him. And suddenly he saw himself as she must and was ashamed.

He stopped, not because he wanted to, but because he'd been raised a gentleman, and gentlemen did stupid things like that.

Mirym frowned, the way his brothers would when they heard his thoughts and disapproved. Her hand dropped from his sleeve, her fingers curved into interlocking circles, her sign for Anheliaa, and she tilted her head in question.

"Immersed," he answered shortly.

Her puzzled frown deepened. A forefinger traced a circle around her mouth, inappropriate though the sign now was.

"*Mikhyel's* fine."

Her shoulders lifted, her hands fanned outward.

"I don't *know* where he is. I don't *know* where Deymorin is. I don't *care*!"

He started up the stairs, she grabbed his sleeve, firmly this time, and he spun, sweeping his arm through the air to free it. The back of his hand caught her face and she staggered, falling a handful of steps before she caught the railing and steadied herself.

{*Nikki! Damn you—*}

That was Khyel. And Mirym's head jerked as if she, too, had heard. Maybe she did. Maybe there were more secrets between his brother and Anheliaa's servant than just children. Maybe Mirym had taught Mikhyel to hold him captive as he had at dinner the night Anheliaa died. Maybe Mirym had only pretended to be his special friend. Maybe she'd always had her sights set on his older brother. Maybe the two of them planned to take over the Tower. Maybe the whole web, considering what had happened in the hypogeum.

{Nikki!}

{Get out!} he shouted inside.

Mirym swayed and collapsed onto the stair in a not-quite swoon. Nikki took a step down, then actually *heard* his brothers shouting. Cursing them all, he raced up the stairs, headed for the lift that would take him to the one place they dared not follow.

֍   ֍   ֍

"He's gone to the Tower," Deymorin said, staring toward the curve around which Nikki had disappeared.

"I don't give a lightning-blasted damn," Mikhyel snarled. He was kneeling on the stair beside Mirym, who was clinging to the railing as if her life depended on it. Deymorin gave up chasing his fool of a brother and backed down the stairs to Mikhyel's side.

The young woman's mouth was cut and bleeding, her eyes wandering. Obviously trying to hold to consciousness, she transferred her hold from the railing to Mikhyel's convenient neck. Mikhyel slid his hands under her, as if to lift her, a gesture that would have been funny had her state not been quite so delicate. And in peril, should Mikhyel try to lift her. The heaviest object Mikhyel had raised in years had been a glass of wine.

Waiting only for Mikhyel's silent plea, Deymorin moved to take her up, pretending for Mikhyel's sake that it took some effort, for all the young woman weighed little more than a large sack of grain. Mirym settled easily against his shoulder and reached a hand toward Mikhyel, who took it and held it as they moved downstairs to one of the parlors.

While Deymorin crossed to the room's far side and set her on a divan, Mikhyel fetched her a glass of wine. She touched Mikhyel's hand rather than accept it; he nodded and sat down beside her.

"Should we send for Diorak?" Deymorin asked, finding himself at a loss, in this primarily male household, to care for the young woman, who was neither servant nor family, but rather something of a habit.

Mirym managed a tremulous little smile and shook her head.

"Kirstin?" Mikhyel asked, and she nodded, so Deymorin left her to Mikhyel while he sent a servant to locate Kirstin.

{Tell him to check the music room,} Mikhyel's thought came to him, and, while dubious, he added that to his list of possibilities.

"Why the music room?" he asked aloud as he returned to the divan, where Mikhyel was dabbing at Mirym's lip with a lace-edged handkerchief.

"Mirym said that's where she last saw her," Mikhyel said almost absently, then: "Sorry," to Mirym, who, other than having a little color back in her face, hadn't seemed to move.

"Mirym *said*?" Deymorin repeated.

{Like this, Deymorin. Didn't you hear her on the stairs?} Mikhyel looked at Mirym, then, and said, "Oh." And to Deymorin again: "She says she tried, but you gave her a headache."

"A headache?—My sincere apologies. I think."

Mirym laughed, silently as always; and Mikhyel explained, "She says it's not all your fault. That damned childish mental outburst of Nikki's almost knocked her cold." And to Mirym, he said, "It certainly *was* childish. *And* cruel. *Especially* after he'd already struck you—and no, it wasn't an accident. It was a temper tantrum."

Mirym shrugged. Mikhyel frowned. Deymorin's head buzzed, and he cursed at Mikhyel. "*Talk*, will you?"

"Sorry. Sometimes I forget which I'm doing."

"Forget." *He* had to make a conscious effort *not* to speak aloud. "How long has this been going on?"

"You mean with Mirym?"

"Unless you've started talking with lizards. Of *course*, Mirym."

"Just since we got back. But it's not quite like with you and Nikki. We have to be touching."

He shook his head. "Brother, we're going to put you under a microscope yet. Spreading leythium all over your face, talking inside your head . . . what next?"

"Nothing, I sincerely hope. —No, Mirym." Mikhyel turned to the young woman, who was jerking his sleeve emphatically. "I'm fine. It didn't hurt me at all." And: {Thanks, brother.}

"Rings, Khyel, you think that's going to remain a secret in this house? *Nikki* is jealous as hell of you. He's not going to keep quiet."

"Jealous? Of *what*?"

"This is Nikki we're talking about, Khyel." And he followed with the image of Mikhyel as he'd seen him, kneeling beside the pool, eyes glowing like the ley itself as the liquid caressed his cheeks. Fey. Magical. Not quite human.

The embodiment of Nikki's most cherished, poetic dreams.

"Good . . . gods . . ." Mikhyel whispered, and Mirym patted his hand. "You saw that?" he asked her, and for a brief time, they sat there, side by side, hand in hand, before she patted his again, and reached for the glass at her side.

And all Deymorin got was a buzz in his head. His brother, whom he'd thought he was finally beginning to understand, was growing stranger by the hour. But he wasn't about to let him drift again, not without a fight.

"Why, Mikhyel?" he asked. "Why'd you take the risk?"

"I . . . Somehow, I think I knew there was no danger. Or, perhaps, I just expected it to part, the way it did for Nikki. The way it avoided our feet when we walked."

"But you're not certain."

Mikhyel shook his head. "Honestly, Deymio? I'm ashamed to admit I had no real control over my own actions. But Nikki—"

"Did it deliberately. I almost wish it *had* eaten a fingertip or two. Would have served him right."

"You don't mean that."

"Don't I? I suppose not. But Nikki's still living in some fantasy otherwhere. That he took such a risk—"

"Perhaps he had no more choice than I."

"You know better, Khyel. You saw his face. It was open defiance of common sense."

Kirstin entered then, a footman carrying a tray of pots and towels in her wake.

Mikhyel stood up. "Will you be all right?" he asked Mirym, who nodded. "Then I'll say good night."

{*Good night?* Where do you think you're going?}

{My room.}

{What about dinner?}

{I'll eat in my room.}

{What about Nikki? What should I tell him?}

Mikhyel paused at the door, turned, and said, "Not a damn thing."

Chapter Two

". . . and then Mikhyel put his hand *into* the pool, and his skin didn't melt! When he raised his hand, it looked like he held a rainbow! And then the rainbow touched his cheek and covered his face, and then . . . it *talked* to him!" Nikki gripped Lidye's hands, squeezing until she protested softly. He relaxed his grip and raised her hands one at a time to kiss them. "I'm sorry, darling. My only thought was . . . Go to Lidye. Lidye will understand."

"Understand what, sweet Nikki?"

"It *talked* to him, Lidye. I heard it. *Felt* it in his head, and it was wonderful. And I wanted it to talk to me, but when I put my hand in the pool—"

She exclaimed softly and turned her attention to his hands, turning them one way and another.

"It's all right. It . . . *rejected* me. No matter where I reached, the ley moved. It was . . ." His voice cracked, useless, as his mind was useless to find words to express his humiliation and pain.

"Poor Nikki," she said softly as she touched his cheek. "You do *so* want to learn, don't you?"

"Of course, I do! And the hell of it is, Mikhyel *doesn't*. All Mikhyel wanted was for *Deymorin* to get him away. It's . . . It's not . . ."

"Fair? No, darling, the ley is never fair. The ley just . . . is."

He balled his hands into fists, but there was nothing to hit.

"I fear there were times that Nethaalye would have echoed your feelings. But Rhomatum wanted *me*, not her. Therefore, I am here and she has returned home in disgrace."

Put that way, he couldn't remain angry. It wasn't *Mikhyel's* fault he was too cowardly to appreciate the gifts offered. But knowing couldn't take all the hurt away. He'd been right to come here. Lidye was sympathetic, as he'd known she'd be. And his brothers' thoughts couldn't reach him here. Couldn't confuse his thinking.

"You, at least, are not in disgrace, Nikki. I love you. I love the fact that you *want to know*."

Soft skin brushed his tight knuckles and slick, manicured fingernails slid inside, urging them open.

"I love the fact that you risked so much to learn. Thank the blessed ley it didn't accept your challenge."

"Challenge?"

"Some people can touch the ley and live, Nikki. That's the way of life. Mikhyel is evidently one of those. It is a physiological protection. Something he was born with. It doesn't make him more or less than anyone else. When it avoided your touch, the ley was *protecting* you, my darling. It didn't *want* to hurt you."

Put that way, the ley's actions didn't sound at all terrible. He smiled at her; she smiled back and raised his hand to her cheek, which seemed to him an altogether agreeable compensation for the ley's rejection.

"What did you mean, Nikki?"

"Mean?" he asked, watching the reflection of the rings in her eyes.

"You said you heard the ley talk to Mikhyel. What did you mean? What did it say?"

"It called to him. It wanted him."

Her smooth brow tightened and her eyes flashed, an angry look that vanished in the next breath. "But Mikhyel rejected its advances, you said?"

Nikki nodded, and Lidye smiled gently.

"Ah. There, you see? The test of a man's character is not what Talent he's given, but how he uses it."

Which seemed, somehow, derogatory to Mikhyel, when she said it, and Nikki looked away, escaping the flash of silver in blue eyes. But her hands drew him back.

"How did it talk to him, Nikki? What did it sound like?"

"I heard it . . . felt it . . . in my head."

"In your head?"

He paused, thinking caution at last, but too late. Lidye cupped his face in her soft hands and brushed his lips with her thumb.

"It's all right, my darling. If there are secrets, you don't have to tell me, but how can I understand? How can I help, if I don't know all there is to know?''

Defiance filled him. His brothers still didn't trust Lidye, because his brothers didn't bother to understand Lidye, as they didn't bother to understand him and this great need to be one with the ley.

"Deymorin, Mikhyel . . . I can hear them in my head, sometimes. And they can hear me.''

She nodded, a calm acceptance that rather disappointed him. He'd thought to amaze her. She must have guessed, because she laughed gently. "Dear Nikki, of course, I'm not altogether surprised. I've seen what Anheliaa does . . . did. How she invaded innocent minds and manipulated them with pain and fear. That you and your brothers speak to each other in this way is, it would seem to me, a kinder, more civilized use of that ability.''

Nikki thought of the night Anheliaa died, of Mikhyel's mind, like a fist holding him immobile, and wondered if Lidye would consider *that* civilized, but he was embarrassed that he'd not been able to break that control, even to protect her honor, and so he said nothing.

"Poor Nikki," she murmured enigmatically, which made him wonder if she could read his mind the way his brothers did. "When did it first happen? Can you tell me that?''

Which she wouldn't have to ask if she could. "I think the first time I felt . . . part . . . of them was on my birthday. When Anheliaa tried to force Deymorin to accept a bride of her choosing.''

Her eyes dropped to her hands, resting now in her lap.

"The night she leythiated him away?''

"You know about that?''

"Of course. Anheliaa told me everything. She was very frightened of your brother, and very fearful of leaving me in his control.''

"You weren't here yet.''

"But she'd already seen me in the rings. She knew she wanted me for you and she very much feared Deymorin would make life difficult, if not dangerous, for both of us.''

"That was stupid of her. Deymorin would never hurt anyone.''

The fingers of her left hand began kneading the knuckles of the right, pulling, twisting, a gesture vaguely familiar, but one he couldn't quite place.

"He hurt her badly that night," she said.

"Deymorin? How?"

"His defiance. The blockade against her that the three of you formed."

"Oh, *that*. Well, that was her own fault, wasn't it? If she'd left him alone, she wouldn't have had the problem. In fact, if she'd left him alone, none of this would have happened."

The knuckle-kneading paused, and her blue eyes gazed rather wistfully at him.

"None of it? Would we have been wed?"

He couldn't answer that. Not truthfully. If Deymorin had been here, he might well have talked him out of marriage to someone like Lidye. But apparently his silence was answer enough.

"Then I can't be altogether sorry it happened, Nikki. I wouldn't want us not to be wed."

"Even though it almost killed him?"

"It wasn't our marriage that almost killed him, Nikki. Please don't equate those two events. It was your family's bullheadedness pitted against itself. And even at that, it brought Mauritum's invasion to our attention. It allowed Anheliaa to stop that lightning machine before it reached Rhomatum. Is that bad?"

"Yes . . . I mean, no . . . I—I suppose . . ."

"And Deymorin wouldn't have his Mauritumin mistress. I don't think he would prefer that, do you?"

He frowned. She was twisting things around. Confusing him.

"I'm sorry. Nikki dear. But it's important that you understand. Events involving the ley happen for reasons. The ley knows what it needs, senses dangers we cannot imagine, and protects itself and so us from those dangers, if only we will listen and not resent the minor prices we must pay in the process."

Suddenly, that absentminded joint-kneading struck a chord: Anheliaa. Not a day had gone by in the Tower that he hadn't seen her doing that, trying to ease the pain of the swollen joints.

"What's wrong with your hand?"

She blinked, glanced down. "Nothing, really, Habit, I suppose."

"Habit?"

"Picked up from Anheliaa, no doubt."

Which made no sense if nothing was wrong. He reached for her right hand, examined the knuckles, looking for swelling, heat, as he would in a horse's overstressed joint. She chuckled, but made no attempt to pull away. If anything, she slid her whole body closer.

"So," she said, and her warm breath caressed his neck. "You first heard them on your birthday. And then? Did you hear Deymorin when he was . . . in transit?"

"N–no . . ." His vision flickered, his senses fluttering from her proximity. The rings' gentle *thrum* echoed his heartbeat.

"When, Nikki? When did you hear him next? How often, dearest Nikaenor?"

He closed his eyes and tipped his head slightly away, anticipating the touch of her lips. "Off and on. Ever since . . ." But he didn't want to think of that, not with those lips so close to his neck.

"Since what?"

He shrugged, the mood vanishing.

"Was it our wedding night, Nikki?"

"How did you know?" He leaned to the side to see her. She met his eyes, close-up as they were, and her hand brushed his hair back from his face.

"It makes sense, my darling. There was so much ley in the air that night. And at one point . . . you seemed . . . different."

"*I* was different!" He grabbed her hand, bending it to display the long, enameled nails, polished and sharpened, as Anheliaa's had been. "My back *still* carries the scars!"

"I'm so sorry, Nikki," she said in a pained whisper, and tears touched her eyes. "I didn't mean to hurt you. I hardly remember that night, except for fleeting nightmare images. And that . . . afterward . . . you were so angry."

She was shaking, inside and out. The delicate fingers turning red within his too-tight and twisted clasp. Appalled and ashamed, he released her, then gathered her into his arms, murmuring apologies.

Her return hold, hesitant at first, tightened when he failed to reject it, and with a sigh, she fit her head to his shoulder. Beyond her pale hair, the rings seemed to beat just a bit faster. Imagination, perhaps. Or perhaps a reflection of their delicate master's own increased heartbeat.

The most wonderful feeling he'd ever felt surged through him, washing away any residual doubt he'd had regarding his beautiful wife.

"What *did* happen that night, Nikki?" she asked.

He tightened his arms, willing those thoughts away. "I don't remember either."

She leaned back to see his face. "You're only saying that to make me feel better."

"I'm saying that because it doesn't matter."

"But it does. You were so . . . very . . . angry."

"I don't think I can explain."

"So show me."

"What?" He couldn't believe what he was hearing. But Lidye smiled, stood and held out her hand.

"Let me teach you one of the great mysteries of the rings."

Beneath him, the comfort of a cushioned chair. Behind him, his wife, her hands on his shoulders, massaging; before him, the rings of Rhomatum. Eighteen concentric, spinning rings, hanging suspended in the air, the nineteenth, the Persitum Ring, lying inert on the patterned-tile floor. The outermost ring, the Cardinal Ring and taller than Nikki himself, spun on an axis perpendicular to the floor, pointing straight into the heart of Rhomatum Node. The others spun on axes only a master could align, a master who could feel the flow of ley energy between Rhomatum and its satellite nodes, and react to its infinitesimal shifts.

Flowing ribbonlike among the spinning rings was the final outer element: the radical, a streamer of pure leythium, that chose its path at random until the master declared otherwise. It was the ultimate tool for manipulation, and the aspect of the ringchamber least often invoked, due to its intrinsically capricious nature.

Legend held that when the rings began spinning above a node, the radical rose of its own accord from the depths of the leythium chambers and began its dance. Nikki had never seen a node capped, never watched rings spun for the first time, so he couldn't say for certain. But without the radical flitting among them, the rings could spin forever and the power umbrella would never manifest.

Or so legend had it. The theory, to Nikki's knowledge, had never been tested.

At the heart of the mechanism, a solid leythium-coated ball spun (or vibrated, he'd never been certain which, only that it lacked hard edges when viewed squarely).

It was on that ball Lidye told him to gaze, and as her fingers massaged their way up his neck and to his temples, the hazy ball disappeared, became his room, as it had been the night of his wedding. And his voice and Jerrik's whispered in the shadows, discussing the upcoming event.

Jerrik's shot: *Tie her up and have someone hold a twitch on her to keep her from kicking . . .*

And his own laughter, which caused him now to blush and turn away, but Lidye's fingers reassured him, and urged his attention back to the sphere, where the image had wavered.

Jerrik again: *This had better go . . .*

As he fingered the chain Nikki wore around his neck. And Lidye's whispered question took him back, making that chain the totality of the image, revealing the Rhomandi Family crest in silver webbing over gold: Deymorin's ring, left behind with his clothes when Anheliaa sent him spinning through time and space.

"So that's what happened to it," Lidye chuckled, and he relaxed. "Anheliaa always wondered. She never thought to suspect you."

He'd taken it from this very room, planning to return it to Deymorin when he finally found him. Instead . . .

On the sphere, a man's face replaced the ring. A Mauritumin priest who had stolen that ring from him . . . and then vanished in the heat of the Boreton Firestorm, taking the ring with him.

"Our wedding, Nikki?"

And obediently, he turned his thoughts to that night, and her room, her body, beautiful and willing beneath her sheer nightdress. And his own utter indifference. Somehow, those feelings came through as surely as the image, as Lidye's feelings also permeated the air. He knew, for instance, that she'd been dreadfully embarrassed, fearful.

And then, she'd changed, grown aggressive and insistent, *Ah, darling, it was not I . . .* and the hum of the rings had filled the room. Despite his indifference, his body had responded, his autonomy had vanished, and he recalled . . .

Fear. And somehow, from somewhere, Mikhyel had been

there, and Mirym, and then only Mirym, and Mikhyel's room.

And always the rings, relentlessly pushing them on.

He closed his eyes, then, not wanting to show her the joy he'd experienced with Mirym, wanting less for her to see the hellcat she'd become in their bed. Besides, for that, there was no image. His body had borne the scratches, but Mikhyel carried the memories.

"Oh, Nikki . . ." Lidye's whisper trembled, and she sank down at his feet, clasping his hand, pressing his fingers to her lips. "I'm so sorry . . . so very . . ."

He brushed her hair, and cupped her chin, urging her to look up. "Not your fault, dearest. You think I don't know that now? And it wasn't so terrible. Just not what I'd dreamed my wedding night would be."

"And how did you see it, Nikki? In your secret dreams?"

He smiled down at her, then looked to the sphere.

Interlude

There was a presence in Mother's web. A shimmering interference of substance where none had been. Substance and a foul stench.

Mother hissed her disapproval to her crystalline drapes and sank beneath the ley's surface, but the stench followed her even there.

Sucks-pond-water the scent taste suggested. The predecessor himself. But he wouldn't dare. Sucks-pond-water *never* left his source. *Couldn't.*

Or so she'd always believed.

Mother sent a searching tendril, touched—and recoiled, disgusted. Then a fleeting, intensely focused thought flung the dropping out, back toward its true owner, the one responsible for its tasteless existence. There was resistance to its return, of course, but she was aware now, and the dropping would not, could not, return to her web.

Surprise, and yet another attempt to force the human excrement upon her. Curiosity and rousing awareness when she laughed and flung it back again.

The predecessor had been complaisantly respinning the same web, over and over, as if that were all he'd been budded for, munching contentedly on the detritus of his humans.

Fat and lazy, that was Sucks-pond-water.

And now he discovered an unpalatable bit and tried to fob it off onto her, thinking, perhaps, in her current depleted state, she hadn't the strength to oppose him.

Depleted, but not for long. The ley flowed steadily again, now Anheliaa's interference was at an end. Mother's strength grew with each passing moment. Soon, very soon now, her time would come, despite the rings spinning overhead, misdirecting her energies into foolish, wasteful tasks.

A third time the progenitor cast.

This time, Mother was waiting.

Chapter Three

(Fingers in his hair, pulling at the braid, ripping the strands free.)

{Tell me, Mikhyel. Tell me you love me . . .}

(Fingernails tracing the line of his cheek, sharpened, enameled fingernails pressing into his flesh, drawing blood.)

{Tell me, Mikhyel. Say it. Tell me you'll miss me when I'm gone.}

"Say it!"

Deymorin's eyes flew open. Kiyrstin, her head heavy on his chest, stirred, murmured a protest and shoved a fist into his bare ribs.

There was no sound, no one in his moonlit suite but Kiyrstin and himself.

Dream—nightmare, more like—and coming from his middle brother, though Mikhyel seemed quiet enough now.

Which only meant Mikhyel was awake.

Deymorin frowned into the dark and closed his eyes, forcing his startled body to relax. And behind his eyelids, in the corner of his bedroom, glowing with an internal light . . .

"Anheliaa . . ." His voice was a tight whisper.

Or Mikhyel's voice.

Not his room: Mikhyel's. And Mikhyel's hoarse voice repeated the name, and Mikhyel struggled to escape the bed's grip, fell out the far side, legs completely entangled in sheets and blankets.

"JD?" Kiyrstin whispered, or perhaps shouted; he could no longer swear to what was in his head and what in his room. "Deymorin!"

He was thrashing, fighting the covers. Or Mikhyel was, in that suite down the hall.

"Dammit, JD, *wake up*!"

And then he was clinging to Kiyrstin, and her hands were clamped on his arms, shaking him back to sanity.

Laughter filled his air, shrill and familiar. He—Mikhyel—cowered, there in the shadow of his bed, covering his ears against sounds that penetrated his pores.

Listening with his—Mikhyel's—fingertips.

"Rings," he whispered aloud, and pushing free of Kiyrstin, flung the sheets back, and bolted into the hall, headed for Mikhyel's room, prepared to break the door down if the fool had locked it.

Raulind was already there. With a key. The valet threw open the door, shouting for Mikhyel. A purple glow emanated from within the room, bathing the hall in eerie light that faded even as Deymorin cleared the doorway.

On the far side of the room, half on, half off the bed, his black hair a spiderweb tangle about his head and shoulders, was Mikhyel.

"Damn you, Anheliaa," he hissed, seemingly oblivious to Deymorin's presence, and he slipped down to his knees, dragging his hands across sheets that pulled loose, following his descent. His head fell forward into his crossed arms and the cushioning mattress. "Couldn't you at least *die* like a normal human being?"

§   §   §

The mountain air tingled with unleashed energy.

{Mother!} Thyerri cried out, caught in half-asleep stupidity, and his arms tangled in his blankets as he reached for that which was no longer his.

He started awake, in time to keep from shouting aloud.

{Mother?} he called again, knowing there would be no answer, for all the air around him said life had returned to Khoratum.

Thyerri buried his head in his arm, shivering. Around him, his fellow employees slept quietly, oblivious to the fact that the world was changing.

The air had been quiet for three days. Three storm-free days in a row. And the lights had held steady in the Tower and beyond. And tonight . . .

Thyerri blinked. The hand he rested on . . . the entire arm . . . glowed with faint green light.

"Mother?" he whispered, aloud this time, but there was

no response, and the glow neither scintillated nor evanesced. He knew then, it wasn't Mother, but only the mountain, calling to whomever could hear.

Needing freedom, needing moonlight and cleansing breezes, he slid free of his pallet and covers, stepped over sleeping bodies and crawled out the window to the alley.

There were ways out of the old village, passages through the stone that were older than the city wall, passages Rhyys' City Guard didn't know about. Thyerri's feet followed one such without benefit of thought, and when next he came to his senses, the mountain was beneath his feet, and moonshadowed forest surrounded him.

He came to the lake and threw himself in, diving deep, feeling the energy tingling through him, dissipating at last into the icy glacier-melt water. And at the edges of his senses, there was a presence that called to him.

{Mother!} he shouted again, begging for an answer, seeking asylum from the wild ebb and flow of energy.

Still, there was nothing, though his mind began to spin for lack of air.

Lungs straining, he pulled at last for the surface. He broke free, gasping, and trod water. Water that glistened green in the silver moonlight. Glowing with energy, as Thyerri himself glowed.

As someone on the shore of the lake glowed.

Someone who was watching him.

The energy ebbed at last, flowed from the air and himself and the lake . . . and that statue-still figure on the shore. And as the last of the glow faded, the moon hid behind a cloud, leaving them all in darkness.

When the moon returned, the figure was gone.

֍   ֍   ֍

"He claims it was just a nightmare." Deymorin cast his robe over a chair and slid under the covers Kiyrstin lifted in welcome. "He says it was brought on by his falling asleep with his . . . *hair* braided." But the shudder that rippled through him revealed more to her than his skeptical words.

"But you don't think so," she said, wrapping her arms around him comfortably.

His broad chest heaved in a sigh. "It makes just enough sense with what I saw in his head when . . ."

Another shiver passed through him and Kiyrstin hugged tighter. His cheek rubbed across her head.

"What was in his mind was no nightmare, Kiyrsti. And— dammit, I *saw* that purple light."

"Could it—" She bit her lip, the thought too bizarre to contemplate. "Still, this *is* Anheliaa we're talking about, JD. Could it actually *be* her?"

"Anheliaa? I suppose we have to face that possibility. But . . . there is the leymother."

Mother. The Tamshi, or so she'd claimed to be, who had taken the form of a man six hours dead to warn Deymorin of danger.

"You think she's here to warn him of something?"

"Warn? Possibly. But what if it was Mikhyel she wanted all along? What if she wasn't warning us, but sending *me* to where Nikki was. To *get* Mikhyel there?"

"She waited long enough to show, if that's the case. He almost died, Deymorin. He wouldn't have been much use to her then, would he?"

He shrugged. "I suppose it depends on what she wanted to do with him."

"You think she might have a special interest in him?"

"I think the ley has. I'm beginning to wonder if there's much difference."

"The ley."

"I don't know if I can explain. In the old stories, the Tamshi and the ley are always interlinked. The way she changed shape, the way she disappeared, it could all be the same thing. All I know is, she appeared out of nowhere and healed Mikhyel. She had no interest in Nikki, none in me. Yesterday, down in the hypogeum . . . Shepherdess, it was—" Another shiver. "There was no sense in Mikhyel's face. No thought. He just reached blindly and buried his hand in the leythium. And I couldn't get to him, couldn't stop him. It was as if every muscle was frozen. There are powers at work that I don't like in the least."

"He's all right now, though?"

"Five stiff drinks later? I suppose. If he forgives me in the morning."

She traced patterns on his chest with her fingertip.

"Why Anheliaa?" she asked.

"What do you mean?"

"Why would Mother take the form of Anheliaa?"

"To terrify him? Because it was convenient? Hell, I don't know." Deymorin's voice was shaking. A long pause, then, "I thought I knew the whole of it."

"Of what?"

"Mikhyel. Mheric. But this . . . rings, Shepherdess, what was in his mind . . . I can't begin to imagine what she did to him over the years. How he stayed sane . . . And I left him here. First, I deserted him to Mheric, then I deserted him to—"

He cursed, and rolled away, driving a fist into a well-stuffed pillow. Once. Twice. And again, harder and harder until feathers poofed out.

Kiyrstin, deciding he'd wallowed long enough, placed a firm hand on his broad shoulder. The pounding stopped.

"Done is done, my friend. Mikhyel doesn't blame you."

"He damnwell should!"

"Maybe. But he doesn't. I can't see where you have the right to blame yourself."

He rolled back, hugged her in harsh desperation.

"I hated her, Kiyrsti," he whispered. "I hated her, and I wanted her dead, more often than I can remember. And *that* was just for her obstinate ego. If I'd known what she was doing to Khyel, I *would* have killed her, and damn the rings. I almost wish that had been her in his room. I wish I could face her down, on whatever battlefield she chose and make her suffer the way she's made him suffer."

"You want to rend a purple ghost into bits of ectoplasmic goo? Rain leythium thunderbolts down upon her insubstantial head?"

That gained her a reluctant laugh.

"Rings, you sound like Nikki," he said.

"So do you."

"Darius save me."

"Darius is hardly in a position to save anyone."

"Who better to take care of a ghost than another ghost?"

"I'd say, forget about ghosts and take care of yourself." She stroked his arm, then smoothed his chest and stomach. "On the other hand, if it is Mother . . ."

"I'm going to have to tell Mikhyel the truth, Kiyrstin, and damn the consequences. He's got a right to know. Not that he'll believe me, of course, but—"

"After all that's happened? After the hypogeum? I think you underestimate him, Deymorin."

"I hope you're right."

She let her hand drift lower and shifted toward him. "Trust me," she said, and set her lips to his.

Chapter Four

Morning sunlight danced in the fountain, sparked colors from dew-touched rose petals.

Four clear days in a row. Four mornings since Anheliaa's death.

Twenty-one before his scheduled departure on a tour that had suddenly acquired more intimate overtones.

Mikhyel walked a familiar route among the roses, out, as had become his habit over the years, before the gardener made his morning rounds. His mind was clearer this morning that it had any right to be, considering the liquor Deymorin had poured down his throat. Possibly it was the tea Raulind had pressed upon him at the last.

And perhaps his head wasn't clear or painfree, but simply numb.

Kharishia's Pride was in full bloom. He paused beside the rose, one of his favorites, to drink in the fresh berry-touched scent. Lavender, shaded to turquoise, with a blush of unnameable color that made it glow. The variety only grew here, at the heart of Rhomatum. Other nodes had tried to import it without success.

Even its growth pattern was different than other roses, sending out runners that sprouted upward.

The origin of the name had been lost to antiquity . . . until Lidye. According to Nikki's strangely knowledgeable wife, Kharishia was the name of Darius' mysterious last wife.

His ancestor.

A suspicious cast to a leaf caught his eye. He knelt down, turned it . . . aphids. He peeled the leaf away from the stem, caught a tiny black eye watching him from the shadows beneath a neighboring bush, and set the leaf down in those shadows.

The instant his hand drew away, the tiny flash-lizard

eased out of the shadows and began devouring the aphids, a tiny tongue-flick at a time.

Mikhyel rested his elbow on his knee and rubbed a hand across his eyes. He wondered, sometimes, if he would ever sleep properly again. His brain seemed to have forgotten how to shut the world out and relax. It had been difficult enough, upon their return to the City, catching up on what amounted to two months' work. Now, with the plans for his upcoming trip, the notes he was accumulating for Nikki while he was gone, arranging for the children . . .

The lizard flitted away. Mikhyel pushed himself to his feet and continued on his path.

Children. Family. It was a problem he'd never envisioned attached to his own duties and obligations. Nikki's duties, perhaps. Deymorin's, certainly. Deymorin had always loved children, and Deymorin and women were so paired in his own mind that children and family were simply a logical by-product.

He scraped his foot across the path, smoothing the fine, white gravel, wondering idly what gardener's tool had left the small trench.

Himself . . . He stopped beside the fountain, propped one leg on the marble ledge and trailed his fingers in the clear chill. Mheric's legacy had been too strong. He hadn't ever really wanted a wife, let alone children.

Nikki had been his child, placed newborn in his nine-year-old arms by their dying mother. And he'd gotten Nikki to manhood, somehow, and by that act assumed his duty to the family web accomplished.

The Rhomandi had never been a prolific family; to have three sons of breeding age at one time was unprecedented. Now, if Lidye were to be believed . . .

He raised a handful of the chill water to cheeks suddenly over-warm, feeling foolish. Blushing, at his age and in the presence of only the long-finned pond fish.

If Lidye had spoken the truth four nights ago, Mirym carried his child. Certainly, it was possible. His body and Mirym's had had as much intimate contact as Nikki's and Lidye's, but why hadn't Mirym said something? There'd been time, surely, during those shared afternoons in Anheliaa's ringchamber. They'd have had the ultimate privacy of their own thoughts, with only a surreptitious touch of their hands.

He had no reason to believe she felt any particular affection for him; he knew he had none for her, had, in fact, reason still to suspect her deepest motives. But he would have thought they were at least adult enough to broach a topic that so intimately involved them both.

He brushed the damp down his face; stubbed skin rasped beneath his touch. He should have shaved, but he hadn't had the heart to rouse Raulind after last night's—

He dropped his hand, staring at fingertips that looked perfectly normal, then explored his chin and lip more carefully.

Pluck them! Destroy them all!

Anheliaa's voice echoed in memory's ear. Anheliaa had hated his growing up, had attacked the hair that marked his puberty, endeavoring to stave off the inevitable, to keep him a child as long as possible. He remembered standing, bare of clothing, skin still tingling from the scrubbing sponge, for Anheliaa's inspection.

Every night.

And nightly, as he grew older, Anheliaa's personal maid would pluck his body free of hair.

Nothing Mheric had ever done had been half so irrational.

Anheliaa had had no husband, no lover, to his knowledge, in all her long life. She'd been an embittered, crippled woman. She'd always wished Mheric had had a daughter, she'd made no secret of that, had frequently cursed him for his ill-considered gender. And after Anheliaa and her rings flung him to the Boreton Turnout, the only hair left on his body had been the hair she'd allowed him to keep as a child, that on his head, his eyebrows and his eyelashes.

And now, she was dead and his beard returned.

Coincidence?

Somehow, he doubted it.

So many questions still, regarding that time following the battle of Boreton. Questions he believed his brothers could answer, if they would, but Deymorin just laughed and said he'd best forget about it, and Nikki glowered and said nothing, but Nikki's mind was a confusion of images of old hags and reptiles, and a cloud of shaded hair framing impossibly beautiful, glowing eyes.

A gust of cool air whipped fountain mist across his face. He shivered.

The sound of heavy skirts displacing gravel swished above the music of the fountain. He glanced up and intercepted Mirym's doe-eyed gaze. She was alone.

He sought words, commonplace pleasantries, but what came out was, "Is it true, Mirym? Are you carrying my child?"

Her smile was tender but secretive. She pressed her hands to her stomach, than crossed them on her bosom and rocked gently. Touched his arm and shrugged.

"You're pregnant, just not certain it's mine?"

She nodded.

"You've been with so many men recently," he chided gently.

She looked generally skyward, her head tilting to one side and the other as she ticked off fingers. When, having used up both hands, she began a second round, he acknowledged defeat. Chuckling in spite of the gravity of the situation, he grasped her hands to stop her.

{Truth, madam. Am I the father?} He thought the words as clearly and forcefully as possible, afraid she wouldn't hear, this far from the ringchamber.

She jumped and pulled her hands away, eyes wide with pain and indignation.

"Forgive me," he said, and reached again, this time to lay his hand lightly on hers, repeating his question, but with rather more civilized intensity.

Her answer was just vague acknowledgment of probability . . . and a reminder that Kiyrstin was also breeding.

"Rings," he whispered, and stood up, feeling a need to move. Three men, three women . . .

{And an old woman's obsessive desire for offspring.} Mirym's thought pursued him, acknowledging his line of thought, and Mirym herself was beside him, hand on his.

"Lidye was so certain, that very night . . ." he said.

{As was I.}

Which assurance defied all he understood about such things.

"I thought it took months to know—"

{I knew.} Mirym's insistence left no room for skepticism. {That night, I felt it quicken within me.}

"Was it Anheliaa? Was it all her doing?"

{Anheliaa was very powerful in her desire. I suspect, yes. But perhaps it was simply meant to be.}

"I can't believe in coincidence that great."

{Did I say coincidence? The ley was involved, Mikhyel dunMheric.}

"Leythium is a substance, Mirym. To deny coincidence implies motivation. Motivation implies self-awareness. Cognizance."

{I said the ley, not leythium. There *is* a difference, as you well know, Mikhyel, son of Mheric, descendant of Darius.}

"The ley is leythium. Crystal that glows and heats within the sphere of its parent node. Liquid that ingests animal flesh and waste and anything else that was once living. It requires the human mind and human-cast rings to direct it to do anything more."

{And was it nothing but light and heat that you experienced in the cavern of spirits? Was it light and heat that visited your room last night?}

This time, it was he who retreated from that revelatory touch. "Who are you? Why— *How* do you know all this?"

She reached, he pulled away; she frowned and held her hand out insistently. Conceding to necessity, he veiled all thought of the cavern and placed his palm with hers.

{I am—was—Anheliaa's servant for two years, Mikhyel. She taught, she tested, oh so many women, but she never asked *me.* I listened and I learned. I felt, and I extrapolated.}

And this silent young woman had shunted power to Barsitum . . . and held the rings steady when Persitum fell and Anheliaa died.

{I will aid; I will *not* be Rhomatum's ringmaster.}

Perhaps she'd plucked that thought from his mind before he was aware his thoughts were headed in that direction.

"I wasn't going to ask that. Would never, but . . ." His choices seemed suddenly confused. She carried his child. He didn't, morally or legally, have to acknowledge it or assume responsibility for it, such was the advantage of his position. But he could no more leave her on her own than he could his own sister, had he one.

"Mirym, do you want me to marry you? I will, immediately and without reservations, if that's what you wish. The contract with Nethaalye's parents would have to be renegotiated, but she'd understand, and we might have to delay long enough . . . I don't believe she'd agree to being second, which is only fair, but . . ."

Laughter, clear and golden in his head. Her hands clasped his this time, and her lips brushed his knuckles.

{Hush, before you explode your poor brain. My dear Mikhyel, thank you, no. I treasure my independence. But if I were you, I'd be careful, cautious about mending your way with Nethaalye. She deserves her own happiness.}

Which insight he didn't need her to explain. He knew he was not the stuff of which a woman dreamed.

He'd never concerned himself about that before, had never cared whether a woman desired him or not. Desire had not been part of his life. Those erotic sensations Deymorin and Nikki sought so eagerly had held only distasteful connotations for him.

Now, for the first time, he thought he might wish that were not the case.

Mirym's eyes crinkled with amusement, picking up his thoughts, or at least traces of them. He smiled back, brushed fine, curling strands back from her face, feeling an urge that, when examined, seemed all his own. A lovely feeling. A temptation he didn't recall having felt before.

He searched that inclination for any trace of his brothers. It seemed important, somehow, that it be his own. He'd been Deymorin's proxy in the Council chambers, Nikki's proxy in bed, he'd acceded to Mheric's demands as a child, to Anheliaa's in his adolescence and to Ganfrion in the Crypt.

Just this once, he *wanted* this simple, uncomplicated human urge to be his alone.

But there was nothing of his brothers surrounding the urge, only himself and his affection for this strange young woman. Sensing only mutual interest through their clasped hands, he leaned forward, seeking her lips—

"Damn you, Mikhyel dunMheric!"

A hand grasped his shoulder and jerked him around. Nikki.

"What's your problem now?" he asked, not the least inclined after last night to tolerate Nikki's histrionics.

"Haven't you done enough?" Nikki asked, and his confused emotions flared through Mikhyel. He'd come here {embarrassment} to apologize to Mikhyel for yesterday, only to find his {shock} austere brother *pawing* Mirym, who {betrayal} had been his *special* friend, and {jealousy} she'd been kissing him back. And a final, unconfused montage of {disappointment} and {anger} and {lust}.

"Go away, Nikki, and duck your head in the fountain." He reached for Mirym's hand.

"Can't keep your lecherous hands off her, can you?" Nikki hissed, and an impact to Mikhyel's shoulder sent him staggering away from Mirym. He came up hard against a stone wall and pushed himself away, only to be slammed back.

His head snapped backward, struck hard, and his vision faded. He blinked his eyes, clearing them to Mheric's fury.

Nikki! his mind screamed insistently. But a deeper portion, a portion forged so early it saw beyond the blond hair and blue eyes that said *mother* to the black essence below, that said *Mheric.*

Nikki screamed something unintelligible, and struck him, a backhanded blow that blacked out his vision a second time. He flailed blindly, seeking a handhold to keep upright, lost it when a battering ram in his gut doubled him over and turned his legs to water.

His fingers slid down that unseen brother, his knees shot with pain as they struck the ground.

Images flooded his mind of Ganfrion and the prison—his own thoughts or Nikki's—and his hands curled into unfamiliar shapes. Fists. He wasn't a child any longer. It wasn't Mheric. He could fight back.

Another portion of his mind screamed this was *Nikki!* and still another recalled Nikki's birthday and Nikki sprawled unconscious on the floor, victim of his brother's hand. *His* hand.

And a vow he'd made that day. A vow that he would *not* end like Mheric.

And another portion stated coldly, as the blows landed and he raised his arms to protect his face, that *he* had not.

๑   ๑   ๑

"Nikki wants to see him," Deymorin said softly to Kiyrstin, trying not to disturb Mikhyel, who was sleeping at last.

"Tell him to go to hell," was Kiyrstin's answer, and while she was probably right, it was not precisely the answer to set Nikki's mind—on the far side of Mikhyel's bedroom door—at rest.

"He was upset, Kiyrstin," Deymorin said in reluctant support of that remote plea for understanding. "He didn't—"

"Think? I rest my case."

"You're too hard on him, Kiyrsti," Mikhyel whispered, and Deymorin stifled a curse.

"I thought you were asleep," he said, and crossed the room to sit next to the bed.

"I was." Mikhyel pushed himself upright. He rubbed his jaw and winced.

"Rings, Khyel, I'm sorry. How's Nikki's jaw feel?"

"Like hell, thanks. Are you sure you didn't break it?"

"No, more's the pity." Deymorin's fists clenched again at the memory of Nikki's black anger flooding his mind, of Nikki himself standing over Mikhyel's senseless body. And then, it hadn't been Nikki, but Mheric, and for once he'd been there to stop his father's brutality. "I've never been so mad."

"Caught up in the past, Deymorin. We all were." Mikhyel sighed and rubbed his jaw again. A jaw darkening with stubble for the first time in a month. A face amazingly untouched, though Mikhyel had, according to the physician, at least one cracked rib.

"Let it go, Mikhyel. You do him no favor."

Mikhyel's thin throat worked in a hard swallow. "I can't stop it, Deymorin. I've tried, but he wants so badly to forget. For everything to be back . . . the way it used to be."

Kiyrstin muttered something under her breath, the gist of which they could both imagine.

"He doesn't realize what he's doing," Mikhyel said.

"He just wants to be the center of everyone's attention," Kiyrstin snapped, and Deymorin didn't argue. It needed to be verbally acknowledged, which neither he nor Mikhyel seemed able to do. "In the past week, Mikhyel has been currying him to take Mikhyel's place here in Rhomatum, a position he looks upon as necessary but overall rather boring. Now, the ley itself speaks to Mikhyel? Calls Mikhyel to it? Mikhyel, the barrister? What could be more romantic, and who less deserving of the honor?"

Deymorin stifled an objection; Mikhyel's brow was furrowed in concentration and his presence beneath was impenetrable stone.

"Nikki's spoiled," Kiyrstin continued, obviously developing a theme held too long in reserve. "He's spoiled and his head is full of clouds. He *needs* a thump now and again to get his attention."

"I've 'thumped' him more than anyone deserves," Mikhyel said, and Deymorin nearly choked on the self-condemnation that flowed to him from Mikhyel.

"And always turned about and apologized and said how sorry and wrong you were, I'll wager."

"Well, yes, of course I did. I—"

"Did you ever just thump him because he'd been an ass, and tell him to straighten up or you'd thump him again?"

"No!" Mikhyel's voice was strengthening with each pass Kiyrstin made at him. "I'd *never* do that!"

Kiyrstin gave an exaggerated harrumph. "I rest my case, Councillor."

She cupped Mikhyel's face in both hands and kissed him lightly.

"You're his brother, Khyel, not his father. You've done your best. Nikki knows that, but he's using your own guilt against you now, whether he means to or not. He's feeling sorry for himself and he's dragging you both into his midden heap with him. He lives in a real world of high stakes risk and wants to solve its problems with Tamshi tales."

"Not his fault," Mikhyel said slowly, and his hand clasped Kiyrstin's, as if he was using her to keep his thoughts focused. "When Mheric would . . . When we were in the closet, I'd distract him, keep him quiet with promises of the Tamshi. We'd accredit every noise to a Tamshi in hiding."

"That's fine, for a child. And many children will seek magical answers. Adults know the answers lie in themselves. That transition from one way of thinking to the other comes harder in some. You may have thumped Nikki a few times—maybe even harder than you meant. And I wouldn't say you were right or wrong to do that. Can't. I wasn't there, now was I? But I see the result, and Nikki is far from cowed."

"I struck him in anger, Kiyrstin. Always in anger, always too hard."

"Maybe. And maybe not. How would you know? You didn't have much of an example, now did you?"

"Perhaps Mheric's father's example was worse even than the example he supplied us," Mikhyel answered, his tone gaining a healthy touch of humor. "By your reckoning, would that not absolve Mheric's actions?"

"Absolve?" Kiyrstin repeated, and seemed to turn that over in her own mind. "No, I don't think so. I don't *absolve* anyone's actions, Khyel. I just don't lump all situations into one category."

"Ah, but you're the woman who tried to kill her husband with a manicure knife. You *would* think all guilt is circumstantially unique."

"I would. And I do. Besides, it was Deymorin who thumped him, not you."

"This time."

"Details. The important thing is, Nikki didn't run off this morning because he'd been physically hurt, as you'd realize, if you weren't so involved. He'd been a fool and a brute, and he didn't want to face that fact in company. Nothing unusual in that. I didn't know Mheric, but I do know his sons, one of whom is the most self-confident ragman I've ever met, one of whom carries the weight of the world on his shoulders, and one of whom, raised by the other two, is a self-important seventeen-year-old, not all that different from other spoiled seventeen-year-olds I've known. That's all I really know about Mheric's skills as a father."

"Not much to go on, is it?"

"It's everything." Her look sobered. "The point I'm trying to make, Khyel, is that there comes a time when it's not the father, not the brother, but the basic substance of the individual. You want to feel sorry for someone, ask Zandy sometime about his father and masters. You don't catch him sniveling about his treatment. He wouldn't know how. Wouldn't think of it."

"Z–Zandy?" Mikhyel's voice stumbled and panic returned to that other sense.

"You remember Zandy, Mikhyel," Deymorin said, stemming his own rising alarm. "The boy Kiyrstin brought with her from Mauritum? We left him at Armayel with his static potentiator."

Mikhyel relaxed, and his smile was warm, easy. "And the puppy."

"Rings," Deymorin laughed weakly. "And the puppy."

But he wasn't feeling like laughing. He'd thought they were beyond this. Since their return to Rhomatum, Mikhyel had done all they could ask and more. But since Anheliaa's death—more, since the funeral yesterday, he'd seemed to be coming apart again.

According to Mirym's indignant written account, Mikhyel had made no move to defend himself against Nikki's attack, apparently convinced, from the impressions that even now leaked through to Deymorin, that Nikki's anger was utterly justified, though Mirym claimed otherwise.

The arrogance, the self-confidence and conviction that had bolstered Mikhyel dunMheric's actions for years had been shattered at the time he most needed it. He required a keeper here, in his own home; how in the name of Darius was he going to survive seventeen potentially hostile node cities on his own in what was now a crisis, not an agenda?

They needed him to remember everything, Zandy, the potentiator, Anheliaa's actions . . . everything that had happened in the recent past. The web was counting on the keen-witted negotiator, the lawyer, the politician, not a feeble-minded—

"Keep your concerns to yourself, Rhomandi," Mikhyel muttered bitterly. "I'm here. I'll *be* here when the time comes. I wouldn't have agreed to the tour if I wasn't *certain* I could do it."

"I know that. Sorry. It seems Nikki's not the only one casting unwarranted thoughts about."

"Thoughts? Was that all? I could have sworn . . ." Mikhyel rubbed a shaking hand across his forehead. "It's getting worse, Deymio. Sometimes, I can hear you more clearly than when you speak. Sometimes, it's as if words only . . ."

"Confuse the meaning?" Deymorin finished for him. "I know what you mean. I suppose we'll become accustomed to it."

"Or, please the nonexistent gods, the link will wither and fade away entirely."

"Not very likely, considering."

"No? My beard's coming back."

Stated as if the two facts were connected. And perhaps, to Mikhyel, they were joined in some strange way. And if Mikhyel truly ceased to believe in it, might the link vanish?

The possibility startled and disturbed Deymorin. The unnatural communication seemed in some ways the most natural aspect of his existence now. To have it disappear would leave an emptiness inside him nothing could ever possibly fill.

Of course, he didn't have to contend with the ramifications that unquestionably plagued Mikhyel.

"Do you really wish for that?" he asked finally, simultaneously reaching for that internal reassurance, but he couldn't claim surprise when Mikhyel refused to answer in either form.

However, since the ability to change history did not lie within his newly-discovered talents, he took Mikhyel's other hand in his own, deliberately seeking Nikki's aching jaw, deliberately absorbing every bruise Nikki had given Mikhyel, blindly attempting what Mikhyel seemed to achieve without conscious thought.

His reward was a bodyful of annoying aches—and a brother who gave a deep sigh and relaxed, possibly for the first time since they'd brought him here that morning. And up Deymorin's arm, along with that stream of physical sensation, came a hint of gratitude: acknowledgment (via that very means Mikhyel wished eliminated) of Deymorin's good intentions.

{No sense wasting a useful tool,} came Mikhyel's wry answer, before his wearied mind faded into silence.

Chapter Five

{Hello, Mikhyel.}

Anheliaa. Again.

"Go away." Mikhyel moaned and rolled over, ignoring the purple glow illuminating the armchair in the corner of his room.

{Oh, stop it. Rings, such a baby. Whimper, whimper, whimper. I never saw so many tears.}

"Liar," he whispered, and discovered his voice hoarse and ragged. "You *never* made me cry. *Never!*"

A purple chuckle. *{True enough. So, boy, when are you going to come see me?}*

"Never. You're a figment of my imagination. An ugly, noxious irritation of repulsive memories. Go away!"

{A figment?} Prick of sharp nails across his neck. *{Are you so certain of that?}*

He refused to listen, refused to react as those enameled daggers traced his cheek.

{Rings, the damned brush is back.} A sharp tiny pain. And another. *{Pluck it out, boy. Get rid of it!}*

He squeezed his eyes shut, ignored the momentary sparks of pain, knowing imagination for an immensely powerful disseminator of lies, fully capable of supplying both voice and sensation. And for a moment, as the prickling pain ended abruptly, he believed he'd won.

But those sharp nails returned, trickled over his shoulders and down his chest, insinuating themselves into his nightshirt, raking patterns—rings—that dripped, warm and damp, along his ribs.

He cursed at the memory, and wrapped his arms around a pillow, pressing it to his chest. But the sensation pursued him, as surely as if the pillow weren't there. And a massive weight depressed the mattress behind him, rolling him backward into a waiting, smothering embrace.

His mind screamed denial: memory held nothing of this. Anheliaa had never invaded his bed, couldn't, were she still alive, have walked even that short distance between the armchair and his bed without help.

{*Perhaps, child, that inability was all that prevented me. Who knows?*}

{Go away!} he shouted within his head. {Go back to the sewers where you belong!}

{*Unkind, sweet Mikhyel. Besides—*} A smell of indignation, a color of pique. {*Besides,* he doesn't want me either. He *wants* you. For which, one can hardly blame him, can one, sweet, tender, tasty Mikhyel?}

He? Who did she mean: he?

{*You were my downfall, pretty Mikhyel. You and your brothers. I knew you were different. I did my best to keep you apart. But you're the one the ley wants, not the others. Did you know that?*}

{Go—away!} Mikhyel buried his head in the pillow.

{*Perhaps sending you through . . .*} The voice in his head took on a taste of speculation. And all the while, the nails traced bleeding patterns . . . {*Perhaps that intimate contact with the ley triggered some latent ability. You have the power, child. You lack the drive. You could be the greatest of all time . . . with my help. Let me in, child. Pretty Mikhyel. Sweet, sweet, Mikhyel . . .*}

Mikhyel forced his eyes open to a faint purple glow emanating from his chest, forced himself to admit this was not just an overactive imagination. He pressed his elbow deep into the mattress, struggling to turn over.

Laughter, shrill and mocking filled his head; fingernails held him steady by the simple expedient of digging straight into his skin.

"Damn you!" he shouted aloud and struck backward, encountering nothing but purple mist.

And there was banging at his door. And voices, shouting. He screamed back and fought the all-too-substantial hold.

The door burst open.

The mass behind him vanished.

He tumbled backward, slipping half out of bed, the blankets tangling about his legs. He was hanging headfirst when steel-banded fingers clasped his shoulders and hauled him upright.

Ⴐ   Ⴐ   Ⴐ

Mikhyel was covered in sweat and streaked with blood,
but from the volume of his curses, and the strength with
which he sought to free himself, he wasn't seriously injured.

In fact, Deymorin, with his head still ringing from the
power (reeking of Mikhyel's anger and Mikhyel's denial)
that had flooded his sleeping mind, found himself struggling
just to contain his markedly smaller brother's flailing arms.

To avoid servant-generated gossip, he ordered everyone save Raulind from the room. Once they were alone,
Deymorin lifted Mikhyel bodily into the air, while Raulind
worked his thrashing legs free of the blankets. When words
and mind proved equally unable to penetrate whatever
madness surrounded Mikhyel, they simply man-handled
him into the bathing room, and flung him into the pool,
tattered, bloodstained nightshirt and all.

He burst free in a spray of water, striking blows at invisible opponents, sputtering curses that rose into a single, furi-
ous scream of denial. The words were incoherent, but his
mind writhed in black hatred, emotions that nearly blinded
Deymorin in their intensity.

Finally, Mikhyel's energy faded, his arms stilled and he
sank into the water, limp as a child's rag doll. The current
of the cycling water drew his hair in a black stream toward
the outlet, seemingly determined to pull Mikhyel's entire
body with it.

Deymorin was about to go in after him when the cords
in Mikhyel's neck strained and dragged his head clear of
the water. "Get *out*!" he shouted, and with an angry sweep
of his arm that staggered him, sent a spray of water over
the bath's tile floor.

Deymorin stepped back, out of range, but no farther, and
between one heartbeat and the next, the madness faded
from Mikhyel's eyes. His body drooped, as if that sustaining
anger had flowed out the drain, and he swayed to the side
of the pool, catching himself on the tiled edge, and buried
his face in his crossed arms, still cursing softly.

Scratches marked the bony arms cradling Mikhyel's dark
head. Deep gouges that matched bloody marks on Mikhyel's chest and throat.

Fresh wounds.

And a man had to wonder, whose future had been entrusted to those bony arms, whether those wounds were self-inflicted, and if not, then who had put them there, and to where he, or she, or it, had disappeared.

"I'm leaving, Deymio," came a low, bitter murmur.

"Of course you are. Next month—"

"Not soon enough. Tomorrow . . . the day after . . . as fast as I can make the arrangements."

"Why the sudden hurry?"

"You're driving me insane."

"*I'm* driving you insane? What have *I* done?"

"You. Nikki . . . Anheliaa. What's the difference?"

"More dreams, brother?" Deymorin asked, refusing to take offense.

Silence, then: "Leave us, Raulind." It was a cold order from the midst of Mikhyel's arms. Raulind hesitated, and, again from that arm pillow, softly, "Please."

With a look that reluctantly entrusted Mikhyel to Deymorin's care, Raulind left. At the sound of the outer bedroom door closing, Mikhyel's eyes gleamed up at him through a veil of dripping black hair. "She *is* dead, Deymorin. Tell me that much is true."

He said nothing.

"Tell me!"

Deymorin squatted on the edge beside Mikhyel. "Perhaps there's dead and . . . dead. This *is* Anheliaa we're speaking of."

Mikhyel sighed, heaved upward, and raised his hands to dig his palms into his eyes. He was shaking. Above the water line his flesh pebbled with chill or shock or both. Deymorin rose to fetch a bathsheet from the cupboard, blinked his eyes against the warm, dry air that blasted him from the cabinet, and returned to stand at the top of the steps, cradling the towel against his chest to retain its heat.

"Come, brother. Out with you."

Mikhyel stepped from the pool, his tattered, soaked nightshirt trailing unnoticed off his shoulders, his grip on the handrail white-knuckled and imperative. Pride kept his chin high, though he avoided Deymorin's eyes, but nothing could conceal the mortification at his own behavior that echoed between them as Deymorin pulled the shirt from him and wrapped the towel around his shoulders.

Mikhyel stumbled twice on the way to the grooming couch. Rings knew he had reason enough.

Sounds from the main bedroom, a flip of sheeting, a scuff of slippered foot on carpeting, and a marked lack of gossiping female voices indicated Raulind had taken it upon himself to repair the damage to Mikhyel's bed, this second night running. Deymorin left Mikhyel's side to shut the connecting door. When he turned, Mikhyel was scrubbing at his arms with the towel as if he could rub the bloody scratches into nonexistence.

"Easy on, brother," Deymorin cautioned, and paused at the grooming table for the salve every man kept at hand to seal and protect razor cuts.

Mikhyel's head fell back onto the padded headrest. He seemed oblivious to the blood seeping from his nose. Deymorin rolled a small towel and tucked it under Mikhyel's neck, ran cold water over a second cloth and settled it gently across Mikhyel's high-bridged nose.

"Hold," he ordered, and placed Mikhyel's near hand over the cloth.

In the mirror, Mikhyel's image, eyes at half-mast above the white cloth, stared into the shadowed corners of the bath. Inside, however, he seethed. Like a tiny shock every time Deymorin's fingers brushed so much as a strand of Mikhyel's hair, there came anger—bitterness against an all too celibate life, a life constructed around denial of life's most basic instincts.

And coloring it all, an intense hatred of Anheliaa.

"She was back, wasn't she?" Deymorin asked, as he spread Mikhyel's hair to hang in the warm outflow of a heating register.

Mikhyel's cold stare didn't waver.

Deymorin scooped a two-fingered glob of ointment from the jar, captured Mikhyel's arm and began applying it to the ragged scrapes, working his way up over one shoulder to the deeper wounds on Mikhyel's chest.

Mikhyel hissed; possibly it was the sting of the ointment on the deepest gouge. "Nightmare," he stated flatly, and his eyes closed.

"Did this to yourself, did you?"

Mikhyel shuddered. "I must have."

"With what?" Deymorin reached for his hand, held the close-trimmed nails to a close inspection.

"No one else here."

"Now."

"See someone leave?"

"Door's not the only way out."

Mikhyel's eyes slitted open, sought his in the mirror. "What do you know that you aren't telling me, Deymio?"

Resentment, distrust—they'd had enough of that in this family.

"Remember the day you popped out of the sky and landed on Nikki's head?" he asked.

"Not when I can avoid it."

He smoothed another dollop over the wounds. "We had help."

"Help?" For once, he seemed to be getting more from Mikhyel than Mikhyel from him; and Mikhyel was confused by—or resisting—the images pressing for acknowledgment within his own mind.

"Nothing we had would have saved you. Truth, brother. You were dying. An old woman came out of the forest. An old woman whose eyes burned with a green fire. *She* saved you—"

"With parnicci salve," Mikhyel interrupted firmly, as if determined to prove he remembered.

"No, Khyel. Not parnicci. And she wasn't just any old woman." He finished smearing the last cut and turned to wipe his hands off, before meeting Mikhyel's gaze squarely. "Laugh at me, brother, and I *will* break your nose. She was Tamshi."

Mikhyel, who should have been outraged at Deymorin's apparent soft-headedness when so much relied on them, nodded slowly, his face devoid of emotion.

"Less than an hour earlier," Deymorin continued, "Ben had hailed me from the forest."

"Ben was dead." Mikhyel's voice was flat, as barren as his expression.

Deymorin nodded, a single dip of his chin. "*That* Ben's eyes also glowed—with green fire."

"Shapeshifter?" Coldly stated, as if the ancient myth were a common occurrence.

"Or illusionist," Deymorin temporized.

"Somehow, I don't think so."

"Says the man who always insists there's a rational explanation for such things."

"I still believe that. If this . . . Tamshi can appear in various forms, there's a logical reason. It's just a matter of knowing all the facts." Mikhyel's brow tightened and his mouth pressed to a thin line. "Why didn't you tell me about this before?"

"*She* said not to. I thought it was for your sake. I thought your sanity had been pressed so hard already, that this might send you over the edge."

"And now?"

"I suspect she—or something like her—is behind these nightmare appearances of yours."

"And so might have had other reasons for keeping me ignorant."

"I just don't know, brother. She'd saved your life. I did what I thought best—for all of us."

"She." Mikhyel repeated, then looked away. "Anhe— the thing said, 'he' didn't want it . . . her . . . Anheliaa. That 'he' wanted . . . me."

And from Mikhyel's mind came flashes of the Rhomandi hypogeum, of the lure cast only to Mikhyel.

Deymorin asked, "What really happened to you?"

A gray-green flicker, quickly hidden beneath dark lashes. A noncommittal shrug. "I was tired. The pool seemed an attractive option to thinking, I suppose."

"It called to you, brother. Loud and clear. I heard it, but it wasn't the least bit interested in my humble self. And it actively rejected Nikki's wanton advances."

Another shrug. Denial permeated the room, thick and heavy. But curiosity was there as well, about Deymorin's revelations, about the creature's words and a beard-stubble's mysterious reappearance.

"Don't you dare go down there alone, Khyel. Do you hear me?"

Mikhyel's silence, inside and out, terrified Deymorin.

"Dammit, brother, promise me!"

A level gaze held his. "What if that really is Anheliaa?"

"Khyel—"

"Think about it. Think about that . . . feeling down in the hypogeum. That wasn't Anheliaa, I'll swear to it. This . . . felt like her."

"So she can sink back into the ooze where she belongs. Mikhyel, don't give her—or it, or *whatever* a foothold in your head!"

"Foothold in my head? Why do you put it that way?"

"I—I just . . ." Except he had no answer. The impression had just come to him.

"But that's what *she* wanted! She wanted *in*. She said, together we, she and I, could be the greatest of all time."

"The greatest what? Ringmaster?"

"I . . . I don't know. We're on the verge of learning something here, Deymorin. More about the ley than has ever been known. More than Darius brought out of Mauritum. More than our very expensive researchers have come up with in three hundred years."

"At what cost, brother? That . . . *thing* invading your mind? I think not."

To which Mikhyel said nothing.

"Dammit, Khyel," Deymorin said slowly, "I'll kill you first. And to hell with the web, the Syndicate and Rhomatum! There's *got* to be another way."

And still, the uncertain oscillations in Mikhyel's mind swung wildly.

"Need I remind you, it's not *your* mind alone it would be in?"

Relief. A deciding factor to tip Mikhyel's mental scale.

"Thank you, Deymorin."

He grinned. "Does this mean I let you live?"

"For a time, at least."

"Good. I'd hate to have to explain myself to the Syndicate." He replaced the lid on the ointment jar, and held out his hand. "All right, brat, time for bed."

Mikhyel's mouth twitched into a reluctant grin, and he limped slowly into the bedroom. Deymorin followed, making an elaborate show of tucking Mikhyel in like a child, deliberate nonsense that soon had Mikhyel cursing him roundly.

Deymorin laughed and nodded toward the couch on the far side of the room. "Just for the record, I'm sleeping right over there for the rest of the night."

Mikhyel grunted his disgust. "Which half of you gets the floor? Go to your own bed, Deymorin."

"Do I really need to list the arguments, Mikhyel? I'd like to keep you sane and in one piece at least until you get on the road."

Mikhyel lay quietly, his emotions masked behind thought. "And if I let you stay now? Where will it end, Deymorin? You worried about me in the Crypt. You're worried about me now. Will you insist on coming along on the tour? Will you sleep at my feet in Shatum? In Giephaetum? Khoratum? What about Barsitum? Are the brothers there suspect as well? I've got work to do, brother. Work *I* do well and *you* detest. Politics, Deymorin. Remember?"

"Point made, Barrister." Deymorin sat on the edge of the bed and stared at his clasped hands. "Still, I could wish you weren't going alone."

"*Alone?* I've eleven men to account for. Raulind. Three secretaries. Coachmen, grooms—"

" 'To account for' being the significant phrase, brother."

"I've fifteen guards to watch over us twelve fools. What else do I need?"

"The guardsmen you've chosen are good men. I'd trust Ori with my own life. They'll be sufficient against the obvious emergencies on the road. It's the not-so-obvious I'm concerned about. A true back-man who understands the streets. Who can read the wind and know of attempts on your well-being *before* they happen."

"Someone without scruples, who can get to the places I can't."

"That's *not* what I mean."

"No? But it's what I want. Thank you for the suggestion, Deymio; I'll find someone."

"You don't know anyone!"

Mikhyel's mouth twitched, and his mind was solidly blocked to Deymorin. "Go to bed, Deymorin. Not on the couch. Your own bed. With Kiyrstin. I promise you, I fear *her* wrath far more than that of some insubstantial ghost."

"She wasn't insubstantial!"

"I'll be all right. Anheliaa's . . . gone for the night."

"How the hell do you know?"

"Dammit, brother. Get *out* of my bedroom!"

"All right!" He pressed Mikhyel's shoulder, sending him the love and concern that boiled within him, the knowledge that he was a heartbeat away, and left the room. Nonetheless, he waited, just outside the door, until that inner sense indicated peaceful slumber, before, still against his better judgment, he returned to Kiyrstin's ready arms.

Chapter Six

This time, he was waiting.

"Hello, Anheliaa."

"Aha, the child's awake."

Mikhyel pushed his back into the pillows and drew a knee up to prop an elbow. Anheliaa was seated in an armchair, lounging actually, as if the arthritis that had plagued her since puberty was nonexistent. And, indeed, the hand she waved through the air was not the least misshapen.

But then, he supposed a ghost had no bones.

"You lied to your brother, you naughty child."

She stated only the truth. He'd known she'd return; he'd planted the lie of slumber into Deymorin's head so that he'd leave, had surprised himself when the ploy worked.

He was gaining all manner of talents these days.

But Deymorin's revelations had suggested a path to him, an answer to the weakest link in his planned tour. He'd been prepared to approach the satellite node ringmasters with vague theories and untested strategies. Anheliaa or Deymorin's Tamshi, this creature was linked in some manner to the ley, and might well be capable of answering all his questions.

"What are you doing here, Anheliaa?" he asked. "You are Anheliaa, aren't you?"

"Of course, I'm Anheliaa. I'm bored, darling. I want company."

"*Company?* You're dead!"

"Well, there is that, I suppose. It's not at all what I expected."

"Expec—" Mikhyel's throat constricted with unexpected laughter. "Tell me, aunt, what—exactly—did you expect?"

"Why, to become one with the ley, naturally, boy." Her ethereal hand fanned through the air. "My spirit joined with the ancestors. Don't you remember your catechism?"

"I remember you told me to learn it and reject it."

"Yes, well, experience changes us all, I suppose . . . I nearly got you, you know, the day that you and your brothers returned to Rhomatum. I sent the lightning at you, but you got inside the City too fast. Perhaps, if you had not, perhaps if you had preceded me into the ley, I might have released my hold on life sooner. Who knows?"

"You tried to kill us?"

"Of course. Silly, I suppose. Petty. But I was angry. Particularly at you, my darling. I'd expected problems from that bull-headed brother of yours, but you . . . you were mine, formed to my specifications. When *you* turned on me, you had to be punished—preferably eliminated. I'd hoped Bro would take care of you . . . after. But I didn't realize your potential. And that Shatumin whore proved more clever than I supposed. Poor Bro . . . Ah, well, he was an ass. They killed me, you know."

"Killed you?" Mikhyel struggled to sort the disjointed fragments to hold them for later analysis. "Who? *Brolucci?*"

Always assuming he had a "later."

"*Bro?*" Shrill laughter filled the air and his head. "Hardly. Those damn fool second-rate ringspinners. So set on protecting their little puddles of energy. If they'd *helped* me, I'd be alive now and Persitum would still be ours. Fools, I tell you. All of them."

A rant was brewing. In that, this creature, whether real or impersonation, echoed Anheliaa's manner to perfection. It was a familiar pattern. One, Mikhyel judged, it was time to break.

"Enough of this." He threw back the covers and sat up.

Anheliaa straightened, her eyes widening with interest. "Yes, nephew? What would you suggest instead?"

"Who are you really? What do you want?"

"Anheliaa, darling, obviously."

"Anheliaa's dead."

"You are redundant, child. The point was made. Reality argues. What now?"

He frowned and sank back on the edge of the bed. "How are you getting in here?"

"Why—" She blinked. "I don't know."

"Don't know? Or aren't admitting. You said before 'he' didn't want you. Who is 'he'? Why *should* he want you?"

"He didn't. Neither did she! I feel like a damned shuttle-cock. Flipped here. Flipped there. I suppose, darling, I landed here because I could always count on you. And because he—I—want—wanted you."

She rose with a control and grace she'd never had in life. And it was Anheliaa, but Anheliaa as he imagined she'd wished to be: strong, lithe, physically imposing, mesmerizing in her confidence.

"I want you, darling. I want to *be* what you can be. Make you what you were meant to become." She sank down beside him, embracing him.

He controlled his reflexive flinch. Bend to the one in power, the one with the knowledge you sought. He'd learned that lesson in a hard school. But there was a reason for the insistent pull he'd felt in the hypogeum, a reason for Anheliaa's appearances here.

And he had been chosen to uncover those reasons. If his sanity was the price, his sanity would be forfeit.

He reminded himself of that necessity as nails raked his throat and down past his nightshirt's collar, flicking the buttons off one by one, those nails severing the threads as effectively as a honed blade.

Breath that smelled of fire-blossom tea puffed into his mouth. His eyelids drooped, shuttering him from her image; his head fell back, too heavy to hold upright.

{Damn you, let him go!}

Deymorin's voice in his head along with Deymorin's vision: himself in the arms of a creature that bore superficial resemblance to Anheliaa, past the decaying flesh. The creature raised its face from Mikhyel's—his—neck, snarled at him—at Deymorin—and bent again, to a sickening, noisy nuzzling.

But that repulsive creature couldn't be the source of the smooth, powerful arms supporting him, and that limp, twitching body surely could not belong to him. He was soaring in the air, drifting in an ocean of purple sensuality. . . .

A purple halo shimmered around the entwined bodies of Deymorin's vision, and Mikhyel knew that shimmer, felt it enter his fingertips with the scent of fire-blossom tea, heavy with honey—the way Anheliaa preferred it.

And somewhere, some part of him saw Deymorin lunge, sensed the creature's snarl, the swipe of the creature's clawed hand. Deymorin swayed out of reach, grabbed the creature's wrist and jerked. The arm parted at the elbow, and the stench of decaying flesh filled Mikhyel's—Deymorin's—nostrils.

For Mikhyel there was only the scent of fire-blossom tea. The glimmer deepened, widened. Mikhyel heard Deymorin's denial, inside and out, knew Deymorin's intense desire to follow . . . to protect his brother.

As Mikhyel had wanted to protect Nikki.

And a bridge formed between them, a glimmering web of iridescence. A bridge reminiscent of the force that had drawn him inexorably to Nikki and to Boreton nearly two months ago.

Mikhyel deafened himself to both internal and external voices. He fought to destroy that bridge, to contain Deymorin, to cast a net over him. Or a web. A web to confine Deymorin and his potent desire in a cocoon.

Like a spider's prey. He fought Deymorin's call, knowing that to listen was to draw Deymorin with him into whatever hell awaited him on the far side of the purple haze.

It was the hypogeum—or at least, a cave.

Mikhyel pushed himself up, away from ground that shifted beneath his palms like the softest sand, and confronted a cavern that could contain the Rhomandi hypogeum several times over.

Miles of shifting, billowing leythium crystal draperies camouflaged the true depths of the ceiling. Thick, viscous leythium formed a living sea in which islands rose and subsided even as he watched. A sea whose subtly mutating shores fluxed in and out of sight, extending at times to depths his rational mind refused to accept.

Rational. Mikhyel stifled the laughter that threatened. Logic—the accepted rules of existence with which he'd grown up—had little bearing on his present situation.

In the center of the lake, something burned: multicolored flames without smoke, without scent, unless that flame was the source of the aroma of fire-blossom tea that filled the air. Free, this time, of the cloyingly sweet honey.

Radiating from this seemingly boundless cavern, seemingly infinite corridors led to points of throbbing, pulsating color. Eighteen in all, each glimmering in a spectrum that centered about a different color . . . blue-green here, spring green there, deep, blood red. . . .

Infinite. Boundless. The concepts *were* crazed, but those were the words his mind supplied. He rubbed his hand across his eyes, wondering for the briefest instant, if Anheliaa's ghost had, in fact, dragged him with it into death. And then, on the floor near him, he saw the decomposing corpse of Deymorin's final imaging.

Its left arm was missing.

That final touch of the macabre lent a compelling reality to an inherently unreal event, an oddly common touch to an uncommon scene, and restored his faith in his own senses.

He staggered to his feet and stood swaying, feet wide apart. He examined his arms for burns, for anything reminiscent of that other near-disastrous transportation to Boreton, but there was nothing. Rather, he felt energized. The all-consuming weariness, even the lingering aches from Nikki's attack were simply—gone.

A color of satisfaction. A scent of lazy curiosity. Belonging—he'd swear to it—to that presence he'd felt in the hypogeum. He recognized it as surely as he recognized the individual signatures of his brothers.

"Who are you?" he shouted. "Where are you, and what do you *want*?"

{Want, want, want—}

The word echoed in his head, carrying with it that sense of welcome, of open arms waiting to draw him to some liquified fate.

{No, no. No!} he heard, and *that* protest reeked of Deymorin. So, he wasn't entirely alone.

{Here?} he sent out into that strange aether.

{*No!* Dammit.} And with that denial, came an image of his own room, empty.

Mikhyel smiled to himself. Deymorin had not been drawn after him; in that, at least, he'd won.

And still that sense of welcome surrounded him. He turned slowly, allowing Deymorin to keep his mental foothold, seeking that presence that was not, definitely *not* Anheliaa. In fact, all sense of Anheliaa had vanished; only the corpse remained as a reminder of how he'd come here.

The entire cavern pulsed with light and color of leythium. Leythium lace draperies billowed in an unfelt breeze, as if the ley itself were breathing. Light rippled and pulsed down those corridors to the distant light sources, like blood passing down arteries. All around him, a forest of glowing pillars oozed up from the floor to meet and merge with the lace draperies.

He reached a curious fingertip to the nearest leythium trunk. His finger sank into a substance that was neither liquid nor solid. He had no sense of texture, only of warmth and a rhythmic throb . . . like a heartbeat. He pressed deeper. His entire hand disappeared.

He closed his eyes, realized, in a half-awake way, that he'd sunk to his knees, and he leaned toward that welcoming warmth, feeling it creep up his arm to his elbow and higher. His other hand rose, without conscious thought.

{No! Khyel, *stop!*}

Nikki. This time it was Nikki calling him. Wanting him. Needing . . .

{Dammit, Khyel, how often do we have to go through this? Get back here. Now! I want to go back to bed!}

It was as if both brothers were there, pulling him away from that pillar, slapping his face as if he were hysterical. He could hear them, feel them, though they were far, far, far away. . . .

But that warmth slid away from him, down his arm and off his fingertip, leaving no sensation at all, no sense of residual substance, only a memory.

{Well . . . *damn!*}

For the first time, that inexplicable presence took firm mental form. Directly before him, the substance that seemed so firm beneath his feet liquified and began turning slowly, then expanded upward, twisting, contorting into a vaguely, humanlike form.

Arms . . . legs. Three of the latter, until that third appendage gradually took the shape of a tail that swept around the forming body and tapered to a tip that twitched just a finger's breadth from Mikhyel's bare foot.

He was enraptured. A detached part of Mikhyel's mind reached that conclusion when he found himself unable to look away from that twitching flash of iridescent scales. His eyes followed that line upward, past slender curves of waist and shoulder, up a long, swanlike neck to a face that defied description.

Fangs, scales—or perhaps the crystalline webbing that

fluttered so freely all around them—faceted eyes . . . utterly inhuman, utterly beautiful.

Mikhyel gazed into those huge eyes, his neck painfully bent as he strained to take in a creature half again as tall as Deymorin, until, as if in response to that observation, the creature diminuated, took on proportions and features more like his own, until they faced one another, eye to eye, man to . . . almost man.

The creature extended a graceful hand, palm upward. A sense of attraction. Interest . . . Hunger. *This* was the source of interest.

{Come . . .}

"No . . ." Mikhyel whispered, having no breath for more, and he took a blind step backward. The ground gave beneath his bare foot, but insubstantial brotherly hands steadied him, and brotherly anger shouted at the creature to leave Mikhyel alone.

Fangs appeared, shrank to blunt, manlike teeth in a purely human smile. *{You have associations.}*

"I have brothers," Mikhyel stated aloud, knowing he could answer with that inner voice, but determinedly human in the face of this inhuman entity.

A creature of the ley. Tamshi, perhaps. A part of him burned with unanswered questions, but he resisted that curiosity and the vulnerability it exposed. This creature had drawn him here. This creature wanted him, not the other way around. *He* would dictate the terms of this encounter, not this creature of Rhomatum Node.

And with that decision, his fear vanished along with the shrinking uncertainty.

Humor filled the air, his mind, his body. Rich, internal, full-bodied laughter. Intrigue.

{Where have you been?} the creature's mind asked.

"Right overhead."

"And why . . ." The voice that reached his human ears from that long throat was a soft, sibilant hiss. Uncertain at first, gaining confidence with each syllable. ". . . have you not been brought to me before?"

One gliding step bridged the space between them and the creature reached a graceful hand to touch Mikhyel's face. Tasting him. Mikhyel, forcing himself to indifference, discovered, to his mild surprise, that he was fighting curiosity, not fear.

"Why," the creature continued, "have *you* not danced with the rings?"

"Danced?" Mikhyel laughed, the image of his graceless self flitting among the whirling dance rings too insanely humorous to ignore.

"Silly child, not those rings." The fingers drifted to his forehead and the hum and flash of the ringchamber filled his head.

"I've no talent—"

"What fool told you that?"

"I tried, but the rings wouldn't respond."

"I suppose not." The creature's chest rose in a heavy sigh. "Darius, you are not."

You have the power, child. You lack the drive. . . .

"Oh, yes, Anheliaa. Get rid of her, will you?" The creature waved a disinterested hand in the direction of the corpse. "I can't expel her beyond the web, and she's *such* a pollutant."

"But . . ." Anheliaa's body should just disappear, as his mother had, as all those other bodies had through the years.

But the ley wasn't supposed to rise up into this amazing creature and converse with him.

Neither were corpses supposed to visit you in your room. Was he truly going mad?

{Not at all, child. She's just been as stubborn in death as she was in life. She retained enough vitality within the web to pull these little tricks. Likely she's still here, if I cared to seek her out. But the body . . .} A sense of delicate revulsion permeated the thought. *{I did think that youngest child of mine might take her . . . she seems to eat positively anything . . . and Anheliaa did control her wild tendencies at the last . . . but even she drew the line at Anheliaa. . . .}*

Body. Vitality. As if that which had accosted him in his room and Anheliaa were two different, however related, entities. And the "youngest child" who had rejected Anheliaa . . . whom Anheliaa had "controlled at last" . . . did the creature mean Khoratum? Was there another creature like this one beneath Khoratum?

Deymorin's "Mother" perhaps?

Laughter. *{Mother. Is that how she calls herself? I've been away . . . too . . . long. . . .}*

The creature had wandered off, or dissolved and reformed elsewhere, Mikhyel couldn't swear what exactly he'd seen. But weariness floated like a cloud about it, and it reclined in a graceful lizardlike swirl on a leythium ledge that rose to meet and surround its body.

{I'm tired, child. It's been . . . so very long since I've taken form.}

It raised a hand to him, gesturing desire, but without that internal pressure to comply, and Mikhyel rewarded its tempered approach, moving to kneel beside the leythium couch. The creature's fingers wove through his hair, and through that touch came a sense of pure pleasure, simple delight in the feeling of the strands slipping through fingers that hadn't felt anything for a long, long time.

"Who are you?" Mikhyel whispered, giving in at last to those innermost drives. "What are you?"

{I am . . . what you would have me. Before that . . .}

A sense of age that staggered human understanding. Mikhyel closed his eyes as the unearthly cavern shifted about him, images of geological ages as reflected in the cavern superimposed over his own sense of the world above—

{We call it the surface world, child.}

Teaching, as was the way with this creature, its nature driving it as surely as Mikhyel's own nature drove him to question, neverminding common sense dictated it was safer not to know.

Mikhyel fought back a surge of hope. As he'd suspected, the answers to their dilemma were here, if only he could . . .

"The web," he murmured, and gazed up into eyes that had no discernible pupils, but only color glittering from beneath half-cast lids.

{Yes, child? You're concerned. Fear. You shouldn't be. Time . . . time will heal.}

Mirym's words echoed in his mind. But they didn't have time. The Syndicate didn't.

"Is it Khoratum . . . sir? My lord of Rhomatum? Is that the source of the problem?"

"My . . . lord." Gentle laughter. "Call me . . . call me Father, son of Darius. Perhaps my silly bud had the right of it. . . . Khoratum? Yessss. How did you . . ." Fingers brushed his mind, and his fears about the web, the plans for the trip rose and bubbled to the forefront of his mind. "Ah, how *clever* you are, child."

And in his mind, Anheliaa's purple essence flared: *{Yes, by all means, go to the fools, make them work as one, my golden-tongued love. Promise them anything, but get them to repair Khoratum, and then force Persitum back into the web. And then, my darling, come back to me and—}*

The creature of Rhomatum snarled and Anheliaa's presence shattered like crystal against stone. And the shards of her essence pierced Mikhyel's mind like tiny needles.

He cried out, protesting. The next moment, the creature's mind brushed his and the pain vanished.

{Forgive, son of Darius. I forgot the fragile nature of your mind.}

This time the creature's presence filled him, exploring, curious. Invasive. Mikhyel tried to push it out, tried to raise protections such as he built against his brothers, but to no avail.

"Damn you, get out!"

Light flared all around him, and he was alone again. Faceted eyes widened with interest.

{Darius you most definitely are not, child.}

"I never claimed to be. And I'm *not* your child! *Is* it Khoratum? If the masters unite, *can* they repair the damage?"

Fangs glittered as the smile ceased to mimic his own. *{Do I answer, oh, wise one? Or leave you to your fate?}*

"And if I judge incorrectly? If it destroys you?"

{Destruction. I wonder . . . is that possible? Curious . . .}

"If it is, you won't be left with much time to ponder the sensation, now will you?"

Laughter. *{Oh, I know the answer well enough, child of the surface world. But you . . . I think, perhaps . . .}*

And an image filled him, of the web and the strands permeating the landscape, the taproots leading to each satellite, the damage, like a collapsed tunnel in the area of Boreton, on the Khoratum line. Not a bleeding wound. A . . . clogged pipe.

Laughter came. A sense of acknowledgment.

{Together, child, they could tunnel through with ease. Give them the picture, tell them to blow as one, and your problem is no longer.}

And abandoning that thought, the creature exuded an overwhelming curiosity. About him. And the creature's desire for him to stay, a need to teach, to impart the knowledge of the ages into a receptive mind. An answering passion surged within himself, but:

{I can't. I'm . . . I'm sorry. I can't stay.}

And his mind was filled with all he had to do, uniting the nodes, raising the armies, providing for the children. . . .

{Children. Yes. Children.}

But that which his mind interpreted as child did not carry a sense of a mother's womb, but rather an image of buds, strands of personal substance oozing between cracks in the stone, sending tendrils deep into the earth. Growing.

{Growing old. Growing away. Go to the children. Tell them their source remembers them. Then come back to me, Darius.}

"I'm not . . ." Mikhyel's throat constricted on the admission. The creature had known Darius. Wanted . . . Darius, not Darius' inadequate several generations removed grandson.

{No . . . not Darius. Son of Darius' son. Father of Darius' son. Child of the Mother who is a child.}

The words made no sense. The images echoing behind them were equally disjointed. The creature's awareness was shattering, shimmering as was its form, both, Mikhyel realized, taken for his sake, for his limited ability to understand.

{Come back to me, child. We'll find the answers together. . . .}

Mikhyel grasped the boneless hand, knew despair when it turned to liquid and seeped between his fingers.

{I'll be back—}

But the creature was beyond hearing, and as the glow surrounded him, Mikhyel bent his head into his arms, not wanting to see the cavern disappear.

Anheliaa's body, partially decomposed, was waiting for him in his room.

§ § §

Mikhyel's disappearance had left Deymorin with an aching head and a feeling of utter helplessness, feelings only partially alleviated when Nikki's mental arrival allowed them to reach into that cavern and free Mikhyel's mind from the ley's enticing web.

But they'd achieved only a temporary freedom. Through

Mikhyel's eyes, he and Nikki had seen the creature rise
from the ley, had heard its advice. And within Mikhyel's
mind, he'd sensed the fascination, the trust the creature
engendered.

He'd called to Mikhyel, but Mikhyel hadn't heard—or
Mikhyel had ignored him. When the creature had tapped
Mikhyel's insatiable curiosity, nothing he or Nikki could do
had been able to shatter the barrier that supernatural promise had imposed between them and Mikhyel.

They could only wait, hoping, until first Mikhyel's mind
and then Mikhyel himself returned, cloaked in an iridescent
shimmer, reconciled, possibly even content.

But not happy.

"Get out," Mikhyel said aloud as soon as he was able,
and he shied away from Deymorin's hand. "I said, *out*!"

And a different sort of barrier formed between them.

"And take *that* with you!"

With a jut of his stubbled chin, Mikhyel indicated the
lump that had materialized with him, a reeking corpse that
matched the reeking arm he'd thrown out the window
nearly an hour ago.

"Just a damn minute," Deymorin hissed, and cornered
Mikhyel, grabbing his arm, forcing the inner communication.

Bitterness. Anger. Frustration. All those came through.
Not directed at Deymorin, not at Nikki, but at life. At
circumstances that forced Mikhyel dunMheric once again
from taking a preferred route toward personal fulfillment.

"I'm *sorry,* Khyel. I'm *sorry* our mother died and left
you with Nikki and Mheric. I'm *sorry* Anheliaa used you.
I'm *sorry* I left you with the Syndicate. I'm *sorry* the web
is down and the Syndicate needs you now. But the web *is*
down and we *do* need you and damned if I'd let you incarcerate yourself in the ground with a talking rock even if
we *didn't*. As for your stinking corpse—" He waved at what
remained of Anheliaa dunMoren. "We *got* rid of it once.
What are we supposed to do with it now? Eat it?"

Mikhyel's eyes narrowed to angry slits, the greenish tint
flashing in a stray beam of light. Then, for no apparent
reason, the anger faded, his brows lifted, and the narrow
shoulders beneath Deymorin's hands shook with silent
laughter.

"I'm . . . not quite certain. If we eat her, it comes out
the other end, doesn't it? And that goes into the ley as

well, and if he doesn't want her in the one form, I doubt he wants her in the other, and I don't think we want *that* lining the halls of Rhomandi." He met Deymorin's open-mouthed disbelief and laughed aloud. "Try breathing, Deymio. It's . . . salubrious. —I think we're supposed to bury her, someplace beyond the web. He doesn't want her . . . polluting his node."

The tension that had sustained him for the past hour slid away, and Deymorin grinned back. "Can't blame him for that. What then, brother? What do we do now?"

"Sleep. I think, I want to . . ." Mikhyel's eyes closed, standing upright as he was, and he slumped, limp as death. But it was sleep, not death, Deymorin knew that before he caught him and eased him onto the waiting bed. Sound, deep sleep as he'd not had for weeks, possibly even for years.

Chapter Seven

"Deymorin says you're leaving early," Nikki said, breaking the silence that had filled the room since Mikhyel let him in.

Mikhyel nodded, and continued sorting through the items on his vanity. Needless fussing, Nikki could tell. Excuse not to talk to him.

Nikki swallowed hard. "Is it . . . is it because of yesterday morning?"

"What do you think?" Mikhyel shoved back from the vanity, rose, and went to get a cravat from his dresser.

"Khyel, I'm sorry. I—"

"Sorry? You don't know the meaning of the word."

This interview was going as badly as Nikki had feared. Worse, if possible. He tried desperately to regroup.

"Khyel, it's not . . . I *am* sorry. It's just . . . you didn't apologize to her. And then I saw you kissing her and—"

"I didn't apologize because I don't damn well regret it! *Any* of it!"

Nikki shook his head, confused. "Any of what, Mikhyel?"

"It's *not* just yesterday. It's not just Mirym, don't you see that? You're a hypocrite, Nikaenor. You make allowances for Lidye, for yourself, even for Deymorin and Kiyrstin, but somehow, Mirym is *my* doing. What happened in the hypogeum . . . what happened last night is all *my* doing. And somehow, in *doing* I'm *cheating* you."

Mikhyel turned to face the mirror, struggled for a moment with his cravat, but his visibly trembling fingers fouled even the simplest folds, and with a curse, he ripped it off and threw it to join two others on the rumpled bed.

Then he leaned on the vanity, hands flat, elbows locked, his eyes pressed shut. When he continued, it was with greater control. "I don't regret what happened, and I thank every god we supposedly do not believe in that Mirym apparently does not regret it either. But if you recall, I was in there with Lidye's claws, not you."

"It's *my* body that bears the scars!"

"And my mind. I'll trade you the distinction any time, brother. You were making love to Mirym—"

"It was your seed planted in her! Your child she carries now."

Mikhyel's jaw clenched, he turned back to the mirror and another cravat. "Get out, Nikki."

"But—"

"Get out, before we say things we really prefer to leave unsaid."

Nikki caught his breath, recognizing, almost too late, the anger shattering his own thoughts as bleedover from Mikhyel. Or perhaps not. Perhaps they'd both entered into this conversation with a little anger, a little fear, and their small concerns had fed each other until now, they were somehow near blows all over again.

Agreement and remorse. That was Mikhyel. Clearly.

He met Mikhyel's eyes in the mirror. Eyes in a face that looked increasingly like the old Mikhyel: dark-haired, cool-eyed, a bit mysterious, even to those who knew him best. Part of it was the return of his beard—nearly full-grown already and lacking the gray it had acquired in recent months, a near-miraculous return that only added to his mystery.

The beard was part of it, but the hard set to jaw and eyes was another part.

"I'm sorry, Mikhyel. I did want to apologize for yesterday. I didn't want you leaving without—"

"You came, Nikaenor, for absolution. I don't know why, I can't read that behind the muddled emotions you radiate constantly. If I were hopelessly cynical, I'd say it was because you're hoping I'll be able to take you down into that cavern I was in last night. Well, you won't get absolution from me. Not today. Perhaps never. Despite all your protestations to the contrary, you have special feelings for Mirym. Anheliaa's influence notwithstanding, the simple fact is that on your wedding night, *I* lay with the woman you really wanted, *because* you wanted her, and I, fool that I am, hadn't the moral fortitude to deny that need. Or my own need, for that matter. Now, in the inevitable aftermath, you choose to take exception to that fact, you choose to blame me, personally. I don't appreciate that. I don't appreciate your laying me out cold because I happened to be talking to the young woman—"

"You weren't talking!"

"—who bears the child of my body," Mikhyel completed without a pause. "No, I wasn't. And I'll tell you something else, Nikaenor dunMheric, I was enjoying it! For the first time in my life, I felt the urge to kiss a pretty woman. I'm twenty-six years old, little brother. Only weeks short of twenty-seven. How many times have you had that urge and acted on it, you who treated yourself to a brothel on your seventeenth birthday?"

"Khyel, I'm sorry! I didn't mean—"

"I know what you meant."

"Of course," Nikki said, feeling the bitter resentment that was a constant in his life now rising. "You always have, haven't you?"

Mikhyel said nothing.

"I was just— Dammit, Khyel, it's as if you know what I'm thinking before I even think it and I don't like that. You know *everything.* It's not fair. I can't hear you. How can *I* know what you were doing with her? I'm just trying to sort things out, and then you and Deymorin make me feel—"

"You're right, Nikki, I can. If you think I *want* it that way, you're out of your mind. I know you're trying to sort feelings every seventeen-year-old would prefer to keep private, and you feel as if they're exposed to the world. Ringfire, boy, I know what you're thinking and feeling even as we speak! I can hardly sort your thoughts from my own. I have to *ask* what you're *wanting* to talk about, and then try to answer based on what we've *said* to each other, not all the other scattered bits I've picked up from you."

"Why bother?" Nikki asked bitterly.

"Because, dammit, I respect you. I respect your need and desire to be understood and to sort out your own feelings. But I'm *tired,* boy. *Tired* of understanding and making excuses, for you, for Anheliaa, even for myself. I'm tired of trying to hold my thoughts clear of yours and of Deymorin's. Thanks to this cursed link, there's not a moment in the day that I don't question my judgment." Mikhyel's voice was shaking, beyond his control, and that last control, more than his words and that underneath sense, shook Nikki.

"I *meant*, Nikki, that events have opened my eyes these past few days. And I'm not about to close them again. I love you, Nikki. Deymorin loves you. But nothing we say or do will convince you of that. Ever. If you would hear . . . but you won't."

"Can't," he protested weakly.

"You hear well enough when you want to hear. But I'm not talking about that inner voice. I'm talking about a lifetime of commitment—mine and Deymorin's—to *you*. At the moment, harsh as it sounds, you're reveling in being misunderstood. That happens at seventeen. I trust you'll get over it. Most of us do. But I can't wait for that."

"What do you mean?" Nikki asked, fearful of Mikhyel's unequivocal language.

"I mean I can't handle your confusion and uncertainty—your damned whining and wallowing—any longer; I can't afford it. I've a job to do. Dammit, I've got my *own* life to live!"

Their eyes met, and Mikhyel's were still hard, still dry, though Nikki sensed at last the effort it took to maintain that facade.

"I'm leaving in three days. You can find your own peace. Pretend the past weeks never happened, if that's what you want. But remember, eventually I'll be back. And *I* won't pretend it never happened, because if I let you delude yourself with the idea that it's all right, that I forgive you, you'll continue to fool yourself, and I'll continue having to pretend, and that's too hard, Nikki. It's just too . . . damned . . . hard."

Nikki stared at his boot toes, carefully polished, as he'd carefully prepared the rest of himself for this meeting—on the outside.

But Mikhyel didn't care about the outside. It was . . . hard . . . to hear what Mikhyel was saying, hard to admit there was any truth whatsoever to it, but even without that underneath feeling, he knew Mikhyel wouldn't lie to him, not about this. They'd had serious talks over the years; Mikhyel expected him to listen, expected him to judge for himself the right and wrong of it. Mikhyel had taught him to ask questions, and consider all the answers.

Of course, Mikhyel himself hadn't been very good at that where Deymorin was concerned. He and Deymorin had—

Nikki caught that thought and worried it about in his head, wondering was he using *Mikhyel's* previous shortcomings to excuse his own current ones, and decided maybe he was, and that maybe he should look only at himself and his own reasoning.

At least for now.

"What *were* you talking about?" he asked.

"I offered to marry her," Mikhyel replied promptly, without questioning who Nikki meant, leading him to wonder if Mikhyel had been following his every thought. "She declined. Politely, but quite pointedly."

"Why?"

"I didn't get a chance to ask. I don't know that I would if I could. Her life is her own. Her choices are. But I'll tell you this, Nikaenor, whatever happens, to any of us, she and her child will be cared for. I've seen to it, set the paperwork in motion and if anyone—*anyone*—stands in the way of that paperwork or compromises her future, I'll take her and the child and leave Rhomatum forever."

"But you don't love her."

"No? But then, you didn't love Lidye when you married her."

"I don't love her now."

"No?"

"I . . . Well . . ."

Mikhyel laughed, and it was an easy sound, not a painful one. "It's all right, Nikki. She's different, now Anheliaa's gone. Perhaps we all are. Perhaps we need to get to know each other. Perhaps we need to know ourselves first. I'll be gone at least two months. Deymorin will likely be longer. You'll be in charge. You've done well, Nikki. You've made very good impressions. I've had several Syndics stop me specifically to commend you on your deference and willingness to listen. They're ready to be on your side. Use that talent you've developed over the years for compromising between your two bull-headed brothers. And remember, Mauritum isn't our only threat. A month ago, you were planning a dam. Have you forgotten that already?"

He had forgotten, because it didn't involve him. It was an Outside problem: changing weather patterns that were turning parts of the fertile Rhomatum Valley into bogs and other parts into near-desert. Older, more experienced men had wrestled with the problem without success. The dam was his idea, one Mikhyel had had vetted by engineers and geologists. The experts were enthusiastic, Mikhyel had said. The Council and the Syndicate were less so.

{Convince them.}

{I—}

{Can't, little brother?}

Their eyes met again, directly this time, not in the mirror, and Nikki grinned.

"Will."

The door closed behind Nikki, quietly, as Nikki's mind was quiet at last. Mikhyel waited until his awareness of Nikki had faded, before he relaxed his own internal controls and sank wearily into the nearest chair, shaking inside and out.

He'd known Nikki would come this morning. He'd had to. He wouldn't be Nikki, otherwise. Nikki had to make everything right.

And Lidye wanted to know more about that creature beneath Rhomatum.

Which interest at least answered one of the infinity of questions roiling about his brain when he awoke this morning: If Anheliaa had known about Rhomatum's resident . . . god, she hadn't told Lidye about it, hadn't taken her to meet it. But Nikki had been there with him. Nikki knew as much as Nikki needed to know. Somehow, he suspected that if it became important that Lidye meet it . . . him . . . the creature . . . *he* would draw her down to his lair himself.

{Yes-s-s . . .}

The echo in his mind faded, and as it withdrew, it removed from him the palsy residual from his confrontation with Nikki, and left warmth in the palsy's stead. Warmth, and a reminder that, when *he* cared to come, *he* would be welcome.

Likely he wouldn't tell Nikki about that either.

Ringmasters spoke of "introducing" prospective apprentices to the rings. After that, each individual seemed to find his or her own way of coaxing the rings to their bidding.

He wondered if they knew how literally that term might be taken.

A knock on his door, a blessedly blank presence on the far side.

"Come," he said, and he stood eagerly when Raulind entered the room. "Save me?" he pleaded, with a gesture toward the ruined cravats on the bed, and Raulind silently blessed his throat with a fresh tie, then gestured toward the chair beside the open window.

Mikhyel sat passively. Raulind smoothed the tangles from his hair, then braided it in the complex pattern that would both hold his slippery hair all day *and* not give him a headache. It had taken Raul a week of trial to develop that pattern, and in the ten years since, not a month of days had gone by that they hadn't performed this particular morning ritual.

"Your brother left this morning," Raulind spoke at last. "Quite early."

"Deymorin?"

"Obviously, sir." Gently chastising, reminder that Raulind knew precisely who had entered and left his employer's bedroom only moments ago. "He and the lady Kiyrstine."

The holding pin of the hair clip slipped past his scalp, and Mikhyel knew it was safe to move. He twisted around.

"What are you saying, Raul? They've gone to the stables every morning for two weeks."

"A sizable bundle preceded them to the stable."

Mikhyel felt his mouth twitch.

"And did my brother say what this bundle was?"

"I believe, sir, he indicated it was, if you will, fertilizer."

᭡   ᭡   ᭡

"This is Shtolis," Bharlori said, tapping the youngest of the new employees on the head. And with a nod to the others, "And Khonno, Frivori, Asthif, and Berghis."

Five new employees, all male, all somewhere between sixteen and twenty. They were necessary, Bharlori explained, because Bharlori had plans. Bharlori's was expanding, and they needed to be ready.

That they could use the help went without saying. Strangers continued to pour into Khoratum, and they all seemed to drift eventually to Bharlori's, either as customers or, like this lot, hillers from a distant valley who had come to Khoratum to take advantage of that local growth. These five—cousins, brothers, and friend—had come to the city, Bharlori explained, as a group. And they carried with them a group's brash confidence, eying the girls with open interest, and swaggering when they walked.

And as one, they laughed when Bharlori pulled Thyerri to the front and introduced him as the tavern's prime entertainment, and as one scowled when told they were to be ready at all times to cover his tables.

Apparently oblivious to the dissension he had just seeded within the ranks of his employees, Bharlori cheerfully ordered Sakhithe to show the "new boys" where they'd sleep, telling them all to "squeeze tight" for the next few nights, promising as he retreated to his office, that they'd have more space . . . soon.

"Looks like it's back to hard beds," Sakhithe murmured, and she cast Thyerri a resigned grin, before leading the way to the back room they all shared.

Extra pallets had arrived the day before, and blankets and pillows. Thyerri and the girls, not realizing they were intended for new employees, had quite happily distributed the largesse among themselves, doubling their padding and their comfort for a single night.

Which meant they now had to separate pallets and blankets, and arrange them about the room, the girls' to one side, the new employees to the other. Besho, having fallen immediately in with Shtolis, threw his pallet beside the new boy's. Thyerri, without giving the matter a second thought, placed his between Sakhithe's and Khani's.

"What's this?" Asthif asked. "Are we welcome as well?"

"What's wrong with you, Thif?" Frivori sneered, "That's girls only."

Thyerri blushed and gathered his blanket.

"It's all right, Thy," Sakhithe said firmly. "You can stay right there."

Thyerri just shook his head and set his blanket among the new pallets, then returned for the pallet. As he picked up the pallet, Frivori kicked the blanket aside, knocking free the purse that held his share of the dance money.

Frivori snatched the purse up and tossed it in one hand. "And what sort of 'entertainment' *do* you provide, Thyerri-boy?" The sneer remained.

"He's a dancer," Mishthi said, and the sneer widened.

Thyerri said nothing, but dropped the pallet and held out his hand expectantly.

Frivori's thin mouth stretched in a tight smile, and he crouched slightly, holding the purse out like a lure. "Come and get it, Dancer-boy."

"I'm going to get Bharlo." Sakhithe headed for the door.

"Wait, Sakhi," Thyerri said, and Sakhithe stopped, looked around at Thyerri, then nodded.

Frivori's grin widened.

"Okay, Dancer-boy. Let's dance."

Chapter Eight

"You're hiring *whom?*" Deymorin whirled from the window, where he'd been contemplating the neighboring building's marble facade, to contemplate his obviously demented brother.

"You heard me," Mikhyel responded, serene and untouchable behind the massive desk. Borrowed, as this office was borrowed. "Neutral ground," the demented brother had called it. Neutral, not for his sake, or even for Mikhyel's, but for a piece of scum who, if Deymorin had had his way three weeks ago, would be fertilizing the leythium growth chambers.

Mikhyel had been gone from the house before Deymorin had returned from burying Annheliaa that morning. Gone from the house and at his office, finalizing plans, maintaining his determination to leave within three days.

But he was moving too fast, making dangerously precipitous decisions.

"Khyel, forget about the tour."

"Don't be ridiculous."

"You never wanted to go anyway."

"What I *want* is hardly the issue."

"Then let *me* handle the tour."

Mikhyel laughed. "You'd hate every moment. Besides, you already *have* a job."

"Must I state the obvious? I *can't* let you go. Not after last night."

"*Thanks* to last night, I finally know exactly what we need to accomplish."

"You *know* nothing. That creature merely confirmed your own damned suspicions."

"He wasn't lying to me, Deymorin."

"How in hell do you know?"

"He had no reason to lie, and every reason to tell the truth."

Deymorin drew a steadying breath. "All right, brother, explain."

"He is *of* the ley, Deymorin, in ways Anheliaa couldn't even have imagined. The web is damaged. That means *he* is. His interests *are* ours . . . at least for now."

"So you're going to act on the opinion of a rock?"

"That's not even remotely funny, Deymorin."

"I didn't intend it to be."

"And what do you suggest we do? Challenge him to a duel? I'm acting on the information I have, Deymorin. That information accounts for the observed symptoms. It's a starting point, nothing more."

"And what will you tell the ringmasters? That a burning lump of leythium imparted the secrets of the universe to you?"

"I'll tell them it comes from Anheliaa."

"Anheliaa's ghost."

Mikhyel shrugged. "They don't need to know the sequence of events. The point is to convince them to trust long enough to try. If it doesn't work, we'll try something else. But if it does, *if* my information is right and *if* I can get the ringmasters to agree to direct their energies simultaneously toward Khoratum, we could have the web returned to full strength in a matter of days. That should surprise Mauritum and anyone else watching us and give *you* ample time to secure those borders."

"And if you're wrong?"

"It's all we've got to go on right now. If I'm wrong, if the web doesn't improve, at least we tried. We go then on what more we can learn."

"All right, Khyel, all right. I'll concede on that part of your plan. But this other notion—"

"I don't know why you're complaining, Deymorin. It was your idea."

"My idea? To hire *Ganfrion* as your personal body-guard? Hardly."

"You said to get someone who understood the shadows of the cities to guard my back."

"Ganfrion isn't exactly what I had in mind!"

"No? Perhaps you should read his file. Might change your mind."

"I've better things to do with my time." Deymorin balled his shaking hands into fists. "Have you forgotten what that animal did to you in the Crypt?"

"Irrelevant."

"Ir—" Deymorin threw himself into the chair opposite Mikhyel's. "Nothing is *more* relevant."

"Circumstances being what they were—"

"Circumstances be *damned!* It's *your* frame of mind *today* that's in question."

"I know exactly what I'm doing."

"Do you?" Deymorin tried to force all the caution and concern he was feeling into the front of his mind and down Mikhyel's mental throat. "And what about blackmail, dun-Mheric of Rhomatum Tower? What about simple, nasty rumor? *Everything* we hope to accomplish depends on *your* image."

"I've faced that particular specter for fifteen years, Deymorin. Mheric saw to that."

Deymorin leaned forward, elbows on knees, laced fingers hanging between. "I'm worried about you, Khy. You've been pushed so close to the edge—"

"Several times, recently."

"Exactly. And you've changed—"

"We all have. Deymorin, if you'd just look at his file—"

"I don't give a *damn* about a Crypt-bait's resume. He's an assassin and a rapist, that's *all* I need to know."

"Actually, he's *not* an assassin."

"*Not?* You're the one who said—"

"No, *he* said. He lied. Read the file, Deymorin."

"I don't need to read a damned file. I *saw* him. I saw you with him. And now, you expect me to entrust *your* welfare to him?"

"No, not at all."

"Well, that's a relief."

"*You've* no part in the decision. Which has not yet been made, incidentally."

"He's not likely to turn you down."

"He's not yet been asked."

"Fine."

Deymorin shoved himself out of the chair, and headed for the door.

"Rhomandi!"

He stopped.

"Don't do it."

{What happened to my privacy?} Deymorin demanded silently and had the satisfaction of seeing his devious brother wince.

{Not where it intersects *my* interests.} Mikhyel's response came at a far more civilized volume, and Mikhyel continued aloud. "This is *my* decision, Deymorin. You keep away from him."

"You should never have told me, then."

"I should have left you with hearsay, perhaps? I wanted to know you knew, Deymorin. I didn't want you thinking I was keeping significant plans to myself. I hoped you would do *me* the courtesy of reading the file—*before* questioning my judgment."

Deymorin clenched his jaw on the retort that rose. Mikhyel's detached expression didn't change, but he stood up and moved to Deymorin's abandoned spot by the window, gazed outward for a moment, and then turned, a shadow figure against sunlit marble. "I'm alive because of him."

"I doubt that."

"Everyone knew, after Brolucci's men came for you." Mikhyel paused, as though expecting comment, and when Deymorin refused to oblige him: "He claimed first rights. *Made* them exclusive rights."

"Damned if I want the details. I've reason enough without them to question your sanity in even *contemplating* including him in your entourage. If you want a man to warm your bed, we'll *find* you one. But—"

{My bed is, and always will be, my own!}

"Not this time, it's not. I've said nothing, Mikhyel. I believed you when you said you weren't interested. I've blamed Mheric and I've blamed Anheliaa for turning you into a monk; I've mourned your lack of a relationship of the kind that has brought so much personal joy to me. But if you want someone like *that,* I've *got* to question your fitness for—"

His voice froze. And Mikhyel's emphatic but formless objection, laced heavily with resentment and anger, pierced his head. Deymorin flared back, and Mikhyel's hold crumbled.

"All right!" Deymorin said through teeth clenched against the pain and frustration resonating between them. "Make your point or let me go."

"He didn't touch me."

"Bullshit. You forget, I saw you, *felt* him with you when I picked you up. You were a bloody mess."

"I was alive. Three days after you got me out, Ganfrion nearly wasn't."

"And I'm to feel sorry for him? So he shat in his own lair, and his creatures turned. Has nothing to do with you. You don't *owe* him, Khyel!"

"Owe him? No, I don't suppose I do. But I can use him."

Deymorin forced his hands to relax, moved a step closer, wishing he dared touch his brother, to get past all the personal inhibitions. "What happened . . . after I left?"

A shrug. "I fought . . . well, resisted. You'd have been amused."

"I doubt it."

Another shrug. "*They* were. Ganfrion stepped in before it became anything more than mauling and shoving. He stopped it. Laid claim—at some personal cost. It ended. He took me into his bolt hole, then left me alone."

"So he's got good survival instincts."

"If you believe that, you don't know the prisons as well as you thought."

"And you do."

"Even before I spent a night in the Crypt. I've sent men there, Deymorin. I knew. It was my job to know."

"So why'd he do it? Why protect *you*, of all people?"

"Why didn't he kill you? He had the chance."

"That's what this interview is about, then?" Deymorin asked. "Scruples?"

Mikhyel tipped his head.

"And if his answers satisfy you, you'll hire him?"

"If he's physically able, yes. I was a bit late getting him out. I might just send him to Barsitum."

Deymorin, still far from convinced, probed underneath for enlightenment and met rebuff. He scowled, thinking he was going to do some investigating of his own into Ganfrion of Sparingate Crypt, but doubted he'd gain anything other than unwilling acceptance of the logic behind Mikhyel's actions today.

He was learning slowly that Mikhyel never made arbitrary decisions, even one as radical and grotesquely absurd as this one.

Mikhyel's mouth twitched, and acknowledgment warmed

him from within. Deymorin resisted that warmth, suspecting—because of that warmth—the origin of the thought
that inspired it.

"At times," he said slowly, "I can truly sympathize with
Nikki. Getting too damned subtle, brother."

The warmth vanished, along with the twitch.

"Watch your backside, Mikhyel dunMheric," Deymorin
said, and jerked the door open. "Rhomatum can't afford
to lose you now."

ら   ら   ら

The door closed with a soft thud; Mikhyel sighed deeply
and relaxed the fists he held clenched at his back.

He'd been expecting a bill for the glass.

If only Deymorin had taken the time to look at the file.
Certainly, Sparingate was a repository for the worst elements in the web—it was part of the price Rhomatum paid
for being the capital—but this particular villain had a most
interesting background. Scholar, mercenary, assassin . . .
the details of the fate that had driven the man called Ganfrion ever deeper into the morass of human existence were
only alluded to, but those specifics might make the difference, might allow the man a . . . Mikhyel mentally reviewed
the file, and decided it would be at least Ganfrion's ninth
chance at an honest life.

But there had been no assassinations. No *unwarranted*
evil deeds, for all Ganfrion would like him to believe otherwise. Deeds of dubious legality, without question, but with
a common thread of equity, justice in the purest sense.

Ganfrion might be a man who believed in causes and
fought for them. Mikhyel wasn't interested in altruism. He
wasn't interested in blind obedience. He believed in his
own cause. In a tower rife with Farricci guards and with
remnants of Brolucci's interests—in a country wracked with
civil rivalries, he wanted a man with *one* loyalty, and a
home in *no* city.

He turned back to the window, leaning his shoulder on
the side frame to look past the neighboring building and
out across the rooftops of Rhomatum. It was a singularly
beautiful view—at least, to him it was beautiful. He had no
referent, had seen no other city. Another few months and
he'd have seventeen referents, but even if there were other

beautiful cities, their beauty couldn't detract from Rhomatum's.

"Well, well, well, Suds, a final audience with the prince before the beheading?" Bold tone, brash words, but the voice of a man nervous, uncertain, caught in a milieu not of his choosing.

Mikhyel turned from the window, slowly, deliberately, and faced the man he'd last viewed from the topmost stair in Sparingate Crypt. He'd not heard the door open, lost in his thoughts the way he'd been. Neither had he heard Paulis' announcement.

And even now, Paulis was not in the room, as he'd been ordered.

"Off after a glass of water, Suds."

He slid his attention from the door to Ganfrion, standing at his case in the middle of the office.

"I was just . . . parched. I'd forgotten how . . . dry the surface air is."

"Dry," Mikhyel repeated, and when Ganfrion coughed obligingly: "Of course."

Came a frantic knocking at the door, and Mikhyel bade Paulis enter. The bespectacled clerk entered, flustered and angry.

"Did you find his water?" Mikhyel asked calmly, into Paulis' verbal stream of self-condemnation, which stopped the stream on a puzzled squeak.

"Water?" Mikhyel repeated.

Paulis snapped his mouth closed and went back out, to return immediately with a silver pitcher and goblet on a silver tray. Mikhyel raised his eyebrows, and Paulis blushed bright red.

"Sorry, sir. It was all I could find."

"No matter. You did well, Paulis. Thank you. You may go now."

The black look Paulis cast Ganfrion sat as oddly on his boyish face as the mustache he was trying to cultivate. Ganfrion, who, with a cut above one eye and puffed and bruised lower lip was likely the most disreputable sort Paulis had ever encountered, merely nodded, simple civility for which Mikhyel was duly thankful.

"It's all right, Paulis," he said. "We're . . . old friends."

Paulis' revised look was one of reverent awe, and too late Mikhyel realized the new heights to which that casual claim thrust him. Not only was Mikhyel dunMheric able to draw on the resources of the Syndicate and the City, but he had contacts among . . . men of dubious honor as well.

The thought lent an appropriately insane note to the upcoming interview.

Mikhyel nodded Paulis to leave, then turned back to the window, waiting until the door closed, then turned to study Ganfrion.

He nodded to the chair; Ganfrion remained standing.

"To whom have you talked?" Mikhyel asked at last.

"Why, I've talked to a lot of people, Suds. I've spent a lifetime talking."

"No doubt. How many people know what passed between us in the prison? Have you talked, man? Because if you have, you're no use to me. And if you lie about that fact, I *shall* find out and you *will* regret it. Now, I ask again, to whom have you talked?"

A slow smile just short of a sneer twisted the man's upper lip. "No one, Suds. I'm no fool. If the lads knew I'd consciously kept Mikhyel dunMheric from their hands that first night, I'd be dead. Are you happy?"

"And yet, I understand you were removed from the prison in less than pristine condition."

Ganfrion shrugged. "You got away. I remained. The lads had to take out their frustrations somewhere."

Mikhyel nodded briefly. "I suspected as much. Your hold there was precarious. Now, I had to wonder, once I was out and had time to piece the facts together, why you acted as you did. Why you took such a risk."

"Why? For your pretty gray eyes, Suds. Why else?"

His back stiffened, he frowned, but he controlled the anger and instead nodded again to the chair. Ganfrion shrugged, sauntered first to the side table where the Syndic whose office this rightfully was kept wine at hand to soften his opponents.

It was a challenge, of the simplest sort, and Mikhyel let it pass, accepted the goblet Ganfrion handed him, and even raised it in a silent salute before sitting behind the desk.

Mikhyel made a show of sorting papers that weren't his, leafed through a bound report that was, and signed a blank piece of paper before returning his attention to Ganfrion. The man had settled at last, his booted legs crossed. No shifting about, no apparent tension, just a sipping assessment of the wine that ended when he caught Mikhyel's eyes on him.

"Pritian Valley, ten years tops. Very mediocre. Briandi had better find himself a better bribe than this."

"Briandi?" Mikhyel repeated. "Why do you mention him?"

"Come, come, dunMheric. It's not your office. Not your style at all, and *much* too far Downhill." Ganfrion lifted his goblet. "Pritian Valley wine, dunGorshi law texts, Persitumin pulled-work—" he indicated the intricate armrest cover of the chair he occupied, "—and a note on the desk to contact Syndic dunSkahtkhi. Who else?"

Astute observations which simply confirmed Mikhyel's suspicions about the man.

"What node?" he asked.

"Briandi? Don't you know? Not much of a Rhomandi statesman, are you?" Ganfrion paused, laughed into the silence Mikhyel left hanging between them. "Originally, dunMheric?"

Mikhyel dipped his head, acknowledgment of Ganfrion's capitulation.

Ganfrion shrugged. "Take your pick. Most, at one time or another."

"Where were you born? To what City do you owe allegiance?"

"Born? That was a long time ago, my friend. A long . . . *long* time ago." He laughed. "Who knows? Perhaps I was hatched."

"Have you loyalties now?"

"Only to freedom."

"Freedom? Not gold?"

"One's not much good without the other, dunMheric."

"And both? How procurable are your loyalties?"

"Prison-bait? Come, dunMheric, let us not mince words."

"I'm not so inclined. You were uncommonly good at avoiding Sparingate before you crossed Anheliaa's path."

"Is this a private trial? Going to put me away forever thanks to that?" Ganfrion nodded to Brolucci's file on himself.

"You've a villainous history. Those who have hired you treated you like a villain. Are you?"

Another shrug, small, contemptuous. "I'm a believer in

fair trade. They were villains, both sides. They treated me as one of them. I returned the favor."

And a man raised with better expectations than life had granted him.

"A man who would survive can't always choose his preferred weapons; he has to be ready with a variety of answers—in any debate."

"You would know, Suds."

"You fought with the options available, there in the prison. You chose your path then. Now I invite you to another."

"I trusted Rhomatum Tower once before."

"I'm not my aunt."

A slow smile.

"No, you most definitely are not."

"I'm prepared to arrange your freedom. I'm prepared to do more for your future."

"Why?"

"Why isn't Deymorin dead?"

The smile pulled, lopsided and wry. "I am that most unfortunate of creatures: a discriminating assassin."

"Meaning?"

"I prefer to judge my prey *before* I eliminate them."

"And you judged Deymorin the lesser of two evils?"

Ganfrion shrugged. "If I'd so judged, he'd be dead, Suds. Evil is evil. I don't quibble over degree."

"Fair trade?"

"Fair trade."

"I thought as much. Your . . . business associates turned you in?"

Another shrug.

Not a man to defend himself. Not one to make excuses. Take the cards as they fell and play them for the moment. And yet . . . "Why didn't you recognize him?"

"In the Crypt?"

Mikhyel dipped his head.

Ganfrion shrugged.

"Dark? There'd been imposters already? Take your pick. Maybe I *did* recognize him, and didn't give a damn."

"And myself? That first time in the Crypt—"

Ganfrion shifted in his seat, and the smile turned sour. "Brought it on yourself, Suds. Should have played along. Let me stake a claim right off. One-on's easier."

"Perhaps."

Narrow dark eyes glimmered through a fall of ragged hair. The scarred mouth twitched. "I like my privacy, Suds. Take you off in a corner, all by ourselves . . . skinny thing that you are, I rather suspect I'd've lost interest fast. No one the wiser."

"Why?"

"Obvious. I wanted out."

"You didn't know who I was. Not at first."

Another shrug.

Mikhyel tapped the file. "You've a record, Ganfrion. Preferences. Were those others you've claimed too skinny as well?"

Ganfrion was a big man, large-boned and iron-hard beneath his prison-ragged clothing. But the hand that cupped the wineglass was mostly clean, the nails no worse than prison life would have them. He wore his hair short-cropped, hanging ragged to his shoulders, like most Persitumin, and the rest of the Northern Crescent. But that might well be an attempt toward personal maintenance, demands of prison life.

There were scars on the backs of his hands, and a scar traced his cheekbone to disappear into his mustache, and pull his mouth into a permanent sneer. Dark eyes stared at him from under heavy black brows.

"Beard's coming back, then, Suds?"

"As you see."

"Interesting. I was raised in the Khoramali, Suds. I don't like to see the hillers persecuted. You've the look about you . . . without the beard."

"And afterward? Once you did know? Once Deymorin was gone? You could have let them have me. You didn't."

Ganfrion scratched his temple idly, then up under his tangled hair with greater purpose. Scraping the grime thus accumulated from under his nails, he wiped his hand clean on his patched breeches and leaned back.

"Don't kid yourself, dunMheric, nephew of Anheliaa dunMoren. I was tempted. At first. I thought you were Anheliaa's. That being the case, the boys would have been a fitting end for you."

"You decided otherwise. Why?"

A long pause, and another of those careless shrugs.

"I was once part of Pasri dunHaulpin's personal guard," Ganfrion said at last.

Mikhyel flinched. It was a name he hadn't thought of in years, and wondered how he'd missed it in the file on the desk.

"I thought you'd recognize the name." The scar twitched. "I didn't tell old Bro about that. It's an association I prefer to forget myself. DunHaulpin's preferences were hardly a secret about the barracks. Rumor held the Rhomandi secured dunHaulpin's signature on the Bartishi venture using his son as collateral."

The Rhomandi. Mheric, at the time of the Bartishi plan. This time, Mikhyel controlled his reaction.

"Barrack rumor also said that same son used the same bargaining power to secure dunHauplin's loyalties to his own cause in the months following Mheric's death. Among the barracks, this was generally considered one of the most audacious bargains ever perpetrated."

Mikhyel said nothing.

"Rumor implied it was Mheric's eldest, that of Mheric's sons only Deymorin Rhomandi would have the cold-blooded balls to stand up to dunHaulpin that way." Ganfrion's lip lifted in a half-smile that held nothing of its former sneer. "Having met Mheric's sons, I decided that perhaps rumor had judged too soon."

A pause, for a swallow of wine, and head-tilted study of Mikhyel's face.

"Why did I step in? I honestly can't say for certain. Respect, perhaps, for the lad who got the best of dunHaulpin at last. Self-preservation, more likely. I don't think I'd want that cold-assed determination pitted directly against me—in prison or out."

The details of Ganfrion's reasoning weren't important. The end result was.

"Anheliaa is dead," Mikhyel said flatly.

"I don't think I want to hear this."

"I'm quite certain you do not. However, she is, you know; and it's worth your life if that information leaks out of this room."

The sneer returned. "Oh, you are your aunt's nephew."

"On the contrary. Anheliaa is dead. She's no longer a threat or a future for you. I want practical, self-serving men, not blindly loyal men who will lose their common sense the first time someone badmouths a Rhomandi."

"Your acumen surprises me."

"I'm not a fool, Ganfrion. I know the Rhomandi are not the most popular family in the web these days. I hope to change that general opinion, but that will take time. And it will take knowledge. I want more than a personal guard. I want someone who can spot assassins, and can find out who those assassins work for and why they want me dead. I want to know, on the streets, who wouldn't care if those assassins succeeded in their attempts."

"Why? To eliminate the problem?"

"At its source—yes. And if that source is Rhomandi ignorance, then the Rhomandi will become less so. You might be that man, if you choose. If you prefer otherwise, I shall simply have you isolated until such time as the information you hold is no longer inflammable, and then you'll serve out your sentence. In a different ward."

Ganfrion drained his glass and poured another, taking the decanter back to the chair with him.

"And your brother? How does he feel about this notion of yours? Where does he come into this gambit?"

"*Deymorin* isn't hiring you."

Narrow eyes assessed him above the glass rim, then dropped to stare into the wine.

"I was pulled a week ago," Ganfrion said. "Your doing?"

"I would have sooner, but I had no power."

"Soon enough." The sneer broke on a bark of laughter. "Bastisti's balls, man, I'm still alive. What more do I need?" Then, with a dark glower, and a set jaw: "Why?"

"Your silence kept me alive in prison. Your common sense kept your hands to yourself at the last. I appreciate a healthy sense of self-preservation, I appreciate logic over passion. Revenge would have gained you nothing. Self-control . . . well, it might."

He paced the room slowly. "I'm about to embark on a fool's venture, man of no city. I'm going to visit every node in the web, to prepare the leaders for the news of Anheliaa's death, to unite the ringmasters, and to rouse the citizens to defend their borders against Mauritum."

"Mauritum?" the man repeated, intrigued for all his attempts to disguise the fact. If Mikhyel was correct in his assessment, Ganfrion had an active intelligence, too lively to handle the boredom of prison for long. "Why? . . . Of course. Anheliaa. No one to mind the store, Rhomandi?"

"As you say. I need men I can trust, men who can infiltrate areas of those cities that I cannot, who can hear and investigate those rumors and factions closed to me. The Rhomandi have grown out of touch—"

"Grown? Man, they've never been in touch. All old Darius ever wanted was a node to call his own. Once the Rhomatum satellites were capped, he didn't care shit who sat on them or what they did with them. And his damned offspring have been no better."

"I want to change that. I can find out what their leaders think. I want to know how the . . ." He smiled to himself, thinking of that moment in the prison latrine and the thoughts he'd had. "How the man on the streets thinks about the web, Rhomatum, the Rhomandi."

"You'll never survive, Towerman."

"That's where you might prove useful. Convince me, Ganfrion of no node. Convince me you'd be useful to me."

SECTION FIVE

Chapter One

There was a new poster on prominent display on the posting wall outside Bharlori's Tavern. Even so, Thyerri very nearly missed it in his rush for the door.

He was late, very late; his fellow employees were not going to be happy with him. But it had been too long—far, far too long—since the goat trails and high meadows had called. When, early that morning—for the first time since the Collapse—the mountain winds had whispered in his ear, he'd chased that ancient enchantress deeper and deeper through the false dawn, into the rocky crevasses, farther and farther from the City and his growing responsibilities there.

He'd thought at first it was Mother calling him. Ever since the night the mountain had come back to life, he'd waited for her summons, but for all the mountain's increased vitality, Mother's voice had never echoed in his dreams.

As he'd chased the wind this morning, he'd called and called and called—to no effect. But his cries had been as much a song of joy as a plea for attention, a song to assure Mother that this child at least had found a home.

Not the home he'd dreamed of years ago when the rijhili first raised the dance rings, but a contentment that Thyerri would never have believed possible only a few short weeks ago.

Because Thyerri no longer merely survived; Thyerri danced now, whenever he felt the urge. And as word of his dance had filtered through the city, Bharlori's business had taken yet another forward surge as rijhili, hungry for entertainment, flocked to this newest diversion.

Sometimes he danced alone, sometimes with Sakhithe. And sometimes he danced with other hiller dancers who, hearing of the coins being flung about, came to display their skills.

But those other dancers rarely returned. Sakhithe insisted it was because they couldn't stand the comparison, that once they saw Thyerri dance, they realized a level they could never achieve, and pride kept them from taking his leavings.

Thyerri didn't know, didn't really care. Thyerri cared that Bharlori, who had given him this job, was happy. Sakhithe was. And if Bharlo's new help were occasionally jealous, and if Sakhi had had to find a loose stone in the kitchen floor under which to hide his purse from those jealous eyes, it was a price worth paying.

Shifting shadows and warming air had warned him of a day more than half gone. His return to the city had been arrow-straight and breakneck, leaving scratches on his arms and legs where he'd chosen to leap into a tree's embrace rather than take the long route down a steep hill.

He darted past the sleepy guard on duty at Khrishim Gate, and dodged between the late afternoon bartering crowd along Farmer's Row South, waved at Zelin, carrying baskets for Cook, and sprinted the final stretch to Bharlori's—

Only to find his passage blocked at the tavern entrance.

A small knot of men had gathered beside the posting board, and none were inclined to notice a dirty hiller wanting past. Thyerri skidded to a halt, made a dart for the alley, only to find his way blocked by a second group.

"So, the cub has emerged from the lair at last," one valley voice said, and another:

"And Rhyys is going to sharpen up the rings to celebrate, eh?"

Rings?

Thyerri strained to see past the massive bodies, all dressed as if it were the dead of winter instead of a fresh spring day.

" 'Bout time we got to see this fancy-dance."

"Says here they're gonna pick a new radical. What happened to the old one?"

"Dead," a grim and goulish voice declared. "On the rings when the web crashed. Sliced 'er right in half. Blood all over the sand."

Which wasn't the truth. Betania, the last radical dancer

of Khoratum, had quit the dance when her sexual interests exceeded her desire to dance. The web had gone down in the middle of the last competition, before a new radical had been declared.

It had been Mavis who died on the rings the day of the collapse. But she had been a competitor—just like Thyerri—not the radical.

"What's Rhyys plan to do? Kill another? We haven't got lights half the time. How can they trust the dance rings?"

"Just adds that much more spice, Prillin," someone said. "Half the appeal up here is the blood count at the end."

"Oh."

Thyerri wanted to say that it wasn't true, that no one went to the competition to see someone hurt, but in truth, he didn't know. He knew that "half the appeal" for the true competitors was laughing in death's face. But that was the thrill and the challenge of the dance itself. He couldn't imagine what the spectators derived from watching.

Himself, he hated to watch. Watching only made him jealous, made his body writhe with the desire to flit among the rings in the dancer's stead.

"When's he due here?" someone asked.

"Three—almost four weeks. We're dead last, lads. Places us, doesn't it?"

Thyerri wondered who was coming and why, caught a glimpse of the schedule as bodies shifted. A list of seventeen nodes. Khoratum was at the bottom. Persitum wasn't listed at all.

Thyerri wondered whether that lack was oversight on the part of the printer, or deliberate exclusion, wondered whether that dire threat voiced in a private upstairs parlor had been carried out, wondered if Persitum was gone from the Rhomatum Web.

Considering the energy that had surged through the mountains that night two weeks ago, it certainly seemed possible that catastrophic changes *had* occurred in the web.

Perhaps Persitum's loss was the reason for this "cub's" upcoming visit—a cub of such importance that Rhyys was willing to risk ringdancers' lives with problematic dance rings in order to impress him.

Thyerri himself would take that risk, if only Rhyys would let him compete.

But the renewed vitality within the mountain would seem to indicate a healthier web, not a diminished one.

Mother would know about the state of the web, of course, but Mother wasn't talking to him. As for the other, this visiting person of importance . . . for the first time since the Collapse, Thyerri longed to be back in Rhyys' court, where speculation would be rife.

The bodies between himself and the poster shifted again and painted eyes stared right at him. Gray eyes, rimmed with green. Eyes painfully familiar to the person Thyerri had once been. Eyes that reached between that past life and this one and gripped Thyerri's soul and refused to release it.

Eyes of the sort that stared back at Thyerri from Sakhi's cracked mirror.

Zelin's Tamshi eyes, for certain. Eyes that could enthrall, that could, according to Zelin, capture a soul to their bidding. But the thin bearded face was that of a valley-man. Middle-aged or older, grim-faced and crafty. Not the face he expected to see, certainly not the expression. A rijhili with Tamshi eyes was coming to Khoratum. Perhaps even to Bharlori's Tavern.

And then he saw the name: Mikhyel Rhomandi dun-mheric. Thyerri shivered, and forced his way past the men crowding up behind him, forced himself away from those eyes, no longer caring why that man was coming here, wanting only to be far away when he arrived.

§ § §

In the distance, a floating sheep wilted and sank.

Elsewhere on the section of the Shatum Leyroad visible through the carriage window, other balloons, some creatures, some simple, brightly colored mushrooms bearing company logos, bobbed in the steady breeze.

Not so long ago, the sight of the cargo-hauler lift balloons had been a constant curiosity; now, five nodes into his trip, Mikhyel found himself in agreement with Deymorin: as eyesores, they were amazingly effective.

He had noted at least three shipping companies that he was considering prosecuting for patent misuse of ley-energy in a time of limited availability. The garish, elaborate constructions had undoubtedly required as much, if not more, hot air to lift themselves than they ever supplied to the relief of the wagon axles.

An avarice you silk-sheep would undoubtedly protest.

He'd seen too much of that on this trip as well. Every time a registered balloon collapsed in transit, the web was liable. There were guarantees. Hauler permits were issued on the assumption of available power. When that power proved insufficient, and a leythium heater failed, someone had to cover the damages.

And right now, that someone's name was increasingly Rhomandi.

"Master Khyel—" Raulind's voice drew him back to the interior of the coach. "Regarding your promise to the Venitumin House of Lords, will you write your brother, or shall I?"

Mikhyel winced. "I'd better write to him, Raul, though I appreciate the offer."

Raulind nodded, placing the note from yesterday's meeting on the stack of notes destined to consume Mikhyel's evening.

Venitum. Not the largest of the nodes they'd stopped at thus far, but the only one to provide him any real concern. Not that Venitum hadn't had reason for their antagonism. Venitum was a small node compared to Giephaetum or Shatum, but within its small umbrella, its dense leythium crystals glowed with unrivaled intensity.

Venitum was a city of metalworkers. The best weapons were made there; artists from all over the web sent their waxes and their plasters to the rather inaccessible mountain node for final casting. Wax and plaster entered the city, the finest jewelry and larger-than-life statues came out. Thanks to the failing web, their production and so their economy, had ground to a near halt in recent weeks.

And for a node that imported all their food and clothing, extended problems with the energy flow could well prove devastating.

When Mikhyel had explained the problem with the Khoratum line, Juminari, the Venitum Ringmaster, had advocated dropping Khoratum altogether, had, in fact, expressed a real desire to return to the pre-Khoratum days when the lightning belt had kept the Kirish'lani raiders at bay. Only a promised visit from the Princeps of Rhomatum to discuss Venitum's *special* security needs had reconciled

the master smiths who ruled in Venitum to the other Rhomandi proposals.

Deymorin, who was, even as Mikhyel had made that
promise, headed for the coastal holdings several days' journey to the west of the Southern Kharatas and Venitum.

Deymorin was going to be so pleased.

"Ganfrion says some of the most seasoned fighters in the
web are the farmers on the east side of the Khoramali,"
Raulind said in Raulind's most imperturbable voice.

"*Ganfrion* says?" Mikhyel echoed. "And since when
have you been talking to Ganfrion?"

Raulind's calm demeanor didn't flicker. But then,
Raulind's calm demeanor never flickered. "Frequently,
m'lord Mikhyel. Ganfrion knows the Khoramali and suggests perhaps those farmers could be assets to the border
patrol in this region."

Mikhyel laid his pen down, and crossed his arms on the
table. "You fascinate me, Raul. And why would the farmers leave their farms?"

"Perhaps you would do better to discuss that with Ganfrion, m'lord. I merely repeat what he said to me, and might
well misrepresent the situation."

"If Ganfrion has useful information, Ganfrion can come
to me," Mikhyel said, and reclaimed his pen.

"Then perhaps you should speak to Captain Ori," Raulind said.

And that was all he'd get out of Raulind. But that was
enough. Ori, captain of his guard, and a man he'd hired on
Deymorin's recommendation, didn't approve of Ganfrion.

"I might just do that, Raul."

"As you will, Master Khyel. Now, about this request for
increasing the Harriisidumin hot baths?"

And so, having made his point, Raulind moved ahead.

Raulind was proving endlessly versatile these days, particularly since the staff Mikhyel had brought along had reluctantly declared themselves unable to work in the moving
carriage. They did their best to make up the deficiency
when they stopped for the night, and had offered to work
around the clock while at the nodes, but Raulind's ability
to work, as did Mikhyel, en route, was making that well-
intended sacrifice unnecessary.

"Acceptance pile," Mikhyel answered. "And urgent. I
know there are disbelievers, Raul, but the Barsitumin baths

have saved my life twice. I have to assume others find them as effective. Because the ley baths don't work for everyone, doesn't mean we have the right to deprive anyone for whom they might work."

"My sister was equally fortunate, though at Harriisidum, of course. I queried only because I feared that personal experience might cloud my judgment in the matter."

Not to mention he'd been a Barsitumin bath attendant before he'd moved to Rhomatum. Even so . . . "At your foggiest, Raul, you're fairer-headed than any Syndic I know."

A back-handed compliment Raul knew full well how to interpret. The valet dipped his head in phlegmatic acknowledgment, and noted the order on the auto-accept cross-file.

After that, there was silence, as it had been mostly silent in the carriage for days. Mikhyel worked on his personal notes, rewriting them for clarity, expanding them before his memory impressions faded; Raul took the letters and requests accumulated at every stop, rewriting those he deemed illegible, and then added them to a summarized listing, filing the original for later referral.

But Venitum was behind him now, as were Harriisidum and Incarodum and Merdum, and even as Mikhyel dealt with the accumulated past, thoughts of upcoming days at Shatum and the thickest of Nikki's reports intruded.

They'd be stopping soon within the hour, if he judged correctly—for all it was still light out, and for all they were running ahead of schedule and might actually have made Shatum before midnight. But he had rooms reserved at the Eagle's Nest, and looked forward to a quiet evening of reflection and review of Nikki's report, a good night's sleep and an easy stage into Shatum tomorrow.

So far, the tours of the Node Cities had been little more than formalities. Save for that momentary dissension at Venitum, all the ringmasters had been quite amenable to his proposals . . . provided Talin Pasingarim, the senior Ringmaster of Shatum, agreed to them. And the various leaders all thought the border watch was a marvelous notion . . .

Provided the Shatumin Twelve agreed.

Without doubt, Shatum would set the tone for the entire trip. But he'd known that all along.

Shatum was the second oldest Node City in the Rhomatum Web. Only Rhomatum herself was older—excepting, of course, Persitum. But, historically speaking, Persitum was part of the Mauritum Web, and since Persitum had dropped so precipitously from the Rhomatum Web, Shatum could now claim her second-born status without qualification.

Shatum was also second largest, and that was true even including Persitum. Not second in power-umbrella radius—in that sense, Giephaetum was slightly larger—but in population. And in *that* sense, Shatum would soon outstrip Rhomatum herself, whose citizens voluntarily limited their population growth.

Most importantly, Shatum, as the primary interchange on the sole sanctioned trade route between the Rhomatum Syndicate and the Kirish'lan Empire, was the undisputed leader of the Southern Crescent of Nodes, a fact Anheliaa had considered carefully in choosing Lidye dunTarim as her successor in Rhomatum Tower.

And thanks in no small part to that decision, Shatum, fifth of the seventeen scheduled stops for the Rhomatumin entourage, would be the first major test of Mikhyel dunmheric's persuasive abilities.

Not that he had any particular reason for concern, only the natural caution one maintained when heading into negotiations with master merchants. The Alliance of Twelve Guilds would agree to Rhomatum's proposals because the proposals made good common sense, but they would drive a hard bargain. Of that, Mikhyel was certain.

Mikhyel had decided it was a very good thing Anheliaa had had the grace to depart this world before he'd had to embark on this tour. The ringmasters were much relieved to have the steady leeching from Rhomatum at an end, and his ability to reassure them that the worst was over and that a healthy Shatumin woman was in charge in Rhomatum seemed to set all minds at ease.

At least, all these Southern Crescent minds. He had to wonder if the Northern Crescent would respond quite so favorably.

A twinge in his left hand advised him to set the pen aside before the twinge became a cramp. Kneading the tired muscles of one hand with the only slightly less tired muscles of the other, he leaned his head back against the cushions and closed his eyes against the light.

He worried at times that the lightning blasted trip to

Boreton had caused permanent damage to his eyes. He wasn't conscious of diminished capacity, just oversensitivity, and he wondered if the dark-tinted protective glasses some of the Venitumin factory workers had worn would help.

Of course, he'd look rather silly, walking down a market-place with his eyes hidden behind two blackened circles of glass.

A rustle of papers from the table's far side; Mikhyel cracked his eyelids, found Raulind watching him, a look of advised concern on his face. Mikhyel twitched an eyebrow; Raulind nodded, and returned to his cataloging.

Mikhyel smiled and let his head drift to the side, swaying with the easy movement of the coach.

Considering how much he'd dreaded leaving Rhomatum, he was finding the trip very much to his liking. He had a defined schedule, a defined goal at each stop, and a defined procedure between times.

He also enjoyed the absence of his brothers. Both of them. Distance had cleared them at last from his mind. At each node, couriered letters had reassured him regarding the situation in Rhomatum, as well as the developing situation on the coast.

Deymorin should be well on his way to Mandriisin's estate on the coast, which was to be his base of operations for the next month; Nikki was pursuing the dam; the rings were stable. . . .

Overall, he had little to concern him. For once.

The link between himself and his brothers that had so completely ruled his life for a time seemed remote now, almost a thing of dreams. If he tried, he could conjure the memory, recall the sensations.

There was a different cramp in his left hand, and his fingertips burned from the bite of guitar strings. Not his fingers: Nikki's. Nikki the poet, Nikki the singer, whose calluses had vanished from disuse.

And Deymorin, the sway and lurch, the stretch of leg around solid muscle and bone, the creak of leather . . . Deymorin on horseback. Such were his associations of his brothers.

Associations, or had they returned to his head? He began a more concentrated search for them, sensed Nikki's frustration, heard the sudden discord of a loose string. And Deymorin—

An explosion of power beneath him, a surge that had nothing to do with the carriage. Mikhyel jumped; the table tipped; and Raulind grabbed the stacks, saving a day's work.

Mikhyel pulled the cord that would signal the driver to stop the coach. A moment later, pounding hoofbeats pulled up beside them in a clattering spray of gravel.

Thud of feet, a cheerful greeting, and a moment later, Deymorin's face filled the window and Deymorin's cheerful greeting filled the coach.

Chapter Two

The city spreading out from this Tower-Hill observation deck shimmered with almost painful intensity beneath the Agoran Plains sun. Pale stone and concrete, whitewashed stucco—every square foot within the power umbrella had been developed, and every square inch reflected that relentless sunlight.

Along the western horizon, Lake Yakhimarrha shimmered with deceptive purity.

Shatum was a city bursting with prosperity.

Shatum's founders had been grain farmers, who had been drawn to the fertile Agoran Plains, and shipbuilders, attracted to the protected harbors of Lake Yakhimarrha. For such as they, large families had been an asset.

In subsequent years, a flourishing textile industry and the fact that Shatum lay on the one reliably storm-safe overland trade route had assured the southern node's affluence, as well as the current strain on her resources.

Shatumins seemed fond of their crowded streets, and didn't seem to notice when the odd eastern breeze wafted the stench of the sewers through the crowded markets, sewers that did little more than hold the city's waste, waiting for the overtaxed leythium growth chambers to accept it.

City engineers added constantly to those growth chambers, excavating beneath the city to create pockets where the crystals could grow. Enterprising citizens leased space in those chambers, growing and tending the crystals to their own specifications, controlling the growth of the crystal to form everything from engine cores to exquisitely fine lace.

And still, the waste produced by the ever-growing population outstripped their ability to dispose of it.

Much to the disgust of the privately-owned resorts scattered along the shores of Lake Yakhimarrha, a handful of districts simply washed their sewage out into the popular vacation spot. The water quality of the lake was (according to Nikki's notes) the focus of much bitter debate within the halls of Shatum's bureaucratic chambers these days.

All for want of a little self-control in their bedchambers.

Mikhyel shook his head in disbelief and deserted the train station's observation window to claim a newly-vacated front row seat in this elevated waiting room. The chair's previous occupant had joined a half-dozen others waiting at the door at the back of the room, anticipating the arrival of their train, trusting, as these Shatumin seemed inclined to trust, the schedule posted on the chalk board beside that door.

And indeed, only moments later, the chime that announced the vehicle's arrival rang from the dock below, and the passengers gathered at the back of the room pushed their way out the door and clattered down the steps.

But the train that was about to pull in wasn't the train he awaited—the inner sense assured him of that—so he remained where he was, affecting an indifference he in no wise felt.

Within the hour, Mikhyel was scheduled to face the Guild Alliance of Shatum, the most influential force in the Southern Crescent, an already difficult, delicate task made infinitely more difficult by Deymorin's unexpected addition to his entourage three days ago.

"Courtesy stop," Deymorin called his unannounced change in plans. An eight-day detour from his planned route to say *Hello* to his brother's wife's family.

Gross interference, Mikhyel called it.

Mikhyel pushed himself to his feet, and returned to the window, compelled to check, even though that inner sense told him Deymorin was not—as he'd promised he would be when he'd left an hour ago—on the train that was pulling in.

Deymorin, whose mere presence here in Shatum dictated he be included in the upcoming meeting, was late. Deymorin, who could have bowed out gracefully simply by *leaving* yesterday, or even this morning, was going to single-handedly destroy this vital first impression on the Elders of the Twelve Guilds.

Leaning his forehead against the cool glass, Mikhyel closed his eyes against that painful light, and called silently, imperatively. The images he received back, vague impressions of control panels and steam-engine schematics, were only marginally reassuring. But Deymorin was on his way. Deymorin *was* aboard one of these machines, somewhere out among the chaos of Shatumin streets, and Deymorin *would* be here in time, or so he silently claimed.

But then, Deymorin trusted these steam-driven vehicles and their exacting schedules.

The previously announced train pulled in to the dock below, venting steam rising in puffs above the engine, and the people milling below surged forward, some to board its open-sided cars, and others to greet the passengers disembarking.

They'd arrived in Shatum late in the evening, two nights ago. Since then, their every movement, every schedule had been dictated by these mechanisms. Official tour of the Shatum Tower, dinner with the newly-elected Princeps, Rekharin dunPwirriin, or the celebrated Shatumin Opera, those events had, beginning and end, coincided with the arrival of one of these strange vehicles at the nearest dock.

Everyone seemed dependent upon the schedules, and for all the streets were crowded, few individuals seemed to walk farther than the nearest station. A cultural adaptation that, to his eyes, had been less than beneficial to the populations' health.

Rhomatumins walked. Some took the pedal-cabs, particularly following a shopping expedition, but for simply getting about, they trusted their own feet. Rhomatum was, by and large, a sleek and slender city.

Here in Shatum, the prosperity that threatened its waste disposal equally threatened its fabricated seams.

A grimly diverting thought wondered how long and how hard Lidye, coming out of this environment, must have labored to make herself attractive to Rhomatumin eyes, and what would happen to her slender form, now the contract with the Rhomandi was complete. He hoped, for Nikki's sake, that the transformation would prove permanent.

Exactly on schedule, the bell rang three times, and with a puff of steam, the train pulled free of the dock and vanished down a side tunnel.

They reminded Mikhyel of snakes slipping surreptitiously from one hiding spot to the next.

From this second-story, upper Tower-Hill vantage, he could detect no evidence of Shatum's twelve leylines. Unlike Rhomatum, where those lines were kept clear for the floater-cabs' brightly colored balloons, here, they'd been built over, spanned with businesses and homes. The trains needed no such air space above them, and frequently slipped under and within buildings.

According to Nikki's notes, thirteen of the eighteen satellites now operated similar systems.

But not Rhomatum. He'd read the proposals to introduce the new technology into the capital city. He'd been mildly intrigued, probably he would have supported the promoters had they come to him, but he'd had other, more immediate concerns, and the floaters and transport lobbies had proved overwhelming. The Rhomatum City Council had refused to accept the proposal for debate, and so his opinion had gone unheard.

According to those reports, one such steam-powered engine could transport five times the cargo—human or otherwise—of one of the floater-cabs, twice as much as the balloon-assisted cargo-haulers that operated on the lines between nodes. But the Syndicate of Nodes was based in Rhomatum, and subject to those same, organized pressures, and thus far none of the proposed internode rail systems had found support either.

He was sorry now that he hadn't pursued his initial interest. Despite his personal aesthetic reaction to the trains, despite his reservations about their effect on the people who relied too heavily on them, their efficiency was undeniable, and with the current reduction in available ley energy, efficiency might be precisely the incentive for the Syndicate at least to give the steam engines a trial.

He made a mental note to have Paulis look into it while they were here, to track down the current usage patterns and the efficiency ratings, and comparatives to the pre-collapse numbers.

Always supposing, of course, that Deymorin didn't take over this trip entirely.

His left hand tightened into a fist around the folio's shoulder strap. A ring glittered in the bright sun. A Rhomandi ring. A copy of that one lost at Boreton; duplicate of one Deymorin wore and a third on Nikki's left hand.

Deymorin had presented his brothers with those rings the morning Mikhyel had left Rhomatum. A gesture of solidarity and equality, or so Deymorin had claimed that morning in front of the collected household.

He relaxed his fist, twisted the ring around his finger with his thumb, wondering why he felt less an equal and more a sworn man—Mikhyel *gor*Deymorin. There could be worse fates, but he preferred honesty in oathtaking.

He believed in freedom of choice.

Deymorin's generous gesture, coming without warning and in front of witnesses had left him without that option. Thanks to that underneath sense, he *knew* that such a subjugating oath had not been in Deymorin's surface thoughts as he placed the ring on Mikhyel's hand, but the underneath sense did not necessarily penetrate to Deymorin's deepest thoughts, and the granting of a family ring *was* the oldest expression of that singular relationship between two men.

Deymorin knew the history of the gesture as well as Mikhyel. Better, he'd wager.

Suspicions—of a sort he'd hoped never to harbor again about his brother. Mikhyel sighed, raised the ring momentarily to press against his lips, and wondered, given the choice, how he would have responded.

He let the hand drop.

A puff of steam rising from beyond the Muradashi Building heralded the arrival of another train, one that inner sense declared to be Deymorin's. Releasing his unconsciously held breath, Mikhyel shifted the briefcase shoulder strap to a different bruise and dropped down onto the chair, his knees simply giving out with his relief.

"What if he's not on this one either?" a guttural voice asked from the row behind him.

"He is," Mikhyel answered, without turning back.

A snap of paper underscored Ganfrion's disbelieving grunt.

Mikhyel debated explaining the unconventional link between himself and Deymorin to his unconventional bodyguard. The question had been moot until Deymorin had showed up, but he found he had an unreasoning desire for Ganfrion's good opinion.

Or perhaps it was simply a desire to ruffle the inmate's arrogant conceit.

Not that personal opinion should make any difference. As long as Ganfrion accepted his paycheck, Mikhyel dunMheric was the most sagacious individual in the universe. The realization that one day Ganfrion might *not* show up for the paycheck caused Mikhyel to keep his peace about certain strengths—and weaknesses—in the Rhomandi arsenal.

Another puff of steam and the cheerful, light bell announced the imminent arrival. The bulk of those waiting gathered their belongings and headed for that back door.

When they'd arrived late last night, the train had carried them from the stables outside the perimeter wall to the Hilltop Inn where they had spent the night in regal splendor, a last-minute change of venue he suspected he owed to Deymorin's presence.

Not that he'd spent much time in the large and comfortable bed, having been far too busy preparing for this upcoming meeting.

But looking out across those tightly packed roofs, splendor was not the norm, here in Shatum. Like Rhomatum, Shatum had had a power-umbrella increase when Khoratum had been added to the web, new territory into which their Families' younger generations had expanded eagerly, expansion that now had their populace scrambling, so Nikki's report said, to accommodate their energy-dispossessed homeowners, and their next generation.

He was certain, if that was indeed the case, that he'd hear all about it in the coming hours.

"Stay where you are," Mikhyel murmured to the rustling paper in the next row back, and joined those gathering at the window.

Impatient passengers poured from the open-sided cars as the train coasted to a halt, but Deymorin was not among them. Mikhyel refused to be anxious. Four of Deymorin's men, inconspicuously dressed and seemingly at ease, had been the first to step free of the forwardmost car; the sense told him Deymorin was near and well; beyond that, he kept his mind resolutely isolate.

Eventually, after the reverse wave of boarding passengers had cleared the dock, when Mikhyel was the last individual left standing at the window, Deymorin did appear, swinging free of the engine, a wide grin on his face.

Mikhyel relaxed, knowing now not only where his brother had been, but why his mind had been so unobtrusive: Deymorin and Nikki shared a fascination with machines not even that inner link could inspire in Mikhyel.

As his grinning guardsmen fell in on either side, Deymorin waved a farewell salute to the engineer, skip-walking backward like an adolescent. The small engine answered with a burst of steam and a cheerful whistle as it pulled out.

Deymorin skipped about and took the lower stairs two at a time, throwing his head back to catch Mikhyel's eyes and broadcasting a cheerful mental announcement. But the sense turned dark and ill-tasting, Deymorin's hand fell, and his grin vanished into a black scowl, before he disappeared into the shadows below.

"All hail Prince Deymio, savior of Rhomatum, leader of the combined forces of the Rhomatum Syndicate. Who stopped Mauritum with sweets and toys." It was the guttural voice again, this time at his shoulder.

"I told you to stay back," Mikhyel said, knowing Ganfrion for the source of Deymorin's black humor.

Ganfrion shrugged. "I finished the paper." He folded the sheets with an economical flip, and tossed the paper to Mikhyel's abandoned chair. The room was empty now, save for themselves and a person of indeterminate age snoring quietly on a corner couch.

"You may go now."

Ganfrion slouched about, leaning against the window, arms crossed. "I better wait until the farm-boy gets here."

Despite his better sense, Mikhyel bristled. "Deymorin's no farm-boy."

"No?" Ganfrion's narrow, dark eyes rounded on him. "He followed me last night, Suds. Subtle as a bull moose in a glass house. Call him what you will, soldiers won't follow him."

"Deymorin's men would follow him to hell and back."

"Farmers." Ganfrion's scarred upper lip lifted. "I'm talking soldiers, Suds. Mercenaries. Swords, guns, and death for hire."

"Men like you."

"Men like me."

Deymorin appeared at the door, scowling.

"You are dismissed," Mikhyel repeated firmly. He steadied the shoulder strap and headed for the door, determined, should Ganfrion press him further, to turn him over to Deymorin's charge, to let him see what kind of leader Deymorin was or was not.

That way, he'd be free of them both.

He'd hired Ganfrion in part because the inmate re-

minded him of Deymorin; it was, he thought in retrospect
as he brushed past Deymorin and headed down the hall, a
very stupid reason.

§   §   §

For once, Deymorin thought sourly, Ganfrion displayed
a modicum of sense. The jail-rot remained at the window—
where he'd been standing too damned close to Mikhyel—
and nodded almost civilly to Deymorin, who dipped his
own head a calculated degree, and followed Mikhyel.

His men were waiting in the hall, their eyes flitting between himself and Mikhyel, who was already halfway
toward the staircase that led to the station's main entrance.
Deymorin hurried after Mikhyel, all too aware of the angry
silence closing his brother's mind off from him.

He'd read Ganfrion's file (compiled through his own
sources), and, he would admit, with his node-wandering history, and underworld contacts, Ganfrion could have been
a useful adjunct.

To another man's entourage.

Pacing Mikhyel as they passed from one building to the
next, he caught the flicker of eye, the half-twist of Mikhyel's
dark head that indicated he was under covert inspection.
Laughing, he held out his hands, first palm up, then down.

"Greaseless, I assure you, brother. Would you like to
check behind my ears?"

Which neither gained him the laughter he hoped for nor
eased that inward tension. Mikhyel's jaw set, his face
turned firmly to the front and grim.

"Trust me, Mikhyel."

"The way you trust me?"

"Of course I trust you."

"So much so, you insisted on attending this meeting."

"I didn't insist, they obviously expected it. I thought it
would be rude not to."

"You weren't supposed to be here at all."

"I *thought* you'd appreciate the support."

Mikhyel said nothing, and Mikhyel kept that mental distance that had a vague tendency to chill Deymorin's heart
with an ice that could spread clear to his fingertips if he
allowed it go unchallenged.

"Ganfrion's not coming?" Deymorin asked, fighting that chill, seeking the root of this argument.

"No."

"I read his file."

"I know."

And Mikhyel didn't care what Deymorin thought. Not now. That came through clearly, just in his silence.

"You should have Ori with you. And a couple of his men."

"I *had* Ganfrion."

"And *you* told *me* that Ganfrion was *not* one of your guard. You were quite specific on that point."

Mikhyel flung him a look that swept past him to his men. "How large a guard do you think I can flaunt before the locals take offense? This *is* Shatum, brother. Not Mauritum. Just in case you've forgotten."

Deymorin set his jaw on the retort that rose. The issue wasn't that simple, but Mikhyel knew that. Mikhyel knew there were those throughout the web who would happily see the end of the Rhomandi era in Rhomatum. Wasn't that why he'd hired Ganfrion in the first place? To ferret out that information and discover its roots? He should let his spies do their job and in the meantime, keep a sensible protective layer between himself and people he damnwell didn't know.

"Is that why you were in the engine? Alone?" Mikhyel asked, out of his thoughts.

"I had my men with me." He nodded to Belnh and Ghestrovii walking to their front.

"As did I. Until you arrived with yours."

"And if we get separated? They'll come with *me,* Khyel, regardless of what I tell them."

"And were they with you last night when you were trailing Ganfrion?"

His teeth grated, one on the other. Mikhyel knew damn well he didn't trust Ganfrion. The fact that he'd followed the inmate into some of the darker shadows of Shatum was *his* business. Besides:

"I can—" *Take care of myself,* he caught the words before voicing them, but it didn't take the link for Mikhyel to complete the sentiment.

"I see. Different rules for the Rhomandi than for his brother."

"I *had* my men."

"And who in addition to Ganfrion spotted you? Perhaps you should reexamine your own wisdom, Rhomandi."

Deymorin pressed his lips tight. Mikhyel was angry. Mikhyel was making deliberately provocative statements. More than likely Mikhyel was nervous about this meeting.

Unnecessarily, Deymorin was certain. These past nights, long after Deymorin had flung himself exhausted into bed, he would wake to images in his head of candlelight and notes and maps spread about a table, and Mikhyel's long-fingered hands, the newly cast Rhomandi ring glittering in the flickering light as the hand bearing it turned a page.

No, his concerns now had nothing to do with Mikhyel's persuasive abilities in the civilized arenas his eloquent and elegant brother was accustomed to treading. It was this notion Mikhyel had taken of probing more deeply into the underground factions within the nodes. He feared that Mikhyel's strange new obsession would lead him into situations far beyond Mikhyel's ability to survive.

Mikhyel called him a hypocrite, and cut him off cold when he tried to discuss it. But there was a helplessness to Mikhyel that frightened him. A vulnerability that went beyond his physical frailty. Deymorin was haunted by images of Mikhyel lying crumpled on the ground at Boreton, beside his bed, limp in the arms of that animated corpse, in the garden with Nikki flailing at him. . . .

And that vision in Mikhyel's head of Mheric Rhomandi's crop-wielding hand bearing down on him. Mikhyel denied the link, rejected the possibility that Mheric's actions had so deeply affected him, but Deymorin recalled the prison, Mikhyel's passivity with Ganfrion and five other—

"Damn you!" Mikhyel hissed at him, and Mikhyel increased his pace, pulling ahead of Deymorin's limping stride, and Deymorin made no attempt to catch him up. His leg throbbed like a rotted tooth; he'd twisted his back trying to see the underside of the engine's control panel, and without Kiyrstin available to work her ten-fingered magic, he saw no reason to aggravate it for a brother determined to ignore him.

{Deymorin Rhomandi dunMheric, if you can't get your mind on the meeting, get the *hell* out of Shatum!}

By the time his head stopped ringing and his vision cleared, they had arrived at the conference chamber.

Chapter Three

Introductions were a droning formality, a matter of Princeps Rekharin dunPwirriin apologizing for the sudden change in schedule, and explaining how the Rhomandi would enlighten them all as to the reason for that change.

Nine men and three women, chosen advocates of the twelve Shatumin guilds. Primary among those guilds was, of course, the Leythium Guild that included all handlers of the ley, from the growth-chamber attendants to Talin Pasingarim, the senior Shatumin Ringmaster, who was, naturally, their advocate at this meeting. Lawyers and accountants—in this city that was the major trade conduit for the Kirish'lan Empire, those guilds were second only to the Leythium Guild.

Except, possibly, for old Kharl Varishmondi, standing next to the window, staring out at his beloved Lake Yakhimarrha. The patriarch of the Varishmondi shipbuilders, who formed a guild unto themselves, the old man's opinion undoubtedly carried more weight than any five others, should he care to make that opinion known.

Kharl had been a frequent visitor to Darhaven when Mheric was alive. Since Mheric's death, Deymorin hadn't seen him.

Beyond that, if he wanted to know the names, Deymorin had the list, Mikhyel had seen to that, but he was here to observe only, moral support for his brother, and once the introductions were complete, he was more than willing to nod pleasantly, and sit down, tacitly declaring Mikhyel in charge.

Mikhyel remained standing, neither by word nor glance acknowledging his gesture.

Resentment flared, until he noticed the silent looks being passed about the table, and realized Mikhyel could not afford to register gratitude, could not even *think* gratitude.

Mikhyel would concede to no one in this room—including Mikhyel himself—that so important a moment was being abdicated to the lesser Rhomandi.

Mikhyel opened with a general statement of appreciation for them gathering on such short notice and with so little explanation, and an apology for any inconvenience their changed schedules might have caused them.

In a delivery that never hinted of rehearsal, Mikhyel shifted smoothly into a personal greeting to each guild advocate, including in that greeting some recognition of the guild's work in general and the advocate's personal accomplishments in particular. Deymorin resisted the temptation to stare, knowing that three days ago, Mikhyel hadn't known a yardarm from a beater bar.

If ever Deymorin had doubted the wisdom of sending Mikhyel on this tour, it vanished then. Even had Deymorin tried to make similar use of Nikki's notes, he'd never have matched Mikhyel's near-intimate delivery.

Neither could he match Mikhyel's sense of timing. While the first mentioned still preened, those yet to hear their own tributes were leaning slightly forward, and all of them surreptitiously eyed their fellows, evaluating the relative prestige of their acts, making sure their fellows were equally cognizant of their efforts as this perceptive foreigner.

He could appreciate that talent now, in a way he couldn't when they'd matched verbal blades before the Syndicate in Rhomatum.

Even old Varishmondi turned slowly from his window, as Mikhyel's litany reached him at last. His gray head tilted as he made a shaggy-browed assessment of Mikhyel, then slowly, deliberately, the big man's backbone relaxed, his arms crossed and he leaned his broad shoulders back into the window frame, one leg rising to prop in casual ease on the sill.

Mikhyel tipped his head in acknowledgment, then, with another smooth feint, shifted his attack.

"I also apologize for the lack of information you have been given. That was, I freely admit, at my request, so blame me, not your honorable princeps. I thought impatience might be better than speculation based on insufficient information. I wanted to be available to answer those speculations as they arose."

"Is Anheliaa dead?" Abrupt, rude, without preamble, the question came from one of the advocates. Which, Deymorin wasn't sure.

But Mikhyel—staring straight at a man half-again his size—obviously did know.

Mikhyel, in fact, answered as abruptly, "Yes."

A forthrightness that obviously rocked the large man, who blinked and sat back in his chair.

"If I may, dunMheric?" a more reasonable voice interjected, and Mikhyel nodded. "When did she die?"

"The eighteenth day of the third month."

A moment's silence, then a third voice commented, "The day the storms subsided." The ringmaster, Deymorin thought, Pasingarim. "The day the power returned."

And another: "The day Persitum dropped from the web."

Mikhyel stood quietly as those observations took root. Then, he said, "I will be happy, honorable advocates, to answer your questions, but if you will allow me a few moments to lay the groundwork . . ."

"One question only." Pasingarim again. "Who has been master in Rhomatum Tower since Anheliaa's death?"

"Lidye Fericci romNikaenor."

The individuals about the table searched that name for significance. Personal name, family, and wife of Nikaenor. Acknowledgment of self, of her Shatumin family, but allied, irrevocably, to the House Rhomandi.

At last the ringmaster said, in a tone that augured no argument, "Proceed, Mikhyel dunMheric. We shall hold our piece."

And for the next two hours, Mikhyel held them riveted— hell, he had Deymorin riveted, and he'd been there. He explained the historical rift between the brothers, the efforts of Anheliaa to promote that rift in order to control the web to her own purposes. And he described the growing unrest in the Outside territories of Rhomatum as Anheliaa's purposes ran counter to their needs.

That admission drew the attention of the two Shatumin Outsiders on this panel: Food Production and Weavers. Between their own operations and imports from Kirish'lan, Shatum provided the bulk of the grain, cotton, and linen for the entire web. Those guilds had to maintain a constant balance between local production and import goods, and

could well sympathize with their counterparts in the Rhomatum Valley.

Mikhyel moved on to the events of the previous fall, and
Anheliaa's attempts (well known to these leaders of Lidye's
home city) to find a new master for the Rhomatum Rings.

"As you also know," Mikhyel said, "Anheliaa hoped to
revitalize web relations through our marriages, hence Nikaenor's marriage to your own esteemed Lidye dunTarim,
and my own, still pending, union with Nethaalye dunErrif
of Giephaetum Node."

"And what of your other brother," Peri Fericci dunBren-
nin, Lawyers advocate, and Lidye's second cousin called
out. "What of the man who sits silently beside you, the
Princeps of Rhomatum who refused the lady Lidye's hand?
To whom was he pledged? He, who was too fine for a
Shatumin woman?"

Deymorin frowned, and sent a silent query to Mikhyel,
who answered with similar confusion:

"Mistress Lidye was my brother Nikaenor's choice, Advocate dunBrennin."

"Not by our first agreement! Anheliaa promised us the
Princeps of Rhomatum for Lidye."

{Anheliaa's secret agreements,} Mikhyel's voice whispered in Deymorin's mind. Aloud, Mikhyel said, "The contract read otherwise, Lord Advocate. Neither I nor my
brother was privy to whatever private verbal agreements
you made with my aunt. The signed contract was between
Nikaenor Rhomandi dunMheric and the Shatumin Twelve.
The practical contract is between Nikaenor and Lidye, and
both those parties are, I assure you, quite satisfied."

"That does not explain why Deymorin Rhomandi refused Lidye!"

"If I may, Mikhyel?" Deymorin spoke for the first time,
and Mikhyel nodded, but qualified with a silent warning
against temper. "What Mikhyel has failed to tell you, is
that Anheliaa's methods of petition began not with logic
or reason, but with force. Who among you would agree to
marriage—or any other life-contract—under violent coer-
cion? It was not the lady Lidye's hand I rejected, it was
Anheliaa's proposal."

A statement of half-fact that was close enough to the
truth for this meeting.

"Are we to infer, then, that your youngest brother was weak in his acceptance of Lidye?" dunBrennin asked. "And that this weak man is left in power in Rhomatum while you two wander about making pretty speeches?"

"Infer, rather," Mikhyel slid in smoothly, "that Anheliaa's methods improved after they failed so utterly with Deymorin. More than that, Anheliaa actively sought, it is my firm belief in retrospect, to drive Deymorin out. Anheliaa feared that, should we three brothers reconcile, her reign was at an end."

He paused, and all those seated at the table leaned forward.

Mikhyel's mouth twitched. "Gentlemen, we have reconciled."

"And Anheliaa's reign is at an end."

"Even before she died. Yes."

"Even though you could, none of you, control the rings."

"There comes a time when tyrants must be stopped. Anheliaa was mad, honorable advocates, there is no other explanation for her actions. I bear the responsibility for keeping that madness from the Syndicate for as long as I did. But I saw no choice. She failed to settle on another to succeed her, and to have her true nature generally known might well have instilled panic and anarchy throughout the Syndicate."

"You sought to protect us from reality," Varishmondi's deep voice filled the room. "As your father did before you. You, who were all of . . . what, thirteen? . . . when he died, knew better then the Syndicates what was best for the web. Is that what we are to believe?"

There was turmoil underneath as Mikhyel struggled with his own past uncertainties regarding his fitness for the task he'd accepted in his youth. But the face Mikhyel turned toward Varishmondi was cold, hard, and absolute.

"At thirteen, no," Mikhyel answered firmly. "By the time I reached seventeen, yes. Absolutely. I knew the danger of crossing Anheliaa Rhomandi better than any one living. There *was* no other way to both end her tyranny *and* protect the web until she accepted the lady Lidye as her successor."

Varishmondi's mouth tightened, but whether in humor or anger, Deymorin would not wager a lump of coal.

420 *Jane S. Fancher*

Turning his attention to include all the advocates, Mikhyel continued, "Your fellow Shatumin's ability to control the Rhomatum Rings *and* to insinuate herself into Anheliaa's good graces gave me options I had not had in ten years."

That pleased them. And Varishmondi, never taking his eyes from Mikhyel, settled into his designated seat at last.

"About your brother's exile into Persitum . . ." the ringmaster interjected, referencing an event Mikhyel had mentioned but not yet explained in detail.

Deymorin believed that oversight had been made by design and opened his mouth to protest, only to find his voice frozen in his throat.

"Yes, Ringmaster Pasingarim?" Mikhyel answered.

"Is it true? Has Anheliaa, in fact, perfected the legendary art of instant leyportation?"

"I wouldn't call it perfected," Mikhyel said smoothly, and that paralysis in Deymorin's throat eased, leaving him little doubt as to its origin.

"But she can do it."

"Could."

"And did. To you—both."

Mikhyel faltered. Mikhyel had kept reference to himself minimal, maintaining, Deymorin was certain, a buffering distance between himself and the events he was describing.

"What was it like?" the ringmaster asked, possibly out of genuine curiosity, possibly smelling blood.

What was it like. . . . No one had ever asked him that.

It was falling—endlessly. And it was sudden pain. And fear. And it was Kiyrstin, which rendered all the other associations harmless.

But the thoughts that breached the barrier between himself and Mikhyel were very different. There was no Kiyrstin to temper the ordeal. Falling as well, but fierce light, burning, a sense of being pulled apart, stretched from one horizon to the other.

And horror. Horror that made his brother's naturally pale face turn a sickly shade of white. And Deymorin feared for him, feared for the control he'd held over his audience, who watched him now with hawklike intensity.

Deymorin, throwing surreptition to the wind of necessity, gripped Mikhyel's elbow, and through that hold, sensed

Mikhyel's mortification, his struggle for control, his anger at his own weakness, and the knowledge he'd been outmaneuvered; and Deymorin sent back bolstering reassurance, and an image of the ringmaster rude enough to bring the color back to Mikhyel's face, and a near-hysterical silent laughter.

"Unpleasant, Ringmaster Pasingarim," Mikhyel answered firmly. "Most unpleasant. Not an experience I'd recommend. If we are fortunate, the secret died with her."

And not a sentiment, from his expression, which the honorable Ringmaster of Shatum shared, for all he let the matter drop.

But Deymorin continued to worry, his confidence in Mikhyel shaken. And, indeed, Mikhyel's eloquence did not return in full, and his hold over his audience appeared markedly diminished. While they listened, it was not with the enraptured attention they'd shown before.

"We've heard rumors," the princeps said, "that link the honorable Princeps of Rhomatum with an invading force out of Mauritum."

"Hardly an invasion, sir," Mikhyel said. "And his association was accidental, a result of his precipitous expulsion from Rhomatum."

Mikhyel went on to explain how Deymorin's exile had placed him in the hands of a Mauritumin scouting party that had brought with it a machine capable of destroying Rhomatum Tower. Wood creaked as weight shifted in the elaborately carved chairs, and disbelief permeated the room.

But Mikhyel looked pointedly at the ringmaster and said, "The machine controlled lightning. I remind you of the Aslimarin incident."

All eyes followed Mikhyel's, and the ringmaster, his own veracity now challenged, nodded. "Such a machine is known. Aslimarin was a small subsidiary of Orenum. Thirty years ago, one of these . . . lightning generators . . . was presented to that tiny bud's ringspinner. The demonstration destroyed the bud, and nearly everyone involved in the demonstration. Such a machine set into action within a ringchamber the size of Rhomatum could indeed cause a chain reaction that might destroy the Tower, if not the entire web. But," the ringmaster qualified, casting Mikhyel a chal-

lenging glance, "it would have to be employed within the
chamber itself."

Mikhyel tipped his head. "They planned to gain access
to Rhomatum Tower through Deymorin."

"Willing participation?"

It was not Mikhyel's most diplomatic explanation: anger
didn't begin to cover the emotion that flared in the room,
this time aimed directly at himself.

"Not willing, no," Mikhyel said, facing that anger without
flinching. "Deymorin thought, and still maintains, that the
technology has theoretical validity—for the Outside. With
proper controls. That, however, is for the future. The point
at issue is that it was a deliberately aggressive move on
Mauritum's part—"

"But if, as you suggested, that aggression was in response
to Anheliaa's failing health and the potential vacuum in
Rhomatum Tower, the fact that the lady Lidye is obviously
in control there should eliminate both their temptation and
our need to arm a defense."

"Rhomatum is under control now. How would you judge
the quality and health of the web, Ringmaster Pasingarim?"

The ringmaster slouched in his chair, frowning, but he
didn't contradict Mikhyel's analysis.

"The damage has been done, honorable advocates. In
the end, it was not necessary to access the Tower. In the
end, Anheliaa sacrificed her own life in order to bridge the
gap to the machine and destroy it, before it could destroy
her rings. But even so, the web was degraded. The web
needs time to renew itself. How long that will take is beyond our reckoning. In the meantime, Mauritum knows our
weakened state and may well try again. We must look to
the old sources to protect the border."

And what, Deymorin started to ask, had happened to
Mikhyel's prime concern, the united efforts of the ring-
chambers to renew the Khoratum line? But the question
froze in his throat and:

{Separate issue, Deymorin. With the ringmaster alone.
Don't give them an excuse to wait on the border patrol act.}

"And those in the Mauritumin party?" The ringmaster
persisted. "What happened to them?"

"Most were killed in the firestorm that destroyed the
machine," Mikhyel answered.

"And the others?"

"Innocents who, by sheer luck, happened to be separated from the others."

"Innocents. Like Garetti's wife?" said one voice.

"Garetti's whore, more like," came from another.

The freeze began again in Deymorin's throat, only to melt in the flare of Deymorin's anger. {Damn you, Khyel!}

Mikhyel turned green and swayed; Deymorin clenched his jaw and sent an additional silent, though gentler, warning to his brother, that he'd better clear this one up—immediately.

"I see rumor has, indeed, preceded us," Mikhyel said, finally, but his voice was hoarse and ragged. "However, rumor only speculates. Without the lady romGaretti's assistance and cooperation, we'd none of us be here. She has continued to share with us the extent of her knowledge regarding contemporary Mauritum and Mauritumin politics. Unfortunately, her knowledge did not extend to the planned invasion of the Rhomatum Web. She was as taken by surprise as we were."

"So she claims—"

"Truth," Deymorin stated flatly, coldly, and all eyes were once again on him. This time, he was content to note, with a touch of fear.

And on that conversation-ending note, Mikhyel opened his briefcase, heretofore lying unregarded on the table before him. He took out bound volumes, and moving about the table, placed one before each advocate, squared precisely with the table's edge.

Deymorin didn't get one.

{Copies were made, brother. One for each member of each meeting we'll be conducting. Yours are in your luggage.}

At Mandriisin's. Deymorin thought as loud and outraged a silence as he could imagine.

Mikhyel, unmoved, said to the advocates, "This contains all I've told you and more. I have included unedited depositions from all members of the Syndicate special investigation committee. As you will discover, through the lady romGaretti's efforts, and those of my brothers, the Mauritum threat was, at least for the time being, blocked.

"There is, however, no reason to believe they will stop at that one subversive act. No reason to believe they haven't already spies drifting among us. Anheliaa *is* dead.

There is no acknowledged successor. No one properly trained. Anheliaa had delusions of immortality that blinded her to the inevitable until too late."

Mikhyel paused. The flip of papers slowed and stopped. Advocate eyes returned to Mikhyel.

"And without Anheliaa," Mikhyel continued, "without the full power of the rings, Rhomatum is helpless against the forces of Mauritum, the entire web ripe for takeover. Or so Garetti believes." Mikhyel lifted his copy of the report. "Honorable advocates, I suggest we prove Garetti of Mauritum woefully uninformed."

Chapter Four

"So, my fellow conspirators, have we at least a verbal understanding?"

Mikhyel gathered the unsigned contracts into a pile and placed them in the center of the table that nearly filled the small room. Elsewhere, a Shatumin celebration feast was in progress, in a grand hall filled with light and laughter, music and dance.

And food. A great deal of food. And drink.

He hoped to all the nonexistent gods that Deymorin was leaving the wine in his cup.

"To the extent that *we* can make promises, dunMheric, yes." Shamrii dunKharec held out her hand and Mikhyel gripped it. "We will speak to our respective seniors, and advise them of the situation. Luck of the radical, we'll have your contracts signed and back in your possession before you leave."

Here, ambience was limited to muted leylight and the strong scent of brewing pachii.

"I regret the necessity of dealing in such a back-room manner," Mikhyel said. "However, under the circumstances—"

"No need to explain further, dunMheric," Kharlo dun-Uchra said, and he gave a light laugh. "We've all of us had to deal with obstructive seniors before."

"My brother," Mikhyel countered firmly, "is not obstructive. Neither, let it be understood, is he my senior where it regards these matters. Not legally, not personally. He is Princeps, but on these documents, his signature cannot override mine. This is a legally binding agreement between the two of us. He does, however, tend to operate on a system of personal integrity that does not hold up well in a court of law."

"Meaning he's a trusting sod."

"Meaning he, himself, would never go back on the spirit of a promise."

"Meaning our seniors might," dunKharec said.

Mikhyel just lifted an eyebrow.

DunKharec laughed. "You're absolutely correct in that assessment, dunMheric. We'll get you those signatures. Would that you'd been Anheliaa's adviser when the first Khoratum contracts were signed."

"I've no argument there, madam. But these new agreements should clear some long-muddied waters. The main thing is, we must look to the future, near as well as far. We cannot afford to be operating at cross-purposes for personal gain. The Rhomandi fortune is now dedicated to the security of the web, but beggaring the Rhomandi will not ensure that end. If I can rely on you all to keep me apprised of the situation here in Shatum—"

"You are as naive as your brother, sir."

"On the contrary, I *hope* for integrity on the part of those I deal with. I *hope* that problems will be dealt with as they arise, not after the fact. If those I *expect* to deal with me honestly fail to do so, I have, as you may well imagine, other sources of information."

"As have we, dunMheric."

"I would be disappointed if it were otherwise."

Mikhyel smiled, nodded, and left the small room. Outside the door, Ringmaster Pasingarim's second awaited him.

ᔕ   ᔕ   ᔕ

Mikhyel was missing the party.

Even as he smiled and chatted with the various dignitaries and their families, Deymorin searched the edges of the great hall for signs of the true guest of honor.

He'd last seen his brother following the meeting, and parted from him on the understanding that they would meet here. Mikhyel was awake and near—and well—the inner sense assured him of that much, but little else. And now, the bulk of the organized festivities were over, and the attendees were settling into serious debauchery.

"So, Rhomandi, did you ever get your sea voyage?"

"Kharl!" Deymorin rose from the low couch to greet the Varishmondi with something approaching real enthusiasm. "Please, sit down." And as they settled opposite one another, on the u-shaped couch: "No, more's the pity. Lake sailing is the best I've ever managed."

"Well, still plenty of time." The big man leaned forward to help himself from the common trays on the low round table between them.

The odd couches had been set in a rather freeform pattern around three sides of the room, leaving the center clear for the various performers who had come and gone all evening. The food trays presented a constantly changing array of choices, and the wine never stopped flowing.

Ten years ago, he'd have been in real trouble; many of the guests tonight hadn't yet learned their lesson.

But Kharl had. Kharl was quite sober.

"I'm relieved you're speaking to me," Deymorin said, by way of opening.

"And why wouldn't I speak with the son of my old friend, Mheric?"

"From the way you looked this afternoon, I'd have judged the friendship died along with my father. We haven't seen much of you in Rhomatum these past years."

"I'd not been invited."

"I wasn't aware my father ever extended an invitation."

"Our understanding was an old one. I had no reason to believe Anheliaa's nephews would welcome my presence."

"Anheliaa's nephews. Ah, we have created a false image. My apologies, Lord Varishmondi. Let me extend, here and now, a standing invitation—to Rhomatum or Darhaven."

The Varishmondi dipped his head in easy acknowledgment. "My thanks, Rhomandi. And I extend the same to you." A sip of wine, a casual, "False image, you said. And your brother, this afternoon, implied similar internal friction. Am I to understand that the two of you are *not* of her expansionist tendencies?"

Deymorin gave a short laugh. "I should think my stand on that was made clear years ago. I disapproved of the Khoratum expansion."

"Ah, yes. For the sake of the farmers who lost their land with the expanding umbrella, as I recall."

"That, mainly, yes. But Khoratum is done now, an accomplished fact. I think we must protect what we have, get it running smoothly, and discuss the future when the past is secure."

"And your brothers are of similar opinion?"

"Definitely."

"Your brother, Mikhyel, is not here."

"I expected him to be. It's possible he's not feeling well. He's been on the road now for several days."

"He did seem rather . . . shaken at times this afternoon."

Deymorin answered cautiously, "He's been ill. The ley-portation that your ringmaster so blithely inquired about puts an . . . unusual strain on the body. And since his ordeal, there's been the Collapse, and Anheliaa's death . . . he's had no real time to rest."

"And yet, you have been under similar strain . . . ?"

"Mikhyel is not, as you can see, the most robust of men. That he is still on his feet is, at times, a marvel to me. And I stand in awe of his abilities to handle a meeting such as he faced this afternoon."

"He always has . . . spoken well. You've both grown up quite effectively."

The joys of dealing with one's father's old friends. Deymorin felt the smile on his face grow rigid, and he reached for the wine carafe to refill both their goblets.

᧔ ᧔ ᧔

With Ringmaster Pasingarim's cautiously worded advisement to his fellow ringmasters safely pressed in his pocket, Mikhyel made his way at last to the banquet hall.

While he'd been reluctant to begin this tour, sessions such as the meeting just concluded increasingly reconciled him to his fate. The intricate maneuverings, the second-guessing of his opponents . . . he'd spent a lifetime preparing for this night and he now reveled in his sense of achievement.

He paused in the shadows, reluctant to enter a room where music and swirling skirts and strongly-spiced food overloaded a sober man's senses.

Deymorin was sprawled on one of the low Shatumin dinner couches, opposite (Darius save them all) Kharl Varishmandi.

"They're talking about you, Suds," Ganfrion's voice, pitched for his ears only, arose out of even deeper shadows.

"Tell me something I don't know," Mikhyel muttered, without looking back.

"How about, they're wondering who's been running Rhomatum all these years."

"Who's wondering?"

"Take your pick. Kitchen. Stables. Board rooms. Word is you lost it today. Word is you recite from a script. Word is, big brother's here because baby Mikhyel needs him. Word is, baby Mikhyel nearly lost it this afternoon. Word is, the two of you together still don't match Anheliaa. Word is, you were Anheliaa's parrot, not a brain."

He closed his eyes on the dizzying swirl, realized, when that didn't stop the images, that his discomfiture came from his brother's wine-scewed vision, and cursed.

"You might say that," Ganfrion murmured. "DunHaulpin used to say Mheric's brat was the best trained monkey he'd ever seen."

In the four years between his mother's death and Mheric's, Mikhyel had served many functions for his father: servant to romPetikh's fancy teas, performer (sometimes complete to having strings attached to his limbs so that Mheric could manipulate him like a puppet) . . .

"DunHaulpin used to say you couldn't possibly understand what you were saying."

Orator for dunBisin's overwritten plays. He'd been good with words. Mheric and his friends had thought it amusing to hear a child spout rhetoric he couldn't possibly comprehend.

But he *had* understood. He'd understood the words he used, and he'd understood the words underlying the laughter of the men and women watching. And he'd used that knowledge to his own advantage after Mheric's death, just as he'd later used the oratory skills addressing the Syndicate and the Council.

"Have to wonder who all dunHaulpin talked to."

Nothing new in that. As he'd told Deymorin, he'd fought those rumors his entire career. But perhaps he was only now facing them for truth. Varishmondi had been his father's friend. Varishmondi had seen the puppet spout those ill-written lines and make them convincing.

"You convinced dunHaulpin differently," Ganfrion's maddening voice continued. "How're you going to convince this lot, eh?"

"Go tap your kitchen maids," Mikhyel muttered back, slipping into the room.

Deymorin caught sight of him immediately and waved him over to his side. As he approached, Deymorin laughed and swung upright to give him sitting space on his couch.

"Kharl, this is my brother, Mikhyel," Deymorin said, wrapping an arm around Mikhyel's shoulders. "Fry, this is Kharl. He's taking us sailing tomorrow, so be nice."

Kharl Varishmandi was not drunk. Kharl Varishmandi was looking at him, wondering what kind of man would put up with such treatment in public.

Mikhyel stiffened, humiliated, tempted to tell Deymorin exactly what he thought of his behavior. But to challenge him openly would solve nothing and might possibly undermine the good he'd accomplished in the past few hours. Deymorin's mind was hazed with drink—exactly as he'd feared would happen. He'd seen it often enough in the past.

He'd thought Deymorin had outgrown such behavior.

Obviously, he'd thought wrong.

But to chastise Deymorin now would gain him nothing, and would almost certainly hurt their cause. The men and women in the hall, most of them at least as drunk as Deymorin, were not likely to remember anything clearly in the morning, so rather than cause a scene, he smiled, and greeted the Varishmandi patriarch and said he would be delighted to join him on a tour of the lake tomorrow.

ॐ   ॐ   ॐ

"Did you *see* that creature at table five?"

A rude sound responded out of the darkness that was Thyerri's new bedroom.

"She elbowed m' privates ever' time I had t' squeeze past 'er!" Shtolis' youngish voice continued. "Pinched me comin' an' goin', I tell ye. Had me soundin' like Mishthi by th' time she left!"

"She wanted you, Shtolis," someone said, in a low, suggestive voice. "She needed your hot, young—"

Another rude sound. A loud pretense of someone being sick. A laughing comment about faces and being flat as a cold balloon.

Thyerri tried to ignore them all.

The new sleeping room was one of the smaller halls in Bharlori's newest investment. True to his promise, Bharlo

had expanded into a neighboring building. His new roommates were the five hillers Bharlori had hired to wait tables.

The girls had their own quarters.

Thyerri wasn't certain he liked the arrangement, he'd
grown rather fond of Mishthi's silly chatter. And the easy
sharing of warmth to which he'd become accustomed was
out of the question with the strangers who now shared
his nights.

Male strangers who filled the room, in the dark moments
before sleep, with coarse language and coarser imagery.

"What's your problem, boy?" The low voice again—Frivori, Thyerri thought—and mocking. "Her money's as good
as any beauty's. Better, likely, 'cuz there'll be more of it.
And they're all the same in the dark."

Loud protests interrupted, and Thyerri pulled his pillow
over his head, trying to block out the sounds.

His new roommates only served to remind him of the
distance between himself and those who should be his
peers. As a child not much younger than Shtolis he'd
roamed the mountain meadows, more wild than the goats
and sheep he chased. He'd watched them mate, seen count-
less births, but never equated those natural acts to his
own life.

Radical dancers never spoke among themselves of love
or lust or children. It was bad luck and stupid. One thought
only of the dance, rarely even of one's physical differences,
except to compare the relative value of muscle and bulk,
and to wish for that person's wrists, or another's flexibility.

Waiting tables, he heard the talk of the men and women
he served, and he learned to avoid the inevitable bids for
his attention. But he never thought beyond the sheer logis-
tics of avoiding probing, clutching fingers while balancing a
tray and without antagonizing the customer.

He knew, in a distant way, the effect his dancing had on
the viewers, and why it had become so popular in the late
hours of the evening here, and why he'd become so significant to Bharlori that the owner had posted signs warning
against groping the dancers.

But it had all been a distant, detached knowledge, for all
his new roommates believed otherwise, and for all they
grumbled about bedroom favorites when Bharlori failed to
chastise him when he was clearly in the wrong.

Fortunately, there had always been work enough to exhaust the strongest body until the need for sleep could muffle the most raucous laughter.

Until recently. Until that damnable poster appeared outside the tavern. These nights, in those dim moments before sleep, with the poster and the upcoming competition reminding him of all that could never be, and his own reconciliation with his present life asking why he persisted with impossible dreams of the past, those other images, images with Tamshi eyes, seeped inexorably past the newly rediscovered mountain music, striking chords of an altogether different melody within his body.

৯   ৯   ৯

Music echoed in Mikhyel's ears as he fell into the grooming chair, exhausted. Evidently Deymorin *hadn't* gone to bed as he'd said were his intentions.

Mikhyel groaned and tried to blank his mind of everything except the rhythmic stroking of Raulind's brushes through his hair.

"Do you want to talk about it?" Raulind asked.

"It's Deymio."

"You feel him now?"

"I think so. He's actually very quiet, for a change. Perhaps I should get him drunk more often."

"Oh, dear."

"I can't understand what's gotten into him."

Years ago, it had been Deymorin's greatest fault. He was friendly, enthusiastic, and could be induced to overindulge. When that happened, his companions had had an exceedingly easy, exceedingly wealthy, mark.

And here in Shatum, it was all those behaviors back again, but in a grown man.

"I'd convinced myself he'd grown past it all; evidently, I was wrong."

A long silence filled with even strokes of the brush, then Raulind said, "As I hear it, Deymorin wasn't the only man acting out of character today."

Mikhyel frowned. Then leaned forward to look at Raulind, whose calm demeanor gave him no more clue than his words.

But he didn't need more clues. Raulind was right. Deymorin had feared Mikhyel would crack, and Mikhyel had obligingly cracked. He had feared Deymorin would regress to old behaviors, and Deymorin had regressed.

"I think," he said, settling back into the couch, "that Deymorin and I had best part company."

"That sounds wise, sir," Raulind said, setting the brush aside. "Would you like the window open or closed tonight?"

ᔕ ᔕ ᔕ

Pale eyes, green-rimmed and black-lashed, flickered close, expanding, shapeshifting to an all-consuming haze of mist and spring-green.

There was warmth, a presence at his back: welcome ease for muscles aching from long hours twisting and turning through crowded rooms, from laden trays held high, above harm's way.

Thyerri sighed and stretched, curling slightly about his pillow, exposing his lower back more fully to that friendly warmth.

Silken strands slithered over his shoulder and across his chest to tangle under his arm and downward, like a spider-web. The tendrils gained bone and muscle, became long fingers that stroked his chin and down his neck, where they intercepted moist warmth nuzzling his shoulder, then tread delicate patterns down his breast and across his ribs.

Thyerri sighed again, and buried his face in the pillow, too tired to object, even when the fingertips flattened into heated palms that pressed upward, crossing over his stomach and chest, drawing him closer to the unknown presence at his back.

Though helpless in sleep's lassitude, he wasn't frightened. A response occurred, deep, deep within. Recognition. Yearning. A sense of . . . need, of . . . desire. Those palms stroked downward in a clean thrust that veered at the last moment, around his groin to tickle his inner thighs with a light, fingertip brush.

He groaned and shifted. But those fingers shifted with him, teasing, tempting, then drawing back, building the tension within until his pulse pounded.

The presence at his back began to move, lifting him with it, leading, falling away and leading again, until their two bodies danced as one, danced to a rhythm as primal as the rings whirling in the Tower uphill.

A subtle shift, a pause, an unexpected thrust, and the presence was within him as well as without. The tension eased slightly, only to leap to greater heights as the rhythm resumed, an ever-increasing tempo. He was sobbing, mindlessly reaching, seeking. . . .

Release. Exquisite and complete. An ecstasy matched only by the dance itself.

§   §   §

Mikhyel awoke with a start, wondered for a moment where he was, remembered in the next and as chill air touched his sweat-dampened back, that he was in the Hilltop Inn, courtesy of the Shatumin Guilds.

And in the room next door, his hypersexed older brother was dreaming about his equally sensual woman; dreams that, had Deymorin a shred of common consideration, he'd keep in his own damned head.

Or wherever such dreams lurked.

Mikhyel drew himself wearily upright, seeking the sleeping shirt he'd somehow cast aside. Deymorin again, he imagined, as he drew the fine linen around his shoulders.

At least Deymorin was quiet now, sated . . . he hoped. Mikhyel shifted to another area of the large and comfortable bed, beat the pillows into a more welcoming configuration, and drew the covers high, beginning the night over, wishing, in passing, that he had his own lascivious dreams to penetrate and disrupt Deymorin's sleep as Deymorin had disrupted his.

Except that Deymorin would thank him, then tease him mercilessly about the source.

Out of his admittedly limited experience, he sought a mental picture of the woman he would deliberately inject into Deymorin's dreams. Something the antithesis of Kiyrstin. Reed-slender. And quiet. Fragile.

Shy. Mikhyel grinned into the pillow warming his nose. Better yet, inhibited. That would do it. Frustrate his brother to awareness. *Keep* him awake—until he departed Shatum in utter desperation.

Then maybe, just maybe, someone *else* might get some

sleep. Mikhyel groaned, slammed a fist into his pillow, and threw himself to the other side.

If only Demorin would leave tomorrow, go about his own, equally important business. Both of them here only confused the issue, made people wonder who to address, whose the authority. If he thought it would do any good, he'd send a message via that silent communication, shift Deymorin's thinking toward leaving.

But he'd tried that last night; Deymorin had not been amused.

Arms encircling his ribs. A scent that said {Kiyrstin . . .}
Mikhyel cursed—and buried his head in the pillow.

§ § §

The first faint light of dawn touched the walls, and limned the bodies lying peacefully on their pallets.

Alone. All of them. As Thyerri himself was alone. Unquestionably alone. Curled about his pillows, his hands clamped between his thighs.

Slowly, he straightened his back. His hair, captured under his arm, pulled free, a thousand tiny pinpricks in his scalp, then slithered along his chest: the spiderweb of his dream. He drew his hands free of the blanket. They were sticky, glistening in the dawn creeping in the windows, and he knew them for the hands of his dream.

Horrified, he began to shake. He struggled to free himself of blankets and pillows. He stumbled over sleeping bodies, raising shrill protests that he ignored in his blind dash for freedom.

Gray eyes, green-rimmed met him. Mocked him. He ripped at the eyes, the poster came away in pieces and drifted into the mud.

Running, then, down streets littered with a city's detritus, filthy, as cities were; blindly seeking the anonymous tranquillity of his mountain, certain those around him would know the instant they laid eyes on him, would know the depths to which he had plunged, the shame, the failure, that were his.

Wet. Cold. It was his mountain surrounding him, filling him as the icy chill of glacier melt swept over him, washing the taint downstream. Changing nothing. Nothing could obliterate the facts; nothing could deny what he had done.

Nothing could unmake what he had become.

Tears swept down the mountain along with those other fluids. Tears for the dancer who'd never been. Tears for the dancer who never could be. Tears for the dancer banished forever in an insidious, carnal dream.

Chapter Five

Deymorin jerked the girth strap tight and flipped the stir-rup iron down.

"Walk him a bit, and try again," he ordered the groom. "He's an accomplished puffer." He gave the gelding a slap on his hard rump, and headed inside for a final draft to bolster his spirits before facing a day in the saddle at a slow carriage pace.

The Rose Garden was one of the better cross-ley inns, lying, as it did, equidistant between Shatum, Mekh'narum on the coast and the spa node of Barsitum. Spacious, with a dozen or more large rooms to let, visiting servants' quarters, three private parlors, a crystal-appointed dining hall, servants enough for three large households crowding the halls . . . it was almost as uncomfortable as Rhomandi House during Reformation Week.

And one couldn't forget the small, glass-enclosed rose garden, from which the inn derived its name: a little touch of home for those traveling between nodes.

All windows were heavily draped against the outside, of course. But then, The Rose Garden's clientele didn't want to see those exquisite snow-capped peaks outside their windows of a morning. They didn't want anything to remind them that they were beyond the boundaries of their little rose-covered havens within city walls.

But Mikhyel had been right in scheduling The Rose Garden as their stopover—as he'd been in all other arrangements he'd made for this trip. None of the cozier inns of the sort Deymorin patronized could have handled the entourage Mikhyel brought with him. Certainly they couldn't have accommodated the unexpected addition of Deymorin and his guard.

Mikhyel was waiting just inside, the portmanteau he used

for these single night stops packed and ready on a low bench near the door, his folded cloak draped over it.

"We need to talk," Mikhyel said.

Deymorin raised a hand toward the sitting room, followed Mikhyel in, and closed the door.

"Your men are saddled and ready?" Mikhyel asked, abruptly.

Deymorin nodded.

"To go where?"

"Well, let's see, what *is* next on the list?" Deymorin made a show of remembering the schedule, hoping to ease past that cold wall. "Shatum, Fedranum, Mekh'narum . . . Barsitum? I believe that was it."

"Fine." Mikhyel threw himself into a chair, plucked a paper from a nearby table, and snapped it open. "Have a good trip."

"And where are you headed?" Deymorin asked the paper.

"I've no idea. It makes no difference."

"Difference? Of course it does."

He reached for Mikhyel's wrist, seeking that deeper understanding; Mikhyel, with an indignant curse, jerked out of reach.

Deymorin held up his hands.

"Khyel, I'm sorry. But would you mind telling me what's going on?"

Eyes that glittered more green than gray beneath angrily lowered brows met his. "Do I really need to say it? Deymorin, *get out!* Go! Do your job, or do mine. Or do them both, if you're so gods-blessed-talented and I'll go to . . . to *Darhaven* and sit on my tail sipping brandywine for the next six weeks or six months or six *years.* Whatever it takes for you to stop hovering and start minding your own affairs!"

Mikhyel threw the paper to the floor, thrust himself out of the chair, and paced the room.

"Khyel, I've just been trying to—"

"Help? Obviously. And thanks to you, everyone in the Southern Crescent now believes I *require* that help. Every Councillor, every Syndic, every advocate, every damnable *innkeeper* believes I'm incompetent."

"That's nonsense. I've *stayed* in the background. When asked, I've told them—"

"It makes no difference what you do or do not tell them. You're *there,* big as life—which in itself is damned unnerving. But— Rings, man, you're the Rhomandi, Princeps of Rhomatum—"

Deymorin opened his mouth to object, but Mikhyel continued. "*Look* at what happened at Fedranum! Poor old dunGardhiin spent the entire two days apologizing for not being prepared for you!"

"I told him—"

"*I* was *supposed* to be touring his plants, talking to the foremen—"

"You *did* go along."

"So did dunGardhiin's secretary. *And* a boy to fetch and carry for him. Tell me, Rhomandi, which function was I to fulfill for you?"

"Neither! As you damnwell know!"

"Do I?"

"This is nonsense." Deymorin slapped his gloves into his hand and headed back for the door. "Get your bag, brother. We're wasting time."

"Good-bye, Deymorin."

He swung around. Mikhyel was staring out the far window. Pointedly not coming.

"What do you *want* out of me, Khyel?"

"I've been trying to demonstrate that we're a team. Hell, I've been *trying* to show them all I'm not the incompetent I appeared when I fought the Khoratum expansion."

"No politician remembers that day—*certainly* not the way you dwell on it! You're as good or as bad as your last effort, Rhomandi, and your current proposals are very much to the advantage of everyone we've met. Besides, the Southern Crescent cities were always your spiritual allies in that battle."

"I *had* no allies in the Syndicate." Deymorin pointed out, the old bitterness rising. "They're all node men and all any of them care about is whether they have their lights, and their toys and a guaranteed rain-free evening for their poolside party!"

"And *you* lost that gods-be-forever-damned debate because you never got it through your thick head that not all cities were Rhomatum! Shatum *never* wanted Khoratum capped. They *knew* it would make Rhomatum immeasurably more powerful, and the ringmaster doesn't exist that trusts another ringmaster, *especially* Anheliaa of Rhomatum!"

"Then why the *hell* did they sign Anheliaa's fucking contracts?"

"I don't damnwell *know*!"

Mikhyel had stopped pacing to face him. They were shouting at one another now, as they hadn't for years.

"I don't . . . damnwell know," Mikhyel repeated in a quieter tone, and he began pacing again. "It makes no sense. It never *has* made sense. Anheliaa promised someone something somewhere. I was *hoping* to find some clue in Shatum. I kept *waiting* for someone to ask specifically, but there was nothing. And there *should* have been. The Southern Crescent historically depended on the strength of the storm belt to help keep the Kirish'lan raiders at bay."

"Raiders, hell," Deymorin broke in. "Shatum wanted to be the solitary overland funnel for the Kirish'lan traders. I was fighting for the rights of farmers and timbermen; the Shatumin Ringmaster wanted the graft from the trading caravans, guaranteeing crossings. Once the storms eased, free traders began making solo passages, taking their chances and more often than not surviving, and cutting into Shatumin profits."

"What *difference* did it make? Their *goal* was the same as yours. You both wanted Khoratum left open. You've *never* understood the difference between motivation and action—"

"What good is the one without the other?"

"It gets the damn job done."

"While compromising a man's soul."

Mikhyel spun about in mid-stride to face him. "Deymorin, there's a world of difference between a man's soul and the moral compromises he makes for the sake of a nation."

Deymorin frowned. Then asked, quietly, "Khyel, what the hell are we arguing about?"

Breaths, deep and trembling, fluttered the lace at Mikhyel's throat.

Deymorin held out his hand, offering that solution, and Mikhyel's hand lifted . . . reached . . . then jerked back.

A rejection more painful than a fist to his face.

"We're *discussing* the efficacy of your presence during

my negotiations," Mikhyel said firmly. "Yours is a . . . a difficult presence to transcend."

"Is *that* why you damned near choked me in Shatum?"

"What are you talking about?"

"Nikki warned me to be careful of that power of yours. Just how much did you learn from Anheliaa, *little brother*? You damned near froze my throat solid. If you want me to let you talk, you can damn well ask in a civilized manner! Otherwise, I don't see a lick of difference between your tactics and Anheliaa's except *you* don't need the fucking rings to do your dirty work for you!"

"Neither do you," Mikhyel said, his face as blank as virgin marble. And Deymorin remembered that same meeting in Shatum, recalled Mikhyel staggering in mid-sentence, wasn't certain whether it was Mikhyel supplying the memory or not.

"If that answer matters to you, Deymorin, we might as well give up now. I'll not be accounting for myself and my actions during an invasion of *my* territory, and a disruption of *my* preplanned attack. I'll not apologize, not for what I say or do with determination, not for the collateral consequences of this curse we carry."

" 'Collateral consequences.' Is *that* what you call damn near choking me?"

"I didn't know, Deymorin. I just knew I needed you not to talk."

And what he didn't say . . . that the attack had been both ways. He told Deymorin not to condemn him. What Deymorin should note, Kiyrstin would say, was that Mikhyel did not condemn him for nearly knocking him cold in mid-argument, and then ordering him to get them both out of the situation.

"What was I supposed to do?" Mikhyel asked. "Stop in the middle of a meeting to chastise abject stupidity? What was I going to say? Shut up, fool?"

"Yes."

A two-beat pause, then a flat, "Shut up, fool."

"Is that a joke?" Deymorin responded hopefully. "Should I laugh?"

"Deymorin, what does it take to get through to you? What must I say to get you *out* of my life and on with your own?"

"I'm just trying to—"

"What makes you think I *need* help? And what's to stop all those people from assuming I need you there when you cut my meat for me at the dining table?"

Deymorin tried a teasing grin. "Well, you weren't eating enough to keep a newt alive."

Mikhyel uttered a frustrated curse and threw his hands in the air.

"What was *I* supposed to do?" Deymorin asked. "You think I've *wanted* to dance attendance on you? You've been one step short of a cliff edge ever since Anheliaa died. *You're* the one who put your faith in a killer. *You're* the one who's been attracting animated corpses. *You're* the one who nearly cracked in Shatum at the mere *mention* of Anheliaa and Boreton! You're the one who's been stumbling over your words like a pubescent whose voice hasn't changed. I don't know what's happened to you, but—"

"*You've* happened, *big brother!*"

"But—"

"And when you're *quiet* in my head, I'm making excuses for what you're saying *aloud*!"

"Now wait just one damned—"

"I doubt you'll like their assessment of you any better than mine. Bad enough to face them as the proxy of the mythical eldest Rhomandi. Now I'm speaking for you with you sitting beside me, with your friendly, all-encompassing grin and massive presence, everybody's best friend."

"What's wrong with that?"

Mikhyel scowled at him, lips pressed together. When he answered, it was one, short word. "Provincial."

Deymorin lifted his chin, refusing to snap.

"Learn to talk less and observe more, *big brother*! You're too damned open. Too obvious. You get them happy drunk, they smile and say exactly what you want them to say, agree to anything you propose, and you find out *nothing*. Settle nothing. Get nothing on paper. Maybe you can operate on a handshake and a promise Outside. In the City limits—any City limits—I guarantee, they'll deny it as soon as they're sober."

"They didn't."

"Because *I* got it on paper. With their secretaries as witness. *Before* they were sober."

"And while I was pouring the wine."

Mikhyel shrugged.

"But that doesn't gain you the respect you need, is that what you're saying?"

"Nor you, Deymorin. We're supposed to be presenting a viable partnership. We're supposed to be reassuring them of Rhomatum's continued strength. We're not doing very well so far."

Old suspicions. Old schisms. And old habits. As he considered Mikhyel's words, he wondered at his own recent behavior. He'd not been in the habit of overindulgence for some years.

But he hadn't been drunk—not at Shatum. Not until Mikhyel showed up. And then he'd swallowed as fast as Varishmandi had poured. Because Mikhyel had expected it.

They'd acknowledged his interference with Mikhyel's thoughts, but they'd not considered the effect of Mikhyel's expectations over *his* actions.

Even so, he had to wonder whether his own actions were the result not so much Mikhyel's expectations, but of old, old patterns, the old challenges to each other's behavior that had driven a wedge between them for years.

A niggling pressure in his head: acquiescence from Mikhyel. He grinned wryly.

"It may be a good thing I wasn't around all those years."

"Maybe it is."

Time and separation had allowed them both to mature. It would take more time and careful exposure to eradicate those entrenched and mutually destructive habits and expectations.

But in cold blood, he knew Mikhyel was right. And that was *his* thought, and none of Mikhyel.

He held out his hand, clasped Mikhyel's arm wrist to wrist in the intimate farewell of closest trust, and realized as his fingers touched, easily encircling Mikhyel's thin forearm, another reason for his reluctance to leave his physically delicate brother.

Like the tingling in the air before a storm, Mikhyel's frustration permeated his skin through that pulse-to-pulse touch.

"Rings, Deymio, I can't imagine how I ever survived without you."

"I can't help worrying, Khyel. You're not halfway through this trip. You're already showing the effects of too little sleep and not enough food—"

Mikhyel avoided his gaze, but touch revealed a wry choice that was no choice at all. Of a stomach unwilling to hold anything down.

"Funny, I never took you for the nervous type."

"Nervous? Not really. Terrified might begin to cover it. But I always am, Deymorin. I spent the entire night before I faced you in Council over the Khoratum affair, throwing up. It's never gotten any better."

And Deymorin had never seen a colder visage than his brother had worn that day.

"It keeps my wits sharp."

"So that's your secret."

Mikhyel grinned at last. "Only one of them, brother. Only one." He released Deymorin and jerked his head toward the door. "I promise you, I won't starve. Raul won't let me. Now get out of here, will you? I want to make Barsitum before midnight."

"If they don't get you there—"

"Don't worry. Ganfrion knows this country well."

Deymorin paused at the door, one glove on, the other balanced in his hand. "I can't believe you made a deal with that man, Khyel."

"He's exactly what I need."

"You really trust his honor?"

"His honor? No, not in the least."

"Khyel, dammit—"

Mikhyel laughed. "Get *out*, Deymio. If my judgment proves at fault, well, I'll leave you Ganfrion in my will."

Deymorin eyed him a moment, stretched an imperative hand, which Mikhyel accepted without hesitation. What came through to Deymorin now was anticipation. Determination. Even a hint of excitement. And most importantly, confidence in himself and his abilities.

Deymorin chuckled. "About time, fry. Keep in touch." And with a parting jab at Mikhyel's shoulder, he was out the door.

§　　§　　§

Mikhyel stood on the veranda rubbing feeling back into his shoulder, while Deymorin and his men mounted and sorted themselves into pairs. Deymorin's horse seemed in a particularly foul mood, bucking and twisting under him, and good-natured shouts filled the air—laughter, and offers of a grandmother's pregnant mare.

Deymorin sat quietly, as if the world erupting beneath him were an everyday occurrence, and only Mikhyel, of all those watching, knew the jolt of pain that accompanied each stiff-legged impact.

Deymorin had been too long away from his Kiyrstin's hands: his old back injury was flaring. But the creature finally settled, and Deymorin lifted his hand to Mikhyel in farewell, his grin unabated, and rode out the stableyard gate at what appeared a most energetic bouncing step.

With every jogging stride, Mikhyel's sense of Deymorin faded.

"About time."

It was an almost-echo of Deymorin's words, and Mikhyel turned half about to discover a body nearly as large as Deymorin's blocking the entrance to the inn.

"You're a spineless ass when he's around," Ganfrion continued, staring at the double column exiting the stableyard.

Mikhyel stiffened. Deymorin had his reservations about Ganfrion; Mikhyel had his own.

"Tell Captain Ori to get the men mounted," he said, brushing past him. "We're leaving immediately."

"Why, sure, Suds."

Mikhyel swung around; Ganfrion took a step backward and snapped to a somewhat startled attention. He touched fingertips to forehead, breast, and sword hilt in a martial salute, the origin of which Nikki had damnwell *better* have included in some brief, and was down the stairs and out in the stableyard shouting orders . . .

Leaving Mikhyel to wonder what he'd done right.

Chapter Six

Ocarshi smoke hung in the air above the low, heavily-laden table. Thick and cloying, the smoke coated eyelashes and lungs as it coated the brocades and velvets and sheerest gauze draped about the room and covering the individuals sprawled on tasseled cushions within lazy arm's-reach of the table. Their forms masked in voluminous robes, faces hidden behind elaborate paint and jewelry, only the hands that reached for the pipes, the source of the noxious smoke, revealed an occasional, unequivocal, male structure of bone and muscle and coarse hair.

Thyerri smothered a gooey cough and picked his way among the bodies to replace a depleted platter. The inescapable smoke dulled his reflexes and impeded his balance. It even seemed to muffle his hearing—or perhaps it actually altered the sound as it came off the lute strings and clogged the flute's holes.

The thump of the drum was simply listless and disinterested.

When it wasn't tangling with his arms, his hair, free of its braid and held off his brow with a length of gold-shot silk, alternately smothered and blinded him at every twist and dip of his head. The knee-length silk fringe hanging from his vest caught on every rough surface and exposed more than it concealed every time he inhaled.

He supposed he should be thankful the official mandate for the evening's festivities had allowed him a loincloth for decency. Sakhithe and Mishthi had to depend on their own movements to protect their modesty. Their vests were short—Mishthi's heavy breasts had a tendency to peek out the bottom when she stretched her arms across the table— and their fringe was suspended from a wide hip belt. Thicker fringe, but nothing underneath. Sakhithe had been practicing for days hoping to avoid both groping hands and prying eyes.

But it had been master the skill or lose her job. Bharlori had made that clear to them all from the beginning: this was the night to set Bharlori's above every other eating establishment in Khoratum.

Loose hair, revealing garments . . . he and the other attendants looked like the inventory of the Agoran Plains slavers of Partiniac fable. Not coincidentally the hall had been dressed to parody those fantastical merchants' richly appointed tents, whose tasteless opulence was said to overwhelm their clients' good sense and put them in a spending mood.

One had to wonder what the man who had ordered this evening's festivities intended to sell to his guests. Not that it was any of it Thyerri's business. His business was to serve the food, itself prepared to specifications that had made Cook blanch.

Those same written specifications had guided them for decorating the hall, a five-day task it had taken these patrons less than an hour to pollute so thoroughly the props would have to be discarded after tonight's festivities.

But Bharlori wouldn't mind the senseless waste. Bharlori had boasted earlier that for compensation already received, lightning could strike his entire establishment tomorrow and he would still see a profit. And, he had added sternly, he expected gratuities for the evening's service to double that profit.

Thyerri had shivered and wished those words unsaid. It was the second time Bharlori had tempted Rakshi. But Thyerri's fears were too late, the statement had already been cast into the wind.

And it appeared, perhaps, that Rakshi was disinclined to take advantage of so innocent a challenge: thus far, and well into the evening's rituals, for all the oily smoke and burning lamps and candles that might have threatened the fringe and gauze, only food and drink had spilled; and while he doubted any of the guests were awake enough to register the fact, their service had been impeccable.

The platter Thyerri sought even now to replace was far from empty, but the pattern of fruits and sauces had been mauled from the passage of uncaring sleeves. If he could rescue it, the fruits could be washed and reused in the replacement tray.

Bodies sprawled at every conceivable angle about the

table. To reach the platter in question, Thyerri was forced
to kneel and stretch across one of the guests, a technique
he'd mastered early in the evening, but which now had the
added challenge of not disturbing the man's ocarshi dream.

Nails stroked his ribs, in a casual, half-considered gesture.
Thyerri's hair-obscured glance intercepted distended pupils
within half-lidded eyes.

"Do I know you?" the guest asked, and behind the mask,
the skin tightened, as if trying to draw drug-hazed eyes
into focus.

Thyerri hesitated to answer, hesitated even to move away
from the hand, for fear of disrupting the drugged languor.
However unpleasant the man's touch, its very negligence
made it insignificant.

As for knowing, this man was masked and painted, as
were all the guests, either in keeping with the evening's
theme or for real purposes of secrecy. In all the hours,
Thyerri had heard no names.

But he did know. As an apprentice dancer, he'd lived in
the Khoratum Tower, eaten in the great dining hall, been
paraded among the city leaders and visiting dignitaries from
other nodes. He recognized many of the voices behind the
masks, and Rhyys dunTarec's nasal tones and coarse, blunt-
fingered hands were unmistakable.

For himself, as was the way with failed radicals, he'd
taken a new name, dyed his hair an even, nondescript velvet black, but Rhyys could remember—if Rhyys cared to
remember him. Rhyys had many reasons to remember the
person Thyerri had been, but Rhyys would never admit to
knowing anyone like Thyerri of Bharlori's Tavern.

He certainly didn't want Thyerri of Bharlori's spreading
it about that Rhyys of Khoratum Tower had demeaned
himself by attending a party in such a place. Rhyys never
came to Lesser Khoratum. Rhyys had often enough made
it perfectly clear *nothing* would induce him to come to
lesser Khoratum.

But something *had* gotten him down here, and one need
look no farther than at one's own outrageous garb to know
what that something was.

It was, of course, all nonsense. But the drapes, the pillows, the ocarshi, even the affectation of the finger-forks
each guest wore on the index finger of the right hand, all
were imports from the south, and all were very much in

keeping with Rhyys' fantasies, every detail lifted from the murals Rhyys had had commissioned for the Tower's great hall.

Someone who sought to curry favor with the Khoratumin Ringmaster had masterminded the evening's festivities.

Someone who, like Rhyys, preferred anonymity.

Rhyys, apparently in no particular hurry for his answer, followed Thyerri's exposed ribs with his fingertips, the finger-fork's double tine, intended for spearing and dipping delicacies from the platters, traced a pattern upward, slipping past the loose vest to explore by touch alone the bare skin of his chest.

"Ah, the illusion ends," murmured the Khoratum Ringmaster. "How sad."

"M'lord?" Mishthi asked, and her voice trembled with the fear of disappointing this important customer. "In what way? We followed the instructions—"

"Child, you've done quite adequately." Rhyys' hand flattened on Thyerri's chest, idly twisting a nipple between two knuckles. "Outside, all is as it should be. It's the underneath, the hidden wonders. You should be prepared, decorated for pleasure. Ours, and yours. . . ."

Tines replaced the knuckles and pressed, with that same detached negligence. Thyerri waited, unflinching, as liquid warmth oozed from the point of contact. The dark eyes behind the jeweled mask flickered into focus, staring with new interest at Thyerri's face.

The pressure increased. Tears filmed his vision, but he refused to blink, as he refused to move or react, and eventually the tines, denied their objective, relaxed and scraped their way down to rest on his bare thigh.

Decimated platter in hand, Thyerri shifted his weight back over his heels.

"I asked you a question, boy." Cognizance began to color Rhyys' voice.

Burning with anger and humiliation, Thyerri ignored him, but the man grasped his hair, using that hold to jerk him back down, while hauling himself upright. Blunt fingers squeezed Thyerri's face, the finger-tines bit into his cheek, drawing blood a second time.

"Do I?"

"I—" He struggled to speak against that muscle-warping grip, knowing he dared not speak the truth, dared not challenge the farce as his heart desired. His tongue had severed a dunKarlon from Bharlori's guest list; he did not think Bharlori would as easily forgive severing a dunTarec.

"I can't say, m'lord mask," he whispered at last. "How *could* I know?"

A short bark of laughter blew ocarshi-fouled breath in his face. "But of course," the man whispered back, and he pulled Thyerri to him for a rough, penetrating kiss. The platter fell, smearing the remnants of sauce and fruit across the tasseled, brocade pillows, and Rhyys himself.

With a hissing curse, the ringmaster thrust Thyerri away; he fell backward into the arms of another man, who caught and held him prisoner. But the ringmaster simply shook the remnants from his robe and shouted at them to remove the platter and clean up the mess and to bring more wine.

Mishthi scrambled over with cleaning rags and Sakhithe brought wine; Thyerri escaped, platter in hand, out the servants' entrance, down the dimly-lit hall, and across the alley to the tavern's kitchen where he threw the porcelain platter at the stone hearth. It shattered, terrifying Khorey, the stove-boy, rousing Cook's wrath, and doing little to eradicate the anger and tension seething in Thyerri's gut.

"I don't *care!*" he shouted at Cook's screeches about crockery in the soup, and he crossed to kick the large cauldron simmering beside the fire, setting it swinging wildly, scattering soup-drops in all directions. Cook screeched again, and Thyerri shouted: "Send it to Rhyys! By Mother's grace, he'll swallow it and choke!"

Cook's screeching ended abruptly. She stared at him, slack-jawed. The stove-boy hunkered outside after more wood, and the transients hired to cover in the tavern so that he and the other regulars could be humiliated, took one look in the kitchen and scampered back out to the floor.

Cook, Besho, Khorey . . . they'd done nothing to him, did not deserve the anger he longed to discharge, and so Thyerri stood there, quivering, the emotions piling up inside him, disgracing himself further with each passing moment.

His hand felt wet. He examined it as if it belonged to someone else. Blood. And slivers, gained in his wild flight from the hall. And as he watched, that hand made a fist and struck the fire-heated stone, and struck again. Stone already stained with his blood.

Cook caught his hand, exclaiming in a different tone, but he jerked free, and ran for the door and the clear air of the alleyway.

Wide eyes reflected the light from the doorway: Khorey the stove-boy, cowering beside the woodpile. A frantic scrambling toppled the pile, and the boy darted past him, back to the light and warmth of the kitchen, shedding wood with every third step.

Mortally ashamed, Thyerri retreated to the pump, and plunged his hands deep into the cool water.

He'd acted the fool in more ways than he could count. Rhyys knew he'd run away. Instead of facing his attacker, he'd run, and attacked others who'd come to trust his easy nature.

What do you want, boy? To run? To hurt?

To kill?

He shuddered, knowing at that moment how close he was to wanting that end for Rhyys. Rhyys had determined his competition days at an end. Rhyys had ruled his life for years, had controlled his training and his time on the rings. And Rhyys chose those who would have another chance to compete.

And now, Rhyys controlled a new arena, in ways he could never rule the competitors, whose success ultimately depended upon their individual pride and ability. Something had changed. Rhyys was heady with power—a power that ranged beyond Khoratum—and getting worse, if tonight was any indication.

But there was nothing Thyerri of Bharlori's kitchen could do to change Rhyys dunTarec, Ringmaster of Khoratum, except not give him satisfaction.

He lifted the icy water to his cheeks, chasing the blood away, hating the remembered touch of those fingers, hating the tingle that ran through him as his fingers washed the cuts on his cheek and the vest brushed the hardening mounds of flesh on his chest.

The dreams came nightly, now, and the most casual waking touch roused myriad sensations he despised. Though he hated Rhyys for this deliberate assault, he hated his own body more, for the hard nubs on his chest, the tingling skin . . . the tightening in his groin.

He swore, and plunged his hands again into the freezing water, this time to drive away the salty tears. There in the shadowed privacy of the alleyway, he unlaced the vest to examine the shallow cuts at his breast.

"Thyerri! Are you out here, boy?"

Bharlori, sounding anxious and a bit frustrated.

"They're asking for you, lad. Best finish your business and get back."

"I'm not going back." Thyerri lifted a handful of water to his chest, caught his breath at the sudden intimate chill, and scrubbed with the flat of his hand to both warm the spot and erase the memory of Rhyys' fingers—and to punish his own flesh.

"What are you talking about? Of course you're going back in. They've hired our services for the night—into tomorrow, if they so choose. *If* they're happy and content. Perhaps they'll ask you to dance. *Think* what that could bring in from this lot. They've no idea what things cost outside their Towers. They've paid handsomely from the start. Dance well, and you may never have to work again!"

Thyerri jerked the laces tight, and turned to face his employer. Bharlori fell back a step as the light hit his face.

He brushed past Bharlori without answering. No amount of bonus pay could exculpate the abuse he and the others had had to endure already. It would be months before the taste of that searing kiss had left his mouth.

Inside, he appropriated a wineglass destined for that damnable party and drained it, coughed as the unfamiliar sensation flooded his palate, uncertain which was worse, the taste of the alcohol or the taste of Rhyys.

"You will go back, won't you, Thyerri lad? Do this, and by the gods, I'll make you my partner. You're my luck, you know that, don't you? Everything turned face-about for me after you began working here. And your dancing—"

By the gods . . . Thyerri raised his hand to stem the flow of words. His fate was sealed. Had been from the moment Bharlori had issued that first challenge to Rakshi weeks ago. Bharlori had said no one would hurt Thyerri while he was alive. Bharlori had said, lightning could strike his establishment and he would still turn a profit from this night.

And a failed radical dancer was no one's *good* luck.

A wise man never celebrated before the transaction with fate was complete.

He bent his head in acknowledgment of his employer's orders, and relieved a passing boy of the wine jug that was destined, as was Thyerri himself, for the outrageous assemblage.

§   §   §

Mikhyel eased himself into the welcoming warmth of the Barsitumin leythium pool and settled next to Raulind, in a curve of stone worn human-shape by centuries of continuous use. The faintly phosphorescent froth oozed around him, bubbling into his very pores, eliminating the aches and weariness of the past days.

Barsitum and Harriisitum, Barsitum's sister node in the Khoramali Range to the east, were unique among the Rhomatum Web nodes. Above ground, all plant life thrived. Below, the liquid leythium harmed no one, and healed some of those who came to bathe in them.

It wasn't the first time Barsitum's baths had worked their magic for Mikhyel; he'd spent several months here, following his thirteenth birthday, and much of that time had been spent in this very pool.

Raulind had been here, too, that first time, one of the monks who tended the pools, as well as those who came to take advantage of the healing leythium. Afterward, responding to some unspoken agreement between them, he'd accompanied Mikhyel to Rhomatum.

He'd never returned. Mikhyel had never thought to ask if he'd given up his monkish vows. Certainly he'd been welcomed warmly by the monks, but so had Mikhyel been greeted, and those they brought with them.

He would swear the monks recognized Ganfrion.

But then, Ganfrion might well have come here before. The brothers charged little for the use of the node and turned no one in need away. According to local legend, those not in need who tried to abuse the brothers' generosity found themselves overcome with guilt, kept awake in fear of their dreams, and soon they departed of their own free will.

Mikhyel had always believed that legend to be one of the more effective pieces of mass hysteria ever perpetrated.

After having met the creature beneath Rhomatum, he had rather a different perspective.

And he wondered who or what ruled here beneath Barsitum Tower.

That the creature beneath Rhomatum was unique, Mikhyel did not for an instant believe. Deymorin had spoken of "Mother." The creature had spoken of his "children" and asked Mikhyel to tell them their father loved them.

He leaned back into the swirling liquid and . . . called, with that inner voice. There was no answer of the sort he'd come to expect, but the leythium surrounding him glimmered, and an increased sense of well-being seeped into his skin.

Curious.

"Welcome." Raulind's serene voice recalled him to the pool. "Have you come to join us?"

Mikhyel slitted his eyes open, let his eyelash-hazed vision slide toward the path leading into the pool.

Ganfrion.

He shoved himself upright. "What do you want?"

Ganfrion's stance shifted ever so slightly, assuming the careless insolence it had, for a moment, lacked. The dark eyes that had been drawn and (Mikhyel realized in retrospect) a bit uncertain, raked him now with exaggerated interest.

"Nothing I can get here, Suds. I like a bit more meat on the bones I chew. Raul, thanks, but no thanks. I fear this pool would not prove salutary to my ignoble flesh. I'll seek something a bit less rich farther down line."

Ganfrion slung his bathing towel over his shoulder and strode away, down a passage, the soft leylight gleaming on numerous scars beneath the dark hair on his arms and legs, a long scar across the large muscles of a less-hairy back.

He was limping.

"It's good that he get time in the baths," Raulind said. "He's suffered recently, I believe."

"As long as it's not mine."

"Has he, then, correctly judged your attitude? Should I depart to a lesser pool?"

"You know better."

"Do I?"

Chapter Seven

"The time to move is now. The web is dissolving beneath us. If in fact Mikhyel dunMheric is forming a secret union among the Southern Crescent Nodes, it could only be to force the Northern Crescent into accepting this Shatumin witch as the Rhomatumin Ringmaster."

Relieved that, from Rhyys' comment, *his* actions were no longer the center of attention, Thyerri slipped through the shadows to a corner vantage where he could monitor the levels in the wineglasses without himself being noticed.

"Lidye of Shatum cannot control Rhomatum, much less the entire web," Rhyys continued, lecturing as Rhyys was inclined to do. "All our understanding of the ley suggests that, and the current chaos in the power stream supports it."

"And yet, our ringmaster claims the web has stabilized since Persitum dropped out. That the depletion of our node has eased. If, in fact, Anheliaa is dead or dying, as our southern informants suggest, would that not indicate Lidye of Shatum *is* capable?"

"If that were the case, there would be no reason for all this maneuvering on the part of the Rhomandi. These are the acts of desperate men. We must take Rhomatum before the southern radicals gain control of it and through it, destroy every node in the web."

"And if not this Shatumin woman," a red-painted face asked, "if not the Rhomandi, then who? The Shatumin has, at least, the benefit of Anheliaa's training, if not Rhomandi blood. Whom, of Rhomatumin birth, would you set in her place? Inept is better than no control, isn't it?"

"Hardly," Rhyys answered, in the patronizing tone every dancer had learned to hate. "A figurehead all the nodes can respect and trust would mean the ringmasters working as a unified force to create a stable perimeter. The merest technician has been known to monitor the Rhomatum rings since Khoratum's capping."

"But that was before Persitum cut us off," red-face pointed out.

"Precisely." The smooth, new voice emanated from the deep shadows at the table's far end, where a dark-cloaked, hooded figure reclined, a black moth among gaudy butterflies, a mysterious figure that was invariably included in Rhyys' commissioned fantastical paintings. "But with the right master in Rhomatum, who is to say Mauritum will not open its borders to Rhomatum? Perhaps even greet the Syndicate with open arms? With Persitum stable, with Mauritum and Rhomatum united into one great state, who can imagine the heights to which we might rise?"

"Pretty words," another nameless voice said, "but the problems began when Mauritum invaded. The resultant chaos ebbed when Persitum dropped from the web. Is it such a stretch of imagination to hypothesize that Mauritum was the source of the malignancy deteriorating the web?"

"So," the moth replied, "from this, I take it you believe the reports out of Shatum."

A cloth-draped head dipped in acknowledgment.

"And do you also believe, as does this Southern Alliance, that the Rhomandi are clay to be shaped and fired to *your* liking?"

To that, there was no answer ventured.

"At your peril, sirs, at your peril," Rhyys, never one to remain out of a conversation for long, said. "I say Shatum will fall victim to her own naivete."

The moth lifted the ocarshi pipe to the shadows beneath his hood. The food before the shadow-figure lay virtually untouched, his drinking had been moderate, but his ocarshi pipe had never left his hand. Not surprisingly, considering the ugly scars on the fingers cradling that pipe, the only visible skin within the shadow. Ocarshi clouded a man's mind, masking pain with insidious pleasure.

"You sound very certain of that, Khoratum." The words drifted out on a cloud of oily smoke, but the moth's voice was steady, the words clear. "And yet the Shatumin reports of Mikhyel and Deymorin dunMheric have little in common with those individuals you have described."

It happened that way sometimes. Common belief held that ocarshi attacked a man's pain first and his wits after, that if a man in pain could balance consumption, he was overall clearer-headed under the drug's influence.

From the cloud around him, evidently this man's pain was great.

"The Rhomandi are playing us for fools with this talk of Mauritumin invasions," Rhyys said. "Since they've been forced to abdicate the Tower to a non-Rhomandi, they must diminish the importance of the web, if they are to maintain their power within the Syndicate. They are creating fears of outside invaders in order to unite the Syndicate militarily under *their* leadership."

"From what you say," the moth interposed smoothly, "it seems possible, perhaps even probable, that this machine the Rhomandi blame for the collapse was not brought in from Mauritum, but was a Rhomandi ploy to destroy the web—or at least gain time. Another generation, perhaps, with the web in chaotic ebb, to breed another Rhomandi master?"

"Quite." Rhyys' mouth stretched in a wolfish baring of teeth. "If Mikhyel dunMheric plays the fool, it is to lure those he would control to a false sense of superiority. Regardless of what the Shatumin say, Mikhyel dunMheric is not and never was a puppet for Anheliaa. She feared him."

"But if something damaged those much-vaunted wits?" The moth persisted. "There were rumors of illness, you said, even before the Collapse."

"I would not operate on such an assumption. Even were that the case, they have allies Anheliaa feared. She feared Deymorin's Outsider friends and she feared Mikhyel's influence within the Council Hall. Were it the youngest these reports spoke of, Nikaenor, I'd believe them. Anheliaa declared Nikki Princeps precisely because he *was* a fool and she could control him long enough to gain control of his offspring. That's what she planned two years ago, it's what she repeated to me the day of his wedding."

"And why would Anheliaa want a fool in charge of her city? Why would she choose an incompetent to control her precious web?"

"Anheliaa wanted the Shatumin as a broodmare for a Rhomandi child, nothing more. She planned to live long enough to raise that child as her replacement."

"She took her time about it."

"She'd planned for the eldest to marry years ago and

produce an heir for the Tower. She finally had to force the issue last fall. At Nikaenor's wedding, she believed she had succeeded in separating Nikaenor from the others. That Deymorin and Mikhyel left Nikaenor in charge at home, indicates a solidarity of purpose among the Rhomandi brothers and with the Rhomatum Council that would indeed ignite Anheliaa's greatest anger—and fear."

"Fear? Why should Anheliaa fear anything?"

"She risked death capping Khoratum to seal the web against them and their ley-blind influence. She'd risk death again rather than release control to them while she was alive, and she'd risk no few other lives to keep the web safe from them after her death. Do you think it an accident that Anheliaa chose wives for them who could both keep the Rhomatum Rings spinning and ally House Rhomandi with the greatest Houses of Shatum and Giephaetum? She knew the rift beginning in the web. *She* knew there was greater danger from within than from without. She could feel it in the rings, and wanted to ensure the nodes would remain loyal."

"And yet, Nethaalye returned home unwed," another voice cried out angrily. "Anheliaa chose a Shatumin as her heir, and insulted the Northern Crescent. Is this the act of a woman intending to solidify the web?"

"Your cousin returned home on her own, Giephaetum," Rhyys sneered. "Had she had more sense, she'd have stayed there and ministered to a Shatumin witch, if that was required to stay in Rhomatum Tower."

"Damn your—"

"I thought we were here to celebrate our solidarity," the moth's voice, still soft, managed nonetheless to overpower the other two. "Might I suggest we avoid insulting one another?"

The Giephaetumin leaned back, eyes closed, breathing heavily. Rhyys drained his glass, then gestured angrily for its replenishment.

"You are right to chastise," the Giephaetum said at last and with a nod toward the moth. "It is the Rhomandi we must depose, not one another. Not even Shatum."

"And if the Rhomandi are correct?" red-face asked. "If Mauritum *is* making a move to control the Rhomatum Web, wouldn't it make sense for us to unite against Mauritum?"

"Under the Rhomandi?" Rhyys sniggered. "The breed has died out. We must take Rhomatum now, unite the web under a powerful leader. *That* will stop any notions Mauritum may have. Which I do not for a moment entertain. Mauritum will support us. The Rhomandi have always been the source of opposition to Mauritum. Anheliaa was the final Rhomandi gasp for survival, and now she's gone. The time to move is now. If Giephaetum joins with us, if we can bring Persitum back in, we'll have by far the majority of the web and the Southern Crescent won't stand a chance. They'll know that. They'll bend to wisdom and join us, and *we'll* choose who rules Rhomatum. We'll choose a princeps with the power to rule the rings, not cater to special interests."

"And who would you set in that exalted position, Khoratum? Yourself?"

"Hardly. *I* am master of Khoratum. But there are those—"

"Who?"

"The ringmasters of the satellites will choose."

"Ah. Then you intend for the ringmasters to rule us."

"I didn't say—"

"Any such appointment will, I am quite certain, be subject to Syndicate approval, Orenum," the moth cut in smoothly. "And, ultimately, I should imagine Rhomatum herself—the rings, not the city—will make the choice. You speak in past tense of the Rhomatum Ringmaster, Khoratum. Do you, then, believe that part of the rumor?"

"Painful as that loss is, I believe she must be." Rhyys' voice caught, and he dabbed at his eyes with a stained finger towel. "I thought I would know for certain when she fell from the web, but it seems otherwise."

Thyerri stared into the locarshi smoke that was said to hold images of lost ones to one who would see them. It was also said that when a person died and was immersed in the ley, their soul became a part of the web. But perhaps that was only to appease the grieving souls yet living.

The smoke made his eyes burn. He blinked them free of cleansing tears, only to realize everyone was staring at him.

"What did you say?" Rhyys asked, and Thyerri realized he must have spoken aloud.

He bent his head and answered quickly, quietly, "Forgive

me, honorables, I meant no disrespect. I was only thinking—"

"I asked *what* you said, dolt, not why you said it!"

Thyerri's hands clenched on the double-handled ewer. "It's the ancient wisdom, sir. If the scent of Anheliaa remains in the web, it might be because her body has been consumed, but not her soul." He kept his voice low, hoping it would not betray the contempt he felt.

"Anheliaa's . . . scent?" Rhyys rose slowly to his feet, and Thyerri looked up, realized his mistake when he couldn't look away, wouldn't deny the challenging gaze. "Why do you describe it that way?"

Thyerri backed away, seeking the limits of his territory, discovered the table much too close.

"Please, m'lord, Thyerri didn't mean anything by it!" Sakhithe ran between them. "He's of the hills and they talk that way all the time. Please, m'lord, don't be—"

Rhyys turned his glower on her; she blanched and staggered back a step, but caught herself and stood her ground, lifting her chin defiantly. Thyerri put her gently behind him, facing Rhyys alone, resigned to whatever fate was his. He'd known since Bharlori first boasted about his fortune that tonight was doomed.

"Sit down, dunTarec," a slurred voice ordered. "The boy's just spouting hiller nonsense."

Rhyys turned on his company. "Don't tell me what to do, dunErrif. That's *exactly* what it's like. Anheliaa's *scent* is still in the web. Tell me how a damned servant knows such a thing!"

"The girl explained that. Besides, I thought we were celebrating tonight."

"A point well taken, Giephaetum," the moth murmured. "So, do we celebrate Giephaetum's alliance? *Will* your sire join the Northern Crescent against the Rhomandi?"

"He arrives tomorrow, sir, to partake fully of this Radical Dance Festival our host is sponsoring. You can ask him yourself."

Casting Thyerri a final intimidating glance, Rhyys threw himself back into his pillows, snatched the ocarshi pipe from his neighbor's hand and took a long pull, holding the potent smoke in his lungs for several long seconds, eyes closed, before expelling it very slowly, pausing to reinhale through his nose that which he had exhaled from his mouth.

Thyerri turned his face to the shadows to mask his revulsion. Addicts came in many forms. Those like the moth, who indulged to keep pain at bay, dancers who had lost the dance, to keep the memories at bay. Rhyys' life contained no such pain, either physical or mental. Those like Rhyys simply gloried in the expanded sense of power the smoke gave them.

"To the alliance!" Rhyys' voice rose, and a chorus of voices answered him, and goblets crashed and shattered throughout the room.

"Another round!" The shout filled the room. And as Thyerri and the others hurried to replace the discarded goblets: "To innocent dupes!" Which roused laughter and a response: "To Mauritum!" And: "To the Rhomandi coastal watch."

The laughter and the toasts grew increasingly outrageous, and for a time, Thyerri and the others were kept busy refilling cups and chasing after more wine. For everyone but the moth. The man in the dark cloak sat back, raising his cup, but not drinking. And soon, he ceased making even that gesture, turning instead to his pipe.

"Where are those dancers Bharlori promised?" someone shouted.

Another voice added, "Tell him to send in the boy. Tobinsi said he's better than a Varkisin window whore."

Thyerri stiffened. Bharlori had said nothing about promises, and *he* had no desire to perform for this drug-stupid audience.

But before he could slip out, Mishthi, in an attempt to bring them back into grace with the man paying the gratuity, dropped to the floor beside Rhyys, in a cloud of silver-and-rose silk, and whispered breathlessly: "We *are* the dancers, m'lord. And Thyerri, he's the most wonderful of all."

Thyerri swallowed his protest, and took another step toward the bead-obscured passageway.

But Rhyys seemed interested only in Mishthi. Rhyys cupped her chin in one hand and turned her this way and that. "I'll take your word for it, girl." He released her and sat back. "Stand up. Let's have a look at you." She hurried to obey; he traced a circle with his finger through the air and she turned slowly. "Well, let's see what you can do."

He waved his hand at the musicians. Mishthi searched

the room, smiled when she saw Thyerri and rushed to his side, hands held out.

"No," he said flatly and strode openly toward the doorway. But two large men barred his escape. Two men attired as outrageously as he, only in steel and leather, and bearing swords and knives they undoubtedly knew how to use.

He whirled, outraged. "I'm no slave, Rhyys dunTarec," he hissed, not caring if he destroyed their illusions. "I dance when I please."

"Not tonight, my feisty little friend," the velvet voice from under the hood answered him, and something in that tone chilled Thyerri in a way Rhyys could never have done.

"I don't understand," he muttered, and though the quiver in his voice shamed him, he couldn't cure it. "Bharlo said—"

"Bharlori sold you for the night, child. For tonight, you *are*, for all intents and purposes, our slave."

"Bharlori!" Thyerri shouted and bolted for the door. A bold move that might have worked, had it not been for the gods-be-damned fringe and his ocarshi-dulled reflexes. One guard caught a handful of fringe, a well-timed jerk made him stumble into the hold of the second, and in another heartbeat, he was immobilized between them, facing a derisive, laughing Rhyys.

"Bharlo!" he shouted again, and Rhyys snarled and back-handed him across the face. But Thyerri only fought harder, letting the man-mountains support his weight, kicking at anything his sandaled feet could encounter, convinced if he made enough noise, Bharlori would come and end this farce once and finally.

"Settle down, boy, I'm here." Bharlori's voice, weary and chagrined. "Please, m'lord, release him. He'll behave. *Won't* you, Thyerri?"

"No . . ." he whispered, shaking his head in disbelief. "I mean, yes, of course, I will. I just want to leave." His voice trailed off as he realized that his freedom was not Bharlori's first priority. The pressure on his arms eased, and he could have escaped. Instead, he stood there, shaking in anger and betrayal.

"Is it true, then?" he asked in the whisper that was all the voice he could find.

"Just to dance, lad. It's a game. Play it well, and I'll make it worth your while, I promise you."

For a moment, Thyerri had no voice at all. Then: "And my pride? Can you buy that back for me as well?"

Bharlori frowned, then turned to Rhyys. "Please, m'lord, may I talk with him in private a moment?"

"You know what it means if he doesn't come back?"

"Of course, m'lord."

Rhyys shrugged, and turned away. "Make it fast, ale-slinger."

Bharlori's frown darkened, but he took Thyerri's elbow in a numbing grip and pulled him into the passage.

"Ale-slinger?" Thyerri's anger exploded in the word. "Are you just going to take that from—"

"Understand, boy. Pride is a luxury only the powerful can afford. You and I, we have no power, therefore we have no pride. Survival, a modicum of comfort. *That's* what the likes of us hope for. If you refuse now, it's over for both of us. These men came here because of you. The reputation *your* dancing has given Bharlori's Tavern. Now, either you deliver, or we're both ruined."

Betrayed twice in a single evening. He shuddered, fearing what the third might be. A pattern had begun, budded in that careless challenge to Rakshi, and he feared nothing could halt its fruition.

Bharlori searched his face, then turned away, slumped and broken. Bharlori, who had given Thyerri a home, a haven, when the rest of the world rejected him, who had fed him, clothed him, and given him back his dance. His soul.

Thyerri placed a hand on the old man's shoulder, intending to head down the passage in his stead, then hesitated as Bharlori's paw covered it. And Bharlori's face was bright with relief.

"It's just a dance, Thyerri."

Thyerri stared at him. "Just a dance? Bharlo, I'm a *dancer*."

But the words meant nothing to an old man, who had worked hard all his life, had played more than fair with his employees, and saw a means now to secure all their futures.

Thyerri clenched his jaw against the anger, or perhaps it was tears that threatened, and slid his hand free.

ᘜ   ᘜ   ᘜ

(The cloaked figure slunk toward him. Dark, enigmatic . . .
(Deadly. Instinct warned.

(Fate, closing in, reflected in a thousand iridescent mirrors.)

"M'lord? Khyel!" A hand on his shoulder gently wakened him.

He jumped: a spasm that encompassed his entire body. Raulind. Not . . . fate.

"My apologies, sir," Raulind said, his voice very low. "You fell asleep. Would you care to go to bed?"

He nodded, his throat too tight for words. He let Raulind's hands guide him from the pool, stood passively while Raulind set the robe about his shoulders.

But as he left the pool cavern, as he rounded a curve in the path, something drew his attention back to the pool . . .

And a figure. Dark-cloaked. With glints of green where the eyes should be.

"Raul?" he whispered. "Do you see him?"

"Dreams, master Khyel. Come to bed."

Mikhyel blinked, and the figure was gone.

He shuddered, and let Raulind draw him up the stairs.

Chapter Eight

The musicians saw him first.

They'd been trying to shift the mood with the sultry *Karlindra,* an amorphous melody that had the women oozing about the floor. Thyerri picked it up, reluctantly, feeling nothing, his heart deaf to the flute's breathy seduction.

But the flute mocked him, weaving its tones in and around his awkward, listless movements, sending a fluttering trill across the room to infiltrate his arm and turn muscle and bone to rippling water; the drum insinuated a muted but insistent rhythm, and Thyerri was lost. He could no more stop his body from responding to that musical temptation than he could stop his heart from beating.

The music shepherded him gently around the room's perimeter; he eddied in and oozed back out of the central mound of cloth, pillows and bodies, like a stream seeking passage.

He teased the edge of the mountain, but he didn't wend among its living folds. He wasn't a torrent, to deluge them in sensation and run downhill. He was a spring-fed stream, irresistibly eroding, certain, in the end, to find his own way to wherever he wanted to go.

And as he turned, dipped and slipped away, all other motion within the room slowed and stopped; all eyes shifted toward him.

Power. Pride. Bharlori had said those weren't his. But what was this, if not power? What drove him now, except pride?

And as he tempted and refused, demanded and denied, he sensed a shifting response in his own body, a heated desire akin to those hated, late-night dreams. Akin, but not the same. This desire, this arousal was of the mind, not of the body. Driven by anger, not lust.

Thyerri had never danced in anger before. And out of

anger grew cold intent. Determination to prove to Rhyys and that shadowed moth that they didn't own him, could never own him, and certainly could never control that which made him alive.

And that was *his* power, he realized as he swayed backward over that hooded moth, sending the strands of his hair to infiltrate the shadow beneath the hood: he was alive as they would not, could not be. And his body mocked them, his movements grew increasingly complex, contorted in ways he knew were awesome, yet beautiful.

You can't buy this, his actions cried out. You've committed your life to lesser pursuits, you've stifled your body and your soul with petty goals, and you'll never be what I am. Never have what I have. Never *feel* what this body can feel.

Desire permeated the room. Self-loathing did. Strangely, rather than assuage Thyerri's anger, his petty triumph fed it.

To use his talent to cause pain and arouse desire was to prostitute it as surely as those window-whores they'd compared him to. But it was Rhyys' self-hate and Rhyys' bitterness tearing Rhyys apart, and Rhyys had denied him the life he'd been born to live, had forced him to waste that gift the Ley Mother had given him. Rhyys had brought him to this. If prostituting his dance could destroy Rhyys, it was well worth the sacrifice.

But it was himself he destroyed, something deep within him cried, not Rhyys, not the moth nor any of these others. They already *knew* their fetid depths. They were consumers of life, not creators, and they were content with that role. *Proud* of it.

On that realization, he drew himself upright, a writhing undulation that ended in a snap and extended clear to his fingertips. Tightening his body, he caught the drumbeat between his hands and reformed it, finger-snapping it into a faster, more complex rhythm.

And without his conscious willing, that rhythm took the form of the challenge dance of the half-mad folk of Goshtari Valley. A challenge, man to man, woman to woman, man to woman—or just oneself against the gods. Power against power. Skill against skill. Daring against daring.

Thyerri had heard the rhythms frequently as a child, had seen others dance, proud and tall, silhouettes against bonfires. He'd never danced those rhythms, though the musi-

cians had teased him nightly with its tantalizing
complexities. But his feet and his body responded now with
instincts evolved out of the mountains themselves.

A whirl. A stomp. A sudden pose that held the music in
suspension. *He* drove the music. *He* controlled the room.

This was no seduction, the most drug-blind man in the
room knew that. The mood changed, darkened. The viewers were still captives of his visual spell, but the men recognized the challenge, and as men, responded. Their hands
created new rhythms, tried to seize control, to punish, but
Thyerri's feet stole it back. Their voices tried to break his
concentration, grasping hands tried to trip him.

He denied them all.

Until at last, hands and voices conceded, and he controlled the room, utterly and without compromise. He had
won, honestly, as the gods measured such things.

And even as his mind reveled in that realization, his own
human frailty brought him down. Muscle and bone had
limitations the spirit did not always acknowledge. He knew,
a heartbeat away, that the end had come, whirled into an
open spot and with a shout of sheer triumph, collapsed.

Exhaustion, total and debilitating. The vitality flowed out
of him, leaving him empty, and he was consumed with a
lassitude horribly reminiscent of the dreams, a satiation that
distorted his victory, warped it away from his purpose.

And in that distortion he knew, as he lay there, twisted,
joints screaming from the contorted position, unable to
move, the only sound in the room his own harsh gasps
after breath, that what he'd just done was terribly, horribly,
unforgivably wrong.

🌀   🌀   🌀

Shame engulfed him. Guilt, overwhelming guilt, unfocused and painful.

Mikhyel groaned and rolled upright on the sleeping
pallet.

"M'lord? Are you well?" Raulind's voice, from the shadowed depths.

"I'm . . . fine," he murmured, for all he wasn't certain
that was true.

Overhead, the curved ceiling of the Barsitumin caves
glowed silver, light reflected off the bathing pools. There

were no buildings in Barsitum. Not even a Tower. The rings were in the deepest cavern, the monks, and all their visitors slept within the caves.

The mother's womb, the brothers called it.

He shuddered.

"I don't, you know," he said to Raul.

"Don't what, sir?"

"Think I'm better than you. Or Ganfrion."

"I know, sir. So does Gan. Go to sleep, sir. Morning comes early for the brothers."

�S   �S   �S

"Interesting," the velvet voice caressed the air of the room, and stole back the moment. "Is this a common talent among your hill-folk?"

A choking sound that might have been Rhyys, a rustling of cloth and clinking of pottery and metal as the guests strove to return some normalcy to the moment.

Thyerri made an effort, managed to straighten one leg, but no more. He curled over, crossed arms pressed to his aching middle, terrified at what he might have done to his own body in that mindless battle.

Once, legend held, challenges had been to the death.

"Remove him," Rhyys' nasal tones cut through the ringing in Thyerri's ears, and before he'd registered the sounds' meaning, the huge vices he associated with the manmountains' hands had jerked him upright. They dragged him to the perimeter, where he tried to take his own weight as they released him, but his numb legs failed, and he went down again.

He'd have curled there, gladly, and slept, or passed out, but Sakhithe was beside him, urging him to sit up and drink something he couldn't identify, his mouth being as senseless as the rest of him.

Somewhere in the room, Rhyys was shouting for the musicians to play and the women to dance. "Something entertaining this time," he added sullenly, and Sakhithe, with a whispered, *"Sorry, Thyerri,"* left him.

The guards had dropped him near the servant passage and the only chilling draft in the close air of the room. He curled into a ball and tucked his face into his elbow, shivering, trying to forget what he'd done, knowing the fact that he *had* done it, the fact that he'd allowed his darkest inner self to drive his dance proved what he'd feared every morning since that first dream.

A radical dancer could never lose control like that. Lives were lost that way. A radical dance captivated an audience and glorified the dance and Rakshi and the very essence of life. A radical dancer never willfully used the gift to conquer those darker sides and rouse those other senses.

"I don't know, Khoratum. Even a mediocre horse gets a blanket after a hard ride."

It was the velvet voice, and speaking from directly overhead. Thyerri started awake and struggled to rise to his feet, but a heavy darkness fell over him in smothering folds and the added weight was more than his chilled muscles could fight. Ocarshi-laden though it was, the cloak was warm, and he huddled in that warmth, trying to feel gratitude and finding that civilized emotion too far from his reach.

"Well?" A booted toe found him through the folds, nudged him, pressed deeper into his gut when he ignored it, and gave a vicious jab before leaving him. "Ungrateful bastard."

Thyerri raised his head. The man's face, what he could see past the tangle of his own hair and the near-full mask the man wore, was as deeply scarred as his hands.

"Which should I do, scarface?" he croaked, his voice rough and sore. "Snort, whinny, or stomp?"

An audible gasp: anticipation of the scarred man's response. And indeed, he did scowl for a long moment, but then, his mouth stretched in what must have been a painful smile.

"Where did you come from, dancer?"

Thyerri winced. But it was a cavalier jibe, the velvet voice was not native, could have no idea what being a dancer meant here in the Khoramali heights.

But then, neither had Bharlori known. Zelin had said no one truly knew. No one, except the dancers themselves.

"I arose from the ley," he hissed bitterly.

Scarred laughter sounded as pained as the smile. "Is that how the local whores explain their accidents?"

"You'd have to ask them."

"Oh, leave the sewage be," Rhyys snarled impatiently. "Stand up, ley-child. You're out of place down there."

Thyerri tried again, and discovering cloak-warmed muscles more inclined to obey, even managed to rise with some grace.

"Join me." Without looking to see if his command was obeyed, the scarred man returned to his shadowed niche. Thyerri, in defiance of Rhyys, followed, and sank onto the pillow a wave of scarred hand vacated for him.

Rhyys glowered, and threw himself back into a nest of pillows and snarled at the musicians, who, after a false start or two, settled into a standard court set piece.

Scarface lifted a finger toward the food. "Help yourself, dancer." And when Thyerri hesitated: "Renew yourself." Which was far more order than invitation. "I would see more of your talent before I leave."

He tried a handful of the strange foods, but found few to his liking. His mouth was miserably dry, but he rarely drank wine, and the heavy drink being served tonight clung to his tongue like the ocarshi clung to velvet.

A goblet appeared over his shoulder, pewter, cool to the touch, its contents fresh to nose and palate: his favorite fruit juice. He twisted and found, as he'd thought he would, Sakhithe.

"I'm sorry," he began, but she stopped him with a fingertip on his lips and an eager smile. "Didn't Mishthi say they'd like you, Thyerri?"

He caught her hand. "Dance with me? Later, when my legs are back?"

"Any time," she whispered back. "Any time at all, with or without legs."

Angry demands from further down the table called her away, eliminating the need to answer.

"Your lover?" the velvet voice asked.

"No!"

"Why so shocked? You're a handsome lad. I'd think you had a dozen such awaiting your pleasure."

"Because we're both—" Except they weren't. And he supposed, if he were to have a lover, Sakhithe might be his first choice. The thought shocked him anew with the pleasant feelings the thought of her, skin against skin, aroused.

He was too raw tonight, the insidious dreams become too frequent, the horror of his dance too fresh in his mind.

"Your interests lie, perhaps, in other directions?"

"You might say that."

"And is your affection rewarded?"

Thyerri thought of the rings and the stadium, vaguely aware they spoke at cross-purposes, but the pain of inaccessibility was real either way, and he shook his head.

"The one who rejects you is a fool, lad." That velvet voice stripped him more effectively than Rhyys' insidious hands. "Were you willing, man, woman, or beast would find you, I think, a memorable partner."

Thyerri twitched, concentrated only on keeping the cup in his hands steady.

"Perhaps unwilling would be even better." This time, the velvet was so deep, so soft, Thyerri doubted anyone heard but himself. He swallowed hard, suspecting bait, but deep in a game for which he had no rules.

"You overreact," Rhyys snarled. "He's adequate, I'll grant you that, but for real dancing, wait until you see Tabinth dance the rings. She'll have your loins in an uproar, I grant you."

"And when will that be, Khoratum?" a voice rang out. "When will the rings once again dance the Khoratum skies?"

"Soon, Orenum, very soon. We await only the arrival of our guest of honor."

"The Rhomandi?"

"Mikhyel dunMheric," the moth said. "We would do well not to mistake the level of the honor we are being granted."

"His may be the lesser power," the Giephaetumin said, "but Mikhyel dunMheric is the more insightful individual. We must be cautious."

"The celebration will keep him distracted," Rhyys declared loftily. "And when it is done, we'll have a new radical dancer, and you'll see I'm right: Tabinth will take the vote. But you can't touch her." Rhyys gave a theatrical sigh and inhaled deeply on his pipe, blew the smoke out across his wine, and drank with exaggerated pleasure. "Can't touch any of the ringdancers. No one can. Not even Khoratum's master." Another sip. "Sometimes I truly hate the traditions."

Thyerri added one more count against Rhyys.

"I should think," the scarred man murmured, "that the inaccessibility would be half her charm. Absent that, what is she but simply another body with clever moves?"

But he was looking at Thyerri, not Rhyys, as he spoke, and the bread in Thyerri's mouth turned to sawdust. He choked, blindly sought relief, felt his goblet pressed into his hand, and gulped—

Only to discover not the fruit juice he'd expected, but the cloying spiced wine.

He cast the goblet away, not caring where it landed, found his own cup, and finished the juice. His head cleared to another shocked silence.

Freezing in mid-swallow, he scanned the immediate vicinity over the pewter rim of his cup, coming finally to scarred fingers swinging a bronze goblet by its base. Upside-down.

But again the obviously important man failed to provide the anticipated explosion. "I should have known better," was all he said, and the spell was broken. Sakhithe rushed over with towels, and when the worst of the wine had been blotted from his robes, the moth's scarred hand caught her wrist, keeping her at his side. "Well, boy, have your legs recovered?"

ଜ   ଜ   ଜ

Music flowed through him, lifting, caressing, as perfect, in its way, as the ley in which his body drifted.

{Yes-s-s, Mikhyel, son of Darius . . .}

{Where?} he asked, in a dream that smelled of raspberries and cinnamon and fireblossom-tea.

{Feel the music, human spawn, dance the rings, fly with the rhythm of the ley . . .}

{Who?}

{All and none. Tell them, I love them. Come to me . . .}

The voice faded. The music swelled.

And the dance began.

ଜ   ଜ   ଜ

This time, like the musicians, he and Sakhithe chose a safe course, a standard piece that told a simple tale of love lost and found. It was a choreography all the dancers, radical or troupe, learned, and a piece he and Sakhithe had practiced for fun in the off-hours.

But if Thyerri no longer challenged his audience, his audience remembered their defeat. They sensed his weakened resolve, his lowered defenses, and as the final strains of the familiar music wove themselves around him, and Sakhithe "died" in his arms, a hand caught his ankle and a leg swept his feet from under him.

He crashed to the floor, angling his body to protect Sakhithe. She squealed, and fought for balance and freedom, caught his face with her elbow, and his groin with her heel.

For a moment, the world blackened. By the time it cleared, he was adrift in a sea of mauling hands and glittering robes. Shrill cries in every direction indicated others in similar jeopardy. Sticky hands roamed across him, leaving honey-sauce in their passing. Laughter and lewd suggestions, and the heated potion dribbled over his stomach.

It was as if he were caught in that endless instant between sleep and waking. He wanted to move. Wanted to run, to escape the sensations building inside him, and lacked the ability to twitch so much as an eyelid. The dreams chased him, swallowed him in green mist.

And he knew that if anything of himself was to survive this night, he had to conquer that lassitude. But the green mist rose, and the Tamshi eyes claimed him, and the hands were the hands of his dreams. . . .

Then, a hand smeared the sauce across his flank and under his loincloth. The Tamshi eyes widened, and a voice screamed denial—

And the immobility vanished. Thyerri scrambled across the table, scattering plates and food, seeking freedom, not caring what he struck, kicked or ran over to find it. His fingers found and flung plates, closed on a knife, that bit into soft folds and stuck. He left it and sought other weapons, finding a rhythm like the dance, counterbalances to the various objects that became weapons in his hands.

His feet struck bare floor somewhere near the disguised door, and he staggered to a halt, a floor candelabra balanced in both hands. A man groaned and cried for help. Red-face. A knife with a jeweled hilt rose and fell with his shuddering breaths; a pool of red spread beneath him.

The others backed away, Sakhithe and Mishthi held captive, silent in their arms.

A guard took a crouched half-step toward him. Thyerri swung the base of the stand in a warding arc before him, and the man straightened, hands raised in surrender.

Then, all in a time-stopped moment, Rhyys' gaze looked

beyond him; an angry voice growled: *"What's going on—"* and a hand gripped his elbow. Thyerri jerked, dodged and swept the iron stand in an arc around him.

With a halt that numbed his hands and elbows, the cast-iron legs encountered an obstacle at once hard and yielding. The stand fell from his fingers. A shrill, female cry filled the room, and Bharlori, his face a barely recognizable mass of bloodied flesh, staggered and fell, his clutching hands seeking purchase, finding brocade draperies, carrying them down with him.

Drapes toppled, one after another, a cascade of brocades, velvets and filmy cotton gauze, scattering oil lamps, ocarshi stands and candles. Gauze flared, and in an instant, flames erupted throughout the room.

ᔕ   ᔕ   ᔕ

(Lightning arced.
(Flames consumed.
(Pain and darkness, fear and panic, horror and—
(Guilt.)
Patricide.
Mikhyel jerked awake, shuddering, his throat sore.

"Khyel?" Raulind's voice, and Raulind's arms surrounded him, as they had all those years ago, when he'd awakened screaming, in pain, in fear, and with the certain knowledge that but for him, Mheric, his father, would still be alive.

And Mikhyel wondered, was it Barsitum, renowned for healing, that was sending him these reminders of his own culpability, or his own unforgiving nature. And he remembered those legends of this place, of the fate of those who took advantage of it, and wondered if he'd been judged . . .

And found lacking.

Chapter Nine

("Murderer!"

(Blood and flames. Flaming blood. Face of blood and bone. Glint of gold. Spark of blue. Stone-set hilt rising, falling—keeping time with labored breath.

("Murderer!"

(Flame flaring, wave upon obscuring wave.

(Face of blood and bone. Hands pulling, pushing.

("Murderer!"

(Face of blood and bone.

("I can't leave him!"

("He's dead, Thyerri."

("Murderer!"

(Flood of water.

(Protection. Panacea for the body . . .

(But nothing for the soul.

("Murderer!")

"Murder . . ."

The accusation filled the air, a whisper whipped back to him in the roaring wind.

A sob, buried in a shivering crook of arm. Rough stone riddled his back, bit deeper as he pushed back, fighting to escape the wind—and the memories.

He told himself it was over. Bharlori's was gone. Bharlo was. And dead meant gone forever, never mind the dreams.

("Murderer!")

He jumped, searching wildly. But the scream rose out of his dreams, not the streets below.

Dreams. He'd let his guard slip, let himself drift off. That was stupid. He hadn't seen or heard a search party in hours, but that didn't mean Rhyys had given up.

Murderer. He didn't know how many had died at his hands. Bharlo, was certain. The man he'd knifed in his mad rush to the door, that was likely as well. Of the others, of the fire, it didn't matter. Rhyys wanted someone to blame; that someone might as well be Thyerri, ex-dancer of Bharlori's.

And Thyerri *was* to blame. That was the true horror. Bharlo was dead, and by his hand, no one else's. He'd tried, tried so hard to save the man that was the closest thing to a father he'd ever known. His back still throbbed with the pain of trying to carry the owner's large body from the flames.

But Sakhithe had thrown a cloak that reeked of ocarshi over him and Sakhithe had made him leave Bharlo, the flames . . . made him leave . . . everything. And she'd been with him, but then she was gone, ripped from his clinging fingers, and Rhyys was screaming invective and accusations at him, through the smoke and the fire that had spread to other buildings.

He'd run, then, mindless in his panic, seeking only to escape those who had responded to Rhyys, those seeking someone to blame for the devastation around them.

He'd struck and thrust. Perhaps killed again: there was a knife hilt in his hand now. Not the jeweled one, just plain leather and seviceable steel. Though it might as well have been that other knife. He'd pulled that free, but dropped it when the blood had fountained and he'd tried to stanch it with his hands.

Perhaps he'd killed, perhaps just intended to kill himself. There was blood on the plain knife, and a wound in his side that throbbed in the cold wind and with his every shuddering breath.

The glacial wind whipped hair and fringe until the ends shredded him like a flail's lash. He tightened his hold on the plain hilt and slashed mindlessly until nothing touched his body except the ruthlessly honest wind that carried away hair and fringe alike.

The long dark strands flying away failed to rouse any sense of loss. He'd dyed his hair after the competition, made it black as night, trying to become something he was not. Trying to hide who and what he'd been, but to cut it, that had been admitting too much, admitting he'd never dance the rings again.

Now, it just didn't seem to matter.

Nothing seemed to matter any more.

Bharlo was dead.

Perhaps Sakhithe was, as well.

He'd found a home, only to lose it again. Except he hadn't lost it. He'd destroyed it.

The cloak lay beside him, useless where it was, except that by its absence from his shoulders, he might freeze to his death. But most likely, he'd only become increasingly uncomfortable, unable to move, until They found him and dragged him away and refused to ever let him die, forcing him to remember all he'd been and all he'd done.

Except that the fire *wasn't* his fault. The *fire* never had been his fault, and he wouldn't let them make it that way, wouldn't passively accept the sentence of lifelong guilt they intended to lay upon his soul.

Bharlori had challenged Rakshi and lost. Bharlori had made a pact with a cruel and evil and stupid man, and tragedy had occurred.

His guilt lay elsewhere. His guilt lay in anger and pride. He should never have danced. Should never have gone back into that room, knowing his soul was already compromised.

Fighting the wind for possession, he got the heavy fabric over his shoulders, and curled the flapping edges over his knees, and himself around his quivering, empty gut.

The fire was out. The shouting had stopped. Bharlo was dead, his gamble with Rakshi's whim was over.

But Thyerri's own challenge, his desecration of his gift . . . would Rakshi consider that debt settled? If so, perhaps now it would be safe to sleep.

Perhaps now, the nightmares would stay away.

§ § §

"He's bolted." The smug, dry tone could have been Deymorin, but it wasn't. "Consider yourself fortunate, m'lord dunMheric, and hope he keeps his mouth shut on your business."

Mikhyel pressed his lips over the retort that rose instinctively to the Deymorin-like provocation, replied instead and calmly: "It certainly appears that way, Ori. Nonetheless, instruct the stable manager to watch for him, and to send him to Brother Riner for direction." He threw his Guard Captain what he hoped was a knowing glance. "In case he's been . . . held up again."

"Held up? In *Barsitum*? M'lord, there's not a brothel within a day's ride of here!"

So much for knowing. Mikhyel clamped his jaw, and hoped the heat in his face wasn't visible here in the shadowed opening of the cave.

"Get the men mounted," he ordered and retreated inside to tell his own small staff that they were, indeed, leaving, and to give his final respects to the monks who had saved his life years ago, and whose small, but vital node had been his rejuvenating home for the past few days.

Ganfrion was gone. According to Ori, the mercenary had disappeared two days ago, a fact Ori had kept to himself until this morning, when the time came to leave and Ganfrion still hadn't returned.

But Mikhyel couldn't blame the captain for that omission. By his own order, Ganfrion had been free to roam as he pleased, his only duty to wander the streets—or in the case of Barsitum, the underground baths—and listen. If that duty kept him out of the barracks late, or even overnight, Ori had been under instructions not to challenge him.

The captain hadn't liked that. Hadn't *liked* including Ganfrion in the entourage any more than Deymorin had. And likely he was right. Likely Deymorin was. Likely Ganfrion *was* a liability, with his attitudes that bordered on disrespect and highly questionable contacts—attributes which had, of course, been his primary value. Now he was gone, in all likelihood selling who-knew-what information to who-knew-whom.

Mikhyel didn't know why he should expect otherwise; he'd always known gut instinct made a bad adviser.

Of course, even if he *had* judged Ganfrion correctly, Ganfrion's leaving *still* made a certain sense. He'd hired the man to look into shadows, to be his eyes and ears in places he couldn't go.

Hired him, and then ignored him . . . even, truthfully, shunned his company.

Before Shatum, there'd been no time. And then, Deymorin had joined them and Deymorin and Ori had made it eminently clear to Ganfrion that he wasn't going to be trusted, regardless of what Mikhyel had promised. His brother's ability to come between Ganfrion and himself must have made it all too obvious to Ganfrion that the man who had hired him had no power to enforce his plans.

He'd had his chance, that first night here in Barsitum. He *could* have offered Ganfrion a friendly invitation. Instead, he'd made it clear to Ganfrion with every comment, every suspicious glance, that his presence was merely tolerated among civilized men, not welcomed.

Civilized. He imagined Ganfrion had a much different term for his employer and his ilk.

After the incident in the baths, there'd been no reason for Ganfrion to see his employer as anything other than another too-rich, too-self-centered Syndic he could bend to his advantage, to free himself from prison (yet again), to put money in his pocket, and give him a free ride to his next den of iniquity.

Under the circumstances, he'd leave himself.

He supposed he should organize a search party, issue a warrant. But he wouldn't. He'd not penalize Ganfrion for *his* bad judgment.

The odds had been long, Mikhyel had known that from the start, and when one gambled, one had to be prepared to lose. One simply reminded oneself that the primary function of this trip had been official posing, not true information, and one proceeded with the posing and the passing about of papers and was content.

Or so he told the disillusion that tightened his throat and sharpened his voice as he made his good-byes to the good monks of Barsitum, and climbed into the carriage that would take him across Persitum ley and on into the Northern Crescent.

And as the carriage lurched into motion, he found himself searching the distance, questioning his judgment again, wondering if Ganfrion hadn't bolted but gotten into serious trouble . . . somewhere. He couldn't see Ganfrion simply leaving. Ganfrion would have a point to make, a final insult to throw.

On the other hand, possibly he'd been overly influenced by Ganfrion's diverse and colorful history and had imbued the man with qualities of his own desire rather than made a rational analysis of character.

Mikhyel cursed softly and pulled the shade across the back window, cutting off the retreating view.

"Not your concern, master Khyel," Raulind said, from his forward seat. "Gan has been on his own from the beginning. You made that perfectly clear, and he was more than content with that autonomy. If he's in trouble now, it's his *job* to extricate himself."

Mikhyel laughed wryly. "Tell me, Raul, how long have you been able to read my mind?"

"Since the day I carried you into the womb, child."

It was an old joke between them, but this time, the answer had new meaning. Even the remote humor vanished as suspicion swelled.

"No, Khyel," Raul assured him gently, "Not as you hear your brothers. Just as someone who cared enough to listen and watch and remember. The half-dead man-child they brought to me that day had no secrets left, only self-proclaimed caretakers who refused to see the truth."

"Truth? What *truth*?"

"That it wasn't a battered and broken child they brought to Barsitum, but a brave soldier, wounded in the line of duty. That it wasn't pity they should accord him, but respect."

Respect, perhaps, for the lad who got the best of dunHaulpin . . . Pity and respect. The difference between Deymorin's response to the past . . . and Ganfrion's.

"Once again, Raul," he said slowly, "you give me insight into myself."

"Very good, master Khyel —Now, about Moisaiidum's import taxes . . ."

ᔕ   ᔕ   ᔕ

By the time Sakhithe arrived with the Tower scavengers, most of Bharlori's was already gone. The charred timbers had been cut up for firewood, the stones hauled off for use elsewhere, even the ashes had been sifted for coins and jewels. Only the stone flooring and ovens of the kitchen remained.

Thyerri had watched the desecration, sometimes from the shadows between buildings, sometimes from rooftops. He wasn't sure how long it had been since the fire. Hours. Days. Weeks. Time seemed not to matter any longer.

He thought, perhaps, hunger had made him just a bit mad.

He wandered the hills when it grew dark out, seeking food. He'd known how to do that once, had survived happily outside the city walls. But he was lost in the hills now, and Bharlo's spirit haunted him at night, regardless of where he slept, and so he came back, waiting for the activity around the area to end, hoping to lay Bharlori's spirit to rest.

Somehow.

The scavengers who came with Sakhithe had come with purpose. She pointed to places, and they dug and pried stones from the floor, sometimes without result, other time pulling small bags or even boxes from the holes thus revealed.

The employees' personal hoards, Thyerri realized slowly. His own lay untouched beneath the ashes near the ovens. He'd forgotten about his money, had always thought it should be Bharlo's, for all he'd hidden it. Sakhithe had shown him where.

As she must have similarly advised the other employees, from her actions now.

Thyerri thought, perhaps, he should feel betrayed, but he did not think Sakhithe was a willing participant. Sakhithe did not look well. Her shoulders were slumped, her head bowed, and when she directed the scavengers, it was with a word and a listlessly raised finger.

One man, in particular, stood beside her, and his hand was always on her, keeping her close, touching her in ways that made Thyerri think that, perhaps, he hated that man.

Only after they had gone, taking Sakhithe with them, did he realize that she'd never pointed the diggers to that ash-filled corner that contained his cache, for all it was obviously undisturbed.

Helping him, even now, in the only way she could. Hoping he was alive and able to make use of his earnings. And in gratitude and friendship, he wished her well, for all he knew that was useless, for she was in the Tower now, and she'd been a dancer.

Rhyys needed no more incentive to destroy her.

When night closed around him, Thyerri slunk out onto Bharlo's tomb and wept, as he'd not done since the fire. He cried for Bharlo, who was gone, and for the others whose fates he didn't know. And he cried for Sakhithe, who would be happier dead, and who had saved his life and protected his tiny hoard, on the chance he still lived.

And when the tears were gone, and there was nothing left inside him, neither sorrow nor guilt nor hope, he pried the stone up, and lifted out his life.

That night, Bharlo did not visit him.

Chapter Ten

The hours passed in welcome monotony.

Mikhyel and Raulind worked in amiable silence, rocking easily with the movement of the coach, their reflexes having learned, over the days, to tell a minor irregularity in the road from a major rut, and to lift pens free *before* disfigurement occurred.

But only quick thinking saved their labor when, with a popping crack, one corner of the carriage suddenly collapsed.

"*Ink!*" Mikhyel yelled.

"Capped, m'lord," came Raul's calm reply, and Mikhyel silently blessed the officially nonexistent gods for Raulind's meticulous nature, that made Raulind's employer seem slovenly in comparison.

Shouts outside requested them to stay quiet and assured them the door would soon be open. He and Raulind collected the pages they could reach without moving from the spots to which they'd been thrown, and by the time the carriage was pronounced stable and hands reached in to help them out, they had all but a few strayed sheets secure, if in no particular order.

"Don't try to help overmuch, m'lord," Ori's voice said, from beyond the upward-tilted door. "We've got 'er stable, but a wrong-placed foot could throw 'er off again."

Not in the least inclined to argue, Mikhyel let the two burly guards lift him free, then stood out of range as they disentangled long-limbed Raul from the underside of the table, and hauled him out as well.

Outside the carriage, the sun burned painfully bright to eyes accustomed to the muted tones within, and downslope, beyond the briar-rose hedge marking the edge of ley-sterile ground, he could see the glimmer of running water. The wind buffeted fiercely, as it was inclined to do along the mountain leyroads, but the air was warm enough on the downwind side of the coach.

He wished for his greatcoat, forgotten inside the coach . . . but, no, with Raulind came both their coats, and the reassurance that the precious papers were safely stowed within the traveling case.

The damage to the carriage was—the captain assured Mikhyel, as Raulind helped him into the welcoming warmth of heavy wool—repairable, and would m'lord care to wait in another coach?

"Thank you, Captain Ori, but I think I'll walk a bit."

Leaving Raulind to stand by, lest any overlooked papers find their way out of the coach while the repairs were in progress, he wandered along the steep bank until he found a spot where the slope eased, giving a less hazardous access to the river's rocky shore.

He could, if he cared to, believe himself utterly alone here. The rush of water obscured all sounds of his party, as the roll and dip of land, the shrubbery, even a small copse of trees, hid them from sight. And he found that isolation surprisingly appealing.

He might have hesitated, were he completely alone—he wasn't a fool—but he wasn't alone, for all he saw no one following him. Ori would send at least one, if not two men to guard his precious self.

But not the man he'd hired for that express purpose.

Annoying, to have Ganfrion disappear just as fate was about to give him this opportunistic break in routine. This impartial setting would have made an ideal conference hall. Ganfrion was from the Khoramali—at least, that's what he'd said in that one interview—had indicated links with the Northern Crescent that might have proven . . . interesting.

But Ganfrion wasn't here, and Mikhyel would just have to count on Nikki's research, which had, thus far, proven meticulously accurate and complete, if a bit academic.

He ran his hand over the rough bark of one of the small trees, the sensation, like so much else Outside, resonating with his deepest memories of childhood, of the time before his mother's death, before Nikki.

Unusual, to his understanding, that sizable plants should grow this close to a leyroad. Small and twisted, but trees nonetheless. The major leyroads out of Rhomatum had a barren strip a good half-mile wide. But Barsitum was a small node, all its lines, save for its link to Rhomatum, undeveloped buds. He supposed the ground-sterilizing effects of the ley might correlate with that fact.

He also supposed that Anheliaa had known, but it was one of those questions he'd never thought to ask.

A prudent man had to wonder how much Anheliaa *had* known, and how much had been lost because she took so long to acknowledge her own mortality and begin training an heir.

Anheliaa hadn't presented Lidye to the Rhomatumin creature, but it was possible that Anheliaa herself had never been introduced.

That Anheliaa had known something of the mind-manipulating possibilities was obvious: he'd seen her use them for years. She'd used such pressures against all of them at one time or another.

It was evidence of her awesome presence that they'd never compared their own strange link to Anheliaa's actions against them, and yet he himself according to Deymorin, prevented his brothers from speaking simply by willing it so.

To have the ability was disturbing, but he was more concerned at his own lack of guilt regarding his use of that talent. And he still felt his actions had been justified. Had those abilities been under his conscious control, he might well have done the same—*would* do the same tomorrow.

Could anyone be so certain of his own principles, his own purpose, that he should overpower another's right to be heard—just because he could?

It was a disturbing thought. He had to wonder how often Anheliaa had questioned her own actions—and more importantly, when she had ceased to question.

His wandering had brought him to a wider point in the river. The water was quieter, the white-frothed rapids flattened into swiftly running water. Mikhyel picked up a handful of pebbles, and cast them, one at a time, into that rapid flow.

The action tweaked some far-off memory, of two boys, standing beside a deep, reflective pool, trying to hit a single pink water lily, it being the only distinguishable target in a sea of white and green.

Deymorin had always had the stronger arm, he, the better aim, as he'd reminded Deymorin during that game of *Dancers in the Maze* played on a prison floor. But the years, he discovered, trying for a jagged-topped rock rising above the rushing water, had taken their toll.

The first attempt fell short. *Far* short. The second and third were better as he regained some modicum of coordination, but miserably far off the mark. Too much thinking, he could almost hear Deymorin say, and concentrated on his throw, hearing child-Deymorin's laughter and child-Deymorin's advice: hold your arm so, use your shoulder . . . elbow . . . wrist . . .

With each throw, his aim and his confidence grew. Then his fingers encircled and recognized the perfect stone. Without looking at it, he fit his fingertips into place, reared back, and let fly.

Arrow-straight, right on target.

An instant before it struck, a second stone, a sunlit flash, struck it aside, deflecting *his* rock into the water, itself into the jagged rock.

"Dammit, Deymio—" he shouted, caught between now and then, and whirled to face a Deymorin-massive silhouette, realizing even as he turned that *Deymorin* couldn't be responsible. Deymorin wasn't here. And if it *were* Deymorin, he'd have known without ever looking.

Besides, Deymorin should be almost as out of practice at rock-tossing as he.

"Not bad, Suds," the shadow said, and sauntered forward, booted feet finding purchase in the steep bank. Without pausing, Ganfrion flipped another stone across the water, clipping the topmost spike of that rock, and another, a side-armed snap of a flat stone that skipped three times before disappearing.

"You came back," Mikhyel said. Stupidly.

Ganfrion laughed.

"Brilliant, Suds. Come, you can do better."

"Better?"

A double-footed hop carried Ganfrion the final stage. His cloak flipped up and snapped down behind him.

"Like: where the hell have you been, you double-dealing bucket of pond slime?"

Mikhyel turned back to the water, tossing the rest of the pebbles at random into the shimmering flow.

"Well?" he said, staring into the sparkling liquid that ate

the stones without a ripple, so different from that mirror-like pond of memory.

"Did better this time, Suds."

"Better?"

"Not real vocabularic, are you? Understood you did pretty well with the good brothers of Barsitum."

Ganfrion was baiting him, and he wasn't prepared, with memories of childhood foremost in his mind, to deal with Ganfrion's well-honed tongue. Ganfrion had been off playing and run out of money, that was obvious. He came back now to challenge his spineless employer to fire him.

He picked up another handful of stones. Began tossing them idly.

"Shit. Forget it, Suds." Ganfrion set foot to the bank, and the haze of the past suddenly lifted.

"Stop right there."

The man stopped, looking down on him, in every sense, and at a greater vantage than usual, being several steps uphill. But Mikhyel was accustomed to men of greater stature trying to use that advantage to intimidate him. Had grown accustomed long before his own body ceased striving to catch up.

Deymorin wasn't in the way now. His own acts had caused whatever rift might exist between himself and Ganfrion, and if ever he was to make use of Ganfrion's past, he had to take control now.

"Where the hell have you been?"

"Too late."

"Where?"

Shaggy brows lifted. "Shatum."

"Why?"

"Heard talk."

"What kind of—"

"What kind do you think?"

"I asked—"

"Something damnwell significant enough to kill one horse going and founder a second getting back!"

A horse or two wasn't all Ganfrion had overtaxed. The man was dead on his feet, swaying as he stood, so determined not to show weakness, he had to take the most difficult route up the bank.

How like Deymorin.

And they were yelling at each other. Just as he and

Deymorin would. Clever of him—get rid of one older brother, just to saddle himself with another. But Ganfrion was *his* man, under *his* pay.

And Ganfrion had been a soldier.

"Report," he said sharply, and Ganfrion jerked as if he'd been struck with a lash. He stepped down even again with Mikhyel.

"Heard two men talking in the pools."

Mikhyel nodded, a single dip of his chin. "And?"

"Varishmandi men."

"*The* Varishmandi?"

"The old sailor himself. Varishmandi's not pleased. Seems the bottom's about to fall out of the shipping market."

"Why?"

"Seems Auntie Liia was making deals on the side, Suds. Seems in order to cap Khoratum, Anheliaa promised to cap some big-ass node down in Kirish'lani land, on the far side of one of Shatum's little babes. Seems the trade's all coming overland, real soon now. Seems Shatum's gonna rule the world, but not via the sea routes."

The hidden promise.

"Heard about a little meeting down Shatum-way, a few of the locals and some Kirish'lan reps, and thought I should check it out. Got down there, just in time, invited myself in, and, funny thing, they seem to figure that, even though Anheliaa reneged, well, they've got Papa Fericci's little Miss Lidye in there, and she'll do the deed and within a generation, Shatum will be the biggest damn trade-dump in the world. That Rhomatum will have to dance to her tune or starve."

"Meeting with the locals. Who?"

"GorTarim, among other, lesser souls."

GorTarim. Lidye's father's most trusted man. And Tarim owned ruling stock in Shatum Tower.

"That's what you wanted to tell me, that night in Barsitum, isn't it? That you were leaving?"

Ganfrion shrugged.

Damned if he'd apologize, still . . . "I learn from my mistakes."

Another shrug. "Better you than farmboy."

"Deymorin knows what he's doing."

"I'll reserve judgment on your improving self. *Deymio's* an overeager puppy."

"Deymorin's not a child!" he objected, then cursed silently. He was snapping at Ganfrion's bait exactly as he snapped at Deymorin's.

A snort of disbelief, a raised lip that might be disdain, and might just be the scar that twisted the ex-convict's mouth. "No? He's—what? Thirty-six? -seven? And still running races on the way to war."

"Thirty," Mikhyel admitted reluctantly.

"Really?" Ganfrion's voice hinted at some surprise. "And yet, he spoke of the Gerinandum Uprising as if he'd been there."

"Possible." Mikhyel searched his memory for the event. "That was some disagreement between Governor Ashriini of Gerinandum and an Outsider . . . taxes, wasn't it? Ten, twelve years ago? Deymorin would have been a senior cadet. I believe he did serve as aide to Erinal."

"A disagreement over taxes," Ganfrion repeated, the sneer profound and indisputable. He shook his head and started again to leave, this time along Mikhyel's easier route. But as he brushed past, Mikhyel caught a muttered: "Rhomatumin *khysswi*."

"Hold!" Mikhyel barked, and the man turned a sullen eye toward him. "Explain yourself!"

Ganfrion shrugged. "Khysswi. It's a little lizard, m'lord Rhomandi. When the world displeases it, it burrows into the sand. Only once its front is buried, it deems itself safe and ceases to burrow, leaving its ass high and dry for the next passing predator's lunch."

"And my ass is similarly at risk?"

Ganfrion leaned back as if to check that appropriate anatomical component. "Possibly. If not, you'd be a decided anomaly among Insider Rhomatumin, now wouldn't you?"

"Would I?"

"Mauritum isn't the first threat to your borders, Rhomatumin Khysswi. Every time the storms cycle into dormancy, the Panidori threaten Orenum in the north, Kirish'lan pushes the entire south. Auntie Liia capped Khoratum, and all of a sudden, the storms stopped and all hell broke loose on the borderlands. There in your valley, surrounded by your satellites, you ignore everything. You treat such activity as 'disagreements.' Where do you think men like me come from? Who do you think your brother's hiring to buttress that coastline? What does *he* think he's going to be leading?"

All the while he talked, Ganfrion scowled and slapped his palm with his riding crop. Suddenly, that crop snapped to a quivering halt, gloved fingers curling around it.

"Wasting my time, Suds," he said, and the passion faded from his voice and his face, leaving only the face of a man weary in every sense of the word. "More comfortable living in your fantasy world. And that fantasy will probably survive your lifetime, though ignorance may well shorten the lifetime."

"I'd prefer to face my ignorance head on."

Ganfrion's dark, narrow eyes flickered toward Mikhyel in an unreadable assessment. "That could be arranged."

"Ride in the carriage with me."

"That an order, Suds?"

"Damn right it is. And the name's dunMheric."

The crooked mouth twitched, the dark eyes narrowed to black slits beneath shaggy brows. One broad shoulder lifted in acknowledgment.

Perhaps.

If he was lucky.

Chapter Eleven

The quill tip caught on the parchment, and snapped free. Fine specks of ink spattered across both printed page and the marble-topped desk Nikki had personally designed for his new office.

With a faint curse, Councillor Merl dunPendac dropped the pen in a flustered search for something to wipe the mess.

"It's all right," Nikki said soothingly as he produced a handkerchief to blot the desk, knowing better than to worry about the dots staining the contract itself. So long as they didn't smear, they'd do nothing to the document's legibility or, more importantly, viability.

"My apologies, Rhomandi," dunPendac muttered, and slid forward again on his chair to finish signing the document. A second search, this time for the pen, found a much larger stain penetrating the carpet beneath the Councillor's chair.

DunPendac's face blanched. Nikki laughed, hoping to set the elderly statesman at his ease, and held out another pen—a modern capillary pen. "My fault, sir, for providing a defective, not to mention antiquated, tool."

A historical touch which he'd thought would make the moment memorable. Special. Well, it had at least half-succeeded. He doubted dunPendac would soon forget this moment.

His efforts to minimize the wealthy citizen's guilt fell on disapproving ears. "That's a two-hundred-year-old carpet. Possibly a civic treasure. Certainly paid for by citizen taxes. Aren't you the least concerned? Aren't you at least going to charge me for the cleaning? Replacement, should cleaning prove impossible?"

"It's still a carpet. Meant to be used. Certainly, I'll have it seen to. If it would make you feel better to pay for the cleaning—"

"Rings, boy—" dunPendac broke off. "My apologies, m'lord. An expert is needed." He dipped the quill and signed the document with cursory efficiency, relaxed, Nikki thought sourly, now he could patronize the ex-Princeps of Rhomatum. "I'll send someone over."

"Thank you, Councillor," Nikki said, schooling both voice and face. "For your signature and your . . . assistance."

"Certainly." DunPendac stood up. "If that will be all?"

"Yes, sir, of course. Thank you very much for your cooperation in this matter. All of Rhomatum will benefit."

"Yes, yes, we've been through all that. Good day."

"Good day, sir. —Renfrii!"

But even as he called to the footman, the door to his office swung open and Lidye flowed into the room. In the months before Boreton, she'd have billowed or floated, depending on her childish mood. And she'd have burst in without ceremony, uncaring who or what she'd interrupted.

She still entered without preliminaries, but her timing was invariably exquisite, and her movements were slow without being languid, graceful without being insipid.

Even her style of dress had changed. Long, elegant lines that emphasized her height and made her seem subtly taller, subtly more mature—and infinitely more alluring than the ruffles and lace and corsets she'd worn before.

Kiyrstin claimed it was vanity, to keep her from showing the child growing in her belly. But Nikki noticed that Kiyrstin herself had adopted the look, when she deigned to wear women's clothes. When he challenged her on her hypocrisy, Kiyrstin only laughed and said good for him, and he was right.

Kiyrstin confused him.

Lidye, on the other hand, mesmerized him. He couldn't keep his eyes from her, her every move reminding him of that graceful body moving against his in the privacy of their bedroom.

Her bedroom. The Ringmaster of Rhomatum's suite. Where Darius the first and his beloved Kharishia had slept. And loved.

He shivered. Lidye smiled, a tiny, intimate smile just for him, then raised her hand to dunPendac.

"Patron Modhisharhi, a pleasure."

"Lady Rhomandi," dunPendac said flatly, most formal of her possible addresses—as Lidye's had been formal to him. He touched her hand lightly, dipping his head just low enough for propriety.

DunPendac, like so many in the Council, still resented and mistrusted the Southern-born ringmaster. Nikki stirred, wanting to object, but a flicker of eyelash, a slight tilt of Lidye's head, kept him silent, and, indeed, even as he watched, dunPendac relaxed and by the time he released her hand, his parting nod appeared almost pleasant.

"What did you do to him?" Nikki asked, when the door was securely closed behind dunPendac.

His answer was a flirtatious twitch of her mouth, half-hidden by her slim shoulder. She pivoted about to face him, halting her dramatic swirl of skirts prematurely, one fold short of the stain on the floor. She frowned at the stain, then glared at the innocent doorway.

"It was an accident, Liddi. *My* fault. I'm sorry."

The tension in her shoulders disappeared, and her smile was sweet. "Of course it was, darling. Don't worry, I know a solution that will lift the stain quite harmlessly. An old family recipe, you know. Just don't let the maids touch it for the next several hours. It must be perfectly dry."

"Is there anything you don't know, Liddi?" he asked, unable to keep the awe from his voice.

Her musical laughter filled the room. "Oh, many, many things, darling." She moved in behind his chair and wrapped her arms lightly around his neck, staring down at the contract. "Good meeting?"

"Very." Nikki's voice vibrated with excitement. "Two more, Liddi, that's all we need, and we'll be in business. We'll have that dam halfway completed before Mikhyel returns!"

Her arms tightened. "Congratulations, darling. See? I told you, you could do it."

He twisted in her hold to look up at her, and covered her hands with his own. "Yes, you did. And I don't think I could have done it without you."

She smiled, a secretive, tantalizing bend of rose-tinted lips. "Now what sort of woman would I be to deny it? To say, of course you could have?" She slid her hands free, tracing his neck to cup his face, her fingers winding in amongst his hair, and leaned that fraction closer, until he had to close his eyes against her dizzying image. "Whatever help I've been, I promise you, it was my pleasure, sweet, sweet Nikki."

Her whisper brushed his mouth with warm breath. Eyes still closed, he strained toward the promised kiss.

{Deymorin? *Nikki?* Damn, if only you could hear—}

"Khyel?" Nikki whispered and his eyes opened. Lidye pulled back, became a sleek-edged woman again.

{Khyel? Is that you?}

Nikki shook his head. *That* was Deymorin.

{I'm here, too!} he shouted into that brother-filled netherworld, and for a moment, it was as if they were all three pounding and hugging each other in greeting.

A confusion of images and words filled him. Deymorin, in a bedroom in the Tower of Mekh'narum near the coast. Mikhyel, in an office at Moisaiidum on the sound. A rumpled bed, a desk of papers. A letter Mikhyel had truly not wished to entrust to a courier's hands.

And a haze of speculations as to why they could hear one another, that settled on nothing except maybe because Mikhyel wanted it so badly and the stars were right, which made Mikhyel laugh in his head, in a way he never laughed on the outside.

{All right, Barrister, what's this all about? Why'd you wake me up?}

{Napping again, Rags?}

A mental growl from Deymorin, edged with humor and concern. And weariness. Deymorin was sleeping when he could, which wasn't often enough. {Don't waste time, Khyel.}

{Right. The situation is rather more involved than we thought. Ganfrion has uncovered—}

{Who?} Nikki asked.

Anger from Deymorin. An image of the scar-faced Crypt inmate.

{*He's* with you, Mikhyel?} Nikki asked. {Why?}

{I'll explain later. Just listen to me.}

A blast of images flared inside Nikki's head, information flooding into him faster than words. A sense of borders far less secure than he'd always believed. Of factions Inside and Out, those with reason to prefer the status quo and those who fiercely desired change.

And at the center of those factions' differences: a deal made with Shatum, Lidye's home node. The secret at the heart of the Southern Crescent's agreement to aid in capping Khoratum—and that resonated with fears Mikhyel had harbored for years, that he was glad to finally have out in the open where he could deal with it.

Images of another node to the south, connected to Shatum through an already capped satellite. A node possibly comparable to Rhomatum herself. A node of which Anheliaa and her predecessors had been well aware; a node they'd refused to consider capping until the Rhomatum Web was secure.

A node that, when capped, could theoretically wreak chaos in the weather along the southern coast, while securing a storm-channeled overland trade route right through Shatum.

{That should delight the Giephaetum buds.} Deymorin's grim thought referencing the seaside satellites of the northern node superimposed over Mikhyel's wordless images.

Those satellites' commerce depended on the sea-going trade.

{Not only Giephaetum.} That was Mikhyel. {According to Gan, the Varishmondi are livid. It will cut the bottom out of their shipping empire.}

{No wonder Kharl looked ready to throttle you, brother.} Images from Deymorin: a meeting in Shatum, and Kharl Varishmondi, aloof and bitter, refusing to sit with the other leaders.

{According to Gan, Kharl believes we're party to Anheliaa's expansionist notions.}

{This must have been brewing since Mheric's time. Kharl was *always* visiting back then.}

{And after Mheric died, he never came back.}

{I'd abdicated to you . . .}

{And I was Anheliaa's. Rings, Deymorin, we've been fools.}

{Don't dwell, Khyel. *I'll* handle Kharl. I'll leave tomorrow—}

{I was counting on it.}

{But! . . .} Nikki interrupted, frantically. {The Varishmondi are Shatumin. You said Shatum *wants* the expansion.}

{Not all of Shatum, Nikki.}

{Then who—} And then, he realized: {Tarim.}
Lidye's father.
Agreement. Sympathy.

{Mikhyel?} Nikki asked hesitantly. {Did you hear *anything* yourself. Not just in Shatum, I mean. If they had a contract with Anheliaa, why didn't they press it before?}

{She couldn't have done anything for years after Khoratum anyway. I imagine they've been dealing with Anheliaa for some time. More recently, well, perhaps they said nothing because they knew Anheliaa would die and someone else, someone hopefully more amenable to their cause was going to be in charge of the Rhomatum rings.}

{Lidye.} Deymorin's thoughts tasted grim.

{Lidye won't do *anything* wrong!} Nikki's head hurt with the force he put behind that mental scream.

{No one's accusing her, Nikki. But her supporters in Shatum are *expecting* her to act in their behalf. They will consider the right thing to be capping that node. She might agree. But the Syndicate *must* discuss it first. But tempers are rising. There are Kirish'lani who insist they have proof that Shatum agreed to assist the Khoratum expansion *only* on the agreement that *their* node would be capped. Lidye may feel forced to comply. She may be in danger if she does not.}

She could be in danger either way, Nikki realized in some horror, and remembering that capping nodes was very dangerous; even a small, willing node like Barsitum had forced Darius II into bed for months afterward. A large node, with only one controlled satellite . . .

He shuddered.

{She might try anyway, Nikki, and we can't let her.} Deymorin's thought came to him. {Such a decision *must* be a web-wide agreement. Anheliaa had *no right* to make private guarantees of that nature. And Anheliaa chose Lidye. And Lidye's family *is* Shatum! Lidye's father owns a ruling interest in Shatum Tower!}

{Lidye will do what's best!} Nikki shouted into that pessimism.

{I hope you're right, Nikki.} Calm thoughts. Mikhyel. {But watch her. Remember whose guards took us to the prison, and watch your back.}

{You're a fine one to be giving advice, brother. Look what you've got at *your* back.}

{And I'm damned glad he is! We'd know nothing about this, if it weren't for him. But we don't know how thoroughly she's involved, Nikki. Don't accuse her. Be careful—for both your sakes.}

{How do you know? Are you certain about Tarim?} He needed to have the details, in case Lidye didn't know. In case she didn't believe her father was involved.

More images, then, of the scar-faced felon gathering hints in several dark and filthy places; suspicions only until an overheard conversation in the baths of Baristum. Talk of a meeting in Shatum, a meeting he raced cross-country to attend, killing a horse in mid-stride to get there and back before Mikhyel left Barsitum—and then missed him anyway, which had made Mikhyel angry and suspicious.

It was all very tangled.

{What meeting!} Nikki shouted into the mental clamor.

{Sorry, Nik. The Southern Crescent alliance against Rhomatum. There are factions who believe that if they combine forces, they can force Rhomatum to cap that node. There's Kirish'lan money in it, you can bet your future on that.}

{Why?}

{The Kirish'lan plan to occupy the node. They've made the noises, greased the proper palms—}

{How does this Ganfrion know all this? How did *he* get into the meeting?}

Images of death, of a guard replaced. Of standing in shadows and hearing everything.

{Murderer.}

{Would you rather ignorance?}

No, he wouldn't, and Mikhyel knew that. Still: {And Tarim's involvement?}

{Sironi gorTarim was in charge of the meeting.}

Which meant Tarim himself might as well have been.

{Do you think the Northern Crescent nodes are aware of all this?} Deymorin asked.

{I'm virtually certain of it. Governor Haulsini here has been dancing about the point quite deftly.}

{I'm coming up there—}

{Why?}

{To help explain—}

{Don't be ridiculous. This new development doesn't negate the need for the border patrol. Besides, you need to talk with Kharl. Make certain he knows nothing precipitous

is about to happen regarding that southern node. I'm going
directly to Giephaetum—}

{Changing schedule again?}

{I want to speak with Nethaalye, get her down to Rhomatum as soon as possible. *Anything* to offset this growing
rift. I've got Pasingarim's signed agreement to aid in repairing the Khoratum line, which is to everyone's advantage. Pasingarim carries the entire Southern Crescent.
Giephaetum is the key to the Northern Crescent and Nethaalye's brother is one of the junior ring spinners in Giephaetum Tower. If I can convince them, I've got the
North . . . at least long enough to heal the web and for
Lidye's loyalties—not to mention our own—to come
clear . . . to everyone.}

{All right, Khyel, all right.} Deymorin's reluctance colored the thought. {But keep in touch.}

{Naturally.}

{And, Khyel . . .} Greater reluctance. A sense of embarrassment, a sense of having been guilty of an injustice. And
humor, but that was from Mikhyel.

Nikki had a momentary sense of ostracism, but Mikhyel said:

{Reconciling personal differences, Nikki. I made a decision with which Deymorin justifiably argued. This time, I
was right.}

{I didn't say that!} Deymorin protested—loudly.

Nikki laughed.

{There's a lot of resentment in the Towers. I'm going
downhill tomorrow and do some checking—}

{You mean Ganfrion is.} Deymorin interrupted.

Mikhyel's answer came in impressions, a desire to hear
for himself, a sense of excitement. Of—

{*Adventure?*} Deymorin's shout echoed painfully in
Nikki's head. {Have you lost what little sense you had left?}

A mental chuckle. {That's what Ganfrion said.}

The sense of Deymorin faded away in aimless, frustrated,
distorted images, then returned, suddenly and very
forcefully:

{Rings! Nikki, tell Kiyrstin! Tell her *everything*. About
the southern node, about Lidye. *Everything*.}

Before he could stop himself, Nikki's impression of Kiyrstin flooded the link, and between one blink and the next,
Deymorin's anger flared, then Deymorin disappeared from

his mind. And immediately after, Mikhyel vanished, and nothing he could do would bring them back.

"Nikki? Nikki, darling, are you all right?"

Lidye's hands, soft yet secure, held his face.

"Nikki, what's happening? Talk to me, darling."

"Deymorin? Khyel!" Shouted thoughts became shouted words. "Where'd you—"

Nikki bit his tongue on the rest, coming to his senses at last, as Lidye's gaze bore straight into his heart.

"Your brothers. You're hearing them now? Nikki, how is that possible?"

He shuddered, drowning in his brothers' thoughts and suspicions. "I should never have told you," he whispered, horrified now at his own indiscretion, even though Mikhyel *must* have known he'd told her, and had said nothing.

"About your brothers? About your fascinating connection? How unkind, Nikki. I thought we were exploring the ley together?"

"It's not—" He broke off, more confused than ever, thinking about Anheliaa making independent decisions that affected the whole web, and wondering, had he been equally at fault. "It's not my secret alone. I should have consulted them first."

"And they'd have said no. They don't trust me." Her delicate eyebrows drew together in a sad and weary pucker. "And you don't either, do you? Not anymore. And yet, if trust is an issue, you alone know how terribly ignorant Anheliaa left me. You alone know how much help I require every day."

"Do I? And what did Anheliaa tell you about a node to the south of Shatum? What did your *father* tell you, when he agreed to our marriage?"

She backed away, turning slowly, gracefully, moving in an unhurried path to the chair dunPendac had occupied earlier. But there was neither guilt nor shock nor evasion apparent in her face.

"I know that what Father expected and what I intend to do no longer coincide, and have not since the instant Anheliaa died and the heritage of the Rhomatum rings passed into my hands. I know I'd never do anything to threaten the Rhomandi hold over the rings. I know that the child I carry in my belly is the most important creature ever spawned in the world, and I know that no paternal order will supersede my loyalty to that child. Does that set your soul at ease, dear Nikki?"

"Why do you call me that?" he asked, past a tightness in his throat. "Why pretend to care for me? Why do you *look* at me the way you do? Touch me the way you do? Make . . ."

"Love to you? Perhaps because I do love you, Nikki. Is that so difficult to believe?"

"What kind of fool do you think I am? I look at you, and I see . . . I see the sort of woman who might find Deymorin, or even Mikhyel stimulating, but—"

"Mikhyel? Goodness, Nikaenor, don't be silly. You're everything a woman could want."

He snorted, painfully aware at that moment of his own shortcomings. "A woman such as you appeared to be at the first, perhaps. Flighty, shallow. A bit childish. Much as I hated to admit it, I could see why the rings considered us a match. Now . . ."

"You said it yourself, Nikki. The rings considered us a match. You chose the words to describe me. Perhaps it's your image of yourself you need to reconsider."

A drought on his tongue made him realize his mouth was hanging unbecomingly open. He closed it, worked to produce enough saliva to swallow. Seeking to see himself through her eyes.

He had, after all, changed as surely as she had in the past weeks. He'd secured the allegiance of some powerful men and set a complex project in motion. Perhaps he was more than he thought.

The rings had, after all, paired him with Lidye.

SECTION
SIX

SECTION
SIX

Chapter One

In all probability, Deymorin was right. Ganfrion was: Mikhyel dunMheric had lost what little common sense remained with him.

Hands—ragged, scratched, and filthy hands—rested on either side of the cracked ale mug on the knife-scarred surface before him. Hands that should, by proximity, belong to him. Mikhyel considered lifting his right index finger, and the appropriate digit rose and fell again, which was either extreme coincidence, or Raulind was likely to end his years-long service on the morrow.

Well, he'd asked for it. He chuckled ruefully and lifted the mug to his lips, succeeding this time in keeping his face blank while the bitter brew destroyed the handful of taste buds that had survived his first swallow.

His right instep still throbbed from Ganfrion's last warning on the etiquette of the Ramblin' Rosie.

Ganfrion had laughed when Mikhyel had first suggested this joint venture into the Moisaiidum dockside, scowled and said he wasn't risking his neck for a rich man's fantasy when Mikhyel had persisted.

There'd been, of course, no real argument.

In cold-blooded logic, he had to admit there simply was no logical reason for him to have come to the Rosie with Ganfrion. He'd hired Ganfrion specifically *to* enter places like this for him.

But that "for him" was precisely why he'd insisted on coming here himself. Ever since that night in the Crypt, he'd grown increasingly aware of the fact that he'd begun to live his life *through* and *for* other people.

In the Crypt, Deymorin had worried about *him*. Not about Nikki, not about Deymorin himself, but *him*. Because Mikhyel dunMheric didn't know how to handle real life, or so Deymorin was convinced. And for all the proof *he* had

to the contrary, Deymorin's assessment was absolutely on
target.

He never did his own dirty work. When it was safe, when
taking action was a matter of public speaking, or filling out
papers, or changing the lives of thousands with a penstroke,
he acted willingly enough. When it was his personal self at
risk, when he actually *needed* something physically done,
he hired someone—like Ganfrion—to complete the job for
him. He hadn't even helped Deymorin bury Anheliaa.

That night in Barsitum he'd been forced to wonder why
he didn't handle his own problems. He *didn't* consider himself superior to Ganfrion, certainly not to Raulind. He
didn't *think* he considered himself *superior* to anyone.

That simple truth was, Mikhyel dunMheric was afraid—
not of death, not of injury, but of incompetence. All his
childhood with Mheric and Anheliaa had proven was that
he was stubborn. He'd shown the world time and again that
he was intelligent and manipulative.

But there'd always been a safe distance between himself
and his opponents. He'd been a child to Mheric's adult
power. In politics, he'd been the Rhomandi, a position he'd
had to prove his right to hold, but a position of intrinsic
stature. Man to man, equal to equal, man to life . . . he'd
never tested that side of himself.

He'd never faced life as himself and won.

Somehow, when Ganfrion had suggested this foray into
the dockside, it had seemed his chance to show them all,
to prove to Ganfrion, to Nikki, to Deymorin—and most of
all to himself—that he neither despised them or their world,
nor placed a higher value on his life than on theirs.

Which sounded dangerously like proving to them all he
was as much a man as they were, which sounded dangerously like stupid and foolhardy, under the circumstances.
But Ganfrion had armed him with clothing and a story to
tell should he have to open his mouth, and then told him
to keep it closed, or he'd close it for him—permanently.

Hence the unfamiliar hands resting before him, the clothing that scratched his skin raw in places, while tickling with
suspect mobility in others. Fortunately, he'd changed in
Ganfrion's quarters and not his own room; with luck, he'd
shed the creatures that had taken up residence with him
when he changed back to his own clothing.

Provided, of course, he lived that long.

Not that the men milling shoulder to shoulder about the tavern concerned him; it was his own so-called bodyguard. Granted, he had established the rules, had given Ganfrion leave to signal in any way Ganfrion deemed necessary, but it was an agreement he was rapidly (considering bruised ribs, a crippled foot and insect bites in places he couldn't possibly reach) reevaluating.

He'd found it suspicious, when they'd first entered the tavern, that while *his* clothing and general appearance reflected the low end of the surrounding spectrum, Ganfrion was undoubtedly the best-dressed man in the room. However, as all eyes in the tavern skewed to Ganfrion wherever he went, Mikhyel rapidly ceased to resent the fact.

In one sense his crazed notion was proving immensely enlightening: no sardonic report could match watching Ganfrion operate in person. The man had no shame, would draw attention and spin a tale so outrageous, no one dared challenge his veracity.

And overall, since the crawling creature (whose identity remained a back-creeping mystery) seemed to have fled his personal premises, and since his remaining foot was temporarily secure (Ganfrion having spotted an "old friend" on the far side of the crowded establishment), Mikhyel decided he was perfectly content to stand, elbows on the bar, throbbing foot propped on a rail, and just listen to rough, northern accents discussing tomorrow's weather, and whether it would affect the shipment scheduled to arrive.

Much of the talk seemed at first aimless and repetitive, but eventually it began to achieve a rhythm with all the subtlety of a fencing match between old friends. Mikhyel had watched Deymorin engage in such impromptu meetings in the fencing salle. There was a distinctive flicker of a smile, a grunt of surprise as a previously known quantity revealed a new skill.

Here, each new arrival added a piece of a growing puzzle that began with wives and children and the day's work and grew to encompass world commerce. And within the casual speech, tidbits of information would rouse similar flickers and grunts.

Quite, quite different from political meetings of his experience, where the greatest surprise was finding out your opponent *didn't* know key information.

One thing was quite clear, there was no love lost between

these men and their Southern Crescent counterparts. While they made no mention of new webs to the south, their economy was suffering, and they set the blame squarely on Shatumin shoulders.

"Heard tell as how Giephaetum is plannin' t' hop inta bed with Mauritum, if this keeps up," someone said down the bar.

"Yeah, and m' mother's entertainin' Garetti hisself t'morrow," said another.

"And what's she entertainin' him to? Tea? Or crumpets?"

"Crumpets, a'course, Blendini. Never nothin' less fer ol' mum."

"Don't gotta worry 'bout Garetti, then, do we?"

"Not for at least another month, laddy. Gots stayin' power, does mum."

General laughter then, and Mikhyel wished they hadn't strayed. Mauritum and Giephaetum?

"Where you from, stranger?"

Such was Mikhyel's limited local fluency, it took him several heartbeats, and an irritated repetition of the question to realize the speaker had addressed him.

"South," he responded, striving for the rough tone Ganfrion had coached into him. "Terslingam." It was a small town on the far end of the Pandiini Sound, known for its fine garments.

"Waiting for Pobriichi's linen shipment, then." Said as a statement of fact: a man who knew his importers.

Mikhyel nodded. "And Peristan wool, if the gods have favored us."

"Long wait, stranger." A hint of suspicion colored the man's tones now. "Been months since Pobriichi come in here. Gotta deal with the Shatumin thieves these days."

"That's strange." Mikhyel frowned, hoping he looked properly taken aback. "The old man's always used Pobriichi, and Pobriichi docks—"

"Not since last fall. —Just who the hell are you, *stranger*?"

Ears pricked around them. Conversations lulled. Sidewise glances missed nothing.

Mikhyel held up his hands, hoping to deflect the man's anger, and beginning to improvise on Ganfrion's scant story as rapidly as he could. "Just repeating what the old man told me. *He* sent me here. Said it was his first order in a year. Why isn't Pobriichi coming in here?"

"Pobriichi's out. Gods-be-cursed Varishmandi stole all four ships right out from under 'im. Broke, thanks to the Rhomandi swindler brothers."

"The Rhomandi? I thought you said Varishmandi bought him out."

"I *said* he *stole* 'em."

"But you said Pobriichi was 'broke,' " Mikhyel said, trying to sort out the man's words. The Varishmandi were astute and even ruthless businessmen, but far from criminals. "The Varishmandi did pay fairly for the boats, did he not?"

The man drew back, staring at him, then waved for another drink. Yelled at Ganfrion's "friend" when she failed to respond immediately. She cursed back, but swung her legs across the counter (a scenic move that momentarily diverted the local man's attention) and drew his drink, actions that prompted a dozen more demands for refills.

"Pay, did he yes," the man answered when his ale arrived. "Fair, did he not."

Mikhyel shifted his attention to the dark brew in his mug, and the flecks floating across the surface, wondering if this was a strange local saying, or if he was being mocked.

One of the flecks appeared to be swimming.

He should have kept his mouth shut.

"I hear you mention Pobriichi?" Ganfrion leaned between Mikhyel and the local to claim his mug—and an extended kiss. In the middle of that kiss, his boot aimed for Mikhyel's remaining foot—and missed, Mikhyel being inclined to learn from experience.

Ganfrion grunted, frustration to one who understood the under-the-counter transaction, and released the barmaid. He thrust back from the counter, casting Mikhyel a scowl, and said to the local, "Hell of a situation, eh? What's become of 'Briichi's family?"

"Wife's holdin'. Kid's in Sparingate—"

"Sparingate? Why?"

"Went after the Shatumin thief. Got caught. Shoulda been 'tother way 'round, I say."

"Absolutely. Helluva fate fer your old man."

"Dunno what I'd do, were m' da to do hisself in like that. But I can't hardly blame the lad fer goin' after old

Varsh'di like that. Only wisht he'd a' got him afore he was caught."

"The boy's father committed suicide?" Mikhyel asked, trying to piece the snippets together with any case he'd reviewed, which, if the boy were in Sparingate, he would have.

"Where's this 'un from, friend?" the local asked Ganfrion.

"Hell if I know."

"Come in with you."

"By whim of Rakshi."

"From the hills, then."

"Long ago, m'friend. Very long ago. You?"

"Orenum, born and raised."

"But if the boy's crime were committed under the circumstances you describe," Mikhyel persisted, "he'd have had a valid defense. He shouldn't be . . . in . . ."

All the surrounding locals were staring at him now, and Ganfrion shot him a look that said in no uncertain terms that it was time to depart. And even as he muttered a purposefully unintelligible pardon and laid a coin on the counter, Ganfrion's look shifted—

To one of recognition—and outrage.

"Now I know you!" Ganfrion cried. "Mekh'narumin bastard! *Where's my sister*?"

Mikhyel had only an instant to register the fist flying toward his face—

A second to fling himself backward—

Into the middle of a dice game.

Dice flew. Curses did; and coins and notes. And then fists, feet and bodies. Appalled at the chaos he'd inadvertently wrought, Mikhyel dodged one way and another, his actions utterly lacking in conscious purpose. He stumbled and rebounded, tossed from one melee to another, but none of those flying fists intercepted him. Somehow Ganfrion invariably appeared between him and the worst. Protecting, he suddenly realized. Giving him the opportunity to escape.

Mikhyel took a step toward the door, and another—

A shout—an answer—and as one, angry eyes turned on him, and as one, the mob swirled inward, with himself as the eye of the storm.

Panic struck. He bolted for the door, though a cold part

of him knew he had no chance, and called him a fool. A hand clasped his shoulder and spun him around. His arms lifted, childhood instincts striving to protect his head, but this time, his opponent wasn't Nikki, or even Mheric.

His guard was swept ruthlessly aside.

This time, he never even saw the fist.

Chapter Two

"And today, Mikhyel plans to go directly to Giephaetum." Nikki completed his explanation of yesterday afternoon's revelations. "But he can't do it all. Deymorin can't. They didn't say anything, but there must be something *we* can do about this situation in the south."

Kiyrstin was sitting back in her chair, elbows propped on the arms, her breeched and booted legs crossed, chin balanced on steepled fingers. She'd come directly from the stables, never pausing except to wash her hands and face and to exchange her riding coat for a house robe.

He certainly couldn't accuse her of indifference to Rhomatum's situation. She'd been in Armayel yesterday, when his brothers spoke to him, visiting the Mauritumin boy, Alizant. He'd debated whether to send for her, and finally, late that morning and at Lidye's insistence, he'd sent a messenger asking her to return to Rhomatum.

No more than that: just a request to return.

And on no more than that, she'd returned immediately, riding, with a minimum escort—and arrived before dinner.

For a woman who had never straddled a horse before she encountered Deymorin, he had to admit, she did . . . all right.

And she'd listened to him. Without comment. Without condemnation.

Kiyrstin's eyes flickered to Lidye. Speculating.

"How long have you known?" She asked Lidye, not him.

"Long enough," Lidye answered calmly.

Which left Nikki utterly confused. "Known what?"

"About your silent communication with your brothers, Nikki." Lidye smiled, a brief, quirky, near-grin, at Kiyrstin. "She's trying to figure what else I know, what I've told my family, whether or not I can be trusted. Am I right, lady romGaretti?"

Kiyrstin dipped her head ever so slightly. But Nikki still suspected there was a different sort of silent communication going on in the room, leaving him as ignorant as his brothers could.

"If you don't mind, ladies," he said defensively, "may we please speak freely? This is nonsense. Of course Lidye can be trusted."

Kiyrstin's green eyes flickered to him, a frown tightening her brow.

"Nikki, my dear," Lidye said, "thank you, but there *is* no 'of course' about it. There is a great need for you all to be absolutely certain where a woman of the Southern Crescent who is now in charge of the Rhomatum Rings stands."

Kiyrstin's eyes flicked back to Lidye.

"Kiyrstin," Lidye said, "If I may call you that—"

Kiyrstin nodded. A quick, irritated motion.

"I won't endeavor to convince you one way or the other. Trust comes not from words, but from actions over time. I have not, since Nikki returned to me, spoken with anyone in my family, *nor*—" She lifted her hand as though forestalling Kiyrstin's unspoken argument. "Nor have I sent messages of any sort. Not to my family, nor to anyone in Shatum. That is, I suspect, why there is some unrest there now. I hesitated to mention the matter, because I knew there was much distrust of me already. I'd hoped to prove myself somehow before it became an issue."

Kiyrstin . . . grunted. There was no other expression for the sound she made. "Then I suggest," she said firmly, "that we call these Shatumin dissidents' bluff."

"Huh?" Nikki said, once again utterly lost.

"She means, Nikki, that we should invite them here, to the Tower."

"Them?"

"My father. The Kirish'lani, Orakan, also, if we can. The forces opposed to the expansion . . . the Varishmandi, for one. And the Khandirri. I . . . know the names, Nikki."

Kiyrstin's mouth twitched. He thought, perhaps, in a smile.

"*We* will explain to them that we know their plans," Lidye continued. "And their wishes. That I am *not* their pawn, and that Anheliaa's promises notwithstanding, now is not the time to proceed with the southern expansion. We will make it clear to them that we understand their desire for the expansion, that we see full well the advantages to them, and that we do not outright begrudge them those advantages, but since they made those agreements in secret and with Anheliaa, we do not feel obliged to honor them."

"And then, see what they do? Once they know we are, without question, united in our immediate goals. Is that what you're suggesting?"

Lidye and Kiyrstin both nodded.

"And we'd do this, the *three* of us?"

This time, the two women looked long and hard at one another, in that mysterious, insightful way of women. And just when Nikki was about to interrupt:

"Well?" Lidye asked, and Kiyrstin said:

"Which of us is going to write the letter to Orakan?"

§   §   §

The smell that greeted Mikhyel upon his return to consciousness was enough to drive him back to the darkness. But damp cold on his face and a rough, low-voiced command denied him that retreat.

Lumps, of indeterminate density, dug into his spine. The surface beneath him shifted with his weight, creaked and groaned in protest, and his heel, when he strove to ease the pressure under one hip, burst through that unidentified substance to strike solid wood below.

"Hold still, idiot," the rough voice muttered, and pulled the foot back to level with the rest of him, though the (one hazarded a guess) bed now had a decided list.

Memory returned in a rush, putting face to the voice, and identity to the fist that had knocked him cold. He cursed and swiped hand and rag aside, then tried to swing his legs free.

But a wave of nausea and the snap of another supporting strap quickly changed his mind.

"Damn. Nothing for it, Suds. Hold steady or I'll put your lights out again." And before he could object, Ganfrion had grabbed him under the shoulders and knees and heaved him free. One glance behind him assured him he needed no closer acquaintance with the object upon which he'd lain.

"Where are we?"

"Not in Ramblin' Rosie's. What more do you want?"

Mikhyel grunted, worked his jaw, and grabbed the rag from the floor. The water in the basin beside the . . . bed did not bear any closer examination than the rest of the room, but it was cool, and the rag, when rinsed and squeezed dripless, did provide some relief to the swelling on his lip.

The only other piece of furniture in the room, a rough chair beside the teetering bedside table, appeared at least as capable of supporting his weight as his knees currently were. He sat, rather more abruptly than he intended.

Ganfrion, arms akimbo, leaned against the wall. Waiting.

Tempting, to lose his temper, to blame the man for stepping above his place, to say that "anything" did *not* include breaking your employer's jaw.

Particularly after setting him up.

"You knew, didn't you?" he asked, holding his temper in check.

"About Pobriichi?"

Mikhyel just stared. Ganfrion shrugged, but in that, confirmed Mikhyel's belief that he knew full well that he'd set his employer up with a potentially lethal story.

"Who were those men?"

"Gicphactum watchdogs."

"To watch for strangers. Like us."

"Like *you*, yes."

"Why?"

"Why what? Why didn't I warn you? Why didn't I prepare you a pretty little story without any holes? Something you could spout like an actor repeating lines in a play?" Ganfrion lurched free of the wall, scowling. "Because this isn't a damned play, Suds, get that through your thick aristocratic skull. No matter how good a story you start out with, you play it simple, you play it ambiguous until you know the local climate. You think you're so damned clever, so superior to us. You think a little half-assed instruction is all you needed to survive in places I've spent a lifetime learning to tread. You've no damn *business* invading my world."

Mikhyel clenched his teeth, but that only hurt his jaw. He'd argue the man's final point—he didn't think Ganfrion had been born to that world any more than he had been—but resentment for perceived disrespect . . . *that* Mikhyel could appreciate.

And yet: "How do I know you didn't set the whole thing up?"

"You don't."

Moreover, Ganfrion wasn't about to defend himself. Mikhyel either took the lesson at face value, or he challenged Ganfrion's domain again. And next time, he doubted Ganfrion would be there to pick up the pieces.

On the other hand: *You play it simple, play it ambiguous until you know* . . .

And he remembered Ganfrion's adroit exchange, in which he'd never made a committed statement, but had led the conversation into revealing significant information.

And perhaps he *hadn't* known any more than he'd told Mikhyel. He had, after all, spent some months in Sparingate. Perhaps he hadn't set his intrusive employer up. Certainly, the new cuts on Ganfrion's hands and face hadn't been planned. And they'd been gained saving Ganfrion's employer's . . . thick aristocratic skull.

It wasn't just the invasion of his world Ganfrion resented. It was the betrayal of trust. Ganfrion had declared his commitment to his mission in that mad run to Shatum and back. To bring Mikhyel what he believed to be vital information, he'd spent himself, and his horses—as bitter a sacrifice for him, Mikhyel suspected, as it would have been for Deymorin or for Nikki.

And Mikhyel had thrown that commitment and sacrifice in his face when he had insisted on this personal validation of that information. Never mind *Mikhyel* knew he'd used Ganfrion and Rosie's not because he disbelieved Ganfrion, but as an opportunity to break his own mold—in pursuing a silly fantasy, he'd risked his real window into this grimy otherworld. And in risking Ganfrion, he'd risked the mission, and the future of the web.

He looked down at the rag in his hands, hands that, despite the dirt, didn't belong here. Nothing could eliminate the indentations around joints that had worn rings for years, nothing could create scars overnight. Inside or out. His, or Ganfrion's.

Whether or not Ganfrion had been born to this world, he'd learned to tread here safely, as Mikhyel had learned to tread the strange paths of his father's associates.

By his record, this was not the first time Ganfrion had had his extended loyalty betrayed. It was the key, the elusive quality he'd sensed in those records, but had not been able to elucidate.

He'd told Deymorin he didn't trust Ganfrion's honor.

He'd been wrong.

"I'm only going to say this once," he said, in a voice tight with embarrassment. "So listen well. I apologize for tonight. It was an insult to your sacrifice, your loyalty, and your honor. For that, I was wrong. Very wrong. The error will not be repeated. Until you give me cause to doubt it, your word on it, whatever 'it' might be, will suffice."

He met Ganfrion's expressionless gaze.

"But I give you fair warning. Give me that cause, make me sorry I spoke tonight, and you'd best be prepared for a long and extremely unpleasant life. You're not the only man who knows how to repay debt in like coin. Do I make myself clear?"

He wouldn't swear to it, but he thought, perhaps, there was the slightest softening about the dark eyes. But it could have been just the flickering of the lamp flame.

"Well?" he prompted, the single word harsh with tension, and Ganfrion blinked.

"Perfectly, m'lord Rhomandi. Perfectly."

Chapter Three

. . . and so, my beloved Rag'n'bones, while I miss you terribly, and would dearly love to urge you home, post haste, I believe you may rest easy tonight. I've read the letters Lidye has sent to her father, and she has read mine to His Imperial Highness Orakan (and yes, darling, I do know him). While I still have reservations regarding Lidye, those reservations do not extend to her loyalty to the Rhomatum Web.

No one is that good an actor.

Between the two of us, I assure you, we can outmaneuver any agreement of Auntie Liia's making.

With love and a disgusting number of hugs and kisses and decidedly lewd thoughts.

—Your Shepherdess

Deymorin folded the letter carefully, and refused to feel like a fool when he raised it to his lips before placing it on top of Nikki's painfully proper account of his intentions.

He couldn't fault them. Not Nikki, not Lidye . . . he wouldn't *dare* fault Kiyrstin. And with luck, they could accomplish a fair amount of good. He'd already written to Kharl Varishmandi, and suggested a similar meeting. If Kiyrstin, Nikki, and Nikki's Shatumin bride could lay the groundwork, so much the better.

At this point, any action he didn't personally have to make was welcome.

He set his elbows on the low table, and buried his face in his hands, rubbing his temples hard, then squeezing his eyeballs into his skull with the heels of his hands.

Tired. He was very, very . . . hell, he was fucking exhausted.

The watchtowers along the Amaidi Channel were . . . functional. The individuals manning them were . . . enthusiastic. With time, they might even approximate soldiers. But they had good men in charge, men with Kirish'lan border experience, and if anyone could train such raw recruits, they could.

Feeding them was another matter. There were farms around most of the forts. And those farmers had been induced to extend their fields—given the free labor of the would-be soldiers for clearing and the promise of a ready market.

He wasn't certain that they all didn't consider the whole thing a game.

Couriers from the northern end of the Maurislan Channel carried a different message. They had felt the pressure of Mauritum for years. The black market trade was alive and well, there where a person could swim between island and mainland, if he were fool enough to risk the icy waters.

The northern border watch had never truly ended; it had simply lost official sanction and shifted its priorities. Deymorin doubted the renewed sanction would affect trade, although it might raise the "import tariffs" paid for temporarily blind watchmen. And those looking out for shipwrecks might as well also keep their eyes out for Mauritumin armed with weapons rather than perfume.

He could, if he so desired, take a few days off. He'd stopped here in Barsitum for precisely that purpose, only to discover the local magic no more effective for his aches and pains than it had been ten years ago, after he'd taken a flying leap from a Rhomatum Tower balcony. Ten years ago, he'd come here with great expectations, following Mikhyel's experience, and he supposed some would say that had he not come, the infection in his leg wouldn't have healed, and he'd never have walked again.

But he'd seen others, as badly injured as he had been, who had recovered without benefit of Barsitum, and couldn't say he necessarily attributed his recovery to the node.

Unlike Mikhyel. Mikhyel should have died. Mikhyel certainly should have been a twisted cripple for life. He'd come home from Barsitum without a single (visible) scar.

The ley seemed universally to favor his middle brother.

Four days since Mikhyel's "adventure." Three days since Mikhyel should have arrived in Giephaetum, and nothing, no word from him, not on paper, not in his head. Nothing even to assure them he had survived his downhill foray.

Deymorin had tried to contact Nikki, tried to force Mikhyel into their three-way communication, but Mikhyel hadn't answered, and neither had Nikki, other than a brief, fluttering awareness.

Obviously, only Mikhyel could instigate their far-flung communication.

There did seem to be an inherent bias in that arrangement.

Deymorin stretched backward in the odd baglike chair the brothers favored: leather, stuffed with dried beans. Odd, but comfortable, in the way it shifted to fit his body.

But nothing could ease the sharp pain in his back, growing worse with each passing day, until he'd been reduced, when he had to walk for any distance or over rough footing, to once again using a cane for balance.

Kiyrstin could fix it. Kiyrstin's hands could have him virtually pain-free in minutes. And a night with Kiyrstin in his own bed would undoubtedly prove more efficacious than a dozen nights soaking in the brothers' pools.

And Nikki's meeting, if all went well, would be in two days. Perhaps three. Time enough for him to get to Rhomatum, without pushing himself or his horse. One didn't want to intrude on one's brother's moment of glory, still, if one were there . . . just in case . . .

He locked the letters in his case, gathered up a towel and headed for the baths. Ley or water, the heat and pummeling jets eased a man's muscles.

And tonight, with the promise of Rhomatum on the horizon, he might just sleep.

Even if he *didn't* hear from his recalcitrant middle brother.

§   §   §

"The lady Nethaalye is not receiving guests at this time." Neither the philosopher nor the magistrate had been graduated that could match a lifelong servant's capacity for pompous.

Mikhyel dipped his head, thanked the Giebhaidii House butler, and gave him a sealed letter, which the elderly man placed on the table with four other untouched envelopes—

his also, from previous visits. Mikhyel left without protest, there being nothing to protest, and wandered down the front steps of the tall house, and out into the surrounding garden, frustratingly aimless for yet one more day.

His fourth day in Giephaetum, his fourth attempt to see Nethaalye, his fourth unequivocal rejection from the house. He was being, there was no other word for it, snubbed. Nethaalye was . . . unavailable, her father was . . . just there, but stepped out . . . in a meeting . . . at lunch. In fact, every official in the city was busy. He'd arrived a week early, and, well, they were extremely sorry, but their schedules were filled. They'd rearranged their schedules to accommodate him once, they couldn't possibly be expected to do so again.

Snubbed. No doubt about it.

"Stood up again?" Ganfrion's dry tones wafted to him on a breeze, and Ganfrion himself stepped free of the shadows, clean-shaven and immaculate in a long black coat and tailored cuffs. "Can't imagine what you do to women, Suds."

Mikhyel had decided, over the past several days, that that ridiculous nickname wasn't worth fighting. Besides, it had a certain value as an indicator of his odd bodyguard's current mood.

At least, he'd never used it in public. Yet.

"I can't blame her," he answered, feeling oddly empty. "I just wish I knew if her silence is by her choice, or her family's."

"You put off marrying her for years, then deserted her to Anheliaa, after getting another woman pregnant, and you can't imagine why she wouldn't want to see your face? By the ancient's balls, man, you're amazing."

"How do you know all that?"

"Fly on the kitchen wall, Rhomandi-lad." Meaning he was romancing the Giebhaidii kitchen staff.

"Rings," Mikhyel muttered, "be careful!"

"Always. O, lord of mine." Ganfrion strolled a few paces away and paused, hands clasped at his back, staring up at the house. "That's her room, you know." And tossed him an over-the-shoulder look. "Third floor. Balcony. Salmon-colored curtains."

"Salmon curtains." Mikhyel chuckled, in spite of his better sense, and asked, with similar disregard to prudence: "And how do you know that?"

"Fly on the—"

"—kitchen wall."

"Actually, the laundry."

Mikhyel cupped his forehead in his hand, and shook his head.

"There is a way," Ganfrion said, slowly, and Mikhyel could almost hear the scheme forming.

"To do what?" he asked, with some trepidation:

"Do you really want to know if she wants your guts for garters?"

"Lovely. How?"

"I could get her a message."

"Through kitchen maids? Or laundry?"

"Actually—" Again, his eyes scanned that window. "I was thinking of something a bit more direct."

"You're joking, surely."

"I'm joking, surely not. Suds, you've got to loosen up. You want to send her a message, she'll get it tonight."

"You know what troubles me most about you? I'm actually considering accepting your suggestion."

"Of course, you are. I'll need something of yours—or something to tell her only you would know. Something to convince her I'm your true messenger."

"Just give her the letter. She'll recognize my handwriting."

"You're joking, right?"

"No." But the disgusted look on Ganfrion's face prompted him to qualify: "I don't think so."

"No special memory? No name? No ring?"

Mikhyel shook his head.

"Well, I give up on you, then. You don't *need* to ask. The answer's obvious. I'd leave you, too, you romantically-deficient boor."

"Our relationship wasn't like that."

"What is she? A dog-faced termagant?"

"Not at all! She's quite handsome!"

"Then you *had* no relationship."

"We were friends."

Ganfrion looked at him as if he were out of his mind.

"There *are* other ways to deal with women, Ganfrion."

"Women you're not engaged to wed, perhaps. Suds,

you're more hopeless than I thought. Well, I'll think of something. You just write your note."

"I've changed my mind."

"Not a chance. You've intrigued me. Obviously, I must meet this lady, with—or without—your leave."

"I'll write the damned letter. But you watch yourself around her, do I make myself clear?"

"Why, Suds, you wound my pride."

"Touch her, Crypt-bait, and more than your pride will be wounded."

"Crypt-bait. Rhomandi, there's hope for you yet."

⑨　⑨　⑨

The fine white sand of the practice field glimmered in the afternoon sunlight. Across that white expanse, dancers of all skill levels and ages gathered in groups, stretching, swaying, spinning and tumbling in time to the music that drifted through the cool mountain air.

A Khoratumin dancer's life was filled with music, morning to night. Music of all sorts, from every known corner of the world—as the dancers themselves came from all over to train with the Khoratumin instructors.

In their brief history, the Khoratum radical dancers had already captured the attention of the civilized world. Visitors from throughout the web and its neighbors had come to watch the Khoratum ringdancers, and carried tales home, along with promises from Rhyys regarding the Khoratum training program.

And so the foreign dancers came to Khoratum, sent here by sponsors to learn the exotic forms of the hiller dances, and the secrets the dancers were said to harbor, thinking that by training alone they could attain that unique quality that set the Khoratum radical dancer apart from all others, with or without the rings.

And in their blind arrogance, they filled Rhyys' coffers with wasted coins, and expanded Rhyys' already outsized ego with delusions of his own significance in the world. Because Rhyys denied the old beliefs and punished those who spoke of them with expulsion, yet the simple truth was that without the spirit of Rakshi guiding you, the dance was nothing more than trained motions.

With the upcoming visit of Mikhyel dunMheric, training

had been stepped up, preparations were underway for a massive celebration showcasing the students, a celebration that would end with the competition for the new radical dancer.

For Thyerri, watching from a rooftop, the sight was painful, but he seemed compelled to return here, day after day. He should be down there, practicing with that elite handful preparing for the competition. He'd been among those still to compete when the rings had gone down. Afterward, his petition to Rhyys for a second chance had been ignored, for no other reason than that Rhyys *could* deny him that chance.

Rhyys dunTarec was obsessed with controlling his dancers' lives. For all he frequently called the dance frivolous, for all he had been gone to Rhomatum for Nikaenor dun-Mheric's wedding at the time of the last fateful competition, Rhyys recognized the political advantages of his city's unique approach to the imported entertainment and paraded his dancers before visiting dignitaries like a breeder of exotic beasts showing off his prize stock.

It was humiliating. But then, so was much of life for a Khoratumin dancer.

Suddenly the music—and the exercises—stopped, and a form the size of three dancers combined flowed out across the white sand. Rhyys, dressed in billowing red-and-gold robes. And behind Rhyys, in simple black, was the scar-faced moth.

Thyerri drew back instinctively, for all the chances of their noticing him were small and of their doing anything about him if they did were nil. The excitement over the destruction of Bharlori's had passed by. Those who had died had been, like Bharlori himself, without importance to any but their closest friends.

The patrons who once shouted for Thyerri, had shifted their loyalties to Bharlori's former competition. Those taverns now thrived, with dancers of their own. Thyerri survived on his small stash of coins and the occasional odd job.

Thyerri hadn't danced since the night of the fire. Wouldn't, even without the threat of arrest. He wasn't even tempted: *Rakshi's* price for the night of the fire. And so, lacking other direction, he came up here to torment himself with images of the past and what could never be. Not even if Rhyys were to personally invite him back into the program could he find that person he once had been.

The dreams had become too much a part of him.

Rhyys had begun to call up the dancers, a group at a time, to perform their exercises for his scrutiny. After each demonstration, he would select one or sometimes two to perform a solo.

It was, so Rhyys claimed, his way of creating a competitive edge within the group. It was also, so he claimed, his way of maintaining control over the quality of the dance.

For the most part, the person Thyerri had been in that former life had been spared these ordeals. That person had not been a favorite of Rhyys', had, in fact, frequently been banned from this exercise field. He'd been declared too different, had joined the program too old ever to be able to move properly.

When Rhyys came to the radical competitors, he ordered them to go through the entire routines of all other levels, and finally, to perform individually. Two among them, who had been engaged in a strenuous routine when Rhyys interrupted, collapsed before the set patterns were completed.

Flaring with rage, Rhyys had them thrown out of the stadium, possibly from the program itself—certainly Rhyys was capable of such capricious acts. Even so, if their sponsors greased Rhyys' palm sufficiently well, they *might* still be allowed to compete.

Such was Rhyys' power, such were his principles.

Those remaining were ordered to begin solo routines, improvised to a piece ordered by Rhyys and chosen at random. Rhyys wandered among them as they danced. It was an all-too-common conceit for him, but one the competitors learned to ignore.

This time, perhaps to impress the moth, Rhyys edged closer to the dancers than usual, close enough, at times, to touch them. Particularly his favorite, Tabinth, whose virtues he'd extolled at that fateful dinner.

And when Tabinth, in an elegant display of flexibility, lifted her leg high above her head, and spun, she brought the leg down to discover Rhyys there. Too late to adjust the angle, her foot caught on his shoulder, and she staggered off-balance.

Rhyys laughed and grabbed her, holding her upright, with all the pretense of good will and aid. Tabinth stood rigid in his hold. Fearful. Certain, as Thyerri himself would have been, that Rhyys was about to throw her out as well.

But Rhyys cupped her face between his hands, and smoothed her hair back . . .

And kissed her.

Thyerri hissed and leaned forward, thinking how he wished Rhyys had died in that fire, not Bharlori, and how, if it were he down there, with Rhyys' mouth on his, he would bite Rhyys' tongue off.

A dreadful shivering consumed him and he thought at first it was in horror at his own violent and vengeful thoughts. But the shivers wouldn't go away, and he pulled the cloak tightly around his shoulders, wondering if he was taking ill. Down on the sand, the moth turned from the spectacle and stared upward . . . directly into Thyerri's shadow.

The shivers intensified—and in that moment, Thyerri knew who had watched him from the lake's edge that night the mountain returned to life.

Terrified, he slipped back into the shadows until the sand was far beyond his vision, then leaped to his feet and ran.

Chapter Four

My dearest friend, the note began, and it ended: ... *until sunset tomorrow* ...

Sunset. Now a good two hours past.

Mikhyel crumpled Nethaalye's note and his own pain-stakingly composed letter into his gloved fist, and thrust them into his coat pocket.

Strange, he didn't feel as if his mind were going. From recent decisions, however, it did appear that such was the case. First, Ramblin' Rosie's, now ...

Whatever had possessed him to entrust Nethaalye to Ganfrion's coarse methods? Nethaalye had, Ganfrion insisted, been eager to see him, had chosen the meeting time and place herself, and written the note to reassure Mikhyel on that point.

In retrospect, she'd obviously told Ganfrion whatever it had taken to get him out of her room the previous night.

One could scarcely blame her for that.

But Nethaalye's expediency put him here, waiting—like a love-struck simpleton—beside a garden fountain in the full moon's light, and destined for the common fate for such simpletons.

Nethaalye wasn't coming. Nethaalye had told her father that Mikhyel dunMheric had lost his mind and was dealing with . . . Crypt-bait.

He removed the thick envelope from his pocket, smoothed and folded it, and slid it into a different, more secure pocket, resisting the temptation to tear it through and throw the pieces in the fountain: a grand gesture that would allow the pieces to possibly retain enough legibility in the morning to start rumors of a nature he'd never unmake.

He'd burn it, when he was back in his room.

Though it was a good hour past his last real hope of her appearance, he began one more slow circuit of the garden's interweaving path, hoping against hope he'd simply misunderstood her very clear instructions.

The public garden *would* have been an excellent meeting spot: when he'd arrived, it had been well-populated by young couples, most, though by no means all, meeting under the watchful gaze of a chaperon.

Their chaperon was to have been Ganfrion, so Ganfrion had claimed, which had given new meaning to the phrase "a show of propriety."

He was disappointed, but not surprised. His relationship with the Giephaetum heiress had never been simple. Nethaalye had originally been matched with Deymorin, until Deymorin grew old enough to know the fate their parents had planned over his bassinet; what might have been a stimulating, comfortable friendship between in-laws had been marred and confused when Deymorin's role of future husband had ceded to Mikhyel.

The first of many such abdications. But Mikhyel had never allowed resentment of Deymorin's irresponsibility to his birthright to rule his actions before, and he wasn't about to start now. If he had to wait until facing the open Giephaetum Senate to request Nethaalye's aid in Rhomatum Tower, for the sake of the web and the cohesion of the Syndicate he'd wait.

Never mind he'd *hoped* to secure her willing partnership in private. Never mind he'd *hoped* to placate, if not heal, this growing rift between the Northern and Southern Crescents, virtually overnight with such a fait accompli.

But that was not to be.

His wanderings had brought him back to the fountain, where two cloaked figures brought momentary hope, dashed in the next instant by the wide-skirted profiles.

Mikhyel nodded to the moon-shadowed ladies, and passed quickly, giving every signal that he was looking elsewhere, keeping his own face bent beneath the velvet hood of his evening cloak. Best to just go back to his rented rooms, to wait in abject boredom for Gan—

"My, my, my, Sudsly." The broken falsetto whisper caught him in midstride. "How rude. Isn't that just like a Southerner, my dear?"

He stumbled.

"Clumsy, too. Best we leave him, child. He's hopeless." The voice broke completely.

Mikhyel turned cautiously, peering into the shadows. But there were only the two skirted silhouettes, one, he realized on closer inspection, rather on the large side. The smaller of the two had risen and now crossed the pebbled walkway with a natural, gliding grace.

"Khyel?" Gloveless hands, pearly-white in the moonlight, extended toward him. "I'm so sorry. I tried to get away sooner, but Verti, my brother, you know, chose tonight of all nights to start railing again about power fluctuations in the web, and once he begins, the only thing for it is to let him wear himself out. I'm surprised to find you still here. Please say you forgive me?"

He accepted the white hands with relief. "There's nothing to forgive, Talli, as you know." He turned her face to the light. "But you *are* here willingly? Ganfrion didn't, well, coerce you, did he?"

She laughed, lightly. "Oh, I wouldn't call it that, but—" She cast a sidewise glance at her large companion. "I must say, you are looking rather more robust than I'd been led to expect."

"I assure you, child," the squeaky falsetto arrived, along with the voluminous cloak, "pining was certainly the appropriate term, when last *I* saw him." Two lace-gloved hands appeared from the folds to cup Neethaalye's face, and the hood descended, then rose. "I'll leave you two lovebirds to talk, but mind you, I'll be watching. So *behave* yourselves!"

The large shadow floated off to settle on the nearby stone bench, arranging its skirts with, Mikhyel had to admit, a fair grace. A gloved hand waved them off, then settled with its mate in the voluminous lap.

Nethaalye's laughter again sparkled in the night air like the leylight on the fountain. "Where *did* you find her—him, Khyel?"

"Don't ask."

"All right, I won't. Now. But I intend to have the full story one day soon, I promise you. Either from you . . . or from him. Your choice."

"Rings," he cursed softly. "If it means I'll have the chance to tell you, I shall indeed regale you with stories."

"Of course you'll have the chance, dear Mikhyel. I'm terribly sorry about the letters; I didn't realize they were for me. Verti said they were for Father, and he's not here. I thought little of it, though I was disappointed that you were here and not asking to see me. But I do try not to judge you on such matters; you know that."

"You are, if anything, too reticent to judge, my dear." He glanced about. "Would you like to sit? Walk?"

"Walk, please. I spend far too much time sitting these days. One of the hazards of growing older that no one ever warns you about."

He held out his arm, she placed her hand on it, and they started slowly along the moonlit path.

"I hope you don't mind the subterfuge of meeting here. When your Ganfrion appeared in my window, along with your letter, I realized, of course, what Verti had been up to. I thought, perhaps, it would be best to consult with you before letting him know."

"Verti is the other ringspinner in your family, isn't he?" She nodded. "Second, now, to Ioniia, as he's *ever* quick to remind me."

"I thought I remembered that correctly. And your father? Where is he?"

"They haven't told you?"

"Only that he's been unavailable to see me."

"He's . . . " She stopped, turned slightly, hiding what little he could see of her face. When the light again touched her cheek, her expression was as calmly impassive as ever. "Tell me one thing, Mikhyel—and please, on our friendship, don't lie to me."

"I notice you do not ask me to swear on our betrothal."

"That was of our parents' forging. Our friendship—that's unqualifiably dear to me."

He squeezed her hand, fingerlinked, now, in his. "Anything."

"*Are* there plans to cap the southern node? Is *that*, in fact what is disrupting the web? Was *that* the cause of the firestorm and the power drain now?"

"Is that what your senators believe? Is that why they're avoiding me?"

"I would imagine. It's certainly what my father believes."

"I see . . ." And such concerns might well inhibit useful dialogue. "Truth, Talli, the firestorm had nothing to do with that node, and everything to do with Mauritum and a dangerous technology the ringspinners have been keeping secret from all of us for years. The current power drain is, we believe, due to damage that occured to the Khoratum line during that firestorm. My primary objective on this trip was to quietly alert the ringmasters and organize a unified attempt to repair the line and get the web stable again."

"And you wouldn't want that public, because there was so much resentment about capping Khoratum in the first place. *Particularly* in the Southern Crescent."

"Precisely. I wanted their guaranteed support in writing before I came up here."

"And you have that?"

"I do."

"And the node to the south?"

"Talli, a month ago I'd never *heard* of that southern node. I find its existence interesting, its potential—for disaster as well as use—interesting, but *no* one will cap *anything* that affects the Rhomatum Web without full knowledge of the Towers and proper debate in the Syndicate, if we have to put Lidye in Sparingate to prevent it. But I don't believe that will be necessary. The agreement was of Anheliaa's making, and Anheliaa is dead."

Her breath caught. Then she lifted a hand to his cheek. "You must be so relieved."

That surprised a short laugh out of him. "That's not exactly the reaction of most people."

"Barring outside malpractice, any half-competent spinner should be able to hold the Rhomatum rings. Anheliaa was . . . obsessively possessive." She began walking again. "And what Anheliaa looked for in her successor lay far beyond web stability. I must be honest with you, Mikhyel. I do not think Rhomatum got that in Lidye."

"But we could in you?"

"No."

"No, you won't? Or no, you can't?"

"I can stabilize them. I could reset them if I truly had to, but little else. Certainly not what Anheliaa planned."

"Were you privy to those plans?"

She shook her head. "Only surmising from things she did say. That was reserved for Lidye . . . if she even got the full truth before Anheliaa died."

"Would you," he asked slowly, "be willing to return to Rhomatum? To help in the Tower?"

"For the sake of web solidarity? I believe, my friend, it will require more than my gesture."

"Solidarity, yes. But more because Lidye truly could use relief. And because I trust you."

"Are you certain that's wise, Mikhyel?"

"Why wouldn't it be?"

"I think, perhaps, you should ask again where my father is."

A cough interrupted them. "*There* you are, darlings." And that poor, hoarse woman flowed in from a side path, through an arbor heavy with blooms. Ganfrion slid between them, a mountain of fabric with arms that engulfed both their waists and guided them firmly down a different path.

"Sorry, Suds," Ganfrion murmured in his normal voice and next his ear. "The lady's dragons are on the prowl. There's a pedal-cab waiting for you at the gate. The lad will take you and the lady to her home the long way, slow and sweet. I'll meet you there."

"The dragons—"

"Won't trouble you."

They were at the side exit, and Ganfrion, shifting to the broken falsetto, whispered, "Have fun, darlings."

A stubbled lip pressed noisily in front of his ear, and the mountain of fabric turned to Nethaalye, whispered something that made her laugh again, an easy, delighted sound Mikhyel would have given much to inspire. But humor, which had never been a large part of his life, was even less so tonight.

When they were safely ensconced within the pedal-cab, he asked, "Your father, Nethaalye?"

"Has gone to Khoratum. There are leaders, and those who would be leaders from all across the Northern Crescent converging there."

"For?"

"I don't know specifically, Khyel, and that's the truth. Ostensibly, Khoratum is celebrating the return of the radical dance following the Collapse. But they're planning something more, and it's not innocent."

"Why do you say that?"

"Many reasons. The simplest? Father took his entire guard with him. Others have done the same."

That surprised a laugh out of him. "What do they plan to do? March on Rhomatum?"

"I don't know." She did not, he noted, echo his laughter.

"If I'd been more clever, if I'd played along with Father's notions, then I'd be more use—"

"You are invaluable, my dear. How could you have known?"

"I should have, Khyel. We all should have. But it's not just the guard. Ioniia went as well."

"Your senior spinner?"

She nodded.

"Why Khoratum?" he wondered aloud. "Why not here? Or Orenum?"

"It was at Rhyys' invitation, is all I know. Ostensibly, he's planning a festival in honor of your visit. A combining of events with a hiller summer festival, or some such."

"And why didn't you go?"

"I wasn't invited."

A world of meaning in that. Errif loved his daughter. Would protect her from any possible harm.

Errif also knew his daughter's pro-Rhomandi views, and her intelligence and insight.

There were many reasons Errif might leave his daughter at home.

On the other hand, Giephaetum's ringmaster had gone with him. And the Khoratum line was the source of the web's problem. "Perhaps they're just planning to do alone that which I've been organizing. If I can get to them, convince them that we're all ready to work together—"

"Perhaps, Mikhyel, but . . ."

"Yes?"

"It's difficult to explain. I've no real specifics, you understand. No solid support of my conjecture."

This time, he waited, knowing she would speak when she was ready. For a while, the silence in the cab was broken only by the creak of a wheel and the rustle of cloth as Ncthaalye rearranged her skirts.

At last, she said, "The Southern Crescent is on the leading edge of imports. They specialize in making deals. Because we of the North are workers, because our primary function is to create a product, not manipulate the greed of others, the tacit assumption is that we're gullible, childish, and in need of . . . patronization. Leadership—in everything from fashion to politics. And it's not just Shatum who treats us this way, Mikhyel."

There was no good answer. There *was* a difference between

the people of the Northern Crescent and those of the Southern—as there was a difference between himself and Deymorin. And as with Deymorin and himself, the difference was a clash of style, motivation, and immediate purpose.

Or perhaps more properly, between Nikki and himself. Tempting, these days, to judge all relationships according to his recent self-evaluations, but in this case, the comparison did seem justified.

Just as *he* had served as a buffer between Nikki and Mheric, the Southern Crescent had acted, over the years, as a protective buffer for the Northern Crescent, economically speaking. Not because they set out believing themselves superior, but by virtue of their geographical location.

And by that accident of fate—whim of Rakshi, Ganfrion said—the Southern Crescent had learned a whole different set of survival skills. Having grown up protected from the true deceivers of the world, the Northern Crescent, like Nikki, weren't yet ready to match the Kirish'lani head to proverbial head.

Accidents of nature. Position and timing. Such factors shaped the character of societies as well as individuals.

The temptation was to assume that the end goal for all citizens of the Rhomatum Web was the same, that what everyone within the web most desired was a strong and viable web with healthy, productive citizens. Working together, they could complement one another, but they had to recognize and respect their differences first.

But such thinking presupposed against human nature. Presupposed that everyone placed such sensible, long-term goals above individual power and individual accumulation of wealth. Presupposition that was, in cold light of truth, folly indeed.

"I don't know," he said at last, "that there's anything *I* could do to change that, Nethaalye, other than open debate."

"One person can't change the attitudes of entire cities," Nethaalye said. "Certainly not now. The distrust has been planted and nourished. Something will be decided in Khoratum, issues *will* be raised. We can only deal with what comes down to us from others and not lose our own sense of what's important."

A subject with which, from her tone, Nethaalye had already had to deal.

"I knew, of course, that if I became ringmaster, I'd be expected to be sympathetic to the Northern Crescent, that I'd have duties. Whatever is underway, Father held back, waiting, I suppose, to find out if I was to be the next ringmaster of Rhomatum."

"And did you want to be, Talli? You never said, and when Anheliaa explained the dangers—that her own crippling was due to the Rings, I wasn't certain . . . except that *I* wouldn't want to condemn you to a similar fate. And then you left . . ."

"I was to be your wife, Mikhyel. If that duty to my family and the web included controlling the rings of Rhomatum, of course I would. I was not particularly concerned over that aspect of which you speak. I suspect that much of Anheliaa's crippling was linked to her . . . warped use of the ley, though I could, of course, be very wrong. However, that the honor of replacing her went to Lidye did not and does not affect me. I was afraid only that Anheliaa's decision played a part in *your* disappearance. That you were disappointed in me for cheating you out of your rightful inheritance."

"Never. As for my 'inheritance.' *I* suspect Anheliaa chose Lidye over you at least in part because she *wanted* Nikki over myself as the Rhomandi, although he didn't particularly want it either. We've already eliminated Anheliaa's meddling. The title belongs with Deymorin, no question about it. When he was with me in the south—"

"What . . ." She lifted her hands to her mouth as if to stop even that one word from escaping. "Excuse me. I promised myself I wouldn't ask."

"Talli, you can *ask* me anything. I can't promise I can answer, but you shouldn't hesitate to ask."

"Khyel, you know I think very highly of you. That I've a great deal of respect for your intelligence . . ."

"Are you trying to ask why I acted like the resident idiot to my brother's pubescent lead?"

Her bent head and tiny shrug was answer enough.

"I'm not certain I can explain. It has to do with too many years of being brothers, I suppose. Being too close and not close enough. We weren't *supposed* to *be* together. But I'd . . . been ill. He was worried about me, and we got in each other's way. I'm sorry if it's been an embarrassment for you. We were in the middle of the situation before we realized—"

"Not for me, Khyel. For you. They . . . They're saying that this is the real Mikhyel dunMheric. That without Anheliaa, you're nothing. That Anheliaa has kept you in Rhomatum all these years because once you were out, the truth would be known. That the Rhomandi will fall because they are none of them capable of . . . of wiping their own noses without Anheliaa to guide their hands."

He clenched his fist and tapped his knee lightly, when what he truly wanted was to put it through the side of the cab.

He didn't think the lad pedaling the bike would appreciate the defacement of his property.

"And is that what you believe?"

Her hand covered his fist. "I know better, my dear friend. You've always seemed to me the cleverest man I know. If I believed those cruel rumors, I would surely have to consider myself a fool as well, and I know that I am not. I was, however, concerned for what might have happened. I feared that Anheliaa's cruelty might finally have broken you. It is . . . it is a great relief to see that that is not the case."

Without looking at her, he lifted her hand to his lips.

"But my father does believe. As do others. It's easier, I believe, for some people to mock those who might outsmart them. To be physically outfought, that's an easily defined accomplishment. But to be outmaneuvered—some would much rather credit someone like Anheliaa, who had the power to destroy, than someone like yourself."

Darius, you are not . . .

One did begin to wonder precisely what one was, under the circumstances.

"When you disappeared, my father lost all expectation. He made me come home. Last week, when the first reports came in from Shatum about your . . . public appearances with your brother, he decided the rumors regarding your inadequacies were correct and that . . . that the Rhomandi were no longer suited to lead the Syndicate. That's when he left for Khoratum."

"He *made* you come home?" He took out of that statement the most immediately significant revelation, the rest being no more than validation of his own suspicions. "You didn't demand to leave when you found out about . . ." The words wouldn't come, somehow, they seemed to solidify so great a personal betrayal.

"Only a father's command could have made me leave Rhomatum when I did. Only a fool could believe that Anheliaa wasn't dying. I feared for the web, with Lidye in charge, her moods seemed to be fluctuating so wildly, and there was no one to control her, with Anheliaa down and you—all of you, gone."

And Mirym. She so carefully failed to mention the greatest provocation for her to leave. He doubted a man could even imagine how betrayed she must have felt.

And yet, she'd been willing, or so she'd implied, to stay in Rhomatum, *despite* the personal humiliation, *for* the sake of the web. He *wanted* her support. He *wanted* her to go back to Rhomatum, to join with the Rhomandi efforts to restore the web. They needed her.

And he'd come so close to turning her into an enemy.

"Not by my will, Talli," he said, and his voice must have been even lower than he'd intended, by the way she leaned toward him, the way she had to reach a hand to his arm to catch her balance.

He searched after the letter that had consumed his entire day to write and rewrite. It contained everything that had happened in the past months, even to the link he shared with his brothers. For a frantic moment, he feared he'd lost it, back there in an all too public park. Finally, he found it in a different pocket and, with a sigh of relief, pressed it into her hand.

"I hope this explains sufficiently. If, after reading it, you're willing—able—to forgive . . . me, I—we all—would very much appreciate it if you would return to Rhomatum."

She smoothed the wrinkles from the letter, then held it to her breast. "I'll read it, Khyel, and be thankful for your trust. But I will return to Rhomatum, and I'll help in whatever way I can, now I know you are safe and that you ask it. I cannot agree that with internal division lies anything but disaster for us all. I know you, I know your dedication to the web. I cannot believe anyone else could provide better leadership for us."

Relief filled him, from tensions he'd had no idea he was carrying. He closed his eyes, and drew a deep breath, letting it out slowly. Then taking her hand in both of his: "Words cannot express my gratitude, my dear."

"Under what pretext do I return?" For the first time, the calm in her voice wavered. "Marriage?"

His heart stopped. The question hanging between them could no longer be ignored.

"After what happened with Mirym?"

"Mirym isn't why I left, Mikhyel. I'd hoped I'd made that clear. She's a servant. A pleasant servant. An intelligent one. Men have always relieved their urges with such women—though I admit to being somewhat surprised in her."

"In her?" He laughed, ruefully acknowledging the shortcoming he'd always known. "Don't question her taste, Talli. It was I who—"

She laughed gently. "Oh, Khyel, you don't understand at all, do you? That's one reason I . . ."

He glanced up. She was looking at him. Just . . . looking. Strangely. Or perhaps it was the silver-dusted shadows from the city street leylamps that made her seem suddenly . . . different.

"Mirym was so very quiet, so eminently practical," she said at last. "It's not her bedding with you that surprised me. It was the fact she got pregnant. That seemed out of character. As for what happened between you, I'd be a fool to let it affect our situation. Other factors, however . . ."

That strange look hadn't left her face. She seemed to be measuring him for something. Finally, she said, "Must I be the one to ask, Mikhyel?"

In a sudden panic, he realized he had no idea what she was talking about.

Her eyes fell; she touched his hand, a gentle, lingering stroke. He turned it over and clasped hers, hoping that answered her need. She smiled, but not, he thought, in humor. Her other hand lifted to his cheek, her body leaning toward him, of necessity.

And only a fool could fail to read those signals. Only a greater fool would feel the confusion that gripped his stomach as violently as the tension before a major debate.

A sensible man—Deymorin—would lean the fraction necessary to match lips to lips, accepting easily the gift offered in such kindly humor and willing appreciation, not thinking beyond that. Or he would have before he'd found Kiyrstin.

But *he* had no Kiyrstin; no hold, moral, legal or emotional, on him. And this was Nethaalye, the woman he would, quite willingly, take to wife.

Would he, however, as willingly take her to bed? To bed, yes, as would his duty to his family and hers dictate. And he would perform, on cue, as duty also dictated.

And duty to her. He'd never thought about that part. Never considered that she might want—and deserve— more.

And he wondered, in some panic, if she did, in fact love him. And if, on that love, hinged the fate of the web. Because he very much feared that he could never feel for her what . . . what Deymorin felt for Kiyrstin, or even what Nikki felt for Lidye.

He steeled his stomach and leaned. Lips touched lightly. His tension remained. He drew back, or she did, and he saw, at this close range, a distinct, moist glimmer in her eyes, though her face remained as serene as before.

Freeing his hand, he cupped that serenity and tried again, seeking that elusive drive he'd felt on occasion with Mirym, albeit in general with the help of his randy brothers. He closed his eyes, seeking sensation first, trusting association would solve its own problem. And for a moment, he thought the necessary response was there, that . . . desire . . . might be possible. Lips softened, formed to one another, and explored with mutual respect.

But the gentle touch disengaged with a shuddery little breath, and dark, satiny hair replaced it against his lips. Nethaalye's hand left his neck to rest lightly on his chest, but for balance only, for all the pressure exerted.

"Oh, I do envy the woman you eventually take to wife, Mikhyel dunMheric," she said on a fluttering breath, and a whisper of a tremor rippled through her.

While he was still turning that over in his head, she sat back, utterly composed.

"But that woman is not I, my dear friend."

"Nethaalye, I—"

She pressed his hand.

They'd arrived at her father's empty house.

"Just let me know when to be ready to leave," she murmured, and stepped out into Ganfrion's waiting hands.

Chapter Five

For a woman who so vehemently resisted donning them, Kiyrstin chose her women's clothing well.

The cool shadows of the north garden formed a fitting frame for her overdress of deep maroon and soft tangerine orange. Her shapely shoulders and long neck rising from the pale blue, beaded undergown were enough to set any man's heart to racing. For Deymorin Rhomandi, too long without the feel of that skin beneath his fingers, the sight was sufficient to set more than his heart rate up.

She stood beside a small pool, one hand supporting the opposite elbow, the other cupping her chin in a familiar, deep-thought gesture.

His boots padding silently along the cedar-bark pathway, he slipped up behind her. Arms spread wide he surrounded her, in one hand, the enormous bouquet he'd brought into Rhomatum with him, in the other, a single rose. As he bent to press his lips to that bare right shoulder, his left hand drew the soft petals of the rose bud along her throat.

As an assassin would draw a blade across his victim's jugular.

Calm as a spring day, she tipped her head to the left, opening more territory to his exploring lips.

"Lucky for you, my husband is away," she said.

He lifted his head, strangely hurt. "Husband?"

Her rich chuckle eased the hurt, as she turned in the circle of his arms. "In all eyes but Garetti's and the law," she murmured, and molded her lips to his.

When Garetti's day had been thoroughly ruined, in absentia, and the bouquet restored to something vaguely resembling the Armayel florist's original effort, Kiyrstin asked, "So what *are* you doing here?"

"Missed my nonwife."

"Good start. And?"

"I'm running a bit ahead of schedule, I was in Barsitum, as close to Rhomatum as I'll be in the next month, so I thought I'd drop in for a visit."

"Drop in. Just like that."

"Well, I'm worried about Khyel."

"Ha. Now we're getting somewhere. When are you going to let the poor lad sink or swim on his own, JD?"

The bench on which they'd settled had a curve that followed the pond's edge and allowed an intimate near face-on conversation. And her face left no doubt regarding her feelings on this topic.

She thought him an interfering, energy-wasting idiot.

"Did Nikki tell you what he's up to?" he asked, feeling rather on the defensive.

"Yes. So?"

"I haven't heard a word from him, haven't felt anything since that wild scheme supposedly took place."

"Yes. So?"

"So, I'm worried."

"Yes. So?"

"Dammit, Kiyrsti, say something useful!"

"Yes. So?"

He glared at her. At length. *She* refused to elucidate. *He* relented.

Welcome to the world of normal people, eh?"

She nodded. "And?"

"Thanks to this *thing* we share, I'd know if he'd gotten into serious trouble."

"And?"

"I'll wait until he's ready to tell me what happened."

She leaned over and kissed his nose. He grunted and swiped the kiss away, figuratively speaking.

"*And* what in the name of Darius' balls are you doing in that outfit? Not," he hastened to add, "that I've any objections, mind you."

"I'm entertaining, this afternoon."

"You're *always* entertaining, m'love. Anyone I know, and do I trade my rose in for the real thing?"

"Keep your toys in their sheaths, laddybuck. We've guests from Shatum."

"Ah. Early."

"You got the letters."

He shrugged. "Thought I'd be here, just in case."

"Just never you mind. And you stay quiet and out of sight. Let Nikki and the ladies handle this one."

"Hadn't intended otherwise. Just wanted to be here for a firsthand viewing. What exactly are you up to? Who all came?"

"Damned if I'll recite the list. Everyone and their cousins. Kirish'lani, Shatumin, and a few who have yet to speak a civilized language."

Suddenly, the day was no longer quite so bright.

"Kiyrstin—"

"Oh, hush, Rhomandi, I'm joking. By the time we're through with them, they'll realize their only option is to sit and wait—unless they care to do it Darius' way, and then, well, we won't have to worry about them, will we?"

He rubbed an already ruined petal between two fingers. He thought of Mikhyel and what Kiyrstin had said, he thought about what would be happening here, if he hadn't come back, and interfering with plans already in motion, and decided, perhaps, he had to trust someone some time.

Besides, if things went wrong, she could—and would—come for him.

"I'll sneak into the house, let my little brother know I'm here, then wait for you in the room, where you can tell me all about it this evening." He yawned. "Darius knows, I could use the sleep."

"How long can you stay?"

"Since you don't need me, I'll be gone tomorrow morning before you wake up."

"Want to lay a wager on that?"

He chuckled. "Which—"

{*Deymorin?*}

His throat constricted. His vision faded. His ears rang.

And his body was soaked.

{Deymorin, are you there?}

{Shit, Khyel!} He waved Kiyrstin's hands away, and pulled himself out of the pond. {Back off.}

{Sorry.}

{Mikhyel? *Deymorin!* You're *here*?} Confusion. Elation. All that and more from an enthusiastic Nikki.

{Nikki, save your reunion for later, please.} Khyel, of course, holding Nikki at bay.

{Where the hell are you, Khy?} Deymorin asked. {You're as clear as if you were standing right here.}

{The Tower of Giephaetum—or near enough it makes no difference.}

{Made contact, then?}

Acknowledgment. {Nethaalye's returning to Rhomantum tomorrow. Nikki, is it safe?}

{Yes. I'll tell Lidye. I'm certain she'll welcome the help.}

{I hope so. Deymorin, Kiyrstin—}

{Is right here. I'll tell her.}

{Here? You're in Rhomatum? That explains . . .} The balance was garbled. {There's trouble here in the north.}

{Want help?} Deymorin asked and thought about heading north.

{Not yet. I'll let you know. But it wouldn't hurt to have a few men prepared to move about the board.}

{To where?}

{Not certain yet. But I'm certain Venitum wouldn't mind some maneuvers in their direction. I'll be continuing on from here, but I'm setting word out that I'm returning with Nethaalye, and I didn't want you to worry. I'm saying it's because I'm ill.}

{Are you?}

{No!}

{Where to?}

{Khoratum.}

Deymorin's heart skipped, and he asked, while trying not to think of what he'd *been* thinking about for the past week: {How's the spy business, brother?}

{It went exactly as you imagined, Deymio, so go ahead and gloat. But I survived and learned a good lesson.}

{I should hope—} He caught that thought. Caught Kiyrstin staring at him, and remembered her lesson about letting brothers live their own lives and revised: {I'm just glad you're all right, Mikhyel. Honestly.}

Laughter that rang lightly in his mind. {Tell Kiyrstin I love her, will you?}

{Fuck off.}

More laughter. Then Nikki's voice, tentative: {We started work on the dam.}

{Already?}

{Two days ago.}

{Nikki, that's *wonderful*! I look forward to seeing it on my way back from Khoratum.}

Satisfaction from Nikki. And pride, shy, but utterly real, in his own accomplishment, and on that final word, his brothers faded from his mind.

§   §   §

"You'll accompany the lady Nethaalye back to Rhomatum. Ostensibly, so shall I." Mikhyel laid his shirts out on the bed, narrowing the selection one more time, choosing the plainest, most serviceable of the lot.

"Ostensibly?" Raulind, from his tone, was less than excited at the prospect Mikhyel offered.

"I'm going to Khoratum. You'll be in charge of the entourage."

"I'll have only a token assemblage, then."

"No. I'm going alone. You'll have the lot. It's got to appear as if I'm going back with you. We'll put it out that I've taken ill—again. The web ought to be accustomed to that news by now. No one will question. I'll go to Khoratum on the public carrier."

"Khyel . . ."

Raulind's protest didn't extend beyond the single word. Mikhyel smiled, setting his hand on his friend's shoulder. "Get Ganfrion, will you?"

The tense muscle relaxed beneath his fingers. "You're taking *him* with you, then. Good enough."

Raulind left in renewed spirits. Strange, that those two should have joined forces. Following the night at Ramblin' Rosie's, Ganfrion had delivered him, bruised, filthy and bleeding, to Raulind, who had simply scrubbed him to presentability and declared him now content to leave spying to those that knew what they were about.

If he were a suspicious sort, he'd have believed the two men in collusion from the start.

He folded another shirt and maneuvered it into the edge of the portmanteau he intended to carry with him on the public coach. He'd be a student . . . better yet, an underprofessor from Bernoi Judiciary Academy. On sabbatical. *Hoping* to better his position. Studying legal systems firsthand.

Strange, how youthful dreams insinuated themselves even at twenty-almost-seven.

A knock on the door interrupted his formative scheme. "Enter."

Raul, of course, with Ganfrion in tow. And Raul left, closing the door behind him, not giving Mikhyel even the illusion of a second. He frowned at the door, then shifted the look to Ganfrion, who met him, frown for line.

"I'm leaving for Khoratum tonight."

"Yeah."

"You're headed for Rhomatum tomorrow, with the lady Nethaalye."

"Try again, Rhomandi."

"I said—"

"I heard what you said."

"You just don't believe I meant it."

"I thought you were smarter than this, Rhomandi. I *thought* you'd learned your damned lesson! Surely Rhomatum has ears and ears in Khoratum. Why not have them investigate the woman's allegations?"

"If they were doing their job, we'd already know, now wouldn't we?"

"Or your woman's lying."

"She's not."

"Sound real sure of yourself, Suds."

"Don't *call* me that. —I am. Sure."

"I'll stop calling you that when you consistently act as though you've something else in your skull besides bubbles! Dammit, Rhomandi, every time I think I've got you figured, you go and pull something like this! What the *hell* do you think you're doing? *Go*, if you must, but take me with you! Dammit, Khyel, you're going to get yourself killed!"

He blinked, quite . . . *quite* unprepared for such impassioned anger.

"I assure you, that's the last thing on my agenda."

"Agendas don't matter, not when the agend*izer's* a fool."

"I'm not a fool."

"Saying doesn't make it so."

"I need no one with me, damn you. People travel about the web constantly, men and women, alone and with impunity."

"People aren't Mikhyel Rhomandi dunMheric of Rhomatum Tower."

"I'm not going to be Mikhyel dunMheric. I'm going to

be Korelli dunKharin, underprofessor of social liberties, Bernoi Judiciary Academy, on sabbatical."

Ganfrion's jaw dropped . . .

"I've thought it through. It's *my* world, this time. Secretaries and accountants and lawyers. *Believe* me. You wouldn't fit in."

. . . and snapped back, then he frowned, tipping his head to one side, looking Mikhyel up and down.

"I want you with Nethaalye. She'll need you most of all."

The frown deepened.

"You make her laugh."

A grunt.

"Rings, Gan, an underprofessor of social liberties! There's no brain more full of bubbles in the web. I'll be right in my element!"

A snort that might well be laughter.

"I *need* to do this myself, Ganfrion," Mikhyel said, and wondered that he didn't sound or feel as if he were pleading. But Ganfrion was listening, now, and Ganfrion understood the need to be trusted, the need to have his own judgment respected.

And finally: "Shave the beard."

Mikhyel sighed, knowing the battle won. "Thank you. I will."

Ganfrion poked his way one-handed through the portmanteau. Critiquing his choices, no doubt.

"So, I make her laugh, do I?" he asked, turning to the discarded shirts still on the bed.

"You know you do."

A grunt, and one shirt pulled free. A judicious rip or two of the lace and it joined the portmanteau. "Secondhand— for dressup," Ganfrion muttered. "Why should she need to laugh?"

"It's good for what ails?"

That got him a raised eyebrow. "So I've been telling you, Suds. Why?"

"She's going into potentially hostile surroundings. She could be nervous en route. Once she's there, Deymorin will set her at ease—"

"Deymorin? Your *brother's* back in Rhomatum? Forget it, Suds."

"That doesn't matter. *I* ordered you to return."

"Right. You think I'm going to Rhomatum and tell your

large, hot-tempered brother who patently hates my interior
that I let you go into the heart of the storm alone, because
you told me to? Thank you, no."

"Dammit, Ganfrion, if it takes arresting you, I'll order it
done! Ori's been waiting for weeks to hear me authorize
it! I'm going *alone*."

The big man's jaw worked, while his broad chest heaved
with suppressed anger. Then:

"I want a letter."

"Letter? What *kind* of *letter*?"

"I want a full pardon. I want my freedom, Rhomandi.
No questions. No conditions. No ties or obligations to the
Rhomandi. I want absolution from any responsibility where
your fate is concerned. I want my ass covered, you self-
serving, narrow-minded son of a money-wallowing
bastard!"

"*Fine!* If that's what it takes—" Mikhyel threw himself
down at his desk and wrote furiously, ignoring the sound of
the door opening, of soft footfalls arriving behind his chair.

"Khyel, I can't allow this." It was Raulind, two-faced
traitor that he was. Mikhyel ignored him, and set his seal
to the hot wax.

"There!" He thrust the official parchment at Ganfrion,
who accepted it with an almost cheerful smile. But then,
he had all he wanted now. Free, he was, to go and milk
some other man's purse, to defy some other man's authority. Free to land one more time in the Crypt.

"Don't worry, Raul," Ganfrion said. "I'll see you and
the mistress to Rhomatum." And without a pause: "And
then I'm off for Khoratum to save his arrogant ass."

"Hell, if you—"

"Can't stop me, Suds," he said softly, and waved the
parchment. "Not now."

Interlude

Life was . . . getting better. Mother stretched, long and hard, until her fingertips brushed the topmost edges of the clouds, and her toes tickled the bottom of the deepest ley-thium pool beneath Khoratum. Then she contracted again, the misty essence of her body condensing to its preferred, scaled form.

Easier to move, each time she tried, and the inclination seemed to come more often. Soon, she might be inclined to walk the surface world.

At times such as this, when her very scales itched for activity, she wondered how her siblings could rest content, aeon after aeon, beneath their mountains, how they could resist the urge to walk among the surface creatures, to run with the four-legged ones, to eat, to breathe, to procreate. . . .

Mother was especially fond of that, and her special children had proven masters of the art. Unlike the other creatures, who tended to feel the urge and act on it at once, her human children understood anticipation. Her human children took their time, tempting, teasing (which Mother well understood) stimulating body and mind before the culmination.

It was all very interesting, and endlessly creative, among the true connoisseurs. Of all the changes humans had made in her existence, love-making was the most recent. It required great amounts of energy, adaptation, study . . . and practice.

She'd really only begun to comprehend its complexities when the progenitor threw his most recent snit and landed her here indefinitely.

One of her most special children called overhead, asleep and in lonely misery. It pained Mother greatly not to answer, but that child, as had others in the past had grown too like its Mother, and Mother had grown . . . concerned . . . that it develop as one with its own world. She had seen a future for it, in a dream, and that future would not come to pass if it retreated into her caverns of mists and dreams.

Other children had, in the past, those whom the cave welcomed, and Mother had watched them fade into their own oblivions, and eventually had been forced to absorb them, but such were her failures, and she tried to learn from them, wishing to enrich her favorites' lives, not to entrap them.

Sometimes, as with the one who called, she simply started the process too young. But the one above had been so close, from the moment she first brought it here, the ley had engulfed it, nourished it, treasured it, until its scent and sweet taste permeated the cavern as none before it.

Mother had had plans for her current special children, had been forced into modifying those plans when Anheliaa had set the rings spinning overhead, and her siblings and progenitor had insisted she fall into *their* pattern.

Not all her special children had weathered that pattern change well.

Another child brushed her perimeters. A mind of a far different scent, an almost familiar flavor. But her memory still inclined toward unreliable. She reached toward it, curious, hungry for something new. . . .

SECTION
Seven

Chapter One

"Whoa-oa-oa-oa."

The public coach rumbled, swayed, and creaked to a halt. Mikhyel, after his second day of fighting frozen feet, sunburned face, and the overwhelming battle of his companions' perfumes, had the door unlatched and the stairs extended before the vehicle had finished moving.

Cool mountain air rushed in, driving out the overused molecules within. The youngest woman squealed, as she had when he'd tried to lower the window earlier that afternoon, and drew a length of scarf up over her nose, protecting herself from the Evil Outside Humors.

One had to wonder *why* such dainty pieces were on their way to Khoratum, but one truly did not want to ask, because one might find oneself obliged to listen to the answer.

The entire answer.

Mikhyel eased down the stairs—the slightest movement jarred his pounding head—then turned to help his fair companions out. At least, he assumed they were fair. From the way they were bundled against those Humors, one of them could be Ganfrion in his newest guise. Hunched over double, but even that was possible.

Words came out of those mounds of fabric; a plethora of words, as a matter of fact. And at least two of the three found him and his fabricated life endlessly fascinating. Fortunately, their curiosities frequently took varying directions and they'd spent more time arguing over what to ask him than in expectations of answers.

And as they disengaged from the coach, each clasped his hand in vociferously heartfelt gratitude. He'd smile, pry one set of fingers loose, only to find himself captured again by the next lady to descend.

The possibility existed that by the time they reached Khoratum, he would come to hate the young man, whose

name he didn't know, but whose experienced, quick thinking had landed him the sole outside seat beside the
coachman.

He picked up the portmanteau that thudded into the dust
beside him, hefted one of the women's bags, whose weight
threatened the limits of his strength, held on to it with grim
determination and pride, and limped into the staging inn
on feet barely able to feel the ground through his thin-
soled shoes.

Somewhere, Ganfrion was laughing while he sipped his
brandy.

He set the woman's bag down inside the door, where the
coachman would pile the rest, and went to sign his name
on the register and get his key—his own key, this time,
please the gods; the quick-thinking young man had snored
the previous night through, after staggering in reeking of
spirits.

The young man complained, having counted on the reduced rate of a shared room, but Mikhyel assured him the
innkeeper had generously offered otherwise, not telling him
the offer was: if Mikhyel wanted separate rooms, Mikhyel
paid the full rate, plus half. It would be worth the extra
expense for a decent night's sleep.

Supper was a delight not to be contemplated, with breakfast still heavy on his stomach and his afternoon bread and
cheese still wrapped, untouched, in his pocket. The ladies
made much of his obviously failing health, exclaiming over
his need of a separate room, his impaired appetite, the
"pain that furrowed his beautiful brow," until all he could
think of was that well-sprung bed, the room filled with
mountain freshness, awaiting him.

The bed was lumpy, and the window nailed shut.

The portmanteau slipped from fingers gone numb. Mikhyel's shoulders slumped, along with every other bone and
muscle, and he sank onto the hard, wooden stool beside
the rough carved table.

The stool . . . rocked.

From somewhere deep inside him, laughter happened,
helpless, but with a real sense of his own foolishness, the
crazed situation he found himself in, all of his own
deliberation.

He rubbed his eyes, then drew the hand down over his clean-shaven face, encountering the tiny bandage from this morning's worst mistake, wondering if tomorrow, he'd manage to slit his throat with his razor.

And he laughed some more.

Until his hands began to glow.

Leythium chandeliers, leythium-lace drapes, liquid leythium bubbling in sweet-smelling pools . . . It appeared he was back in the caverns beneath Rhomatum.

"Damn," he muttered, then said aloud, "Sir? Your, uh, lordship? Forgive me, I . . . I don't know how to address you, but I can't *be* here."

{Ooo-oo-oo, do I know you?} Mikhyel spun on his heel. His *bare* heel. Bare . . . as the rest of him was exposed.

"Sir, *please* might I have my clothes back?"

{Clothes? Why? Certainly not for my sake.}

He turned again, and there he was. Or perhaps not the same creature, for this one was as female as the other had been male.

Which seemed a silly conclusion, for something he'd seen form out of the ley itself, then shift shape even as he watched. This could as easily be a different manifestation of the same being, chosen out of whimsy.

Still there was something in the . . . flavor . . . of the thoughts that had floated through his mind that suggested, if not female, then at least youth, a facile agility of thought the Rhomatum being had lacked.

And the scent that filled the air here was not fireblossom-tea, but . . . raspberries.

Almost as if in response to his thoughts, the creature changed form subtly as it glided across the cavern toward him, gaining humanlike, feminine curves. But if it catered to his sensibilities in that shift, it only compromised: the iridescent, scaled skin, the fanged, elongated face, and the bare, webbed feet were many things, of which humanlike was not one.

And though she declared clothing unnecessary for him, she was herself covered in lacy leythium gauze, that trailed off in floating tendrils and connected, weblike, to the surrounding leythium formations.

A sort of sleepy curiosity encompassed him like a cloud as the creature made a slow, drifting circuit around him.

"I thought," her voice whispered through the tendrils, setting them fluttering, "that I knew you. But I . . ."

She seemed puzzled, but Mikhyel hesitated to place any human value on what such a creature might feel. That they *had* emotions, he didn't—*couldn't*—doubt following his session with the Rhomatum creature.

Self-preservation dictated caution, and healthy fear of these strange beings, but curiosity overpowered all sensible faculties.

"Did you bring me down here?" he asked.

"Naturally . . ."

Her voice held none of the Rhomatumin creature's sibilance, and it, as well as her form, seemed more easily maintained.

"Why?"

"I told you . . ."

She drifted near, and her webbed, talon-tipped fingers cupped his face. Instinct dictated avoidance. Escape. Logic scoffed, and asked: Where would he go?

"Welcome home, my darling . . ." Her fanged face leaned close, her eyes closed. She seemed to be smelling him.

He held himself very still, vaguely disturbed that calm acceptance came so easily, particularly when very womanlike lips pressed his, more so when his lips opened willingly—*her* will, a voice deep within him objected—and a strange, delicate flickering investigated the inside of his mouth.

He should, a different part of him pointed out, feel violated. He should be fearful of such intimate contact with a being composed of a substance that in at least one form absorbed human flesh. He should be wondering whether these creatures considered him a viable candidate for supper's main course.

But none of those fears reached maturity. Only love and curiosity coursed through him in the wake of that flickering exploration. Love, curiosity . . . and memories of the caves beneath the Rhomandi hypogeum.

"Ee-ee-eck!" She pulled her hands away as though stung,

and her—forked—tongue flicked out between her lips, over and over as though ridding them of some foul taste. "You've been with *him!*"

Free at last of her influence, those remote fears blossomed to full flower. He fought them down, determined that panic would not rule his thinking. He had nowhere to run, no way to escape this place except through the same agency that had brought him here.

Besides, he reasoned with himself as he backed slowly away, compared to Anheliaa or Mheric, this creature's touch was exemplary, and the ley had never threatened him, had, in fact, welcomed him with its cool-warm touch at both Rhomatum and Barsitum. Had, in fact, saved his life.

This creature was, he had to believe, responsible for the unnatural calm that had held him steady for her examination. Anheliaa had used her own desires to manipulate his thinking, he and Deymorin affected one another even without consciously willing it. It seemed reasonable to assume that these creatures, made of the ley itself, might project eminently more compelling desires.

And yet, it was difficult to find threat in either being.

These creatures. He was increasingly certain this was *not* Rhomatum. But if not Rhomatum, where...?

He'd been on a cross-ley road about halfway between Khoratum and Giephaetum. If each node had one—or more—of these creatures beneath it, wouldn't Giephaetum have "spoken" sooner?

They'd crossed the Orenum line, but the Orenum Node itself was quite distant, far to the north.

Khoratum...?

{How clever you are . . .} The thought drifted into his mind and the creature floated up to him again, cautiously, or so it seemed, examining his face. Her fingertip, a talon every bit as sharp as Anheliaa's honed nails, traced his jaw. And again, foolishly, he felt no desire to avoid that touch.

But it was a feather's gentle caress, not Anheliaa's vicious torment.

A slow smile split her undeniably beautiful, though utterly inhuman, face. "Ah, darling, I did a good job on you."

"Job?" He blinked, wondering what she meant.

She disappeared. A finger traced his backbone, followed the handful of near-invisible scars remaining from the terrible burns he only half-recalled.

"I told them there'd be scars-s-s-s." And with that came the first hint of the sibilant hiss he associated with the Rhomatum creature's speech.

The webbed fingers smoothed his shoulders and down his ribs. "Skinny, child. Chickens. You must eat more chickens." And absently: "Did you bring one for your mother? She grows thin with hunger these days-s-s-s."

Delicate fingers cupped and caressed his buttocks, slid around his waist and down his flanks. He shifted. "Uh . . . excuse me . . ."

Laughter, light as the breeze, full as a storm-fed gale, and she was back in front of him, her hands once again on his face, soothing, reassuring. Until . . .

"Ptah! Fuzz!" Her hands jerked away. "*His* doing, isn't it?"

"Excuse me?"

"Such a bother. Scrape it off it just comes back, scrape it off, it's back, scrape it off . . . I could *fix* that for you . . . again."

Her fingers entwined in his and she pulled him, with a child's eager delight, toward the nearest pool.

"Thank you, no." He tried to jerk free, and in the next instant discovered himself captive, his arm twisted behind his back, forcing him into her solid as stone body.

Anger. It permeated the air around him, and the leythium pulsed a deeper and deeper red. But he refused to be frightened. Neither she nor Rhomatum had given him any reason to believe his life was in danger from them. Instead, he sought, and found, fascination within himself, just as he had beneath the Rhomandi hypogeum.

Slowly—in the face of that curiosity or perhaps in response to his indifference to her implied threat—the creature relaxed. The stone clamping him regained the warm pliability of living flesh, and the red cooled, shifting to its former iridescence.

"Darling, *don't* fight Mother. *Never* fight Mother. She doesn't want to hurt her children, but when they fight, sometimes it's hard . . . so very hard . . ."

Her tongue flickered out again, touching his face, soothing him with her strange fluttering kisses.

[Not so bad. You taste of him, but you temper his flavor. Make him quite . . . quite palatable.]

It was that other being she referenced, he slowly realized. The one beneath Rhomatum.

[Of course, darling. You do hear me, don't you? And very well. Oh, you are clever. I'm not surprised he couldn't resist. —But Mother *found you first. Don't you remember?]* Her thought tasted wistful. And he wished that he could make that sadness go away, but—

(Pain.)

It was sensation born out of a memory as vivid as the day it had happened.

(Deymorin! Nikki!)

His brothers' desperate situation. Near, in his head, yet far distant.

(A sense of being stretched, horizon to horizon.

(A snap—

(Light. Pain. Falling. Pain. Burning. Pain.

(Dying.

(Mother.

(And another face, green eyes framed in a cloud of shaded hair.)

[Oh, we do remember! And did you bring your mother a chicken?]

He was lying on the floor, curled on his side, so consumed with the memories, he had to check his own exposed flesh to convince himself he was not once again burning. The creature—Mother—was squatting next to him, her bright eyes following his every move.

He pulled himself up, wrapped his arms around his knees, not yet ready to trust himself to stand. The remembered pain was gone, but his muscles were trembling. Cramped.

From fighting memories.

"Oh, dear." Mother touched his forehead, and the pain stopped. Instantly. The trembling did. Mother tipped her head to one side, lifted a graceful shoulder in a lopsided shrug. "Sorry."

Mother. Deymorin's shapeshifter; Nikki's Tamshi.

His . . . savior.

"Yes-s-s-s. Keep remembering, darling. Remember for us both . . ."

He drifted, then, in a sea of memory, of childhood and on, of Deymorin and Nikki, Anheliaa, and finally, those months leading to the Boreton Firestorm.

"Yes-s-s-s . . ."

But the events after he'd fallen from the sky were broken, shattered sensation. His eyes (he suspected, and Mother's thought confirmed) had been sealed shut in that burning transfer.

And Mother supplied images then, of himself on the ground, of Deymorin and Nikki and Kiyrstin, and a slender humanlike creature spreading an oil over his repulsive burns, burns that vanished with the oil's passing.

And he sensed excitement, an eagerness for the rest of the story, for what had happened since that time of healing. And his mind carried them both, moment by moment, through his life, from then to the present, including what he understood about the state of the web, and Khoratum's line and Rhomatum and Anheliaa. . . .

{Thank you, my darling child,} and the touch on his forehead slipped away.

"Why?" he whispered, "What happened to you?"

She seemed . . . different now. Vitalized.

"I was tired, child."

Her speech and thought crisp and focused.

"Very, very tired. Had I known at the time how fractured the web had become, I'd never have healed you."

"Forgive me if I don't say I'm sorry."

Her laughter filled the chamber with music. "You'd be a fool, darling. And that, obviously, you are not. No, it would have been . . . irresponsible of me, had I known. It weakened me, at a moment in the course of time that I would most have desired to be strong. I transferred back to my source, and I've drifted here ever since, renewing my essence."

"And are you . . .?"

"Quite well, darling, thank you, and thanks to you. I'd . . . lost touch with my surface world. You have helped me to regain it. But there were others . . ."

Her voice faded, her eyes closed, and her head rolled

back. Her seated figure seemed to dissipate, and to float.

"Ah, child," she whispered, but not, he thought, to himself. And when she opened her eyes, it was as if she'd never drifted off.

"So, where were you headed, child of Mheric?"

"I'd prefer it if you don't call me that."

"And do you prefer child of Darius?"

"I prefer my name, madam."

"And I prefer mine."

"Mother?"

"Quite. Mikhyel?"

"Quite."

"Not a common name."

"My mother chose it."

"Of course. Mothers always name their children."

"Mheric chose Deymorin. And Nikaenor."

"Only because your mother agreed."

He laughed and threw up his hands in defeat, and her delight with his impertinence filled that under-sense.

"So, Mikhyel-darling-child, where *are* you headed?"

"You already know that."

"Of course, but conversation is *such* fun, and how am I to offer to help you if we don't know what I'm talking about?"

Even repeated in his head several times, he wasn't certain that made much sense; however, there seemed no reason not to admit: he answered, "Khoratum."

"Of course. Where? The Tower?"

"Why?"

"I'll send you there."

"Like this?"

"Well, if you're that bashful . . ." She flourished a hand, and a green-blue glow hazed the air about him, solidified into the clothing he'd been wearing before she transferred him here.

"You must be feeling better," he commented.

"The least you can say is thank you."

"Thank you."

"You're welcome. So, where in Khoratum?"

"Thank you, no. The room you pulled me from will be fine. I'm going to have enough explaining to do."

"Explaining? Why? They've already left, you know."

"Who? Left where?"

"Those silly humans who think you're not-Mikhyel."

"*Left?* How do you know?"

A floating shrug. "Mother knows."

His heart raced, then stopped. He thought of tales of people disappearing . . . for years at a time, to appear again, unchanged. And he thought of Deymorin, who had simply . . . lost half a year.

"How long have I been here?" he whispered.

"Long enough. Not too long."

"What's *that* supposed to mean?"

"You can still beat the post to Khoratum."

"How can you be certain?"

"Mother *never* loses."

He clamped his lips on the retort that rose; Mother grinned, a very sharp-toothed stretch of scaled lips.

"Tell me, Mikhyel-child, why *are* you pretending to be someone you're not?"

"Because I—" Feel like it, he almost said, then he sighed, and resigned himself to his fate. "Because there are those who won't speak honestly to Mikhyel dunMheric."

"Oh." Her eyes glowed with excitement. "Have you a good story to tell?"

"You sound like Ganfrion."

"Mother sounds like no one. Others may sound like Mother. Have you a good story?"

"Sufficiently so."

She fluffed out her leythium skirts and wiggled downward, as if preparing a nest. And indeed, the leythium beneath her molded upward into at least the appearance of comfortable pillows. "Let me hear it."

"Don't be ridiculous. I must get back. I've had no sleep—"

"Plenty of time." She waved a hand airily. "I'll deposit you inside."

"Inside? Inside *what?*"

"The town. The Tower. The public bath . . . How about a brothel? Wherever you like, Mikhyel-child. It's just overhead, you know. It'll be fine. I want to hear your story."

He made a final attempt: "What about my baggage?"

"What do you need baggage for?"

"My razor, among other things!"

"I told you, I can take care of that for you."

"You and Anheliaa."

"Oo-oo, how disgusting. Keep the fur, then, by all means. Now, about that story . . ."

Chapter Two

There was a commotion outside in the Riverview Inn's stableyard: a large entourage arriving. Little doubting who it was, Deymorin descended the stairs to greet them. Kiyrstin was already in the front parlor, waiting for him and her dinner.

Kiyrstin had insisted on coming along. Kiyrstin had said Nethaalye needed an ally. Kiyrstin had said the drive back to Rhomatum would give her and Nethaalye time to get to know one another.

Kiyrstin had come because Kiyrstin wanted *out* of Rhomatum, even for just a day or two.

He rounded the final corner just as the front door opened. Nethaalye dunErrif entered first, laughing and shaking her hair free of a spattering of raindrops. Behind her—

"What the hell are *you* doing here?" Deymorin barked, and the smile vanished from Nethaalye's companion's face. Dark, deep-set eyes lifted slowly to meet Deymorin's.

"Hello there, unfriend," Ganfrion said without the least hint of confusion. He shifted position, but only giving to pressure from those behind him wanting inside. His eyes never dropped from Deymorin.

"Deymorin!" Nethaalye moved to the bottom step and smiled up at him. "Have you come to meet me? How kind of you."

"Nethaalye," he acknowledged, and dipped his head politely, but his gaze, likewise, never left the scar-faced inmate. "Where's my brother?"

"The fop? Why? Have you lost him?"

"Gan," Nethaalye said, and placed a hand on the prison scut's arm. "What's going on?"

Ganfrion shifted again, as more rain-spattered bodies demanded entrance. The servants pressed past him, then squeezed past Deymorin, hauling luggage up the narrow staircase, muttering obscenities to large fools who clogged the passageway.

"For the love of Maurii, Rhomandi, don't just stand there like a lordish lump." *That* was Kiyrstin, coming out of the parlor. And Kiyrstin's bright, canny gaze seemed to take in the situation at a glance. "Lady Nethaalye?" she said, "I'm Kiyrstine romGaretti. I don't believe we've met, but I've heard a great deal about you."

"A–and I you, madam," Nethaalye said, obviously confused and quite out of her depth.

Kiyrstin, who swam extremely well in a variety of waters, tapped Ganfrion's arm, demanding attention. He turned a scowling face to her; Deymorin took another step down.

"You, I take it, are Ganfrion." She smiled blithely and held out her hand. "I've heard about you, too." Her glance flickered toward Deymorin; he frowned. "From *several* sources."

And while Deymorin pondered the multiple layers of *that* revelation, Ganfrion's scowl faltered. He accepted Kiyrstin's hand gingerly, wrist to wrist, as she'd offered. Her hand closed firmly, and Ganfrion, after a start, returned the grip.

Her smile deepened, and she gave a little nod. "You'll do." And with that cryptic remark, she took Nethaalye's arm and steered her toward the parlor door.

Nethaalye protested softly.

"Don't worry, child," Kiyrstin said. "They'll growl and spit a great deal, and compare biceps and other anatomical parts, but nothing will come of it." And as she closed the parlor doors between them, she called back, "Try not to break anything, boys."

The thin wood did nothing to muffle her laughter.

Ganfrion, mouth slightly open, stared at the door, then gave an answering shout of laugher. Deymorin, more accustomed to Kiyrstin's tactics, ignored her and took the final handful of steps to confront Ganfrion eye to eye.

"Why aren't you with him?"

Before Ganfrion could answer, the door opened again, and fear replaced every other emotion.

"Raulind?" Deymorin asked, "*is* Khyel here, then? Is he truly ill?" And in the next instant knew that couldn't be the case. He'd *know* if Mikhyel were near. Dead, or alive.

"M'lord Rhomandi," Raulind said. "How pleasant to see you. Sooner than we expected. Ganfrion, have you not explained? How exceedingly wicked of you."

"Raulind, dammit—"

"Well on his way to Khoratum by now, I should imagine, sir. Might I suggest we retire to the smoking room and discuss the matter in a somewhat less—" He hopped forward as another portmanteau swung through the doorway, "trafficked locale?"

Imperturbable as always, Raulind headed in the opposite direction from Kiyrstin's parlor. Just as if he knew where he was going. Which, like as not, Raulind did. Somehow.

Deymorin scowled at Ganfrion.

Ganfrion glared back—until his rain-spattered shoulders began to shake. His mouth twitched, resisting his obvious efforts to control it.

"M'lord?" Raulind prompted.

And Ganfrion with a grand wave of his hand toward the door, added, "Shall we go, uh, compare biceps . . . *m'lord?*"

Deymorin, with the ominous feeling he'd been caught between three experts, preceded Ganfrion down the hall.

§   §   §

The wind whistled out of the northeast, off the Gai'tishii-lari glacier, cold enough to penetrate to Khoratum Tower itself. An alleyway on the very edge of the umbrella provided no refuge whatsoever.

Thyerri huddled in the stolen cloak, that retained only the faintest hint of ocarshi in its deepest folds, and tried to ignore the cold as he tried to ignore the protests of his empty belly.

The bulk of his hoard had gone for replacement clothing (one could hardly term them "new" garments where patches outweighed original material). He'd been grossly overcharged by a merchant who had sized up his customer's surreptitious ways in the first exchange, and judged his capacity to bargain accordingly.

But then, considering the ridiculous clothing he'd been wearing—clothing included in the description on the warrants posted throughout the district, clothing which, short of theft, he could do nothing about—Thyerri's manner might not ever have been at issue. And if he'd been willing to steal, he'd never have had to go through that umbrella-skirting thief of a secondhand merchant.

At least now, with his hair washed free of the black dye, and dressed in the plainest of hill clothing, he could walk the streets, buy a meal, and even gain the odd coin or two without risking imminent arrest.

Besides, Rhyys seemed to have lost interest, for all the warrants had not yet been officially removed. But when one blew away, or was posted over, no one came along to replace it, the way they had at the first.

Another gust. He pulled the edges of the hood closer and let the shivers rattle his joints, hoping by that means to generate the heat needed to warm the air within the heavy wool folds. He had to leave the cloak, which was far too fine and would be noticed, when he went after food, or to perform one of the small jobs that kept his pockets from going completely flat. That meant getting chilled, on evenings such as this, and getting chilled to his bones meant spending the rest of the night getting warm.

Better than the alternatives, or so those other alley-rats he sometimes huddled with claimed. Himself, he wasn't yet convinced. He'd share no bed, rijhili or otherwise, just to survive, but there were times he truly wished the wind would simply steal him away as he slept.

The shiver became a steady vibration in his back. His feet, fingers, even his nose tingled. He buried his face in his crossed arms, saving the warmth of his exhaled breath within the cloak. Behind the darkness of closed eyelids, hunger made sparkling patterns, a myriad of colors in a spring-green glow.

His dream, coming to haunt him even in waking.

He cursed softly, tearfully, wishing the dream away, hating it and the disaster it had wrought in his life, until at last, it began to fade, for once without consequence.

"What about my—" A voice said, out of the dream.

A glittering tingle, a flash blinding to his dark-accustomed eyes.

Thyerri smothered a cry and hid his face again, convinced hunger had brought back the old delusions, the waking dreams that had haunted him in the days following the collapse of the web, like memories that weren't his own.

"Thank you."

That voice was no dream.

Thyerri scrambled to his feet, blinking himself awake.

A man stood in *his* alley. A man whose clothing, even in leylit silhouette, declared him unwelcome in this elite spot of destitution.

"Who are you?" Thyerri asked. His cold-hoarse voice was barely audible, even to his own ears, but the man seemed to hear him.

"Uh, hello." Another invader from the valley, from the accent. "Where did you come from?"

But Thyerri had no intention of *answering* questions. "What are *you* doing here?"

"I'm sorry. I'm . . . lost. I was . . . looking for a place to stay."

Precise, his low tones; from the valley, but not of the sort that had most frequently patronized Bharlori's. This man might well have been one of Rhyys's guests that god-forsaken night, were he not here now.

"You'll be wanting Tower Hill."

"By no means! That's where . . . I mean, the coach left me off, and the place was much too expensive, and they said to follow Steachli Lane, and I would find something in my range, but there was nothing . . ." The narration floundered to a non-end, and the man muttered something, then picked up a large bag lying at his feet, and turned back toward the light.

Thyerri laughed, a short, bitter laugh. Steachli was on the far north side of Khoratum. Lost, indeed.

"Rijhili." He spat the word out, making no attempt to conceal all the hatred, old and new, that word held for him.

The shadow paused and turned.

"Did you say something?"

He certainly wasn't about to repeat himself, not with this shadow-man out of dreams walking the wrong damned way again. Thyerri took a step back, seeking deeper shadows, cursing his own stupid tongue.

"Did I offend you? I'm sorry. I've just arrived, and I fear I am quite woefully ignorant of local manners."

"Go away."

"Please, it would be very helpful to know what I did, since I'd like not to repeat the mistake with someone else. Could I . . . buy you a warm drink? Dinner, perhaps? Any-where you like? So that we might discuss it?"

"Sure, why not? Bonnechhii's?"

A graceful gesture of the hand. "Lead on!"

Harsh laughter hurt Thyerri's throat. "You can't afford a room on Upper Steachli. Dinner for two at Bonnechhii's would *buy* you Minta's Place."

The rijhili's responsive chuckle sounded easy and unoffended. "Very good, my friend." Another step closer to Thyerri. An extended hand. "Compromise?"

"No!" Thyerri stumbled back another half-step. Into stone. Trapped. His heart began to race.

"I'd honestly appreciate—"

"I said, *go away!*" Thyerri's voice broke, as fear, and cold, and panic took over.

The shadow leaned its head forward, as if trying to see better. "How old *are* you?"

"As old as the hills. Go away!"

The shadow stopped encroaching, but it didn't go away either.

"I'd be quite happy to oblige, but . . . well . . . Do *you* know a place with good, inexpensive lodging?"

"If I did, I would be there, wouldn't I?"

"I don't know. Would you?" The shadow shrugged. "Ah, well, I've no more time to waste. It's getting late, and damned cold. Certainly wish I could find someone who might give me a hand with this bag. Maybe guide me to a place that won't steal from an honest man. There'd be a double bulli in it. If you see such a person, tell them to look for the . . . rijhili . . . wandering the streets like a damn fool, will you?"

The damnfool rijili swung the bag about and began a slow, slump-shouldered amble toward the leylights of the street. Thyerri sighed, thinking of the offered prize that meant meals for a week, and sighed again and knew he intended to snatch the proffered bait.

ဢ ဢ ဢ

"Here." The cold-husky voice arrived first, as Mikhyel had reckoned it would, and a thin, cold hand closed on the handle next to his. As their skin touched, he sensed a tingling ripple of . . . what? Recognition? Certainly, that touch carried an awareness similar to that sense he shared with his brothers.

Startled, Mikhyel stopped short and stared at the hood-

568 Jane S. Fancher

shadowed face. The boy, or perhaps young man, as they were nearly of a height, seemed similarly startled. His pale eyes, the only feature visible within the shadow, went wide, then narrowed and his cold fingers released the bag.

"Follow me," he muttered, and flowed down the street with unnatural grace. Or perhaps the heavy cloak, draping from his narrow shoulders, dragging a bit on the ground behind him, made it seem unnatural to the imagination of a man who'd just spent some untold hours with a creature made of leythium and dressed in leythium lace.

He did know that keeping up with the boy required an effort that challenged his chilling knees, particularly with the added weight of the portmanteau. "Boy, wait! Please!"

The figure's halt was as graceful as its movement, and the heavy cloak formed a sweeping curve up to the shadowed hood, as the boy twisted to watch him lumber up to his side.

"Rijhili!" Again, that muttered epithet, which Mikhyel needed no interpreter to fathom. But he had no guide other than this proud local, Mother having landed him in an area not covered on his mental map, and he could not afford to take offense.

Besides, he could hardly ignore that moment of perception. He and his brothers were the not only ones with this strange gift. Mirym, at least, shared it—and Mirym was also from Khoratum.

He wanted to learn more about this boy.

So when the boy stopped and nodded toward a doorway beneath a carved and painted sign, Mikhyel urged him come in with him, to share a meal at least. But the boy refused, and when the hostler arrived in answer to his bell, the boy disappeared, without demanding so much as a copper pildic for his trouble.

Chapter Three

{Khyel? Mikhyel Rhomandi dunMheric, damn you, *wake up!*}

Mikhyel groaned, and rolled upright, holding his head against the throbbing pain of intrusive siblings.

Deymorin must have seen Ganfrion's letter.

{Damn right I saw it. —Nikki, steady on, lad, no time to lose your balance. —Khyel, where the hell are you?}

He ground his palms against his eyes, trying to remember. {Khoratum . . . I think.}

{Think?}

He yawned and looked about the small room. Mountain air flowed in through the window; the remains of a simple supper covered the small (but sound) table; his razor and comb . . . he recalled laying them out on a small vanity, next to a perfectly adequate bowl and pitcher of clear, sweet-tasting water. There was even (this room's particular luxury) a small, private bath with running water.

Compared to the last prospect, it was the next best thing to his own bedroom back in Rhomatum. Particularly the mattress pressing up against his tired legs, a surprisingly firm, lumpless haven his tired back had been busily consulting only moments before.

"Deymorin," he moaned aloud. "I hate you."

{If you expect sympathy—}

{Deymorin, shut up!}

Surprise. Anger. And a dash of laughter. It was a taste of his brother increasingly familiar. But Deymorin shut up, save for a distinct sense of waiting.

He could almost feel Deymorin's foot tapping.

Mikhyel swept the hair back off his face, then shoved himself off the tempting mattress to splash cool water on his face.

{Nikki, are you there, too?}

{Yes. Are you really in Khoratum, Khyel?}

{Last time I looked.}

{How?} And a sense of confusion, of only three days passed out of a seven-day trip. Three days. So, Mother, had kept him only a day. But he wasn't about to get into that explanation. Not with Nikki. Not at the moment. Nikki would want to know about Mother, would want answers he didn't have.

And Nikki, he noted with relief and no small brotherly pride, didn't push for that explanation.

He broke a piece of bread off the loaf, and threw himself down in the simple wooden chair. Simple, but it had a back, unlike other rented chairs of recent acquaintance.

A back—*and* stable. Luxury, indeed.

{All right, Deymio, get to it.}

It was nothing more than he'd expected the moment Deymorin's anger shattered his dreams: Deymorin, suspicious and anxious, had gone to meet Mikhyel's entourage.

{And why, brother, didn't you just get back to the coast?} Mikhyel asked.

{The same reason you aren't where you're supposed to be! Things have come up—}

{Don't you dare blame my change of plans.}

{And don't you flatter yourself. It's under control, thank you.}

{So am I. Thank you.}

Long silence.

{He's got a point, Deymorin.}

Hesitant input from Nikki that—tasted—of real understanding. Mikhyel sent his younger brother heartfelt gratitude with all the power his throbbing head could generate, and on a return pulse, like a hand fumbling in the dark to stroke his hair, Nikki sent sympathy, and a desire for the headache to go away.

A wish that threatened to suck his hold on consciousness right out of him.

Mikhyel severed the attempt with a thought that felt as if he clasped that fumbling, searching hand, and held it steady, but "free" of his head, and sent back to Nikki that he was feeling much better now, thank you.

{You're coddling each other.} Deymorin's thoughts

floated over their hands, more soothing, in his dry humor, than Nikki's well-meant attempt had been.

{Yes, I am. You shouldn't have yelled so loud, Deymorin.}

{And I'm supposed to know what it takes to wake him up? Would you mind telling me how? Last time I tried—}

Mikhyel laughed. {Forget it, both of you. I'm *fine*. I'm more than fine. —Deymorin, tell me you didn't kill Ganfrion.}

{Kill him? I got him drunk. Poor man deserved at least that.}

Ganfrion and Deymorin allied. Perhaps he'd best concede.

{Bet on it! Don't move. I'll have Ganfrion take Nethaalye and Kiyrstin back to Rhomatum. I'll gather some men at Darhaven and—}

{No! Dammit, Deymorin, don't you dare! I'm *fine*. If I need help, I'll *call*. We know I can, now, and I'm promising you I *will*. I'm in a good position to listen for a while, so don't you dare foul things up for me by sending an army out looking for me.}

{You sound as if you're enjoying this.}

He blinked into the near dark of the room, and realized, {Yes. Yes, I am.}

A pause, during which he could almost see the room in which Deymorin sat, the golden glow of a heating candle beneath the amber sheen of brandy. {I can't stop Ganfrion, you made certain of that.]

{*He* made certain.}

Laughter, that bounced off the walls of that far-distant inn.

{That he did. I begin to comprehend your fascination with the jail-bait. If I promise to leave you alone unless you call, will you accept him bringing your men to within spitting distance of Khoratum, for when and if you decide to make a proper appearance in Rhyys' court?}

Or a fast escape. Mikhyel smiled into the empty room. It was no less than he'd expected when he sent Ganfrion off with Nethaalye.

And it was more. If Nikki was learning to think beyond his own needs, Deymorin was learning the art of graceful compromise.

{I'll go you one better, Deymio. I'll check in every—"
He considered the promise he'd been about to make and
revised it on the fly. {"—*other* night. Deal?}
  {Deal!}

Chapter Four

He supposed some would call it charmingly old-fashioned, this Node City perched precariously on a mountainside, just below the timber line. Like something out of a Tamshi tale, but sufficiently endowed with modern amenities for the discomforts to be picturesque rather than annoying.

For Mikhyel dunMheric, it nourished a bit too much squalor for the fantasy to overcome. Or perhaps, for some, that *was* the fantasy, to know there were destitute folk on the verge of starvation, and knowing you were not among them, that a coin from your pocket could provide them one more meal, or that same coin, mercifully withheld, could expedite their sad, but unavoidable descent into the ley.

It was an arrogance to sicken the healthiest mind.

He could well understand, in retrospect, the young local's antipathy toward him that first night. To that boy, Mikhyel dunMheric had been just one more rich man giving a poor hiller one more meal.

On this, the third day since Mother had transferred him to the surface, Mikhyel drifted through a market that was not the open stalls of Rhomatum, or the massive, covered shopping complexes of Shatum, but cozy, enclosed single units with carved and painted signs in place of flapping banners.

Creatures roamed the streets apparently at will: goats, sheep, chickens, even a loose pony or two, though from the way quadruped ears pricked at the sound of certain voices, he'd judge they rarely strayed far.

Wandering the outer perimeter streets, those areas of the city farthest from the Tower complex and modern buildings looming uphill, he grew accustomed to the local dialect, learned to tell locals from those who had moved in with the capping, from those newly-imported, and all from those just-visiting.

A great number of the latter. And too many groups traveling about in what appeared to be uniforms for a visiting Rhomandi's piece of mind.

The common talk centered around the upcoming radical dancer competition and the festivities surrounding it. One might assume, even without Nethaalye's advisement, that these guards, or at least their employers, were here for that celebration. One might also assume that that influx of visitors was quite normal: at least one shop owner, who carried leather and fur garments produced by local hiller families, said the week or so before a competition were always her most profitable.

Considering the cold mountain winds that regularly crept past Khoratum's weather perimeter, a man from the temperate valley could well understand the popularity of her merchandise among similarly thin-blooded visitors. He had, himself, picked up a pair of fur-lined gloves.

One *might* assume the visitors here for the festival, were it not for the fact that the advertisements for the event that met him at every posting board carried Mikhyel dunMheric's visage as well, and one might wonder why those signs (apologetically) proclaimed the date of the competition as subject to change depending on that particular dignitary's schedule.

At no other node had his visit been made public knowledge.

A suspicious man might think Rhyys wanted to make certain the city was in maximum turmoil while Mikhyel dunMheric was in Khoratum.

That suspicious man might also note that the portrait used on the poster was one he'd never seen before and one he had to examine twice before recognizing himself. Not a face *he'd* be inclined to trust, and that suspicious man had to wonder what Rhyys intended, whether that unapproachable Rhomandi was a purposeful representation . . . or simply substandard artwork.

He'd never particularly cared for Rhyys. Rhyys, like Lidye, had been Anheliaa's personal choice for the new node's first ringmaster. And Rhyys, like Lidye, had always pandered, to Mikhyel's way of thinking, to Anheliaa's worst egotisms.

But so might some say of Mikhyel dunMheric.

For all he knew, Rhyys had been as much Anheliaa's

pawn as Lidye—and as Mikhyel himself had been. Perhaps, like Lidye, now that Anheliaa was dead, Rhyys was finally free to think his own thoughts.

It was possible Rhyys was as distrustful of Mikhyel as Mikhyel was of him. He could be gathering reinforcements, thinking Mikhyel dunMheric was on the way to Khoratum to disinherit him. Possibly Rhyys believed Mikhyel blamed *him* for the Collapse in the web.

And if Rhyys was indeed gathering the Northern Crescent leaders to create a unified agenda, Mikhyel dunMheric wasn't necessarily adverse to that. It rather well depended on what the Khoratum ringmaster's intentions were in creating that union.

Sunset caught him by surprise, coming early and with startling rapidity as the sun ducked behind the hills. One of those cold mountain breezes wriggling past Rhyys' weather perimeter set his teeth to chattering, and he ducked into the nearest tavern, just as thunder grumbled in the distance.

He lifted three fingers to the bartender, the mountain sign (so Deymorin had assured him during last night's conference) for the reputation-at-stake homebrew, and settled into a corner booth from which he could watch the patrons without himself drawing notice.

The tavern had a curiously elusive ambience. Not at all like Rosie's but equally unlike any of the restaurants of Khomatum he had patronized. If he sought a word to describe it, and for that matter, all of this older district of Khoratum, he supposed that word would be innocent.

But the frightening innocence of a child toddling among wolves.

As a town, let alone a node city, Khoratum was young, not far removed from a tiny village community. Those natives still living here radiated a trust that could frighten a man not inclined to take advantage of them.

And attract those who were.

Even those who must have learned otherwise—like the young alley-rat who had greeted him upon his arrival, or the owner of the small hotel who had refused to take more than a single night's rent in advance—seemed determined to make each individual prove himself unworthy of that trust.

A double-edged sword of righteousness that could only hurt the innocent wielder. No matter how wrong it was,

how essentially unfair, the unscrupulous would never truly
be hurt. The honor, the self-respect that was gold to such
as that boy in the alley was so much sand to the ruthless.

At the moment, the vast majority of Khoratumin power
and wealth resided in foreign node hands. Mostly it was in
the hands of those Northern Crescent businessmen who
complained of the Southern Crescent's tendency to take
advantage of *their* trusting natures.

Khoratum must grow up and take care of its own interests. The Northern Crescent in general must care for theirs.
Not by power of arms, not by crying foul and creating laws
to punish those who preyed, but by realizing that, fair or
not, their world was now larger than their own small community and that *they* must learn to protect themselves,
rather than expect the wolves not to hunt.

On the other hand, while encouraging the young states
to grow up, the Syndicate, in fairness and self-protection,
should help ease that transition—for both sides. Every node
in the Rhomatum Web had benefited from the capping of
Khoratum. (Even Shatum, for all certain factions would like
to see the case otherwise.) They owed their child at least
the time to reach maturity.

Somehow, he doubted these were quite the insights the
Syndics had hoped he'd gain when they demanded this
tour.

Thunder again, and lightning. Moments later, rain descended in large, very loud, wind-driven drops. They were
on the perimeter here, and the storm seemed practically
atop them.

He'd never been this exposed before, not to a true, natural storm, and for one insane instant, as the drenching
stream flowed down the windows, he had the strangest inclination to run outside into that storm and let those drops
pummel his body.

Fortunately, common sense prevailed.

A young man came over and set a mug on the table.
Like the other servers in this tavern he was a local, one of
the natives from before the capping. A high-cheekboned
face, naturally beard-free, small, to a Rhomatumin's eye,
and slight, dark, almost black hair . . . Mikhyel could well
understand the mistake the inmates of Sparingate Crypt
had made regarding his own origins.

"That'll be ten p, sir," the serving boy said, his voice low, diffident.

When Mikhyel asked for an open tab, the fellow bit his lip, looked over at the owner behind the bar, whose attention was elsewhere, nodded, and left.

Too late, Mikhyel wondered if the lad had understood him.

Among themselves, the servers spoke the native dialect that was so deceptively similar to the language of Maurislan, which all the descendants of the Exodus spoke. The two languages were similar enough that a Rhomatumin could believe them the same, once long ago; similar enough that, if said Rhomatumin didn't really work at listening, he could convince himself he understood every word—until he tried to respond, and realized he had no idea what the hiller had just asked.

He took a cautious sip from the mug, and discovered the ale more drinkable than most, which was something of a relief, as (according to Deymorin) a man did not, in the hills, order anything less potent.

Of the patrons he could see, most were male, all, from their dress and accents, from the Northern Crescent. And most wore uniforms. Evidently he'd happened on an upper-common meeting spot: too rich for the locals, not good enough for the masters.

The sole nonmartial group were all on the adolescent side of twenty, and evinced the capacity to become members of a mindless mob. As happened, there were only a handful of them, thus their failure to attain mob status here, but if a mob were in the making, they'd be certain to join in.

They had the look and sound of Giephaetum. Possibly offspring of those who had come in to help settle the new city. More likely they were just visitors, *attachments* to those personages flooding upper Khoratum. They were offensively out of place here, with their rude handling of the slight-bodied servers and their loudly voiced opinions about hill-folk and Khoratum and the mountains in general.

One, not the eldest, he would judge, but the largest, provided the thinking, such as they could handle. The rest were nodders, those who would endorse whatever the thinker thought—so long as that thought wasn't *too* challenging.

It was a pattern he recognized well, and one hardly limited to the young of Giephaetum. He'd seen it often enough in the lobbies outside the Rhomatum Council Hall.

The mob's rather pretty waitress teased and taunted them, seemingly in full control, and flaunting her unavailability in their faces. The more frustrated they became, the more outrageously she flirted. It remained in tolerably good humor, but to Mikhyel's way of thinking, no good could come of it.

As the waitress swayed her way back toward the kitchen, another employee, an exceedingly slender young woman, emerged. She was carrying a closed container of some apparent weight, and moved through the room like a pale shadow, eyes downcast, her face hidden behind a fall of dark hair that lightened toward the ends as if bleached in last summer's sun.

The leader of the would-be mob, bored without his waitress to harass, grabbed as she passed. A smooth sideslip foiled the attempt, and she was beyond range before he could do more than curse at her.

Without so much as lifting her head, she aimed for the side door near Mikhyel's table. Mikhyel reached the door before her, and swung it open, then stepped back to let her pass. Pale eyes flickered up at him through a veil of sweat-streaked hair.

Up, but most of that height difference came from the bend of her body around the large container.

"May I help you?" he asked.

She blinked, long lashes tangling in that shaded hair, then looked toward the owner, polishing glasses behind the bar, and shook her head. Mikhyel bowed slightly and returned to his table. Moments later, she returned, the container notably lighter, the rope handle suspended now from one slender hand.

He smiled at her, but that hair remained a veil between herself and the world and he had no idea if she noticed. Though dressed in hiller clothing, she was tallish for a hiller—which still meant below average height for a Rhomatumin: Lower Khoratum was the first place *Mikhyel* had ever felt *tall*. Her extremely slender build, which seemed natural as opposed to emaciation, enhanced her apparent height.

Perhaps it was that build that made her every movement, as she made her way back to the kitchen, almost mesmeriz-

ing in its grace. Curiosity piqued, Mikhyel raised his hand
for another ale, and caught the serving lad's eye to order
supper, intending now to stay.

Musicians arrived: guitar, lute, drummer, and a flautist
whose face and hands were so badly scarred, Mikhyel wondered whether the instrument belonged to another. But the
lute player smoothed a clear ointment over the scars, and
the flautist flexed lips and hands, and tried a few practice
runs which slowly gained confidence and speed.

He stopped for another coating, and tried again.

The young woman came out from the kitchen, carrying
a bowl and a pewter mug, and slid into a small, dark nook,
where she would be invisible to the majority in the room.

But not to Mikhyel. He wondered, briefly, if that exception was conscious, decided it was personal vanity—his—
wishing she'd noticed him, and if she was oblivious to his
interest.

She ate and drank slowly, with the care and attention a
connoisseur would grant marsh chicken and fine wine. Only
the thin, shaking hand that lifted the spoon betrayed how
rare that meal might be.

His ale arrived, and the bowl of stew. Mikhyel paid the
announced price plus ten, which generosity got him a sly
sizing, then a politely eager, "Thankee, sir." But he never
took his attention from that dark little booth.

The music began, guitar and lute first.

The young woman paused in her meal, folded her hands
quietly in her lap. When the flute began to ripple among
the strings, her head swayed and dropped forward, her rag-
gedly cropped hair once again masking her expression.

She lifted her napkin to her lips, folded it carefully, and
left it on the table before she headed for the door.

Taken by surprise, as he was certain she had yet to finish,
he sought another bite of the stew, and washed it down
with the ale, torn between the desire to follow her, and the
sure knowledge he was being a fool.

"I said, let me by!"

Anger set uncomfortably on the musical voice. The
young woman had been cornered near the main door by
the handful of Giephaetumin, and the oversized leader was
forcing her into an empty booth.

Mikhyel was outraged. The other patrons, either truly or
selectively deaf, had evidently chosen to ignore the assault

taking place. But even as he ached for the young woman and wondered what he could possibly do that wouldn't bring extremely unwelcome attention to himself, the young woman brushed the groping hands aside, darted like quicksilver through the huddle closing in around her, and slipped out the door, the ill-mannered pack hot on her trail.

The music never even faltered, the conversations about the room never paused. It was all Mikhyel could do not to stand up and demand an explanation. Instead, he drained the ale, nodded his approval to the owner, and followed as unobtrusively as possible.

They'd disappeared by the time he reached the evening-quiet street, but he heard them, and he followed that laughter and the hissed objections into a twilight-shadowed alleyway. There, under dripping eaves, they had the girl facedown in the mud; two were holding her captive, the leader was standing over her, his breeches half-pulled.

The pack had, however, suffered in the pursuit. Two bleeding lips that he could see, one out cold, and another rolling in a puddle and moaning.

"Here, constable," Mikhyel called with all the force in his lungs, and waved his hands wildly at his fictitious law-keeping authority, deliberately choosing the Giephaetumin term. "I told you there was trouble. Hurry!"

The pack froze, the leader half-turned, his face twisted in disbelief.

The young woman rolled, curled, and struck. Her heel contacted its delicate and highly exposed target in a lightning fast snap; the leader howled. A second snap flipped her feet over her head in a roll that had her free in one moment, and at Mikhyel's side in the next.

The now-mindless ruffians scattered, as they were able. The staggering leader disappeared between two buildings, at least one companion close on his heels. Two others shuffled away, dragging their semiconscious companion.

The young woman made a fast, down-the-street assessment that undoubtedly took in the lack of impending aid, and a second that assessed him. Then, she snorted and dodged away—*after* the group's leader.

With a swallowed curse, Mikhyel ran after her, caught her when she had to pause at a branching and seized her arm, holding her despite her protests.

Her hair hung in mud-soaked rattails, the simple wrap-around shirt hung loose on one side, pulled nearly free of the strip of ragged cloth that acted as a sash, exposing a heaving chest and one practically nonexistent breast. Poor skinny thing was not exactly the sort one would expect to find on the receiving end of such a group activity.

In the next moment, all thoughts of her physical attractions vanished as through that hold on her elbow, and for the second time since arriving in Khoratum, he had that sense of awareness, of almost-recognition. This time, clearer-headed, he blocked it off the instant he suspected it: the last complication he needed was some local recognizing him.

Still, he wondered *where* he could he have met her, then knew that he had not. He'd never have forgotten such haunted eyes.

"Let me go," the girl spat, breaking the silence, and those haunted and haunting eyes narrowed in anger. She jerked her arm, trying to pull free.

"Let the law handle it, mistress, please."

"Mistress." Her eyes scanned him. "Like that, is it? Well, the law doesn't exist for me, rijhili. And *no* one challenges that lot."

"You know them?"

"The leader . . . he's Giebhaidii."

Giebhaidii. Nethaalye's family. Mikhyel no longer wondered at the selective deafness in the tavern.

"They've threatened me before," the young woman continued, "but this was the first time they followed. *Now* I have to take care of it myself, if tomorrow's not to be a repetition of today, and that means making that *berinjhili* useless for a month."

Berinjhili—the mountain equivalent of bastard, but it implied much about the recipient's genitalia as well. He'd learned any number of useful bits from Deymorin last night. Bits not found anywhere in Nikki's notes.

He controlled a smile. "I think you probably took care of his love life for the next year."

"Rakshi should be so kind." She shivered, and the elbow in his relaxed hold jerked free.

"Where's your home?" he asked. "Would you like me to see you there?"

"You? What good would you be, you who can do nothing more than call for nonexistent authorities?"

She tugged her shirt into alignment and stormed past him, bound for the main street. But she was shaken, the blindest man could see that, and limping.

"Mistress, please wait."

Her steps never faltered. Feeling a fool, he chased after her, fell into step beside her and pulled out his purse, wishing he'd brought more with him.

"Here."

He held it out to her, received the briefest, disdainful glance.

"At least let me buy you a decent meal."

"Then what? What about tomorrow? Or the next day? or the next? My stomach knows its allowance. I'll not lie to it to satisfy your altruistic-deed-for-the-day quota."

He lifted the purse. "There's enough here to satisfy your stomach for a month."

She plucked it from his hold, bounced it lightly in her hand. "At least a year, valley-man." She tossed it back at him, not looking to see if he caught it.

Not caring.

"Dammit, girl." He grabbed her arm and planted his feet, forcing her to stop and face him. "*I'm* not the one who attacked you. I'm *sorry* everyone in there ignored what was happening to you. I didn't know why. I *don't* know why. I don't *care*. I'm just trying to help someone who doesn't seem to deserve the fate she's been handed. Explain, if you will, how that makes *me* the villain?"

Her eyes raked him up and down.

"In return for *what*, you who call me 'mistress.'"

"*Nothing.*"

"You see? Even to yourself, you lie. You offer because it makes you feel superior to think you can help one of us. Our lives were so *meager* before you arrived."

He winced, hearing his own evaluation of the situation here applied once again and so ruthlessly to his own actions.

"Well, fuck you!" she hissed, using the lowest, commonest of those words Deymorin's mind had supplied. "I'm not your mistress! I'm *nobody's* mistress!"

And in one smooth motion, she whipped around, pulling free and flinging a bare foot in his direction. But her exhausted reflexes robbed the move of its earlier snap. He stepped back, caught the flying foot, sending her off-balance, released the foot for her wrist and, flung an arm around her tiny waist to keep her upright.

He meticulously released her the instant her balance was back, but not before he felt the chill permeating her thin body.

"Please, come back to my rooms with me." He held up a hand to stop her protest. "Just to get warm. And a small meal. I'll not lay another hand on you. I certainly won't force you. Not here, not in my room. But I assure you, I've no designs on your virtue. I'm just protecting myself."

She frowned suspiciously. "How?"

"I'll not get any sleep for the rest of my stay wondering what happened to you."

Her eyes dropped, her head angled down and away, and the thick fall of muddy hair obscured any expression.

"My room has a private bath," he persisted, sensing a weakening resolve.

With a faint hint of laughter edging her voice, she asked: "Who are you, lowlander, and where are you from, that you persist so?"

"Who? I— My name's Mikhyel." The truth was out before he remembered, and once committed, he realized that, deep within, he wanted no lies between them. "I'm from Rhomatum."

She stared at him a moment. Then took a step closer, and stared, and laughed again, a heart-lurching, half sobbing sound. "Well, who am I to say no to Mikhyel of Rhomatum?"

Despite her brave front, the young woman was stumbling with exhaustion by the time they reached his rented room. The manager looked at him strangely when he requested a cot and more towels, but didn't question his personal addition to his room's . . . accoutrements.

At least not to his face. The rumors would undoubtedly be flying by morning—but nothing more than Korelli dun-Kharin's reputation could handle.

"Bath?" he asked, when they'd reached the room.

The young woman, standing in the middle of the room, arms wrapped around her, nodded, and in a tiny voice answered: "Please."

The claustrophobic bath cubical contained only a footed tub, a simple drying tube, and the towel-warmer. Hardly

the private pool he had at home, but it had running water
and a door with a lock. For the young woman waiting outside on legs that could barely keep her upright, it meant
privacy, warmth, and an end to the mud in her hair and
clothing, and he doubted she'd seen better.

At least, not recently. Before . . . as with Ganfrion, he
didn't think she'd been born to her current lifestyle. She
had about her the air of survival, not acceptance.

On his return, he discovered the cot had arrived along
with a maid bearing extra towels and a voluminous robe.
Older, with a plump, motherly face that smiled at the world
in general, the maid bustled about the room, changing the
sheets on the cot, then into the bath. She emerged and
pronounced the room ready whenever Miss desired, and if
Miss would just hand out her clothes, she'd see they were
washed and ready by morning.

"Miss will damnwell see to miss' self," was the hissed
response.

The maid nodded calmly and went off to see to the dinner for two Mikhyel had requested. The moment the door
closed behind her, Mikhyel hissed back, "That was unkind
and unnecessary! Act however you like to me, but—"

"Oh, shut up," she said wearily, and she slipped into the
bathing room. "I'm already sorry enough."

"I'll tell her."

"Not just her. For agreeing to come here in the first
place." She turned and leaned her head against the doorframe, and she looked so sad and weary he was hard put
not to take her into his arms . . .

As he would a child. Or one of his brothers, he assured
his conscience.

"I'll use your bath, and thank you sincerely for the opportunity, Mikhyel of Rhomatum, but then I'll leave. I've
no wish to abuse your hospitality."

"That's not necessary. I didn't bring you here to . . ."
And then he wondered exactly why he had brought her
here. It seemed quite probable that she had a home and
family far safer than a stranger's rental rooms.

But she wanted the bath, and considering her lack of real
resistance to accompanying him here, Mikhyel suspected
that she, like the boy who had met him that first night,
spent her nights in those shadowed alleys.

She smiled, though that stretch of lips failed to wipe the

sadness away, and wilted backward, closing the door softly between them.

And slid the bolt to. Noisily.

Food arrived before the bolt slid back again, simple fare of cheese, fruit, and bread, with a pleasant, local wine. But the young woman, in an opinion stated through the closed door, adamantly refused to join him.

Wisdom of experience, he supposed recalling her earlier protests regarding her stomach and lies, but still Mikhyel found himself unable to swallow. She was going to finish her bath and leave, and nothing he could say would stop her.

He was a fool to care, but some part of him had assumed responsibility for her the first time their eyes met. Collecting stray dogs, Deymorin would say. Habits of a lifetime, his own logic mocked.

Something deeper said neither Deymorin nor logic had the right of it. He wanted her to stay to prove—to himself as well as her that he was not the . . . *rijhli* she and the boy accused him of being.

Inside the bathing room, she'd begun, from the sounds, to dry her hair in the warm pressurized air flowing up from the heating caves, the final luxury of this unpretentious room. But that shoulder-length mass, thick as it was, shouldn't take as long to dry as she spent, and he wasn't surprised when she emerged dressed in clothing stained and wrinkled, but overall clean and mostly dry.

She stood just inside the room, pleating her hem between nervous fingertips. "I want to thank you, Mikhyel of Rhomatum. I know you didn't intend me any harm, and I want you to understand my leaving is not because I don't trust your word or your honor. Unfortunately, if I stay here, I'll bring trouble on you, and I don't want that to happen. So, thank you, and fare—"

"Well? I don't think that's possible, if I let you leave like this."

He'd stood when she entered, wineglass forgotten in his hand. He set the glass down, and crossed to stand in front of her, cupped her chin in his hand and raised it, until she relented and met his gaze.

At this close range, her eyes took on a familiar cast; the gray, like his own eyes, was streaked with a tiny webwork of spring-green. Unlike his, hers held a melancholy, a wild, tender innocence.

He was more loath than ever to condemn her again to the streets.

"Please, stay here tonight," he said. "You'll have the bed to yourself, and I'll not come near you. I've . . . not much appetite for such activity under the best of circumstances, and my health lately has not been the best, which leaves me with little energy to spare. Certainly none for such . . . athletic endeavors."

Her uncertain look deepened.

"I just want to know you're safe for tonight, child. That you've not taken ill from their treatment, and that you've had one good night's sleep before I send you out to face those ill-mannered street-scum again. I wish I could convince you to eat something . . ." He looked suggestively toward the small table, had the satisfaction of seeing those fine eyes blink away dampness, and the mouth quiver with obvious desire. "Please?"

Her hands clenched white-knuckled on the pleats. Then her shoulders dropped, and the wrinkled hem fell free. She edged over to the table, and lifted a small apple with hands that shook pitifully to a mouth that forced itself to take just one small bite. Long-lashed lids obscured her haunting eyes as she chewed and swallowed deliberately.

Another small bite, similarly savored.

Then the eyes opened wide and her head dipped as though a decision had been reached.

"All right. But just tonight. And *you* take the bed."

"But—"

"It's not negotiable, Rhomatum. Argue, and your conscience can find another cure."

He found a smile happening from some devilish person inside him. "But you've already eaten my apple."

"So I have." She dug in her sash, surfaced with a tiny packet, a many-folded strip of cloth. Producing a coin from within this makeshift purse, she laid it on the table, and, chin determinedly thrust out, surveyed the rest of the meal, and wrapped a loaf and sizable chunk of cheese into a napkin, tied the corners and tucked it as well through the rag-belt. "I think you come out somewhat ahead, Barrister." She brushed past him, reaching for the door.

An altogether different internal devil grabbed her elbow and forced her around.

"*What* did you call me?"

"Barrister? You are, aren't you, Mikhyel dunMheric?"

"Yes, but . . ." Only after a fashion. And no one *called* him that except Deymorin. "How long have you known?"

She shrugged. "Your picture's posted all over. I suppose your clean-shaven face might throw some in passing, and you're early . . ." She shrugged again. But the memory of that sense of *something* that had passed between them when they first touched, flared anew.

"Why didn't you say something before now?" he asked.

"Who am I to interfere with the whims of the rich?"

And yet, she'd not called him dunMheric—not first. She'd called him *Barrister*. How could this starved waif know . . .

But, of course, she couldn't. And the challenge in her eyes was just that. He picked up the coin, tucked it in her belt when she wouldn't take it.

Ignoring her, he stripped, as freely as if she weren't standing in the room, put on his sleeping shirt, and retreated to the bed.

"Get the light before you go to bed, will you?" he said, and turned to face the wall, striving for sleep he by no means wanted. He tried, and failed, to ignore the sigh and the rustle of blankets.

And when the muffled sobs began, he was quite irrevocably awake.

The quiet sobs continued long after consciousness had left them, became the lonely sounds of a lost and lonely child. A child too tired to stay awake, too frightened to truly sleep. Sounds that cut deeply into the memory of Mheric Rhomandi's child.

And Mheric Rhomandi's child knew he could not leave that loneliness unanswered.

Mikhyel laid back the covers and crossed to the shadowy corner where the young woman had curled under a single blanket, scorning the cot. Evidently she was not of a mind to lie to her bones and muscle any more than to her abused stomach.

". . . home, Mother . . ." A shaking, sleep-muffled whimper rose from the shadow. "Let me come—"

He knelt beside her, and the mutter ended in a swallowed exclamation. A moment later, the shadowed profile turned, burying itself in the pillowing arm, the other hand tucked up under, and the shoulders shook with soul-deep, fully conscious sobs.

"Mistress," Mikhyel whispered, and touched her shoulder ever-so-lightly. "Please, let me help you."

Her shoulder stiffened. Her hidden hand appeared to brush his touch away.

There were teeth marks, oozing blood, on her wrist, attempts at control Mheric Rhomandi's child also recognized.

"Oh, child." Disregarding her protests, he pulled her up and into his arms, was unspeakably relieved when, despite her verbal protests, her arms wrapped around his waist, holding onto him as a drowning swimmer would clutch a floating log.

Every muscle was tight as a drumhead, and she felt as if she were frozen through. Reaction, he was certain: it wasn't *that* cold in the room.

He tried to lift her, found his strength, never outstanding, utterly inadequate for the task and had to admit, humiliated: "You'll have to walk, child. I'm sorry."

She nodded wearily against his neck. Once on her feet, she startled him by turning toward the door, startled him more when she didn't object at having that course angled toward the bed.

And the ultimate surprise: once in bed, she pulled him to her and kissed him, a fluttering, uncertain brush of lips, then tucked her face, damp with tears, against his neck while her hands moved blindly to his shirt buttons.

"No, child, that's not—"

"No?" And her hand traveled lower, touched him where his body gave lie to his protest.

"Never mind that," he said firmly, and gently removed her hand, hating his body for its betrayal, disgusted that it could find anything exciting in the current situation. "My head's firmly in control, and I've no wish to have a relationship of that nature with a woman whose name I don't know. Especially one I'm trying very hard to protect from such a fate."

"Hardly matters now, anyway."

Which made little sense to him, but he didn't ask. She sighed and curled into him, pent-up sobs still very much

alive within her tense body, however silent. Tense, hard . . .
strong. Her slender body had no sharp corners, but a sleek
covering of solid muscle.

Such a body was no accident. Hard work had created it,
and hard work kept it. He recalled a night in the Crypt
with Deymorin's arm about him, a sense of Deymorin in
his head, and Deymorin's dismay at his brother's bony
shoulders, and was embarrassed to have her touch
him . . . anywhere.

She was blinking up at him again, her brow tight, and
her long-fingered, work-roughened hand touched his jaw.
"S-so, payment pending, Barrister?"

He forced a smile. "Not at all, child. I—cheated you.
I promised an undisturbed night. So far, I've failed quite
miserably. You've every right to stay until I get it right."

Her head tucked back down, and a ripple passed through
her body.

"And if you don't?"

He barely caught the tiny whisper.

"I suppose I'd be stuck with you for life."

One of those sobs escaped, and he rocked her gently,
patting her back, the way Raulind had once done for him,
and he wished, just for the moment, that it were possible.

They were, he would judge, much of an age, although
she could be anywhere between seventeen and twice that,
but she was like all of Khoratum: an innocent's ability to
trust lurking behind a facade of maturity. She deserved, at
least once, not to have that trust betrayed.

He'd adopt her in an instant, if she'd have it.

But she had family somewhere. A mother, at least. One
she wanted very much to be with. Perhaps, somehow, he
might be able to reunite them. Which led him to wonder
what so young a woman could possibly have done to warrant such a hideous exile, wondered if she *had* sold herself,
and whether her determination to avoid him might not
have to do with her ability to return home.

A soft mutter against his chest.

He drew back, and she looked up at him, her eyes seeming to glow with an inner fire, though logic said it was only
the light filtering in from the streetlamp.

"Did you say something?" he whispered.

"T-Temorii, Khy," she said, and suddenly it was he who
shook with suppressed emotion. "My name is Temorii."

Interlude

Mother laughed. And the sound shivered among the infinity of leythium stars. One star, among all the others, shimmered with renewed joy.

She was awake, now, as she hadn't been for far too long. Awake and able to enjoy her children.

All her children.

The newest pattern neared completion, and Mother, though she could read its destiny if such was her desire, enjoyed the suspense of wondering, savored the sense of danger.

For within its intricate webbing her own fate lay waiting.

Chapter Five

Kiyrstin rolled in his arms and pressed her backside against his lazy, early morning erection, and arched backward as his hands sought her familiar curves.

She'd lost weight, was his first, marginally coherent thought, and without opening his eyes, and at the same lazy pace, he explored more fully.

Slender, hard-muscled, ribs his fingers could count—

And flat-chested.

His second thought was: *Kiyrstin* was in Rhomatum. *He* was not.

His third thought was: Kiyrstin is going to kill me.

$$\mathfrak{S} \quad \mathfrak{S} \quad \mathfrak{S}$$

{Khyol? Khyol! If you love me, wake up and tell me you're with a woman!}

{I'm with a woman,} Mikhyel answered, out of love, then realized, when the pillow he hugged to his chest squeaked and protested, that he told Deymorin nothing but the truth.

Relief, and a sense of brotherly surprise echoed from the distance, and Deymorin sent back a hazy, {Have fun . . .} and drifted away.

Meanwhile, the young woman—Temorii, he recalled the name with mixed emotions—flopped about, precarious activity on the narrow bed, but settled as soon as she again faced him, having somehow, in the miracles of sleeper's survival, managed to turn away during the night.

Have fun, Deymorin had so blithely advised.

He supposed that his actions last night, what he did now, as he eased her into comfort and safety against him, did constitute fun, though not, perhaps, the fun Deymorin proposed. Together, he and Temorii had also, however inadvertently, paid his brother back for all those disturbed nights back in Shatum.

He balanced Temorii against him, pressed his back to the wall to give her as much room as possible, and let his mind wander aimlessly, taking unabashed pleasure in the feel of her body against his.

That she was asleep, he had no doubt in his mind. That it was a restless sleep became increasingly clear. Her hands slithered around him, and her body began to ripple against his in a rhythmic sway he could in no fashion blame on a search for warmth. Any doubts he retained vanished when her leg slid over him to draw them still closer together. Her face buried in his neck as her body strained against him.

Dreams, he told himself, there in the faint glow of dawn, and as his own blood began to race. Dreams of the sort that Deymorin had and that occasionally plagued his own sleep.

Morning dreams, he reminded himself fiercely, as her movements sparked answering ripples through his own nervous system, and he held himself quiet, certain that, should he awaken her, she'd be mortally embarrassed.

Hell, *he* would be, he thought in personal disgust. But he fought his own response to morning and her wanton, but painfully innocent actions, shifted to keep her from encountering the manifestation of his losing battle until, as he hoped it would, her nature-driven—and blind—need eased, and she relaxed in his arms.

His legs and shirt were damp, but it had gone no further than that, for all he could wish nature had spared them both. With luck, she'd sleep soundly yet a time, and awake none the wiser.

For himself . . . he wished she'd not been asleep, and in that admission, he abandoned all thoughts of adoption.

A groan, and a shift of the narrow mattress pulled Mikhyel up out of a comfortable doze.

Temorii sat on the side of the bed, holding her head with all the unequivocal signs of an eye-crossing headache. Not a hangover—she'd had nothing to drink last night, but considering the pent-up emotion, the tension in her body as she'd fallen asleep, not to mention the awkward-for-two bed, he wasn't surprised.

"I suppose 'Good morning' is not in particularly good

taste," Mikhyel murmured. "Stay still. I've just the thing, being prone to them myself."

He eased himself along the wall to escape the bed without disturbing her, got the pill box from his bag, and poured her a glass of water from the pitcher. When he turned to face her, she was staring at him.

In horror.

But not at his face.

He didn't have to ask what was wrong. Didn't have to look down at his clothing to know what she saw.

"Nothing happened, Temorii. I promise you, *nothing happened*."

Her luminous eyes lifted to stare blankly, as if she didn't even remember coming here or ever having seen him before. Then, she stood, slowly, looked down at the bed, and with a wordless cry, ran from the room.

ⓢ ⓢ ⓢ

"Temorii?"

It was a hushed call, imperative, yet discreet, and dunMheric ran halfway down the alley, then stopped, panting heavily.

Thyerri edged farther into the shadow, pulling the cloak's folds in, trying to ignore his empty gut that twisted painfully this morning.

Precision elegance would not describe Mikhyel dunMheric this morning, but striking, with his raven's wing hair hanging loose, his bare throat rising from a hastily buttoned shirt . . . Yes, striking covered his appearance quite well.

"Dammit, girl—" The Rhomatumin's voice broke on the soft curse.

Thyerri supposed he should make himself known, should tell dunMheric where the girl he sought had gone, but Thyerri was embarrassed not to have recognized dunMheric right from the start. Of course the posters, with the beard and the grim expression, had not done the Rhomatumin justice, and over the weeks, that image had overpowered hazy memory.

Except for the eyes. And now, in the early morning light, those Tamshi eyes that had haunted Thyerri's dreams for weeks searched for the young woman who had run down this alley moments before.

The Rhomatumin's shoulders slumped, he searched the shadows a final, hopeless time, and turned slowly. His pain, his fear permeated the very air, even to Thyerri's deadened senses.

Thyerri sighed, knowing himself a fool, and stepped free of the shadows.

"Khy?" He called softly, using the mountain diminutive of the Rhomatumin's mountain name, helping, should any be watching, to keep dunMheric's secret.

"Tem—?" DunMheric whirled, saw him, and paused.

Thyerri pulled the hood more closely around his face.

"I'm—" Thyerri's protest was smothered as dunMheric's arms closed about him, and dunMheric's lips closed on his, and for a startled moment, the cursed dream returned, full force, and Thyerri returned the kisses with a passion that at once thrilled and terrified him.

"Is this what you want, Khy?" he whispered on the heels of that terror, kissing the Rhomatumin mouth, eyes, the Rhomatumin throat, trying to remember who this man was, what he had done, why he must be here, and what he would do to Temorii, striving for indignation to force his reeling emotions back into control. "Is this? —And this?"

"Oh, dear gods . . . " DunMheric's groan rippled down Thyerri's throat, past his cramping gut, all the way to his toes. And dunMheric pulled his mouth away to press Thyerri tightly to him. "Tem, I'm sorry, whatever I did . . . I'm . . ."

Mikhyel dunMheric's pain and guilt broke the spell between them, succeeding where Thyerri's own methods had failed. He shook himself free of dunMheric's arms, though he could not free himself entirely of dunMheric's insidious attraction.

"Sorry, Khy?" He flipped the hood back up over his head to conceal his own uncertain expression, and from within its concealing shadows said, with forced indifference: "Oh, you are cruel."

"Cruel?" DunMheric, for all his hands lifted, seemingly inclined to reach of their own will, didn't pursue Thyerri's retreat. Instead, breathing harder than ever, in an admirable fight of his own, he clenched his fists and forced his hands to his sides.

At least, it would be admirable if Thyerri were inclined to be generous.

Which he was not. In point of fact, Thyerri, at that moment, could wish Mikhyel dunMheric dead and buried, far—*very* far—from Khoratum. Thyerri had found the source of his dreams, and traced his own internal subversion directly to that damnable poster's first appearance outside Bharlori's Tavern.

And if Temorii weren't careful, this Rhomatumin, with his Tamshi eyes and hot rijhili blood, would do the same to her.

"Who?" dunMheric asked when he seemed to have himself under control. He tipped his head, trying to see Thyerri's face beneath the hood. The black hair slid forward in a silken wave. "Rings." He turned his head, hiding his face in that black silk. "You're the lad who helped me that first night, aren't you?"

Aloof. Embarrassed.

"Obviously," Thyerri responded, "you believed otherwise."

"Obviously." DunMheric's narrow shoulders heaved beneath his dark coat, and his head came up, though he still didn't really look at Thyerri. "My *extreme* apologies."

Thyerri dipped his chin.

"What . . ." dunMheric began, seemed to reconsider, then repeated: "What did you mean, *I'm* cruel? You, who allowed me to believe *you* were someone else?"

Tempting, to let him wonder, to let him suffer as he'd caused others to suffer. But he *hadn't* known. And who could imagine the confusion that must dwell within a rijhili with Tamshi eyes.

But to explain . . . Bharlo hadn't understood. Rhyys mocked. How could a rijhili possibly understand?

"The girl you followed? The girl you would maul so casual—"

"There's nothing *casual* about my feelings for Temorii," dunMheric interrupted, and his eyes flared with suppressed passion.

"No?" Thyerri mocked that passion as well as his own. "Is so deep an understanding possible in three days? Or do I mistake my time for your arrival? Perhaps you knew her before you arrived and came here specifically to pursue your acquaintance?"

DunMheric shook his head, slowly at first, then emphatically, until that beautiful hair rippled in the early sunlight. All the time he refused to meet Thyerri's challenging stare.

"Well, then, let me tell you something about Temorii."

"You know her?" dunMheric's head came up, his eyes wide, excited. "Help me find her! I'll make it worth your while."

"Why?"

"What do you mean, why? I'm *worried* about her."

"Then leave her alone."

"Why?"

"Why was she running away?"

"I don't *know*."

"Not? Obviously, she was demented, and you're well rid of her. I'll be going then." Thyerri took two steps down the alley before:

"Wait! There . . . there was blood . . ." A cursing pause that hid, Thyerri suspected, an embarrassed search for words. "I encountered her in a tavern yesterday evening. I took her to my room—*Not* for what you think—"

"You've no idea what I'm thinking, rijhili. What then?"

"We . . . we slept in the same bed—but that's all I did! I just . . . slept."

"So defensive, Khy," Thyerri mocked. "Then?"

Appearing somewhat taken aback, dunMheric finished in a rush. "This morning, she woke up with a headache; I got up to fix her a tonic; she cried out—I thought in fear—and ran out."

"Fear of what? A medicinal tonic? That's foolish. Demented, I tell you."

"I . . . I don't believe . . . There was blood on my shirt, you see, and on the sheets. Her . . ."

"Obviously, the girl was a virgin."

"Nothing happened! At least, not with me. But yesterday . . . She was assaulted, and if one of *them* . . . well, I'm truly concerned. You see, I must find her. Make certain she's all right!"

"There is," Thyerri said cautiously, "another possible explanation."

"What? What could there be that a doctor's exam could not improve?"

"Many things, I assure you, rijhili! —But Temorii . . . That name means dancer, did you know that?"

DunMheric shook his head. "What would that have to do with—"

"Possibly nothing. Possibly a great deal. Would you know more?"

"Of *course*."

"No 'of course' about it, rijhili. Most don't care. Was her

hair cropped? Like . . ." He pulled the ends of his own hair free with the tips of his fingers.

"Yes. And sunbleached, like yours. That was one reason I, well, mistook . . ."

"Ah."

"What do you mean 'Ah'? Stop *playing* with me. Do you know something about her or don't you?"

"It's possible that this young woman you seek has aspirations of dancing, perhaps the rings."

"I still don't—"

"You *are* ignorant, rijhili. Khoratumin ringdancers cannot also be lovers. Ideally, they think of nothing but the dance, and most specifically, they do not think of those acts lovers perform."

It was Thyerri's turn to hide his embarrassment, to stumble after words to express that which he, himself, was experiencing for the first time in his life. Confusions this hot-blooded Rijhili had undoubtedly long since forgotten.

"For some dancers, such denial . . . stunts . . . sexual . . ."

"Maturity?" DunMheric finished for him, and Thyerri nodded, grudgingly thankful.

"Are you trying to tell me she might simply have begun her menses?" Said without embarrassment. As a physician would.

Or as a man would who had no concept of the true meaning of such bodily changes.

"That could explain the headache," dunMheric continued musingly.

"And you, a bachelor without sisters, have such *vast* knowledge," Thyerri mocked him.

"I—" Those Tamshi eyes flashed with sudden intensity. "How do you know I haven't a *dozen* sisters?"

"A dozen." Thyerri folded his arms. "Nikkitia, Demoria . . . Who else?"

From the long, cold silence that greeted his deliberate taunt, the challenge had not passed unnoticed. But dunMheric's reply clung stubbornly to the illusion of anonymity. "I had an aunt . . . who hated that particular aspect of her . . . existence." DunMheric's voice was tight with emotion and Thyerri wanted no more details. "So . . ." A deep-drawn breath. "She was embarrassed. But why just . . . disappear?"

"Don't you see? If it *was* her first time, in—in her own mind . . ." Thyerri had to swallow hard, before he could continue. "She might feel she's lost the rings forever. She might feel that just *lying* with you could, well . . ."

"And that is why you call me cruel: for pursuing her."

"For exuding desire, dunMher—" Thyerri caught himself, but not in time.

Another long silence. At last, "So. You *do* know as well." Thyerri shrugged.

"Rather silly to continue the charade, I suppose."

Thyerri shrugged again. Hardly his place to judge.

"All right, lad. I'll . . . let her go. But . . . you said . . . Do you know her?"

"Farewell, Khy." Thyerri turned to go.

"Wait."

He paused.

"If you— If you see her, tell her, please, to come back. Tell her, I'll keep my promise."

"To do what?"

"Just *tell* her."

"Perhaps. If I see her."

"Fair enough." DunMheric half-turned. "About what I did . . ."

"I'll tell her, dunMheric," Thyerri interrupted. "*If* I chance across her."

DunMheric nodded and left slowly. Defeated.

Thyerri sank down to squat on his heels, arms pressed to his aching gut, hungry, yet convinced anything he ate would run right through without pausing to make more than passing acquaintance with his stomach. Which sounded to him like ill health, which frequently meant, for one living on the streets, death.

Perhaps he should see if dunMheric's invitation might extend to include himself. Somehow, he doubted it would, not when dunMheric knew all there was to know, and what one Thyerri of Bharlori's had done to those who last extended him the hand of friendship.

Thyerri was waiting for the cramps to ease, or lay him flat, when a hand clamped on his shoulder, heavy enough, strong enough, that he had no hope of breaking free of it.

"In the name of Rhyys dunTarec, Ringmaster of Khoratum, you're under arrest."

Chapter Six

Exuding desire . . . one did have to laugh. Certainly Dey-morin would.

Mikhyel tied off the end of his braid, and flipped it back behind his shoulders. The strands around his face were certain to work loose the moment he stepped into the mountain winds, but a disheveled appearance would only make him that much less like his poster.

The simple woolen greatcoat and colorful muffler the re-doubtable Ganfrion had supplied, completed his non-Rhomandi look. Perhaps that explained the street-boy's cryptic remark. Perhaps "Korelli dunKarin" *was* . . .

He struck an appropriate pose before the mirror . . . and decided the boy had unquestionably been making fun of him, as he had with the remark about his sisters. Nikkitia, Demoria . . . he'd known all along.

But either the others in this strange almost-city were less astute, or they also took delight in baiting him. They were free enough with their opinions. Particularly of the upcoming visit of Mikhyel dunMheric and the ill-health that had placed a DELAYED banner across the posters, putting their festival on hold yet again.

Today, as he had for the past several days, he would roam the streets of Khoratum, listening, observing. Like yesterday, he'd also be looking for Temorii. Hopefully, he could avoid assaulting any more alley-rats.

A full day after the fact and his face still grew hot just thinking about that encounter. Even had the young man *been* Temorii, Mikhyel's actions would have been uncon-scionable. He certainly hadn't chased her in order to . . .

Or had he? He could not deny she roused feelings in him he'd never had to deal with before. His relief, when he believed he'd found her, had expressed itself . . . ener-

getically. Perhaps, had the young man not called him
"Khy," as *she* had, perhaps had he not responded . . .

But he couldn't blame the boy. *His* was the behavior
in question.

And yet, the boy's response was a curiosity in itself.
From their first meeting, he'd obviously resented Mikhyel's
presence in Khoratum, Mikhyel's and all *rijhili*. Likely he
had encouraged Mikhyel's outrageous behavior in order to
mock him, as he mocked him with that personal assessment.

Exuding desire . . .

He should be thankful, he supposed, that the fellow had
also deigned to give him valuable insight into Temorii.

Such a simple explanation, though obviously, not simple
to Temorii. Or the young man. The motherly maid, who
was, it turned out, the proprietor's good wife, had listened
to his embarrassed explanation, and confirmed the likely
harmless nature of the stains (though how she could know
was beyond his male comprehension). She'd clucked with
understanding, called him a good laddy and told him not
to worry about the Poor Young Thing, and lamented how
many there were on the streets and in the alleys these days.

When the woman had left, he'd added her name to the
list of Khoratumin business owners the Rhomandi intended
to support in the future.

It was a very short list. One thing had become abundantly clear in his daily tours: Rhyys dunTarec did *not* deserve to be in power in Khoratum. Neither did those who
endorsed him. Rhyys had bullied his people into considering him something like the old kings of Maurislan, but gave
them nothing in return. The outside investors he'd lured
in, Nethaalye's father included, were so obsessed with their
own short-term gain, they'd willingly supported his despo-
tism to the detriment of the natives.

From Nikki's reports, one would assume Khoratum pros-
perous and developing right on track for a new node. However those analyses were purely theoretical. There had *been*
no nodes capped in recent history. The original satellites
had all been similarly struggling and intersupportive in the
first century after the Founding.

Not so Khoratum.

Khoratum was being raped by her elder siblings. Her
mineral-rich mines were being stripped, her fur-trapping

and sheep-herding natives were being robbed (he'd seen what their wool and furs brought elsewhere in the web—particularly on the Shatumin export tables) and the money was going into the pockets of the Northern Crescent rich—and Rhyys dunTarec in particular.

He'd learned enough to start asking more pointed questions, and he no longer fooled himself that Rhyys' intents were defensive. If he understood correctly the gossip of the uniformed individuals crowding the streets, he'd learned yesterday that this petty demagogue was urging revolt against Rhomatum—or at least, the Rhomandi.

But Rhyys, so the most vindictive claimed, needed to do *something*. Rhyys had ruled by virtue of Anheliaa's backing; and with Anheliaa gone, the guards maintained, Rhyys would be deposed within the year.

Mikhyel settled the scarf around his neck, and headed out the door.

Today, with luck, he'd learn the details of that revolt.

With a bit more luck, he'd find a certain, rather skinny native girl with a headache.

§   §   §

"Now, where have I seen this before?"

The scarred hand stroked the heavy wool weighing Thyerri's shoulders down, then jerked back the cloak's hood, grabbing a fistful of hair in the process, exposing Thyerri's anger-flushed cheeks to the chill of winter, that radiated still from the stone walls of the old fortress.

Scarface stepped back to Rhyys' side, a puzzled expression twisting his already twisted features. Rhyys just looked bored, one leg propped on the prison-master's battered table.

As a dog lifted its leg to mark territory, was Thyerri's sullen thought.

Thyerri had spent the night in a cell as black as death and empty except for himself and the rats. He'd been taken there without explanation, and this morning—at least he thought it was morning—he'd been brought to this place.

He was cold, he was tired, he was hungry . . . and he was scared.

Without giving Thyerri more than a cursory glance, Rhyys said, "This is a waste of time. Street-scut won't find us dunMheric. Besides, it can't *be* dunMheric. This dun-Kharin has been in Khoratum for at least four days; dun-Mheric was in Giephaetum seven days ago at *most*. There have been no private entries into Khoratum in two days, and the common coach takes at *least* six days—frequently seven. It's so annoying the Syndicate hasn't financed that new road—"

"Rule one of a ringmaster, dunTarec," Scarface interrupted. "Never base *your* sense of what is possible on the experiences of the masses."

And how, Thyerri wondered bitterly, did this *Scarface* know so much?

"The tavern owner claimed resemblance," Scarface continued. "Captain Eelanghi heard this . . . charming young creature *call* him dunMheric, to which he responded. Think what you will, I believe your street scut might indeed help us follow his movements. —Well, scut?"

Thyerri said, in the language of the hills: "May the ley-mother eat your flesh and piss it to the twelve winds."

Rhyys lurched upright and signaled Thyerri's guard, who struck Thyerri a backhanded blow that spun him to the stone floor.

Stupid, he thought, pushing himself up with arms whose elbows seemed to bend every way but normal, and he wondered how the gods had ever allowed so great an idiot to survive as long as he had.

But Rhyys and Scarface roused hatred in him. Hatred and anger, the two emotions more destructive to a dancer's gift than lust. Emotions he'd been trained to control.

Further proof, as if he needed it, that the rings were lost to him forever.

Hands pulled him up and to his feet, and recognition dawned in Scarface's eyes, so close now to his. "You cut your hair." Those scarred fingers combed through the ragged tangle. "How sad. The fire perhaps? One does trust the flames damaged nothing essential."

Thyerri said nothing.

"I think, dunTarec, you've a valuable asset here. I suggest you don't waste it."

Rhyys approached him then, scanning him down the length of his prominent nose. Then he grabbed Thyerri's chin and held him for a different kind of examination. And suddenly, his eyes narrowed, his mouth hardened, and he turned abruptly away.

"Remove the cloak," he commanded the guard, who jerked the garment free, letting it drop to the floor. "And the rest."

"No!" Thyerri protested, but he had no real hope against the guards, and within moments, they had him stripped and spread on the floor, like a beast for gelding. Eyes closed, Rhyys knelt on one knee beside him, dragging a hand over his naked, chilling flesh. Face, neck, hands and arms . . . a dehumanizing, intimate examination that extended to his toes.

All without ever looking at what he touched.

It wasn't the first time Thyerri had been forced to endure this type of inspection. Rhyys claimed that after such a tour of their bodies, he would always know them. They all endured it once: it was one of the prices to pay for the dance. They universally hated Rhyys.

Without a word, Rhyys rose to his feet and moved out of Thyerri's limited view. Someone threw the cloak across Thyerri's body, but the guards at his wrists and ankles still held him immobile.

"Are you quite finished?" Scarface drawled, and Rhyys returned to Thyerri's range of sight, wiping his hands delicately on an embroidered cloth.

"Do what you want," Rhyys said. "Make what promises you choose. It will avail you nothing. I've dealt with this person before."

He strode abruptly from the room.

"Leave us," Scarface said, and when the guards hesitated, "*Now!*"

Thyerri was free. He jerked upright, fighting stiffening limbs to grab his clothing. He was decent again before the door closed behind the final guard.

"Now," Scarface said, handing him the cloak, which he pulled on against the room's chill and Scarface's flagrant interest. "Let's talk."

Thyerri threw himself into a plain wooden chair, drew his bare feet up and huddled in the cloak's concealing folds.

"That was Mikhyel dunMheric in the alley with you, was it not?"

Thyerri refused to meet the scar-rimmed eyes. He knew. He didn't need a street-scut's endorsement.

"And have you enchanted the middle Rhomandi the way you enchanted us? Is he keeping you?"

Thyerri shook his head, a brief, fierce denial.

"Ah. Then who *did* he follow into that alleyway, directly from his room?"

So, they'd been tailing dunMheric all along. They didn't need him at all.

A back-handed slap rocked his head to the side. *"Who?"*

"Temorii." If they'd been following dunMheric, they already knew anyway.

"A young woman?"

Thyerri shrugged.

"How disappointing for you."

Thyerri jerked to his feet and paced the room. "Dun-Mheric's interests mean nothing to me. They mean disaster for Temorii."

"Because she would be a dancer?"

More insightful than Rhyys, this scarfaced man.

"Well. What *is* your name?"

"Thyerri," he answered sullenly, past a lip already swelling from his last insolence.

"Well, Thyerri," his name was clipped and ugly in this foreigner's speaking, "I think you would do well to encourage this young woman to return to dunMheric, in whatever capacity he wants her."

Thyerri spun to face him. "You can't be serious!"

"Oh, but I am, child. I think you will do this because I think you want, above all else, to live."

Before Thyerri could avoid him, Scarface reached out and clamped his long fingers around Thyerri's head, holding him in a flesh-and-bone vise. And it was as if those fingers grew right through his skull, sending tendrils throughout his body. A touch more horrifying and base than Rhyys' crude methods could hope to match.

Worst of all, he couldn't move, couldn't escape that invasion, until the tendrils retreated, and the hands left him. The moment he was able, he jerked away, toward the door, knowing, all the while, that escape was impossible. Ever.

"I *do* know you now, child," Scarface's velvet voice confirmed his fears. "You can't hide anywhere within the web, that the Khoratum Rings can't find you."

"You're not Khoratum's master."

"No? Perhaps you are right. Perhaps you are wrong. It's

your life you wager. You are wanted for murder, child, and for arson. And for attempting to assassinate the Khoratum Ringmaster."

Thyerri tried to conquer his shaking limbs, found his only safety in the wedge between floor and wall.

"Wh—what do you want of me?"

"Very good, Thyerri." That velvet approbation made his gut quiver in horrified objection. "It's quite simple, really. I want to know where dunMheric goes and why he goes there. I want to know why he's living in squalor when he could be living in Khoratum Tower luxury, sampling Rhyys' hospitality."

"I— All right. I—I'll try."

"Good child. And, I want a hold on him. Emotional, rational, whatever and as much as you can get. I want control over him, sweet Thyerri, as I have control over you. Do you understand?"

Thyerri did understand. All too well.

Chapter Seven

"A—and then, Ringmaster Ioniia, sh—she began screaming." Though the rather lumpish Orenumin kept his voice to a near-whisper, nothing could hide the tremor completely. "We could hear her even through those great thick doors, saying they were all crazy and dunTarec was going to land us all in Sparingate, if they didn't destroy the web and all the nodes in the process!"

Urichi dunRondri reached a shaking hand for his mug. It was empty. Mikhyel caught the eye of the waiter, who brought replacements for both their mugs, for all Mikhyel's was untouched.

It maintained the illusion, for anyone sober enough to take note.

This was Mikhyel's third encounter with the assistant to the Orenum governor's legal advisor's secretary. The first, a chance meeting in a small inter-node bookstore in Greater Khoratum, had led to supper in this tavern rather farther downhill, during which they'd compared notes on Bernoi professors. (Mikhyel hadn't mentioned to the much older dunRondri that those same professors had been *his* private tutors.) By the close of their second shared meal in as many days, dunRondri had ceased to think of Korelli dunKharin as anything but a fellow traveler through the maze of a world grown too complex.

Tonight, the man was shaking with the ramifications of what his superiors were concocting in upper Khoratum's back rooms.

"It's enough to drive a man mad." Mikhyel kept his voice hushed, conspiratorial. "They treat us as if we're furniture. As if we have no consciences. They say anything, *do* anything and *we* must live with the knowing, the wondering when the powers will come down on *our* heads because *theirs* are so well-protected!"

DunRondri's head nodded mournfully.

Mikhyel dropped his voice to a near-whisper and dun-Rondri's head bent closer. "I used to work outside old Peneriiac's office. He'd be raging inside, saying things I knew I didn't want to know about, but if I left my desk, it would mean my job." He took a sip of his ale and set the mug down, letting it rattle a bit, then hid his hands beneath the table. "And the students who came to 'conference' . . . rings, if I didn't care if I never worked again, I could tell the admin a thing or two about their favorites. But somehow, I doubt Peneriiac's neck would be the one cut."

A hand touched his sleeve under the cover of the table. "And I'll bet it wasn't just students who had to conference with old Pen, was it?"

He hadn't considered that interpretation of his comment, and wondered briefly, and in some irritation, what it was about *him* that inspired such notions. Careless of him, Ganfrion would say. Ganfrion would say *of course* he should have expected it, along with many other possibilities.

But he saw no reason to deny it. It wasn't as if he was maligning an innocent man's name. He flicked a glance up at the compassionate, round face, and lifted his shoulders in a slight shrug.

"Hardly matters now. I'll finish my paper, defend it before the board, and then I'll be free of him forever."

"Surely he's not still employed at the academy?"

Mikhyel shrugged. "He did nothing illegal."

"That could be proven."

Mikhyel shrugged again. "He's a damn fine lawyer and professor. Perhaps the students considered it a fair exchange."

"And Korelli? Did he consider it a fair exchange?"

Exasperated, Mikhyel dropped his eyes. When he looked up again, the small, tired eyes behind the thick spectacles had gone misty with sympathy.

"Poor lad. Well, we'll just have to get this paper of yours written, now won't we?"

With a sense of filth about him, inside and out, Mikhyel dragged himself up the narrow stairwell and limped down the hallway to his room.

DunRondri had been his best opportunity. He'd hoped, with that softening over supper, that the information would be more forthcoming, but all the assistant secretary had said was that the general consensus held that the era of the Rhomandi was over. That the Southern Crescent had to be put in its place and that everything was pending Mikhyel dunMheric's visit, which had been delayed due to illness, which everyone knew was a lie, and everyone was getting damned antsy about the situation, saying Mikhyel dun-Mheric wasn't coming at all, because he'd made such a fool of himself in the south that the Rhomandi had recalled him.

He'd become amazingly adept at calmly hearing himself denigrated in the past handful of days.

Listening to conversations not his own, milking information from a stranger on a topic regarding which he knew absolutely nothing, pretending to be someone he wasn't . . . such prevarication had become second nature to him. Ganfrion would be proud.

Listened, milked, but learned little of substance regarding Nethaalye's presumed caucus, other than something was, without question, drawing significant numbers of significant individuals from all over the Northern Crescent, and that something was enough to drive the likes of dunRondri to drink and indiscretion. But overall, he'd gotten nothing, likely, worth the risk to his influential neck.

Or at least, nothing an impartial observer would consider worthwhile; for himself, he'd never felt more alive, certainly never felt more in control of his own life. He'd foiled three robbery attempts (two on himself, thanks in part to Deymorin's advice about where to *keep* his money), two assaults, and numerous shoplifting attempts.

Deymorin would also say that if he'd kept to the areas of Khoratum the individuals he most wished to tap tended to frequent, his life would have been far less exciting.

He'd had, he would be the first to admit, a secondary agenda over these past five days. There wasn't a spot in all of Lesser Khoratum that he hadn't investigated, not a strange food he hadn't tried, not a store he hadn't browsed, not an alley he hadn't searched.

All that experience, including examining the stables of three different brothels, and he'd found no sign of either Temorii or the young man in the cloak. He was a fool. An obsessed, guilt-ridden idiot. He could wish . . .

But no, that was *too* selfish. Temorii, the street-lad and the truth behind that illusive perception would have to wait.

If the political climate in Khoratum awaited the arrival of Mikhyel dunMheric, it was time Mikhyel dunMheric entered Khoratum.

Tonight, he'd contact Deymorin and set the final plans into motion.

Ganfrion was, according to Deymorin's last report, camped a day's ride outside of Khoratum. Deymorin himself was on maneuvers on the Harriisidumin line, two days' ride to the south. He'd contact Deymorin, Deymorin would send word to Ganfrion, and he'd be gone, free of Khoratum in three days.

He set the key in the lock and turned. It resisted with a grating noise that had set his nerves on edge the first day, and the effect had only worsened with familiarity. But the lock worked; a man's privacy didn't need anything more.

He stumbled into the dark room, the only light a shaft of leylight seeping through a gap in the curtains. Blindly weary, he dropped scarf, greatcoat, and dress coat in a pile he'd regret in the morning, and dropped himself onto the mattress, kicking his shoes one at a time onto the floor.

His braid made a lump at the base of his skull. Expending his final bit of energy, he pulled the clip free and flipped it across the room in the general direction of the table.

A pale hand reached into the shaft of light and caught it. Mikhyel, discovering a hidden reservoir of vigor, jerked upright.

"Who's there?"

"Matron let me in." A ghostly shadow rose from the chair. "You told Thyerri you were concerned for me," the shadow continued, and the voice was as beautiful as he remembered, and he wondered how he could ever have mistaken anyone else's for it.

"Thyerri?" he whispered back. "The street-lad?"

Like a ghost, Temorii drifted into the shaft of silver light. Her shoulder lifted in a graceful shrug. "I am, as you see, well enough." She turned toward the door. "I should, I suppose, apologize for any distress I caused." And one pale eye glittered back at him. "I . . . I am sorry, Khy."

Her hand was on the doorlatch before his aching legs could carry him across the room to her side. He covered her fingers with his own.

"Where are you going?" he asked.

"Does it matter?"

"Of *course* it matters. I've been all over this city looking for you!"

"Why?"

"Because—" Fool that he was, he had no sound answer, settled on, "Because I want to help you."

"Help *me*. That's rather miserly of you."

"Miserly? I . . . don't understand."

"The entire web is in need of help, Mikhyel Rhomandi dunMheric, and you want to waste time on one lone beggar."

"I've spent my life helping the web; I don't intend to stop now."

"Ah. I'll be going, then." She turned the lock with her free hand.

He tightened his hold on her other hand. "Does dedicating my life to the web mean I'm not allowed to help a friend?"

"I'm not your friend, Mikhyel dunMheric."

Simply said. Coldly enough said to make him wince. He should have known. She and the boy—Thyerri, she'd called him—were of a kind. Proud. Resentful of any valley-born man's interference in their lives. He was *rijhili*. The intruder. No different than the rapacious investors. Never mind he meant better.

"Forgive my presumption," he said, weary to his bones, and let her hand slip free. She jerked the door open.

He turned and slumped into the nearest chair, not wanting to see her leave, only then realizing just how much the hope of seeing her again, of solving the puzzle that was Temorii, had sustained him these past days. His exhaustion returned tenfold; he propped his elbow on the table, closed his eyes, and propped his forehead in his palm.

The noisy latch slid into place; he crossed his arms on the table and let his head fall forward, thinking maybe he'd just fall asleep right there.

"Help me what?"

He jumped; the chair beneath him slid, tipped and crashed to the floor. Her hand on his elbow was all that kept him from following it down in an ungainly sprawl.

Heart racing, he got his feet under him, and stood straight. Temorii quite matter-of-factly set the chair right and pushed him down in it, before settling herself into the other chair. She leaned her elbows on the table and stared at him.

Waiting.

He ran a shaking hand through his hair, trying to resurrect all the times he'd thought of her over the past days, what he'd planned to say when they met again, though this interview in no way resembled that fantasy encounter.

Searching for something approaching composure, he got to his feet, and twisted the overhead lamp into alignment. He got no more from the leybulb than the faint glimmer that said all other lights were on in the building, but that shimmer was sufficient to highlight her face.

He poured himself a glass of water, a second for her, set it on the table between them when she refused to take it from him.

"Never mind," she said, and placing both hands flat on the table, shoved herself to her feet. "Farewell, Mikhyel dun—"

"F–find your mother." He steadied his voice and continued. "If that's what you want. Go home, wherever that is."

A startled look vanished between one breath and the next. "In my sleep?" She asked.

He nodded.

"You're cruel to use it against me now, dunMheric. Mother is long ago. Past history. There was only one thing I ever wanted, and it's closed to me now. Not even Rhomatum's premier barrister can change that fact. So best you forget me."

This time he didn't try to intercept her dash for freedom. Physically.

"Is it the dance you want?" he asked.

She froze, her hand poised above the latch.

"The street-lad—Thyerri—implied as much."

Her breath caught; her head dropped.

"It doesn't matter," she said, and the music in her voice soured. "Rhyys determines who competes, and my opportunity passed."

"Are you too old?"

"Hardly."

"Incompetent?"

She turned slowly. "I'm the best damned radical to ever challenge the Khoratum Rings."

"Then why'd you lose?"

"I didn't."

"Then why aren't you dancing?"

"I never got a chance to compete."

"Why not?"

"Because the damned web went down and the rings crashed!"

"Oh. Well, then, I guess we'd better get you another chance to compete."

Her mouth opened, closed. "You can't." She said flatly.

He grinned, relieved at having breached her cold indifference at last. "Never tell a lawyer 'can't,' Temorii."

She drew a deep, shaking breath and hissed: "I missed my chance, damn you!"

"Only one?"

"For me, yes."

"Not for others?"

"I'm not others."

"Temorii, do you *want* to compete?"

"Yes!"

"Then stop giving me unsubstantiated conjecture, and answer my questions!"

Her mouth set, lips pressed tight in anger. Unimpressed, Mikhyel grinned, his blood moving faster with each passing moment, now that he had a specific goal. He pulled his notebook and a pen from the outside pocket of the case on the floor behind his chair, tested the pen's cartridge, and began taking notes.

"The next competition is scheduled for—"

"Canceled." Still sullen, but she hadn't gone out the door.

"Canceled?"

"Delayed at least." Her mouth twitched. "You're ill, remember?"

The public announcement. He'd forgotten.

"So—" Mikhyel raised an eyebrow and made a note. "First: Mikhyel recovers. I can manage that." And with a flourish, checked off the line. "Then, we find out the new date." He sensed her proximity, made a point not to look up. "Third: practice. Are you in . . ." He thought of that thin body, and poverty and obviously short rations, and wondered: "How soon could you . . . I mean . . ."

"You get me in, Barrister, I'll be ready." Her breath was short, quick. Frightened.

Afraid to hope.

He dropped the pen and twisted around to face her. "What happened, Temorii? Why shouldn't *you* get another chance, if others will?"

Her eyes flickered away from his to stare at her toes, and one shoulder lifted in a half-shrug. "It's hard to explain."

"I'm not going anywhere. But if it's a long story, would you mind sitting back down, before my neck is permanently kinked?"

She swallowed hard, blinked, but rather than return to her chair, she sank down where she stood, as if her knees had given out beneath her. Her fingers began that nervous pleating of her patched and dirty tunic. And when she began, he wasn't certain she remembered the question, but he didn't interrupt, content for the moment, that she hadn't run away again.

"The competition is more than the dance. First, there's the maze. You're led blindfolded into the courtyard, and there, you await your turn to compete. Staying warmed up and ready—sometimes for all day—that's part of the challenge."

She leaned against his chair until her shoulder and hair brushed his thigh. Her hands were folded—clenched—in her lap.

"When they call your number, you try to reach the dance stadium. The maze is . . . more than a puzzle to test logic. It's full of hidden traps—most potentially lethal. Some of the most expensive seats are the hidden viewing areas for those traps."

"Dancers in the maze," Mikhyel murmured, and she looked up through the ragged fall of hair, her expression puzzled. He smiled, and brushed the strands free of her improbably long lashes. "A game I used to play. A child's game of sticks and stones. I never thought where it came from."

"Oh," she said, though he didn't think she truly understood. She was staring at him, eyes wide, unseeing, and he realized, somewhat belatedly, that his hand was still in her hair, finger-combing the tangles out of the sunbleached strands. He felt his face grow hot, but before he could think what to say, her shoulders heaved, and she relaxed, settling down onto the floor, letting her head rest full against his knee.

"I waited all day," she murmured, talking into the shadows. "I waited for the arbiter to call my number. But he never did. There were three still to compete when the rings went down . . . as I later discovered."

"So you never got to run the maze, never danced . . ."

She nodded. "From the time he accepted my application, Rhyys had said I was to be led in once only. I'd have one chance to run the maze, and one chance to dance. I sent Rhyys a petition to try again . . . after, but Rhyys says I chose the competition I'd take part in. Rhyys says I lost my chance. Rhyys says, obviously Rakshi doesn't want me to dance for him, or Rakshi would have made my number rise to the surface before the rings went down."

"Rakshi? Is Rhyys a believer in the old gods, then?"

"Not that he will admit."

"But you are?"

A shrug. "I'm a dancer."

As if that explained everything.

"And he uses that belief against you?"

No answer.

"What about the others left to compete? Did Rakshi also frown on them? Will they get another trial?"

"Probably, though I can't swear to that. Rhyys delights in controlling our . . . the dancers' lives. But it's rare that he doesn't let them try again. He . . . likes having the students and trainees around."

"Why would he single you out?"

She shrugged. "Because I am a child of the mountain and not his precious Khoratum? Because I was a better dancer than his favorite? Because he dislikes the color of my eyes? Rhyys dunTarec doesn't need logical reasons to wield his whip."

An analysis that certainly corresponded to his sense of the petty tyrant Anheliaa had chosen to control Khoratum Tower. A petty tyrant he would enjoy outwitting. And there might be a way, though not one Korelli dunKharin could use to advantage.

"It appears," he said slowly, "that the time has come for Mikhyel dunMheric to make an official entry into Khoratum."

She tilted her head back to look up at him.

"Care to become part of his entourage?"

🌀 🌀 🌀

"He's taking Temorii with him to join his men, some-where outside the city wall."

"Where?"

Thyerri shrugged, hating himself already, then staggered as the scarred hand reminded him that insolence would not be tolerated in this elegant Tower room.

"I don't *know*," he protested, dabbing blood from his lip with the back of his hand. "They'll take the Orenum stage and then leave it—somewhere. Someone will pick them up and then he's to come back to Khoratum. Officially."

"When?"

"I don't *know*."

Scarface raised his hand again, but the blow didn't come, and Thyerri stared dully at the hand that glinted with gold and silver in the leylight. Rings, several per finger. One, at least, bore Rhyys' crest. Scarface gorRhyys, then, though Thyerri doubted Rhyys was the real master.

The beringed hand fell.

"Where did he go today?"

"Downhill. All day."

The brocade-clad shoulders shook with silent laughter. "Looking for his Temorii."

Thyerri said nothing. Scarface began pacing, a wild cat's impatient prowl.

"And did he meet again with the Orenumin?"

Thyerri began to nod. Caught himself and muttered, "Yes. At Louinnii's again."

"Why?"

Thyerri controlled his shoulders in mid-shrug. "He said something about a gathering here, and some concern that the Northern Crescent nodes are unhappy. I think he wants to find out why, is all, and that's why he was just . . . here."

Scarface scowled. "I'm not asking you to think. How does he intend to get Temorii this second chance at the dance?"

Thyerri shook his head. "I wish I knew."

Scarface paused in mid-prowl. "Why?"

A shudder ran through him, and he thought of those holds over people that this man treasured so highly. "Just . . . curious, that's all. It does seem an impossible task, don't you think?"

Scarface grunted, but he continued to watch Thyerri with a hawk's interest in a field mouse.

"I think, perhaps, I will tell Rhyys about this plan. And you will tell Temorii that Rhyys knows and is prepared and that when she returns to the Tower, she had best play along with whatever Rhyys does."

"Temorii wants to compete."

"I can't guarantee that."

"Then I can't guarantee her cooperation."

"No? And you, Thyerri. What do *you* want."

"You can't guarantee it."

Scarface laughed, a long, hard, cruel laugh.

"May I go now, sir?" Thyerri asked.

"I think I'd like you to stay a while. I'm in a festive mood. As I recall, you were a competent dancer."

"Please, sir, I'd rather not."

"I don't care what you'd rather. Dance for me, Thyerri of Khoratum."

"I will try, sir," Thyerri answered slowly, "but I fear you will be much disappointed. You asked that first night, whether anything essential had been damaged in the fire. The fact is, sir, the answer was 'yes.' "

"You will, nonetheless, try."

In the end, even Scarface admitted it was a meaningless exercise and sent Thyerri on his way, untouched. As he rushed through the back corridors of the Tower, and into the streets, Thyerri hoped he was in time: Temorii had promised dunMheric she'd be back by midnight.

Thyerri slipped out the door that barely opened, stuck now as it was between old and new construction. He squeezed down the narrow space between the buildings, paused behind the hedgerose to listen for passing guards, then slipped out into the open.

And a vast mountain of a man.

Thyerri ducked back between the buildings, but a huge paw gripped his arm and hauled him out. The next instant, the living mountain had him backed up against a building, and a knife point pricked his throat.

"Who are you and what's your connection with Mikhyel dunMheric?" the mountain hissed in his ear.

"W–who?"

"Don't try to play the innocent with me, hiller. I know

you. I know your kind. I've been following you for three days now, and I don't like what I'm seeing. Who are you selling him to?"

"I—I can't . . ." Thyerri let his words and eyes drift, let his body wilt, as if he were about to collapse.

The mountain cursed. The vast weight shifted, and Thyerri shoved off the stone wall with his feet, driving his shoulder into the mountain, sending him staggering farther off balance.

Thyerri tapped and jumped, as those days with Zelin had taught him, driving his hands, then his feet off the huge shoulders, gaining the height and the loft to make a nearby roof. The mountain's fingers brushed his ankle, caught and nearly pulled him back.

He snapped free, hauled himself to his feet, and ran.

Chapter Eight

"There." Mikhyel gave the cravat's top fold one final tug and stepped to the side. "Well?"

Temorii swallowed and lifted her chin as if trying to avoid the lace, then met his mirrored eyes suspiciously. "Why is *yours* so plain?"

He grinned. "Your father's a timber baron and I'm your humble tutor, remember?"

She made a face at his reflection, then stepped back, to fit more of herself in the mirror. She tugged the coat lapels and struck a pose so reminiscent of Nikki at his most self-aware, that Mikhyel almost choked on his stifled laughter.

"You'll do," he said, and threw his grooming kit into the portmanteau and buckled the bag closed.

By the whim of Rakshi (as Ganfrion would say) under-professor dunKharin had escaped Bernoi forever. He'd been hired as companion and tutor to one Thyerri dunMatrii of Orenum (which Mikhyel complained showed a marked lack of imagination; Temorii said Thyerri wouldn't mind, that it was a common enough name in the Northern Khoramali and easier than remembering a new name). Young dunMatrii, having declared himself bored with Khoratum, was being sent home following an Embarrassing Incident with a local heiress.

A (Ganfrion would say) far too elaborate story, and one Temorii had endlessly embellished over the past days. In fact, once he'd convinced her to trust him (a formidable task in itself) Temorii's enthusiasm for her role had flourished. Temorii had wandered about the Khoratum market wearing *his* spare clothing, spending *his* money on items *he* pointed out, because (she insisted, and he soon conceded) she could get a better price.

They were, as he'd noted the first day, much of a height, though he had the slight edge, and his clothing, though tailored to his measurements, seemed somehow to fit her better than ever it fit his too-bony frame. In fact, in his clothes, with her hair pulled back into a simple queue, she cut a figure well able to turn a variety of heads wherever they went.

Or perhaps it was just his increasingly prejudiced eyes that interpreted her effect on people.

Time and familiarity had done nothing to diminish his fascination with her. He'd tried to hire a second room, but that had proven impossible, thanks to the growing number of outsiders coming in for the festival. He'd had the cot brought back in, and a sheet hung between the beds for privacy, but while he was awake, he remained conscious of her every action on that far side, and twice he'd waked to discover her curled at the foot of his bed.

Both times, morning had found her back in the cot, which she claimed was quite comfortable.

She didn't mention the late night shifting about, therefore neither did he, but he'd seen her eyes widen when he left her alone to go "listen" in Greater Khoratum, and he'd noted the eagerness with which she followed him about the market, and he wondered whether having thrown her trust into him, she feared that trust would be betrayed and he would desert her, and whether that fear ruled her late-night actions.

It would be too much to hope that her motives bore any resemblance to the insane urge he felt simply to be close to her. And it was undoubtedly best for her if they did not. Fortunately for them both, she felt at times such as this more like a younger brother than a young woman.

Best, he told himself, to encourage *that* relationship—in both of them.

Either way, in an hour, they'd be on the coach to Orenum and by tonight, (thanks to late night conversations with his brothers) a long-lost cousin would have met them and carried them off for a family reunion.

And hopefully, he thought as he pulled the door closed for a final time and followed a haughty Thyerri dunMatrii down the hallway, along with that family reunion would come a return of his old serenity of mind.

It was evening when the cart pulled into the camp. Campfires dotted the darkness like a painting of the original Darian Exodus. Rather more numerous than Deymorin had led him to expect, those dots of light lay in orderly rows, along a black mass of hillside that, according to Deymorin's thought picture, should have caves where the men could shelter in the event of a lightning storm.

As the cart bumped and rattled to a halt near the central-most fire, Mikhyel slid off the open back amid a small cascade of straw. He turned and held his hands out to Temorii, but she harrumphed and jumped down alone, with a muttered: *"You wouldn't help Thyerri, would you?"*

In answer, he hoisted the valise from the cart bed and heaved it at her; she caught it with greater ease than he had thrown it, grinned, and set it down gently.

"Well, Rhomandi, I see you survived."

He swung around to face the owner of the distinctive, gritty voice. "Rhomandi?" he echoed, and before he could prevent it, an idiotic grin stretched his face. "I'm coming up in the world!"

Ganfrion's large paw surrounded his hand and he realized a ridiculous satisfaction when Ganfrion's other hand gripped his shoulder.

"*I* see *you* brought backup for your backup," he said, and waved his arm to indicate the campfires.

"Just in case, Khyel. Just in . . ."

Through that double hold, he sensed Ganfrion's sudden tension, and Ganfrion looked beyond him to where Thyerri—*Temorii* stood waiting. The lace-edged cravat hadn't endured beyond the last sight of the posting inn. Her coat hung free, her shirt lay open halfway to her cummerbund, her hair was straggling free of the queue and with her hip-cocked, hands-on-hips stance, she looked like a would-be rakehell-in-training a good half-year short of his first real shave.

"And who is this?" Ganfrion asked, in his most unwelcoming tone.

While Mikhyel hesitated, Temorii stepped boldly forward, into Ganfrion's fire-cast shadow, and held out her hand.

"Name's Thyerri," she announced cockily. "Thyerri dun-Matrii. And you?"

Ganfrion frowned and shifted, taking his shadow with him, casting Temorii into full firelight. Temorii shied backward, blinking, but then moved willingly enough into the light.

Ganfrion grunted and took her offered hand. "Call me Gan."

"Yessir!" Temorii snapped into a salute rather like the most pompous of the guards crowding Lesser Khoratum, then hefted Mikhyel's portmanteau to her shoulder. "And where should I take this, m'lord Khy?"

"Over here, lad," a cool voice answered her from the largest tent's open flap, and Mikhyel felt the last of his tension slip away, as he crossed the firelit camp to greet Raulind.

Temorii's attempted deception lasted no longer than Raulind's decision that "Thyerri" should share Mikhyel's tent rather than sleep outside with the men. Temorii watched Mikhyel like an eager puppy, waiting.

Mikhyel took Raulind inside the tent and explained, to Raul *and* to Ganfrion. Raulind said he'd suspected as much; Ganfrion said nothing.

And, in fact, over the course of the following days, Ganfrion proved less thrilled overall about the sudden addition to Mikhyel's personal entourage. The ex-inmate, ex-guard, ex-soldier said nothing overt, but the way he watched Temorii's every move left little doubt that his interest had nothing to do with her femininity, and everything to do with her city of origin and the circumstances under which she'd come into Mikhyel dunMheric's life.

Raulind, on the other hand, had obviously decided she was a much needed addition to Mikhyel's life. And since the last thing Mikhyel could claim was impartiality where Temorii was concerned, he tried very hard to listen more to Ganfrion's caution than to Raulind's smiles.

If he was a fool to trust her, he'd rather know that *before* entering Khoratum Tower than after.

They spent two weeks there in the mountainside camp. Eighteen days for the official announcement of his revised plans to arrive in Khoratum, and to allow for fictitious travel time from Rhomatum. Eighteen days for Mikhyel to answer the accumulated mail and paperwork—and eighteen days for his beard to grow back, a surprisingly tedious task, lacking the influence of Rhomatum's leythium pool.

And he had time to acquaint himself with the additional

men Ganfrion had brought. Ganfrion was not, he was relieved to discover, actually in charge of the small army. Ganfrion was—by his own choice, according to Raulind—fulfilling the exact function Mikhyel had hired him to perform, taking independent forays, keeping track of Mikhyel's interests and Mikhyel's safety.

And in fact, during that time of waiting, Ganfrion twice disappeared, to return bringing updates on who was newly in Khoratum and with what agenda and what forces.

Temorii arose early, exercised, ate, exercised, ate, exercised and ate again. Mikhyel heard stories about her activities, but he had work to do, and endeavored not to give in to her allure. Besides, he imagined the last thing she wanted was him for an audience, although that excuse might well be wish fulfillment on his part.

Halfway through the fourth day, however, his hand cramping with fatigue, he excused himself to Paulis, who, like Raulind, had come of his own will to assist Mikhyel, and escaped into the mountain sunshine. He stretched and inhaled the brisk air . . . and wondered if he dare commandeer Raulind's hands for a rubdown in the middle of the morning.

But the stiff joints were merely the result of too much sitting. Even in Rhomatum, he'd spend much of the day walking, and in Khoratum, he'd grown accustomed to a great deal more activity. He had insisted Paulis take exercise with the men, but hadn't dared expose himself so closely to Temorii's presence.

That, he knew, was foolishness indeed. And so, this morning, rather than disturb Raulind, he wandered down a goat path widened and trampled by hundreds of human footsteps.

Somewhere the path met a river . . . or so he'd been told. The farthest he'd been from his tent was the officer's latrine.

Some small creature darted across the path in front of him and he paused, watching it scamper up a tree. A breeze rustled down through the trees and tried to insinuate itself inside his coat, blowing strands of hair in his eyes. His attempts to lodge the strands back into the simple braid succeeded only in setting more strands free.

On a whim, he pulled the pin from his hair and let the braid slither free. The wind infiltrated the strands like the slenderest of fingers and lifted it from his scalp. It was a wild feeling. A feeling of freedom. A minor freedom, without doubt, but an accomplishment, even so.

He leaned his shoulder against a tree and closed his eyes, feeling the strain seep out of his body into the tree's sturdy bole, receiving, in his turn, a strength and vitality, almost as though from the earth itself.

Slowly, around the edges of the breeze, came a sound so like the wind and the birds in the trees that it took a moment for him to realize it was man-made.

A flute.

Curious, he followed the sweet sound to its source and found a group of about a dozen trainees on their midday break. They were lounging about the edges of a clearing, where the torn and trampled ground, the practice weapons and padding stacked at one end of the grass indicated they'd spent the morning practicing.

The sound of the flute came from a slight figure dressed in hiller garb and sitting among the men. Farther down the hill, sheep dotted the grass.

In the center of the clearing . . .

Mikhyel's heart stopped. His head grew light. He reached a hand to the nearest tree and braced himself against its solid mass, seeking, without success, that earlier stability.

Like a bird in flight, Temorii leaped and dived, swooped and twisted in and around the flute's light melody. She was everything of beauty he'd ever seen and like nothing he'd seen before.

He told himself firmly he'd seen dancers before, dancers of all varieties, and the best always had this ability to hold an audience breathless. And ringdancers, with their gymnastic twisting flights among the rings were some of the most spectacular.

But none had ever made his heart soar with them.

And this ringdancer had no rings, only her slender body clothed in little more than a loincloth and one of his old shirts—and a rope. She carried a short length of rope that sometimes whipped—like a dance ring—around her as she soared through the air, and sometimes snaked around her body in undulating paths—the way the radical streamer slithered among the Tower rings. And at times the rope floated high into the air, seemingly forgotten, until a toe caught it and returned it to her waiting hand.

Like a child—an impossibly skilled and beautiful child—playing with a toy.

It was common knowledge that in Khoratum the radical dance was different from all other nodes, but he'd been led to believe, by the legal arguments, that it was the Khoratum dance rings with their sharpened edges that created that difference, not the dancers themselves.

For the last three years there had been ongoing debate over whether or not the Khoratumin radical dance should be outlawed. There were those who said the Khoratum rings with their sharpened leading edges were too dangerous, and that the mystery surrounding the dance training held too much religious connotation.

No one ever mentioned the magic that lay within the dancers themselves. Seeing Temorii, he could well understand why others might fear the standard such a dancer might set.

Or perhaps it was only Temorii who could cast this particular spell. And perhaps only Mikhyel dunMheric who could be so mesmerized.

{Oh, Tem . . .} he thought, and bit his lip to keep from saying her name aloud. Her head twisted up and around, and he thought, for a moment, she'd heard him, the way his brothers could. But her eyes flitted past his shadow, the flute shifted to a more sultry mood, and her dance flowed to a different pace.

He rested his head against the tree, unable to pull himself from the view. Only he, Deymorin would say, would fall in love with the one person he knew he couldn't have. And yet that inaccessibility was probably her greatest charm, his most cynical self pointed out. She was safe for Mikhyel dunMheric to love: she *couldn't* return his affection, and by her very birth, she was utterly unsuitable for a Rhomandi to wed.

He was (horrifying thought) as blindly, foolishly romantic as Nikki.

But here in the trees, he could indulge, just for a moment, the sort of foolish dreams he'd never even thought to have before.

Cheers rang out. She'd finished. He was free.

While the lounging men thronged about her, laughing and exclaiming, and throwing "Thyerri" high in the air, Mikhyel pushed away from the tree and began walking back toward the camp. With half the distance yet to go, the men began to rush past him, running, laughing, challenging one another to foot races.

Mikhyel stepped well off the path, moving slowly, savoring his fleeting images.

"Khy? Khy, *wait!*" The voice of his dream cried out. A voice that made a song of his name. "It came back today! Khy, did you see? It was back!" And in the next moment, light footfalls ran up behind him, and a hand grabbed his arm. "Did you see, Khy? Did you?"

Her voice was breathless as she skipped along beside him, the smile on her face wide and bright.

He nodded, not trusting his voice.

The smile dimmed, a line appeared between her brows. "Well?"

It was Thyerri's cheeky demand, and Temorii's uncertain plea all wrapped into one word.

He sought the control and the words, and neither came. Temorii blinked and bit her lip. Then her face hardened, the lower lip pouted ever so slightly, and his little brother Thyerri said, "Never *mind*. I don't—"

He stopped and caught her arm, interrupting her, forcing her to face him.

"I think—" His voice came out in a hoarse rush. "I think that you lied to me."

Her eyes went wide, her face blanched. "I—"

"You said," he continued, "that you were the best damned radical to ever challenge the Khoratum rings."

"I *am*."

He shook his head. "If *that*—" He tipped his head back toward the clearing. "—is *any* indication, you're the best damned radical to ever challenge *any* rings."

Her mouth snapped shut. Her head tipped, and then sunlight again ruled her face. She laughed and grabbed his hands and began swinging him about.

He protested and pulled her to a stop. *He* was gasping.

She stood staring at him. His hair had wrapped fine tendrils around their clasped hands as they whirled, keeping them close. Without looking down, she freed the strands, then twisted her fingers in and around them, absently playing with his hair as she'd played with the rope, slowly adding new strands to those she already held captive.

Breath came shallow and shaken. He opened his mouth,

wanting to free himself of her, but, eyes still locked on his, she took a step uphill, away from the camp, and tugged gently on the hair bridge between them.

"Come with me?" she pleaded. "Just to walk."

He thought of Paulis, and the letters, and what Ganfrion would say about his going off alone . . . And then, he saw Ganfrion, standing deep in the shadows of the trees . . . which meant, Ganfrion *wanted* him to see. Which also meant, Ganfrion would follow him.

And he could follow his . . . hand.

From that time on, it became a tacit agreement. Twice a day, dressed in simple clothing of Ganfrion's provision, he'd follow her up the mountain slopes. She teased him into running, albeit for very short distances, and showed him exercises that had him finding muscles he'd never dreamed existed.

Finding, but not debilitating them, as Ganfrion (from the wicked jibes leveled at him across an evening fire) obviously anticipated. Thanks to Raulind's nightly massage and healing oils, Ganfrion's anticipation was doomed to disappointment.

It wasn't as if he'd led a sedentary life. Every city dweller knew the dangers of growing too lazy. There was walking, swimming, even the occasional workout in the gymnasium with the Tower trainers. He wasn't Deymorin, who despite his leg could challenge the best horsemen and fencers in Rhomatum, and he certainly wasn't Nikki, whose youthful vigor and enthusiasm more than made up for any lack in talent or training. But he was healthy, in an average sort of way, his body sufficient for the tasks he'd set it.

Compared to Temorii, he was an unformed child.

Temorii danced, even without music. Or her movement was . . . visual music. Or she made *any* sound *into* music. There were no words to describe that which the sight of her skipping and tumbling and spinning along a mountain trail created inside him. His greatest difficulty in following her instructions was the constant temptation simply to watch her move.

For himself, he considered it an accomplishment when, on the morning before they were scheduled to leave for Khoratum, he finally managed thirty pushups with some ease. Even as he congratulated himself, Temonii laughed and crawled onto his back, hugging him, and ordered ten more.

He struggled through two, collapsed, and cursed.

She laughed. "You're too easy on yourself, Khy."

"So why don't *you* try it?"

She poised on hands and toes; he stared at her.

"Climb aboard," she said.

"Tem, for—"

She jerked her head toward her back. He knew, by now, better than to argue with her.

The first few she managed without noticeable strain. At seven, she struggled far more than he had at two, and by nine, she was shaking so badly he feared for her joints. But she refused to stop, and he dared not move. She'd taught him how vital balance was, and he wasn't confident enough of his own skill to get off without ruining one of those thin, straining wrists.

And she, who had taught him that precaution, straightened her arms for the tenth time, and lowered again, her body all the while tight as a drumhead beneath him.

"Now, Khy," she whispered, and he was off.

She collapsed, sobbing with effort. And cursing. Vehemently.

He stroked her back and her hair, fighting the desire to take her into his arms. "I'm sorry, Tem," he said, "I should never have challenged you."

"I sh-should have b-been able to . . ." Her whisper caught, and she buried her face in an arm.

"Should, maybe, but to push yourself too hard . . . to risk permanent damage. Nothing can be worth that, Tem."

"And *that* was nothing compared to the challenges we used to make to one another in practice."

She rolled over and lifted herself cautiously, seeming to check each joint and muscle, rising clear to her feet, stretching, testing, until she was satisfied. Then she settled beside him, legs crossed, back straight but relaxed.

"*Risk*, Khy, is attacking the rings with insufficient strength. Risk is not being willing to challenge death with each and every breath, because uncommitted moves are the essence of failure, and failure on the rings is synonymous with death."

Real death, or figurative—to a dancer like Temorii, there was no difference. He'd watched, with his heart in his throat as she tumbled along a sheer cliff edge, or jumped an abyss without a second thought to the death that lay a misstep away. For Temorii, to dance was to live. It was also to defy death.

A fact of which he reminded himself as his longing flared without warning. But it was easier, now, than it had been a week ago, to tame his passion. He knew now that whatever happened in Khoratum, *he* could not be responsible for preventing so great a talent from fulfilling its obvious destiny.

Which altruism did *not* mean he didn't regret the loss. Just his luck, to finally find those elusive urges in himself, only to have to deny they existed.

A callused hand covered his. A hand that, save for her calluses and his manicure was not so different. She was an illiterate entertainer from the Khoramali Hills, he was from the center of the civilized world, beneficiary of the greatest tutors of the age, and yet they had the same long, thin fingers, the same prominent knuckles and veins.

Who knew what else they might share?

Almost without conscious thought, he turned his hand to clasp hers and reached for that inner spark he believed he'd sensed the first time they met, the awareness he himself had shut down. And for the first time since they'd left Khoratum, he realized how . . . empty he felt, that he actually missed that sense of {Deymorin} and {Nikki} underneath his skin.

And for a moment, he thought he did sense a shimmering on the other side, her side. A shimmer, but no more, and even that much could have just been imagination. Too much of wishing, perhaps, for that ability to exist beyond himself and his brothers, too much of hoping for that kind of similarity, that level of . . . sharing.

He retreated to discover her luminous eyes fastened on him. Wide, unblinking. The tinge of spring green pulsed deeper with each passing moment. He couldn't move, couldn't look away, and Temorii seemed similarly transfixed. She gripped her lower lip between her teeth, and her hand clenched his.

Then her other hand lifted, trembling, and touched his face, traced the narrow line of his close-cropped beard. Her index finger brushed along his lips—

With a painful inner strain, he wrenched free—enough

at least to close his own eyes. She gave a soft cry and collapsed against him.

Somewhere, he found an ice within himself that held him steady and kept his arms from encircling her until she gathered herself together, jumped to her feet, and raced down the hill.

By the time he caught up with her, they were in camp, and swept up in the flurry of packing for Khoratum.

Chapter Nine

Mikhyel sat passively beside the open window while Raulind combed the morning tangles from his hair and braided it in the old, familiar pattern.

On his own, Mikhyel had settled for less. Far less.

Outside that open window of the third-story Khoratum Tower complex ranged a vastly different view of Khoratum than the one he'd grown to know in those foot-flattening treks. From here, the alleyways, and trash-ridden wind-eddies of Lesser Khoratum where those like young Thyerri fought to survive, were nothing more than blue mountain shadows among multitextured rooftops.

Clustered in a band around the Khoratum Tower complex, and insinuating tendrils outward into those relatively crude structures of the previous mountain village, were buildings more familiar to a Rhomatumin eye. Large buildings, with impressive, complex facades, but somehow out of place here in the wild beauty of the Khoramali.

Closest to his window were the oldest structures in Khoratum: the final remnant of a pre-Rhomatum fortress. Local legend, according to Nikki's notes, provided no clues to the original owners of the fortress. Like many similar ruins scattered about the Rhomatum Web, Rhomatum-bred historians attributed the fortress to an unknown people who had abandoned their massive stone fortresses long before the Darian exodus and the capping of Rhomatum.

The current, most popular theory, placed the blame for that withdrawal on the capping of Persitum, an act that made the Rhomatum Valley the perimeter of the Mauritum Web, and subject to violent, uncontrolled storms. Seeing a sample of those ruins restored here, Mikhyel questioned that theory. The massive, solid stone structure would have provided their makers protection as effective as those caves Ganfrion's men had camped near.

A man whose window on history was confined to one man's viewpoint had to wonder if that one man had allowed the entire truth to survive living memory, had to wonder whether Darius' high-handed bid for independence hadn't affected the lives of far more individuals than those who had followed him out of Mauritum.

It made a man anxious, who wanted to be a good lawmaker, who wanted only the best for his own City, made him wonder what *his* valley shadows concealed, made him wonder who his own ancestors had summarily displaced in the name of personal exigency.

From here, the native Khoratumin were simply tiny bodies bobbing about the streets in seemingly aimless patterns. From here, it was all too easy to believe one's own way of life superior, and those bodies downhill mere sheep in need of herding.

Mikhyel understood now, in a way he never had before, why Deymorin had so vehemently fought the capping of Khoratum. Deymorin had fought for the rights of the valley farmers who had owned and worked the land closest to Rhomatum and who had been displaced when the Rhomatum umbrella expanded, but their situation was not all that different than the villagers of this once-thriving community.

In the way of node umbrellas, the capping of Khoratum had caused once vital soil to go infertile within the vicinity of the node. Developers had moved in and built, ready to take advantage of the new and growing market, as miners moved in, ready to tap the surrounding hills.

But the village and farms that had occupied these lands before Anheliaa's expansionist supporters had taken control of them had supported hundreds of people, honest, unsophisticated people who either adapted to the city life or tried to relocate in a land already well populated. Forcing that choice arbitrarily upon people, he was willing now to make the judgment, was wrong.

Deymorin would be amused. Deymorin was also going to gloat for at least a month after he admitted that.

He pulled his dressing robe more securely against a sudden breeze, but had no inclination to close the window. Deymorin would also be amused at this preference he'd developed for the scent of the wind off Mount Khoratum.

It wasn't, he decided, that he believed progress in and of itself was wrong, it was the destructive employment of that progress to which he objected. There was nothing the Syndicate could do for those long-dead victims of their ancestors' actions, but for those victimized by the Syndicate's own actions—those like Thyerri and those other dots wandering about Khoratum's streets through no fault of their own—for those, there had to be a fair and new beginning.

A beginning that could not include Rhyys dunTarec; of that, he was certain.

Mikhyel dunMheric had arrived in Khoratum five days ago. He'd arrived on schedule, with a very small entourage, and an utter lack of fanfare. A minor attendant to Rhyys had seen them settled here in the Tower Complex, had handed Mikhyel an itinerary of tours that Rhyys had arranged in his honor, and a list of those individuals currently in residence within Khoratum that he might care to contact, and that was the last they'd seen of Rhyys' personal staff.

Of Rhyys himself, they'd seen nothing. The official word from Rhyys' staff to Mikhyel's was that Rhyys had been thrown off-schedule by Mikhyel's early (according to his *original* itinerary) arrival. The plans for the celebrations that were to precede the dance competition that was to be the highlight of Mikhyel's visit were all of them falling apart, and Rhyys was too distraught to see him.

It was a tactic, Ganfrion assured him, familiar to Rhyys' household staff. Rhyys, according to his staff, would drop out of sight for days at a time to give the appearance of great demands on his time. Sometimes, this retreat took place into the Tower, more often than not, these days, into his bedroom.

When asked who minded the Tower at such times, the staff had no answer, except to say that since the energy flow from the Tower improved, no one complained. Apparently the Khoratum Rings, like the Khoratum Tower staff, were more efficient without, than with, their hand-picked master.

A fact Mikhyel dunMheric conscientiously recorded in his notebook.

Considering the length of the list he was compiling against the Khoratumin ringmaster, he was increasingly perplexed at Anheliaa's selection of Rhyys in the first place. Anheliaa might have enjoyed those who catered to her vanity, but her first and foremost consideration had always been for the web.

He had to wonder whether this Rhyys was the same one she'd trained, or if something—perhaps even just the handling of so much power—had changed him.

History notwithstanding, while Anheliaa had chosen Rhyys and recommended him as the first ringmaster, his appointment had been ratified by all the stockholders of the young City. No Rhomandi could depose Rhyys, but those same investors might well be induced to get rid of him should he be exposed as incompetent in terms businessmen understood.

However with leaders and ringmasters from all over the Northern Crescent crowding into tiny Khoratum as Rhyys' personal guests, now was hardly the optimum moment to challenge Rhyys' hold over his little pocket kingdom.

In every sense, Rhyys was the weak link in their plan to restore the Khoratum line. For the time being and in the interest of the web, he had to convince Rhyys to cooperate with *all* the other ringmasters, Northern and Southern, long enough to repair the Khoratum line. Keep things calm, keep them cooperative until the web was at full strength. Prove to themselves and the web that Rhomatum was under control, and he would be able to legally request Rhyys' replacement.

On the other hand, perhaps, a simple bribe—

"Breakfast!" The cheerful announcement accompanied an organized chaos that took over his sitting room. Mikhyel sat back and enjoyed the performance of the young man authoritatively arranging the items to his satisfaction. When the harried footmen finally departed, the lad hopped over to Mikhyel's chair, bowed deeply over an exceedingly shapely leg, and announced, through an unruly flop of hair:

"Your breakfast is served, m'lord dunMheric."

Mikhyel laughed, and rose from the grooming chair to settle into the imperiously indicated throne at the head of the table. But when the cocky brat flipped a napkin into a neat triangle and spread it across Mikhyel's lap, he grabbed the cloth up and snapped the lad with a technique his fingers remembered from childhood with Deymorin, though his mind had long since forgotten.

"Thyerri, sit!" he demanded, and the brat, rather like one of Deymorin's well-trained hounds, flopped to the floor beside his chair, to stare up at him with a puppy's adoring, and rather vacant expression.

He buried his face in his hands and strove for control.
He nearly achieved it—then he made the mistake of again
looking down.

Raulind had settled at Mikhyel's right (the same side as
the puppy) and was helping himself to a hearty breakfast
(Mikhyel having long ago established that he'd rather have
company for breakfast than a servant hovering about in the
corners) and the fact that Raulind ignored the puppy made
its behavior increasingly outrageous.

But when Raulind tossed "it" a scrap of ham (which it
caught, amazingly, in its mouth) Mikhyel shoved his chair
back, hauled the youngster up, and plunked him into his
chair on the left hand side of the table.

"Behave," he said firmly, and the puppy miraculously
transformed into the young woman he'd spirited out of
Khoratum thirteen days before.

Raulind passed her the basket of hot, hard-crusted rolls.

Mikhyel laughed and began dishing up his own breakfast.

So much depended on factors as yet opaque to him. The
men Deymorin had sent with Ganfrion had joined the
ranks of the other armed guards encamped at various
points around the lake that spread southward outside Khoratum's city wall.

There was, Ganfrion reported, an uneasy truce among
the various companies. Men hired and trained for
peacekeeping within their home territory, suddenly and
without explanation drawn into close association with other
trained men, from other nodes, were naturally suspicious
of one another. They'd been left to wonder if they'd been
brought to Khoratum to protect their employer from these
men camped to either side of them or to join forces with
them against some as yet unspecified common enemy.

The largest contingent was out of Giephaetum, and no
small part of it were Giebhaidii men. Nethaalye's father,
Errif, was indeed in Khoratum, along with several of Nethaalye's cousins and uncles. One of those cousins had been
the leader of the pack that attacked Temorii.

Such coincidences did make a man at least wonder about
Temorii's Rakshi, and whether or not that fickle godling
did indeed rule this area of the world.

Ganfrion had obtained revised estimates on the private
guards gathering outside the Khoratum perimeter, and
while substantial, Ganfrion felt they couldn't really pose a

meaningful threat to Rhomatum, decentralized as they were. Which analysis had not stopped Mikhyel from reporting to Deymorin, via that internal link, that transferring his training maneuvers to the Mount Khoratum district might not be a bad notion. To which Deymorin agreed.

Mikhyel pretended not to notice that Deymorin was already on the Khoratum leyline. Pretended as well that the thoughts of messengers already sent to several coastal camps had not seeped through.

Such forethought and maneuvering was, after all, why Deymorin was sleeping out under the stars and he was here in the rather cumbersome Tower of Khoratum, smiling politely at men who patently distrusted him.

While Mikhyel had not avoided Nethaalye's father, neither had he sought him out, having decided he was here primarily to react, not to act. He'd have preferred as well to watch, not be watched, but that was a forlorn hope indeed. He was quite certain his every public exhalation made it into at least one notebook.

He'd seen Errif at a formal dinner in the house of one Mosharni dunSharn, originally of Giephactum, and one of the few valley investors who actually maintained a household here in Khoratum. As there had been some fifty-odd guests and nearly as many servants to attend them, and as Errif always chanced to have his back to Mikhyel whenever the crush eased between them, it was possible no one noticed that they never exchanged so much as a nod.

Possible, but not highly probable.

For the most part, he was ignored. Ostensibly. The fact was, these men *didn't* know how much he knew, or how much of his image was conjecture and how much an accurate assessment of his affiliations. He was here to meet with Rhyys, and their actions, it appeared, were geared toward that meeting: their animosity was not likely to change until he could meet face-to-face with Rhyys. When that encounter finally materialized, he might, with luck, gain Rhyys' confidence. If he could convince Rhyys they were *both* Anheliaa's men, he might uncover all their sordid plans.

And he had a secondary reason for pressing a meeting with Rhyys. He was still no closer to fulfilling his personal promise to Temorii. He was, he feared, a fool to worry about such a minor failing, when there were so many greater problems to be solved, but it wasn't a minor failing to Temorii.

And he had promised to try.

Temorii insisted that he shouldn't worry. She left each day and went into the hills alone to exercise. When he asked how she got in and out, she laughed and said that, considering the warren of passages beneath the old fortress that comprised half the Tower complex, he shouldn't be surprised if he should one day wake up inside the mountain and beneath a pile of rubble.

But even as she laughed, her eyes would drift toward the northwestern wall of the room, beyond which lay the dance stadium. Her face would grow somber and that haunted look that was the first thing he'd noticed about her returned to her eyes.

Temorii believed in him and in his intentions, but she didn't trust him, didn't expect the miracle to happen.

There was still time. The precise date for the competition was still pending—the integrity of the dance rings themselves now being in question. But that problem would soon be solved, the competition would be scheduled, and Temorii's opposition, who even now trained daily on the practice rings, would soon be given time on the dance rings themselves.

If she was to have any chance at all, she would have to join their ranks soon.

But Rhyys had ignored his attempts to see him, and without facing Rhyys directly, he had no leverage to get her included in the upcoming competition. Somehow—today—he had to get in to see Rhyys.

As if in answer to that thought (except that similar thoughts had come to him several times a day since he'd entered Khoratum) the door to his guest suite crashed open, and without so much as a by your leave, Rhyys dun-Tarec himself strode through.

Rhyys looked older than Mikhyel had expected. The last time he'd seen the Khoratumin Ringmaster had been at Nikki's wedding, only some three months ago. It might have been thirty years. But Rhyys, according to Nikki's notes, was an ocarshi addict, and the experts said, after a certain point, the narcotic never quite left your system, and your muscles and nerves never quite worked again.

Considering the way Rhyys slouched there in the doorway, considering the pouty sneer that appeared a permanent fixture on his face, and the heavy-lidded eyes that sluggishly took in the room, Mikhyel could believe that assessment. And in that assessment, could also believe he saw the source of Rhyys' decay from the man Anheliaa had chosen to rule Khoratum.

Like an actor, Rhyys waited until all eyes in the theater were upon him, then slammed the door shut on the guards waiting to follow him into the room. There came no protest from the guards still in the hall. Neither did they reopen the door. Which made Mikhyel wonder whether they cared if anything happened to their exalted employer.

"Hello, dunTarec," Mikhyel said blandly. "Joining us for breakfast?"

But Rhyys ignored him, assuming Rhyys heard him. Rhyys addressed Temorii directly.

"So," he hissed, "the kitchen-scut was telling the truth. I thought I told you never to come in here again."

Temorii's chin raised proudly. "Since when has it been polite to ignore a visiting dignitary's request for dinner?"

"Dinner? A bit early for that, isn't it?"

"You know very well when I came in."

"More importantly, I know when you're leaving. Guards!"

The door opened—more politely than Rhyys had done. The two surly guards stepped in and posed on either side of the door, arms akimbo, staring straight ahead.

For a moment, Mikhyel thought Temorii was going to resist, but then, her eyes flickered toward him, and her shoulders slumped.

She stood up and faced Mikhyel. "Farewell, m'lord. And thank you for the meals and the bath, and . . . well, thank you. This creature will try to embarrass you over my being here, and I'm sorry for that. I tried to warn you."

"Creature? *I'm* a creature?"

Temorii flushed. "M'lord Rhyys, please, I'm—sorry."

Mikhyel could tell she nearly choked on the apology.

"Let it be enough," she continued, and the defeated note in her voice ripped at Mikhyel's heart. "I was filthy and cold. Lord dunMheric offered me a bath and a place to stay—"

"He has none of those things to give! They were *mine*. Not his."

"Rings, man, I'll pay you for them," Mikhyel broke in, "you unfeeling—"

He caught himself, rather appalled at his lack of control. Antagonizing Rhyys was by no means his intention.

"Don't say something you'll regret later, dunMheric." Rhyys stared down his nose at them both. "You've no idea what this individual did."

"I'm certain you intend to enlighten me, so why not get on with it?"

"I gave this uncivilized hill creature a safe harbor for years, *gave* it time on the rings—out of the goodness of my heart. Just because it *might* be a distant relative."

"You *gave* me nothing, Rhyys. *Nothing.* I worked—"

"When it suited you. When you were not off roaming the hillside like the wild goat you are. And in the end, it was all for nothing. Talent you might have. But courage, cleverness . . . those, you lack in *embarrassing* proportions. I lost a great deal of money, that day, not to mention the humiliation."

Temorii just stared at Rhyys as if he'd gone mad. But to Mikhyel Rhyys always sounded rather as if he were speaking from a script. It would be perfectly well in character for Rhyys to have spent the past several days editing and practicing the script for this moment, particularly if Rhyys had known all along, as Temorii had accused, that Temorii was here with him.

"Money?" Mikhyel repeated. "Humiliation? Would you care to explain?"

"This *individual* to whom you gave safe haven, dun-Mheric, is a would-have-been ringdancer."

"Yes," Mikhyel answered. "So?"

"On the day of the trials, one after another of the competitors made it through the maze. Some faster than others, but all made it through. All but one. The arbiter called number thirteen. I held my breath until I nearly passed out, the suspense was thrilling, I assure you. And we waited. And waited. And waited. Until well into darkness. But no number seventeen. All my bets lost, because this creature was too stupid and too cowardly to confront the maze. Days later, it showed up at the Tower door, starving, demanding entry . . ."

"Lies . . ." Temorii's whisper brushed the air. "I *never* came back here. The rings had crashed—"

DunTarec's hate and scorn raked Temorii's determinedly straight figure. "*After* the competition was complete."

And not even you can get it for me, Barrister.

"Lies," Temorii's response was a breath deep in her throat.

"I *have* your petition. . . . It's in the files somewhere— as if I'd ever let such an ungrateful creature beneath my roof again."

Temorii's mouth curled in a snarl, but her head bowed, and she took a step for the door, but Mikhyel placed a hand on her arm. He had all he needed to know on which side truth balanced. Rhyys had been in Rhomatum for Nikki's wedding. The web had collapsed two days later following the Boreton Firestorm. Without Mother's help, Rhyys could *not* have been here for the competition.

And something told him Mother would not welcome Rhyys within her lair, even had she had been able, with the damage to the Khoratum line.

"You say Temorii showed up at your front door, not at the gateway to the arena," Mikhyel said, assuming a modified court-voice. "Is that correct?"

"Yes."

"No one saw her leave the maze?"

"Of course not. As I said, it was days later—"

"As I understand the arrangement you made with Temorii, she was to be led in once, and come through the maze and into the arena once, on her own."

Rhyys frowned impatiently. "Yes. Yes! *Once.* One time only!"

"And you say no one saw her exit into the maze?"

"No! Coward, I say!"

"Since no one *saw* Tem walk into the arena, who can say she did? And if she can enter the courtyard, without being led in, shouldn't she be allowed to dance?"

"Khy—"

"It is what you want, isn't it, Tem?"

"Yes, but—"

He shook his head, a quick jerk, and she shut up, but the hand she reached to ease herself into the chair was shaking.

Rhyys was watching them with narrowed eyes, taking in gods knew what. Then, in a run that had the sound of a rehearsed speech, Rhyys said:

"I see why Rhomatum Council jumps to your call, dun-

Mheric. You make even the impossible sound plausible. Fine. Keep your bed warmer here. Enjoy it while you can."

He turned to leave, paused with his hand on the door, and swung back with a theatrical flourish. "By the way," he said, in a thoroughly pleasant tone, "welcome to Khoratum, Mikhyel. I do hope you enjoy your stay."

And then they were alone.

Temorii was shaking.

"*That* was your great solution?" She thrust herself from the chair and paced the room. "I can't *believe* I let myself trust you."

She slammed across the room and into the antechamber in which she slept. Doors slammed. Drawers did. She appeared moments later, wrapping a sash about the hiller clothing she wore in her outside excusions.

"Tem, please, sit down. Talk sense with me."

"No! I've listened to you too much already."

"Tem, dammit, it was too easy! We've *got* to talk—"

She shook her head, a violent wrenching motion. Tears were streaming down her face, and shaking fingers made her movements with the sash awkward. He tried to still her hands, tried to calm her, but she jerked free, cursed at him, and fled out the door.

He stared at Raulind, who, for once, *looked* as confounded as Mikhyel felt.

§ § §

"I want to dance," Thyerri said. He sat cross-legged in one of Scarface's best chairs, his elbows propped on his thighs, his chin propped on his clenched fists.

"I told you the scut would come," Rhyys said, not to Thyerri, but to Scarface, sitting at his ease in another chair.

"I *want* to dance!" Thyerri hissed.

"So . . . dance!" Scarface waved a languid hand. The ocarshi was thick here today: Scarface must be in greater pain than usual.

Good, Thyerri thought, and then threw that anger away. Cool head. Confidence. That was what he needed to dance. Not anger. Not thoughts of Tamshi eyes and rijhili thieves and rijhili lies.

"I *want* to compete."

"Oh, now that's different, isn't it, Rhyys?"

"You'll compete again when I'm reborn a woman," Rhyys sneered.

"Then you'll get no more from me."

Thyerri snapped his feet free and jumped out of the chair. An explosion inside his head sent him reeling back. When his vision and mind cleared, he was sprawled awkwardly across the chair, and a scarred hand gripped his neck, holding him there.

"I warned you, boy," Scarface said.

"Go ahead," Thyerri spat. "Kill me. If I can't dance, dead is better."

"Has dunMheric bedded her yet?"

"No! Nor will!"

The hand released him and cracked across his face. For a moment, he couldn't hear past the ringing in his ears. When he could, he hauled himself straight in the chair.

"So, dunMheric's lost interest."

Thyerri shrugged.

Rhyys laughed. "Don't believe it, Mauritum. *I* saw him this morning."

"Interested, but chaste. How noble. And if I said that's the price of your competing?"

"No!" Rhyys shouted. "I told you, I wouldn't allow—"

Scarface turned that smile on Rhyys. Rhyys blanched, then muttered, "What difference does it make?" And left the room.

"Now, boy," Scarface said, "let's talk about you . . ."

§   §   §

A gilt-edged invitation to dinner arrived from Rhyys. Mikhyel sent his own card back declining, politely. He had the headache.

Which was only the truth. But if he hadn't had, he'd have cultivated one; let Rhyys explain his absence to his fine friends.

Of course, he might have felt differently if Ganfrion hadn't shown up well into the evening with a fancy variety platter of breads and fruits and cheeses from a kitchen supposedly too busy to come up with a bowl of soup.

"Did you find her?" Mikhyel asked as he settled into a chair, wine on one side, the bread and cheese on the other.

On the far side of the cheese, Ganfrion lounged side-ways, one leg thrown over the chair arm. He accepted a wineglass from Raulind, took a sip before he answered: "No."

"Rings, she's been gone for hours. She *must* have gone outside."

Ganfrion shrugged. "You got her her competition, didn't you?"

"She doesn't believe I can make good on my side of the bargain."

"Can you?"

"I think so."

"She'll return."

Mikhyel didn't dispute. Likely she would. But he'd not be surprised if she didn't. Temorii, for all she captivated him, was in every way the wildest creature he'd ever been near.

Besides, there were more important issues in his life than who would be the next radical dancer of Khoratum.

"I've a question for you, Gan."

Ganfrion lifted his glass in invitation.

"When Rhyys came in this morning, his attitude was . . . well, just a bit too . . . He's always seemed rather melodra-matic, so I might be reading something into his perfor-mance that wasn't there, but it felt as if he came in ready to perform a role. And when he agreed to my terms, it was too pat. Could he have known what I planned to ask? I mean, regarding Temorii. Or did he even care? Would he have agreed to *any* request? Is he setting us all up with the competition, refusing her so arbitrarily? Rings—" He nearly choked on the thought. "Could *she* be part of his plan?"

This time, it was Ganfrion's eyebrows that lifted. And Ganfrion's eyes shifted to Raulind. "Did you say something to him?"

Raulind shook his head. Raulind did not look happy.

"Very good, Suds."

"What's that all about?"

"Only that Raul and I were discussing that very possibil-ity earlier. Raul, it seems, had the same impression. Just complimenting you on your growing acuity."

"And?"

"I'd say—" Another glance toward Raulind, and a sigh. "Yes, Rhomandi, there's a damned good chance he knew."

"How?" He steeled himself to hear Temorii had been planted on him, but:

"The . . . street-boy, Thyerri? I've been following him."

"Thyerri? Why? How long?"

"Off and on. Since before you came out."

"Checking up on me, were you?"

Ganfrion shrugged.

Mikhyel grunted. "Why Thyerri?"

"Followed him from your hidey to the Tower. Several times. He's been a regular visitor. Both sides, unless I miss my bet. I think . . ." Ganfrion shifted, dropped his foot down and leaned forward to balance his elbows on his knees. Glanced again at Raul, then faced Mikhyel straightly. "Just be careful, Khyel. I'll watch Thyerri. You watch Temorii. I'm . . . impressed that you are even able to suspect her. But by Rakshi, man, be careful what you say and do. You're talking about a true dancer. And nothing stands between a dancer and a chance to dance."

"Experience, Gan?"

"Experience." Ganfrion drained his glass and stood up. "I think I'll be going now."

"Aren't you going to help me with this?" Mikhyel asked, gesturing toward the food.

Ganfrion shook his head. "Got plenty while I was talking them out of yours. Save it for Temorii. The mountains make a man hungry."

Mikhyel nodded.

"Just in case you're interested," Ganfrion added, hand on the door. "I've a lead on what these rijhili might be up to."

"Damn you, Ganfrion. Why didn't you say so?"

"Didn't ask, did you?"

"Too fixed on the woman?" Mikhyel asked, and Ganfrion shrugged.

"They're planning a demonstration. Involving the nodes. When, where, and exactly what, I don't know for certain. I *suspect* they're going to coordinate all right. Maybe a shutdown. Whole Northern Crescent."

"Complete what Persitum started?" Mikhyel asked, and Ganfrion nodded.

"I'm also quite certain at least one Mauritumin *is* in-

volved. High up. *Very* high up." He nodded and opened
the door. "I'll be in touch."

Mikhyel glared after him, tempted to follow and demand
a better explanation, but knowing there *was* no more. Rumors passed on, that's all it was. But rumors Ganfrion had
a great deal of confidence in, else he would have said
more—or less.

Ganfrion was trusting *him* to be able to put two and
three together and figure the possibilities on his own. If
Mauritum was involved, they might be planning something
far more ambitious than a shutdown. With Persitum back
in line, they'd have the entire Northern half of the web,
and ten of the eighteen nodes. One of them directly connected to Mauritum.

And Garetti wanted Rhomatum. Ruined or healthy, he
wanted Rhomatum.

He'd contact his brothers later—after his head stopped
pounding—and warn them, such as there was to be
warned against.

In the meantime . . . "What was *that* all about?" he
asked Raulind.

"The web, sir. I believe he was saying the Northern Crescent plans to shut out Rhomatum. Which seems suicidal to
me, but—"

"Not that, Raul. Temorii. Thyerri. Gan was lying to me."

"Not lying, m'lord."

"Not telling all he knows! Or, rather, not telling *me*."

"He did speak to me first, sir. And rightly, under the
circumstances, I believe. He doesn't know anything. He conjectures. I suggested he keep his conjectures to himself."

"You suggested."

"Yes, sir."

"Conjectures. Regarding Temorii? And her involvement
with Rhyys' conspiracy?"

"Indirectly, sir."

"Directly?"

"I'd rather not say, sir."

Mikhyel wasn't certain whether to laugh or dismiss his
oldest companion.

"Is this mutiny, Raul?"

"No, sir. Equity."

"And if I ordered you to explain?"

"I'm afraid I'd have to quit, sir."

"Quit. Just like that."

"Yes, sir."

Suddenly, the conversation lost any hint of humor. Temorii had been a personal project, an indulgence. Now, she seemed to be encroaching directly on the safety of his real purpose here.

"Who are you protecting, Raul?"

"*You*, m'lord Mikhyel."

"Explain."

"If Gan is correct, and you are not told, no one is hurt when the truth comes out—and it will, if Gan is correct. If I am correct, and he tells you his suspicions, I might never recover a friend I've come to hold very dear."

"Meaning, whatever Thyerri and Temorii are involved in, I should allow them to play it out for a while."

"Something like that, m'lord."

"Damn it, Raul, this isn't a game!"

"I'm well aware of that, m'lord."

And Raulind knew as much about web politics as Mikhyel dunMheric. And far more about people.

He pressed fingers into his eyes, striving to counteract the pounding, internal pressure. Whatever Ganfrion suspected, whatever Raulind did, it could wait until morning. Perhaps longer. He could order Ganfrion to explain, and Ganfrion would, but he would lose Raulind if he did ask. Raulind didn't make meaningless threats.

And it was too soon—much too soon—for that sacrifice.

"Do me a favor?" he asked.

"Of course, m'lord."

"Help me get rid of this damnable headache."

He was lying facedown on the grooming table, half-asleep, with Raulind's spidery fingers working their magic on the knots in his back and shoulders when the entry bell rang. Insistently.

"I'll see who it is, sir," Raulind murmured, and draped a bathing sheet over him.

He kept his face buried in his crossed arms, trusting Raulind to get rid of whoever it was. After some unmarked time, Raulind returned and was once again working on his back. Tentatively at first, then hard enough to wake him up.

"Raul, what—"

A murmur and fingers poked his ribs. He yelped and struggled upright, still groggy. But the tickling fingers pursued him, and giggles filled the room.

"Dammit!" He swung his legs over the side of the table, swept his blinding fall of hair back, while simultaneously defending his ribs from Temorii's relentless pursuit. Eventually, he got his hands on her wrists and held them away long enough to catch his breath. *She* was still giggling.

He thought, from the smell of her breath, she might be drunk. When she collapsed forward against his chest, he was certain of it. He cursed softly, put his arm around her shoulders, and brushed the hair off her face.

Her head fell back, she smiled up at him, for all she couldn't see him, not with those distended, half-crossed pupils. Her fingers tickled his ribs again; he jumped, she giggled, and wrapped her arms around his neck.

He searched the room desperately for Raulind, but Raulind had deserted him, gone to his own peripheral room and shut the door.

"Tem," he said, "I think we should—"

Her mouth stopped him. He groaned and fought the inclination to crush her to him. She was fully clothed and drunk. He was bare beneath the sheet and too damned sober.

"I came back, Khy," she whispered against his lips. "I wasn't going to, but I came back." She pressed against him and buried her fingers in his hair. "You lied to me. Said you'd get me the dance, and you can't. But you didn't mean to lie to me, did you, Khy? You didn't mean to be cruel and make me hope?"

"Tem, please." He held her back, and for a moment she hung between his hands, swaying, then she wrenched free with a cry, and flung herself at his waist, holding as if for her very life.

"You do want me, Khy, don't you?" she murmured into his side, and one hand ran up under the sheet to caress his thigh.

"More than life itself," he said, and his voice sounded hoarse, even to his ears, but he pulled free of her, never mind it left the sheet behind, found his quilted-satin robe and buttoned it securely, as she sank to the floor in a ball.

If she *was* Rhyys' plant, it was only the offer of the dance that had driven her to this action, only the excess of wine that made it possible. Rhyys might well hope to establish some hold over Mikhyel dunMheric through this painfully vulnerable conduit.

Painful indeed—for both of them. He wanted her, he couldn't deny that fact, but not this way. She thought she had no options.

He knew better.

When he had himself under control, he returned to her and drew her to her feet.

"More than life itself," he repeated. "More than *my* life. But not more than yours."

She put her arms back around his neck; he pulled them free.

"Listen to me, Tem." And when her mouth sought his again, he shook her. "Listen to me! I *wasn't* lying to Rhyys. We *can* get you inside without anyone seeing—at least, I think we can."

The momentary spark of hope faded from her eyes and her head fell forward to lie against his chest.

"I should have warned you before I brought it up with Rhyys. I'm sorry. I'd simply lost track of what I'd told you and what I had not. There is a way, but I haven't been able to test it yet. If not? What have you lost?"

Her head came up, and her tear-filled eyes said: everything.

He brushed the hair back from her face. "I want to go with you into the hills tomorrow."

Chapter Ten

"It's getting late, Nikki," Lidye's breath brushed his ear; he nodded—and added another figure to the growing column.

"You must sleep, darling."

"And Deymorin needed these supplies yesterday. It's early in the season. We've had two indifferent crops here in the valley, so even if we could afford to buy food indefinitely, the supply might not be there. There's the City's supply, but if Kirish'lan takes offense, as your father threatened—"

"He didn't threaten, Nikki. That was a warning of what promises had been made."

"Well, Kirish'lan expected part interest in a Tower that might not happen for years, if at all. They supply half our grain and dairy supplies."

He dropped the pen and buried his face in his hands, rubbing his eyes fiercely.

"I simply had no idea, Liddi, how dependent we'd become."

"How could you, when Shatum has been the clearing house. You—all the nodes—buy grain from Shatum. That Shatumin fields have not produced the grain they sold was not their responsibility to reveal. Their profit margin was better on silk worms."

Nikki grunted. "I wonder if they're edible."

"What?"

"Silk worms," he answered, but his attention drifted back to the papers in front of him. "Perhaps, if we trained the men, then let them return home, keeping only token forces in the watchtowers . . . We'd need reliable quick-muster procedures, but—"

"Nikki, come to bed. You can't solve it all tonight."

He sighed, and pushed back from the table still staring

at the maps and columns of figures, knowing the perfect solution existed, somewhere in the mass of information.

Except, they didn't have all the information. Not the givens, not the variables. The Northern Crescent situation needed resolution. They needed to know they weren't fighting two battles . . . or three, if Kirish'lan truly took offense and attacked.

Supposedly, Mikhyel was investigating that situation, and they received daily reports from his men encamped just outside Khoratum. Reports delivered through a highly efficient mounted relay system of Ganfrion's establishment. Deymorin said Ganfrion was just full of surprises.

But rumor out of Khoratum, nearly as fast as Ganfrion's system, maintained a different vision of their brother's doings. Rumor claimed Mikhyel dunMheric was making a fool of himself over a Khoratum ringdancer, which even *he* knew was beyond measure stupid.

And because Mikhyel was being stupid, Deymorin had moved his training maneuvers to a point partway between Khoratum and Rhomatum, and *he* was having to find the means to feed those troops.

"Come, Nikki," Lidye said, and drew him to his feet.

"At least you have Nethaalye now," he said, and as if she'd been following his every thought, she nodded.

"And grateful to have her, my darling," she said. "Please, come to bed."

They started for the office door.

Lidye had spent time in the Tower with Nethaalye and expressed confidence in Nethaalye's good will and basic ability. With Mirym for backup, Lidye said, the possibility of stable prosperity and regrowth was very real.

If they were given that chance. The meeting with the Kirish'lani and Shatumin had gone as well as could be expected. They had time . . . at least until the attempt to repair Khoratum had been made. But if that attempt failed—

{*Nikki? Deymorin?* Can you hear me, brothers?}

"Khyel," he whispered aloud, and Lidye stopped; he already had.

{I'm here, Khyel,} Deymorin's thought whispered in his head; their communication grew easier, clearer, with each use.

{I think we know at least what Rhyys *wants* to do.}

{Rhyys *is* behind a conspiracy then?} Nikki asked.

{Ostensibly. Ganfrion claims there's another man, a Mauritumin, so he believes.}

{Mauritumin? Who?}

{Ganfrion has no names yet. They're being remarkably discreet.}

And maybe this Ganfrion was making it all up, Nikki thought.

{*I* trust him.} Mikhyel's thought chastised, with the implication that if he did not, he was petty and stupid.

{Who's the stupid one, brother? Who's the one flirting with a ringdancer?}

Silence, and a blackness in the area of his head that was Mikhyel. Then:

{I haven't the time, Nikki. —Deymorin, we think they're planning a shutdown.}

{What kind of shutdown?}

{The entire Northern Crescent. The way Persitum did.}

"The idiots!" Lidye hissed beside Nikki, and he realized she was holding his hand, and must be getting at least some of the conversation. "That's *suicide*."

{Quite,} Mikhyel answered. {Hello, Lidye. I'm glad you're here. It's possible they just plan to initiate a blackout, to shut Rhomatum out at a coordinated time to make a point of some kind.}

"Perhaps we can hold them . . . if we know the exact time. . . ."

{I'll try to find out. I assume Khoratum will instigate, but I'm not even certain of that. With the talk of Mauritum and Garetti's involvement . . .}

"Garetti might be trying to take Rhomatum down."

{That's what I fear as well. By what I've heard and what Nethaalye said, I'd like to believe they intend it as a demonstration only, to intimidate us into some as yet unspecified agreement, but even so, the ramifications—}

"Are completely unknown," Lidye said. "Nikki, tell him, we'll do what we can. I have an idea. I've been wanting to run some tests . . . It's possible that, among us, we can force them to stay aligned from here."

{I heard that. —Nikki, keep that lady around. —Deymorin, are you as close as you feel?}

{On your doorstep, fry.}

{Thank the gods. I'll see you soon.}

{Looking forward to it. Life's been too dull here.}

{I don't know. I think I'm ready for dull.}

{Had enough adventuring?}

{I'm . . . tired, Deymio. Very tired.}

{So, why aren't you asleep? You damn well woke me up.}

Sense of sorrow, of impending loss, of a cherished body held close.

{So it is true,} Nikki sent. {Rings, Khyel, do you realize—}

{More than you can possibly imagine, Nikki. —Good night, brothers.}

ꙅ   ꙅ   ꙅ

As if the feel of Temorii in his arms hadn't been enough, Nikki's accusations kept him awake.

Rumors. Of himself and a Khoratumin radical dancer. Rumors undoubtedly designed to further undermine Mikhyel dunMheric's already faltering image. And in Rhomatum already. Damned difficult to explain unless someone deliberately started them, *before* the deal was made.

And Rhyys had known Temorii was with him.

It was a setup. It had to be, and willing or not, Temorii was a part of it.

. . . *nothing stands between a dancer and a chance to dance* . . .

Temorii believed Mikhyel had failed her.

Temorii believed Rhyys was her key, now, to the dance. She'd come here, drunk, to make love with him.

Rhyys' city was the source of the rumors regarding Mikhyel dunMheric and a Khoratumin radical competitor.

{Oh, Tem . . .} he whispered, in his mind where it was safe, and she sighed and snuggled closer. That she was a dancer, there could be no doubt. What else she might be, might still be, mutable, given the right stimulus.

Perhaps, a little ley-driven magic might provide that stimulus.

{Mother . . .} he called tentatively, wondering whether she would hear.

{Ah . . . Mikhyel-child. Where have you been?}

Temorii stirred again and whimpered. He spoke softly to her, and when she was quiet, he continued.

{Mother, might I come visit you?}

{But of course, Mikhyel-child. I told you just to call . . .}
His hand on Temorii's arm began to glimmer.
{No, Mother! Not yet. Tomorrow . . .}
{Ah! Subterfuge/stealth/deception. How delightful. Of course, my child. Just . . . call . . .}
Mikhyel sighed, startled and relieved at the ease with which contact had been made. His mind at last at peace, his eyes grew heavy. Suddenly, as he hovered on the very edge of sleep, Mother's voice returned. *{And try to remember a chicken, this time . . .}*

Temorii awakened the next morning to the effects of her first major battle with a wine bottle. She groaned and accepted Raulind's tea, and groaned and tacitly ignored the fact that she'd come to, fully clothed, wrapped in a blanket and his arms.

He ordered Raulind to cancel his meetings for the day (he still had the headache), took a light meal, then went with Temorii down a narrow hallway and into the dark tunnels beneath Khoratum. Mikhyel thought, as he followed, his hand in hers, that perhaps Rhyys had not altogether misrepresented Temorii's tenure within the Khoratum Tower. Certainly, she knew how to escape without detection.

Within an amazingly short time, following passages of dubious origin and great age, they were outside the city, on the uphill side of the Tower complex. Unlike Rhomatum, where Tower Hill was the center of the umbrella, Khoratum spread like a fan, downhill, toward Rhomatum.

But it was small, for what he'd expected, given the size and importance of the node within the web. The umbrella should, by comparative size and number of lines, be comparable to Shatum or Giephaetum, and it was . . . tiny. And the power within the umbrella weak.

He wondered whether that deficiency was another manifestation of Rhyys' improper spinning. Or perhaps it was due to the fact that Khoratum's buds had not yet been capped. There was so much they could be learning by monitoring the development of Khoratum, and instead—

"This was where I first saw them." Temorii crawled under an arch of rocks and settled on her stomach, glanced back and waved Mikhyel forward. Reluctantly, he joined her, though the two of them barely fit, and he wasn't at all certain those very heavy looking rocks would stay put. "See?" She pointed downslope, and nestled in a courtyard behind the Tower, hidden by high walls, were the practice rings.

"I used to sit here for hours and watch them practice. All the village youth did, you know. They were looking for a troupe for the capping ceremony, and wanted it drawn from local talent."

She leaned forward, arms crossed beneath her chin, staring down the narrow viewing channel. He propped sideways on one elbow and with his free hand brushed her hair back from her eyes, drawing an inquisitive glance.

"And that was what drew you down to the city for the first time?" he asked.

She shook her head.

"Then what . . . ?"

"Watching Kashiri dance."

Kashiri. The name was familiar.

"That was the first Khoratumin radical, wasn't it?"

Her eyes widened slightly. "Very good, Barrister."

"You needn't look so surprised. It was in my brother's notes."

"Ah. And did your brother also tell you who and what Kashiri was?"

"If he did, I wouldn't tell you."

She frowned.

"I'd rather hear your version."

"Ah. Meaning, Nikki said: Kashiri was the first Khoratumin radical dancer. He performed once only, on the opening ceremonies, and then he died."

"Well . . ."

"I've read your rijhili texts, Barrister."

"You can read?" The question was asked before he thought.

"*You* needn't look so surprised. *All* Rhyys' dancers learn to read and write. Even those he dislikes. Rhyys likes to show off his dancers . . . like fancy toys, to everyone who visits. He couldn't have them look or sound like fools, now could he?"

She wrinkled her nose in disgust.

"Being a Khoratum dancer—even a dancer in training, means never wanting for *any* creature comfort. You wear beautiful clothing, eat the most delicate foods, drink the

best wines . . . And we learned to read and write . . .
and some of us must learn just to speak, the language of
the invaders."

"The invaders." Mikhyel winced. "Rijhili."

She nodded.

"Like me."

The faintest smile quirked her lips. "Like you, Khy.
Sometimes."

"Not always?"

"Takes more to be rijhili than parents, Khy. Rhyys is
more rijhili than you."

"Rhyys was born in Khoratum."

"Exactly." She shifted about to face him, propped up on
an elbow, her head cradled in her hand. "We learned to
read and write, we learned the history of the web . . .
according to Rhyys' hand-picked tutors. And music and the
arts and court etiquette . . . according to Rhyys' hand-
picked tutors. And politics and economics of other
nodes . . ."

"According to Rhyys' hand-picked tutors." He finished,
and she laughed, though the sound had a bitter edge. "I
begin to understand. And when did you discover the dis-
crepancies?"

"The first time I opened my mouth to one of his cultivated rijhili friends. But I didn't care, not really. None of
us did. We hadn't come to Khoratum Tower to learn about
Venitum's casting methods or Shatumin imports or Orenum's lumber and paper output. We were there to dance."

And they allowed Rhyys to control those other, insignificant aspects of their lives because in return, Rhyys allowed them to dance.

. . . nothing stands between a dancer and the dance . . .

And what, Temorii, does Rhyys control now? he longed
to ask, but instead asked, "And Kashiri?"

"Kashiri, my dear Khyel, was a Rakshi dancer long before he ever mounted the rings."

"I thought the Rakshi dance was outlawed centuries
ago."

"Outlawed. And the dancers were hunted down like animals by their own neighbors, those who had once cheered
them to glory. But the dance would not die, Mikhyel dun-
Mheric. Rakshi's spirit cannot be destroyed."

"Are you . . ."

Her laughter filled the small niche. "Oh, no, my Khy, don't worry about that. No, the spirit of Rakshi fills me, but the old dance . . . no, I don't. I've never met one who has. But their secrets . . . those came down to us from Kashiri."

"That's why you considered it a given that you should believe in Rakshi," he said, mostly to himself.

"You believe, or the dance is only . . . movement. But Rakshi . . . Rakshi touches only a few."

"And Kashiri was one of those few?"

She nodded. "I saw him dance. I saw him die. And I knew I had to dance the rings."

"Rakshi touched you that day, didn't he?" Mikhyel asked gently and her eyes dropped.

She slumped back next to him, her eyes creeping back to the view.

"I would sneak over the wall—easier in those days than it is today, and I didn't know about the tunnels—and watch from the shadows. A young woman, about my age, found me. I was afraid she would say something, bring the wrath of Rhyys down on my head, but she was very kind, and when she discovered I'd come into Khoratum just to watch, asked me if I'd like to try it. We were much of a size, and she had hair about—" Temorii searched a strand of her own hair for a spot near the longest end. "About that color, which my ends were then, so once the helmet and harness were on, the instructor didn't pay much attention."

She settled on her back near—practically underneath—him and shut her eyes, a look of sheer ecstasy on her face. And after a moment, her head began a slow, side-to-side sway.

"It was just like in my dreams. I swooped and twirled among the rings . . . well . . ." A soft chuckle. "Not quite. If it hadn't been for the harness, I'd have died a thousand times over that first time. The instructor, thinking I was the young woman, believed I'd gone berserk. I found out later that she hated the rings, and had seen me as one more means of dodging practice. When I rather fearlessly risked life and limb, the instructors were certain they'd pushed her too far and too hard. But they soon figured out our deception and invited me back. Eventually, they put me into training for the real thing. I lived in the Tower, ate at

Rhyys' table—everything. Just like a real student. That was when Rhyys found out . . .''

Mikhyel was barely listening. His heart was beating hard again, and not from the climb. "What—" He forced his mind to logical processing. "What did Rhyys mean when he said you were a distant relative? Is *that* why he hates you?"

"Hates me? I suppose he does. That was the story the girl gave him. I don't know if it was true. I . . . didn't really care."

She stretched again, and put her hands behind her head. He looked out, down the hill, then closed his eyes, trying to shut out all awareness of her. But closing his eyes didn't lock out the scent of raspberries and cinnamon.

He bit his lip and wished to her Rakshi and any other god that was near to take his mind off that body lying so close to his.

A tug on his hair: her fingers working the braid loose, spreading the strands. She seemed fascinated by it, had claimed the nightly brushing as her own. He didn't argue, taking it as his only *real* concession to his personal obsession.

He pretended not to notice that every tug vibrated him to his fingertips. Instead, he chewed the inside of his lip, and stared down the hill at those rings that had claimed Temorii's soul long before he ever met her.

"Poor Khy," she whispered softly, and smoothed his hair back from his face before she squirmed out of the hidey-hole to begin one of her routines, slowly, in deference to a skull that must still be throbbing.

He followed her out, but had no inclination this morning to do more than watch.

"What happened to her?" he asked, when she paused for breath. "The girl whose place you took."

Temorii stared down at Khoratum, then said, with puzzlement in her voice:

"I don't know. I haven't seen her for at least two years. Since I became—"

She broke off abruptly and rolled up onto her hands, drawing her legs about in an arc to extend them above her head. Three times, she dipped down and pressed back up, but on the fourth, her balance wavered, her right wrist overflexed, and she tumbled down into a heap.

And she lay there, curled around her wrist, panting. And cursing. And crying. Not, he suspected because of the wrist.

"Tem?" Mikhyel crouched beside her, and rested a hand on her shoulder.

Her head came up, and her expression was a confusion of anger, and pain, and betrayal. "Why? Why did you lie to me, Khy?"

"I didn't. I tried to explain, but you ran away."

"That's a locked and guarded *underground* passage that takes us in. You *can't* get me in without anyone seeing."

"No? And how do you think I got into Khoratum in the first place?"

"The public coach," her tear-heavy voice answered. "Walked. Drove. —How should I know?"

Easiest just to call Mother herself, and hope Mother answered.

Mikhyel rested his forehead against Temorii's bowed shoulder and called, as clearly and as imperatively as he could:

{Mother?}

Temorii jumped as if stung. And he recalled their first meeting, and last night, and all those other times she'd seemed to hear. He gave her a light hug and murmured reassurances, then called, more gently:

{Sweet Mother of Khoratum, if you can hear me, I need you. I need you badly.}

Temorii pulled free, staring at him. Disbelieving.

"*She* put you into Khoratum? *She* called to *you*?"

Mikhyel was speechless. They were accusations she threw at him, not questions.

"She welcomed *you*? Why?" Temorii scrambled to her feet and screamed: {*Why*, Mother? Damn you to the highest, most lightning-blasted hells, Mother, *why*?} She paused, eyes wide with anger. Then: {I know you can hear me, Mother. Why? Why? Why? Why? *Wh*—}

{Oh, hush, brat. You don't need to shout.}

And Mother was there, even more exotic in contrast to the rocks and the grasses. She stretched her arms toward the sky, arms that grew abnormally long and tenuous, as if she were reaching for the clouds, then she shrugged, and shook out . . . hair. Long, shimmering hair. As she was otherwise more humanlike than before. But that it was Mother, Mikhyel had no doubt.

"Ah, my children, it's been too . . . long . . ."

Anger. Betrayal. The air reeked with it, and that underneath sense was all raspberries and cinnamon—Temorii.

"I came," Temorii hissed aloud. "I called—so, so often, Mother, and you *never* came! You never even *answered* me. *Why?*"

Mother shrugged. "I was sleeping."

"You were ignoring me."

"Ignoring? No, child. Sleeping." Mother frowned when the anger flared brighter, and her head tipped as if in confusion. Then, she shrugged and opened her arms. "I'm here now, child."

"That's not good enough, *Mother.* Not this time! It's too late! It's too—damn—"

Temorii turned and ran.

Mikhyel started after her, but Mother was there—just there—before Temorii, with her arms wide.

Temorii staggered backward, improbably fast, impossibly agile in that avoidance.

{Child, the web was shriveled/broken/fractured. I was asleep. And deaf. For a very long time, child. Your Khy helped me awaken.} And with a sudden relaxation, a twist of her brow that in a human might indicate contrition, sorrow: *{Please, child. This is my first time to the surface since . . . since the last time.}*

Bitter, reluctant laughter. "Of course it is."

Mother blinked. "Please, child. I've . . . missed you."

"M–missed?" Temorii held a hand to her mouth, trying to stem the incipient tears. "You don't even know what that *means.*"

"Oh, child, but I do. You've taught me the word's meaning. Please. Come?"

With a sob, Temorii fell into that embrace, and the leythium folds enveloped her like a shroud.

The embrace of the Mother she'd despaired of going home to. Bits and pieces began to make some sense. Realization that at once made Mikhyel's task easier, while making him wonder just how much a pawn he'd been.

A pawn not in Rhyys' game, but Mother's.

He wasn't altogether certain he considered that an improvement.

Mother gestured to him. He backed a step, but she was

there, and Temorii was, and Mother's sleeve swallowed them both before he could so much as blink.

When the sleeve dropped . . . or melted, or faded away, any or all of which were possible, they were in Mother's leythium cavern beneath Khoratum.

And as before, his clothes, and Temorii's, had somehow failed to make the transition. He suspected humor.

Mikhyel turned away, embarrassed, and Temorii crouched on the floor, hiding herself. Mother clucked gently and knelt beside her.

{Have you, then, grown so ashamed of your beauty, child?}

{Please, Mother, not now . . .}

Mother placed her hands on Temorii's face, the way she had on Mikhyel's, when she'd shared his memories, and Mikhyel received a rapidly shifting montage of images: Temorii's life, since last Mother had seen her, he would guess. And remembering his own desire to keep certain of his memories inviolate from Deymorin, he tried to shut those images out, tried not to know what Temorii had suffered.

Such secrets were hers to tell, when she chose. If she chose.

Eventually, the images fluttered to a close, to images impossible to ignore. Images of himself, standing nude here in Mother's cavern, his hair drifting in the air, almost as it would in water.

{The hair, child.} Mother's hand stroked Temorii's ragged, shaded locks. {Why?}

Temorii's answer was to bury her face in Mother's shoulder. Mother continued stroking the shaded hair, strokes that took longer and longer to reach ends increasingly less ragged. Mikhyel watched, unable to turn away, as that hair grew to what it must have been before Temorii felt compelled to cut it: long, shaded from the same sable brown at the roots to nearly white on ends that would brush Temorii's hips when she stood again.

And as the hair extended to cover her shoulders, hair-fine tendrils of leythium flowed up her legs and intermingled with one another so that when Mother raised Temorii to her feet and stepped aside to view her handiwork, she left Temorii draped in that luxurious hair and shimmering folds of leythium lace, a heart-stoppingly beautiful sight that made a man trying very hard to convince himself he wasn't in love even more conscious of his now singular state of undress.

Fortunately, Temorii, enthralled with her renewed hair, hadn't yet noticed.

{Mother . . .}

Laughter rippled in his head and through the leythium drapery above. Mother flung a casual gesture in his direction, and a heavy robe of deepest black covered him, neck to toe, a robe of living fabric, that caressed his skin with soothing warmth and velvet's deep cushioning.

"Thank you."

{I liked you better the other way.}

"In that case, I thank you doubly."

"Such a well-mannered child you are," she said aloud.

"I'm not a child, Mother."

"But of course you are. All my children are childs. How can they possibly be anything else when I am so much older and wiser?"

"Are you?" he asked, and realized Temorii was following every word, a slow smile beginning to light her face at last.

{I'm—} A sense of utterly unfathomable age entered him, and Mikhyel staggered under the impact.

{You are, what, human? Twenty-and-bits sun-circuits old? Child, I say.}

"Granted. But are you wiser?"

"Of course. Did you bring your Mother a chicken?"

"No. And *you* are trying to distract me. Was as it wise to put Temorii through such misery? Is she better for it?"

"Khy, wait," Temorii protested at last, but Mother asked him:

"Are *you*?"

"Mother, *please!*"

"That hardly matters," Mikhyel said firmly.

"No? Is Mikhyel-child's happiness not important?"

"No," Mikhyel said, and, "Yes," from Temorii.

Mother shook her head.

"Why do you divide your pattern?"

"I don't understand," Mikhyel said.

"You think by destroying one part of you, you can enhance another? I will never understand you silly humans."

"We're not parts of a whole, Mother," Mikhyel said.

"But of course you are. Parts of a pattern. —Tell him, child."

"Mother, *please*. It's too much . . . too soon."

Mother threw her arms in the air, and the ley fluttered around her. "I give up on you. Mother came home *all alone*. Weak. *Dying*. Mother left you to find your pattern, your happiness. . . . And now you come back, pattern in tow, yet no different than before. Still squawking *Why, why, why?* Well, *why* have *you* not danced the rings, yet? Why have *you* not helped these silly fools fix my web? Why have you not mated a great deal with this hairy but sweet-tasting individual?"

{Mother!}

{*What's wrong? You like/love/lust/rut/identify/recognize/want/need him don't you?*}

{I still hope to dance the rings.}

{*So dance them. Your pattern is set, child. You* will *dance/love the rings. You might as well dance/love him, too. It's all part of the pattern.*}

Temorii set her hands on Mother's arm.

{Mother, of course I care for Khy. Deeply. More deeply than is wise.}

"Bat's poop."

{No, Mother, it's not. What you're implying, that can't be. I *can't* lie with him. It's a . . . a human failing, Mother, but I *am* human. Too many have died. The dance is too dangerous for one whose interests are compromised.}

{*So the child grows too wise for its Mother. As belief goes, so goes reality.*}

{Mother, don't you see? I've *changed*. Loving means . . . I *can't* dance with a child growing in my belly!}

{*And can you dance without one?*}

{You *know* I can.}

{*Has Rhyys, then, miraculously changed his color and given you the rings?*}

{Oh. That. No, but—}

{*Then you've tricked him!*} Mother quite obviously approved of trickery.

{Possibly. Khy has arranged—}

{*Ah. A champion, child. And a clever one; Mother remembers. And has he remembered? Does he do this out of guilt?*}

{No, Mother. He's a good man. A kind man. But he offers, I think, to remedy injustice.}

{*Ah. Altruistic, then. And he'd do this for anyone, I'm sure.*}

Obviously, Temorii believed he couldn't hear them. *Mother* knew differently. It was a cruel game she played on Temorii.

Mikhyel sent into that stream: {Excuse me . . .}

They both looked around at him.

"He hears us," Mother pointed out, as if amazed, and Temorii looked away, blushing.

"I'm afraid so, Tem. I'm sorry. I tried not to."

"Mymymymymymy. Talented child isn't he?" And once again, Mother was looking at him as if he were an object for purchase. {*Pretty too, if a bit hairy. And skinny . . .*}

"Mother, behave!" Temorii hissed, and her eyes flashed brilliant green in this strange leylit air.

Mother laughed again, delight that shimmered through the ley and Mikhyel's own nerves.

{*Aha, my Dancer returns. Come, child, and dance with me. Tell me what it is you want of Mother . . .*}

A veiling cloud descended about Mother and Temorii, a shimmer both visual and mental. Mother's doing, Mikhyel was certain, and a welcome respite. He truly did not relish the constant invasion of private thoughts and conversations.

Tempting to stay here long enough to learn to do . . . whatever it was Mother had just done. If only to be able to deal with his brothers as normal men once again.

Normal. In that, of course, he deluded himself. He could never be normal again . . . if he ever had been. But he must have been. Those early years with Deymorin, when their mother was alive, and Mheric was still sane. When Outside had meant sunshine and swimming ponds, or snow forts and freezing toes, and Deymorin had been a warm body to thaw him out.

Early days that—perhaps—had provided *him* the strength to remain sane in the following years. Early days that had set the pattern for how he and Deymorin responded to each other as adults. Deymorin was older. Deymorin had been Mikhyel's teacher, his protector. Shifting from that role was difficult under the best of circumstances.

Theirs were not and never had been the best of circumstances.

Mother and Temorii had wandered completely out of sight. He sincerely hoped they remembered him.

{Oh, don't worry, darling child. Mother will never forget you . . .}

{A decidedly mixed benediction, Mother.}

Which brazen disrespect seemed to amuse her—as she had preferred Temorii's impertinence. And he recalled that first meeting where fear had triggered one response that nearly killed him and insolence had induced laughter.

Strange, strange being, whatever she was.

Mother and Temorii. It seemed so obvious, now he saw them together, explained so much about Temorii's contrasting moods, her oddly mixed understanding of human nature. If—he scanned the eerily exotic cavern—*this* had raised her, and subsequently rejected her, if Mother had nourished her mind as well as her body, had fed her the way the creature beneath Rhomatum had offered to feed Mikhyel . . .

And then, to lose it all. What must it have been like for her? And why had it happened?

He settled on a rock formation beside a glowing pool, and the formation shifted, conforming to his body.

Had Mother rejected Temorii the moment Temorii saw the practice rings? Or when she'd gone to live in the Tower as a fully acknowledged competitor?

Or had it been later? Their exchanges would indicate Mother knew about the competition, and about Rhyys, and Temorii's life in the Tower. And that Mother had fully expected her to win.

Perhaps the devastation of the failed competition, perhaps the fact she *had* failed . . .

Except, Temorii failed because the rings had gone down. And the rings had gone down because Vandoshin rom-Maurii had brought a dangerous machine into the Rhomatum Valley and Anheliaa used the Rhomatum Rings to blast it out of existence, depleting the Rhomatum Web in the process.

But the machine hadn't been on a node. Hadn't even been on a leyline. In order to complete the attack, Anheliaa had needed a node at or near the machine.

And that node had been himself and his brothers. He'd

been in the Tower one instant, and falling from the sky into his brothers' arms the next. And with *him*, the lightning had arrived.

The lightning that had nearly destroyed the Khoratum line.

They had escaped, but he had been on the edge of death. And Mother had saved him.

With the help of a human who had appeared out of a tunnel of light.

A human Mother had called Dancer.

Temorii. Whose dream had just been shattered.

And the disintegration of the Khoratum line had cut her off from Mother, had condemned her to a life on the Khoratum streets.

Does he do this out of guilt?

He buried his face in his hands, pressing his palms into his eyes, trying to cut out the exotic beauty, the colors, and the past. But nothing could cut away from him his part in Temorii's betrayal.

"Khy?"

That voice had the power to touch every nerve in his body with exquisite anticipation. He lifted his head, blinked at the pain of light and fine puffs of drifting air.

She was there beside him, in all her delicate beauty and steely strength. All the joy, the fierce competitive nature, the defiance, and the need.

"Why don't you hate me?" he whispered, and dismay puckered her brow.

"I could never hate you, Khy, even if I wanted to. Why would I want to?"

"If not for me, you'd have it all. If not for me, the rings wouldn't have failed, the competition would have gone on, you'd *be* Khoratum's radical dancer. Even if the rings *had* gone down, if not for saving me, you'd have been in the court with the others when they came to lead the remaining contestants out. You'd have *had* your second chance without question. You'd never have had to cut your hair. Never have had to put up with the likes of that Giephaetum-scum, never been cold or hungry. You'd never have lost . . ." He swept his hand in a broad curve, taking in that amazing beauty that surrounded them.

"Oh, Khy." She embraced him and cradled his head against her solid middle. "My dear, dear friend. It's possible, even probable, that all you say is true. And perhaps I did hate, a little, at first. When I was bitter and believed Rakshi had deserted me and you were nothing but a rijhili. But not now. Done is done. Rhyys was right in one sense: Rakshi controlled events that day, not you, or I, or even Mother. I might have had the dance. I might have died. Many things might have happened."

And through that touch, a warmth as perfect as child-Deymorin on a winter's day surrounded him. A warmth glowing with raspberries and cinnamon—and a mysterious hint of clove. And on the edge of that scent, a thought, a thought so faint, he wasn't certain he was meant to hear:

{But I wouldn't have *you*.}

Chapter Eleven

Eighteen rings hung suspended in midair. One ring for each active satellite node, each ring's axis aligned on the leyline between its parent and Rhomatum. The axis of the outermost, Cardinal ring was perfectly perpendicular, aligned to Rhomatum node itself.

The nineteenth ring, the Persitum Ring, lay inert on the pattern-tiled floor, as it had since the day Anheliaa died.

Kiyrstine romGaretti had never really trusted the leythium rings. In all her years with Garetti, she'd been into Mauritum Tower only a handful of times, and then only at Garetti's request. She preferred, overall, to simply have the light happen, and hot water to come out of the tap on command. Knowing that those amenities depended upon rings spinning without visible means of support and at the command of someone like Garetti—or Lidye—was rather like knowing what went into your breakfast sausage.

Some things were best left mysteries.

But Lidye wanted to run a test, and Lidye's test required *all* of them, so she claimed. And Mikhyel had told Nikki that the Northern Crescent was threatening a unified shutdown and that Mauritum might be instigating the trouble. So, here she was, once again, in the middle of a place she'd really rather do without.

Thanks ever-so, Deymio-luvvie, she thought, and eased around the rings to settle on a padded bench set along one of the glass walls. Sunlight entered through those glass walls, and struck the slowly spinning rings to send bands of light flashing about the room and its occupants. Nikki, Lidye, Nethaalye, Mirym . . . and herself.

They settled on a variety of seats set randomly about the chamber. Staking out territory, Kiyrstin thought rather cynically.

"I have," Lidye began, "absolutely no idea if what we're

going to try will make any difference whatsoever, but it's a fool who pitches Rakshi's rare gifts to the winds."

"Gifts?" Nethaalye asked, and Kiyrstin asked:

"*What* gifts?"

"Unexpected assets." Lidye's voice took on the singsong quality of a tour guide, or a bored professor, or a religious convert spouting rhetoric. "Most of life is patterns, chance intersections of people and events which eventually come to an ending determined by the pattern they've made."

"Sweet Maurii," Kiyrstin muttered. "Get *on* with it! What do you want us to *do*?"

"Patience, Garetti's wife."

She smiled tightly. "Call me that again, Shatum, and you can spin your own rings."

"Ladies . . . please!" Nikki's voice squeaked slightly, and he looked scared.

"Yes, my darling," Lidye cooed, and Kiyrstin controlled her reflexive gag. She *wished* she could trust Lidye. Certainly the Shatumin woman's recent actions gave her no reason not to. But something about the woman made her teeth ache from clenching. She could not deny the meeting with the Southern Crescent representatives had gone well, but the moment that was over, Lidye had returned to her domineering ways.

Especially offensive was her patronizing manner with Nikki. But Nikki didn't complain, and overall, Nikki seemed very happy.

It was not, to Kiyrstin's way of thinking, Nikki's greatest selling point.

"As I was saying," Lidye continued. "Patterns. Events linked to the greater world have placed Nethaalye and myself here. Kiyrstine romGaretti's presence is related to events beyond the web that placed the web in jeopardy and so brought us to this point of action. Mirym, coming from Khoratum, the complementary node of Kiyrstin's, is our accidental, radical factor. Our true gift from Rakshi."

She smiled at Mirym; Mirym did not return the gesture. Lidye's smile vanished as though it had never been.

"Thanks to Mirym's presence, we have all the major satellite nodes represented here today, as well as Rhomatum itself."

This time, she smiled at Nikki; his shy duck of the head could hardly be called a return smile.

"I'm from Mauritum," Kiyrstin dryly pointed out the obvious, "not Persitum."

"Are you quite certain of that?"

"Quite."

"Curious. However, to get to Mauritum, you must go through Persitum. Perhaps that is your value."

"How nice it must be to have so mutable a theory."

"Not at all. *You* are not here because of talent. You are here to provide *me* a focus by which to stabilize the western quarter of the web."

"You sound very certain of yourself."

"I know what I'm doing."

"*Do* you? You just said you didn't know if it would work."

"It was merely a figure of speech. I am certain of what I know."

"We've got *ten* nodes threatening a unified shutdown. Are we to assume that such an event has become commonplace and you are now an expert?"

"When you've no idea what you're talking about, Kiyrstine romGaretti, perhaps it is best not to speak."

"No idea what *I'm* talking about? *I* know Garetti. If Mauritum is part of this Northern conspiracy, *Mauritum* is spearheading it, not Khoratum. Garetti does *not* willingly play second to anyone. *That's* what *I* know. Suddenly you're so clever. *Suddenly* you've got ideas how to solve all our problems. To *whom* am I talking? Lidye? or Garetti?"

"Ah. A challenge. And at such a time, Kiyrstine of Mauritum." Lidye's mouth twitched. "If I were inclined to take offense, we're in *my* Tower. It's possible I could make you very sorry."

"And *you* haven't come down from here since Nikki talked to his brothers last night. You rather well had the advantage. Besides, if you need these three to stabilize your web for Garetti's takeover, you'd hardly be likely to estrange them by overplaying your hand now, now would you?"

The painted mouth pressed into a hard line; Nikki, usually quick to leap to Lidye's defense, hadn't said anything. He was, instead, intently watching both Lidye and herself.

"I am," Lidye said tightly, "Lidye romNikaenor, Ringmaster of Rhomatum."

"And is Lidye romNikaenor also Lidye dunTarim?"

"No."

"GorPasingarim? gorRhyys? Garetti? or any other damned egomaniac?"

"I take such a pledge to no one, man or woman, Kiyrstine romGaretti."

Kiyrstin folded her arms and glowered. It was a situation without a clearcut solution, but damned if she'd simply trust this woman. Not with the possibility of Garetti sitting on the sidelines *waiting* to leap in.

Nikki cast Lidye an apologetic look and crossed the room to kneel at Kiyrstin's side.

"Please, Kiyrstin, I think she's got a good plan, but it can't work if we're angry with each other. Won't you just listen to her plan? Just try it . . . once?"

He wheedled like a twelve-year-old, but he was scared, of that there was no doubt, looking into those blue eyes. She wondered what had passed between him and Lidye last night, after he talked with Deymorin and Mikhyel, wondered just how deep the water he was trying to swim in, and wished, somehow, that he could find it in him to be more open with her. But their pattern had been set as well, and trust of that nature would not come easily.

She forced a grin and flipped a wayward curl off his forehead. "All right, fry. Just for you." She waved a hand in the air. "Go ahead, spinner."

Lidye's brow tightened, but otherwise appeared impervious. Which restraint only made Kiyrstin distrust her that much more. She didn't trust anyone who, like a chameleon, so easily shifted behavior and coloration to fit her needs.

Lidye began pacing slowly about them as she spoke. "When dealing with the ley, one learns to look for patterns. Not to recognize a pattern is foolish. We have Nikki, male. From Rhomatum. And four females from the four greatest points of the web. The creature below Rhomatum is, Mikhyel says, male. Mother is female, and refers to her 'sisters,' also according to Mikhyel."

"I thought you were Rhomatum's Ringmaster," Kiyrstin said. "Why won't *you* control Rhomatum?"

"I have discovered an . . . affinity between this body of mine and Shatum, as there is one between Giephaetum and Nethaalye, Mirym and Khoratum, and . . . well, suffice to say, you and the others provide a focus for me to reach through to the nodes. My body is the bridge to Shatum.

Nikki's—" Lidye set her hands possessively on Nikki's shoulders. "Nikki is my potent link into Rhomatum." She leaned toward him and murmured, "Think of Rhomatum, my darling. Think of him strong and virile. Keep that Cardinal ring beating as if it were your own heart."

Nikki's eyes widened. And as Lidye spoke, that shimmering outer ring began to speed up.

"No, my love. Gently. Quietly. You are the source, the strength, the character of the web . . ."

The ring faltered, Lidye's eyes widened in alarm.

"Let it go, Nikki. *Let it go now!*"

Nikki's eyes closed. He swayed. Kiyrstin jumped to her feet and steadied him.

"What happened?" she asked, when his eyes fluttered open.

"I don't know!" Lidye answered, her voice harsh, unforgiving.

"I'm not good enough, Liddi," he whispered, and he was shaking. "I t–told you last night it wouldn't work." Mortally embarrassed.

Ashamed.

Kiyrstin squeezed his hand.

"You—you said, *I'm* the strength, the *character* of the web." His blue eyes flitted toward Lidye, then focused on Kiyrstin. "Don't you see, Kiyrstin? If the web has to depend on *me*, on *my* character . . . I'm *not*. I'm *trying*, but I'm *not*."

"Oh, for the—"

Lidye broke off, and Nikki flinched away from the swirl of her skirts. Then he just stared at the patterned tiles.

Kiyrstin didn't pretend to understand what signals passed between Nikki and Lidye these days. More often than not, Nikki seemed enormously happy. At others, like now, he seemed . . . lost.

"Don't you see, Kiyrstin. I *can't* pretend I'm something I'm not. Not when the fates of so many people are at stake. Mikhyel's the one who should be here. The creature down there likes him. But he can't." He scratched his head and then shivered, a study in uncertainty. "Maybe I should contact Deymorin. *He's* the strong one. And Khyel said he set the rings once when they were boys."

"Maybe you should," Kiyrstin said abruptly, and Nikki winced. "And then again, maybe not."

Nikki shook his head and stared at her, obviously confused. His eyes wandered the room, going from one woman to the other, and finally to Lidye, whose back was to him. He dropped his head again. His hands clenched.

Kiyrstin took those hands and gripped hard enough to hurt. "Pay attention to *me*, damnit. It's no disgrace, what you've said. It's no disgrace to have doubts. *That's* what helps us to *build* character. You can't *improve* something until you admit it has faults, now can you?"

He blinked up at her.

"If a reputable engineer looked at the plans for your dam and said it would fail, eventually, at this point, or that one, and you refused to listen to him and didn't rethink those plans and get other opinions, and the dam failed where he predicted, your character would be at fault, wouldn't it?"

"Yes. But I wouldn't—"

"Nikki, your brothers have tried to show you the potential weaknesses in your own structure. Not to destroy you, but to help you fix them. Are you trying to fix them?"

"Yes!"

"You admit they are structural weaknesses, and not just appearance."

"Yes!"

She smiled and squeezed his hands, but not to hurt this time. She no longer needed to force his attention. "Mikhyel told me a long time ago . . . or perhaps it was Deymorin who told me first, that *they* feared they'd destroyed your character. They carry a great deal of guilt on that score."

Nikki shook his head. "No! Whatever's wrong with me isn't *their* fault. It's—"

"If there is, Nikki, they'd be right. They raised you and they were very young. They may have made mistakes. Perhaps many mistakes. Perhaps irreparable mistakes. Did they, Nikki? Are they right?"

He opened his mouth to deny it, but closed it without saying anything. He chewed his lip, then said: "May I ask you something before I answer?"

"Of course."

"Mikhyel says in some ways you see us better than we see ourselves, because you don't have that inner sight, and have had to watch people all your life, and have good common sense."

"I accept that as a compliment."

"I think that's how he meant it. So . . . can I ask you—what do *you* think? *Are* they right?"

She grinned. "I'll answer with a question."

"Like Mikhyel does."

She nodded. "I noticed. Why did the ring falter just now?"

"Because I did."

"And why did you falter?"

"Because if everything was to depend on *my* character, on *my* strength, and that was faulty, then everyone could be hurt, or killed or—"

"I submit, brother of Rhomatum's leading barrister, that if your *character* was in question, you'd never have had that doubt."

"So you don't think I'm a bad person?"

"Does what I think matter?"

He frowned. "May I ask a different question? Will you forget that one?"

"You're trying my patience, Nik. What?"

"Can *we* be friends?"

"Absolutely."

He looked up at Lidye, who was watching, arms folded. Impatient.

"I'm ready to try again, Liddi," he said.

၆   ၆   ၆

This time, Nikki didn't falter. The ring held steady, beating in time with his heart. He was aware, vaguely, of Lidye's anger and impatience with him, but he was even more aware of Nethaalye and Mirym's confidence and admiration.

He thought perhaps that caring about their opinions was a character flaw, and the thrum of the Cardinal faltered. He called up Kiyrstin, then, and what she'd said about Deymorin and Mikhyel, and the ring steadied.

Confidence. Absolute conviction. Those were the hallmarks of ringmasters. Nikaenor dunMheric was no master, but he had Talent of some sort, Talent to be used by a master. And yet, *he* must still have conviction of his own. He *knew* what they did was right. Hold that thought and keep it steady, that's all he had to do.

And at first Nethaalye, then Mirym, in response to Lidye's instructions, concentrated on the Giephaetum and Khoratum Rings, he could *feel* them, not as clearly as he did his brothers, but he knew them. And he felt a bridge strengthening the connections to those nodes. Giephaetum, always strong and stable, throbbed with life; Khoratum, that large, but wobbling ring, began to beat steadily.

And as those two corners, east and north grew stable, Nikki could almost see Lidye reach out to the Persitum Ring. It wobbled from the floor.

"*Think* of Persitum!" Lidye hissed at Kiyrstin, and Kiyrstin hissed back:

"I've never *been* there! How can I—"

"Then think of Mauritum!"

And for a moment, the Persitum Ring rose, held steady an inch off the floor.

Then it dropped.

"Never mind. It's too unstable. I can't endanger the others. We'll do without."

Lidye divided her attention then between him and the Shatum ring.

"Feel one another," she purred. "Feel your source. Draw strength from it . . . and from each other. —Strength, Nikki my love. Hold steady." And it was as if her hands caressed him.

He swayed with the rhythm of the Cardinal, the steady stroking of her voice. He thought of the creature below and those roots of leythium that plunged into the heart of the world itself, and imagined energy flowing up into him.

"Steady, my love . . ." It was a whisper in his head. "That's it, hold steady. Hold strong . . ."

Suddenly—

"Dammit!"

His attention faltered.

Pain. Fierce and blinding.

Someone screamed; Nikki thought it might have been himself.

"Nikki! Nikki, wake up!"

"You incompetent *fool*!"

Hands were holding him upright. He was on the floor, and it was Kiyrstin's hands supporting him, and Mirym's holding his, and Nethaalye was there as well, kneeling beside him, asking was he all right.

Only Lidye was not. Lidye was on the far side of the rings, ignoring him.

There were two rings on the floor.

"Shatum," Nethaalye whispered. And as they watched, the ring rose, weaving carefully past the Cardinal and Khoratum, and steadied on its appropriate axis.

Nikki, light-headed, swayed against Kiyrstin, who pressed his head comfortably against her shoulder and told him to relax.

"Well, that was an abject failure!"

Lidye was not pleased.

"I'm sorry, Liddi—"

"*Don't* call me that!"

He flinched; she swirled away, paced the diameter of the room, then spun back and snarled.

"That, *dear* Nikki, was a *test.*"

He flinched again. A test he'd failed.

"Where I come from, we call it a setup," Kiyrstin snarled back at her.

He blinked and asked, past the pain in his head: "Setup?"

Kiyrstin pressed a note into his hand. A note in silent Mirym's handwriting:

Shatum dropped us. It felt like when Persitum went. Planned?

And the note was snatched from his hand.

"Damned right, planned," Lidye hissed above him, and the torn parts of the note fluttered into his lap. "And *that* was *nothing* compared with the shock of the entire Northern Crescent forcing us out."

"And why weren't *you* holding that Southern quarter?" Kiyrstin responded fiercely. "Was it because you were spending so much energy mauling Nikki? Or because you just couldn't be bothered?"

Nikki realized then his shirt was hanging free, and that more than Lidye's voice had been active. He felt his face grow hot, and the bile rose in his throat.

"I've . . . got to . . ." He pushed himself to his feet and stumbled for the lift. But Lidye was before him.

"We'll try again. Now."

"Liddi—"

"*Now!*"

"No!"

Nikki pushed past her, she grabbed his arm, swung him around—

The impact of her hand was worse than any blow he'd ever taken from one of his brothers. He caught her wrist before she could deal him a second.

Kiyrstin exclaimed aloud, but he shot her a stay-back look and then faced Lidye directly. She scowled and fought for possession of her wrist.

He tightened his hold—no more than that—and she relaxed, for all her breathing grew faster, deeper.

"Will you call the lift, lady wife?" He kept his voice low and even. "Or must I break my way out?"

He was immeasurably relieved when the clunk of gears indicated the lift's engagement.

"The next time," he said quietly as he stepped onto the platform, "Shatum will not fall."

§   §   §

{It was much more successful the next time.} Nikki's internal voice seemed oddly subdued. Quiet. Free of the complex overtones of emotion Deymorin was accustomed to receiving from Nikki.

{Are you all right, Nik?} That was Mikhyel. So, he'd noticed the same thing.

{Tired, Khyel. Just . . . very tired. It was a wearing session. A long session. Lidye and Kiyrstin . . .}

He was worried, Deymorin could tell, of saying something that would insult *him,* perhaps send *him* away.

{It's all right, Nikki.} Deymorin reassured him. {What about Kiyrstin? What did she do?}

{Nothing we can't handle. But Lidye can't get a fix on Persitum. She hoped Kiyrstin could reach through, could connect her somehow to Mauritum, I . . . don't really know what she means. But Kiyrstin . . .}

{Kiyrstin's suspicious of her.}

Acknowledgment. And a feeling of failure.

{Not your fault, fry. Trust me. Can you possibly have Kiyrstin there with you next time?}

{She *is* here, Deymio. Mirym, too. I . . . thought you might want verification.}

{Not for that, Nikki,} Mikhyel sent, and Deymorin concurred: {Your word *is* enough. I just wanted to talk to—}

And Kiyrstin *was* there, then, in all her sensual wonder, and for a moment, the intimacy of her mind in his came close to overwhelming him.

{Excuse me . . .} That was Mikhyel. Effective as a dip in a cold mountain lake.

{Sorry brothers.} Deymorin said, then nearly lost control again as Kiyrstin's husky voice, coming through Nikki, said: {Hello, there, Rags.}

{Rings . .} Nikki, Mikhyel, or himself, he wasn't sure.

{Khyel!}

The cool lake again swirled around them.

{Thanks. —Kiyrsti, can you hear me?}

Acknowledgment.

{Problem with you and Lidye?}

{Easy. I don't trust her. No matter how much I *want* to help, I can't seem to overcome that. I'll try.}

{We can't ask for more.} That was Mikhyel. {Might be our saving grace if she *is* Garetti's pawn.}

It spoke volumes that Nikki didn't object to that suggestion.

{You can be proud of Nikki, Deymorin.} That was Kiyrstin again. {Very proud.}

Nothing more than that, and neither he nor Mikhyel formed a specific thought in response. None seemed needed. But the dark tension hovering beneath the surface of Nikki's thoughts dissipated, along with the weary aches.

{Have we date and time yet, Mikhyel?}

{Nothing certain.}

{I'm not moving from the line. —Nikki, you stay put as well.}

{I'll be here.}

A hint of roses and raspberries floated down Nikki's thoughts, and a shy: {Hello, Ravenhair.}

The next moment, Mikhyel disappeared, and the link faded into mist.

Chapter Twelve

"Khyel? *Mikhyel dunMheric, where are you?*"

The bedroom door slammed shut.

"I'm in—"

Temorii's eager face appeared in the doorway.

"—the bath. Temorii, for the love of Darius—"

"Why should I care about Darius? She's done it, Khy! The date's set! We get to test the rings tomorrow!"

"Temorii, sit down. Get—"

"Each contestant will get *as much* time as they want on the rings, with, or without music. And the contest will *not* be controlled, it will be like the *real* dancing, with live music and *we* get to control the rings."

"Temorii, will you sit—"

"*I* think it's because the controlling mechanism was ruined in the collapse, but *Khyys* won't ever admit that. And *guess* who gets to go first?"

"Thyerri, *sit!*"

Temorii flopped down onto the grooming chair beside his bath, and pulled her knees up to her chin. She radiated excitement, and seemed oblivious to the fact that he was in the middle of his bath.

"Tem, do you mind?" he asked at last.

"Not at all." She waved a hand in the air, disturbingly reminiscent of Mother's grand gestures. "Go right ahead."

He began to protest, thought better of it, and gestured toward his back. "Raul?"

As if bathing with a young woman in the room were an everyday occurrence, Raulind spread the oil and began to scrub his back. But then, it wasn't Temorii in the room. It was Thyerri dunMatrii. Cocky, eager . . . and utterly oblivious to Mikhyel dunMheric's admittedly negligible charms.

"She, who?" Mikhyel asked. "And what's she done?"

"Mother."

Naturally.

"They've been having trouble with the dance rings—ever since the Collapse, you know—and Mother said yesterday . . ."

The rest of the sentence was lost to Mikhyel. Yesterday. Yesterday, Temorii, beautiful, strong, elegant child of the ley, had held him and thought the closest to a declaration of love that had ever crossed his senses.

Granted, she'd *said* nothing. Granted, she probably even regretted *thinking* it, but Mikhyel had heard, and *he* at least couldn't set that moment aside easily.

This was the first time he'd seen her since then. Mother had been behind her and Mother had transferred *him* back to this room. Temorii had stayed with Mother.

And now, she burst in with news of the rings and Mother, as if that . . . moment . . . wasn't.

"Temorii," he interrupted her, and she gave him an indignant look, which he ignored. "Would you mind turning away for a moment?"

She rolled her eyes and flopped around in the chair. "Hurry up."

"Raul?"

A warm towel enfolded him as he stepped free of the small sitting bath. As Raulind proceeded in his normal, efficient manner, Temorii tapped her bare foot impatiently.

"Mikhyel dunMheric, I think you must really be as large as all other rijhili. You just spend so much time in the water, you've shrunk!"

"Don't call me that."

"Rijhili?" A wicked eye twinkled over her shoulder at him. "Rijhili, rijhili, rijhili."

He frowned, and stalked into the bedroom, Raulind at his heels.

"Khyel?" Her voice quivered. She was standing in the doorway, leaning against the elaborately carved frame. "Khy, I'm—"

"Dammit, turn around!" Give him *some* privacy, at least. Raulind's hand on his towel-covered shoulder advised against temper, and he swallowed hard.

Temper was the least of his problems this morning.

He pulled his own clothing on, getting in Raulind's way more than expediting the act, but needing—*needing*—that sense of personal control. Of personally armoring himself against her. When he had his coat safely fastened, he said, "Please leave us, Raulind. I'll call when I'm ready for you."

"Very good, sir," Raulind said, but the squeeze he gave Mikhyel's shoulder as he left counseled: *be careful.*

Mikhyel nodded. When Raulind was gone, Mikhyel pulled the tie off his braid, yanked the strands free, and began pulling a comb ruthlessly through it, welcoming the minor discomfort.

"Can I help?" Temorii's hand touched his where it held the comb.

He jerked away. Pulled a knot free of the comb and flung it in the general direction of the dressing table.

"Khyel, *please*! What's going on? What did I do?"

He wished he knew. He stared down at the comb, tried to still the shaking hand that held it, and decided the hand didn't belong to him, since it kept shaking. But when Temorii's fingers touched the hand and extracted the comb, he felt it like fire running from his hand to his entire body, so perhaps it was his hand after all.

"It doesn't matter, Khyel," her gentle, Temorii voice murmured. "Just sit down."

He shook his head.

"Please?"

It was undoubtedly a weakness in his character that he couldn't resist her request, that if her hand guiding a comb through his hair was all he could have, he'd take it.

But it didn't mean he had to watch her face in the mirror while she did it.

"I love the feel of your hair," she murmured, as she had every night out on the mountainside camp, and indeed her fingers did more of the work than the comb.

Mikhyel said nothing. Talk of hair, talk of rings, talk of the dance . . . it was all irrelevant anyway. If Temorii wanted to dance, she had Mother.

"So she got the rings up." Funny how much easier it was to keep emotion from your voice when dealing with the Syndicate than when dealing with a hiller. "And the maze? Will she transport you in? Or didn't you ever *get* that far in the plans?"

"Of course she will. Is that why you're so testy?"

"I'm not testy."

"Of course not. You always glower and spit and order Raulind out of the room."

He propped his elbow on the chair arm and rubbed his forehead. "Tem, will you just leave me alone? You've got your dance. You've got Mother. They've set the date . . . What more do you want?"

"I want you to be happy for me!"

She flung the comb on the dresser and squatted beside his chair to jerk his hand away from his face.

"Look at me, Khyel," she said, and when he turned his head, letting the hair fall like a veil between them: "*Look* at me, rijhili!"

He flung his head back, felt his mouth pull in a snarl he wasn't conscious of ordering. But Temorii didn't flinch, only raised her chin another notch.

"So, what's *your* problem?" she asked.

He raised a fist between them. Not meant for her. It was himself he wished he could strike, blows such as his father had once dealt, to knock sense into him. To make him think. To remind him only Rhomatum mattered. Always Rhomatum.

. . . and what of Mikhyel-child's happiness . . .

It didn't matter. Couldn't. But he couldn't get himself past the wanting. And Temorii never would. With Mheric gone, with Anheliaa, there was no one left to keep Mikhyel dunMheric's mind from wandering off into frivolous irresponsibility.

Hands surrounded his fist. Warm, strong . . . gentle. "Khyel?"

And eyes, beautiful, worried . . . eyes that had stolen his soul and left him this witless, self-centered idiot.

"Why, Temorii?" he whispered, so that he wouldn't shout. "Why did Mother leave you?"

Confusion clouded her eyes, and she shook her head ever-so-slightly.

"I . . . she said last night, she believed she'd made a bad mistake."

"Mistake? *Mother?*"

"Her words, Khyel. Absolutely. I was . . . obsessed, she says. Out of touch with my self. Becoming . . . not human."

"So she forced you into the worst possible human hands."

Temorii shook her head. "No, Mikhyel dunMheric. Mother left me in *your* hands. I chose to leave."

"Why?" Rings, he could have been with her . . . all this time, he could have had—

"Mother. The dance. Freedom. Mother has plans . . . Mother always has plans, some more sound than others. Some only she can begin to comprehend. But this one . . . hoping to save my humanity, she wove me into the new pattern . . ."

"Pattern?"

She shook her head. "I can't explain. Not here. There's a cave below . . . I call it the world cave, where the patterns in the ley reveal the patterns of the surface world. You and your brothers caused a new pattern to form in the web."

"My brothers and I. And you?"

Her head dipped. "I believe so. Mother is . . . vague on that point." She stroked his fist until his fingers relaxed, then raised his hand to brush the Rhomandi ring with her lips.

His stomach twisted in a sickening knot, but he didn't, *couldn't* pull his hand free.

"I'd . . . known you for months—through the pattern. And I followed the politics and gossip in Rhyys' court. I knew when Anheliaa leythiated Deymorin, and I knew when he came out, and when your Nikki attacked Anheliaa's rings."

"I almost died then."

Temorii nodded. "Anheliaa was in shock and dying. You were trying to pull her down, willing to die, to protect your brother."

Mikhyel said nothing. It was a time he barely remembered. He remembered Nikki challenging her, and Anheliaa trying to force Nikki to comply with her plan. In an amazing act of courage, Nikki had thrown Deymorin's cane into the middle of the Rhomatum rings.

After that came a time of nightmares, a reliving of everything evil that had been his life with Anheliaa. In shame and hatred, he'd wanted to bring them both down . . . And then, a flare of hope. Of light . . . on a scent of raspberries and cinnamon . . . and a hint of clove.

"That was you?" he whispered, and she nodded, her eyes damp.

"I couldn't let you die. Not that way."

So she let him live to destroy him with her indifference.

But he didn't say that. Knew that *that* had never been her choice.

Any more than his feelings for her now were his choice.

"And the day of competition, you and Mother saved me a second time."

"And you saved me, Khyel. That's what Mother was trying to explain last night."

He frowned. "How?"

"Your physical healing was over, but your heart, your soul, still wanted to die. Mother told Deymorin he could change that. Deymorin . . . distrusted. Himself, most of all. He was frightened of what he would find. Frightened of what would drive you to death. Of the truth of the past. But he faced that and more for love of you."

"*You* were there as well?" Embarrassment nearly overwhelmed him. He wasn't proud of what Deymorin had witnessed that day.

"Only as a guide. Only to make the pathways, and even that proved unnecessary. I was to observe, or so I thought." She laced her fingers in his. "Until that day, my life had been Mother and the ley and the dance. What I was, beyond a dancer, meant nothing to me. I think . . . I think that denial limited everything that I might become, Khy. After Deymorin went searching for you . . . I wanted to be like you. I wanted to have it in me to inspire such love, to be capable of feeling so strongly. To find that entity, that pattern, for which I would die to protect and nurture. Thanks to you, I began to find the key to my own soul."

The concept shocked him. She provided a view of himself that was less recognizable than the poster's unflattering portrait.

"After . . . after you woke up, I *thought* I'd found all Mother wanted. That I'd been included to find what it meant to be part of something larger than myself. I left to go back to you, who was the rest of me. But when I came to Khoratum . . . she didn't answer. I thought I'd understood incorrectly, and condemned myself to a life with nothing. Without the dance. Without Mother. Without . . ."

You, he wished she'd say, but she did not, even if that had been her intent. And because she did not, that moment they'd shared, the thought that had haunted him ever since, had to be rejected. Temorii denied it, therefore, Mikhyel dunMheric must deny it as well.

He drew a deep breath.

Then rescued his hand and cupped her chin. "So?" He forced a smile. "When did you say this competition is to be?"

There were harder ways to appear an idle wastrel while your men skulked about the shadows than watching the dancers practice, particularly when one of those powerful, lithe bodies belonged to someone you . . . cherished a great deal.

Word of Mikhyel dunMheric's incompetence had indeed preceded him, and Mikhyel didn't know whether to curse Deymorin or bless him. The men assembled in Khoratum would meet with him behind closed doors, accept his papers, listen to his explanations and plans, then ask where Deymorin was, and how was Mikhyel's ringdancer doing, and did he care to lay a wager on the outcome of the competition.

He'd even met officially with Rhyys. He'd tried to explain his concerns for Khoratum, and especially the Khoratum line and how he had the Southern Crescent Nodes ready to help repair it. And then he suggested what Rhomatum might be willing to do for the young mountain node in the coming years.

Rhyys had smoked his ocarshi and yawned—and asked how his ringdancer was doing and did he care to lay a wager.

That was when he decided on the idle wastrel tactic.

Ganfrion had been amused.

But his reputation had made Ganfrion's job easier, Ganfrion insisted. Ganfrion had been able to confirm his suspicions regarding the shutdown. Ganfrion had also discovered evidence that the Giephaetumin ringmaster, Ioniia, had disappeared following her refusal to cooperate with the plan.

Mikhyel hadn't enjoyed passing that information on to Nikki to tell Nethaalye. But Nethaalye had said, with typical common sense, that Ioniia being dispossessed probably meant her brother was in charge, and from past experience she had no doubt that she could out-stubborn him, should that become necessary, so it was all to the best, wasn't it?

The only question remaining was exactly when.

So it was that Mikhyel dunMheric, the golden-tongued orator of Rhomatum, came to be sitting in the coaching box, along with some thirty or more other men and women, sponsors of the various dancers, while the nine contestants warmed up, preparatory to their only precompetition time on the dance rings.

The excitement that had vibrated Temorii's body an hour ago had, to all outward appearances, disappeared. The warmup routine he'd witnessed a hundred times was as perfect and precise—at least to his untrained eyes—as ever. Certainly, it had the opposing sponsors craning their necks and puckering their brows.

She was, without question, unique. Quiet. Disciplined. Focused on her own movement, and, to all outward appearances, utterly oblivious to the others, all of whom made occasional flights of flashy tumbling moves across the warmup sand.

Sand. A long side strip of it, running between sections of the stadium seating, as the stadium floor itself was covered with a thick layer. On the far side of the sand, across from the half-circle of seating, was the maze, and in the center of the maze, the building into which Mother would place Temorii on the morning of the competition.

Two days from now.

The arbiter called for the first practice to begin, and suddenly, breathing became difficult. When Temorii's slender form climbed to the uppermost platform to receive the safety harness, the effort not to call a halt to the proceeding taxed his control to its limits.

The technology and upkeep of the dance rings was the province of one of the Syndicate's most self-contained and self-policing guilds. It was, the guild maintained, the job of the people to be amazed, not to understand. That their suspension was somehow linked to the ley was certain: for all there were physical connections between the rings, and the central support column, the dance rings would not operate outside a power umbrella.

Or when the umbrella went down, as it had during that last competition. And Khoratum's power umbrella was *still* vastly unpredictable.

All of which became irrelevant the instant that outermost ring, tall as a fourth-story window, began a slow, majestic sway. The one truth was: dancers died on the Khoratum rings. And he didn't want Temorii to die. He most definitely did *not* want Temorii to die.

Temorii, however, obviously did not share his concerns as she leaped from the launch tower in a tumbling dive through the stationary rings to seize a handle on the ponderously swaying outer ring. If the rings were inclined to malfunction, that fierce attack should have settled the issue.

And for the next quarter hour, Mikhyel wouldn't swear to whether or not he breathed. As Temorii's lithe form twisted, tapped and flew between complex and ever-shifting patterns of flashing steel, objectivity eluded him. He found himself in one moment enthralled, disbelieving that any human, let alone one he knew so well, could possibly perform such feats, and in the next controlling an embarrassingly physical response to the sheer beauty of her form and motion, and wondering *when* his mind had begun making such damnable associations.

Until he began to realize his reactions *weren't* arbitrary. In one pass, a child skipped through the rings, making them spin at random, and Mikhyel laughed. In the next pass, a woman in love caressed the rings, riding one after another up to the top, dropping through to catch the next rising swing, and it was his body she embraced. Another pass, and a warrior challenged the rings and his own skill and power, or an elder calmly controlled the rings' actions, with quiet taps from the outside ring.

It was during one of those cerebral respites that Mikhyel became aware of those around him. Of their awe—and their jealous contempt. One said the hair that floated, then whipped behind her was obviously a wig, and should be disallowed. One tried to criticize her technique, another challenged how could she tell when she'd never seen the move, and someone else said half the dance was weaving and unweaving the safety line, and if a dancer couldn't do that, he'd never win.

Horrified, Mikhyel looked to that diving platform, the launchpoint from which the safety line should run. And then to Temorii, riding the outside ring, ready to launch to another . . .

Her slender form utterly unfettered.

Fear consumed him. For all he'd heard her complain of the confining straps, for all she'd argued they simply made the dance more dangerous, he'd never quite convinced himself she was right. He'd seen dancers saved when they miscalculated a trajectory.

Temorii had said, flatly, they shouldn't have missed.

As if she never had.

Watching her now, perhaps she hadn't. Perhaps she simply didn't know what missing meant. But there was a chance. There was *always* a chance. And as she flew from one ring to another, then paused to ride one to the top, he bit his lip on the urge to cry out to her to be careful. That he loved her too dearly to watch her die.

And as she flexed, ready to leap, she seemed to falter. Her eyes flickered to the booth where Mikhyel sat with the coaches. She shook her head, ever-so-slightly, and launched—

—off line.

Mikhyel cried out and surged to his feet, frozen in utter horror as she tumbled through the rings, reaching out, trying to orient her fall through rings sharp enough, spinning fast enough, now, to decapitate her, should she misjudge position.

The instant she struck the ground, Mikhyel was over the edge of the booth, dropping to the lower tier and running for the steps into the arena.

Others were there before him. He tried to thrust his way through, but the physician ordered everyone back, and the crowd carried Mikhyel back with them.

"Khy!" He heard Temorii scream, and called back, but he wasn't certain she heard. She screamed again, this time to someone else, to leave her alone, to get out of her way, and Mikhyel rammed his way through to the front just in time to see her disappear alone down a tunnel beneath the stadium seating.

Mikhyel cursed at the surgeon, who cursed back—something about crazy has-beens who shouldn't be let near the rings and she was lucky an arm was all she'd broken. He ignored the surgeon, and ran after Temorii. By the time he reached the tunnel, she'd disappeared.

୨   ୨   ୨

"Physician Nodio claims dunMheric was crazed with fear for the creature." Rhyys pulled deeply on the ocarshi pipe, held the breath until he had to let it go, then inhaled again, quickly, as if afraid some of the narcotic might escape him.

Thyerri looked away from the sight, hiding his nose

within the folds of the cloak's hood, trying to filter the noxious smoke.

"He also claimed her arm was broken," Scarface said, from his shadowed corner. "Well, Thyerri? *Can* Temorii dance with less than two days' recuperation?"

Thyerri nodded within the hood, without looking up, and he pulled the cloak tighter, fighting the chill that seemed to come so easily these days.

"Obviously, then, the dear surgeon's powers of observation are lacking."

"I saw it myself!" Rhyys cried. "He's obsessed. And he will remain obsessed until he has relieved himself of it within the object of his fascination!"

"And you would know."

"All too well." Rhyys waved his hand through the air. "It's the inaccessibility that holds his interest. Once that impediment is passed, there's nothing to sustain the excitement."

"You are disgusting," Scarface said, as if commenting on the recent lack of rain. "Well, Thyerri, would you agree with that? Will dunMheric, once he's had Temorii, lose all interest? Will he depart Khoratum as if she never existed? Able to continue life without her?"

Thyerri shrugged, still watching his feet. "It doesn't matter. To bed with him is to risk the dance. She won't do that."

"You seem very certain."

"I am."

"She wants the rings, doesn't she? What if I were to say, if she beds dunMheric, she'll win the contest?"

"And die in the winning."

"I think she'll choose the risk, don't you?"

It was the control over dunMheric that Scarface had wanted from the start. If the Rhomatumin truly loved Temorii, she would become his weakness, if he did not, the simple fact he'd bedded a Khoratumin dancer before the competition would be an indiscretion a man who was trying to unify the web would not want known. If she died in the competition, it would simply increase the value of the scandal.

"I think she will win whether you control the vote or not," Thyerri said at last.

"Silly child, any vote that can be high-balanced one way

can as easily be high-balanced another. I promise you. Perhaps that balance could favor . . . well, we wouldn't want to make you self-conscious, now would we?"

"No!" Rhyys swayed upright. "I tell you, I'll not allow you to make *that* promise. We don't *need* proof to arrest dunMheric. The people hate him already. Rumor alone will inspire them to murder. If Mauritum fails to control—"

Rhyys reeled as if he'd been struck. When he swayed back up, his mouth was bleeding. Thyerri, who had felt that blow at a distance himself, knew precisely who was responsible and looked back at his feet, which seemed the safest spot in the room.

"I think, of course," Scarface said mildly, "that your ringmaster raves from the ocarshi. Such a sad affliction."

Thyerri met Scarface's gaze at last. "And I think, sir, that if Temorii beds dunMheric, it will be because she wishes to bed him, not for your threats, not for your promises. She never asked for guarantees, only for a fair chance. I suspect, that once the competition is over, if you stack your vote against her, you might well cause an inquiry not even Rhyys dunTarec can cover up."

"And I can say, murdering arsonist, that if Temorii is still a virgin the morning of the competition, *you* will spend the day of the competition in chains, and the morning after will be your last."

Thyerri stood up, chin high, looking Scarface squarely in the eye. "May I go now?"

Scarface laughed, and jerked his head toward the door.

The man-mountain was waiting in the shadows. Thyerri knew who he was now, and no longer ran.

"Well?" The mountain's gravelly voice implied a cruelty Thyerri knew better than to believe. Ganfrion had intercepted him several times since that first meeting, and Thyerri knew his only concern was for dunMheric's well-being.

In that, they had a shared interest.

Thyerri melted into Ganfrion's corner and said, in a low voice: "They are planning it for after the competition."

"Mauritum?"

"Garetti is definitely involved."

"The South?"

"I don't know."

"DunMheric?"

"I'm afraid for him."

"Why?"

"Arrest. Riots. They want him incarcerated. Perhaps dead."

"And yourself?"

Thyerri shook his head. "I'm to compete."

"You don't sound very excited."

"I *was* a dancer, Ganfrion. I thought I could be one again. Instead, I find myself fighting for a life I don't care to live. Rhyys was bad for Khoratum, anyone of sense knew that. But so were the rings bad. Khoratum itself was from the start. All I cared about was the Dance. At least, that's what I thought."

"But that's changed?"

Thyerri nodded. "With this Mauritumin man in there—"

"Your scarface? Still no name?"

Thyerri shook his head. "But with Mauritum lending him credibility, Rhyys seems to be gaining the support of people who should know better. I don't understand what's happening in the rest of the Syndicate. I don't know why strangers are infesting Khoratum, but I want Rhyys out!" He paused, staring into the night. "And I want dunMheric safe. If securing those two ends means my death, I will consider my life well-spent."

"DunMheric will have to be told "

"Enough to get him to leave."

"He deserves to know everything."

"Temorii will do whatever it takes to get him to leave."

"Before the competition?"

"Temorii would wish otherwise."

"Even after today's accident?"

"Temorii will discuss that with him tomorrow night."

"What's wrong with tonight?"

"Temorii needs time to think. And to rest. Away from dunMheric."

"And will she tell him everything?"

Thyerri shrugged. "That's up to her. And dunMheric. The competition is meaningless. Temorii will win. Rhyys will see to that. It will keep Mikhyel there, keep him close, and somehow, by the end of the competition, Mikhyel will be in custody and by the next day, Rhyys said it wouldn't matter whether he was guilty or not. 'They' would be ready to blame anything on him. Murder was mentioned."

A curse, deep and heartfelt.

"One more thing," Thyerri said, his throat tight with fear.

"Yes?"

"Scarface . . . he wears a ring . . . like Khyel's."

"The Rhomandi ring?"

Thyerri ducked his head.

"Scarface is *not* gorMikhyel . . . or any other Rhomandi's man."

"Anheliaa's?" Thyerri suggested hesitantly.

Another spate of cursing that consigned Anheliaa's soul to frightening areas of the hereafter.

Then: "I'll see what I can find out."

"You'll tell him? You'll tell K—dunMheric about the ring and Scarface?"

"Yes, Rakshi-child, I'll tell him." For the first time, the mountain's rasping voice was almost gentle. "And don't worry. We'll get him out. Will you leave with us?"

"I can't."

"Why not?"

"I have to dance."

"For *what*?"

"For the mountain. For Khoratum. For Bharlo. For Sakhithe . . ." Thyerri shrugged. "And for others."

"For Thyerri?"

"Those things, those people . . . they *are* Thyerri."

Chapter Thirteen

The precompetition banquet was winding to a close. At least, it was as far as Mikhyel dunMheric was concerned. One more side-whiff of Rhyys' gods-be-damned lung pollutant and he'd be too sick to make it to his room alone.

Besides, he *wanted* to get back. He hadn't seen Temorii for almost two days. The word was she'd broken her arm and wasn't going to compete. But no one had seen her—including Ganfrion—and on *Ganfrion's* inability to track her, he was basing all his hope.

She was with Mother. She had to be. Mother wouldn't let her be hurt. Not again.

And whenever he thought that, a feather-touch of reassurance convinced him Mother was aware of the thought, and telling him all was well.

He hoped. That feather could equally well be Mikhyel dunMheric's profoundly active imagination.

"Ah-h-h." Rhyys, seated at the center of the main table, let out a sound that was either a sigh or a wheeze of deflation. "Let us have the parade of dancers, eh?"

Mikhyel let out a sigh of his own. The parade first, then a dissolution of formal tables. They'd begin to mill about, and he'd be free to leave.

There were nine huge tables arranged in a horseshoe shape around the enormous and elaborately decorated room: one (theoretically) for each contestant. The tickets for spaces at those tables were, he understood, quite precious.

He would have *given* his away for dinner in his room and word from Temorii.

He'd been placed at Rhyys' table, though fortunately not immediately beside Rhyys himself, who preferred buxom females about him, as he'd loudly announced at the beginning of the evening, to the mortification of the two well-bred women forced to sit beside him by their well-bred husbands, who were currying favors with Rhyys.

Somehow, the subtle maneuverings Mikhyel had observed and participated in all his life took on the look of petty, here in Khoratum.

The musicians began a standard, unobtrusive ballroom piece with a clear and regular tempo, and the parade of contestants began.

The slender, elegant creatures who entered the room one at a time in answer to their introduction, bore little resemblance to the athletes who had warmed up in the sand the previous morning. Male and female, they were painted and dressed, with their long hair crimped and braided in elaborate styles, their slender, nearly sexless forms hidden behind flounces and drapes, padding and corsets, or flowing robes with padded shoulders.

But while they moved with uniform pride, each made that pass in their own style; however their sponsor-provided coaches had adorned them for the occasion, *they* knew what they were there for, and uniformity was not a preferred commodity in a Khoratumin radical dancer.

Each contestant made a slow circuit of the tables, acknowledging the guests, making a special show at the table of their own backers. The musicians catered to their lead, choosing pieces to enhance that tour of the tables, creating a background that was a constantly shifting medley of familiar ballroom pieces.

"Thyerri of Khoratum."

Mikhyel jerked. Startled. And took his eyes from the competitor bowing before him to seek out the entrance of the lad who had played so strange and fleeting a role in his life.

Laughter began with those nearest the door, and spread as more caught sight of the strange vision entering the room. The figure bore little resemblance to the others. He was dressed in leather, tanned to skin-hugging flexibility. His cropped hair was held back from his face with a band that trailed beads and feathers down his back. There were beads and feathers also at his neck and on his leggings. His face, like the other contestants, was painted, but his was a mask of a different kind, composed of fine lace-patterns of pale blues and greens and purples.

Like the ley itself.

And proud as Mother herself, Thyerri strode down the hall, with the grace and power of an athlete, not the studied glamour of the others. As with the others, the musicians shifted their style to match his. But this time, it was no ballroom piece. It was of a kind with those pieces he'd heard in the Lower Khoratum taverns. Hiller music, with the drums dominant, enhancing Thyerri's solidly placed strides.

That drum, and Thyerri's own determination, the obvious self-confidence that matched the most self-confident of the previous contestants, silenced the laughter.

These rijhili had no idea what they were seeing.

Mikhyel felt his lips twitch, remembering his meetings with Thyerri, and his firsthand introduction to the derogatory term. And seeing Thyerri this way, no longer wondered at his initial confusion between the hiller-lad and Temorii. In many ways, Thyerri *did* remind him of Temorii, ways that went well beyond the physical similarities all the dancers shared.

And it went beyond the strangely-shaded hair, even beyond the similar high cheek bones and finely-sculpted chin, features that he saw for the first time without the cloak's hood.

It was their bearing, a posture that said somehow, *I'm different. Good or bad, you can never be what I am. Never have done what I have done.* And he wondered, remembering that brief sense of contact, whether that bearing came from Mother. Whether Thyerri was another of Mother's children and, if so, what might have dropped him from her favor.

More than ever, he regretted that lost opportunity the first night to get to know the street-lad better. And now it was too late. Now Thyerri's soul belonged to Rhyys.

Thyerri had no table of backers. He'd not been one of the nine on the field yesterday morning. Rhyys must have granted him some sort of special dispensation, possibly as recently as last night. One had to wonder what piece of privacy Thyerri might have sold to get Rhyys to allow him to compete.

. . . nothing stands between a Dancer and a chance to dance . . .

As Thyerri crossed in front of Rhyys' table, that haughty glance slid past them all to seek out one of the servants standing patiently behind Mikhyel. And Thyerri's eyes lit,

his face broke into a smile, and he swept a bow so deep
the feathers flopped forward and brushed his sandal-bared
toe. The feathers flipped back, and the audacious fellow
blew the servant girl a kiss, then whirled and strutted away,
to unison applause of appreciation.

Rhyys turned with a snarl toward the object of Thyerri's
interest. She cowered and dodged his back-handed sweep,
nearly dropping the wine bottle she held.

Mikhyel's upraised palm intercepted Rhyys' heavily jeweled hand in the middle of its wild swing. Rhyys glared at
him; Mikhyel said mildly, "Your guests enjoyed the performance, Rhyys. Make more of it, and you give it a significance it otherwise lacks."

Rhyys cast the servant a disdainful glance, then threw
himself back into place and signaled for the next contestant
to enter. Mikhyel smiled back at the servant, but she was
staring at Rhyys, wide-eyed and very frightened.

She had what was becoming a familiar look to Mikhyel.
Short-cropped hair, though her black mane had the flat
look of dye, and the slender elegance of a dancer, though
she was markedly older than Temorii or any of the contestants. Perhaps Thyerri's older sister. Perhaps, he thought of
the difficulty of telling age with the hillers, even his mother.

He drained then lifted his wineglass, and when the young
woman bent forward to fill the goblet, he murmured, "Follow me out?"

Her nod, if it was a nod at all, was a single dip of the
head that brushed her hair against his cheek.

Thinking he'd done all he could to ensure her immediate
safety, he turned back for the final handful of contestants.

"Temorii dunKhoramali."

Only years of life with Anheliaa prevented him dropping
his wineglass. He set the glass down, and placed his hands
beneath the table where they could shake in private.

Temorii, child of the Khoramali. As audacious, in her
own way, as Thyerri had been. She wore a gown similar to
the one Mother had given her in the cave, and there was
no doubt Mother had provided this one as well.

Spider-fine leythium lace gave the illusion of transpar-
ency, yet revealed nothing, the illusion of all color that was
no color, but a walking shadow of a rainbow.

Grown lace, not manufactured. Grown around a manikin
form over the course of years and under painstakingly con-

trolled conditions; such gowns were available in highly specialized markets, but he'd never seen one that approached what she wore. Considering what just the bodice would cost, he could only imagine what rumors were generating even now behind the silence within the room.

Temorii's upper body was, like so many of the dancers, lean and hard, but rather than hide that unusual characteristic she gloried in it. The gown proclaimed to the world that the one who wore it was different. Special. And proud of the difference.

At least, that's what it said to him.

Below her narrow hips, the skirt flared into heavy folds that flowed behind her in a short train rippling with sparks of color. Her shaded hair was a shimmering veil down her back, shot, like her skirt, with sparks of color. Near her head, where it was deep, almost black, sable, she wore a coronet of leythium crystal.

Her face was bare of any makeup. But her flawless skin, benefit, no doubt of growing up bathing in leythium pools, dark lashes and large, obliquely-set eyes needed no enhancement.

At least, not to his eyes.

The musicians were first to shake off the spell she cast. Following the flautist's lead this time, they began a rippling, flowing, nearly formless melody that sounded more like the wind in the trees and a mountain stream than a song.

And that sound seemed to ripple up her spine and as if she had no will of her own, she began to dip and swirl in response to the rise and fall of notes. She made her circuit, just as all those before her had made the circuit, but she made it as the dancer she was to her core. Fortunately, the alert flautist recognized the spell Temorii was under and brought the music to a cascading climax in front of Rhyys' table.

She whirled to a stop, but before Mikhyel, not Rhyys as had all the others. Whether by her design or accident, he didn't know. But she didn't bow. Not to him, not to Rhyys. Her long, deep breaths made the leythium sparkle on her breast and in the hair that had swirled around to the front of her shoulder.

She dipped her head to Rhyys. To himself, she gave a look that twisted his heart.

Then the music began again, and she was gone.

*   *   *

The servant said her name was Sakhithe, and that she was a friend of Thyerri's once, but that Rhyys had laid claim to her, and she feared for Mikhyel if he tried to help her.

Mikhyel laughed, reminded her that slavery was illegal throughout the web and handed her over to Raulind, and asked Raulind to have Paulis see to the details in the morning.

There were times he truly enjoyed having a completely reliable staff.

Inside his room, Ganfrion was waiting for him.

"You've got to leave. Now. Tonight."

Before he'd even taken off his coat. Reliable was one thing. Interfering—that was another.

He tore the pin from his hair and began pulling the braid loose, anxious for the bath that would eliminate the stench of ocarshi from its strands. After tonight, there was no doubt left in his mind that whatever value Rhyys had once had to Anheliaa and the web, that value had gone up in greasy yellow smoke long ago.

He tossed the pin on the dressing table, then turned to face Ganfrion.

"No," he said flatly.

"Dammit, dunMheric, you're getting bubbles in the brain again!"

Mikhyel paced his room, trying to think how to explain to Ganfrion, enough to ease his concerns without getting into the issue of Mother. Without proof, Ganfrion would simply take it as more evidence of his growing irrationality.

"I can't desert Temorii," he said at last.

"She's not even *here.* For all you know—"

"She was at the parade. You're getting sloppy, Gan."

"I was *busy* elsewhere."

"You didn't see her tonight. The marked hostility they have for her. Because of *me.* If she loses—"

"She won't."

"She's good, Gan. But nothing is that certain."

"If the vote is rigged, it's certain."

"Rigged?"

"Thyerri says—"

Mikhyel swung around to face Ganfrion. "*Thyerri?* What

did you do? Have lunch with him and discuss my business?"

"Yes. —Khyel, *listen* to—"

Mikhyel raised a hand; Ganfrion's mouth closed in a tight bar. Without a word, Mikhyel gestured to a chair. Ganfrion sat. Mikhyel poured two glasses of wine, handed one to Gan and swallowed half the other. He refilled it and sat down.

"All right, Gan, what did Thyerri have to say?"

"He came straight to me after his meeting last night."

"And you're only now coming to me?"

"I wanted to verify his story. And I met him again this afternoon. He found me."

"I see. Go on."

"He didn't even pretend that I wouldn't know what he was talking about."

"He knows you've been following."

"And knows who I'm with."

"All right. And?"

"He says Tomorii is *marked* to win."

"Why?"

"To keep you here. Control you. Perhaps use you as a diversion if their plans go awry and panic breaks out."

"We know when?"

"Tomorrow, after the competition. Sometime."

"When *exactly*?"

"I don't damn well know! If I did, I'd tell you!"

"All right," Mikhyel said. "All right. Of course you would. Mauritum?"

"Definitely involved. There's a man, Thyerri says he's gorRhyys, but that Rhyys is *his* puppet, not the other way around. A scar-faced man out of Mauritum. *He's* the one to watch."

"You've got nothing more on him?"

"Keeps his nose real clean, Suds. *No* one mentions him."

"Except Thyerri."

"Except Thyerri."

"You trust him?"

"Thyerri?" Ganfrion paused and frowned down into his glass. "In this case, yes. Absolutely. Khyel, Thyerri says the Mauritumin has a Rhomandi ring." Ganfrion nodded toward Mikhyel's hand. "Like yours."

"That's impossible."

"Anheliaa's man Brolucci?"

Mikhyel shook his head. "He must be mistaken."

"Just . . . shit, Suds, keep an eye out for him? If it *is* true—"

"I'll keep it in mind, Gan. I promise you." He stared down into his wine, swirled the deep red liquid. "And Temorii? What about your . . . reservations?"

"Irrelevant. Inconclusive."

"And the ringmasters? Demonstration? Or takeover?"

Ganfrion sipped his wine. "By what I *know,* it's to be a brief demonstration. A shutdown to frighten Lidye. By what I suspect . . . *I* think they plan to take over Rhomatum."

Mikhyel nodded. It no more than coincided with his own thoughts.

"Dammit, Khyel, *say* something. If Thyerri heard right, sometime after that damned competition tomorrow, all hell is going to break loose. For all I know, they plan to blame it all on you, and turn you over to the raving masses as a diversion *while* hell breaks loose. You've *got* to leave."

"When we know the time, I'll leave."

"Dammit, you're a Rhomandi! You've got to get back to Rhomatum. Warn the other nodes, prepare Rhomatum Tower."

"Prepare, how?"

"Hell if I know. That's ringspinning, but any fool can see that half of an already crippled system shutting down isn't going to help it run better! If Garetti wants it, he's going to have it!"

"Your arguments are slipping, Gan. What can be done has been done and will be done, whether I'm here or in Rhomatum."

"How the hell do you know?"

"I have my ways, Ganfrion. You're not my only source, you know."

"I know I'm your best one."

Mikhyel chuckled, enjoying for once having useful information Ganfrion lacked. "I assume you've sent messengers to my brothers."

"Of course. But—"

"Did you do a good job on my signature?"

"Of course. But—" Ganfrion broke off. Frowning. But Mikhyel only chuckled. He could see where Ganfrion's methods, while expedient, must have gotten him into a great deal of trouble over the years. Fortunately for Ganfrion, the Rhomandi brothers had ways of backing up the information sent via other methods.

"Then we've done all we can," Mikhyel said at last. "I certainly won't get to Rhomatum faster than a single horseman."

Ganfrion's stare accused, tried and judged him wanting in common sense; but oddly, his voice held a trace of sympathy when he asked: "You've got a bad case, haven't you, Suds?"

The ghostly humor deserted him. "I care deeply for someone whose skill I respect and admire, if that's what you mean."

"You know what I mean. Why don't you just get it over with? You know the feelings are mutual. You'd both feel better. Maybe straighten out your thinking."

He couldn't argue with that. The cold truth was, his desire for Temorii did cloud his thinking. Still: "I can't even consider it. It would be as good as a death sentence for her."

"And living without you won't be?"

"Not if she has her dance."

"Perhaps having you would be an adequate substitute."

"Hardly. And I'd never ask her to make the choice."

"Never ask? Or never give?"

"You cut too fine a line for me."

"Leave now. Tonight. Take your dancer with you—by force, if you must. The poor child hasn't a chance anyway."

"Of course she has."

"Your dancer will win, that's a given. Your dancer will *be* the Khoratum radical. But for how long, once you're gone or in prison . . . or dead? The outcome is rigged! They're *counting* on you sticking around for the ceremonies and celebrations. If you don't, Temorii is doomed."

"I'd never leave, if I believed that to be the case."

"Well, wake up, Suds. Because *that's* the way it *is*."

"And there are facts yet to come into evidence, Cryptbait. Temorii will be safe."

"You're blind, Rhomandi."

"And you don't understand as much as you think you do!"

A hesitant knock on the door interrupted them.

"Come!" Mikhyel barked, and the door inched open revealing pale eyes and long shaded hair.

"Is it safe?" Temorii whispered, eyes wide with theatrical fear.

Mikhyel laughed, and held out a hand. "Come, child. The ogre is in his cage."

She sighed dramatically, and slipped the rest of her inside the room, the mass of skirt sweeping in behind as if it had a mind of its own.

For all he knew, it did.

She was carrying a small pile of clothing that she placed in a chair near the door.

Ganfrion scowled and spun on his heel to leave. He paused beside her. They exchanged a long look that made Mikhyel wonder what new conspiracy Ganfrion was brewing against him.

"See if *you* can talk sense into him," Ganfrion growled, and slammed out the door.

Mikhyel waited until he was certain Ganfrion was gone, and he was himself in control of his emotions. There was so much he couldn't tell the man. From Mother's ability to transport Temorii and himself free of any danger, to the debt he owed the young woman herself. He simply could not be the one to rob her once again of her chance to prove her talent to the world.

And to herself.

More than that, he *wanted* to be at that competition. For his *own* sake. Rhyys would use rumor whether he attended or not. At this point his personal fate was the primary risk and he had every right—

"Khy?" Temorii's voice drew him free of his thoughts.

He held out hands which she took without hesitation. Or pain. He examined both her arms, finding on the left a thin red mark, but no more.

"Mother?" he asked; and she nodded, confirming the suspicions her sudden disappearance had roused. "And tomorrow? You'll be well enough to dance?"

Her head lowered, the mass of hair falling forward to hide her face. But she nodded again.

"I was so worried, when you didn't come back last night. What happened?"

"I went to Mother."

"And does bone take so much longer to heal than skin or hair?"

She shook her head. "It . . . wasn't my arm. It was *why* my arm happened."

"Dancing without the safety lines will do that," he said, gently chastising, but choked on the words when her head came up, and her expression said he didn't know what he was talking about. "What, then?"

"You, Khy. *You* happened."

"What did *I* do? I wanted to yell, but I didn't. I was scared out of my mind, once I realized—"

{And when did you realize, Khy?}

A thought. Clear and sweet as in Mother's cave, carrying the tartness of raspberries and the warm mystery of cinnamon.

"Rings," he whispered. "You heard me?"

She nodded.

"How much do you get?"

"Before Mother transferred us to the cave, only occasional drifts, hardly more than impressions of impressions. I *should* have known you from the very beginning."

"From the time in the woods. After Boreton?"

She nodded.

Mikhyel murmured. "I sensed it, too."

"Did you? I wondered. It cut off so quickly. But I'd changed. Or you had. I know my . . . hearing has been diminished along with the web. Perhaps we both just . . . needed our privacy. Now . . . at times, it's impossible to shut you out."

It was like his conversations with Deymorin reenacted. As his ability to hear and sense his brothers was to Nikki's and Deymorin's, so Temorii's was to his.

"Like Deymorin and Nikki," she confirmed softly.

"You know about them?"

She nodded. But of course she would.

And as with Deymorin and himself, during a moment of crisis, his uncertainty at the key moment had caused her to falter.

"Oh, sweet mother of the ley," he whispered. "Tem, I'm sorry. I'm *so* sorry."

She shrugged. "Mostly, I can block you out—"

"How?" he asked eagerly.

"I can't teach you, Khy. Not in one short night."

One night. So she was part of the conspiracy to spirit him out of Khoratum.

"Then I'll stay here. As long as it takes for me to learn."

She shook her head. "Then *I'll* leave. Perhaps Mother will take me back . . . now."

"*Why?* In your own Rakshi's name, the whole *point* of this was to get you the Dance."

"It's too dangerous for you to stay here, Khyel."

And then he realized, and was ashamed not to have thought of it sooner.

"Of course. I must leave before the competition. I'm a danger to *you*. It's worse than my trying to shut Deymorin out. You can't afford to have your attention distracted in that manner. Tem, I *am* sorry. I . . ."

He lifted a hand, let it drop before it touched her, and feeling suddenly very old, he headed for the door to send for Ganfrion, to tell him to make the arrangements.

But Temorii swirled into his path.

"I didn't mean that. I *can* handle it. You simply startled me, because you'd been so happy, so pleased with the dance until then. Your . . . appreciation simply made it better than I'd ever imagined. So when you . . . changed, I wasn't ready. I'm ready now. I've only one chance to compete, and I . . . I *want* you to be there."

She pressed her injured hand against her stomach, rubbing it with the other. He captured both hands again. "Then what is it?"

"You *must* leave, Mikhyel, right after *my* competition. And if my number comes up too late—"

"It will be last. You *know* it will be the last number called. It's certain to be rigged for *Rhyys'* maximum entertainment."

"And . . . and to make certain you're still there. You must leave before I dance, then, Khyel. You *must*."

Her logical functions were vacillating as wildly as his own tonight. Nerves. Pressure. They were both walking a narrow ledge.

He smiled and shook his head. "Immediately after. You've said you want me there. You've said it won't endanger you. I—dammit, Tem, I *want* to see this through! I *want* to see you dance. Gan can damn well get me out afterward!"

"It . . . it won't be easy. I think Rhyys plans to have you arrested right after."

"I can always get out the same way you'll get in."

She smiled faintly. "That's true, isn't it? She's back . . ." The smile disappeared. "Unless the web disintegrates completely. —Khy, no, it won't work. You must go. They'll arrest you. Ruin you, one way or the other. And if she can't get you out—"

"What do they plan to arrest me for?" he asked, interrupting her.

She blinked, then looked away. "S–seducing a radical competitor."

It was the same nonsense that had buzzed about the room after she'd left. Comments on the dress only a Rhomandi could afford, the tiara, the flaunting of tradition, and that she wouldn't get away with it if she weren't warming *his* bed.

He turned away from her, and paced the room, feeling caged already. "This is ridiculous." And, dammit, unfair. "When I think of how often I've *wanted* to do precisely what they—" He bit his lip and sent a despairing glance across to the shadows where her pale eyes echoed his dilemma. "Tem, I'm sorry. I never meant—"

Her eyes vanished, whatever feelings she might be having hidden behind long-lashed lids. She moved to the chair, and silently held out the pile she'd brought with her.

"What are those?"

"Hill clothes. From the Belisii Valley. They are . . . Mother says they are like what my parents wore. I . . . I'd like you to—to wear them tomorrow."

"I'd be proud to."

"M–more than that. If you leave with your men, they'll follow you." Her eyes came up, hard and sure. "They mean to have you, Khy, make no doubt of it. There's a Belisii trade caravan camped outside Khoratum. They're leaving during the competition tomorrow. I've arranged for you to accompany them."

"I don't—"

"You'll be safe. Far safer than ever you've been here. They'll have a head start, but Ganfrion can get you to them. They're poor folk who've pooled their assets and their products hoping to find a market in Rhomatum. I . . . told them you'd help, in exchange for safe passage."

"I won't go unless you go with me." The declaration escaped before he realized he'd thought it. "If I'm in danger, so are you. Ganfrion says you're playing Rhyys' game, that you and Thyerri have been all along. Well, I don't believe you are now, and if you've double-crossed Rhyys to this extent, it's possible not even Mother could save you."

"She'll protect me."

"She's been just a bit unreliable! It's one thing for me. Time will not exactly be of the essence. But if the rings go down, if the web collapses again, while you're dancing—who's to *say* what you'll be facing?"

"Now who's being unfair? Trying to frighten me into making *your* life simpler, dunMheric? I'll *not* be manipulated—not by Rhyys, not by Mother, and certainly not by you. You want to die—fine. Wait until tomorrow night, go leisurely to your carriage, and see how long you last in Rhyys' tender care. But don't expect me to give up what I've finally gotten. The dance is mine, to win or lose. No *matter* what Rhyys says, *I* will know. The rings will whisper the truth to me. *Rakshi* will. And if I am meant to die, let it be on *my* rings, not on some foreign city street."

"You can dance Rhomatum's Rings!" The thought was said before he realized its ramifications. "Rings! Of course! Temorii, that's it! Come *with* me. Tem, they'll love you. They've never *seen* anything like—"

"Shut up!" She sank to her knees, her hands clenched on the clothing. "Gods, you're stupid sometimes! I can't dance just *any* rings."

She was shaking with anger and fear and frustration—all of it his doing. She was going to dance tomorrow, one way or another, and in this state, it would surely mean her death.

They were both talking nonsense. They'd made one plan and never seen beyond it. If she could have been talked into leaving, the time to convince her was long past.

"I'm sorry, Tem. I'm truly, truly sorry." He crossed to her side, waited until she, very reluctantly, met his gaze. He cupped her chin in one hand, brushed the shaded hair back with the other.

"I should have known. I'm still learning. Gan . . . Ganfrion says they'll kill you, win or lose, after they have me. Or if they lose me. After the dance, *your* dance, will you come with me? You'll have your answer. You'll know . . ."

She was shaking her head slowly. "I . . . I *can't* live anywhere else, Khy. Khoratum . . . Mother . . . I'm—"

He laid a finger on her lips. "All right, I'll go with your caravan. Without—" Despite his determination, his voice broke. "—you. My brothers and I will deal with this little problem. I'll live, but I don't promise to be happy. These days with you . . . Ringfire, I've tried so hard not to feel . . . what I'm feeling. You caught me by surprise, my brave, beautiful dancer."

She jumped within his hold, and her startled gaze searched his face rather frantically.

"Are you all right?"

"Why did you call me that?" she whispered past trembling lips.

"It's what your name means, isn't it? It's what Mother called you. It's—it's what you are." His control broke and he pulled her fiercely up and into his arms. "Sometimes I hate the rings and everything about them." She hissed like an angry snake, but before she could pull away, he tightened his hold and whispered: "But without the dance, you wouldn't be you, and I might never would have known you."

"Maybe you'd be happier if you hadn't. You told Mother—"

"Never." He leaned away to see her face. "I love you, Tem. And that's something I never thought I'd be able to say to any woman—no man, other than my brothers."

"You do mean that, don't you Khy?"

"You can doubt it?"

"And yet you feared for me on the rings."

"That's contradictory?"

"Mother says if you love a dancer, you never fear for them while they are on the rings. If you love a dancer, you know that the rings won't hurt them, and if they die on the rings, they die happy, and if you love them, you won't be frightened for them, because that might make the dancer frightened."

"I was startled. You didn't warn me you were going to perform without the harness."

"Dancers don't perform, Khy."

"I stand corrected. But I didn't know, Tem. There's so much I don't know."

"We can none of us know everything, Khy."

706 *Jane S. Fancher*

They remained motionless for no little time. Then Mikhyel released her reluctantly and picked up the costume.

"When will you join Mother?"

"When I leave here. The competitors are led in at first light. She'll need to leythiate me in before they get there."

"Leythiate. Is that what you call it?"

"It's how I interpret Mother's thought."

"I see," he said, though none of it meant anything. Words, noises, anything to take his mind off her.

He spread the shirt over his arm, admiring the intricate cut and pulled work on the neck and sleeves. Black, with an iridescent leythium-dipped thread, on black. "I've seen Mirym do this. I'd swear it's even the same pattern."

"Mirym?"

"Anheliaa's servant. You'd like her, I think." He didn't mention she carried his child, but a caught breath told him Temorii had picked that image from him. "Tem, I—"

"I th–think, probably, I would," she whispered, and he murmured back:

"She's always stitching something."

"A valuable accomplishment for a mother."

"For a mother, yes," Mikhyel said. Words. Just words. But he thought then of that final interview with Mirym, of her disinclination to be his wife.

"But the child was conceived in love?" Temorii' whisper demanded assurance.

"Yes, in that love is compassion for specific individuals."

"And it will be raised in love?"

"Yes." Without qualification. Of that, he was certain. Mirym would not allow it to be otherwise. *He* would not.

"That's good, Khy. I'm glad you have a child. And you will be a good father, I think."

"Rings, I hope so. I certainly intend to try." He smoothed the patterned sleeve, and said, because he thought she deserved to know he wasn't ashamed of the fact: "I wish it were yours."

Her hand covered his, and that internal sense entreated him to meet her eyes. He was relieved to find them dry. Utterly at peace.

{Put them on, Khy, please. I want to see you in them, and this might well be my only opportunity.}

Hating the sense of urgency, worse, of conclusion, he removed his coat. She went and stood beside the window, looking out, while he changed. Careful of his modesty for once, as he had always been of hers.

Drawstring pants, wide-sleeved, voluminous tunic, open down the front, those were simple. Unfortunately, regardless how he wrapped it, the simple strip cummerbund insisted on falling off at his first deep breath. He cursed softly, and a soft chuckle happened behind him, arms wrapped around his waist to pull the strip of cloth free.

"Turn around."

He did, quickly, unthinking. The tunic fell open. The smile on her face faded as her eyes traveled slowly downward, and the cummerbund fell, unnoticed, to the floor. One trembling hand reached tentatively, brushed his bare chest. His whole body tingled, and he grasped her wrist firmly to stop any further exploration.

"Tem, please. I'm not some curiosity you can—"

"Mother says the traditions are foolish."

He closed his eyes as her callused fingertips made another circuit around his hardening nipple.

"Mother says, loving should only improve the dance, if the lover truly understands and loves the dance as I do."

"And you call me unfair!" He swallowed hard. "Dammit, Tem, your needs have kept me from touching you for what seems ten lifetimes, and now—when I'm leaving, when I'll likely never see you again —"

"Does the when matter? Does the how many times?" Another slow circuit. "I'll not have my life dictated. Mother says I should. Rhyys says I should. But I don't do this for Rhyys. I don't do it for Mother. I do it for me."

"And what about me, *Dancer*?"

She smiled. And that smile cut to his heart like no blow Mheric had ever deal him.

"I don't find this the least humorous. Neither do I care to participate in your—act of independence."

"Is that what you think this is?" And her voice caught.

Her wrist jerked from his hold. But she didn't run away. Her arms circled him, under the shirt, and her head pressed his shoulder, burrowing past the collar. Without asking his preference, his arms enfolded her. And her gown, like the robe Mother had materialized around him in the cavern, caressed his skin like living flesh.

"Perhaps you are right," she whispered. "Perhaps it is independence I seek, but not from Mother, not from Rhyys.

Not even, my sweet Khy, from you. Do you think you alone
have felt the need rising within you? Mother made me part
of your pattern long ago. I don't believe she intended this,
but it has happened. I've tried to resist it, to ignore it, but
to dance in this condition is—unthinkable. And there's only
one cure I know."

Her hands began a tingling journey across his bare skin,
her lips and tongue following the course her fingers charted,
tasting him. He staggered a wobble-kneed step backward,
setting his shoulders against the door. He buried his hands
in her luxuriant hair, unable at that moment, to think of
anything but the wonder of her touch on his body.

Sensations that, until now, had been reserved for dreams.

And dreams were all he had to guide him, when it came
to touching a woman. Dreams and a seventeenth birthday
with a prostitute and that tangled vision of his night with
Mirym.

Beyond that handful of dreams, his *experiences* were the
stuff of nightmares. The last thing he wanted was to con-
taminate this moment with some nightmare-driven mistake,
and that fear of frightening her, of hurting her, of—in any
way—ruining this moment for her, held him helpless in a
cloud of uncertainty, as her callused fingers brushed his
shoulders and down his arms, sliding the tunic free.

The tunic, like the cummerbund before it, fell to the
floor. Unkind, he thought in a dizzy haze, to the hard-
working seamstress who had created such—

Her mouth on his chest eliminated all thoughts of that
seamstress.

"I used to lie beside you in the meadow, watching while
you slept," she whispered, and her shoulder lifted as with
a deep breath, then slowly relaxed. "And sometimes I'd
wake up with my head pillowed on you, and all I could
think was how good you smelled, and when you held me,
and my lips brushed your skin, how good you tasted."

Her hand crept past the simple placket-fly of the loose
pants, and touched him, gently, sweetly, a touch not too
light, not painfully tight. Not shy, nor inhibited, though she
lacked a prostitute's obvious expertise.

His mind reeling, he frantically sought some healthy paradigm, some guideline for what he should and shouldn't
do, and as he fought to keep his knees from buckling, his
body remembered another fight for balance. An under-

ground passage, and shadows, and a red-haired temptress. And an overwhelming passion for life and . . . Deymorin and Kiyrstin . . . the day they'd entered the City.

Temorii's mouth tried to follow where her hand had led, and while his dreams reeled in images and possibilities, his mind thought of where and under what conditions this innocent must have witnessed such tactics. Or perhaps, she simply picked the images of Kiyrstin and Deymorin out of his mind.

Either way, it wasn't what he wanted. Not now. If they were to have only one time together, there would be nothing one-sided about the experience. He'd be an active participant and those actions would be his alone. Not Deymorin's, not Nikk's.

He grasped her shoulders to raise her to her feet, cupped her chin and kissed her, long and deeply, as he had in his most cherished dreams, and deciding, just perhaps, his instincts might be sound, he allowed his hands to seek her slender body beneath her simple gown's heavy folds.

He paused. Perplexed. Her mouth reached for his.

"Wait." He held up his hands, palms out, between them. "Just . . . wait."

Blinking his eyes clear of lust-induced fog, he examined the dress more closely. She giggled and gasped and swayed into his curiously searching hands, making his task that much more difficult.

Finally, laughter welled and spilled out.

{Mother!] he shouted in helpless frustration.

Temorii jumped. "What's wrong?"

"The damned thing has no fastening!" he got out, past the laughter. "Oh, my darling, we've a choice: ripping this beauty to shreds, which considering it's probably pure leythium, I doubt we could do anyway, or—"

"Doesn't bother me," she said, and swayed toward him.

"But I—"

Her breath shuddered into his mouth, she pressed hard against him, the full length of her body until he was pressed full against the wall. Her hands lost the wonder, and pressed deep into muscle. A bit rough. A bit desperate.

He gasped a complaint; she wrapped her arms around him and clung there, shuddering.

"Sweet, sweet, *sweet* Mother," she sobbed into his neck, "I'm sorry, Khy, I—I didn't *know* . . . I want . . . you."

Her arms tightened spasmodically, relaxed in a flare of deliberate denial. "Please?"

There was no sense denying his own desire, but . . . "Tem," his voice was a hoarse whisper. "Rings, are you *sure*?"

"Oh, Khy." Her voice caught on a laugh. "How *can* you wonder?"

And like fingers in his head, she began to separate her own sensations from his, eliminating a duality of thought and desire and feelings he'd had no idea was there.

And without it, he felt . . . naked. Exposed and lonely in a way he'd never imagined.

"Please, Tem . . ." His voice, what little there was, shook uncontrollably. And a sob tightened his throat.

"Please, Tem, what?" She mocked him, but gently.

"Come back to me?"

"Oh, *yes*." And when she returned to his mind, it was with a depth of passion and need that left him dizzy. She drew him to the bed, or he drew her, and they lay down together. And together, they pulled the heavy leythium folds up between them.

But she alone guided him to a softness that had nothing to do with clothing.

All the while, he kept his eyes on her beloved face, waiting for her to change her mind, hoping desperately to be able to give her that option.

Fortunately, the request never came, and there was no denying that internal verification of her wishes and her needs. Releasing all hope of rational control, he pressed into the softness—and very nearly lost all inclination to touch anyone, ever again.

Any remaining doubts he harbored regarding her experience vanished in that instant. No question now, even for his limited experience, that it was her first time, less that his entry hurt her; it wasn't painless for him. And the sense of surprise/fear/pain/curiosity that accompanied her scent could not be fabricated.

But when he would have drawn back—some vague, years-gone warning of Deymio's—she muttered an objection, and withdrew her mind from his, with an abruptness that left him gasping, even as the pain disappeared. Then she twined her legs over his back, and thrust up and around him, while smothering a wordless cry in his shoulder.

For several breathless moments, she clung there, quivering against him and around him, while those old warnings of Deymorin's ran through his head, along with the memory of her pain, and he knew, no matter how much his body wanted it, that it would not be at all kind to—

{Oh, Khy. You *think* too much . . .}

And again she infiltrated his mind and body. The pain, that was still there, but minor, and other sensations that approached pain, in areas of his body that he . . . didn't have. Like, and yet unlike his own.

And within those areas he didn't have, the presence that pressed and thrilled and pained those nerve endings began to change in character. He no longer felt quite so . . . full.

{You're thinking again.}

And she began to move and sway, like the rings themselves, and never had he been more aware of her lithe power as she drew him into the dance with her. And the sense of being filled returned, the pressure increased as Temorii drove them both to a mind-shattering climax.

They collapsed, shuddering, still locked together. When he would have withdrawn, she curled her top leg tighter, holding him steady, and whispered, "Not yet, Khy. Please, just a moment more."

And as that moment stretched into a lifetime, she neither moved nor spoke, she seemed not even to breathe, and he found himself imprinting the feel/sight/taste/smell of her on his memory, knowing he'd never forget how he felt at that instant, never again smell raspberries or cinnamon the same way.

Raspberries, cinnamon, and the slightest hint of clove. A mystical blend that would forever be part of him.

Perhaps, that was her intention.

Then, with a tiny sigh, she slid free.

And all he could think of was . . . never again.

Chapter Fourteen

Mikhyel drifted slowly toward consciousness on the dawn tide. To escape the gentle, but persistent, glow from the window, he buried his nose into Temorii's soft hair.

Except . . . Temorii should be with Mother by now, possibly already deep within the heart of the maze. And upon a startled opening of his eyes, he discovered a Tem-shaped pillow within his arms: Mother's doing, indeed.

Morning. The competition. This evening, he'd leave Khoratum. Forever. Mikhyel groaned and buried his face deep in the Tem-pillow, cursing fate in one breath, praising it in the following.

He had found what poets called the perfect love. Found it, attained it, and in true poetic style, must leave it forever. The one perfect moment. The sweet agony of self-sacrifice.

The poets must all be eunuches.

Tugging the bellpull to notify Raulind his master had come to whatever sense remained his to achieve, Mikhyel hauled himself up and out of bed. As he saw to morning needs, he discovered blood.

Cursing them both for fools, he hurried back to the bedroom, and a sheet that, while not covered in blood, certainly betrayed evidence to make a man horrified at what he'd done on the eve of so important an event.

"Oh, Tem," he murmured, and wished her well. And a stream of satisfied sentience wove through his mind, reassurance that Temorii had awakened without pain, without concern . . . and an annoying case of self-doubt nothing could change.

{Because of what happened?} he sent back up that stream, and as his question reached the source, he had an image of Mother, bored, soaking her feet in a leythium pool.

{Of course. And no.}

Mikhyel laughed. Mother: at her frustratingly ambiguous best.

{Then at what? Dearest Mother, can I help her?}

{At her own ability. Couldn't do the simplest handstand when she awoke.}

{Nerves, Mother. Normal, eminently human nerves. They'll make her dance even better.}

{Is that a promise?}

{Is anything a certainty?}

{Yes, but not those things we choose. Perhaps I should watch.}

{I think Tem would like that, Mother.}

{I'll see if I find the energy. Go hop in the bath, child: your friend called the maids and they're just outside his door.}

The angle on the rings was different, here in the ringmaster's box, where the intent was to be seen as much as to see the dance. But it also afforded one of the best stadium views of the maze that comprised the other half of the stadium crescent. The stadium seating had been cut out of the hillside, the stone-walled maze built up out of the downhill side, angled and leveled for optimum viewing from the stands.

The coaching box was closer to the rings, lower, almost to ground level—and contained better company.

Rhyys had insisted Mikhyel join him in his box. He'd wanted to show the increasingly anti-Rhomatum citizens of Khoratum that their beloved ringmaster and the ruling family of Rhomatum were the best of friends, and that Khoratum could sleep soundly, knowing their interests were covered.

In other words, Rhyys wanted to lie.

The only other individual to join them in the booth for breakfast was a man Rhyys introduced as dunGarshin, an importer from beyond the storm-rim. But unless Khoratum Tower housed two hideously scarred men, this dunGarshin was young Thyerri's ocarshi-smoking Mauritumin.

He said little, ate and drank sparingly, but his eyes never left Mikhyel. His hands, scarred and twisted, bore many rings, but none of them remotely resembling the Rhomandi ring Mikhyel wore.

He'd dismiss the notion out of hand, but if this dunGarshin knew what that ring was, he'd be unlikely to flaunt it in Mikhyel's presence today.

During the mostly silent breakfast, the stands filled steadily, seemingly everyone from the city and the surrounding hills intent on viewing the spectacle. For some, Nikki's notes had explained, it was a religious event: Rakshi's selection of a worldly representative; for others, it was blood sport, eager anticipation of the inevitable wounds, regular maimings and occasional deaths; and for some, it was sheer love of beauty.

For Mikhyel dunMheric, it was nerve-wracking.

He didn't know, couldn't, unless Mother or Temorii chose to inform him, whether the plan was proceeding: whether Temorii was waiting in that simple building at the center of the stone maze, whether Ganfrion had managed to prepare his men to move out during the ceremony, whether his staff would successfully exit the Tower through those passages Temorii had shown them, or whether they would all find themselves arrested by the end of the day.

It was tempting to grow impatient, when regular check-ins were possible. But Temorii was justifiably silent, preparing for the greatest moment of her life. Mother . . . Mother was probably enjoying his incipient panic.

Music filled the air constantly. Down on the white sand, color festivities were already in progress. Student dancers of all ages performed complex choreographed routines, trained animal acts, a magician or two . . . Deymorin and Nikki would have loved it.

As if choreographed, their breakfast's conclusion and the opening ceremony coincided. By the time the announcer introduced Rhyys, the table had been cleared and removed, an ocarshi brazier erected between Rhyys and dunGarshin, and tea arrived for the others who were ushered into the box.

Dignitaries of the Northern Crescent, all. Some of whom Mikhyel had known were here and visited in the past week, others whom he recognized by name only.

Including Nethaalye's father.

Rhyys rose and delivered a disjointed and self-aggrandizing statement to the audience. It was a terrifying ordeal. This *could not* be the same man Anheliaa selected fifteen years ago. Anheliaa, though mad, had never intended to sacrifice Khoratum. Ocarshi and a surfeit of power had destroyed whatever Anehliaa had known.

And opened the way for the scar-faced man's ilk. If it hadn't been Mauritum, it would have been some other lurking hawk. Khoratum and Rhyys had been their weak link for years.

He only hoped they didn't pay dearly for that oversight today.

Rhyys' monologue seemed destined to absorb the entire morning, but he ended abruptly, and with utter incoherence, when a tiny buzzer sounded within the box. He turned, then, to the booth's interior, and introduced, one at a time those seated there.

As if he were pointing to trophies in a case. Polite to outrageous applause greeted each man as he stood, until Rhyys came, finally and at last, to Mikhyel.

He stood to utter silence.

Stunned, he sank back down. Nikki's rumors, his own sheets this morning, and the maids. He cursed again his own stupidity within a web that needed no more division, a situation that required no more volatility. And yet, hypocrite that he was, he found it impossible to regret the events of the previous night.

The organized performances began. More of the student dancers. More music. More . . . everything. All around him, the leaders of the Northern Crescent talked and laughed and shared rumors.

Many of those rumors centered openly around the Rhomandi sitting within easy earshot. They knew. They all knew. They believed he was doomed and used this opportunity to taunt him.

Stupid, petty, and so human. But his mind took him into the future. A future that assumed he and his brothers won everything they hoped, when he would have to face these same individuals across a courtroom and determine their guilt or innocence in a game so much larger than individual pride, and he wondered just how much objectivity he would be able to maintain.

He wondered if any of the men and women sitting here had ever considered the possibility of failure.

If *he* failed, if he was wrong to trust Mother, or if any of a number of variables went against him, he could die.

But he wouldn't have run. He wouldn't have deserted Temorii and he wouldn't have run from a petty tyrant.

Strange, to have so important a decision boil down to something as simple as personal pride.

And suddenly, it was time. The sand was cleared and dragged a final time. A hush fell over the stadium. On his platform on the stand beside the rings, the arbiter pulled a red-and-gold banner from the container and raised it on the staff.

The number thirty-three billowed out and a roar went up from the crowd.

Chosen for luck by the contestants, plucked at random, these numbers meant no more than identification. Within the central courtyard, that number would be announced, and a contestant's perilous journey to the rings would begin.

Each guest in Rhyys' box had been presented elegant, engraved, gold-and-silver viewing glasses. As the music began, Mikhyel trained his on that distant building, to which the contestants had supposedly been led that morning.

The plain doorway sprang into sharper view, and a slim, lithe figure in sparkling red and gold emerged. Five steps forward, to a stone turning. A wooden gate to either side: only one opened. On its far side, a blade swept in an arc at waist level. The audience could see, the contestant could not. The audience had been given a key to the maze, the contestant had not.

The gate swung open, the blade swept toward the contestant. He dropped, flat to the ground, sprang up the moment the blade passed overhead, and dashed for the far end—

Where only solid stone awaited.

Retreat, then, another clash with the blade, and a second attempt at the locked gate, which this time opened smoothly.

But time had been lost on the clock that spun atop the arbiter's tower, ticking off the minutes. Energy had been wasted. The contestant's confidence had been shaken. All of these things, Temorii had told him, could affect the final outcome.

The rest of the maze contained similar tests of endurance and wit. No two tricks were the same, though some were variations on themes. Seemingly solid stone shifted beneath a dancer's feet here, there it was a mirror-made illusion. Blades, falling stones, false avenues . . . all designed to test and exhaust and delay the contestant.

Time was important, but so, Temorii had said, was the style in which one extricated oneself from the dilemmas. No one expected to go freely through, although some could expect easier times than others, as not all took the same route and not all the traps worked every time.

The red-and-gold #33 entered the stadium at last, panting, and staggering . . . and the music began. In an obvious attempt to regain dignity and strength, the contestant followed an undulating path across the sand. By the time he reached the tower ladder, he was able, with some grace, to writhe his way to the top, never losing the intricate rhythms of the accompaniment.

Granted he had no baseline from which to judge, but to Mikhyel, the young man looked very impressive. And his performance on the rings, though perhaps not as inspired as Temorii's practice session, certainly gained the approval of the audience.

When he was finished, the sand was dragged and the next contestant's number announced.

And so it was, with contestant after contestant, each seeming better than the preceding, until you realized it was the uniformity of skill that made the one currently competing appear the best. There were no bad runs, as Temorii insisted he call them, not even mediocre ones. They were all one step short of awesome.

And it was that step, he began to think, that must set the true Rakshi dancers apart.

After each run, the sand was dragged to pristine beauty. The best runs left recognizable patterns in the sand . . . yet one more challenge, one more consideration for the dancer.

And after each run, the successful contestant was presented a golden robe and led with ceremony to a ground-level viewing box to watch their competitors.

Another minor torment Rhyys thrust upon them. Temorii had said more than once that she *hated* watching other dancers on *her* rings. Temorii was, he thought, very possessive.

Six runs complete. Five more to go. The number 00 painted on a rag fluttered out from the pole, and a figure in leather and beads, with shoulder-length, shaded hair stepped from the central courtyard.

Thyerii. And as audacious as he'd been last night. Mikhyel felt a smile tug at his mouth, and settled back in his chair to enjoy the show.

The street-lad's maze time, while not the fastest, compared with the best, and his trip was the most entertaining by far, as he darted and twisted and laughed his way past all obstacles. He seemed indefatigable, entering the stadium at a run and bolting for the rings, scorning the fancy dance across the sand, obviously with a single goal in mind. Leaving only gaps where he leaped the largest rings as they swept past him, his tracks made a direct line to the tower.

His trip up the ladder was one large, swaying arc after another, and at the top, he grabbed the safety lines from the attendant and lunged outward for the rings, fastening them himself as he fell.

The audience went wild.

His performance on the rings proved equally thrilling and energetic, and Mikhyel assumed he'd seen Temorii's competition, when, suddenly, a poorly calculated twist, a too-fast spinning ring, and the line was severed. The young man's body swung crazily through the rings, and he landed in a heap in the sand.

Silence, then, utter and complete, as a red stain spread slowly from beneath him.

Silence, while the surgeon's crew lifted the slight body onto a stretcher and took it from the stadium, and the grounds crew spread new sand to hide the stain.

When Mikhyel came to his senses, he discovered he was on his feet, at the front of the box, straining for a final glimpse of the young man he'd once mistaken for Temorii. As suddenly as the vital, passionate young hiller had entered his life, he was gone.

In shock, he returned to his seat. As he eased into the deep-cushioned seat, his gaze registered Rhyys, and slipped past, appalled and disgusted. Rhyys was smiling, oblivious to the value of the life that had been lost. Or perhaps, he knew exactly what had been lost, and reveled in it.

And Mikhyel wondered whether Raulind and Sakhithe had come, as they'd considered doing, and tried not to imagine what Sakhithe was thinking and feeling now, if she had.

The next number appeared on the tower; Mikhyel couldn't read it, couldn't hear the announcement for the buzzing in his ears. And then, he did know what Sakhithe was feeling:

If you love a dancer, you know that the rings won't hurt them, and if they die on the rings they die happy. . . .

And he hoped Sakhithe *was* here, and had seen Thyerii's dance to Rakshi.

The current contestant, oblivious to the fate of the preceding one, had a pleasant, clean run through the maze, and what had become a fairly standard routine among the rings. And the next was equally innocuous. And Mikhyel wondered if the runs were truly that banal, or if he'd simply lost all enthusiasm for what he watched.

"Excuse me, sir . . ." A servant appeared at his side, with a teapot that wafted a familiar, stomach-settling scent into the air: Raulind *had* seen Thyerri's dance. And Raulind, with Raulind's unerring sense of his master's needs, had sent him exactly what he needed to make it through the rest of the competition.

He offered a silent blessing on Raulind's absent head, and accepted the cup and saucer the servant extended.

A thick napkin beneath made holding the cup awkward. He sipped the level down, then endeavored to extricate the napkin with some grace.

Between its folds was an envelope.

Mikhyel swallowed hard.

Number twenty-seven, in white on black, fluttered out from the pole.

Temorii's number. His choice, at her request. His age. As of tomorrow morning.

The door of the courtyard did not open.

Mikhyel drained the cup of tea, and slipped the envelope into his pocket as he set the cup aside.

The number was called a second time.

A messenger arrived in the booth and whispered in Rhyys' ear. Rhyys smiled, slowly, cruelly.

And a third droning announcement.

"It appears, dunMheric," Rhyys said, "that there is no one left in—"

The door opened. A black figure emerged, and the crowd roared.

Time lost. Mother and her grand gestures. Still, Mikhyel easily returned Rhyys' smile. In triplicate.

Temorii tried one gate, the locked one, tried the other, cracked it . . . and waited. The blade swung, she grinned, a smile that required no viewing glass to see, and took a leaping dive over the locked gate; her shaded hair, pulled up into a tail, whipped behind her head. She rolled on the far side, then skipped and tumbled the length of the passage to the next turn.

A foolish risk: there could have been a different sort of deathtrap on the far side of the locked gate, but it was a flamboyant action that sent the crowd to its feet. If Temorii could see or hear them, she gave no indication. She seemed to have no fear, constantly second-guessing the designers of the maze, sometimes winning the gamble, sometimes losing the gamble, but always winning the game with a show of strength, dexterity, and fast thinking.

But she took her time, using breath-catching lulls to stealthily move along, making a show of great suspicion and overcaution: an illusion she'd shatter the moment her breathing eased. Her actions proclaimed to all and sundry: I only get one chance to do this, and I'm going to enjoy it.

And that thrill spread to those watching.

This was the imp that ordered servants about, then flopped to the floor at his side to catch bits of ham in its mouth. This was the rakehell-in-training who challenged Ganfrion, the crazed fool who tripped lightly along mountain cliffs. This was the essence of life on the edge and the engagingly insane who lived there.

A second message slowly came clear, at least to him. Somehow, Temorii knew what had happened to Thyerri. Twice, three times, her response to the maze exactly duplicated that of Thyerri's fatal run. By the third time, he could almost hear her telling them: remember the run, remember the challenge. Remember the skill and joy with which he faced that challenge—and this one, and this—and won.

And with that realization, the last of Mikhyel's reservations vanished. He sat on the edge of his seat, running that maze with her, jumping, dodging, twisting and spinning, laughing when she laughed, gasping when she gasped. He felt it all. Whether that sharing was deliberate, and only between the two of them, or a by-product of her skill that everyone in the audience shared, he neither knew nor really cared.

No one watched the clock, *no* one cared, except the musicians, who began playing the moment she reached the entrance to the arena.

She paused in the shadow of that opening, then darted back into the maze, as if to stay there and play. A cry of protest erupted from the crowd, and within moments, unison clapping urged her, in time with the music, to come out to them.

The second time she appeared, the daring imp who had laughed her way through the maze had vanished, and in her place was the living embodiment of the music that filled the stadium. The slender, black figure undulated, spun and flitted her way about the white sand. Her iridescent sash came free to float in trailing spirals around her.

Like the radical streamer in the Tower.

Her hair was loose now, and it shimmered, itself almost iridescent in the sunlight.

Ley-touched, he'd heard some people call such an effect, and he wondered if they knew how accurate a description that was.

By the time she reached the stadium seats, her tracks in the groomed sand had left a pattern: a stylized web surrounded by concentric rings. Mikhyel swallowed hard, and wondered if anyone else in the stadium recognized the Rhomandi crest; a chuckle from the area of the ocarshi brazier assured him that at least one other someone had.

And as Temorii passed beneath them, they could all see the trim at her throat and wrists that echoed the leythium-touched cut-work of Mikhyel dunMheric's garment.

Subtlety, he decided, was not his Temorii's long suit.

Laughter reached him, indicating his thoughts were not alone, but Temorii's twisting path spun her away, as the music shifted to a rhythmic staccato, and in a final tumbling run, she struck the bottom, ground-sweeping ring and rode it nearly to the top where she launched herself toward the tower.

Her loft was high, much too high, but before anyone had

time to react, she'd grabbed the central pole of the tower and spun her way downward to land lightly on the platform. The music spun to a close with her.

Surrounded by silence, she stood quietly while the attendant affixed the lines to the light harness that was part of every costume.

Refusing, again, to be hurried.

And then, instead of leaping immediately out among the rings, she took a wrap of the safety line in her hand, and lowered herself slowly from the platform, one foot looped in a length of the line. A light shove carried the swinging boom that supported the line outward.

Then, she began to sway. The music began as a nearly inaudible hum, and rose slowly, matching her pendulum motion's growing intensity and exploded into sound as her ever-increasing arc finally intersected the rings.

From that point, any hope for her competition ended. To that point, all she'd done might have been show, might, the envious would say, have been to delay her getting on the rings, to baffle the audience with early flash so that the true purpose of the competition was forgotten.

She performed what he'd come to think of as the standard moves, showing competence equal to all who had come before, but it was in her variations that her true artistry came to life, and by the time she slipped the harness free and rode the outermost ring down, cradled like a child—or a lover—in its curve, she *was* the radical dancer of Khoratum.

Even after the music's final notes faded, the crowd remained silent. Temorii, free of the ring's support, staggered . . . and collapsed into the sand at the exact spot where Thyerri had fallen. Mikhyel ached for her, longed to be able to pick her up and carry her out. But he couldn't. No one could. He couldn't even reach out with that internal sense to lend her strength; she'd reject it if he tried.

Survival: the final test. The dancer had to walk out of the arena on her own strength.

And as the silence dragged on, one of the other contestants stood slowly and began clapping in rhythm, announcing to all his concession. Temorii pushed herself up to her knees.

One at a time, the other contestants rose to join the first, clapping in unison. Temorii lifted a hand covered with red-stained sand, and touched the sand to her lips.

The crowd picked up the dancers' rhythm, and with their approval, raised Temorii to her feet, and carried her out of the stadium.

He'd waited too long, or perhaps simply been outmaneuvered. When Rhyys invited him to take part in the award ceremony, he knew there was no option.

Foolishly, perhaps, he wasn't truly worried. Let Rhyys arrest them: Mother would get them out. And even though he knew that to count on such a fickle resource was irresponsible in the extreme, *something* had to explain the eagerness with which he followed Rhyys out of the ringmaster's box.

Perhaps his ill-advised confidence had nothing to do with Mother and everything to do with the wild imp who had stolen his heart and taken over his better sense, his excitement now a backlash of the confidence that had sent Temorii flying from one part of the maze to the next.

Confidence that, in the end, she could cope with whatever Rakshi threw at her. Confidence that *he* could. Confidence that this was where he was meant to be.

In the time it took for them to walk down the steps and through the tunnels beneath the stadium and into the arena, an elaborately decorated podium had been wheeled out onto the sand. Standing atop that podium, while the officials droned on about voting rules, historical precedent and ties, Mikhyel found himself hard pressed not to search the area for Temorii.

But the dancers had all been taken away, the official said. They'd be brought up on the podium, one at a time, in the order they'd danced, and the applause of the masses would determine the winner.

The official vote began. One at a time, the contestants came up to stand beside the official pollster, who duly noted the relative volume of the rhythmic applause each incited by adjusting the order of the numbers on the tower.

The ordering seemed rather arbitrary to Mikhyel, and he wondered if that was always the case, and if so, protests must be frequent. But there were no protests today.

The number 00 was called. And a somber man stepped forward to say that the spirit of contestant #00 had joined Rakshi that day, and that the body of contestant #00 would be immersed in three days. There was silence, then deafening applause, acknowledgment of the greatness of the spirit that had touched them that day.

But the name Thyerri was never mentioned. It did seem a rather inhuman approach to loss.

Two more numbers, two more shifts of the numbers on the tower . . .

The final number was lost in the screams of the crowd. In places along the perimeter, guards were forced to physically restrain members of the audience. Temorii, coming up the back stairs as had all the others, hesitated. She appeared stunned, even frightened of the reaction she'd engendered.

Mikhyel, standing at the rear of the podium, edged over and held out a hand—and a thought—to steady her. She took the hand, and her fears and startlement at the audience's actions came through in a breath-stealing rush. There was elation at seeing him, but fear as well, and a dismayed: {You should be gone!} reached him.

And yet, she clung to his hand as if it were the dancer's safety line, as he led her to the center of the stage, where her new subjects could adore her.

{I'm not a queen/king/royal!} came down the line of thought to him, and he answered:

{Tell *them* that. Relax, my darling dancer, enjoy it. *Rakshi knows* you've earned it.}

A chuckle, nervous but real, shook her shoulders. A hand pressed his shoulder, and cold metal touched his hand. A coronet. Another round of silent laughter passed between them: queen, indeed.

He glanced up, discovered the hand on his shoulder was not, as he'd expected, Rhyys', but dunGarshin's. Rhyys stood well down the podium, sulky, angry—and yet not interfering, for all he'd obviously expected to be at center stage for this moment.

And on dunGarshin's hand, the one resting on his shoulder, was the Rhomandi ring. Beyond that ring, the twisted mouth pulled in what might be termed a smile. Mikhyel knew, then, that whatever trap they planned had already sprung and their prey simply hadn't yet felt the bite of cold steel into his flesh.

Dismay, horror, and {All my fault} came down his hold on Temorii's hand.

{Never,} he returned. {I knew the risk, and would do it all again.}

{I felt you with me. Especially when I began to tire.}

{Is *that* why I'm so exhausted?}

But he knew it wasn't true. That she *hadn't* drawn when he willingly would have given. She'd needed to do it on her own . . .

{Not entirely. Did you enjoy the run, my lazy Khy?}

With a completely unforced grin, he released her hand to face her. Taking the coronet into both hands, he lifted it above her head.

The crowd roared.

He settled it on her shaded hair.

A second approving wave of sound surged to engulf them, and surged again. A sound that failed to compete with the pounding in his ears: his heart and hers, beating in synchrony.

Only this morning, they'd shunned him, condemning him for rumors. Now, the facts disproved the rumors, or so the mob believed, and he was acceptable. What they'd witnessed, their mutable logic declared, couldn't be tainted.

So damned fickle. So blindly judgmental. So unmitigatedly cruel.

And as his fingertips brushed the sable hair at her temples and her own breathing quickened, he thought of those stained sheets and the charges soon to be leveled officially against him. Charges Rhyys was certain to use to destroy Temorii as well.

And he wondered would this crowd, who so quickly embraced and forgot, forget again as quickly in order to destroy? Would they, whose lives were so narrowly defined and self-consumed, who condemned him so freely for seeking that which they all took for granted in their lives, destroy her at a madman's whim?

He thought of that mindless, practicing mob who had attacked her the day they met, and knew his answer.

And he thought of the lover he'd never have, and her daring trip through the maze, a trip they'd shared, and the caress of the swinging rings and the caress of her callused fingertips.

And he thought of Nikki attacking him for kissing

Mirym, and of Deymorin, whose infatuation with Kiyrstin
would surround him the rest of his life . . .

A life destined for solitude, even if he survived the upcoming hours. Without his brothers, whose thoughts drove
him mad, without Temorii, whose laughter and fears and
determination had restored *his* humanity, far more than
anything he'd done for her.

And he thought of Mother, whose aid was whimsical and
on her own schedule. And he thought of the impending
shutdown and the suspicion and of Kirish'lan angry in the
south and Mauritum and Garetti, and all the web-
spanning politics . . .

And damning them all, he kissed her.

Silence.

When he would have released her, she wrapped her arms
around his neck and kissed him back. And in the underneath sense, it was last night all over again, and her trip
through the maze and the rings, and the mountains, and
his salvation from the brink of death, and hers from the
brink of despair.

A low hiss, spotted throughout the stands, and growing.
Anger from her subjects. Anger toward the one destroying
the dancer they'd adopted. He heard it, she did, and knew
their moment ended. With a final mental caress they
stepped apart.

Rhyys called, in outraged tones, for his arrest. Leather
gauntleted hands seized his arms, and pulled him away
from Temorii, who, in response to his mental request,
stepped quietly toward the back. The guards, finding passivity where they obviously expected resistance, seemed confused, uncertain, but Rhyys, grandly sweeping to his
coveted center stage, and in a gesture meant for the upper
tiers, drew back his heavily beringed hand and struck Mikhyel across the face.

The crowd roared their approval of a scene increasingly
reminiscent of some melodramatic play, which abhorrent
realization made Mikhyel doubly grateful for the guards
holding him. He'd hate to give the crowd the satisfaction
of seeing him sprawled at Rhyys' feet.

"Remove him!" Rhyys bellowed, and Temorii started
forward; Mikhyel begged her back, wishing her silent and
quiet. For now, she was innocence defiled. In time, Khoratum would embrace her as their radical.

{Not after this!} Her thought followed him down the steps. And: {I don't *want* them. Not any more.}

Wry laughter filled him. Rather late to decide that.

{Just dance again for them, Temorii. They'll be entranced all over.}

{How can I? I didn't dance for *them* in the first place.}

The guards were escorting him into the tunnel beneath the stands, he paused at last, unable to resist a final glance, never minding it simply added to the crowd's sense of melodrama.

{For me, then? Please, Tem, I want to feel you dancing inside me again.}

And he wanted her to stop thinking about him, to think about saving herself. The various officials were leaving the podium, pointedly ignoring her, ready to leave her to the citizens she'd so completely betrayed.

Excitement flowed from her, a sense of possibility—

And in one smooth action, she whirled and leaped for the ring poised quietly beside the podium. Her weight started it moving. A guard moved to stop her, but she leaped for the next ring, and the next, and the next.

Once they were spinning to her satisfaction, she began to dance, to a music everyone watching had to hear within them. It was a challenge she made; daring those unbelievers to consider her gift compromised. Daring them to expect more of anyone than she had been willing and able to give.

Mikhyel ached for her, knowing to his own joints how tired she was, and he wished her the strength to convince them. He sent, along that invisible line between them, all the help she'd refused before. And he felt her willing absorption of it now, draining him, making his head spin as with a sudden loss of blood.

And he sent her more, flinging it down that line: Strength, confidence . . . love.

It was love her dance offered to every individual watching. Love of self, of life, of beauty, of others; it was last night, and all the nights before, the bitter-sweet of self-restraint, the ecstasy of fulfillment, the fear of loss, the joy of having had.

Mikhyel couldn't move. Tears burned his eyes and he couldn't so much as lift a hand to wipe them clear. She'd burn herself out, convincing them. She meant to die on the rings, rather than at the hands of the audience, or Rhyys' planted assassins.

And she meant them to know, before she died, exactly what they'd lost.

"For the love of my sacred mother's womb, Suds, do you expect the poor kid to keep it going forever? —*Wake the fuck up!*"

Ganfrion. Jerking on his elbow, drawing his stumbling feet past guards lying motionless on the ground, pulling him down the dark tunnel. He was numb, near mindless with exhaustion and impending loss.

"Tem?"

"Is saving your ass. Shut up and say thank you, and move!"

"Wait!" He jerked free, swaying, and closed his eyes.

{*Mother!*} He made the call a demand. Mother was the only one who could save Temorii. And he reached deep into those caverns and screamed for acknowledgment. For aid that, *dammitall,* he and Temorii had earned.

Nothing. Cold, dark, uncaring silence.

{*Mother! Damn you!*}

Still, it was silent. And he knew, beyond doubt, he'd destroyed them all. He'd gambled senselessly with his own life and Temorii's.

Ganfrion was pulling him, blindly, down the tunnel. He jerked free again, and staggered back toward the stadium.

Temorii had never stopped dancing. She was weakening. A near miss that made the enthralled audience gasp as one. Again, he poured himself out to her. Everything he had, while screaming for Mother's help, for Mother to leythiate her Dancer to safety.

His vision faded. Hearing did. His only senses were those he shared with her as she soared from one ring to the next, so exhausted, her only thought was for the next jump.

And then, suddenly, painfully, his own body returned to him. He was in the tunnel, with Ganfrion's broad shoulder biting into his stomach and Ganfrion's sword hilt bouncing in front of his nose.

He gasped. Ganfrion swung him down and panted, *"Run, damn you!"*

At the far end of the tunnel, a figure was waiting.

"Thyerri?" Mikhyel whispered, disbelieving. "Alive?"

And mocking laughter, unmistakable. "What do rijhili know? Come. Come!"

"But—" Even Ganfrion, for once, sounded stunned. He glanced back down the tunnel, and then to the cloaked figure, who gestured them again to hurry, shook his head as if to clear it, and hauled on Mikhyel's elbow, moving him in the young man's wake, down alleyways and between buildings, a circuitous route heading generally downhill.

A bell pealed. Others, all about the city, picked up the alarm.

"They're after us now, Rhomandi. Thyerri-lad, look sharp!"

And Thyerri, at the far side of a building, raised an acknowledging arm, but didn't look back, and a moment later, waved them forward again.

Their luck ran out just short of the gate. A handful of guards spotted them down an alley and began closing. Cautiously, as if expecting more than the three of them.

"Give up, Rhomandi," one called. "It's over. The dancer's dead."

His heart stopped . . .

Ganfrion drew his sword.

"Get him out of here, boy."

. . . and started.

"Ganfrion . . ."

"Of all the times in your life, Rhomandi, don't be a fool now."

Without taking his eyes from the approaching guards, Ganfrion transferred his sword to his left hand, reached back with the right. Mikhyel clasped it reflexively, speechless, even while he knew this was, ultimately, Ganfrion's job.

"You're a good man, Rhomandi. If I've got to die for someone, I'm glad Rakshi chose you."

But he didn't *want* it to be Ganfrion's job. He didn't *want* good people dying to save him.

"Gan—"

"Just don't waste it."

Waste it. Ganfrion had committed himself to the Rhomandi cause . . . to Mikhyel's cause, without reservation. Was dying, never knowing . . .

"Dammitall! Get him *out* of here, boy! Get him to his brother!"

730 Jane S. Fancher

Ganfrion pushed him away, into Thyerri's arms. Mikhyel jerked free and pulled the Rhomandi ring free of his middle finger.

"Ganfrion!"

Angry dark eyes glared at him over a broad shoulder. Mikhyel tossed the ring, a flash of silver and gold in the band of sunlight between them.

Ganfrion's quick reflexes intercepted it.

"Damn you, Rhomandi." His deep whisper was more vibration than tone.

"Get out if you can, my friend," Mikhyel said, and by that ring, made that statement Ganfrion's primary directive.

Then he followed Thyerri's impatient pull at last. Around one corner, and a second—into a blind alley.

Thyerri jerked him to a halt.

"The game is over, dunMheric," Thyerri said. "The pattern is set."

Riddles. When a man was dying.

"Are you mad?" Mikhyel tried to push past, but an iron-fingered hand caught his arm and thrust him against the nearest building. "Not necessary, pretty Khy."

"Damn you—" He tried to pull free, to get back to Ganfrion, where the sounds of metal clashing evidenced the fury of the encounter.

Stone-hard arms clamped him tight.

"Ganfrion!" Mikhyel shouted; and Thyerri hissed, "Don't fight me, child."

Child?

He stopped struggling and stared into that hood-shadow.

"Don't worry about him, Khy. He's not the one they want."

"Who are you?"

"Someone who loves you, Mikhyel-child." And within the hood-shadow, light glinted. A faint green glow. And hands clasped his face, freezing him to the marrow as lips closed on his. Lethargy filled him through that kiss, the immobility that had gripped him in his room so many long weeks ago.

Anheliaa, his mind made the connection, and remote panic threatened, though in truth, he knew better.

{Anheliaa! —Hardly. Farewell, sweet Khy.}

And as Mother's spring green essence consumed him—
{Tell your brothers: the demonstration is scheduled for midnight tonight. . . .}
He opened his eyes inches from Deymorin's startled face.

Chapter Fifteen

Midnight. A time for ghosts and goblins, for Tamshi tales and falling stars, for love-making and . . .

. . . Certainly *not* for political grandstanding.

"If Rhyys wanted to make a point," Nikki said, his tension finding outlet in irritation, "why didn't he do it during the day when he could cause meaningful chaos?"

"Obviously," Kiyrstin said dryly, "Rhyys' point is not to cause maximum chaos, but to frighten whoever he expects to be in charge of Rhomatum and the Southern Crescent. He means to startle and frighten, not destroy. He still *needs* Rhomatum."

They waited in the Tower: himself, Lidye, Kiyrstin, Nethaalye, and Mirym. For what, no one truly knew. Lidye had said, after that test, that she could feel the nodes through Nethaalye and Mirym, but wasn't certain what she felt through Kiyrstin.

They'd know soon enough, he supposed.

His brothers had contacted him just hours ago. Mikhyel, according to Deymorin, had appeared on Deymorin's lap in the middle of his supper. Mother's doing, Mikhyel had said, and refused to answer questions, and his mind was darker and more closed than ever to Nikki's tentative probe—to which Mikhyel had snarled at him to mind his own fucking business.

Which nearly convinced him all over again that somewhere, someone—likely Mother—had slipped a changeling in on them.

But Deymorin had caught that real fear and insisted otherwise, and said they should believe when Mikhyel said the Northern Crescent would shut down at midnight tonight, and prepare accordingly, and to be ready, in case Garetti made a grab at Rhomatum itself.

They'd warned the Southern Crescent days ago about the

impending demonstration via carefully worded messages, couriered directly to the node ringmasters. After his contact with his brothers, they'd sent the simple: *Midnight tonight* via the message encoders on the Tower's communication level.

If only the clocks had been similarly affected. If the clocks of the web hadn't continued to synchronize with Rhomatum's Cardinal ring, this coordinated demonstration wouldn't be possible. They'd be in bed instead of—

"It's time," Lidye said.

Nikki's heart skipped a beat. He looked from one woman to the next, each exuding calm confidence, and suddenly realized himself for very young and very foolish.

"I can't . . ." he whispered.

"You must," Lidye answered. Coldly.

"You did it before, Nikki," Kiyrstin said and held out an imperative hand. "And this time, Deymorin and Mikhyel will be there to help. You won't *be* alone."

He stood up, took her hand, and felt strength and confidence flood him.

Lidye said, "Controlling Rhomatum, Nikaenor Rhomandi dunMheric, means being more stubborn than granite—"

"Call on Deymorin for that," Kiyrstin muttered.

Lidye frowned. "And you must be clever—"

"That's Mikhyel," he said.

He didn't think she liked that answer any better than Kiyrstin's.

"Then . . ." He blushed, ashamed he should have to ask. "Then what is my part?"

Kiyrstin chuckled. "Keeping your brothers from murdering each other."

He chuckled, too, and felt his gut relax. "They're past that."

"Never."

He laughed aloud, and reached out for Deymorin . . .

But Deymorin wasn't there.

§   §   §

"Mikhyel, for the love of Darius, it's time! What *is* it?"
Mikhyel held out the paper, silent inside and out.

Rhomatum's faltered. Pasingarim's lost faith. Shatum to back NC.
      —*Shamrii*—

"Shamrii? Who the hell is Shamrii?"

"Shamrii dunKharec. Shatum. One of the secretaries I dealt with. This was delivered to me at the competition. I *couldn't* look at it there, and I'd forgotten about it. She's *trying* to help."

"You trust her?"

"Better than assuming otherwise. If there's even a possibility the Southern Crescent intends to back the Northern, we haven't a chance. We're in trouble, Deymorin."

"Nothing to do but see it through, brother."

Deymorin held out his hand.

                    ᔑ   ᔑ   ᔑ

{Nikki!}

"He's here!" Nikki cried, and relief flooded him along with his brothers' imperative warning. "Pasingarim's lost faith? What's that mean?"

"Because *you* lost Shatum," Lidye said coldly. "Dammit!"

She paced the floor of the ringchamber, fists clenching, then froze.

"Never mind. We'll just have to stop him as well." She held out her hand. "Nikaenor?"

He took her hand.

At first, it seemed almost ridiculously simple. As his attention flowed, one point of the compass to the next, the image on the central viewing orb within the spinning rings shifted.

Through Lidye, he saw Shatum, strong and pure, seemingly all cooperation. Perhaps Pasingarim had changed his mind.

{Don't count on it,} Mikhyel's voice whispered.

Through Nethaalye, Nikki saw her brother in the Giephaetum Tower, second Ringmaster of Giephaetum. He was staring at his clock, waiting for the exact moment.

Through Kiyrstin's touch, he had only a sense of direction, and her own wish for it to be otherwise, could see Mauritum's Ringchamber, but only, he somehow knew, as she visualized it.

From Mirym's Khoratum side, there was nothing.

And as that north-south axis stabilized, Shatum to Giephaetum, he felt Lidye reach through him to Kiyrstin, *seeking* Mauritum, trying to force Persitum back on line.

And he felt Kiyrstin's distrust, a solid wall against Lidye. Lidye screamed, in sheer frustration.

{Kiyrsti?}

Deymorin, in his head. And Kiyrstin jumped, would have jerked free but for Nikki's reflexes.

"Deymio?" she breathed.

{Take *my* hand, Kiyrsti-love. And trust me.}

"Asking a lot, Rags." Her voice was shaking.

{Yes. So?}

She laughed, and reached *through* him directly to Deymorin. He could feel their hands clasping right inside him, and the power that flowed, Deymorin to Kiyrstin. Confidence. Arrogance. Trust.

And the Persitum Ring began to rise. Somehow, without disrupting the others, it began to spin.

Lidye laughed.

This time, it *was* Mauritum's Ringchamber on the viewing sphere, not Kiyrstin's memory, and Garetti himself, or so Kiyrstin's thought acknowledged the hard-faced, gray-bearded man.

Garetti appeared startled. Unlike the other Towers, he seemed aware of their intrusion. Seemed to look straight at them, though Nikki realized then it was at the rings he stared.

In a hiss audible within the Rhomatum Ringchamber, Garetti said: "Kiyrstine!"

Kiyrstin laughed. "Hi, Gari. Wanna wrestle?"

At once, Garetti reached into the Rhomatum Web. The image turned black, and that oily presence spun outward into Giephaetum and Shatum. An answering reflux. But Lidye was waiting. Anger flared back at Shatum. Anger pure and focused and undeniable, and Shatum's line cleared . . . only to have a second oily wave seep in from Mauritum.

On the Giephaetum line, a battle of a different sort raged. Brother against sister, and a battle against hubris. Nethaalye attacked her brother with images of his own behavior, colored with those details of personal inadequacies only siblings could know. And as he wavered, he listened more to her than to Garetti, and the line to Giephaetum, like the line to Shatum ran clear more often than stained.

And still in the West, Kiyrstin and Deymorin fought to block Garetti. Strength against dogged strength, sending wave after wave of oil back at Mauritum.

From Khoratum, there was nothing. And in the end, that lack made the difference. Without the unity of the web, the circuit was incomplete. Without the fourth compass point's assault, the smaller nodes, whose attacks had been mosquitoes to the Mauritumin, Giephaetumin, and Shatumin hawks, dropped out.

Eventually, Nethaalye's brother and Pasingarim relented, dropping out of contention, and the Giephaetum and Shatum rings held steady. Through those rings, Lidye and Rhomatum controlled the nodes.

The attacks from the West ended. The oil cleared, and Garetti appeared again on the viewing sphere.

"So," he said to Kiyrstin. "It's true. You've joined the offspring of the Heretic."

"Better than the alternatives," she replied.

"Are you certain?" Garetti's dark eyes narrowed. An eager look crossed his face, and his hand reached out to them. "Join me, Kiyrstine! Join me now, and we'll have them all."

There was a long, long pause. Nikki felt Lidye battering at his mind, trying to reach Kiyrstin, but he knew, somehow, if he let Lidye in, Kiyrstin would be lost. Whether to Garetti's lure, or simply to anger and distrust.

{Kiyrstin?} Deymorin's voice, in his head, and Garetti didn't react. Perhaps Garetti didn't hear. Nikki strove to keep that part of him private, wanting it for his brother and Kiyrstin alone.

And on a mental breath from Kiyrstin: {Trust me, Rags?} {With my life . . .}

A wavering. A mental hand reaching. "Gari . . ."

Triumph flared in Mauritum. Garetti reached. Kiyrstin clasped. And—

"Now, Lidye!" Kiyrstin shouted, and Nikki opened himself for Lidye to flow through him and through Kiyrstin to Persitum and beyond.

Garetti was gone. The Persitum Ring held steady . . . and responded to Lidye's command.

But the Khoratum Ring was nearly at a standstill within the Rhomatum Ringchamber.

"Mirym?" Nikki asked, and her eyes flickered toward him.

"Give us the Tower, girl," Lidye demanded, and Mirym shrugged. "You said you'd been there. Give us the image!"

Lidye hissed, and anger such as he'd never felt surged through him, and Nikki fought it back, forced Lidye under control, refused the second surge of anger she directed toward him.

{Tend to Shatum!} he yelled at Lidye, and she flinched. Surprise, anger.

He ignored her.

{Mirym?} He sent to her, a plea for reason. But received no response.

An image, then, through Mikhyel, who had seen the Khoratum Tower during a tour, and Lidye's sigh permeated the Tower and the link. The now-familiar bridge formed between Rhomatum and Khoratum, and Lidye's voice demanded: *Now!*

A surge of energy, pure and powerful, through the nodes they controlled, burst through to Khoratum Tower itself. And imaged on the central sphere were two men, combining their efforts to force contact with the other satellites.

One, Nikki recognized as Rhyys dun'Tarec. The other—

"Van," Kiyrstin gasped. "Sweet Maurii, Vandoshin's alive!"

The hideously scarred face tipped toward them, and a deep, seductive chuckle resounded through the rings. "Hello, Kiyrsti-love. So it's *your* doing. Shut us out, have you? Garetti?"

"Gone," Kiyrstin replied. "For the love of Maurii, Van, give up! It's over."

"Well, we shall see . . ."

The face of the man next to Vandoshin—Rhyys, Mikhyel's mind supplied, for all Nikki couldn't recognize him—contorted in pain just before a scarred hand swept between them, and the image shattered.

And the ring stopped.

Mirym whimpered; he could only imagine the tremendous strain on her. She had somehow kept Khoratum out, and by that effort, consciously or not, enabled their success. But now—

"Make the damn thing spin, Nikaenor!" Lidye hissed, and he wondered how he was supposed to do that. "Reach down, fool. The strength is in the ley. *Make* him spin it!"

Him? And Nikki thought, then, of the creature who had spoken to Mikhyel. He closed his eyes and called, furiously, desperately, but there was no answer. And he called again, *thinking* himself down into the depths, into the leythium caverns where the creature dwelled. Deeper. Deeper.

{Deymorin?} he called as his strength faltered, and Deymorin was there, steady as the granite Kiyrstin had likened him to, adding his voice to the demand. Still the creature ignored them.

And finally, Mikhyel slid in, though Deymorin objected, saying they could do it, that the creature would suck Mikhyel down and keep him.

And Mikhyel snarled: {Let him try.}

And plunged down Nikki's extended awareness into the depths below the Tower.

§   §   §

The creature awaited him on a leythium throne.

"You heard, didn't you?" Mikhyel demanded.

It smiled.

"Why didn't you answer?"

{Why didn't you return sooner?}

"I haven't *returned* now."

And he hadn't. For all his senses told him he was below Rhomatum, Mikhyel's mind knew *he* was still with Deymorin. *He* had put himself here, this time. He and Nikki and Deymorin, and he didn't *want* to be here physically.

And he sensed that that determination, coupled with the fierce anger that brought him here in the first place *kept* the Rhomatum creature from pulling him there physically.

{Not completely. Your brother won't let you go. By yourself . . . no you aren't strong enough.}

"No?"

The smile widened.

{Any time you care to try, child. Any time.}

"Not now," he said aloud, through the body that wasn't real. "You've a battle taking place overhead, you realize that."

"Yes-s-s. Rather amusing, isn't it? Children, trying to

break free." The creature . . . yawned. And stretched. As if those creature comforts truly affected it.

"But they do, child. Now, about my children . . ."

"Your *children* are dying. Would you have that? Would you lose them altogether?"

"Children do that. They grow. They strive for independence. They're gone."

"We're not talking independence. We're talking gone forever. Would you have them destroyed?"

"If they destroy themselves, they have grown unwise, and I am well rid of them."

"They are *not* unwise. It's the humans controlling them who are stupid."

"Oh, well, that's different then, isn't it?"

The creature reached out and cupped his chin. "Do *you* want this, bud of Darius?"

"Yes!"

{Then best you leave now. Farewell, child.}

$$\mathfrak{S} \quad \mathfrak{S} \quad \mathfrak{S}$$

Mikhyel raced up through him and back to Deymorin. On his heels, power, such as Nikki couldn't begin to comprehend, surged through the rings. And iridescent lightning arced through the night sky toward Khoratum.

Somewhere between, it exploded in midair, a multicolored fireball.

And Mikhyel and Deymorin disappeared.

{Deymio!} he shouted into the silence, and {Mikhyel!}

And as the fireball faded and another surge of power rumbled the Tower itself—

{Here, Nik. Had to make sure of our heads. That was right—}

Another arc. A second fireball. And he wasn't certain whose eyes he was seeing with.

{—above us. Everyone there all right?}

{So far, but—}

This time, with the lightning came an audible roar of pure anger, the explosion, though miles away, shattered one of the priceless windows of the Tower—blowing it outward.

And still the Khoratum Ring would not move. Nikki felt the creature's efforts flowing through him to Mirym, trying to force it to move, yet, it would not.

Mirym dropped to her knees, searching the floor blindly, then scrambled to her feet and thrust her hand among the spinning rings. A lightning-fast jab.

The Khoratum Ring shattered. And fell. Dust, nothing more.

Mirym collapsed.

And the lightning ended.

§ § §

When Mikhyel's head cleared they were no longer alone. And what had been a perfectly black cave, out of lightning's reach, glowed with a faint purple light emanating from the figure sitting cross-legged across from them.

"That," the Rhomatum creature said, tapping his fang with a long claw, "was no human, bud of Darius."

{Nikki!} Mikhyel called, and received dazed awareness in return.

"Oh, he's all right. You've disturbed my rest, child. Now, are you going to explain why?"

Deymorin stirred, pushed himself upright, clutching his head.

"You should be commanding the rings, you know," the creature said to Deymorin, who blinked, closed his eyes and tried again.

"Oh, you're sane enough. And, no, I don't mean at *all* to be ruled by such as you. *I* am not, I assure you, your silly rings." The creature stretched, and grinned. "A body feels . . . good again. Different . . . or perhaps memory faded. Now, who in the name of the essence that budded me was I just arguing with?"

{Who do you think?} The address was not a name, just an image of something drinking disgusting fluids that no self-respecting entity would touch.

"Naturally," the creature moaned aloud, then: {Get in here, you ill-mannered brat!}

Mother arrived in a magnificent cloud of leythium lace . . . that settled over the Rhomatum creature like a shroud. A single claw caught and dragged the delicate lace down, one deliberate stroke at a time.

"Sorry," Mother said, when his fanged jaws appeared, and she settled herself comfortably on folds that stiffened beneath her like a chair. Or a throne.

{Lazy.} Rhomatum's mind muttered.

{Smart.} Mother responded. *{You're just jealous because you didn't think of it first, and now I've got the height advantage.}*

"What is it you want, brat? I'm hungry."

"You're always hungry. —Freedom."

"Out of the question. You're not old enough."

"Age has nothing to do with it! Who just fought you to a standstill, you old fart?"

"Such language your humans have taught you."

"And such insipid prudery have yours instilled in you. Conservatism does *not* become you, Father."

"Father." He propped his jowl again in his hand. "I suppose I am. How curious, putting such things into human concept. You're still an ill-mannered brat."

"But I'm strong. I'm clever. And I'm bored. I want no more to do with my dull, ridiculous sisters. They do nothing except drain my essence when I most want it, and all so they can grow their buds. Well, I'm not *interested* in their damned buds."

"So you set out to destroy them."

"Not at all. The *humans* did that. I just want free of them."

"And me."

"Can't have one without the other."

"All a matter of perception, bud. You're not as clever as you think. I believe I'll refuse."

"I'll fight again."

"Ah, but will you win?"

"My rings are free."

"You cheated."

"I placed allies in your Tower."

"As I said, you cheated."

"I told you I was clever."

"The human girl is good."

"Of course."

"And clever."

"Like her Mother."

"And Rakshi helped you."

"Rakshi *always* favors Mother."

Rhomatum frowned and tapped his fang again.

"So, you want your freedom. The normal method didn't work. You've still got to form a bud between us. I don't care to go to the effort required to make one. So, clever, cheating brat, what do you intend?"

"I'm so glad you asked." Mother smiled: *{Nikki, darling, come to your Mother.}*

{Will you stop at nothing?}

"I want free!" *{Come, Nikki.}*

"Mother, dammit, *no*!" Mikhyel, sprang up and grabbed her shoulders. She snarled and swiped, a swing strong enough to crush him, with claws sharp enough to gut him. If the blow had landed. Instead, she held him with that bone-fingered grip.

{Khyel, you're mad.} That was Deymorin, which only confirmed his own suspicions.

{Cast-iron balls, though,} Rhomatum answered, which made a madman wonder why a leythium creature would use such an expression.

And Mikhyel began to laugh.

"Well, daughter?" Rhomatum interrupted. "Will you kill him? Or explain?"

Mother released Mikhyel and petted him and said she was sorry, which of course she was.

"Mother," he said. "Why? What do you need with Nikki?"

But Mother was distracted, now, with making certain she hadn't hurt him.

{Well, daughter?}

Rhomatum's internal roar sent Mikhyel to his knees; Mother hissed at Rhomatum and patted Mikhyel and brushed his hair back, taking the pounding in his head with it.

"Still don't see it, do you? You saw what happened when Anheliaa went after Maurii's silly toy. These three will provide a focus for us. A seed. A bud. Have us a baby, we will."

"Will that satisfy you?"

Mother shrugged, sending her veils fluttering. *{For now.}*

Another fang-tapping consideration.

{Tell me, are your rings still spinning?}

{Not at the moment.}

{How pleasant for you. —Go, then, child. But do be careful. They are a delicate species.}

Mother spun about in a swirl of lace.

"Don't worry, my wonderful, my darling papa. I won't let anything happen to them. They are my *special* children."
{Whatever—}
The two strangely elegant creatures evanesced and then vanished altogether. And from the light-blinded darkness in their wake: "Deymorin? *Khyel?* Brothers, are you there?"

§ § §

It began with streams of pure coloi arcing from Rhomatum and Khoratum, to meet and shatter above their camp, and rain in tiny droplets to the ground. Those who sought to catch them discovered hands full of nothingness, but if Mikhyel shut his eyes and turned his face to the sky, they became pinpoint pricks of total sensation—sight, taste, smell as well as touch . . . even his ears rang with sweet, delicate music.

It continued with great fireballs, exploding above them, filling the air with indefinable energy. And it ended with veils of glittering color that appeared destined to proceed well into the night, if not for days to come, as a new node was born.

Mauritum had made their play. They'd pulled the Northern Crescent into their game. They'd wanted proof of who was in charge in Rhomatum; they'd gotten a display of power to put Boreton to shame.

He hoped it satisfied them all for a while.

Whatever value he and his brothers served the leythium creatures, they had little to actually do. They watched the display in silence for a time. Then Deymorin asked Nikki about Kiyrstin, who was fine, and Mirym, who was also fine, but would, he was certain, be under arrest by the time they returned.

Mikhyel wanted to object to that, but it was only prudent. Kiyrstin wouldn't let Lidye do anything stupid. And Mirym . . . *I did what I had to . . . for the safety of* my *node. My source* . . .

It had all been there, if only he'd had eyes to see.

So much had been there, for anyone to see.

Exhausted, Mikhyel sought a bedroll apart from everyone, even his brothers, and stretched out under the light of the budding node, strangely unafraid, though he'd never slept under the open sky before.

Nikki and Deymorin, thankfully, sensed his mood and left him to his thoughts—after he promised to explain everything in the morning.

Morning. It was morning now. Well after midnight.

His twenty-seventh birthday. Or perhaps it wasn't. Could it be tomorrow, if he hadn't yet been to bed?

Just this morning, he'd awakened to an armful of pillow. Just this morning, he'd had breakfast with a man who, if there was any justice in the universe, was dead now. This morning, Ganfrion had been alive.

So had he.

Now he wasn't altogether sure.

Temorii, Ganfrion . . . likely Thyerri was dead, as well, since Mother had taken his shape there in Khoratum. They'd all died helping him escape, or just because they'd known him. Trusted him. Mother had saved him so *easily*. Why couldn't she have saved them as well?

Because they couldn't do this? Couldn't sit in the open with their brothers while demigods used them for target practice? Couldn't sit beneath a sky flaming with blues and greens and purples, so that Mother could be free?

He groaned, knowing sleep was destined to elude him, and pulled himself up to sit with his shoulder to a moss-covered boulder. Someday, as the new node formed deep within the earth—perhaps as early as tomorrow morning—that moss would die, and nothing would grow in its place but roses.

And no one could tell him why.

He'd stay awake, in case the moss died tonight. So someone would note its passing.

He wished he could cry: the tension-relieving tears which had come so easily a few weeks ago had been burned from him again. At the time, he'd thought he would be well rid of them. Now, like so much else, he wasn't certain the convenience was worth the price.

He couldn't blame Mother. Couldn't ask human compassion from any creature so utterly inhuman. Mother played at human actions and human emotions and human reason, but all she'd really wanted was a far more basic drive. Freedom. Recognition as an adult.

Never mind she reminded him of Nikki at times. Perhaps he'd tell her that. Someday.

He couldn't blame Mother. *He* had trusted too much in

Mother to save them. He'd been stupid. Set himself as a target. And in trusting Mother, had killed everything that made him alive.

At least Temorii had died on her beloved rings. At least she'd died happy.

Perhaps one day, he'd believe that.

But neither could he dwell on his personal loss. There'd be much to repair, in the wake of tonight's events. He'd return to Khoratum, if Mother would let him, in her newly achieved independence. He'd have to make the effort. Of them all, she was most likely to answer his call, and there was a whole city up there to account for.

And two bodies, possibly three, who deserved proper immersions.

"Rhomandi?" a low voice called, and he ignored it. Some of the men had begun passing spirits around, toasting the strange and wonderful spectacle.

He wanted none of it.

And that same voice, lower still, turning away. "Dammit, Suds. You'd *better* be asleep."

And a flash of silver flickered from the shadow's left hand: a ring lodged halfway down the smallest finger.

"Gan . . ." Mikhyel's voice caught. He tried again. "Ganfrion? Is that—"

"There you are." Ganfrion's large body eclipsed a fair portion of the sky.

Mikhyel scrambled to his feet to grasp the monster hand and found himself jerked into a smothering embrace, then shoved back.

"That brother of yours said I'd find you somewhere over here. Said you damnwell weren't asleep and that he wished you would get that way fast, though how he knew that—"

"Never mind. How did you get . . . ?" But he knew better than to ask that question. There was only one way Ganfrion could have gotten this far from Khoratum, this fast, and the exhaustion in his voice told a story of its own. Mikhyel clasped the big hand again and said, "Never mind that either. You can explain in the morning. Go get some sleep. Get drunk, if you like. Rakshi knows, you've earned it."

But Ganfrion retained his grip on his hand. "Just one more thing, Suds."

"Gan, please, I'm very tired."

"I think you can handle this."

"All right. I—"

"Owe me? Damn right you do. Heard tell, it was your birthday. Brought you a present."

"Look, Crypt-bait, I don't *want*—"

Cold metal slipped over their clasped hands to encircle Mikhyel's wrist, a feel and weight burned forever into his memory. He caught it with his other hand, as Ganfrion released him at last.

And the hot tears filled his eyes, reminding him why he was glad they'd left him. He controlled them fiercely, only to fight them once again when he raised the cold silver to his lips.

He'd find out tomorrow how the radical dancer's coronet had come to be in Ganfrion's hands. Find out what news he had of Khoratum—and of Temorii's body. For tonight—what was left of it—he wanted, finally, to sleep.

He pressed Ganfrion's upper arm and turned away.

"For the love of my mother's blessed womb, Suds, *wake up!*"

And past the exhaustion lurked laughter and frustration. Mikhyel turned, glared at the shadow-guard. "What *el*—"

And suddenly, the shadow budded. And a scent of raspberries and cinnamon . . . with a hint of clove, filled his head.

{Hello, Khy.}

Jane S. Fancher

The Dance of the Rings

☐ **Ring of Lightning**   UE2653—$5.50

Deymorin, Mikhyel, and Nikaenor are the descendants of Darius Rhomandi, the man who three centuries before rebelled against the ruling priesthood of Mauritum and founded Rhomatum—a new city based upon his dream of democracy. Now the brothers must overcome their personal differences in an attempt to wrest control of their city from the ringmaster, the tyrant who controls the leythium, the magical power that means life for the city.

☐ **Ring of Intrigue**   UE2719—$6.99

The sudden death of the ringmaster of Rhomatum throws the nation-state of Rhomatum into chaos. As Deymorin desperately strives to resurrect defenses that have lain fallow for generations, and Nikaenor struggles to bring order to a city in shock, Mikhyel finds himself following a trail of secret agreements and ancient feuds—a trail which leads him from the depths of Sparingate Prison to the teeming trade city of Shatum and finally to the decadent courts of Khoratum, and a fight for independence that penetrates to the heart of the leythium web itself!

More Top-Flight Science Fiction and Fantasy from
C.J. CHERRYH

SCIENCE FICTION
☐ FOREIGNER (hardcover)   UE2590—$20.00
☐ FOREIGNER   UE2637—$5.99
☐ INVADER (hardcover)   UE2638—$19.95
☐ INVADER   UE2687—$5.99
☐ INHERITOR (hardcover)   UE2689—$21.95
☐ INHERITOR   UE2728—$6.99

THE MORGAINE CYCLE
☐ GATE OF IVREL (BOOK 1)   UE2321—$4.50
☐ WELLS OF SHIUAN (BOOK 2)   UE2322—$4.50
☐ FIRES OF AZEROTH (BOOK 3)   UE2323—$4.50
☐ EXILE'S GATE (BOOK 4)   UE2254—$5.50

FANTASY
The Ealdwood Novels
☐ THE DREAMSTONE   UE2013— $2.95
☐ THE TREE OF SWORDS AND JEWELS
        UE1850—$2.95

Buy them at your local bookstore or use this convenient coupon for ordering.

PENGUIN USA   P.O. Box 999—Dep. #17109, Bergenfield, New Jersey 07621

Please send me the DAW BOOKS I have checked above, for which I am enclosing
$_____ (please add $2.00 to cover postage and handling). Send check or money
order (no cash or C.O.D.'s) or charge by Mastercard or VISA (with a $15.00 minimum). Prices and
numbers are subject to change without notice.

Card #_____ Exp. Date _____
Signature_____
Name_____
Address_____
City _____ State _____ Zip Code _____

For faster service when ordering by credit card call 1-800-253-6476

Allow a minimum of 4-6 weeks for delivery. This offer is subject to change without notice.

Tanya Huff

IRENE RADFORD

☐ **THE GLASS DRAGON**   UE2634—$5.99
Within a realm which has always been protected by its magicians, and in a kingdom whose ruler's own life is intricately linked with that of the dragons, the disappearance of these magical beasts could well see the land fall to invaders.

☐ **THE PERFECT PRINCESS**   UE2678—$5.50
Without the dragons and their magic to back his claim to the throne, Prince Darville—only recently freed from an enchantment that had kept him imprisoned in the form of a wolf—might soon see his realm lost to these enemies.

☐ **THE LONELIEST MAGICIAN**   UE2709—$5.99
The kingdom of Coronnan and its new liege, Darville, are once again threatened by Lord Krej and a magical coven determined to seize the Dragon Crown. And even as Senior Magician Jaylor struggles to protect the king and kingdom from these enemies capable of wielding powerful, long-forbidden magics, the young apprentice Yaakke undertakes a dangerous dragon-filled quest to find and save the dragon Shayla, to learn the truth about his own identity and powers.

Michelle West

The Sacred Hunt:

☐ **HUNTER'S OATH**   UE2681—$5.50
Once a year the Sacred Hunt must be called, in which
the Hunter God's prey would be one of the Lords or his
huntbrother. This was the Hunter's Oath, sworn to by each
Lord and his huntbrother. It was the Oath taken by Gilliam
of Elseth and the orphan boy Stephen—and the fulfillment
of their Oath would prove the kind of destiny from which
legends were made. . . .

☐ **HUNTER'S DEATH**   UE2706—$5.99
Blessed or cursed by their Hunter God and gifted with his
most unique creation, the Hunter Lord Gilliam and his huntbrother Stephen were about to do the unthinkable. Guided
by the seer Yvaine, they would journey beyond the borders
of their kingdom, something no Hunter Lord had ever done.
For only in the ancient city of Averalaan could they find
their true destiny, even if it meant facing the Dark Lord
himself. . . .